THE DEVIL'S PLAYGROUND©

J. Gregory Garrison

Cumberland House

Exclusively published and distributed by:
Cumberland House Publishing Co., Inc.
7399 N. Shadeland Ave., Box 250
Indianapolis, Indiana 46250
U.S.A.

The Devil's Playground©

Copyright © 1999 by J. Gregory Garrison

This is a work of fiction.
All characters and events portrayed in this book are fictional, and any resemblance to real people or incidents is purely coincidental.

Library of Congress Catalog Card Number: 99-93253

ISBN: 9672016-0-8

Scriptural quotations are from the King James version of the Holy Bible.

J. Gregory Garrison
The Devil's Playground©
www.thedevilsplayground.com

ACKNOWLEGEMENTS

When this book suddenly turned into a product, more than just a fantasy of my imagination, the realization hit me very quickly that there was much more to a book than just an idea—more than even a finished manuscript. I was fortunate beyond description to have the friendship and guidance of Greg Segal in turning a rough—and I do mean *rough*—piece of writing into this book. As editor/producer, Greg introduced me to a number of talented and energetic folk who in turn made the whole thing happen. Gene Redding, who edited and proofed the manuscript, did as much as anyone to take the rough edges off and mold my efforts into a product for the presses. John Koonsman designed the web site, consulted on designs and printing, and otherwise provided the kind of encouragement that kept me from pitching the whole thing in the trash. And the quality of the artist is self-evident in the cover design, a piece of work accomplished by Tim Coulon in record time. But through it all, Greg Segal kept after the details, had faith in the end result, and convinced me we could in fact deliver a product that would be worthy of the effort.

Technical help came from several directions, and the assistance of friends from all over the place bears mention. Dr. Dean Hawley, professor of pathology at the I.U. Medical School and one of the best forensics men I've ever known, provided tremendous help in ways that will bear his obvious signature as the reader moves through the story. Special Agent Patrick Donavon, with the Bureau of Alcohol, Tobacco, and Firearms, explained the science and alchemy of explosives in a way that even a lawyer could understand, and my partner, Michael A. Kiefer was always there with the military perspective. His passion for the institution of the National Guard, and his love of the citizen soldier, helped me keep in sight one of the most important lessons of this story. They are, and historically have been, the backbone of liberty for this grand experiment in freedom. My old and dear friend, Chuck Siebold, attorney and confidant over the years, provided the insights necessary to properly understand the incredibly powerful—and vulnerable—network we have come to depend on for the movement of money all over the world. And of course, the fingers behind the work, my secretary, assistant and friend, Cathy Schackel did everything it took to get these words onto these pages.

Although the idea for this book has bubbled in my mind for several years, there was one person who alone was responsible for the writing. My critic, cheerleader, partner, and guiding force, she is the reason The Devil's Playground ever became a reality. To my beloved wife, Phyllis Jean, "thank you." Countless nights of being awakened in the wee hours as cold feet got into bed after writing sessions that lasted far longer than I had intended, reading every section over and over, then refusing to let me give up and chuck the whole idea, she has done it all. We leave the rest to the world's readers, and we hope they will enjoy and benefit from the experience as much has we have from the writing.

Contents

BOOK I

YOU'RE IT

1.

John Wesley Kincaid lay back on the crisp clean pillowcase and tried to focus his burning eyes on the elegant designs in the ceiling of his new bedroom. Not drunk but clearly a bit tipsy, he was tired to the bone. One crazy day at 1600 Pennsylvania Avenue, Washington, D.C., finished, and 1,400 give or take to go. His last thought as he drifted off was nothing cosmic or even particularly creative: "I wonder what's next?" Blurry designs. Then darkness. It was his last thought.

* * * * *

Across town, in the presidential suite of the Washington Hilton, another man fought consciousness. He first felt the commotion, before anything approaching cognitive reaction could begin in his drunken head. Damn it. What's going *on*?! He tried to comprehend. And then, without knowing him how it happened, they were there— Molly, his wife, Nathaniel, the older son, and Brooks, his personal assistant for the entirety of his tenure as a general. Molly was shaking—vibrating, actually and babbling out of control. "Jackie, for godssake, wake up—Jackie—oh my god, he's really loaded! Jackie, please, for Pete's sake, wake up! Jack-"

"Oh all right, woman, I'm only asleep. I'm not *dead*. What is it?" Molly began to vibrate again at once, so Brooks, hand on her shoulder, spoke. His voice had that humble but authoritative Sergeant Major tone—the one reserved for addressing a general at moments when there was no time for protocol, and immediate, appropriate command reaction was required.

"General, sir, *you* may not be dead, but, sir, President Kincaid *is* dead. I just left the private quarters at the White House, sir—saw him with my own eyes, and John Wesley Kincaid is dead. Very dead. General, sir, you're it."

The Devil's Playground

* * * * *

Nobody knew exactly where to start. The place was still strewn with the trappings of the Inaugural and, because it was early in the morning on a Saturday, cleanup had not really begun in earnest. Had it not been for the nagging neurotic tendencies of the new chief of staff, who just had to check on the new president before leaving the White House, the revelation that he was dead would not have occurred until morning. But he had gone in to check, finding the man stone dead in his clean sheets. There had been a quick flurry of frantic activity, people yelling and rushing up and down the stairs to the private quarters, followed by medics with their full regalia and heavily loaded crash carts. Then more yelling, Secret Service agents wide eyed and grim, brand new staff alternately shouting nonsense and staring blankly into their own helplessness. Billie Wilkins, the new president's physician, walked slowly out into that hallway full of anxiety where everyone waited. White hair askew, wire glasses on his forehead, slightly stooped of shoulder and less than large of stature, he stopped, pulling the specs from his head. "People, the President is dead. I am sorry. Looks like his heart, but we won't know 'til autopsy. I am sorry." And with that, the Gunsmoke Doc Adams character parted the astonished sea of gaping faces and walked out. A man, after all, of few words.

Mac Reed, the new—*very* new—White House chief of staff, gathered himself up, looked around the disarray and, seeing Brooks, moved directly toward him. Brooks saw him, waited, and consciously came to a sort of understated position of attention as Reed approached. "Don't have any idea why you're here at this hour, Sergeant Major, but I'm glad you are. Guess we better find Jackie, huh? Come see for yourself."

Brooks had always had a knack for being where the action was, often with dire, violent results. But tonight, after the gala wound down—a kind of event with that he was all too familiar with but not fond of—he had begun to wander. Even at the White House there are certain people who can come and go pretty much with free will; especially if the guards know your name is Jonathan Montgomery Brooks, Sergeant Major of the United States Marine Corps.

They walked back through the litter of lost souls, through the entry way to the private suite, arriving in the bedroom just as the medics were putting away the last of their gear. Those tools of heroism, the defibrillator paddles, i.v. bags, syringes of epinephrine and bicarbonate. Gauze patches and sterile container pieces lay scattered all around the bed and on the night stand, and one section of rubber tubing lay on the floor, dangling out of a presidential shoe. John Wesley Kincaid was still. Blue/gray. Slack. Eyes half shut, mouth agape. Brooks, no stranger to death after 30 years as a Marine, came to it directly. He looked, reached over and pressed Kincaid's neck for a carotid pulse; shook his head. "Sombitch, Mac. . . Shortest presidency in history. General Jackie's not gonna believe this one."

"You better go tell him and get his drunken ass sobered up and squared away—quick. I gotta make notification and tell the media *very soon*. And President Jackie Robinson Webb had better be here." Mac's tone was less harsh than his words, as he looked away from the deathbed. The General, although a hard drinker and one time pure hellraiser, was also pure Marine, and Reed knew from years of experience with him how fast Webb could square up and take command.

"Roger that, Mac . I'm enroute." A glance at his watch, 0400 now. "He'll be here, dressed and STRAC by 0630." (**S**tanding **T**all and **R**eady for **AC**tion)

Reed grunted. "Make it 7, OK? I want to get things cleaned up, find Sarah, remove these zombies from the place before the photogs start firing for effect."

"Done, sir. 0700." Then, muttering as he made his way to the back stairs, expectorating an oath/prayer. "Holy Jesus what now, Lord? General Jackie, you're it."

3

2.

At 41, Jackie Robinson Webb had become the youngest general in the United States Marine Corps. Early and prolonged duty in Vietnam had first wounded, then nearly killed him and, after a too quick return to combat as a captain, he managed to end up in the middle of some of the bloodiest and most intense fighting of the war. Bronze Stars, Silver Stars, Purple Hearts, commendations stacked up in his footlocker at Ben Hoa. It all culminated, finally, in 1969, with a combination combat assault and hostage extraction that left him slumped behind the wheel of a deuce-and-half full of bleeding GIs, while his own wounds bled down the dashboard and into a puddle on the floor. Behind him, in the jungle from that he had just come, lay 51 dead VC and NVA, variously machine-gunned, blown up, or knifed by Webb or one of his zealots. Four more he just ran over with the truck on the way out of the last ambush. And of the 23 men in the back of the truck, one was dead and two more would die in the following hours. But twenty of them—and nobody knew how many others from the two units they went to extract—were alive and pretty much well, and all because Captain Jackie Robinson Webb, Yale grad, Rhodes Scholar, Atlanta-born poor black kid and more recently raving, screaming killer of men, had simply willed himself not to die, nor even to slow down until the enemy on that jungle hillside had been neutralized.

He awoke 48 hours later in the hospital in Da Nang, his body plumbed like a three—story outhouse, sprouting an array of tubes, wires, and bandages. A note pinned to his pillow, signed by General Jason Willoughby, Commanding General of the Marine division to that Webb was assigned, read "Doc—save this man. He has this date been nominated for the Congressional Medal of Honor. You are tending to our best. He must live. That is an order. Jason Willoughby, General, USMC."

Even in an unpopular war, and despite the squeamish stomachs in Congress on the subject of killing 51 men in about 30 minutes, the story quickly became front page news all over the world. Headlines in the Atlanta *Constitution* declared "Atlanta's Own Greatest Hero Since Sgt. York." And

4

the *Washington Post* called him "A Marine of the Old Corps. The Essence of the Warrior." This at a time when the editorial pages virtually steamed with the rhetoric of anti war hype. So when in the Rose Garden Richard Nixon presented Jackie, the poor black kid from Georgia, with the Medal of Honor, every newspaper in Christendom printed the picture. From then on—from captain to major to light colonel, to Full Bull to Brigadier general—took about 12 years. And if the rise to General Staff was quick, it was eclipsed by the rocket shot trip from Chairman of the Joint Chiefs of Staff to Republican candidate for Vice President of the United States.

* * * * *

In an election year that had been characterized by the unorthodox, not to mention at times the unthinkable, the Republican coup of nominating the first black man to run on a major ticket for a presidential-level position had been as fortuitous as it was brilliant. A whirlwind arms campaign against a leftover Communist regime in Central America had been transformed into a military effort of truly great proportions by the entry of Cuba into the fray two years earlier. Supported by a large contribution of arms and manpower from the Chinese, the whole thing turned into an overnight all-out war, culminating again in a stroke of armed genius on the part of Webb and his zealots.

With a joint multidivision coordinated offensive through some of the toughest, wettest terrain in all that part of the world, the general's Vietnam era tacticians successfully resurrected their combined wisdom and experience on jungle warfare. And the sitting president, William Duffy McGinnis, an Irish-Catholic Democrat who knew better than to let the politicians ruin *another* war effort, turned Webb and Co. loose to rain down hellfire and true damnation on the formidable assembled forces of Castro and his Chinese pals. The result was a lightning-style ground and air assault on a total of eleven well-chosen locations at the same time. Because there was no one to start whining about the carnage (they simply didn't tell anyone until it was over just how many of the enemy they were killing per day), the whole thing was over in about a week.

American casualties were remarkably light, about 350 killed and 1,100 injured; the loss of life on the other side had been fifty times that, thanks in large measure to complete control of the skies. This was accomplished by the use of every flying weapons platform known to the American arsenal, from Warthogs and Cheyenne combat helicopters and F-16s to old Huey gun ships and Cobras from a wide array of National Guard units. They also used a dozen ancient B-52s, so demoralizing the fixed emplacements of the occupying forces that most of them, or at least most of the ones still alive by the time of the land attack, greeted the advancing GIs with white flags and promises of immediate assistance in return for safe passage out of hell on earth.

All this was compliments of the United State Air Force strikes that came from such an altitude—mostly at night—that those in the target zones never knew what was coming until their world simply disintegrated around them. And as for the more elite mobile forces that were not treated to the B-52 surprise, there was the agony of defeat before M-1 tanks, roaring through jungles and along hillsides as well, at times over 50 miles per hour. They were accompanied by the birds of death, who made all attempts to shoot back a quick, fiery suicide mission. Add to that mix a web of intelligence sources composed of dozens of deep cover operatives who had been in place ever since the Reagan era and before, all of whom spoke of Castro like he was something they had discovered stuck to the bottom of their shoes, and the results were impressive.

McGinnis was a star, the Democrats looked like world beaters, and General Webb was compared with MacArthur and Eisenhower as the greatest military mind—and leader—of this war filled century. However, the irony on the political front was that Webb and McGinnis were not particularly close. Webb had been chosen by the president, after a bitter congressional fight had bloodied his nose badly. His own first choice was soundly defeated by a Republican senate that disliked McGinnis and hated his first choice for JCS chief. Webb's name had surfaced when the president sought some damage control. With minority support for his upcoming re-election bid tepid at best, McGinnis figured that Webb's raucous past and somewhat unorthodox personal history might be overlooked. Congress itself was eager not to further alienate a black population that had become a wild card, if not a political time bomb, for both parties in the past six years. The gamble was well conceived, and Webb sailed through the Congress and into the Chief's post in record time. Then came Central America and *poof!*—a national military hero,· a black man, and an immediate threat to the Democratic president whose war he had just prosecuted to a resounding success.

McGinnis then did what successful American politicians have always done: He made such a complete mess of the remaining two years of his term that his popularity simply disappeared. He lost his party's nomination for re-election to a snake oil salesman from Alabama by the name of Flint, who had been the only candidate in the whole party to see, two years in advance, that McGinnis was headed for the wall. And with the Republicans asleep at the switch, not to mention embroiled in an internecine squabble with their conservative component, Flint simply slipped in, slicked up to the sleeping public, and became president. The great American dream relived once again, this time by a real prize crook.

* * * * *

Flint's presidency was a study in positions du jour, almost from the first day he was in office. The counterculture radio and TV heads went nuts on his constant, almost dizzying position changes on everything from gays in the military to medical care for the indigent, to tax cuts, to abortion. The only thing sure about Jeffrey Flint was that nothing was for sure. His people got indicted—*and convicted*—of all manner of crimes and misdemeanors; his old girl friends kept turning up on talk shows, on magazine covers, and even in an occasional drainage ditch in some rural Alabama precinct. It finally got so bad that Brokaw, Jennings, and Rather could no longer ignore it.

In a period of about 120 days during the spring of 1996, culminating with the indictment of his wife on a variety of charges stemming from having lied to a federal grand jury, the country's first baby boomer president essentially vanished from the American political scene. Of course, the Democrats quickly distanced themselves from him and his "array of thugs and thieves," as they called his administration, but the problem of replacing him with a candidate of some potential was a real problem.

Enter vice president Allen Dickens. Handsome, smart, also young, and dressed in a much higher quality coat of Teflon than Flint (also sans the carnivorous appetite for everything in a skirt), he began to clutch the high ground as they all watched the president sink from sight. Dickens was quickly, quietly, but suddenly everywhere. Flint got sick; then his wife got sick. Then their kids got sick. Dickens showed up at more and more important functions with the infected president, often *instead of* the president. Then Flint resigned in May. Dickens took the solemn oath and transformed himself into the consummate chief executive in a matter of hours.

The networks went nuts. Integrity dripped from his every utterance, as the media began hitting the "delete" button on all that Flint had done to damage the office, not to mention the Democratic Party, over the past three years. And with the idiots at the top of the Republican Party still beating each other senseless in their never-ending quest to snatch defeat from the jaws of victory at every opportunity, Dickens saw his ratings rise above the 50% mark by the time of the convention.

He was nominated on the first ballot, after a huge fight between the old line liberal establishment (still stinging from the blows suffered at the hand of their boy Flint) and some young, fiscally conservative firebrands from the South. The Democratic convention nominated as Dickens' running mate a Midwesterner named Howley—Boyd Howley—whose biggest claim to the spot was that he had managed not to offend a soul in more than 22 years in the U.S. Senate. Laid back and quick-witted in a Will Rogers sort of style, he well complemented Dickens' smooth "come let us reason—and *spend*—together" persona. The issues—welfare reform, tax reform, and the collapse of American education—seemed well suited to these two clever and adroit men, particularly in view of the slim pickin's on the other side.

3.

If happy days were here again for the Democrats, especially for the *already* President Dickens and his homespun running mate, things were anything but cheerful in Republican dreams during the spring and summer of 1996. The front runner, a long time congressman from Iowa, Willard Jackson was unsuccessfully attempting to sound conservative enough to interest the large right side of the party in supporting him. This in spite of a long record in Congress as a big spender and a master at getting along with the perennial liberal leadership that had controlled the Congress for the better part of 30 years. And he was too old. At 68, the whole image was wrong. He looked bad on TV, he sounded like a crotchety old curmudgeon, his wife was ill and older than he was. But he had won too many primary votes not to be the man to beat. Then he got sick. A slight stroke followed by a trilogy of coronary occurrences left him with his walking papers, courtesy of his own doctors. What a mess.

* * * * *

John Wesley Kincaid had been a pretty good candidate for a while during the early primaries, even beating Jackson in two early spring races. Then his eccentric, Machiavellian personal style sort of soured the public on him, even though the conservatives liked him for his stand on abortion and the abolition of the income tax. Then Willard Jackson swept the big states all at once, and Kincaid faded from view, although not officially withdrawing from the race. But during the time he was eclipsed by Jackson, his people worked on the idea of a vice presidential nomination for him. Several thought Jackson's health would make him a one-term leader, and it seemed like a pretty good way to run as at least a quasi-incumbent, four years hence.

The Kincaid people sandpapered off some of his more obvious edges. They disposed of some of the flannel shirts and toned down the sometimes incendiary rhetoric for that he was occasionally known, particularly when addressing some of the more emotional issues on his agenda. When the docs called the fight from Jackson's corner, the Kincaid team was already in position to advance the new and improved candidate.

The convention was predictable, and much to the relief of the party leadership the candidate packaged himself in a mid-fairway style. Then, in a stroke of ironic, even diabolical genius, Kincaid called Jackie Webb and asked him to be his running mate. And what the world knew but had really never thought much about became the ingredient by that those damned Republicans nominated the first black in the history of the republic to run on either of the major party tickets.

Lt. J.W. Kincaid, A Co. 3rd Batt., 2nd Brigade, U.S. Army, assigned to the combined Marine/Army taskforce, central highlands, Republic of South Vietnam, had been in the back of a certain 2½-ton truck when Capt. J.R. Webb, USMC, drove it out of death's grip in the spring of 1969. Kincaid spent the following 3 months in a variety of hospitals, but recovered quite well from several wounds suffered that bloody day, and he was ever so keenly aware of who it was that had saved him from almost certain death at the hands of a passel of very disagreeable VC.

The war hero who had for several months the year before tantalized the American public with talk and actions consistent with a possible run for the White House reappeared. He never even told anybody what *party* he would run for and then quite suddenly quit the whole idea, but now he was just as suddenly *back* in the fight. A Republican, a black war hero, he was running for office with one of the men whose life he had saved enroute to collecting several wounds and the Medal of Honor himself. Recently retired from the Marine Corps and constantly in the public eye as he spoke at commencements, signed copies of his memoirs, did interviews with Barbara Walters and Diane Sawyer, Webb was ready made for the campaign. His wife was a beautiful, classy woman who had raised their four children while her husband was streaking through the ranks of the military, and the kids had all managed to distinguish themselves in unique and impressive ways. So when he gave his acceptance speech that summer, all the fire and brimstone that had sent his career to the top and his enemies to hell once again launched him headlong into a *non*-military campaign to that he was very well suited.

Book I – You're It

Smoke and steam rose in a pallid plume from the hood and undercarriage of the rusty '82 Dodge truck. The owner, sweaty, dirty, and grim faced, watched as the windows shattered, the tires went flat, and a big orange flash signaled the ignition of the remaining dollar's worth of gas. Motorists backed up for more than a mile, honking their horns in the usual intelligent response to a traffic jam on the expressway around Richland, Iowa, and the smoke began to settle back on them all as the temperature touched the century mark. Standing next to the dejected grease ball, Josh Landry absent-mindedly brushed beads of sweat from his brow with his shirt sleeve, spat dryly into the gravel, and grunted his condolences to the Jed Clampitt caricature who grieved the cremation of his rusty steed on the public thoroughfare. "You'll need a ride, friend, whenever we can finally get out of this mess. C'mon. You got any people to come get you?"

The grease ball grunted in the positive about the "people" question and in the negative about the ride, blew his own plume of smoke from the butt of a Lucky Strike (Josh hadn't seen an unfiltered cigarette since Sonny Crockett quit smoking during the second season of *Miami Vice* some ten years before). He burped something about "M'waf—she be 'long d'rctly. Thanks anaway." And the sweaty Samaritan walked back to his own hot ride.

It was after 7 p.m. when the tired Chevy van pulled into the drive of the Landry residence, rumbling through the dust cloud past the small barn, weed-choked fence, and finally up to the modest farm house quaintly landscaped with red, orange, and John Deere green plastic monsters. Tractors, motorcycles, bikes, and big wheels all stood as dusty proof that kids occupied the place, and Joshua Owen Landry felt a smile crack the grit encasing his tired face. The sprinkler was clacking in the back yard as it revived the vegetable garden from the searing heat of the day, while the scent of smoke from the grill announced the preparation of the evening's fare. A horse nickered from the small pasture behind the barn, the neighbor's rooster crowed his eternal ignorance of the fact that it was *not* morning, and Rusty, the retriever at brother Carl's house down the road, barked at nobody knew what.

11

The familiar sound effects of the nightly edition of *Power Rangers* filtered from inside the old house. Home again.

It was always a new discovery that Jessie Landry could be so easily ambushed in her own kitchen. At least three nights a week, Josh could be counted on to slip in through the mud room, into the back of the kitchen, around the cabinet top that covered the cooking island. Then he would alternately either goose her while entoning a traditional Comanche war whoop or, if the mood was more mellow, simply grab her in a more tender, but no less lecherous manner from behind and plant a series of wet kisses on all available exposed flesh. Tonight the goose was loose and, as always, sweet preoccupied Jess screeched as if groped by Jack the Ripper. A wet dishrag flew wildly over her shoulder at the unseen but well—known attacker, followed by a string of epithets righteously learned from her father, the cop. Elbows flew and, if the reaction were truly one of outrage at the attack, anything within reach on the cabinet might become an instrument of counterattack. Tonight, following the dishrag and one errant shot with half a tomato, the relief of having him home and the joy of feeling his arms around her again won out, and the aggressor was met with a hot, sweaty, wet, and passionate kiss.

A five-year-old boy was the first to respond to Mom's scream, and his was the first hug/tackle of three. One of those three was sister Emily, age seven, the other was a "big kid," Jan, age fourteen. Eventually the other of the "older girls," Sarah, would deign to pass in review, favoring the old man with a peck on the cheek or forehead before returning to the phone or the television.

"The collective I.Q. of all the drivers on the expressway tonight was approximately the square root of the temperature," he offered in response to Jessie's query about the late arrival versus his stated ETA from the office. "Some poor oyster blew up his old piece of cheese on the crossover from the beltway to the interstate. What a barbecue. Dumbest sumbitch I think I ever saw and an excellent argument for mandatory sterilization of the products of all unions between siblings. Nobody could decide whether to try to fight the fire or just cheer the demise of at least *one* moronmobile. So everyone just honked their horns instead. My head is killing me."

Book I – You're It

Grabbing a beer from the fridge while scooping up boy tackler number one, Luke, under his free arm, Josh headed for the sound of the news coming from the television in the family room. "Look, guys, it's President Flint, and he's lying again! Know how I can tell? His—" Three exasperated kids drowned Dad in unison, mocking the now worn out nightly one-liner, "Because his lips are moving!!" Pillows pelted him from several sides, and one of the elegant "older girls" even hurled a wad of dirty clothes from the top of the stair rail that skirted one end of the family room. "Oh," quoth Dad "I guess you already knew that one." Unison groans. Then, almost without a second's passing, Josh lurched forward and bellowed, "QUIET! Shut up guys—QUIET, DAMMIT!!" Silence, as the tone had instantly gone from good ol' jocular Dad to that seldom-heard god-like roar with which nobody argued. Eyes bulging, he fired the remote at the set, raising the volume so high that the neighbor's rooster immediately crowed in retaliation.

My fellow Americans, I appear before you with a heavy heart, but my head high, resolute in the truth of my pure innocence of all the character assassinating accusations that the small minds in the Republican Congress have conjured against me, even to the point of causing the outrageous indictment of my beloved wife, Billie, for crimes of that she knows absolutely nothing.

The thick southern drawl would have seemed comical but for the enormity of the moment, although the man's command of the language was never in doubt. He looked into the camera with a kind of used car salesman/Baptist preacher sincerity that had been successful at insulating him from blame for all manner of misdeeds over the period of his brief administration; the suspense built as he continued.

However, there are times when a man must choose the good of his country over the defense of his own good name, and even that of one so morally true as my beloved Billie. Tonight, I make that choice. So that I may attend to the vanquishment of the scurrilous charges now lodged against both of us, but more, so that our great country might be spared further rending and division at the hands of these scoundrels, I am this day, May 24, 1996, resigning the office of President of the United States of America.

13

The Devil's Playground

Vice President Allen Dickens, a man of the finest character and possessed of the greatest of integrity, will, I guarantee all of you, lead this great country through the remainder of this term, and into the next century. To my enemies I say, I bear you no ill will, though I will defend my sacred honor and that of Billie with the last ounce of energy that I possess, knowing in my heart that my integrity, love of country, and devotion to the office I have been privileged to hold these past three wonderful years will in the end be fully and completely vindicated. Thank you, Godspeed to you all, and God bless America.

Voice cracking with the end of the speech, tears not so discreetly wiped from the eyes of the erstwhile First Lady, the hush of the small crowd outside the White House was punctuated with sniffles, sobs, and the mutterings of reporters. They were trying not to look like buffalo smelling water as they whispered coarsely, excitement choking their voices, spreading the cellular word. The President of the United States had just repeated the ritual of the loathsome Richard Nixon, who had intoned a similar message just 20 years before—then for the first time in American history.

Josh waited, heart racing with a combination of glee and disbelief, followed by the sinking realization that he had just watched Allen Dickens become President. Brokaw appeared, ashen and slackjawed, and began to try to put a face on this huge mud pie that had just hit the liberal presidency in the kisser. Nonsense came from his astonished mouth. The remote fired and there appeared Rather, gaunt, pale, but not speechless, although words were hard to find. A bad phenomenon for a man looking into the camera of a live television show, being seen by some twenty million folks. Fire the remote again, and Jennings appeared. Predictably, he *could* talk, although not particularly well, as he looked at a befuddled and crestfallen Sam Donaldson, across the desk on the set of the ABC news layout. And, as the kids sat looking confused at what they had seen, and Jess stood looking at her husband with a combination of curiosity and cynicism, Josh looked back to speak. But nothing came out of his open mouth.

Finally a sort of prayer "Dear God, what now? I can't believe it. I can*not* be*lieve* it. That rotten snake has turned tail and hauled ass. And left us with Mr. Teflon in his place. GENIUS, dammit. Jess, by damn, it was pure genius! He *knew* his ass was grass, and he *absolutely* knew that Billie's indictment was going to finish him anyway, so they convinced that paper-hanging bastard to take the dive. Damn. Genius, that's all. Genius. Man, they must've promised him the absolute moon to get that hillbilly out of the White House. And Dickens, that shiny screwball, he'll make a better, *exponentially* better candidate than Flint, anyway. I swear. They're gonna come out of this with a winner. Just you watch! Just you wait and see, Jessica Marie Landry. Just you wait and see. Damn it." The phone rang, and the daughter who won the race to answer it groaned dejectedly that "Uncle Carl's on the phone for Dad..." More groaning.

"Well, whatcha think a' *that* shit, boy?! That scamp smelled the meat fryin', now didn't he, baby brother? Huh?! Damn right. Only he just figured out the meat was his own worthless ass heatin' up in federal *court*! Praise the Lord, Joshua, that worthless little thief is *history*!"

"Swell, Carl, only now we got the same lowlife in the top spot, but much smoother, and without all Flint's warts. No broads, no felonies, at least none we know of now, and a package that looks a lot more moderate than Jeff baby produced. You watch. Sixty days from now, Allen Dickens will be 'the people's choice,' better'n Flint was *before* all that crap about the money and the skirts came out. He's good, Carl, I'm here to tell ya, he's *very* good." They talked on to no particular conclusion, ending the conversation without a finish or even a complete "goodbye;" just the half—word, half—thought language of two men who needed little vocabulary to communicate.

Jessie reached around to the front of the television and turned it off; Josh seemed not to notice. He hung up the phone, and they all filed into the dining room for dinner. "Kind and gracious Heavenly Father, we thank Thee for the food we are about to receive, and for the home and family we share. But this night we pray a special prayer for our country, and ask Thy guidance over us all. Amen." Josh looked at the plate, at the floor, at the food, then into Jessie's wonderful green eyes. "Hell, it's just politics," he thought. Then speaking, a distracted, detached statement aimed at no one in particular: "Ninety percent of all the politicians in America could be run out of office, or into the penitentiary, if their true deeds and morality could be exposed." Jess shook

15

her head at this truthful cynicism. He had a crazy vision of political dominoes tumbling down, politicians piled up like cordwood, a big squirming mass, like a bunch of night crawlers in a coffee can. "What a mess. Let's eat."

5.

Saturdays were days of total transformation for the Landry brothers; up no later than 6 a.m., Josh was dressed, at the barn, and saddling his buckskin gelding for the weekly ride to Jericho for breakfast with Carl. In a town with only one paved street and an old fashioned "store front" main drag, the sight of two '90s full grown men riding horses the entire length of the thoroughfare to Fran's Cafe should have created quite a stir, if not a real problem. But Josh and Carl had been born here, raised here and, although educated elsewhere, had come home to marry, work, and raise families on land their family had acquired by federal patent over 150 years earlier. In fact, the tradition of horseback trips to Fran's was anything but novel, with folks from the surrounding countryside having met there for many years; rural Jericho had been horse country as far back as the days when the Army was still raising or buying horses to mount its cavalry for the likes of Pershing and his regiments of sabered soldiers.

Carl had more land than Josh, at least it said so in the Recorder's office, but the horses were usually quartered at younger brother's place, as his was the old homestead that had the stable and pastures surrounded by ancient fence. Carl, having built his field stone edifice on some high ground a quarter mile down the Jericho Road, actually held the larger tract, about 130 acres in all. It included the walnut and black locust woods, the creek bottom, and several lush and remote pastures on that were kept about twenty head of beef and dairy stock.

The elder Landry divided his days between his family medical practice and the gentleman farming operation at home, the 16—hour days of a GP having given way after his fiftieth birthday to a more modest medical schedule. This was due in large measure to two factors: The young woman he had hired as his associate and who had become quite the protege of the master, and the lightning strike heart attack he had suffered three years before. Survival had been a real question mark for several days, but the Landry grit was more than the Devil counted on, and Carl simply stuck his fingernails into the sheets of his bed in coronary critical care and refused to give up the fight. And, if he and Josh had wanted to break at least one of them loose to start the farming operation in earnest before, the events culminating in Carl's attack and recovery made those dreams at least a partial reality.

Now, riding past the front of Fran's on his dapple gray gelding, he was fit and tanned, straight and relaxed, and as resolute as any man could possibly be about the work that now occupied his life. They turned the nags into the alley beside the restaurant, circled to the rear of the building, and tied the horses to the split rail hitching post that still held a special place among the cars and pickup trucks parked loosely around it. Silver gray from the fifty years of heat and cold it had weathered, smooth as marble from the thousands of reins and lead ropes that had been tied to it, the rail silently spoke welcome to the two brothers as they swung down from the saddles and headed for the scent of bacon, ham, and strong coffee.

Entering through the open kitchen door, Carl led, blocking the sun's morning rays with his broad back and wide hat; Josh followed, hat in hand and, brushing past the soft expanse of Fran's back side, snaked an arm around her ample waist and under her equally ample bust, planting a noisy kiss on the back of her neck. Her rosy cheeks flushed bright, she pursed her lips in mock disgust, and then kissed back at the youthful cheeks of this Saturday desperado, her 50 plus year old whiskey tenor bubbling up a lusty laugh and hearty greeting.

" 'od dammit Fran, but you get better lookin' by the week. Look here big brother, but Fran is positively *radiant* this morning! If I wadn't afraid Jess'd beat the livin' bejeses outta me, I'd run off with her *right now!*" Carl looked around absently, half smiled at the renewed line of bullshit his sassy brother was producing, winked shyly at Fran, and disappeared into the dining room. Josh followed, but stole another squeeze from Fran's good graces first.

The heads of the early risers, farmers and retired gents mostly, turned as the Landrys entered, smiles appearing and quiet greetings being exchanged between the doctor and his patients, the farmer and his compatriots. Josh tossed light barbs at a few, crooned a coffee order to the plump waitress, and dropped into a ladder back chair across from Carl. The elder regarded the younger with slightly feigned reproval at

18

his predictable banter, then buried his square face in the steaming coffee mug. And commencing the half grunt, pigeon English, shorthand dialect in that they conversed, they covered again the cataclysm of the presidential events just passed. Soon, however, the talk turned to the farm, to the myriad chores and projects needing attention, and to the preparations. The two men, part business/professional and part cowboy, part cynic, and part zealot, part peace-loving family guys and part throwback to some ancient edition of *Small Farmer Journal*, had a plan.

Things might continue as the world saw them, with the Dow climbing like a Saturn rocket into the next century and the tax burden remaining just short of 50%. If so, they wanted to make enough money between them from their businesses to be able to come home to stay by the time Carl was 60 and Josh was 57 years old. But if, as they feared more with each passing month and year, the incredible stupidity and pure insanity of the current economic and political situation was approaching meltdown, they wanted to be able to care for their large extended families, and as many others as the Good Lord might send up Jericho Road, through whatever might happen.

Although Carl was far more cynical and pessimistic personality of the two, even Josh, with all his blarney and energy, had come to believe that a time might be approaching during that the privations of the '30s would pale by comparison.

After Vietnam, Joshua had spent over a year acting like a lost ball in very high weeds, in and out of school, living with his mother on the family farm but only getting in the way and driving her crazy by coming home drunk, beat up, and once even in some kind of semi-catatonic state. He wandered in the house on that occasion, mumbling about gooks and Claymores, frags and friendly fire, then he had collapsed on the stairs.

Jessica Marie O'Neal had been the medicine that cured the malaise, banished the demons for all time. She had stayed away from the wild-looking, long-haired remains of her high school sweetheart, but when she heard, upon returning home after her junior year in college, that he was hospitalized in the psych ward at Richland Community Hospital, she sucked up her courage and decided to visit him. The stories

19

about his injuries and the brief but awful captivity as a POW had shaken her terribly. They broke her heart and haunted her dreams, so that she could no longer allow herself to imagine his strong, slender body tortured and bleeding, or his infectious laugh silenced by the unspeakable brutality they all knew was the rule in Vietnam. The news that he had escaped, been found and sent home had, for reasons far too complex for her young mind to understand only served to further exacerbate her passionate confusion about *everything* having to do with Josh Landry.

Motivated by what she at first thought to be a need to exorcise the burning memory of her first—and only—real love, she decided that if she could see him in his awful, altered, and hairy state, she could put to rest the fiery memories that still captured many of her late nights and most of her dreams. Wrong. When she walked into the visitors lounge at RCH, she looked around for the apparition previously described to her by so many of her friends. But Charles Manson was notably absent and, instead, Joshua rose, clean shaven and youthful, if a bit sad around the eyes, looked at her with those same gray-blue eyes. He flashed a somewhat muted version of that old kiss-butt smile and, after what seemed like forever, looked down at his shoes briefly and said "Hey Jess, whas'sup?" She looked back, green eyes at first falsely cool, expression thinly casual. Two cautious steps toward him had burst into a unison lunge together, and both stood sobbing quietly in each other's arms for several minutes.

Gentle moans and soft giggles accompanied grateful applause as the two looked around to see patients, nurses, clerks, and aides grinning, even wiping sappy sentimental tears, so rare was it that a moment so joyful and optimistic occurred in that sad place. Josh was already on the road back to the world anyway, and the advent of that beautiful Irish lass simply shot him the rest of the way home, and they never looked back. Surely, the ghosts of Southeast Asia lurked, and the man was more quiet and given to a kind of deadly quickness that had never been evident before the jungles. And, with almost three years gone with no education, no money, and no tools to show for it, the young man had much to do to catch up.

The market for snipers was ever so soft; not much call for those skills in 1973. But marrying a teacher who had a full time job in a college town had been a stroke of sheer genius, or maybe sheer luck anyway, and the years passed with Josh finishing undergrad in two and a half years and law school in two more. Not bad for a brain dead Peter Fonda re-run with an attitude and a voracious appetite for booze, women, and violence. And people say there's no God.

6.

Richland, Iowa, was what the patronizing types who cast word curses on the Midwest called a "nice town." With a metropolitan population of about a million, a GM assembly plant, an international airport, a convention center and domed football stadium seating 65,000, it was a thriving place, with all the pollution, crime, poverty, and political incest that attends a place of such size. Settled initially by the military when the Army first starting "pacifying" the Indians (and later "neutralizing" them), Richland had been an early trail head for buffalo hides, beef on the hoof, and settlers by the tens of thousands as they headed across country on the Oregon Trail. The railroad went right through the middle of the original Main Street, and the town that grew up around it thrived. The rich land turned to the plow and spade of the sodbusters began to flourish after the Indians and the buffalo were gone.

The area provided horses and meat for every Army to fight from the 1870s on, and even the Depression had been less severe in Richland than in other places, due in large measure to the number and quality of the small farms that together produced what the scholars of modern agribusiness would later call "maximum yields." The farmers simply kept working and producing and took everything they didn't need for their own families to town, where they fed the entire population of Richland for about eight years. Then the psychotics in Germany allowed the United States to trade war for depression. Now, in 1996, this fine, flat, hot, boring city was home to a wide diversity of manufacturing and technology. The Air Force had top secret proving grounds and a lab outside of town in the wide plains, and a natural gas pipeline network moved gas from an ugly mess of wells that sprouted out of the ground for a hundred miles around. A great place to raise a family, a fine place to build a business, and a perfect point of attack for anybody who wanted to cripple an economy.

7.

There is an enclave in the South Bronx, just a dead end alley, really, where the junk, garbage, and trash of an entire block of tenements collects. It looks like just another urban cesspool, or a sort of impromptu landfill, and the smell supports that conclusion. Rats scurry in and out of the rotting paper, doing what rats do best: squeaking, multiplying, and stinking things up. Sunlight seldom hits the end of this little garden spot, so the water that collects there seems to take permanent residence in the corners and under the piles of disintegrating paper and plastic trash. It collects in the low spots and festers to a microbiological soup that might make a Carl Sagan think of starting his own new life forms. A real primordial soup, that. And there also resides a collection of some of the most brutal, evil people ever to inhabit the planet.

Behind the big trash pile and under an overhang created by the junction of two tall brick buildings, both empty and falling down, there is, for those brave—and crazy—enough to venture there, a short tunnel—like passageway that leads to a half below-ground level doorway into the basement of one of the two buildings. Visually very dilapidated, the door is actually supported by fresh timbers and massive hinges that are visible only from the inside. The casual observer (if there ever could be one so stupid or naive as to go there uninvited) would never suspect that the door would withstand even the slightest push; however, the thing is impenetrable without (a.) the knowledge that it is locked in three places, (b.) the codes required to operate the locks in the right order and with the correct electronic keying devices, and (c.) a specific invitation from Willie D. Calvert, a/k/a Abdul Salim Alakmah, a/k/a "Sallie." The last one is the most important, as "unauthorized entry" of any kind is a capital offense, unless, of course, you're a rat.

At 5'6" and weighing in at about 118 American pounds, Sallie is not an immediately imposing guy. Light chocolate Afro hair is diminished by a receding hairline, face is pockmarked from a near terminal case of adolescent acne. Those scars are made more severe by a series of knife wounds suffered during the riots that he endured while a guest of the county at a place they call "The Tombs." That's a charming

23

moniker for one of the nastiest jails in North America. His gait is halting, posture stooped and weak, his gaze furtive. But the voice. Holy Mother, the voice. Like an electronically enhanced, synthetically mixed combination of James Earl Jones, Sammy Davis, Jr., and the Wizard of Oz, when he speaks, virtual *thunder* emits from his scrawny throat. The diction is clear, the tenses in perfect agreement, the syntax flawless, and the vocabulary immense. Of course, it is well peppered with all manner of jive, vulgar, profane rap/crap that only NYC can produce, so the complete effect is more than captivating or even riveting. It is *commanding.*

Jonathan Flannery Abdelmanek had just finished negotiating the last of the labyrinth of sewage and garbage while trying not to gag on the fumes from the dead dog lying in the water under a trash pile when he heard the most gawdawful scream ever to pierce his patrician ears, coming from inside the massive door. He was somewhat put off by such a bloodcurdling sound of obviously human origin, coming from a place known for its total concealment, as well as its perpetual silence. He hesitated before running the newly changed litany of dials, key pads, and tumblers to gain admittance to the basement.

From behind the door came the Darth Vadar bellow of Sallie's melodious tones, "Jonny, you half-white camel jockey, what the fuck do *you* want at this *most* inopportune of moments? Take that fancy suit, turn it around, and haul yourself out of this place. *Now.* I am otherwise engaged, as you may just have gleaned from my companion's most recent ejaculation. Beat it."

"Salim, my good man, please reconsider," Jonny responded in as insistent a tone as he dared, knowing the limitless bloody mayhem of that the man was capable. "I really *must* see you at once. This is a matter of the most extreme moment, 'Priority double Alpha,' actually, and I shouldn't want to have to explain to the Committee your truculence at such a serious juncture." The King's English both clipped and rolled from his blue/black lips, the joint product of his Arab lineage (he was Iranian by birth, but raised in Saudi Arabia) and his English public school education, followed by college at Oxford. Silence greeted his plea, as he stood there in the stench of dog death and rotting food, the only visible feature of his face being the glistening of the beads of perspiration on his forehead. No light reached this place after about 6 p.m., and now, well after midnight, the place was the epitome of blackness. No one could ever get there in the dark unless they first *knew* where they were going, and then also had an intimate familiarity with the numerous tripwires, passive surveillance devices, and boobytraps that had been so carefully placed in what appeared, even upon careful examination, as a random pile of urban crap.

"Stand there, please. *Wait*." The eventual response thundered out through the entryway. Jonathan knew he was being watched as he stood there; no expense had been spared in the area of video surveillance at and around the singular entrance to this unique place. When the door opened, Jonathan stepped into a scene straight from Dante's *Inferno*, complete with a wide variety of instruments of torture, a significant quantity of blood spattered about the floor and walls of this filthy place, and the crumpled form of a man—or at least *part* of a man, in a fetal ball beneath the table.

Jonathan Flannery Abdelmanek could never find words to describe his loathing for the place he now occupied or for the man whose company he now kept. It's moniker, "the SPA," or "Sallie's Palestinian Annex," was a nether-legend among the world of terrorists, and that simple expression was typically sufficient to conjure images no one wished to harbor for long. But business was business. And his was to carry the most highly classified of mail and messages in all the world of terrorism between the architects of chaos and all the places like this one, around the world, where their designs became awful realities. And the information he bore this hot summer night could not be delayed in its timely delivery by any personal predisposition held by any of the soldiers of Holy Jihad. The smell of death was intense, as was the diabolical mood of its occupants, at least the ones left alive. Two pale men in long gray coats stood astride the hulk on the floor, their faces impassive, their gaze vacant.

The wobbly old table, about kitchen size, was arrayed with numerous knives and picks. A pair of alligator clips were attached to a 12-volt car battery; they shared the space with several pairs of pliers, tweezers, and some dental tools. There was also a .22 caliber revolver, equipped with a long cylindrical silencer, that gave it a Ned Buntline western appearance.   Seeing it, Jonny immediately identified that *other* smell that had been haunting him as that of gun powder.   That realization in hand, his practiced eye searched at once for the signature of small caliber execution, the little black hole with the purple and black circle concentric with the entrance wound behind an exposed ear.   Not a difficult observation for one so finely tuned in the exotic arts of torture and death, and no more difficult a conclusion than the one that made even his burned-out psyche shudder: The man had only recently been dispatched by the slender weapon, maybe within the seconds that had elapsed after Sallie's last epithet and the moment the door was opened.   And before that, the poor wretch had suffered a broad assortment of "fractuosities," as Sallie called them.   Several teeth lay on and under the table, an ear and the man's nose were missing, and his midsection had been expertly carved.   Tough business, terrorism.

In a supreme effort to hide his revulsion, Abdelmanek turned slowly away and feigned a shallow smile at his carnivorous host.   "Salim, my good man, you *do* practice your chosen trade with such extreme skill—and such obvious pleasure."   The intended insult was either ignored or missed by the perpetrator, as he grunted a sound that seemed to the room's occupants to have come from somewhere below the concrete basement floor.

"Piece of shit decided to visit unannounced.   And without *any* clearance.   Pity, too.   Kind of a nice looking young fellow. However, Jonathan, *in extremis* he provided a somewhat disquieting tidbit.   Apparently, he was not just wandering aimlessly about the Bronx; some person by the name of "Lassiter" seems to have had an interest in what might lie in or behind our somewhat unique foyer.   We shall have to run that name through the database at once, would you not agree, Sherman?"

The shorter of the two men in gray looked up from the grisly cleanup being initiated by the two and spoke with clipped, dignified reverence.

"As you wish, Salim; certainly the search is warranted. And *this* may help in our inquiry."   "This" was a zip lock bag full of freshly severed fingers from the hapless soul on the floor.   "Ah, Sherman, *excellent!*   Of course, the identity of our nosy Mr. Lassiter might make more sense if we knew more

26

about this miserable coward. Do it." Looking back at his guest—the one still alive—he explained. "One of my many warped followers is quite the computer geek. Said he could gain access to the FBI fingerprint files by modem. I told him how lovely that would be. He seemed to work harder after I had Cedric, there, tell him he would be executed if he failed. I *do* so love to provide that extra measure of incentive to my new operatives."

He looked absently at the corpse being dragged on a plastic sheet through the door and into a brightly-lit room where a large iron sink occupied center stage. His yellow/green-eyed gaze now fixed intently on Abdelmanek, and the addition of the extra ingredient that always appeared in his countenance immediately after having so thoroughly performed his artform produced an instant reflexive desire to vomit—and run away. "All right. What is it?"

The messenger looked cautiously at the open door through that the body had just been dragged by the two ghouls, noticing that they were now hoisting the corpse up onto a table to the right of that big sink. Sallie saw the question in Jonathan's look and walked over to shut the door. "There. Out with it. I've got a job to finish in there."

Breathing a deep breath of the heavy air while removing a thick envelope from inside his suit coat, he responded with momentous but understated delivery. "The entire Committee is all in a dither over the Republican ticket. They felt things were well in hand with Dickens and Howley, particularly with Dickens already *in* the White House and that dreadful old man as the odds-on favorite for the Republican nomination. But *this*. Kincaid, all full of conservative claptrap and Zionist pandering, *plus* that damnable general—well, the whole Palestinian operation is afraid of them."

"Bullshit, Jonathan, pure bullshit. One redneck holding up a washed up nigger *leather* neck is hardly a viable choice compared with the savior-faire of an Allen Dickens. Moreover, with all the gains we have accomplished with the assistance of that idiot Flint, we need little help now anyway. Tell 'em to relax. The people of this country are too enamoured with the whole Flint/Dickens mentality to elect a crackpot like Kincaid. Hell, Jackie Webb is as white as George Washington, for crissakes, and any black person with an I.Q. above room temperature knows he means bad things for them. Even if *half* the people this government is paying to get fat and stay home come out and vote, it'll be a fucking landslide."

"Bravo, Ted Koppel. I am confident that our comrades in Beirut will be assuaged by your analysis, which I shall at once convey to them when I return. But, just in case they are not mollified by your political acumen, I had best convey their instructions to you. Here. This is a list of steps to be accomplished at once, along with a detailed outline of the offensive." He said that last word, *offensive*, with hushed intonation, employing a kind of melodramatic bravado that made Sal, the political pundit, stifle a snicker.

"Now, I am to tell you that you are to proceed with all prearranged preparations consistent with a level 2 standby posture. You are to increase security to level one tonight, remove all munitions and ordnance from all storage that is less than maximum secure, and store them by midnight tomorrow in one of the code 1 bunkers. Change all passwords and electronic encryption codes and confirm that this has been accomplished, complete with confirmation of the new codes, by midnight tomorrow by secure microwave transmission. Then remove and store the transmitter on this building until you receive additional orders. Any questions?"

Willie Calvert would probably have sworn a string of South Bronx pornography at such a tall and difficult order; Abdul Salim Alakmah, reborn religious believer and devout citizen of the Nation of Islam, simply roped in the rage and hatred and all the passionate loathing for the oppression created by all authority and said, in a voice soft, aware, and compliant, "It will be done as you have directed." Jonathan stood up, walked to the door and, as the sound of the electric saw whirred from the direction of the sink room, let himself out. The locks reset themselves automatically.

* * * * *

Midnight was not an hour well known to Carl Edward Landry, M.D. Truth be known, 10 p.m. seldom arrived to find him outside the grip of the night's slumber. Years of late night obstetrical duties, usually followed by early morning rounds at RCH, tending his rural/suburban flock of devoted patients, had trained his body to an early bedtime routine.

Book I – You're It

Carl had come back to the Richland area from his internal medicine residency at the University of Chicago, made an unerring straight line for Jericho, and announced to family and friends that he was home to stay. The same day he returned from taking his internal medicine boards he called on the aging doc who had delivered the entire Landry clan, near and far by now, and who had, in his 1954 Studebaker Commander, made house calls routinely for approximately 41 years. Raymond Young had stepped into the waiting room full of his own faithful flock, whipped his hornrimmed glasses from his face with a muted flair, and opened his scrawny arms as if the prodigal had indeed returned. "Jesus, Mary, and Joseph, if this ain't a sight...Carl Edward, *oh—excuse me!...DOCTOR Carl Edward Landry...*(voice now almost imperceptibly quavering) *this is a sight for these tired, sore old eyes.*" Embracing him without a moment's hesitation right there in front of 17 sniffling, hacking, wheezing, baby burping patients, the old country physician wrapped his lanky frame around the mass of the new kid on the block. Stepping back, he clapped him firmly on the shoulder twice and pronounced the rest of the story. "Well, c'mon back here, *Doctor,* and let's get you dressed for work. The place is full, and these sick folks won't heal themselves!" And that had been that—he began, not the next day, or the next week, but right then. He saw five babies, two little old ladies in need of vitamin B12 shots, sewed up two lacerations, and took the evening duty of setting a broken leg suffered by Jimmy McClelland after an ugly dismount from a loaded hay wagon. Welcome home.

But, maybe because of the memories of those very beginnings, or maybe because of the more troublesome thoughts that seemed ever more frequently to creep into his mind late at night, Carl now found himself alone on the screened porch, and like Jacob wrestling with the Spirit through the night, found not his hip, but his heart, out of joint. Ever since having gone to a half time status in the medical practice, but especially over the past few months, Carl Landry had become ever more pensive, quiet, and at times, even more serious than he had always been. Tonight he sat ruminating and eventually actually fuming about what he continued to see as a collision course with disaster for his community, his country, the world.

Now make no mistake; most folks who talked much to "Doc L.," as he was known around Jericho, saw him as just a bit on the *odd* side, a little eccentric, almost *weird* about the trends in world affairs. He sat listening to the concert being offered by the cricket and bullfrog ensemble performing beyond the hedge that circled the pond. And this bright, concerned, competent man fretted about how he would feed the huge extended family for that he and brother Joshua were so clearly responsible—not to mention the community up and down the Jericho Road.

Carl feared a "meltdown," a "crash," even anarchy; and very few people in his circle of friends and acquaintances ever allowed themselves to think in such Draconian tones. He read those screwball counterculture newsletters and listened to the right wing late night radio voices; he studied the fundamentalist books espousing the "end times" predictions culled and synthesized from the Books of Daniel, Isaiah, and Ezekiel in the Old Testament. They all seemed to have made Carl just a little crazy, or at least *very* preoccupied with things for that there was little proof and *absolutely* no audience.

Whenever he got into the Apostle Paul's wild predictions about "rapture" and "the day of the Lord," you could almost predict the slow but resolute exodus from the table or living room. Often his wife, Gail, just went to bed, so irritated did she become with his doom and gloom outlook. She had quite enough of her own, without listening to his fantasies. He brooded about the coming new world order and the evil of those damned blue helmets the U.N. put on the heads of *our* troops when that treasonous bastard Flint kept consigning them to another one of his acts of complicity with the "One Worlders."

So Carl Landry—physician, farmer, intellectual—sat wondering about things, and about himself. Maybe he *was* a crackpot. Maybe he *did* read too much of the things that made so much sense to him, but that so infuriated his wife and so often left him alone at whatever table he occupied. Anyway, he was disquieted in his soul—in his very soul. And the symphony coming from the pond could not calm him. Dawn came, subtle and damp, silent and red, and Doc L. headed downstairs for the coffee pot.

Josh was awakened as always by Luke, the earliest rising child ever to bear the Landry name. Horses awaited feed, the water tank was low at the barn, and the neighbors were on vacation, so their chickens would need to be fed and let out of the hen house. And these were all chores that the nine-year-old had no intention of omitting. Dad was gently shaken awake and rousted from bed, where his jeans, boots, and straw hat stood ready. "C'mon, Dad. Remember, we gotta feed Beasleys' chickens all week! I hate that old rooster, too, Dad, so I can't go alone. I'm 'fraid that ol' devil's gonna peck my bottom or spur me like he did Jan when she was feedin' 'em last year. Remember that, Dad? She had to go see Uncle Carl, and he had'da scrub out the hole with hot soap suds, then give her a *tetanus shot*! She cried like she was shot, Dad. I hated that and I'd *really* hate ta git spurred, Dad. So you gotta come, OK Dad? Huh?"

The excited monologue had not changed a syllable any morning in the past ten days that the Beasleys had been gone. Luke *was* afraid of the rooster, but the litany of the bird's transgressions was mostly just make-weight argument to assure that Dad would do what Dad always did, even on the mornings when earlybird Luke missed Reveille. But Luke *loved* that morning time with his dad, and he was forever preaching the gospel of some overriding consideration that made it imperative that the daily ritual not be altered. It wasn't.

So they went as always, first to the barn, where they turned on the electric pump to begin filling the horse trough, then waited patiently while the six horses traded insults, bites, kicks, and snorts as they vied for pole position at the feed mangers. Of course, there was enough for all, and every one got its full measure every time, but then that's why they call them "dumb animals." Cat food went into the big bowl, where it was attacked by a furry pile of kittens who were quickly pushed aside by two momma cats with enormous appetites; the guys topped off the water tank and headed for Beasleys'. Although he never told Luke, Josh hated that damnable rooster at least as much as did his son. Every entry into the hen house was a true Hitchcock adventure, as one could never know whether the schizophrenic bastard would be lolling back in the dark, already be out through the side gate, or poised for attack when the door came open. Twice Josh had nearly killed the thing; the only reason it had survived spurring Jan had been that Josh couldn't find it when he headed back over there, shotgun in hand. Maybe there were more brains in that tiny ugly head than people thought.

This day there was no confrontation, as the mean old rooster was already up on top of the henhouse, making his ridiculous racket, by the time the boys got there. With him in plain view, sneak attack was unlikely, and if one had occurred, Mr. Rooster might have found himself kicked through the uprights of chicken eternity. Josh had never forgiven the bird's assault on his kid.

Looking down the road from the loft in the barn, Josh could see the faint but telltale flicker of the light in the kitchen at Carl's big house. Only a practiced eye could see such a thing after the sun had started its course across the early sky, but his was *very* practiced, indeed, and lately he had been ever more watchful, as his older brother continued to show more and more signs of stress and lack of rest. One heart attack had been quite enough to suit Josh, and the thought of losing his lifelong best friend and only living brother was nothing less than horrifying. Vietnam had taken their only other brother, a sunny blond nineteen-year-old, in country all of eleven days when his Jeep hit a land mine. Their mother had never really recovered from the shock, having been *in* the hospital when notification had been made. Old Doc. Young had been the man who had told her; the long fight with Lupus had not gone well for at least two years before, and the news that her youngest, Luke Joseph Landry, had been blown to bits on a public road half way around the world was just too much for her. She died eighteen months later.

Josh had been the last to learn of Luke's death; both were in Vietnam at the same time. He had been told in a letter from Carl, almost six weeks after the fact. He was convalescing in the big field hospital at Da Nang, after escaping from the POW camp. Carl waited to determine with certainty that his condition would tolerate such a blow before allowing Josh to hear of Luke's death. And the post-war problems that so tore at him, made so much worse by the reality of Luke's death, only hastened the end for Mom. Now, with the blond, blue-eyed son named Luke beside him, Josh felt the most complete and perfect mix of emotion, looking at an image of his long dead brother so exactly like him as to produce layers of cold chills when father regarded son, and brother saw brother.

Carl was much more radical about things than Josh and had always been much more serious minded, as well. The Good Lord must have known that war would have destroyed the pensive, brooding elder Landry; it was no joy ride for the younger. However, the very cockiness and the facile mind that kept him one step in front of the law and his parents' wrath at his constant taunting of the finer points of small town protocol had served to allow his survival when the VC dropped him into the bowels of hell for 43 days in 1970. There was even a sense, unspoken for sure, in that Carl held Josh in special esteem for having endured what he did—and for having come home afterward. Carl had been in medical school when the worst fighting was decimating the landscape of Southeast Asia. Military service and eventual exposure to the effects of combat awaited every medical student until the war wound down. He just never got that far.

So Carl worried about everything, and Josh worried about Carl, and nobody worried about either one of them, except Jessica Marie Landry, who knew and understood—and loved—both. Gail, the stoic and proper wife of the doctor, portrayed an air of resignation that followed exasperation with her ponderous husband. In fact, with all four children gone from home, he was now under foot far more than when she had known the freedom that his former pace in the medical practice afforded her. She was far less happy and much more prone to closeting herself in the private master suite of their massive fieldstone edifice; actually relating to this mysterious and rigid man had never been an option to her, not from the day she accepted his marriage proposal, five days after they had been graduated from Jericho High School. But Jess, long a fixture in the Landry household while both boys were still at home, was intimately familiar with the vagaries and the complexities of the remaining Landry boys. And although she had never passed so much as a romantic syllable with Carl, she knew him and loved him completely. Even at his most sullen and brooding times, she could sit with him at her kitchen table drinking coffee and listening to his foreboding, never shutting him off or performing the oft—seen "digression two step" so common when he bared his thoughts to everyone else.

So these three shared that unique sense of understanding and family, so uncommon ever, and so very rare in the '90s. And, as Carl grew more brooding, Joshua kept working, earning, and watching out for his brother, knowing how intense the elder's passions ran and being ever more afraid that Carl might *not* be so eccentric, after all.

8.

The country's redneck population had never been in such a fix. Their boy, Kincaid, had been nominated; that hated thief, Flint, had resigned in disgrace, and gun control was again stalled in a huge committee fight in Congress. Kincaid's popularity had soared since the convention and, with six weeks left before the election, the Republican Apocalypse II appeared to be certain. But the screwballs on the fringe—the Klan, the Neo Nazis, the white supremacists, and all the greaseballs who secretly hoped things would go to hell just so they could have some *real* fun—had a problem. Kincaid had chosen a black man, "a goddam nigger," as his running mate. Holy shit, what kind of trick was that? And every self—respecting racist in the United States of America was stumped. They could never become the Republican version of the old "Reagan Democrat," forsaking party affiliation in favor of that that might better suit their various agendae. That would require voting for Allen Dickens, the very nigger-lovin' sumbitch who had fired things up at the federal level during Flint's one term, chasing good American whites out of the workforce in favor of the "new affirmative action," that they all hated.

But Kincaid was a "no bullshit kind of guy," pro-life, a lifelong member of the NRA, a hardliner on federal spending, and absolutely opposed to affirmative action. So he was their man, all right. Then he chose that nigger Marine. Now everybody could understand the connection with the war, and John Wesley having strong feelings for the one who had saved his life and all, but Jeses, Jack, a *nigger* in the White House? What the hell were ya' *thinkin'?* "Well, bygod, if anything ever happens to ol' John Wesley, there'll be hell to pay if that nigger ever gets to be president." So went the "rhetoric" among the unwashed on the political, and cosmic, far right.

While lacking the organization and directed fanatic zeal of their counterparts on the militant left and the crazies to the way out right, they were several million strong, and the current of racial, gender, and religious hatred they bore was much stronger than anyone could know.

There were, however, those on the far right who cared less about the nonsense of race than their ignorant brethren. To them, the idea of a roughneck ex-Marine in the White

House, especially one who spoke so passionately against most of the liberal agenda, made perfect sense, irrespective of his color.   And what *those* people learned, thanks to the candidacy of General Webb, was that there was a very large moderate, even conservative, black constituency. Those folks found, for the first time in the history of the Republic, a voice and a champion who made it less difficult to express their true feelings.   All this combined to make the last few weeks before the election the most interesting political juncture in the history of the United States and the most intrigue-filled sixty days in the Twentieth century.

Nobody could know what the result of a Republican win would be, but everyone knew it would be explosive.   The counter-culturists made bolder statements supporting the Kincaid/Webb ticket, and the militant right found it harder and harder to keep the attention of the less radical following, with the Grand Old Party singing the parts of their songs that made the most sense to the most folks. And besides, Kincaid was young, strong, and ready to govern. He'd be a cinch for two terms and, at fifty years old, he could be counted on to live out both easily.

Book I – You're It

Forty, maybe fifty years of lurching, topsy like change, complete with a kind of unbridled, unashamed lust for all the things this planet can promise—or lie about—seemed to be coalescing into an ever- tightening circle of competing appetites, passions, demands. Everyone—absolutely *everyone*—had an agenda or a litany of what *they* thought was important. The gospel of the politically correct had supplanted most orthodox religion in the conscious minds of the masses, so much so that the passing of almost the entire set of traditional values and institutions seemed not to draw more than a wistful sigh, followed by immediate denial, from folks everywhere. Commonalties had been replaced with idiosyncrasies, shared goals with aggressive competition.

Everywhere the tide of separatism grew, accompanied constantly by an ever—intensifying passion for a kind of clannish supremacy. One of the more ignominious legacies of the Flint era was an almost immediate reopening of the racial barriers and wounds that had always been in the way of American society. The subtle changes that accompanied the decades of the '70s and '80s were quickly and expertly replaced with a new, separatist "us vs. them" attitude that manifested itself all over the place, from the courtroom to the board- room, from City Hall to the Hall of Fame.

Likewise, gays became such a force that even the military was subject to Flint's perfect intellectual dishonesty—"don't ask; don't tell"—as if such an artifice of institutional fraud could remedy, or even hide, a problem of such enormous proportion. Middle America, and particularly the more successful Middle Americans, while constantly the subject of those ridiculous presidential promises about tax breaks and family-oriented social engineering, had found themselves the targets of what amounted to nothing more than income confiscation, as tax rates touched the 50% mark. And the ravenous vultures at the IRS, too lazy to chase real criminals, feasted on the people who were the easiest targets: Good old Middle Americans.

Women fought for all manner of protection from a myriad of perceived wrongs at the hands of men, while people who stayed home, declining employment at all, demanded more and better benefits. They wrapped themselves in the convenient shelter provided by politicians intent on exploiting them into a kind of permanent liberal voting block; everybody wanted—*demanded*—something from everybody else. Everyone began to escalate this demand contest with ever more strident implications, suggesting all manner of dire results if they, whoever "they" might be, were to be disappointed.

As has been the case over the millennia of human experience, the more the idea of "give us what *we* want, and to hell with the rest" began to drive everyone, regardless of what their own special "thing" might be, the more people began to head toward the kind of polarization that had always spelled violence, eventually. This in a culture that had decided that the evils plaguing the rest of the world simply could not happen here. The remaining traditionalists, largely white, mostly churchgoing, predominantly Christian (sort of), did what ruling classes have always done: They shook their heads, mumbled a few "shoulds" and "oughts," and went out to lunch. All the way out to lunch. So the militants moved in. Everything outrageous was at least probationary, if not immediately OK. Platitudes promising vague theorems about fairness, pluralism, and non-judgmentalism appeased the masses and elected thugs like Jeffrey Flint and an army of moral and intellectual degenerates like him.

But underneath it all, behind the slick "We Are the World" veneer and the saccharin lie of concern, was the sinister evil of mankind without any truth greater than the appetites of its loudest, and often self—appointed, spokespersons. To be sure, the Gusto Generation had gone for it and had set a clear example of the ethic to be copied; but it had little or nothing to do with the brotherhood of man, Christian or otherwise.

From the professionals who sought to wring every last dime out of the people who looked to them for medical care, legal advice, technological advancement, or even recreation and entertainment, to the miscreants bent on cramming their perversions down the throats of society, the land was a fertile soil for the seeds of cataclysm and anarchy. All it would take would be the right combination of fear, deprivation, and violence to shatter what so many complacent folk thought to be beyond destruction. But then, this was a time when the impossible had become almost commonplace.

10.

The last weeks before the election were noisy and full of sound and fury as all election campaigns have always been in the U.S., with last minute scandals, late breaking revelations, and ridiculous predictions on all sides. The Kincaid/Webb ticket had pulled ahead slightly in late August, behind the most recent conviction of a pair of Flint cronies. They had first swindled the citizens of Alabama out of several hundred thousand dollars, then tried to fund the "under the table" paybacks with money made from a complicated series of cocaine transactions that had been engineered by some of the ex- president's South American buddies—leftovers from Sandinista days. The guy really had some friends in low places. Dickens did his dead level best to act outraged over the whole scene, but the drama was made more complicated by the fact that he had been closely associated with one of the convicts while employed by an elite Washington, D.C., law firm shortly before the original Flint "Run for the Rose Garden."

Kincaid hit stride with a series of ugly commercials that depicted the opposition visiting several of his best friends at the Alabama penitentiary; the last of the debates, the one between Webb and Senator Howley, had been a real bloodbath. After thirty years of expertly saying absolutely nothing every time he opened his mouth, ol' Boyd was made to wish he had died as a child when General Jackie began to fire for effect. Webb was everything Howley was not. He was incisive, erect, bold, and he was articulate. Howley was amorphous. Webb was aggressive, tough, organized, handsome, and black. Howley was not. The combination of the conviction by the Alabama jury and assault by the Marines was just too much, and the Republican ticket surged to an eight point lead with only 12 days to go until the election. Heartburn rose in the throats of the many Flint liberal client states like bitter gall, and the darkest places in all the nether world of evil began to glow with anxiety and sinister activity.

11.

Sallie was not pleased. The heat of the August night was oppressive, and sweat poured off him in tiny rivulets as he and the two charm school grads in the gray coats grunted and heaved the largest of the microwave components from their positions atop the condemned building. Stout coaxial cable lay in concentric coils around the opening in the roof, piles of wood scraps and pieces of the ancient water tank that had once served the building lay scattered around the work site, evidence of Sallie's haphazard genius for camouflage. Just one of the features of the urban guerrilla that were second to none. He had many such talents, from street intelligence to sophisticated communications devices to the fine art of the disposal of the remains of human beings. Right now he was just sweating up a storm, as the last of the pieces was stacked next to the route down into the dark structure.

The whole tenement building idea had been genius in the first place. The building was long since empty, and one of Salim's trusted operatives with connections in the Department of Public Housing succeeded in expediting the process of causing the place to be condemned as an unsafe place for human habitation. However, having first accomplished that— a feat not too tough in a city full of decay—the real trick was keeping if off the demolition list. The problem was that the demolition of condemned buildings was a major source of revenue for the mob. The contracts were always awarded according to the same indescribably complicated process, involving a myriad of political and turf lord payoffs, with the eventual award going to one of three or four "minority contractors." All of these had nominal minority participation and actual ownership by one of the old line organized crime families who had controlled and ruled the city's bureaucracy for generations. So the business of keeping one of those machines from successfully pushing its way into the assignment of leveling the place was a bit tricky.

The mission was accomplished in the most unlikely of ways. In the Office of Contract Appropriations, Department of Public Housing for the City of New York, Bronx Borough Division, there was a stout young black woman by the name of Willa C. Hathaway. She was not a boss, or even a supervisor. But she did sit at a desk that was strategically located just thirty inches away from the file cabinet that held the "process for demolition" file for the South Bronx Projects. Two feet the other way was the door to the office of the maintenance supervisor for the Bronx Building Authority, a lazy, fat slob by the name of Janus Kataschetsky. "K shit," as he was so affectionately called when he was out of earshot, was responsible for causing the buildings that had been condemned by the building inspectors to be placed on a list in that "process for demolition" file cabinet. And every time he waddled out to the top drawer, about five or six times per year, Willa Calvert Hathaway, only daughter of Willie Calvert, a/k/a Salim Abdul Alakmah, a/k/a Sallie, proprietor of the little shop of horrors down Dead Dog Lane in the South Bronx, performed her little hat trick. Fat man lists the subject building for destruction, plods off for his two hour lunch at the Polish deli down the street, and *voila!* The new entry in the demolition file disappears.

It was important, even critical, for the old tenement to stay just as it was; the Palestinians had invested over three million dollars in invisible improvements to it, all done with meticulous attention to detail, using the most expensive state of the art equipment, and all installed without the slightest attention being drawn to the delivery of the materials or their installation. The sanitary sewer hookup had been completely refurbished and fitted with new, large stainless steel pipe that was slick, clean, non-corrosive, and capable of transporting all manner of grisly effluent without clogging up or retaining evidence of what had gone through it. That plus a large, powerful, industrial strength grinder, like an enormously oversized garbage disposal mounted in the floor under that iron sink in the basement, made disposal of large biodegradable waste—like an occasional human body, in appropriately sized pieces—a real breeze.

The elevator worked; the electricity worked. The water worked. These little public utility conveniences were compliments of a creative billing anomaly that caused the bills to be sent to a post office box in Cleveland, where they were processed and paid out of a small balance checking account drawn on a bank in Chicago. It was funded by monthly cash deposits via a small elderly woman who was well paid to appear at a different branch each month, where she put several hundred dollars in small, wrinkled bills into the

41

account. In fact, there was also an elderly man doing the same thing, and neither knew about the other, so that between them they deposited about three thousand dollars to the account each month. Checks were mailed from Milwaukee, Gary, even Des Moines, in payment of utility bills for Arafat's quaint satellite office. And the whole financial thing, only a tiny part of the funding that accomplished the maintenance of this covert operation, could be dissolved without a shred of paper trail in a matter of minutes. About every three months, that was exactly what was done. New bank, different old folks, changed signatures on the checks, the whole program.

Aside from the technological wizardry that was everywhere apparent inside the nasty exterior, the most awesome feature and best concealed secret of Sallie's Palestinian Annex (hereinafter "SPA") was the huge stockpile of weapons, explosives, and ammunition he held there. And with the order to pull in all offsite stored ordnance, the quantum of deadly devices had burgeoned to near capacity. Hundreds of AK—47s, mostly Chinese—made and still in the oriental version of cosmolene (packing grease), hundreds of 9 millimeter handguns, Glocks, Berettas, and a variety of Chinese makes, plus 150 Mac 10s, Uzis, and similar small submachine pistols filled the lead -lined, climate—controlled storage rooms that comprised the terrorists' urban armory. There were even 100 Hechler and Koch MP5s, the choice of the American military elite for close—in combat.

Grenades, cases of C4 plastic explosive and many cases of LAWs—light anti-tank weapons—pre-loaded, disposable and filled with high explosive charges capable of bringing down large aircraft at low altitudes, gave the place the capability of being vaporized into one big smelly crater, if the right—or wrong—combination of factors was to combine in just the right—or wrong—way, at just the right—well, anyway, the result could be devastating. With the last of Sallie's off-site ammo stashes consolidated into the big house, he could report compliance with the last directive in the most recent communication from the Committee: "Complete all prescribed preparations."

Book I – You're It

* * * * *

The invisible scramble that began in earnest with the last Gallup poll had the look of one of those macabre medieval paintings that depicts peasants running from the attacking hordes of murderous Mongols. Except it was, unless one knew what to look for, invisible. Flint, allegedly back in Alabama, licking his wounds and acting innocent while spending every waking minute trying to raise money for his own defense fund, was travelling more than anyone, including the CIA, knew. From the small cement landing field in the middle of an old family cotton plantation, a small biz jet would land without lights well after dark, at least twice a week. Swishing off into the blackness, it would take him to a variety of interesting places, including, on three occasions over that summer, to Beirut. Not Beirut, Mississippi, but the real place. The one where that Arab scholar had blown himself and all those Marines to bits when Reagan was president.

It was not that he was so powerful, or even that he was involved in their evil plans; it was more like he was the dealer who had lost his merchandise and still owed the suppliers for it. He went for the money, to be sure. Old "Nobel Peace Prize" himself, Yasser the Butcher, had seen to it that the enormous wealth of the Arab world would be channeled to assist in the defeat of those infidel Republicans. Flint had pledged to keep the heat on the Israelis to keep up "the peace process", an interesting euphemism that translated into continuing a diplomatic and financial campaign to force the Jews to keep giving up real estate.

When Jeffrey Flint hit the political wall, the Palestinians were distressed, to say the least. Now they flew him over to the Promised Land to apply pressure, lots of it, reminding him in a variety of ways about all the things he had promised, pumping him for information and predictions about the impending election and pushing him to tell them what the results of a Republican sweep might be. And, of course, with the continuing efforts on the Right to get the ex—president indicted, his need for money in large quantities kept him interested in their attentions.

Most of all, they wanted to know about this Leatherneck vice presidential candidate, who was shortly to become that underemployed guy who was at any given moment just one heartbeat from the Oval Office. But on that subject, Flint was of very little help. The general's personnel file was pretty straight ahead—the only things negative had to do with some messy barroom brawls when he was still a recovering vet with too much piss and vinegar and not enough enemies to vanquish. Marriage had fixed that, and his performance in every one of his assignments, his War College and Command & General Staff school records, and his brilliance as Chairman of the Joint Chiefs during the Central American Offensive were so good, nobody really cared if he occasionally got a bit rowdy with his compatriots. Truth be known, that remaining bit of "loose cannon" imagery was very attractive to the Middle American, working class people who made up such a large percentage of the voting population. All Jeff could tell them was that he was hard to predict, difficult to argue with, and impossible to control. Not the news that hairy old bandit and his murderous entourage wanted to hear.

The real problem with Flint and the Palestinians, or Flint and the Russians, or for that matter, Flint and *any* faction, interest group or fringe element that could get his ear, usually by way of his pocket—or his crotch—had always been that he was not what he appeared to be, or what he might say he was. The idea of power, and the very suggestion that he and Billie might actually occupy that ultimate seat of power, was so intoxicating that he had always been more than happy to say whatever his immediate audience wanted to hear. He was for or against tax breaks, for or against abortion, for or against a balanced budget, for or against "you name it," without regard to what he might truly believe; he would simply say what seemed popular, without compunction.

That was the kind of politician "we the people" had sunk to in the '90s. And it was those opportunistic promises and the view that our enemies were really the folks we should cultivate that had gotten him—and the country—into such a mess of intrigue and trick bags. He was the perfect epitome of the oily politician, the deal maker, the chameleon—a card shark who was happy to deal with the Devil himself if it would help his own quest for power and position. Huge contributions to his campaign, by foreign countries, had been instrumental in the reality of his presidency. Obviously his failure to stay put in the place where his client states had installed him was a big problem for all of them. His conversations with Arafat and Co. were less than pleasant that summer. Unfortunately, they always let him come home. Even a snake like Arafat has standards.

12.

The stoic dignity of Chief Justice William Renquist, his sonorous voice intoning the Oath of Office, the brilliant cold sunlight in the Rose Garden, and the click of cameras and whir of video cameras created a deja vu for the General, sending his memory racing back to 1971. He had stood in this exact same place, felt the exact same sun on his broad shoulders, heard the same sounds, and listened to Richard Nixon's voice awarding him the Medal of Honor. Now, twenty six years and several lifetimes later, they had just made him President of the United States of America.

For the next three days, the new president was sucked through a tornado of activities that kept him so busy, there were times when he actually had no idea where he was, what he was doing, or what was next. In the midst of state appearances and endless events associated with the wake and funeral of his predecessor, there was the business of fielding a team to run the executive branch of the government. Kincaid's choices for most of the cabinet—level positions were fine with Webb; the two men not only shared very similar political philosophies, but they knew many of the same people. Both had long, deep ties with the military, and both had lived in and around Washington for many years.

The White House staff, the people whose job it is to turn orders into action, created a different problem. Kincaid had been eccentric, a sometimes unpredictable personality, and the people who were his choices for top inside positions reflected that. Too young and "pretty" to suit the Marine, they needed to be replaced with people more direct, more down to earth, and less arrogant than some of those chosen by Kincaid.

No such problem existed between the new president and Mac Reed, Kincaid's chief of staff, however. An ex—Marine himself, the two had served together after Vietnam, once in Europe and again as instructors and cadre at Parris Island, that infamous garden spot off the coast of North Carolina where the Marines and the Navy SEALs attempt to drown their young. Reed had also served in Southeast Asia, but he had been a snoop—an intelligence officer, who had "officially" *not* been in Laos, *not* been in Cambodia, and *not* been in Thailand, for an *un*official two and one—half years. While

46

there he had officially *not* killed several of the enemy's upper leadership, in his efforts to slow the flow of men and weapons to the VC. The two men then shared two assignments and, while Webb was racing through the ranks of the USMC, Reed was deciding to go back to law school and skip the ongoing picnics at Parris Island. So when Webb had to make some quick decisions about what to do to build a staff, Reed was an easy choice.

The Inauguration was on a Friday, and Kincaid's funeral was on the following Tuesday. And even though he had only been president for a few hours when he died, he was a well—known figure around the world, and dignitaries from every point of the globe came to pay their respects. As a veteran of the military service, he was entitled to burial at Arlington National Cemetery, and Sarah, his only child, had expressed that desire. So they prepared the whole drill: the cortege drawn by black horses, the riderless stallion with the backward boots in the chrome stirrups, the long procession from the Capitol Rotunda to the burial site, the twenty-one gun salute. The *Navy Hymn* was followed by *Taps*, and the Marine Color Guard snapped and popped Old Glory as they folded it above the plain black casket, turning then to reverently hand it to Sarah. She stood unsteadily beside, and held onto the powerful arm of, the new president. She turned a few degrees, handed the flag to the new First Lady, then collapsed into the arms of the man who had saved the life of her beloved father so long ago and so very far away.

Although Webb and Kincaid had not maintained any kind of close relationship after the war, the name of Jackie Robinson Webb had been a household word to the Kincaid family, spoken always with a combination of awe and good humor. The man was, in a very direct way, responsible for the very existence of that household. Had Webb not saved Kincaid from that jungle death, no household would ever have been possible. Like so many young men who had fought there, Kincaid was young when he left for war, and had no wife or children. Now it only made perfect sense for his only child, a carbon copy of his dead wife, sole representative at the funeral, to seek the strength, dignity, and tenderness of her father's hero to stand by her side at this moment. Around the world, every wire service, television station, newspaper, and magazine printed the image of this grieving young woman sobbing into the sad countenance of the new man who occupied the ultimate seat of power.

The ceremony ended, and the First Family plus Sarah Kincaid rode back to the White House in a huge black Cadillac limousine, complete with Secret Service agents running alongside, helicopters overhead, and thousands of curious faces lining the street. Sarah sat between Molly and the president, a hand in each of theirs, staring blankly through swollen eyes into the emptiness of her shattered dreams. She had been ever so close to her father, and his triumph was shared completely with her. Now she could only hear the hollow ringing in her ears, see the blur of faces and fading color in the cold late—afternoon January air. Somehow, the pomp and dignity of the ceremony had not dulled the pain of his loss, nor even the outpouring of sentiment from around the world. The only comfort came from the gentle voice of Pastor Wilkinson, as he read favorite passages of her father's from the New Testament—Matthew and John—and from the presence of Jackie and Molly Webb. The cellular phone rang in the back of the limo. Webb absently answered "Webb here," as he had for the entirety of his military life. "Mr. President? This is Bill Greeley, at Langley. Sir, what is your ETA back to the White House?" Webb looked out for a street sign. "We're five minutes out. Whatcha got?"

"Better do this on a secure line, sir. We'll have people waiting.

Thank you, sir. Oh, and sir, congratulations. . .I mean. . and sorry about the president—I mean the *other* pres—I mean . . .I'm sorry for him, 'er them, I mean, but, ah. . .but congrats to . . .I mean. . ."

Webb smiled slightly, "*Thank* you, son, I understand." The line went silent.

* * * * *

All weekend, they had been watching a small number of odd circumstances that kept appearing, disappearing, and reappearing, in places far distant from each other, but disquietingly similar. Within four hours of the discovery that the new president was dead in his bed, the White House situation room began receiving the reports. The CIA reported satellite images of large convoys of truck movement in the deserts of Iraq, headed west toward Syria. What was of concern was that nobody had known there were any trucks or *anything* in that entire region until the trucks suddenly appeared moving across the sand. Then intelligence sources in Paris reported an impending assassination plot concerning the new premier of Israel, Benjamin Netenyahou. That report was confirmed by Israeli intelligence, and an attempt to blow up the new man was foiled, but not before a shootout on the streets of Tel Aviv ended with a dozen dead Palestinians and two dead Mossad officers. The Premier was not injured but had the crap scared out of him, along with a large contingent of his personal staff and all his kids.

The British intelligence service, MI 6, had also gotten wind of the Israeli problem, plus a report that an Arab terrorist was seeking asylum in London, claiming he knew about a large cache of C4 explosives and arms somewhere in New York City. Then someone blew up a small electric substation outside a suburb of Dallas, blacking out about 300 homes and a score of businesses. The bomb was believed to have been C4—not a true connection, but strange anyway, in light of the NYC report that had surfaced within a few hours before the blast. And, of course, the new president had died in his sleep, leaving things in a pretty chaotic state in the nerve center of the most powerful, and therefore most vulnerable, capitol in the world.

None of these things, with the possible exception of the trucks in the Iraqi desert, were particularly surprising, but they had a commonality about them—all bore characteristics long associated with the militant terrorist population worldwide that had always been Muslim in root and Palestinian in architecture. "And," thought the new chief executive to himself as he looked at all these like chess pieces, "Jack Kincaid died the night of his inauguration. Interesting coincidence." Now ol' General Jackie had learned a few things from his Jewish buddies in the Mossad, back in the days when they engaged in some top secret joint exercises while he commanded an operation in Germany, before the Bible School experience at Parris Island. One of the first things those crafty bastards had taught him was that "coincidence is not a kosher word." Everything had a reason and a purpose in their world. Jackie liked the ring of that one and had made it his own.

* * * * *

On the Saturday that Kincaid died, a small but very elite crew of forensic pathologists gathered in a secure lab at Andrews Air Force Base to attend what the three of them ghoulishly called "the presidential autopsy party." These were men who spent their lives inside the bodies of people who had died from some unnatural cause, usually violent, and often gruesome.

They were assembled at the order of a man who had not been president long enough for the ink to dry on the signature of the Chief Justice; the erstwhile vice president now *president* had quietly caused things to start getting done his way. Right after sitting down at the end of the actual swearing in, and while William F. Buckley, Jr., spoke of the fallen president, through a serene facial expression that appeared cast from bronze, Webb smiled at Mac Reed and, motioning him closer, growled through motionless lips, "Where is Kincaid's body?"

Reed, still trying hard to maintain some grip on himself and all that had happened in such a short time, looked at him like the new man had just broken wind into his public address microphone. Webb's eyes hardened, his half smile vanished as he bored into the face of the incredulous chief of staff, and he said in a voice audible only to Reed, "Mac! answer me before I jerk you out of that rented tux; where is Jack's body? Where did they take it, and what's been done with it?"

Reed then comprehended that the questioner was not making idle conversation, but was being *very* insistent and extremely focused on this subject. "They took the body to Andrews, I told them to lock it up and keep it under armed military guard. Why?"

Webb relaxed the tensed muscles in his neck only a bit, sighed almost imperceptibly and, leaning slightly forward, addressed Reed again. "That body goes *no place*, OK? *No place.* Confirm that—now. Scramble a forensics team, the best at CIA, and set up an autopsy for this afternoon, if possible. Make it clear that nobody is to *touch* that corpse

50

until the docs and the crime lab people are finished. *Are you clear?"*

The imperious tone was so demanding, and so overwhelming, that Reed found himself coming to attention in his seat, and responding "yes, sir," instantly. Without even breathing first, he excused himself and found a telephone to confirm the President's order.

So the blood and guts squad went to work on the presidential corpse, took it apart from head to toes, weighed its organs, measured its retained fluids, and came to an odd conclusion: The man was fine. No hemorrhage, no stroke, no damage to the heart muscle consistent with myocardial infarction (heart attack), no trauma, normal blood work, the picture of health. Except he was dead. In the average morgue the coroner or death examiner would just call the cause of death "cardiac arrest" because it was in fact obvious that the man's heart had stopped. And these guys, even with all their special skills and experience, said the same things. But seeing a perfectly healthy dead man, who had died without the assistance of any violent or forceful means, left these mad scientists unsatisfied.

They knew what the General would want—to find out what had killed the new president. And that meant some tests that could not be performed at the time of the post mortem examination. So they bagged up all the organs, including the brain, stomach and intestinal tract, heart, liver—the whole mess of innards—and put it in the cold vault at the Andrews morgue. They just wanted the opportunity to see what the lab would say about this body's organs after observing absolutely nothing upon gross examination.

13.

The crisp cold, although intensified in the dark, damp alley that concealed the SPA, at least reduced the smell associated with warmer weather in that garden spot of the Bronx. As usual, the important meetings happened at night, and this one included one of the whitest faces ever to occupy the basement environs, except for those being tortured. This one, a stocky man in his early fifties, wore a scholarly tweed sport coat and heavy pants; he had a thick head of blond hair, flecked with subtle highlights of gray, and he wore wire rimmed glasses that looked like a re-run of the 60s. He sat tensely at the same table that had been covered with the instruments of the unspeakable when Jonathan Abdelmanek had come to call months ago. Only this time, the host was ever so much more hospitable. Because this man, Willard Smalley, MBA from Harvard in finance, MS from MIT in computer science, and paid mercenary spy for the PLO, was also the director of operations for the Wire Transfer Division for the New York branch of the Federal Reserve Bank. Translated, he was a money—smart computer genius who had access to, and control of, one of the largest electronic banking operations in the world. Estimates varied, but it was well known that the operation for that he was responsible moved in excess of five *billion* dollars each day.

As Smalley shifted uncomfortably in the hard chair, at that table, in that basement room of horrors, Abdul Salim Alakmah made every effort to provide a measure of comfort for his guest. Small talk, compliments, dirty jokes, all failed to produce any evidence of a relaxation in Mr. Smalley, so after a few minutes of that effort Sallie approached the subject that had been the reason for the visit in the first place.

"You see, Willard, I—we—the *Committee*—is interested in experimenting with an interruption in the flow of electronic money, targeting the New York Fed operation as the test site. We want to see if an unexplained 'problem' with the big computer that drives the whole program could actually produce results in communities remote from the situs of the actual problem. Can you help, my good man?" Sallie did his best to hide the bloody creature he really was, but poor old Willard was not fooled. His skin crawled and his bowels rumbled, but he nodded affirmatively, thinking at once about the price that would be paid for the chance to perform such an "experiment." He had already decided, before even coming to that awful place, that his silence would be expensive, and his help even more so, if they really wanted to get into the money system without detection.

"The irony of the whole thing, Mr. Alakmah, is that—"

"Please, call me Sallie; we shall see each other often, I hope, so such formality should not be an impediment!" Stiff smile from the guest.

"As you wish, *Sallie*—as I was saying, the whole thing is really not so complex. To be sure, the system operates in a complex environment, with complex results, but the actual machinery that drives the NACHA and CHIPS systems, and really that of the entire Fedwire system, is run from a single room, on a single, very powerful computer, over on Long Island. It is one of the inside jokes in our business that the electronic transmission of funds, *worldwide,* is so deceptively simple, at least in terms of the mechanics of origination." (NACHA is the National Automated Clearinghouse Association, and CHIPS is the Clearinghouse for International Payment Systems.)

"Now, can I cause an interruption in that flow? Absolutely. But you see, the problem with the simplicity is that, because it is so simple, it is also more difficult to conceal an unauthorized entry and the resulting sabotage. That is to say, getting caught, or at least being identified, is extremely likely."

"That is why we have experts, like *you,* Willard. . . to handle such fine points as concealment, timing, and effect. All we really want right now is a test—a subtle little blip on the electronic money radar that will tell us just how vulnerable the whole thing is, and therefore, how effective a major interruption might be. We will then integrate that piece into the architecture of the bigger operation for execution at the appropriate time."

"I understand. However, there is the subject of compensation. There are great risks, security measures to be avoided, and I cannot trust any of that to anyone else. I shall have to do it all myself."

"Of course. We would not expect such assistance for free. I have been authorized to transfer $100,000.00 to you upon completion of the experiment. I am prepared to pay

$25,000.00 at this moment." Silence. More silence. Staring at the floor, the walls, the floor again. More silence. Willard Smalley had other ideas, much bigger goals in the money department, and he was about to say so. But the horrific reputation of his present host, not to mention the host's even more horrific employer, had his heart pounding and his bowels threatening to explode within him.

"With all due respect, Sallie, to you and to the Committee. That is unacceptable." Long pause. Many short breaths unsuccessfully concealed. "I require $1 million for the first experiment. Half now, and the rest in escrow with automatic release provisions upon completion. I can cause the transfer to be electronically initiated upon the execution of the order creating the desired disruption. You will have the capability to reverse the transaction only if the effects on the system do not result. All very safe, very discreet, and extremely effective."

Another pause. Deep breath. Sallie's breathing was also quickening, and his eyes were acquiring that vacant animal quality that came with the awakening of his more carnivorous instincts.

"For the big event, the price is $100 million. All to remote accounts, deposited in the same manner. If all this works, money will become an immediately extinct commodity, and the possibility of moving around with currency will be nonexistent. You understand, I am sure."

A really long pause occurred next. Sallie stood up, much taller than his measly frame would seem to allow, and began to pace. His jaws flexed, his eyes darted around the room over and over. The tools of torture were within his grasp, and the massive door was locked tight. Willie Calvert wanted blood. He wanted screaming, pleading, insane agony. But Abdul Salim Alakmah was obedient to his master.

He turned quickly and spoke in his huge tones. "This is far beyond my authority—to make such an arrangement. I shall consult with my contacts and return. Of course, you cannot leave this place. If they wish to do such business at such an exorbitant rate, I shall arrange it. If they do not, we will burn you alive. Either way, you must wait." He walked over to the other door, leading to the elevators and storage vaults, walked through it, and closed it behind him. The sounds of electronic locking mechanisms, the whirring of arming devices, and the heavy clank of the big iron bar that provided the fail-safe for the whole thing, caused Smalley to jump clear off his chair. He closed his eyes and fought with all his might to resist the urge to soil his pants.

* * * * *

The dull sheen to the hard floors in the basement of the main hospital melded with the ever so beige tile covering the walls and the dirty almost white of the ceiling tiles; there was little to engage the senses or stimulate the imagination when walking through this subterranean tunnel. But Richard Andrew Freeman, M.D., Ph.D., biochemist, cellular biologist, and forensic pathologist, had no such problems. With the thundering black passions of the Mozart *Requiem* roaring in his head, some unrecognizable moaning escaping from his throat as he absently hummed along with himself, an occasional glutteral *pfft!', teeTOM! or PomPomPom. . ."* of his own percussion section punctuating the ensemble, and his yellowish green eyes flitting around the flat surfaces; this guy was a real one man band. And anybody who happened to pass him as he droned along would be sure to remark that "*that* is one weird sonofabitch!" Of course, had they said so, or if they had announced it over the loud speaker, or even if they had screamed it in his oval little face, Dickie Freeman would never have heard them, so loud was the music in his head, and so complex and varied was the conversation being carried on inside it. Dickie *was* weird, *very* weird—always had been. But by the time his face had begun to clear up from his adolescent bout with acne, the kids were figuring out some very important and unique things about this gnomey little guy.

Dickie was basically harmless and, except for the eccentricities associated with people of really huge intellect, and except for being only a little over five feet tall, he was really a very normal, nice person. When the girls in his chemistry class began to realize, quite by accident, that he could balance an equation, recite a formula, and explain why the valances could only be a certain way if the thing was to balance—and that he would explain it clearly and without the least arrogance—his stature began to increase, figuratively at least. Oh, a couple of times some of the jocks tried to get ugly about the attention he got from one of the more buxom cheerleaders (when Dickie sat at his desk in Calculus and Buffy VanMiddlestein, captain of the cheerleading team, stood beside him, he looked directly into the Bosum of Everyman's Dreams, without lifting his eyes two degrees from straight ahead). Dirk Jackson, a thick necked—and even thicker headed—running back who spent a lot of each day with his hands in his pockets as he leered at Buffy, nearly decompensated one day when he looked into the Calculus classroom from his seat across the hallway in General Math. Dickie's round little Charlie Brown head appeared to have completely vanished into mammary oblivion as Buffy stood behind him. Of course, it was only the angle from that he observed them—and the size of Buffy's bust—and the coincidental backlighting from the afternoon sun through the closed blinds, but it was an effect that was too much for poor Dirk.

Dirk was suspended from school after the authorities pieced together the fragments of the story, but Dickie was really unhurt, only shaken a bit by his violent and high speed ride across the hall, down the steps, and into the dumpster outside the Vocational and Career Center's back door. Well, Dickie spoke up for Dirk, the principal relented and let him play in the County Tourney, and Dickie even helped the cretin pass General Math. The jocks invited him to the big Senior picnic and all night party, at the end of their last year. Wandering among the giants, he looked like a forlorn escapee from a daycare center, but that day gave him a lifetime of memories. He would never forget languishing in the drunken clutches of poor sick Buffy VanMiddlestein, as she bewailed her revulsion at all those groping apes from the Athletic Department. Clad in a bikini that was clearly inadequate to the task of supporting her substantial attributes, she had sworn, preached, and finally wept to Dickie about her feminine plight, while dipstick Dickie continued to try to keep up with Buffy in the Beer Department. Problem was that she had about twice the body mass, so a beer to her was worth about 1.6 beers to him. (That had been his biochemical calculation, right before he had passed out.) The last thing Dickie remembered—and he remembered it well and for a long time—had been the sobbing Buffy, cradling his little head against her, at first almost exploding his tender pysche with such sensory and sensual overload, then nearly suffocating him. And Dickie made no move to take unfair advantage; not that he had much choice, pinned in the drunken wreckage of Buffy's sadness. He really was a nice guy—he was just so smart.

So Richard Andrew Freeman made his dizzy way to the morgue, humming, mumbling, and of course, *thinking* all the way. Now this fellow was no stranger to morgues, in general or to this morgue in particular, so the mystery tour into the guts of dead people was nothing out of the ordinary to him. A table full of organs, a string of smelly intestines, even an occasional smushed eyeball on a glass slide was pretty much just another day at the office. But *this*—what the *hell* is *this?*

"*Sir*. Restricted area, sir, sorry, no admittance." Private First Class Ormond, Charles A., U.S. Air Force Military Police, Special Security Detachment, Andrews Air Force Base. The music stopped in Dickie's head, and he looked at the soldier in the blue uniform as if words had just emitted from a urinal. "*What?* What do you mean, 'no admittance'? How the hell am I supposed to do what they asked me to do if I can't go in the freaking morgue? Huh? Whatcha think, soldier? Problem, huh?"

"Sorry, sir, orders. Nobody goes in there without presidential authorization. You'll have to leave."

"Oh. *Oh.* Oh yeah. That. Here." Dickie fumbled around in the side pocket of his lab coat, searched the breast pocket of his shirt, stuffed his hands in both the pockets of his pants, and then began to frisk himself all over. "Shit. It's here someplace. Crissakes, if I lost that goddam letter...*There!*. . . no, that's a laundry ticket. . .maybe in my appointment book. . .shit. . ."

The soldier stifled a smile, copped a particularly military attitude: "Sorry sir, you can't stay here. Orders. No loitering. You'll have to leave the area. *Now.*"

"OK OK—just a second—*OH!* Now I remember. . .*here* it is. . ." He reached into the zippered pocket in the top of his back-pack/napsack/lunch bag and was just pulling out a wrinkled envelope when the security detail descended on him. "*Wait! What the hell*. . . hey you guys, wait just a goddam min. . .*HEY, YOU MISERABLE PIECE OF . . HEY!*"

They had him under the arms, one on each side, and his feet were now approximately thirty inches off the ground, churning bicycle style. His backpack was flapping along, back and forth, as they hauled his tiny ass back in the direction from that it had come, quick time, when Private First Class Ormond, the first guard, the one who had told him to leave, looked down at that shiny floor. There, soiled, smudged, and with a size 13 combat boot print across the front, was an open envelope that bore the Great Seal of the United States of America, and that also carried, in the return address area, the words "The White House, 1600 Pennsylvania Avenue, Washington, D.C." Now the *soldier* gasped, quoth his *own* "Oh shit," and, as soon as his voice came back, called out to the two thugs who were disposing of Dickie. "Schmidt. . *HOLD IT!* Bring the guy back here— *NOW!"* No response. The racket being created by their own grunting and shuffling, plus the noise emitting from the little squirt being hauled off, was too much. The sentry panicked, having spilled the entire contents of the august envelope out onto the floor. As his ashen countenance beheld the letter, the top secret clearance badge, and the multipage briefing materials, marked with several "EYES ONLY" stamps, his pulse seemed about to burst his eyes from their sockets. He leaped forward, screaming, now pleading in a high pitch, "Schmidt, *SCHMIDT!!!* for the love of God, Schmidt, put the little bastard...I mean. . .Holy shit. SCHMIDT!!! He's got orders Schmidt!! He's got fucking orders*!!!* We're about to get our butts court—martialed! Put the guy *DOWN!!!"*

Schmidt heard that last part about orders and court— martials, stopped, turned slowly, and beheld the macabre death look on his buddy's face. The other goon—the one with Dickie's other armpit in his hands, looked at Schmidt, then at Ormond, then at Dickie, who was by now precisely the color of ripe cranberries, then back at Schmidt, at the wad of papers in Ormond's hand, and then back at Dickie again. The two enforcers began a slow and deliberate lowering action—kind of like the stuff the honor guards do when laying a beloved corpse to rest, or setting flowers at the tomb of some unknown soldier—very, *very* carefully.

Dickie's feet gently touched the ground, and he felt the grip on his arm pits released; those little yellow—green eyes saw the whole picture, and Richard Andrew Freeman, M.D., Ph.D., was pissed. Spinning toward the direction of the morgue entrance, he withered Ormond with his gaze alone.

Book I – You're It

The two thugs stepped quietly, quickly back, and the doctor snapped to the closest thing he could get to attention. Straightening his lab coat, adjusting his glasses, he stalked back toward his point of origin.

"Sorry, sir. I didn't know. Orders, sir, you know. They said no one in without clearance from General Jackie—I mean—the President, sir and well, you see, ah, well, and. . . you know. . .you didn't have no ID sir, and well. . .Holy Jeses, sir, I'm sure sorry and . . ."

"*Forget it*. Just forget it, pal. OK? Let's just forget the whole thing, OK? Just let me in the freaking morgue now. Can we do that?" The inflection made the little man roughly the size of Roosevelt Grier, with the voice of the Almighty Himself.

"*Oh yessir, sir,* I mean, sir, er, *SURE!*" He spun around and barked at the giant PFC who stood obscuring the door to the lab. "*Whitson! Open the door and let the doctor in! NOW!*" Whitson did as directed. Instantly. The doors to the ghoulish mystery chamber stood open, with the eyes of all four sentries fixed on it, and on Dickie. For a moment he could hear the Mozart starting up again, and then, before slipping back into genius land, he saw the situation with stark clarity—only for a moment. He willed the smile not to appear on his face; refused to give vent to the giggle in his throat, the snicker in his nose. The old nice guy in him really couldn't get too crazy, or too mean, but the *doctor*, on the other hand, had just been manhandled, berated, and "escorted" out of his own domain. *Some* return fire was required.

He stood erect. His eyes focused on the open door. Then, as though Walter Mitty had just become Douglas MacArthur, he strode with great purpose and dignity through the gaping faces and into the morgue. Stopping, he turned smartly and, smiling only slightly and with condescension dripping from his small countenance, he slammed the door. Hard. He thought for a moment and could not remember ever having *strode* before. It felt good. He liked it. The previously stifled smile broadened across his round face, and he permitted himself a chuckle. His little chest swelled to its scrawny maximum, and he chuckled again. If Buffy could only see him now. Then the *Requiem* kicked in again, and he turned toward the refrigerated body vaults and the work at hand.

14.

Jericho Road was supposedly a paved surface. But as Josh swerved all over the thing in his quest to achieve the driveway, he swore again at the ineptitude of the County Highway dopes who never seemed to have enough goop to fill the potholes all the way up—or enough smarts to discover the horrendous condition of this road at all. Many times he was certain nobody in the bureaucracy even knew Jericho Road was in their jurisdiction at all; then he could hear his older brother opining that the dilapidated condition of the road only served to discourage traffic and to keep the speed down below racetrack pace. Carl often fought fits of apoplexy when "some asshole in a BMW" came roaring past, even honking his arrogant horn if the guys happened to be impeding his imperial path with their horses, or a tractor pulling a hay wagon, or even just standing at the roadside getting the mail.

"I'd give a month's pay for the chance to watch that yuppie break an axle on one of our little tank traps! Sumbitches think they own the goddam roads, anyway. Best reason I can think of to let the road go *completely* to hell—keep those little pencil necks out of the country."

Josh dodged the last of the really big holes, then braced himself for the sheer break in the edge of the pavement at the end of the drive and began to build the billow of dust that would announce his approach. Dust knew no season on the prairie, returning within hours of any precipitation, frozen or otherwise. The evening ambush ritual was suspended, as sweet Jessica was sitting on the porch swing with a pan of fresh green beans in her lap. It was January, so the beans were store bought and flown in from far away, and the porch swing seemed a strange venue for a rest; but the temperature was mild—almost sixty—as they were enjoying one of those odd but welcome midwinter thaws so common but so unpredictable in the Midwest. Everyone knew how quickly the bottom could and *would* fall out again, so Jess was not about to miss the opportunity to pretend it was spring, just for one or two evenings. A heavy sweater and jeans made up for what the low, distant orange sun failed to deliver. Somewhat surprised to see her husband before six o'clock, she smiled.

"Whatsamatter—they run out of booze at the gin mill? Or did you suddenly develop an aversion to women in cellophane tee shirts?" The wise ass gene was working well, as her daddy would have quickly noticed. Ol' Mick woulda' been proud. Richland PD had never had a cop more full of the blarney, or the courage, of Matthew Michael O'Neal, homicide detective, Irish beer drinker through and through, and victim of the advent of gang violence to the Heartland. His murder, in a shootout with a gang of young blacks from the ever-growing housing projects on the near west side of Richland, nearly killed Jess as well; the only man she had ever loved and trusted, besides Josh, had been her—red faced, red—headed father. It had been over three years since his death, and even now the whole ordeal woke her in the dead of night. And just to keep the wound open, they had never caught the kids responsible.

The mayor, a chickenshit little man with all the courage of jello, had decided that the racial problem he faced would not be helped by an aggressive investigation of the problem. So he followed the lead of luminaries like Neville Chamberlain and decided to try appeasement. The leaders of the black community—self proclaimed—had stonewalled the investigation at once, and every time a cop got close to the facts or the killers, they'd raise hell and go marching into the mayor's office claiming more racial invective. Or they might call a news conference and say the same thing for a larger audience. That so terrified the guy that he began to react to their antics almost on command.

The result was twofold: First, the murderers got away with killing a policeman; second, the gangs began to see themselves as bulletproof, and their activities and their violent rhetoric began to accelerate. Fact was, the black community was as terrified of the bloodthirsty bastards as the mayor was. But their spokesmen, a bunch of loudmouthed lay preachers—what and *whom* they were laying was much in doubt, as they all seemed well healed, well oiled, and usually well accompanied by one or more ladies in waiting, gave new meaning to the term "lay ministry."

Anyway, the folks in the black neighborhoods, the ones who were working everyday to support their families and better themselves, took the crap in silence, afraid to speak out against their "spokesmen" and the hoods thus protected from just and merited prosecution. The real problem was that they *had* no voice; and the climate of violence and the rhetoric of separatism that filled the streets only redoubled their well-founded belief that silence was the only protection they had.

Josh reddened at the short fusillade emitting from his wife's quick tongue, smiled briefly, and disappeared into the kitchen. He returned with two beers and, sliding the sack of beans over to the end of the swing, plopped down next to her. "Naw, just got tired of all that flesh, that's all. And besides, like they always say, 'ya seen one, 'ya seen 'em both!' Right?" He ducked a handful of beans, dodged a weak backhand, then stole a kiss. End of match.

They began to visit about home and kids, beans and kittens, new toys and old bikes with flat tires. The sun of late January sank low in the sky, and the clouds around it exploded into one of those orange and red fire shows that only seem to happen in the winter. They grew silent, watching the sunset, while the muffled sounds of the kids inside made for a moment of real peace. Then Jess noticed that her husband was no longer looking at the beauty; his gaze was toward the floor of the porch, distracted, distant. And this woman who knew this man so well—this woman who had seen all those hidden scars, those awful wounds, and that dark passion—immediately knew there was more to this moment than snap beans and a January sunset. The knots in his jaw betrayed the warrior's thoughts.

"Josh, hey. . .Joshua Owen Landry!. . .hey, you're home early. Honey, what *is* it?" Josh looked away, squinting into the light. Back to the floor of the porch. To his hands, knotted in fists, then massaging his scarred knees.

He took a deep breath. "I got a call from Bill Cargil at the FBI today. You know, the guy on that gang taskforce that's been working on Mick's case for the last few months? He's been pretty good about letting me know what they're doing. After that first bunch of assholes who refused to talk to us at all, I guess this is a pretty big improvement. Anyway, even though I've been gone from the Prosecutor's Office for a while, the guy calls me when he has anything to report. Deal is, they've found a lead on LaShawn Mitchell. Apparently he beat feet for Chicago, then Detroit, right after the shooting, and a different chapter of his gang hid him out for a long time.

Now he's been sighted back in Richland, according to Cargil's snitch."

The gang that had killed her father, Jess knew, was still in existence, and Mitchell had been one of the top dogs among those vermin when the shooting started; at least three different sources had told police he had been the trigger man. That, added to the fact he had split instantly afterward and the rumor that he himself was shot in the battle with Mick and his troops, made it ever more likely that he had a good reason for making himself scarce.

Still, such news, although important information, was not earthshaking; similar updates had occurred over the last year or more, and all they really meant was that the investigation had not been closed—no thanks to the gutless wonder in the mayor's office. Nothing in this report could account for her husband's dark countenance as he sat in the fading, now chilly light of evening in the country. She reached out with an upturned hand, fingertips gently under his chin, green eyes like X-ray, voice softly probing. "Josh, I'm glad to hear they continue to work the case. Daddy would be gratified at their efforts. He always thought a lot of the FBI—particularly *'those taskforce bastards'*, he always called them. But Josh. . .that doesn't account for what I see in your face. Your eyes look like one of those old 3 a.m. flashback episodes. Come on. . . Look at me. *Talk* to me. Tell me the rest."

The ghosts of evil and death had long been stilled in his head. The country, the work, and the family had so filled his thoughts, and finally his being, that there was no room for the nightmares and the flashbacks anymore. Hell, just the woman herself was sufficient to have exorcised the demons. Her presence, her scent, her beautiful body, her consuming direct, passionate self so intoxicated him that the whole experience, from that first moment in the psych ward at the hospital to the present moment, was a seamless fabric of joy and satisfaction. From being lovers, to being married, to childbirth and the building of their lives together, she was the complete woman, the complete wife. But nothing had ever happened since she first came to him that threatened her or their family. Not one moment had passed when he sensed danger, felt fear. Until now.

"Mitchell is apparently more than just another punk— more than just one more loudmouthed hood. The Islamic New

World, a western arm of the PLO, apparently hid him and got him treated for some pretty bad gunshot wounds. Took over a year to get him nursed back to health. I guess he was out here from a big cell of this Islamic thing somewhere in New York City. Supposedly teaching 'the brothers' all about fundamentalist Islam, enlightening them to the glories of guerilla warfare, urban terrorism. One of about a hundred highly trained, extremely motivated operatives charged with the mission of building a network of terrorist cells all over the place. Called "the Vanguard," or something like that. He wasn't supposed to get dirty while he was here. Just a sort of bloody 'advisor,' or something. Looks like Mick may have known something about all this when he went after that little bunch of pukes that night.

"His notes were sketchy—unusual for Mick—and the other guys who were involved from RPD really had very little information about what they were getting into. Also unusual for your father. He had a lot of bullshit, but he knew how to conduct a tactical entry, and he always paid a lot of attention to the welfare of his men. That whole incident looked more like the Bay of Pigs than one of Mick's trademark operations.

"Cargil thinks Mick had gotten a hint that something was up with a big time black terrorist, or *something*, and he got in such a hurry, he forgot to be careful. Probably traded some prep time for the element of surprise. And, if Mitchell *was* there, and if he *was* a part of this Vanguard thing, he was probably a lot better prepared, and the whole miserable bunch was probably *much* better armed, than he ever expected. Remember, the guys were sure that there were at least four origins of fire from full automatic weapons—rock 'n roll—and Mick's wounds came from some kind of high powered round, either a .223 or that weird round they fire in the AK47."

Jess was intent, watching and listening with all the acuity her bright Irish mind could muster; it was scary, alright, and infuriating too, not to mention nauseating, thinking about her handsome Daddy all shot full of holes. But *still*—there was more.

"Joshua, that's nice. I'm impressed with the forensic skills and the intelligence network of the FBI taskforce. But there's more. *A lot* more. Now *OUT WITH IT!* I can't breathe, and I'm tired of waiting for the punch line."

He took a deep breath, turned full into her wonderfully freckled face, now softly aglow with the fading orange hue from the clouds, and, slumping forward a bit, hands in his lap, he spoke again. "Mitchell was hit with a shotgun blast. Well, *two* shotgun blasts, actually. Number three buckshot. Mick was the only man there with a shotgun. And, as you know, it was sort of his trademark, like his preparation. That S&W 12-gauge riot gun with the short stock and the seven round magazine extender. And always #3 buck. See? Mick blasted the piss out of one of the Vanguard's chosen few. Not just once, but twice! Put enough holes in him to strain soup broth and dribbled the snake's blood all over the projects. Now it's payback time. Some kind of 'offensive' with national implications, and they want to use retribution against Richland for having spilled the blood of the Vanguard as an excuse for starting some really bad shit here."

His jaws locked, rippled, froze. His hands kneaded his thighs as he stared intently at the silver gray of the porch floor, streaked with fire orange and striped with long shadows. The chill air brushed his hair, and he closed his eyes tight. "The word that got leaked was some Islamic crap about 'the vicious infidel *and all those of his house*' or something like that, and Cargil says the feds are afraid that means you—*us*." He looked up into her face again. "They think we're in danger — big time."

* * * * *

NOTICE. MEN OF SUPREMACY: ALERT. YOUR FREEDOMS AND THE PURITY OF YOUR RACIAL QUALITY ARE IN EMMINENT DANGER.

With the death of President Kincaid, our worst fears are reality. A nigger occupies the white man's chair of sacred honor, and the purity of the white race is ruined. The once proud United States of America are now led by a mere slave, a colored male of low and mean degree. Unless he is removed at once, the Republic is lost. AWAKE! Watch for the signs of increased influence and infiltration. Our own operatives report that the government will soon be awash in black criminals, the confederates of their nigger president, their slave leader. Weapons to the ready! The years of preparation must now be tested by fire. To Arms! God save the United States of America!

So mankind ain't all it's cracked up to be. Bet the Good Lord shakes his head when he hears it. We discover fire, then make napalm; split the atom and build genocidal bombs; and now, a real nineties kind of genius, racial venom via the Internet! Now *that's* progress. A group calling themselves the "Society for the Preservation of White Supremacy," (the SPWS) a sort of confederation of the worst dregs of our time, had a Web page that regularly peddled racial and ethnic hatred for all who cared to turn on, tune in, and get ugly.

The Aryan Nation, the KKK, the Skinheads, and so on, all subscribed to the thing, at WHITESUP.COM. Routinely, it produced news releases and "updates" on the continuing struggle with all those who aren't white, or who came from someplace besides the U.S. As though all those scholars were a bunch of natives themselves. Hell, the guy who wrote the newsletter was named Kowalski—go figure. Anyway, for about five years on the Internet and for several more before that via paper mailers, a constant barrage of vicious crap had been disseminated, including announcements about enclaves, diatribes against every politician who seemed to be to the left of Attilla the Hun, and a daily updated listing of the availability of all manner of guns, ammunition, and explosives. There was also a wide variety of "how to" infomercials for the synthesis and fabrication of homemade bombs and weapons. Nice guys.

All over the country, fringe elements stockpiled weapons and awaited the opportunity to use them. Seems hatred is really pretty undiscriminating. What Yugoslavia proved was that there was nothing about the '90s that had caused Homo sapiens to advance beyond the primal carnage that has always been a part of human history. Torture, random killings, even mass atrocities have always lurked close to the surface of human nature; Jews and Christians have always taught that the evil in mankind is inborn, in need of the Almighty to keep it in check. And luminaries from Hitler and Stalin to the butchers in Bosnia continue to prove it. The Rodney King/Reginald Denny thing should have shown Americans that violence and viciousness are not unique to Eastern Europe. Anyway, the biggest difference between the white supremacists and the black militants—except for the ones who were actually the agents of foreign terrorism—was that the white boys were much better armed. But nobody had a corner on the ugliness market.

As is always the case, amid all this polarized militancy was a huge population truly "in the middle." Black and white, Hispanic, Asian, and all the mixtures thereof, they continued to go to work every day, tend their yards and gardens, try to save for a better day, and hope the government would leave enough for them to enjoy—eventually. As the crazies on both poles continued to heat up the rhetoric, and as crooks like Jeffrey Flint and many like him on both sides of the political aisle continued to pander to those whom they thought could advance their own selfish and often immoral, indecent goals, the rest of the population found themselves essentially without truly reasonable choices. It seemed that every thought or expression *necessarily* stepped on the toes of somebody else. And soon, whites and blacks found themselves looking askance at each other, made ever more uncomfortable with the divisions that were the subject of most of the public debate. So most folks just kept working, mowing the yard, and trying to save a bit for tomorrow. But what they did that was so ironic was to stop thinking at all. If people in the restaurants who were feeling that uncomfortable space separating them from their fellows had reached out, spoken, or made some move to bridge the gaps, the crazies might have had less sway. But they did not. They just finished their meals, drank their coffee, and went home.

* * * * *

When Mick O'Neal was killed, the local chapter of the ultra—rightwing SPWS lost no time in capitalizing on the event. Not that they gave a damn about the death of one Irish homicide dick or about the welfare of cops in general; in fact, these guys were about as antagonistic about the police, what*ever* color they were, as they were about that whole big world out there that was different from them. The FBI dogged them constantly, as did ATF—Alcohol, Tobacco & Firearms— always trying to keep up with their voracious appetites for the instruments of killing. But the fact that Mick had been killed by a black man, a militant gang member, and that he had been killed in a very bad part of town that was almost totally occupied by black citizens, really gave them the kind of vitriolic ammunition they needed to stir up their particular brand of racial invective.

All over Richland, posters, flyers, even a couple of renegade billboards decried the killing and the race of those who had done it. In fact, all over *Iowa* the venom spread, and rednecks everywhere began to listen more intently to the hatred being peddled by the SPWS. And Iowa was certainly not the only place. The seeds of unrest seemed to sprout wherever they were spread. The problem with blue collar America is that they have always been too easy to bullshit—at least for a while. Of course, they ended up fighting and dying first and in the greatest numbers in every war, paying the most taxes to fund every politician's agenda, and enduring the brunt of every resulting economic collapse. But they tend to buy into things that sound like easy answers at first. And some of the good ol' boys—and girls—found it all too easy and convenient to assign the blame for Mick O'Neal's murder to "those worthless blacks" instead of thinking through the less obvious truth that militancy and hatred had killed him and so many others like him who continued to die on American streets everywhere.

The SPWS gained members, as did the Islamic New World and the Nation of Islam, the Black Panthers, and the myriad of gangs growing in the nation's ghettos. Everybody in those camps did what camps have always done: They listened to themselves and not to anyone else. In the late 1850s, the South listened to itself and the North did the same. The result was anarchy. Surprise, surprise. Now the weapons of anger and hatred continued to be stockpiled, as the maniacs at both ends of the spectrum prepared for their chance to get ugly—*really* ugly. In their minds they were paying retribution for insults and wrongs done. Not the folks in that massive and denial—ridden middle, but the wild men on the fringes of reality. *They* were not strangers to the evil, the diabolical, the insanely cruel. There have always been such people, living for the sheer thrill of making reality of ordinary people's nightmares. The West was full of them during the era that knew its heyday after the end of the Civil War. But like always, folks just *couldn't believe* anything like that was still possible. Never mind wizards in the art of horror like Gacy, Bundy, Daumer, Manson. Nothing new. In fact, they were fantasizing atrocities just like Bosnia, Serbia, and Thailand. The devil's own playground, American style.

15.

Cardiac muscle is really interesting stuff. Of course, the human body has very little of it, since it does only very specialized things. Most notable among the cardiac muscles is of course the heart. Weighing about 2 ½ pounds (1,000 grams) in the average adult male, it is a four—chambered miracle of God's genius for high performance, low maintenance machinery. The average heart muscle will beat several billion times in the average lifetime. But for occasional genetic anomalies and the poisons humans give it, like nicotine, huge quantities of animal fats, and magnum quantities of alcohol, it works like a fine Swiss clock. Dickie knew the many intricacies of the heart very well, having dissected thousands of them during his career as a forensic pathologist. He was his usual methodical self, working through the protocol for autopsy of each of the president's organs.

The other guys had done a superb job of post mortem exam of the corpse "in gross," meaning as a whole—more than an apt description of the procedure for taking apart a dead human body. Pretty gross, indeed. But now it was Dickie's turn to find the needle in that biochemical haystack and figure what had caused the totally normal, healthy, and *living* body of John Wesley Kincaid to quit living.

"Liver appears smooth and glistening, lobes well defined and normal upon gross exam. Incising the organ, all lobular walls appear discrete, and the vasculature is intact and unremarkable. There are no nodes, lesions, or visible abnormalities associated with metastatic cell growth; slide samples of all tissues are retained, segregated and marked for microscope." Like all surgeons of the living and the dead alike, Dr. Freeman narrated to himself as he worked, but he also talked to a microphone suspended above the autopsy table. A foot pedal operated the tape, and he recorded his dictation of every detail of the examination. Besides making an immediate verbatim record of what he was doing, this ritual served as a memorized recitation of the outline, called a "protocol" in the biz, for all the steps to be followed in the complete examination of the corpse. Of course, he had less to narrate that usual, as the "gross" work was already done, but given the failure of the rest of the team to discover a cause of death, this soliloquy was no less important.

He proceeded through the grisly business of taking apart the presidential guts and got really tired of telling his mechanical audience what a great specimen Kincaid had been, for a man of fifty-two years on this dirty planet. The notes from the security sources made no mention of any complaints from Kincaid about not feeling well, or not eating, but then nobody had actually been assigned to take note of it.

Back to the heart. Same deal. Fine-looking muscle. No evidence of breakdown in the vasculature that transported the blood through the pump and no signs of even the slightest wall damage, as is expected when myocardial infarction occurs. He cut slide sections for the microscope, drew serum samples from the cardiac sac, the device that holds the organ in place in the chest, and scraped the insides of the vessel walls of all the plumbing. Everything was appropriately marked, separated, and sealed. A very skilled assistant repeated every marking back to the doctor as he identified the various artifacts for further examination, and they did it all again after completing the process at the table.

Ordinarily, the organs would have then been disposed of, the corpse having been already buried. Actually all they buried was what the pathologists call "the canoe," an irreverent bit of gallows humor among these strange people. This was no ordinary autopsy and had resulted in a very extraordinary result, so he ordered that the organs should be frozen at once, kept secure and separate and made available to only those persons he might later designate. He instructed the assistant not to allow the fact that the organs were being retained to get around. He would advise the President in his report, and that would be all. He took off his surgical gown, stripped off his gloves and hat, depositing them in the hamper, and headed off for the microbiology lab and an afternoon with his microscope.

* * * * *

The tumblers spun and the electronic sensors snapped in and out as the locks disengaged themselves from the other side. Willard Smalley's heart raced and his miserable little life flashed before his eyes; he awaited Sallie's shining countenance in the door's opening. The pale green eyes betrayed nothing as the little man entered the basement room. He turned, addressing himself to the business of re-locking the access to the most guarded parts of the mysterious building.

He walked to the table where Willard was seated and, turning toward that awful room where the unspeakable occurred, that *voice* thundered: "Sherman! Get your ass in here. NOW!" Willard fought back the bile in his throat, the pounding in his head. He knew very little about this place or these people, but the lore that had filtered through the few operatives of this charming little group in the Bronx was nothing less than Halloween in character. All he really knew was that people had come here and never been seen again— that they were rumored to have endured unspeakable torture, and that their fates were a total mystery.

"Sherman! Welcome Mr. Smalley. He is our guest, and the Committee has ordered special treatment for him." Smalley felt moisture in his pants, looking into the vacant eyes of the man in the gray coat. "In all my years with them, I have never received such orders for one man. Never. See to him." Sherman's steel eyes riveted themselves to the white man like a SAM lights up when it locks on "target acquisition," the evil in his intentions more obvious with each passing second. Two steps brought the big man to Smalley's side, and, as he arrived, he set an enormous hand on his shoulder. The weight was indescribable. Sallie was obviously enjoying this little preamble, this apparent overture to the Opera of the Macabre, in that he was not only the director and producer, but also the composer of libretto and spoken lines as well. The kind of tension he could create *before* the games began was beyond the imagination of mortal man. Unfortunately for Sallie, but miraculously for Willard, the Committee had other and bigger plans for the greedy computer nerd.

"Take him to the bank, ask for Simonson. You remember him. Call first, and be certain not to be seen. Authorize $500,000.00 to be deposited to the account of our guest's choice now, and allow him to arrange with Simonson the details of a $5,000,000.00 transfer to be confirmed upon the completion of the conditions that Mr. Smalley will describe to you both. Mr. Smalley, you will never know how close you were to the unspeakable. Be grateful. We pride ourselves here at the SPA on a number of things; but among our specialties is our uncanny ability to maintain consciousness in our guests. Your greed was almost your demise. Understand, *Mister* Smalley, that my vote was *not* to comply with your demands. Oh—I realize you got less than you asked for. Don't press your luck. I am still eager to watch you beg for your own death, with*out* the benefit of your tongue."

The eyes ran milky and frigid. Smalley nearly fainted as Sherman led him by the arm to that vault-like door. Several minutes after they left the SPA, Willard Smalley was still having difficulty focusing, hearing, framing thoughts, sentences. The unspeakable is really just that: *Unspeakable.*

* * * * *

Being President was not all it was cracked up to be, in the opinion of Jackie Robinson Webb. Military leadership had been much easier, and far less esoteric. The number of sensibilities inside the Beltway and the quality of the people who had real power were totally different than what he'd known as a general. First of all, there were the spin-doctors from the political side. They were in the way constantly. Nothing could be decided without first assaying the nuance of what it would, or *could,* mean to the "other side of the aisle," the media, or some perceived target of said nuance. To General Jackie, the whole exercise was wasted 90% of the time. Those spin guys gave an awful lot of credit to the intended targets of all that nuance bullshit—a lot more than *any* of them deserved, in his experience. And speaking of experience, the General had hardly been a Potomac gadfly when he was chairman of the Joint Chiefs for Bill McGinnis. He had had a bad habit of hanging out with his leatherneck pals, including Brooks, Mac Reed, and the guys he employed to run the JCS office. And, unlike many of the hotdogs, he tended to go home after work. Molly Webb was not only pretty hard to lie to or hide from, she was also a pretty good reason to go home.

Molly was one of those black women who simply defied the elements. Age, childbearing, stress, tragedy, although they took their toll on her from the *inside*, seemed powerless to hurt her *outside*. Molly, like her husband, was classic black. Her features were bold and almost stark, her coloring deep ebony. She was neither shy nor ashamed of her race or her features. She was just beautiful. Tall, slender, possessed of a dramatically shapely, breathtaking body, she was the kind of woman who spun heads wherever she went; not so much just because of her beauty, but because of the quiet dignity and humble pride that seemed always present wherever she was. And it was not a matter of fashion.

In the '60s, with Afro hair and gauze dress, she was devastating. In Europe in the '80s, in bright colors and sculpted coiffure, she stopped traffic. Now, in Washington in the '90s, elegant and understated, she could easily distract the crowd, and the cameras, from her imposing husband, whether he was dressed in full formal uniform with a chest full of medals or on the podium of some august Ivy League commencement address. Black eyes, a direct, piercing gaze, and a devastating bright smile, her air was part warmth and intellect and part "kiss my ass." No wonder the guy always found himself eager to get home at night.

The business of governing two hundred twenty million people was full time employment; the new president attacked it the way he had always attacked every objective: Full bore and with frontal assault. The people who counseled "wait and see" or who advised half-a-loaf solutions found themselves ignored, if not excluded from the decision making process. Things got done with this new president. And they got done NOW. Jack Kincaid and his entourage of whiz kids had drafted this man in large measure as a political/racial move with the avowed intention of winning the presidential election. He was a flashy personality, a war hero and a proven winner. And he was black. And although Kincaid held him in the highest esteem, for some pretty obvious and personal reasons, the idea that he might have to *work* in the new administration—or God forbid, *take over*—had never been much of a point of discussion. But now he *was* the President, Kincaid was as dead as he was gonna get, and there was real work to be done.

Even though Webb had not really had a lot to do with the formation of the administration, he was inheriting a complete term, minus about 19 hours, so he saw no reason to start one of those Gerry Ford apology acts. He was the only president the country would have until the next election, so the work had to get done. Besides filling an enormous list of positions at and below cabinet level, there was the usual number of major issues and problems to address. The Kincaid platform had been very aggressive with regard to the balancing of the federal budget and the need for drastic tax reform, and these were positions with that Webb had absolutely no problem. He ordered every initiative he could think of to get things moving, taking the position that a strong offensive was needed to get the idiots on Capitol Hill off their huge collective ass on either of those subjects.

Appointments were made, pointed invitations issued to the right committee chairs, and the word quickly got around that there would be no honeymoon, no wasted conferences where a lot of "sharing" of ideas took place. Results were what the man sought, and results were what he required.

And there was the subject of all those coincidences that seemed so—well, so coincidental. The whole idea of vehicles moving where vehicles never moved in the Saudi desert, an attempt on the Israeli Prime Minister's life, intelligence about a big arms and ordnance cache in NYC, and a power substation sabotage in Dallas, of all places, really set his cynical teeth on edge. The last thing he ever expected was for Jack Kincaid to die in his sleep. A round from a sniper rifle would have been much less a shock. And what this new president worried about, all the way down to his size 13 wingtips—what troubled him deep in his soul and kept him awake at night—was the specter of being stuck right in the middle of a crisis for that he could not prepare and against that the people he now governed were ill-equipped to defend themselves.

* * * * *

Josh sat with his back to his messy desk, staring out the thirty-fourth story window of his office. Three years had elapsed since the prosecutor's tongue-in-cheek condemnation of the office Landry shared with investigator Jimmie Whitaker, affectionately christened "the Swamp" by the rest of the homicide staff at the Richland prosecutors office. Three years had also elapsed since leaving the public sector for a *real* job with a civil litigation firm; but he had still not broken the twenty—year habit of living like a combination of pig and packrat. The place was piled with files, stacked with phone messages—some dating back to the Truman administration—strewn with heaps of open law books, notes, yellow stickies, and pages of legal paper drooping from within the mess.

The ever—growing skyline of the old one—horse town never ceased to amaze him, as he watched the insane courage of the beam walkers erecting the crowning story on the newest high rise. The Consolidated Bank building, in that he now sat, was the first of the new generation of commercial structures for the old downtown; at 40 stories, it had been *the* place to be for accounting firms, brokerage houses, and law firms, until it was eclipsed by a 50—story competitor that was built 10 years later by a big regional bank. And now, the "Flying Wallendas" drove the final anchor bolts in the sixty-second story of the newest addition, a six—sided monster with a rotating restaurant inside the top. It was built, nominally, by a consortium of insurance companies, but the real money was all foreign, mostly Arab. Josh refused to permit himself anymore redneck utterances, even to himself, on that subject.

His thoughts were far from the burgeoning skyline and even further from the pile of unanswered discovery that screamed silently at him from the landfill on his desktop. An appellate brief was due in the Iowa Court of Appeals in six days, with most of the research and all the writing left to be done and no grunts to assign to any of it. The ten million-dollar Khan divorce, a bloodbath between two Pakistani doctors, had been a trip into the depths of hell for both lawyers and clients. The issues, legal, equitable, and even cultural, were so complicated, and the facts so convoluted, that the idea of trying to explain it to another lawyer well enough for him or her to be able to make sense of the record of the trial was ridiculous. Like trying to explain the fight between the IRA and the British to a total stranger who knew nothing about the subject, in 25 words or less. So, he had to do it himself. Not one of the more glamorous or attractive aspects of the lucrative, but also exponentially more boring *private* practice of law.

This particular gray February day, Josh Landry's head, heart, and spirit, were at home; his mind had become a mess of twisting, conflicting thoughts and visions, full of competition between fight and flight, between old violent proclivities and the peaceful mentality he had cultivated since the days of torture and killing in that land far away. More with each passing day, this buttoned-down attorney wrestled the sniper within, as images of violence and mayhem crept back into his memory.

Then, as if the mind finally expended itself on the struggle, the fog cleared. No one—*no one*—would challenge, threaten, or harm Jessica Marie or any of their family. No one. And if that meant hauling out the long buried warrior skills and the long since suppressed instincts of aggression and preservation, well, that was OK. He'd gotten past all that before, and he'd just have to get past it again. After all, those very instincts had served him well enough to save him over and over in Vietnam, while sending his enemies to fiery hell in the process; might just need to do some of that again. And if LaShawn Mitchell or a platoon of his murderous emissaries from Yasser Arafat needed convincing, no problem. Of course, adopting such a bloody attitude created a whole host of complications, problems, and required attitude adjustments, but there was also no reason to take out a full page ad in the Richland *Libertaryan* to announce it, either. Just get ready, stay ready, and react as indicated. He stood up, saw that it was 4:41 p.m., dropped his reading glasses on top of the refuse that represented the last volume of the Khan transcript and, pulling his coat from the old sofa by the door, headed for the car. He poked his head into the cubicle of his secretary, a sage, classy woman named Ginger and, having winked and intoned the usual greeting of departure, "See Ya', I'm history," walked out.

Driving home, the landscape seemed a bit less murky, his thinking less muddled, his course more obvious than on the previous evening drives since the last call from Cargil. What had congealed through the last week of brooding was the fundamental truth that, unless he did all he could do to protect Jess and the kids, and unless he committed himself to a "whatever it takes" attitude and course, and unless he and Carl were successful in that endeavor, his life was gone anyway.

Josh began to think about the kinds of things that might produce the greatest risk to her and them, and he also worked through the most efficient, unobtrusive ways of protecting them. And there was more to it than just worrying about his own people. Cargil said that Vanguard outfit was intending to use that little buckshot incident between Mick and Mitchell as an excuse to hit Richland, and that the thing had some kind of national implications. He never realized he had driven within five minutes of home without noticing a single feature of the route; he was so deeply engrossed in trying to examine all these issues and place his own precautions and preparations into some kind of time frame and reasonable factual context, he missed the whole drive home. A couple of things were clear from all this thinking: First, the best way to protect the family was to keep them close to home, where observation was easiest and enemy concealment most difficult; second, Richland was a fat target and an easy mark for anybody who wanted to raise some serious hell.

It was clear from Cargil's report that the Feds were aware of the problems created by the threats against the city in general. It was also clear that he expected Josh to take charge of the protection of his own family. Twenty years in the law enforcement business had made him all too familiar with the realities of "police protection." That was a television term, a figment of the imaginations of authors and Hollywood producers, not a fact for people in the real world who found themselves in danger. Not that the cops have no concern for the plight of the citizen; there is just no way to deliver the product—not enough money, not enough manpower, too many bad guys. A sad, wry smile creased his face as he turned onto Jericho Road. He realized how utterly impossible it would be for organized law enforcement, or even the National Guard, to provide any significant degree of protection to this community. If a real effort to stink things up was mounted by even a relatively small force that was well enough equipped, well enough trained, and mean enough to engage in the right activities, there would be no adequate defense available.

The math would have been funny, if it had not been so true: Richland PD had about 900 uniformed officers; the county sheriff had about 270 more. Of those, at least half were in administrative positions or were otherwise not directly involved in street police work—answering runs, investigating crimes, protecting the citizenry of the community. With just over a million people in the county, and another 150,000 in the surrounding metropolitan area, the ratio of those officers to citizens was about 500 to 1,150,000, or 1 to 2,300. Just imagine the adventure of having a substantial number of each cop's 2,300 folks hollering for help at the same time. Pretty interesting shift, right? "Hi, honey, I'm home. Had a real bitch of a day, Hon, got 1,721 calls from 911! The first one turned out to be a bomb blast that killed about twenty folks, and I don't know what happened to the other 1,720. I just can't *wait* to get in tomorrow!"

Turning in the driveway, Josh laughed another dark laugh, as he found himself thinking about all the armaments he wanted to amass. "Holy Shit!" His mind instantly indicted him for acting like some survivalist nut case, hiding in a hole in a mountain in Idaho. The chuckle bubbling up in his throat was quelled quickly by the sight of Luke rounding the corner from the side door to the stable, flagging down Dad for a ride to the house. "Oh. Well, guess I better decide on doing *something* to protect these guys! Calling the Sheriff seems kind of like a waste of a quarter," he mused, noting that this place was approximately 13 miles from the Sheriff's office. Even the suburbs lived with slow response time in emergency situations; out there, self-help was not a matter of political disposition—it was reality. Another dark smile. "Hello, 911, this is an emergency! There's some nut with a Mac 10 shooting out the windows in my house!" "Please hold. Please hold. . .please hold. . .Thank you sir, we'll have someone there within about 30 minutes. And have a nice day." Great argument for gun control, huh? The only guns that get controlled are the ones the innocent folks should have to protect themselves. Sure can't wait for the police. As they climbed out of the van and headed for the porch, Luke chattering nonstop, Josh resolved that tonight he and brother Carl were going to have a serious conversation.

16.

The bank of monitors that blinked confirmation of the continuous activity running through the central processing unit gave the main control room of the wire transfer department a kind of Cape Canaveral atmosphere; there were gomey little guys moving purposefully around the place, and telephones rang incessantly. Through a glass partition was visible a long bank of young women wearing headsets and talking into more of those same green screens. There was so much sound, but such quiet and monotonous sound, that the place was almost peaceful—a deceptive aura certainly, as the place was very busily moving money. Not just *some* money, but *a lot* of money; not just *moving* it, but moving it at or about the speed of light. This was where the big boys did their high powered business, on an international scale. Nobody says how much money gets sent from one place to another via the wire transfer system that has its heart on Long Island, but it is well into the *billions* of dollars per day.

Willard Smalley was at home here; this was his gym, his tavern, his fishing cabin, his mistress' townhouse, his fantasy. But it was real. With a busted family, ex—wife in Oklahoma someplace, remarried to some small time farmer or something, and a couple of grown kids who called him about once a year, he found little to compete with the power of this place. There were no friends competing for his off—duty time. As far back as the Masters program at MIT, the other guys had opined on occasion that he was about as much of a loner as any of them had ever seen. And *weird.* This from a bunch of boys who were themselves a couple standard deviations off the norm. But more than being a loner, or being weird, was his seldom seen but pronounced proclivity for being a real mean son of a bitch. Ask the kids who call once a year or the wife who moved two thousand miles away the next day after the divorce was final. OK, so he's a loser, a weirdo, a real prick; he just happens to be a wizard in the business of electronic money and how to move a lot of it, very fast. Only today he stands watching with hooded expectancy from his glass-walled office the details of his little experiment into the cyber world of self-destructing viruses, replaying at high speed in his head.

Book I – You're It

Simple, really. Make a change in the cryptographic verification codes that authenticate every transfer from one institution to another. Then program a time delay return to the *real* stuff to occur within a few seconds of a bogus transfer, to the nonexistent account, and then wait for the gurus at both ends to try to figure what the hell happened to a million dollars. A mil is not really so much cash in an environment that moves several thousand times that per day, so it takes a while to even decide there's a problem, once the transaction has been ordered, verified, authenticated, and settled.

The overnight process of settlement, the banking term for debiting and crediting all the appropriate accounts to complete reconciliation of the many transactions that occurred the previous day, will show an out—of—balance condition in the accounts from that the money was removed and an unexplained transfer into the account that Willard targeted to receive the funds. The point? To show the Committee that he can move funds without authorization of the institution that holds them and cause them to be deposited into an account from that they can be removed. He can do it before detection can occur and without leaving an audit trail that eventually causes suspicion or allows the transaction to be reversed. No problem. It happened so easily, he wondered why he had not done it over and over for *himself*, a hundred times before this.

Now for the real coup: To momentarily *stop* the system from operating at all. This requires a little more elaborate virus, but also one that self-destructs after a few seconds, leaving no trace that it has been present and responsible for the little *oops!* that has occurred. The Committee has in mind much bigger objectives than the moving of a few paltry billion dollars to some mystery account. And they want nothing whatever to do with the sticky business of unexplained additions to account balances, attempted transaction reversals, all that formalistic crap. What they want is financial mayhem. Simple. Make the system stop sending money where it's supposed to go, while making it send everyone's money to everyone else—or whatever devious mechanism it takes to create financial havoc for the big boys.

So, for the real proof. This program, one that disappears after doing its thing, creates enough trouble to stop a few hearts for a few seconds, but not enough to create the stink that breeds investigation or gets mentioned in the *Wall Street Journal*. No problem. He reroutes the transfers to German banks—they all go to London, except for a random few, say twenty, that go to the Netherlands. Some of those *appear* to have then been retransferred to Tokyo banks, only to get reversed back to Germany. All are documented by realtime tape of the transactions and verifiable by the Committee, that has its moles watching the appropriate screens in the target banks.

What Smalley cannot show them is his big time trick, that will cause the meltdown of the whole operation when initiated. Can't do that without tipping his hand to the security people inside and compromising his position. The fact that he can cause German money to end up in London and then in Tokyo, only to finally, after his little bugs have vacated the system, arrive in the appropriate German banks, without anyone being able to either identify the problems or attempt to explain them, will have to do. When the experiment goes as predicted, several hundred million in deutschemarks will go zipping around Europe and Japan, at first being credited to the wrong accounts with impunity and then, almost before anyone or any system can recognize that there is a problem, *zap!* it's all fixed. The point is made to the observers: This guy has a way of doing just about whatever he wants, whenever he wants, and nobody is between him and the keystrokes required to turn the world of electronic banking into an inexplicable mess of 0s and 1s—a bunch of binary gibberish—without detection, and in such a way as to preclude timely repair. The phone rings in Willard's glass bowl. "Very well done. Both items observed and effects demonstrated. Proceed."

A deep breath, a sigh, a momentary vision of a faraway place. Willard has always been fascinated with Tahiti. No reason. He's never been there. Just the idea of that black sand. That clear hot air, and those innocent girls wearing nothing above their grass skirts. He knows all about how to get there, when to go, and where to land once the move is made. All it takes is money.

82

Back to reality, and he begins to construct the program for his own little Big Bang. The financial business has attributes of a huge, intercontinental domino board, where one problem causes at least two more, and those create five others. The various pluses and minuses, the debits and credits to the myriad clearing accounts, asset accounts, settlement reconciliations, start to tilt out of balance. But not completely. These guys did not construct the most powerful and efficient money system in the history of mankind by being stupid. The wire system is surprisingly simple fundamentally, operated from only a single—or a very few—computer nerve centers in the U.S., and there is great faith placed in it by the entire financial world. The business runs on faith in the system and trust that all its participants will do all they can to keep it running, that keeping it down, once it falls, is not so easy. That is why he has also plotted to throw a little surprise party for the domestic credit card industry.

* * * * *

Jonathan Abdelmanek and Abdul Salim Alakmah sat together just inside the doorway to the roof of the SPA, attention focused on a small monitor and also on the white sound in their ears, being produced by the headphones they were wearing. Via "Priority Double Alpha" order delivered by the Iranian, the Committee had called a bigtime powwow among its North American annexes, requiring Sallie to reinstall the sophisticated communications devices he had been so careful to remove several weeks earlier. Their absence had left him in a sort of informational vacuum, out of touch with the big boys in the terror business and increasingly reliant on courier, messenger, and his own acumen for their dark business. At least this time he'd have the opportunity to hear from the real hitters, maybe even the head dog, himself, Arafat.

The screen flashed an alpha numeric message, nothing more than hieroglyphics, really, and mostly in Arabic; then the headphones came to life and, after a moment of distortion and a series of high speed electronic tone messages, a voice from Beirut asked for confirmation of their presence in the conversation. The voice was electronic, the product of a marvelous de-encryption device that took the spoken word, scrambled it into the unknowable, then reproduced the actual words by one of those monotonic things like that voice on the subways in the airports of Atlanta, Denver, and Chicago. Not very personable, but secure. Once the whole procedure was completed, the real voices took over, the transmissions now scrambled and coded, then unscrambled and decoded upon receipt. Pretty fancy stuff.

"Good evening, gentlemen. This is the Vice Chairman." Holy Shit!, it's old Yasser's right hand man. This *will* be big. Sallie would have been little more surprised if it had been Arafat himself, so infrequent were the appearances by the Vice Chairman. The bearded butcher, however, *never* got this close to any but the most clandestine, and *in person* meetings, and Sallie, for obvious reasons, had never been to one of those.

"We have called this meeting to discuss, and to decide upon, the most immediate steps to be taken in the commencement of the offensive. The financial disruption appears to be in hand, simply awaiting our order. The difficult parts are at this end, with our efforts to prepare for the operations in Jerusalem proving most complicated. The damned Zionist Americans are *in the way* more than we had anticipated. However, we need to decide upon a course regarding the new American president. Other matters are well set, but he remains a problem. It is the view of the Committee that he must be eliminated before the commencement of the operation in North America. Flint's presence made things simple; Kincaid was unpredictable.

"But Webb is military. He is, by virtue of the way he arrived in the presidency, unbeholden to the usual power brokers. He is very experienced in matters of the use of force, unafraid to employ it where he sees it as necessary. And, at the risk of restating the obvious, I remind everyone that the success of the operation is dependent not only upon swift and violent execution by our forces, but upon the intransigence and inertia of the Americans. This implies a failure of leadership, and Webb simply cannot be counted upon to fail. So, he must die.

"We have examined several possibilities for his removal, but most have appeared unattractive. Plane crash is difficult, as he is travelling very little, and his itinerary is very well guarded. Mac Reed is doing most of the personal stuff himself, and his intelligence background makes Webb a difficult man to follow—or to predict. The more esoteric mechanisms: bombs, poison, close-in hits, all appear problematic at best, given the strict security in place. That crew of ex-Marines with that Webb has surrounded himself presents too many variables for that kind of thing. That leaves us with three options: 1. recoilless rifle, presented via armored van at the side of the White House; 2. suicide airborne explosive attack; and 3. sniper attack at the Conference of Governors in Chicago in two weeks. Of those, Jonathan has advised that the recoilless rifle idea, while extremely effective if the target is in the right place, produces an almost certain capture or casualty to the fire team. The fact that a *team* is required is also a problem, as the likelihood of detection or mistake rises with the number of required participants. The World Trade Center proved that.

"Our operatives in Washington advise that the airplane idea is very workable, especially if we can use a small, high speed aircraft loaded with enough H.E. to disintegrate the whole building and part of the Executive Office Building across the street. But that requires the right zealot, a Shiite with complete devotion to the cause, plus the required flying skills to evade low altitude surveillance. The plane must take off from National and immediately veer into the White House, in order for the fixed emplacements that protect the area to be ineffective. Too many variables, in my opinion. That leaves us with the Chicago option. Salim, my friend, what have you to tell us about the availability of a good sniper?"

Sallie blanched; if the place had not been so dark, Jonnie would have had the rare opportunity of seeing this bloody little ghoul betray real fear. The pause was shorter than it seemed. Finally, he responded. "Mr. Vice Chairman, I apologize for my slow response, but I was quickly running through my cadre in my mind. Ah . . . yes. Ah. . .*yes. Of course.* That should be no problem. I—we will need some detail, and very quickly, we will need to move into place. My choice will be a seasoned veteran, a man who has performed flawlessly for us on four prior occasions. Also, he is an American, at least by appearance, so that he will attract less attention. Only real problem will be the location of the hit."

"Good. Thank you, Salim. Certainly we will forward you the details at once. Where is this man? And how would you propose to get him to the site?"

"He is now in Wyoming, training some right wing fanatics who are interested in their own agenda of anarchy. These people, I might add, although fundamentally antagonistic to us, will make great de facto allies when the festivities actually get rolling. I will need to fly him to New York and then probably have him drive to Chicago, assuming there is time. Travel by car is much more anonymous, and he will be able to transport a wide array of weapons choices without fear of detection or compromise. We will begin at once. How much time do we have?"

"You should have your man in place within seven days." Sallie exhaled slowly. "Very well, Mr. Vice Chairman. How should I make contact again?" He was really sick of this radio silence treatment; he much preferred to have free access to the communications system as he had before Abdelmanek's last visit. "We will reach you by courier within twelve hours. However, you may leave the microwave installation in place for the moment. Gentlemen, I believe that concludes our agenda. Any questions?" Jonathan fidgeted in his uncomfortable top step seat, squirmed a moment, then spoke. "Anwar—Jonathan here, forgive the interruption, but do you really think it wise to attempt the assassination of the sitting president now, what with the ongoing negotiations with the Jews and the presence of so much military in the Golan Heights? I mean, if this operation gets botched, or if his death is attributed to the PLO or the Arab world in general, won't it affect our efforts there?"

"Good point, Jonathan, but the Chairman has made it clear that Webb must be eliminated before the main offensive can begin, and that clock has already begun to tick in earnest, as you well know." Sallie had snapped back as if slapped in the face when his companion spoke. Angered by the suggestion that his people might fail, or botch anything, his blood raced, and his hands sweat. He throttled the urge to rip the camel jockey's throat out with his bare hands—right now. He was well experienced in just such action, and the result was most impressive and gratifying. The victims always displayed such a look of confusion as they gurgled briefly. Instead, he breathed slowly.

"Not a problem, if I might respond. You see, we shall cause attribution for the killing to rest with the Society for the Preservation of White Supremacy. Not only are they a likely choice in the public's eye, but they will probably willingly accept the unearned credit for doing it. And even if our sniper is compromised—an extremely unlikely eventuality—he is white, closely associated with the SPWS, and can be counted on not to say otherwise. Besides, the contingencies include preparations for and placement of a Jack Ruby, just in case. If the shooter appears to be in danger of compromise or capture, he will himself die at once." He looked at Jonnie with a baleful, hideous kind of smugness that left the Iranian weak and shaky. The seconds seemed frozen into eternity before the Vice Chairman spoke again.

"Jonathan, your point is well taken, but I think Sallie states a brilliant plan. And, when the White Supremicists get the blame—or the credit—it will only serve to accelerate the stress on things there. Proceed, gentlemen. Good evening."

The screen again displayed its array of nonsense, went white. The audio ceased, went to that soft sound, went dead. The two men looked at each other, removing their headphones. Sallie quickly disassembled the components, placing them in a cabinet at the top of the steps inside the door to the roof. Again the master of disguise and camouflage, the cabinet was then hidden behind an apparently dilapidated wall of crumbling plaster and lath strips, well secured to the wall studs by fiberglass fasteners. No chance of detection by magnetic search devices. The transmitter dish was then concealed amid the aging debris already on the roof. They did not speak as they descended to the elevator, rode to the basement, entered the secure room. Once there, Sallie summoned ghoul #2, the smaller of the two gray men, Cedric.

"Find Monroe. He's out in the mountains teaching that bunch of idiotic white trash to kill their own people. Mobilize a courier at once and have him on the phone to me via secure line within four hours. And I want him here tomorrow. Clear?" The gray man never blinked. "Done, Salim."

Jonathan wanted to debate, to argue, and to express his profound worries about this whole thing; he also wanted to complain that the SPA was less than totally secure, in his opinion. Bringing Smalley here had been an egregious error,

87

and Jonnie was ever more afraid the place would come under the surveillance of some American agency. He maintained caution, however, still certain that this horrible little man might simply tear him apart. "Sallie, you were simply brilliant with the Committee tonight! I wish you all the best in this operation. Oh—I almost forgot. What did you learn about this 'Lassiter' fellow—the one revealed to you by that young man who met his demise here last fall?"

Sallie froze for an instant, then continued to turn pages in one of the code books.

"Funny you should ask about him. Sort of a convoluted piece of research, in fact. But not to worry. Appears to have been a false alarm."

Jonathan was not assuaged, but he dared not carry the discussion further. Abruptly, he turned toward the door. "Call if you need anything. Good Night, Salim."

* * * * *

February in the Bighorn Mountains is a time of few options. The snow is deep at the higher elevations, sometimes twenty feet or more in the upper reaches of the Cloud Peak Wilderness, where the government has decreed that no motorized vehicles, no chainsaws, and no aircraft are permitted. The only way into the wilderness area is on foot, or riding a horse or mule. Not the kind of place for the company picnic, unless you've a bit of mountain goat in your lineage. Of course, the place is a perfect domain for men on snowmobiles, except, of course, for the fact that they are illegal. Thing is, there aren't too many park rangers, game wardens, or local sheriffs who have a craving for routine patrols in that country, as there is no such thing as a "routine patrol" up there in February.

Although the weather can kill in a matter of minutes out on top, it is possible to co-exist with nasty old Mother Nature at the lower elevations that are still in or close to the wilderness area. And it is there that some of the craziest men in these United States went to hone their warlike skills, to train with some of the most accurate—and deadly—weapons available, legally or otherwise, and to preach their gospel of revolution and anarchy to each other. When the scholars in Washington started banning everything that goes *bang!,* these guys got their own exemption from the new laws; they just bought the good stuff on the black market.

Here, above a frozen creek in a place called, appropriately enough, "Winter Park," a platoon-sized group of these fine folks bivouacked in the tall pines, camouflaged in white and gray tents, burning fires at night only, and then only in enclosed wood stoves. Unless Uncle Sam uses his satellites to scour the Bighorn Mountains, and unless he's looking pretty hard, they're just not there. But they *are* there, learning the fine points of advanced infantry tactics from a true Aryan by the name of Lester James Monroe, Master Sgt., U.S. Army Delta Force, retired; or at least that's what he tells them. Actually, he left the military in sort of a hurry, after a particularly ugly debate with the boys in charge of the place. They got wind of a little weekend retreat he had planned for some of his men. It included an array of illegal sporting events, the poaching of a wide variety of game animals for immediate consumption, a large quantity of untaxed liquor (some kind of moonshine white lightning) and about thirty young women from the red light district of Atlanta.

Well, the Army being such prudes as they are at times wont to be, and Lester being the full time pain in the ass he had become since he had run out of enemies to kill, everybody decided it would be best if Lester made other arrangements. Everybody but Lester, that is; he took direct and severe umbrage at all this moralism over just a few broads, a little booze, and a good time in the mountains. He left, all right— right after a late night visit to the armory, where he cold-cocked a Sp4 who was sleeping on guard duty and relieved the good folks of Fort Gordon of four M60 machineguns, six M79 grenade launchers, as many M16s, and about a dozen 9mm Beretta automatic pistols, plus one old M14 from the back room where they kept the obsolete weapons.

Knowing as he did that ammo would present no problem, and being aware that its weight would only slow him down, he stashed the little acquisition, processed out of the service of his country, and headed west. Since early 1991 when all this occurred, he had lived mostly in these mountainous regions of the Bighorn range and on out toward Yellowstone. And he had had the occasion to provide skilled labor for a wide variety of concerns who had on their agendas the elimination of undesirable persons. Truth be known, Lester James Monroe had killed 13 men in the period between his separation from the service and the election of Jeffrey Flint as president.

Never a fan of explosives, he favored the high—powered rifle over more imprecise and messy media for the delivery of death. Actually, he had a sort of warped sense of propriety about injuring or killing any but the intended target in any of his operations. Some kind of leftover from the chivalry that had no doubt once made his ancestors more noble beasts than he had devolved to. And, unlike so many of the killing elite, he had no use for silencers, exploding bullets, or those puny little high—speed rounds that work only in optimum conditions. The good old .308, the round fired in the M14 (the last "real" military rifle), was his favorite. Oh sure, it had a sort of rainbow trajectory at long range, and it made a lot of noise, but it wasn't nearly as temperamental about little things like wind and glass, even an occasional wall. And boy what an impact! In like a nickel—out like a cash register. He had never had a nonfatal wound in all 13 of his "private" missions, 13 rounds—13 kills—and the same had been his experience in Vietnam, Cambodia, Grenada, and a host of other unmentionable little ops he had completed for whoever it was that issued such orders. Several quick trips to Central America were conspicuously absent from his personnel file.

So the screwballs from the Aryan Race were being treated to warfare, Lester style, on a soggy, 35-degree day just inside the wilderness line in Winter Park, practicing fire and maneuver drills in the sloppy snow. Then the low whine of a powerful snowmobile motor began to compete with the sharp staccato of small arms fire in the live fire version of this particular drill. At first, only the bright crimson flag that whipped in the air behind the machine on a long, flexible rod was visible in the direction from that came crescendoing sound. Lester immediately sounded the shrill whistle that was the signal to cease firing and take instant measures to find concealment. He stepped into the shadows of a low—hanging tree line, perfectly drawn by the deer as they had browsed off the edge of the big meadow before moving to lower elevations in the late fall. Dropping to one knee, he caught sight of the speeding sled as it crested the rise that ended in the open space of the big park. He shouldered his trusty M14, slipped off the safety with his thumb, and took aim at the cloud of snow and steam coming toward him, still out of range at about 600 yards.

He tracked it in, breathing steady and slow, until it was in to about 400. He squeezed the trigger gently, increasing pressure slowly. Just before the weapon would have fired, he relaxed, inhaled, and lowered the heavy weapon. The bright orange coveralls and hood on the operator of the snowmobile were familiar, and Lester stood to meet him.

Fred Snowcloud's growling machine swept up to Lester's position, and he curtly gestured to the mercenary to come close. First looking up and down the huge meadow for signs of any other persons, Lester walked deliberately to the side of the idling snow rocket. The face, obviously that of a full— blooded Indian, was flushed with the chill air, wet with the frozen spray created by the drifts he had exploded en route. His eyes were cold and black, his expression a mat of the unknowable. "This is for you. All I was told was that you were to read it at once and respond by 2100 hours this date. See ya." And with that, he was gone. Sort of like a grumpy Saint Nick, with no personality and no "ho! ho! ho!" Monroe ripped open the envelope, quickly read the note twice and, taking an old Ronson cigarette lighter from his fatigues, first lit a Pall Mall, then set fire to the note. That night, he was back in Story, Wyoming, gassing up his old Blazer, and at noon the next day he was on a plane from Sheridan, Wyoming to Minneapolis, with connection to LaGuardia, and an eventual date with the President of the United States.

BOOK II

THE HOUNDS OF HELL

1.

Among people who have endured terrible events—tornadoes, plane crashes, earthquakes, hurricanes—there are three things that they all say:

1. I never thought it could happen to me.
2. It all happened so fast.
3. My life will never be the same again.

Those words have echoed throughout the twentieth century in England, Germany, France, Italy, the Baltics, and Russia, as what appeared to be the most solid and trustworthy of institutions disintegrated into horrors too monstrous—and tragedies too numerous—to recount or comprehend. Only those who have suffered such devastations can appreciate their terror and consequences. Over and over, again and again, mankind has said: "Oh, that could *never* happen here." Never. . . . Never say never.

* * * * *

Ever since the declaration, premature as it might have been, that communism was dead in Europe, the United States standing Armed Forces had been shrinking. First, William Duffy McGinnis proclaimed the "peace dividend." that would result from the downsizing of the military, based upon the reduced strength needs created by the fall of the Berlin Wall. Then along came old Snake Oil himself, Flint, who did everything in his power to dismantle the whole apparatus, while constantly deploying what was left in one politically correct and militarily stupid conflict after another. But what seemed to evade the attention of the public in general was that, due to his ax murder of the standing forces, the necessary bodies required to tilt at his deadly windmills had to come from reserve units and from the various National Guard units around the country.

Little dances like a U.N. operation in Bosnia and the invasion in Central America were largely staffed by units from a wide variety of Guard units from all over the place; but the only people who seemed to notice that fact or pay much attention to it were the families of those who were taken and the leaders of those Guard operations, who were faced with trying to provide services and security for their own states without the people required to do it.

The results were not often obvious, unless catastrophe struck at home. But if a tornado, a hurricane, or an earthquake hit, or if a whole section of a state got washed away by flooding, suddenly there were not enough personnel to throw at the problems of trying to save lives and property. Not a problem for a sensitive guy like Jeffrey Flint, but a real mess for any governor whose citizens were suddenly homeless, cold, and in immediate danger of all manner of bad news unless the Guard could get to them.

Andrew Whitaker believed in the concept of the citizen soldier. He had been one ever since his return from Vietnam when, unlike so many young people who couldn't get away from the service fast enough, he still wanted to maintain his connections with military life. Something about the methodical attention to detail, the feel and security of being around the weapons and the heavy equipment, and the camaraderie of associating with folks who shared like experiences and just a touch of a taste for danger appealed to him. So, joining the National Guard had been natural.

The folks in the Iowa Guard were tickled to have a real combat veteran in their midst, and the fact that he was willing to share experiences and add a note of realism to their training and exercises only made him a bigger hit. It therefore came as no surprise that he would rise through the ranks of the state militia until he finally became the AG, the Adjutant General, for the whole shebang. And his passion for military leadership and his belief in the importance of the citizen soldier to the people of the State of Iowa found a serious pulpit when he hit the top spot.

The biggest and the most unpleasant surprise the new guy got when he assumed the AG role in 1994 was that the federal demands placed upon the state Guard establishments were more than modest. Turns out, the Department of Defense, in return for the matching funds it provided and the arms and equipment it delivered to the states, required a great deal of obeisance.

There were things like maintaining "ready" status for a large contingent of Guardsmen to respond to any call from the Commander in Chief when he decided to commit American troops to *any* potential conflict. (A "conflict" is a war that a president or a Congress wishes not to recognize for what it is.) The whole "payback" drill, imposed by the DOD, simply reproved the old adage that "he who subsidizes also controls." No surprise that, when the snoops began to record big time troop and vehicle movements in the Iraqi desert, headed both west toward Syria and eventually toward Israel, and east toward Kuwait, the big boys immediately started the wheels in motion to call up a huge contingent of state Guardsmen and active reservists to field a team. Precisely the reaction predicted by Yasser Arafat and his bloodthirsty clone in Iraq, Saddam Hussein, or "SoDamnInsane," to the troops who fought him.

Whitaker had raised hell at the DOD guys who first called him with the advance warning, known as a "warning order" in the biz, that a substantial infantry and armored contribution was anticipated from Iowa, Indiana, California, and Texas, four of the biggest militias in the country. He was hot because he felt the thing was far short of a crisis, first of all, and they wanted so many of the people he routinely called on to help when the inevitable spring tornadoes and floods hit. The same support vehicles used to move infantry and support troops in combat make great tools in those types of situations. And, of course, he had several Engineer battalions attached to his infantry and armored units, and the feds wanted them, too. He also knew that the strength of his and many other units had already been weakened by Flint's commitments to Bosnia and a couple other stupid ideas that appealed only to him.

"Look, Buzz, what the hell am I supposed to use for search and rescue people when the Missouri jumps its banks in April? Huh? And who's gonna move the dirt and sand we need to keep those hundred-year-old levies from caving in? Ever thought a' that? No. 'Course not. Just more cloak and dagger bullshit from the intelligence geeks and the Joint Chiefs, making sure the goddam A-rabs behave themselves, right, Buzz? *RIGHT, Buzz!?*" The liaison officer for the Area Command, Department of the Army, a mere Lt. Colonel, fought back the urge to respond to the AG's tirade in kind. He had been the target of five such speeches in about three hours, as he delivered the warning orders.

"General, I understand; if it makes any difference, I don't blame you—*any* of you— for feeling this way. But, with all due respect, sir, I don't write these orders, OK? I just deliver them. I am sorry. All I can tell you is that DOD has run all this many times, in the Strength and Readiness program, and it is their conclusion that you will still be able to respond as needed, given the climatic conditions now and the statistical likelihood of a dry spring season this year."

"Bullshit, Buzz, more bullshit, and you know it. That crew of computer geniuses has obviously never experienced Iowa in April. There hasn't been a dry spring here in fifty years, because I've been here for all fifty, and I can tell ya' myself! Besides, what about all that spook stuff we got from NSA at the Boston meetings? What about *that*, Buzz? Remember? A whole afternoon about maintaining a Brigade-sized mech infantry force to react to any urban threat that might arise out of all that Muslim shit they got from the Mossad, right?"

The man flinched more acutely at this one. No stranger to this point either, he had heard it from every general who had been present at that briefing. Biggest problem for the messenger now was that there *was* no good response to the point. The man was right. He simply sat there, watching drizzle soak the Pentagon, his stomach churning great quantities of acid. He reached in the top drawer of his desk for the Maalox. Dammit. Empty. He closed his eyes as the general continued.

"Well, guess we'll just hand out rifles and flak jackets to the Quartermaster boys and the grease monkeys at the motor pool, and go kick some militant ass! Holy Mary, Buzz, what the hell are you guys smoking up there, anyway? You know what *I* say—*fuck* those people! I got our own folks to worry about. We've given the goddam Israelis enough air and ground firepower to kick *our* butts! They're so well armed, thanks to us, they can whip any force known to mankind." Whitaker finally took a breath, acknowledged the order and, mercifully for the poor Colonel on the other end of the line, hung up the phone.

Ever since the conflagration in L.A. after the first Rodney King verdict, AGs all over the U.S. had found themselves awakening during the early morning hours in a cold sweat, visions of mass rioting, looting, power source threats, and massive civil disturbances in their urban areas making sleep impossible. The thought of deploying armed troops right in their own communities, the vision of armored personnel carriers roaring through the streets of Middle America, or tanks firing into old buildings to root out snipers, was not the stuff from that Norman Rockwell painted his gentle images.

The Devil's Playground

In November past, Whitaker had sat sipping cognac and smoking a really good cigar, visiting with the commanding officers of a dozen other state militias, at Loch Obers, in Boston. The AG conference was over, and that group, plus the rest of the leadership from the many states in attendance, had spent a solid week in briefings. The information came from the top DOD brass, as well as CIA, National Security Agency, and combined force Criminal Intelligence units from all over the place.

The wonderful old restaurant, with its brass clad bar and high ceilings, had been the site for meetings of great and famous men for the last one hundred years. Sitting there in the midst of those devoted citizen soldiers thrilled Whitaker, stimulated his military soul, and spun his already nervous stomach almost out of control. As snow swirled around the little dead-end alley that cradled the entrance to the place, the men talked in quiet but earnest tones about the fears they shared and the potentially massive problems they faced.

The upshot of the whole gig was that the world was not a particularly stable place; it was not a particularly predictable place and, truth be known, not a very safe place, no matter where the discussion turned. And being without the very units that were crucial to the establishment and maintenance of order in the event of a real and substantial upheaval in any one of the eight Iowa cities for that he was ultimately responsible made him just a little bit crazy. It caused what the boys in the military have always called "a case of the ass"—a really bad and chronic case of the ass. In short, the general was not pleased.

The argument that the only real problems involving domestic upheaval to have occurred in recent memory had happened in California, where there was no real law anyway, and where nobody even pretended that there was any effective control, did little to allay the stomachache he felt. The '90s had proven to be a very violent, abusive decade from his perspective. American troops had landed and spilled blood on at least half a dozen different foreign shores. Time-honored institutions and fundamental mores had been forsaken in favor of a kind of sliding scale morality that depended for its strength and acceptance on its immediate popularity and its tolerance of whatever anybody wanted at the moment. And the realization that many, many factions and interest groups showed ever-increasing willingness— and ability—to enforce their versions of what was right by whatever means they found necessary left the man with a sense of truly dark foreboding.

His unrest knew no tangible or concrete source. He just felt weak, uneasy, like he had felt so many years before when moving off into a familiar piece of jungle he had left only just hours before, but sensing that the whole place had changed, moved, altered itself in the intervening hours. And there was no way to know what might lie ahead in the darkness to follow. Only now the place was not half a world away. It was his own homeland, his own hometown and, quite literally, his own back yard.

2.

"Twin Peaks" was a lovely little establishment, owned and operated by a very large woman by the name of Enchante Weaver, or "Tits" to her many friends. She was quite the sight in her flowing satin gowns, usually white or, in appropriate season, *winter* white, but at times crimson, burnt orange or, when the spring mood struck her, iridescent green. A foundational garment of truly cosmic dimensions propped up her enormous bosom into a bulwark that would have been the envy of Dollie herself, if sweet Dollie were ever to find her unfortunate way to the south Bronx and into this charming gin mill. Her equally enormous laugh, big smile, and huge hair all combined to make her an apparition of frightening proportions. Tits was, or at least *had been*, a hooker of great renown in the neighborhood for many years. That was true until her taste for rich, fatty foods caused her to get so big that even that portion of her clientele that favored their whores a bit on the "plump" side found the task just a little too steep of a climb to be worth the effort.

But this old broad was unusual, if not unique, in the world of NY prostitution, because Enchante had never been a heroine addict, had never been a problem drinker, and had not conceived a huge gaggle of illegitimate young'uns as she continued to practice her evening trade. Having been raised by a mamma who had failed in that ever so important procreation department, she learned from her dear departed mother that, next to heroine and vicious men, pregnancy was her worst enemy.

So, with her first profits, she began to pay religious attention to the simple consumption of birth control pills. *Poof!* No kids, except for three who somehow happened notwithstanding the precautions she took; no drugs, and no—or at least not very many—beatings at the hands of mean Johns.

More importantly, she saved money. See, this was one hell of a good looking woman until the calories began to stack up. At five feet ten inches tall, legs a mile long, and the aforementioned incredible dimensions in front, Tits had had her pick of the whore-chasing men in the community. They included a significant number of well-heeled Johns from other "jurisdictions" who came along to see if the stories about her body—and her substantial bedroom skills—were true. Anyway, all this meant that she saved enough money to buy a liquor license and lease an old drugstore site on the corner of a very busy intersection in the Bronx.

Twin Peaks was the culmination of all Enchante's dreams, complete with "sleeping rooms" upstairs and lovely quarters in back for her own leisure. There was a large bar that even had a small kitchen serving it and room for a couple of pool tables where the men could wait and occupy themselves in anticipation of the delivery of whatever other "services" might be on the menu.

The sign out front had cost her $2,500.00, but its symbolism was *just* what Ol' Tits had always dreamed of. A six foot by four foot neon display depicted a pair of snow covered mountain peaks, coincidentally exactly the same size, draped in a satin-like covering of twinkling snow, slopes descending to a valley of dark trees down below. . . very subtle. It was here, beneath the glittering, alternately flashing, pulsating, letters TPs that men— and women—had come for a decade, to drink, laugh, eat, play and, in recent times, to meet, free from the interference of vice cops, excise policemen, or narcs. One of those three babies had been—surprise, surprise—fruit of the loins of one of New York City's finest, currently head of Bronx Vice Enforcement. What a fortuitous event, that.

Of course, things being the way things are, Tits and her girls had always been pretty free of the untoward interference of law enforcement zealots. This was mostly because of the lineage of her eldest son, a fact subtlety but carefully and thoroughly disseminated throughout the precinct; but also because of her consistent willingness to avoid drugs, violence, and the huge numbers racket that had been ongoing in the area forever. The politics and racial complexities of black gambling had made a frequent war zone out of that neighborhood ever since the boys had come home from WW II. Whenever anybody tried to mix drugs, booze, *or* broads into the program in an effort to upset the time honored power structure, there was always trouble. Inevitably a bunch of folks ended up strewn about the darkened streets, full of enough holes to sink the Queen Mary, their blood making a sticky, stinky mess of the pavement. She was too smart, and too "Enchante," to allow herself or her girls to become embroiled in such a tribal war, so she steered clear.

If ever a member of one of the many law enforcement agencies who themselves fought their own turf wars over the Bronx needed a little help, like a small loan, a place to stay, or even, say, a discreet and anonymous evening's entertainment, the same was always available and forthcoming—of course, at no charge. This was no dumb hooker. As time passed, word got around that TPs was a very safe place for a wide variety of activities, to include just plain old "meeting."

It was there that Enchante Weaver unwittingly hosted some of the most dedicated, skillful, and deadly mercenaries in all the world of terrorism. It was there that the Vanguard, the elite of the New Islamic World, found safe harbor to sit and talk in strange dialect—code really, and to taste from the wide array of delicacies on the proprietor's varied menu. Not a bunch of self-important idiots trying to look like African chieftains in dopey-looking hats and striped robes, but very quiet, confident, normal looking guys who just happened to be extremely competent at and devoted to the art and science of killing. And nobody ever knew it.

* * * * *

James Brown Sanderson was born in the projects of Philadelphia in 1949, son of an unwed woman who died of a heroin overdose when he was eleven. He was kept in food and clothes only because of the thrift, good graces, and fortitude of the woman's Aunt Hattie until he was old enough to choose the Marines over prosecution for a liquor store holdup. The proprietor of that establishment, most unfortunately, had lost not only the evening's cash register receipts and a pint of Calvert's sour mash, but also most of the right side of his head to a shotgun blast that erupted from the barrel of James' sawed-off. It really had been an accident, though, as it was his first such escapade; he had never even held a gun in his hands before and certainly knew nothing about how easily one could be fired.

As the man lay gurgling and bubbling behind the counter, James saw the surveillance camera swinging back in his direction. Instantly, he fired the other barrel of the shotgun, blowing the small device right off its pedestal in a shower of sparks, plaster, glass and smoke. No one was in the place, and he was wearing gloves, so he just dropped the gun behind the counter at the feet of the dying man and nonchalantly walked out. The doors had been shut against the January cold, so the sound was muffled, then all but extinguished by the roar of the expressway that pulsated above the store on its elevated network of concrete, heavy trucks shaking the place constantly.

Book II – The Hounds of Hell

It was just a few minutes before 2 a.m. when he walked out, heart racing, pockets full of cash and whiskey. He walked quickly to the alley behind the storefronts, cut under the elevated highway, crawled through a hole in the chain link fence, and slipped in the basement of a tenement via a broken window. This place was no safer than the street, as anyone he saw there might be expected to attempt to relieve him of his booty or, if they saw the spatters of blood and brains on his sleeve, turn him in, in hopes of a favor from the local cops.

Finally, he found a room—no bigger than a closet, really—where he could sit close to a noisy but warm old radiator, sip his booze, and contemplate his next move. As he sat on the filthy floor in the corner of that little room, shadows and reflections from the highway moving across his young face, three things seemed clear. First, he had to get away from Philadelphia immediately. The shotgun might never be traced to him; James had deftly lifted it from under the bed of a sleeping holdup man while on his nightly burglary rounds, and the man was unlikely to report the theft to the authorities. The surveillance camera presented a different problem, however. If it had caught him on a previous pass, before he blew it to tiny bits, he'd be dead meat within a matter of hours.

Second, although unsettling momentarily, the act and consequence of killing the old Polack had been surprisingly easy. The gun felt natural in his hands, the firing almost instinctive—and very accurate. The results were sort of matter-of-fact. No big deal. Huh. He was a natural born killer.

Third, the fastest and cleanest way out of this place was immediate enlistment. Immediate removal from the problems, and a quick trip to war and the chance to hone his newly discovered killing skills. He knew there were induction physicals scheduled for the next day, because he had an acquaintance who was going in. That did it. He drained the pint, concealed the cash in his socks and underwear, and slipped into the predawn snowfall. Tomorrow he would become a United States Marine and go kill gooks for fun and profit.

Time sort of telescoped itself into a flash of experiences, all in furtherance of his zest for killing, as he sailed from Army basic training and Advanced Infantry Training to a special school for some of the very best students in the art of warfare. Commando school was just what it sounded like it was: A study in how to sneak around in a foreign and dangerous place, under awful conditions, shooting, stabbing, strangling, and blowing people up, then sneaking out to a safe place—only to go back and do it again. What fun. James ended up in Cambodia, spring of 1968.

The day came when even this joy would come to an end. James Brown Sanderson lay dead, horribly mutilated by several rounds from a distant heavy machine gun. His head and chest were pretty much gone after a big shrapnel charge, suspended ten feet above the trail, had detonated right over his head. Well, at least the name on the dog tags said "James Brown Sanderson, 300-21-1139." With no face, only one hand, and generalized burns that had destroyed any unique markings, the guy could have been anybody. In fact, he was James' partner in killing, David Jergenson, a young black sniper from Denver, who just happened to be about the same size and general build as James.

Training paid off, as the two had kept a substantial distance between them as they moved through the jungle. Even with several yards separating him from David, the explosion knocked him down, rendering him unconscious for several minutes. After he came around from the explosion that had so rearranged David's head and torso, James did some quick calculating on the subject of his future. Bleak.

He had grown weary of all this mud and rain and the regimentation imposed by the pompous assholes who seemed committed to keeping him wet for the rest of his life; he considered the realization that he would never be anything more than a totally expendable killer, easily replaced, and probably just as easily discarded when his usefulness waned. Oh, the killing had been grand, and the training excellent. He was competent to hit tiny targets from upwards of five hundred meters with a variety of weapons, to extinguish life silently at close range, even with his bare hands, and he could rig explosive charges that could bring down enormous structures like they were tinker toys.

Only now that all seemed wasted as he lay in the jungle of a far away land, his companion splattered all over the ground and his own body still twitching and aching from the concussion that had knocked him out a few minutes earlier. And the enemy responsible for both the machine gun fire and the booby trap were no doubt en route to his exact location.

Time to assess, as he had done a couple of years before in that cold little room in Philadelphia. Quickly it had become clear that, in addition to the necessity of his immediate withdrawal from this location, he might create his own death, compliments of poor Ol' David. He took the dead soldier's tags, smeared his own with David's blood—there was plenty in the area— draped them around what was left of the corpse's neck. James collected up all the weapons, ammo, David's cash and valuables, and hauled ass for parts unknown. David's tags went to the bottom of the first big river he crossed.

It took James twenty-six days to make his way out of Cambodia, avoiding not only the enemy, but also the half dozen units from his own outfit who had been trying valiantly to find him. If they found the remains of Billie, they would, unless someone had a better recollection of both men than he thought, believe the nasty corpse they found was James Brown Sanderson. And while he was winding his way through the jungles, across rivers, and up into the hill country, he had nothing better to do than to plan, and to create, his new self. The result was Jackson Daniels, or just "J.D." to those who knew him—that, of course, nobody did. At least not then. And it helped him to ponder his new persona as he swam, hiked, climbed, bribed, and killed his way up into Thailand, on to Burma, and eventually to the teeming, steaming streets and docks of Calcutta. From there, after a year of hiding, stealing food and clothing, and telling more lies than a politician running for office, he started for home. The result was an entry into Central America at Panama, a painfully slow trip up into Mexico, and finally, a very illegal crossing of the Rio Grande with a bunch of Mexicans who were headed for those fabled green pastures and golden streets of the good old USA.

Philadelphia was out for obvious reasons, so he migrated to Jersey, eventually landing back across the bridge in the Bronx, where he first met some interesting guys at Twin Peaks; he was drinking some pretty good booze and waiting to meet one of the young ladies. Tits provided. The result—of meeting the interesting guys, not the hookers—had been an introduction to the world of killing for *profit*, not just for fun. After being thoroughly screened, repeatedly tested, and completely indoctrinated into the world of mercenary murder, he eventually rose to the highest levels among his peers. Not bad for a dead guy. And it was here, at TPs, that he first became familiar with the whole Islamic thing, initially as his employer, then as doctrine, and finally as a way of life. James Brown Sanderson, a/k/a Jackson Daniels, a/k/a J.D., a/k/a "Whiskey Jack," was so good at what he did, especially with explosives, and he was so quick, so quiet, and so efficient, that he became a member and later a leader of The Vanguard, the elite among terrorists for the PLO in North America.

If Enchante only knew what she had encouraged. There, in a rundown little dive called Twin Peaks, on a corner in the Bronx, a small but elite group of fanatics prepared to execute part of a plan called by their leaders simply the Offensive. It would destroy a major portion of the structure by that most of the people in the United States obtained their electricity. They would lead small squads of experts in the field of demolitions, and they would set in place a chain of explosions that would change the lives of *at least* one hundred fifty million Americans. And they would do it very soon.

3.

Yasser Arafat was really quite a guy. That is, if you like your heroes a bit on the bloodthirsty side. Awarding that thug the Nobel Peace Prize was about as appropriate as recognizing Adolph Hitler for his contributions to population control. Over an illustrious thirty-year career, the guy had ordered and overseen the murder of thousands of innocent men, women, and children, mostly Jewish, but many Muslim, just like him. Prosecution for war crimes would have been a more appropriate recompense for his deeds, rather than fawning over him like Flint had done, and in the *Rose Garden, no less!*

Ordering the bellies of pregnant women slit open in front of their horrified husbands, hanging his enemies up on butchers' hooks, bombing whole busloads of tourists, even engineering the awful killing spree at the Olympics in Munich, demonstrated the kind of "peace" he favored. But—give the devil his due—he had quite a following and an enormous popularity among militant Muslims around the world. He was also chairman of an elite little group of powerful, wealthy, and very dangerous Shiites known only as the Committee. Shiites were the most militant and most aggressive Jew haters in the world.

"Gentlemen, the Chairman has only a brief time with us tonight, and the danger he faces meeting with us like this is beyond calculation, so let us begin. Jonathan has returned from his Western rounds, and his report is that commencement is very close.

Jonathan—?" Anwar Solkirstan was an amiable man, Egyptian by birth and heritage and a man of the most passionate hatred for everything Jewish. His gentle firmness fit well in contrast to the bombastic brutality of Arafat, and he had been at the operational helm of the Committee for several years. He turned to Jonathan Abdelmanek for this report, and, although most cordial in his demeanor, Jonathan knew the accuracy that was now required of him. No room for conjecture, and absolutely no margin for error. Death would be far easier than the consequences of a mistake before this group.

"Thank you, Anwar. . .good evening Mr. Chairman. Gentlemen. I am just so honored to be here and to have the privilege of addressing the Chairman in person, I—"

"SPEAK, man! Do not waste our time in such groveling!" Arafat's face reddened as he jolted Abdelmanek—and the rest of

the eleven men in the room—with the speed and volume of his verbal assault.

"As you wish, Mr. Chairman. . ." The man was nearly apoplectic, and he besought Allah to give him courage to continue—quickly. "Both the financial aspects and the sabotage of the electrical system are well in hand. The operative in charge of the wire transfer effort advises that the viruses are ready, available for introduction into the Fedwire system, as well as the entire overseas wire transfer system, upon command. The present scenario calls for implementation at the same time as the interruptions planned for the credit card networks.

"The electrical operation is in the process of final deployment, with all units—twenty in all—each led by a Vanguardsman, ready and in possession of all necessary explosives and attendant devices. Targets number between two and three hundred in all, and Mr. Alakmah advises that setting the completed devices will take ten days. We have allowed for twelve, due to the area being spanned and the number of man-hours required to set and properly conceal the charges at so many locations. As you are aware, our study indicates that the destruction of this number of the larger substations will have a shock-wave effect on the entire network, so that power can be expected to cease to exponentially more users than the simple number actually served by the stations that we destroy.

"Our engineers are confident that the whole interconnected electrical power network, throughout the country, will be affected by this technique, at least interrupting service for a period of several months, if not actually so overloading the remaining lines and network relationships as to cause complete collapse. In fact, my own review of the proposed sites and their placement in the electrical network suggests resulting long term blackout nationwide."

As they all knew, the plan called for the destruction of many of the larger substations, with the targets being chosen on site by the explosives experts from a larger list of installations that provided power to the most populous areas. The man took a breath, just one breath, and looked around the room, through the thick smoke emanating from a dozen cigars and pipes. The faces were taciturn, phlegmatic, the voices silent. Anwar spoke.

"Excellent, Jonathan, and quite in line with what we have been planning. Obviously, the timing of the actual explosions is critical, as each team must have precise instructions as to when the devices are to be detonated. All must go off at or about the same time, nation-wide, in order to avoid the possibility of tampering or attempted disarming of any of the bombs, once the word gets around that such events have transpired in various places. I believe the time is presently set for 3 a.m. EST on March 21, is it not?"

Jonathan nodded his affirmation and started to speak. Solkirstan continued too quickly. "Now, as to the electronic banking area, has it been coordinated with the bombings?"

The reporter spoke without hesitation now, relieved to be asked about an area about which he was well versed. "Absolutely, Anwar. Three hours earlier, on the morning of the explosions, the New York Fed will stop transmitting wired funds, the funds it attempts to transfer will all go to the wrong accounts, and the credit card system will simply stop working." They continued to discuss a few details regarding the potential impact of this two-pronged attack, and then the conversation turned to the American President.

"Tell us, Jonathan, we know you were concerned about the decision to take out the new man with something so risky as a sniper. Are you now in your comfort zone, and how are those plans progressing?"

Now he started sweating. The whole idea was insanity to him; he had always hated such direct and traceable actions. And the fact that Sallie was really *in charge* of the whole thing because of his sole connection with the shooter made him even more uncomfortable. The man was a perfect loose cannon—a vicious, bloodlusting lunatic—and the idea of him having control over a mission of the magnitude of a presidential assassination was incomprehensible. But such an attitude could be quickly fatal at this point. That madman had the ear and the confidence of both the Chairman and Solkirstan, mostly based upon his accomplishments in the intelligence and ordnance areas, and they placed great store by his opinions as well as his accomplishments.

"The operative has arrived in New York and has been provided all necessary assistance. He will drive to Chicago day after tomorrow, as there is far less chance of detection by car. He will set up his procedures on location, cache his weapon well in advance, and await final word. The Governors' Conference is in ten days, that fits well with the other two prongs of the offensive. The 'Jack Ruby' operative has been put in place already, so the shooter will never leave the location alive. The hit is scheduled for the afternoon of March 20, some twelve hours before the electrical explosions occur. The financial portion will be implemented during the evening hours, with the results confirmed by midnight." He could only hope he had been suitably positive about the whole thing and that his grave concerns were not apparent.

They continued for several minutes, second-guessing, questioning, and at times arguing, until Arafat suddenly arose, raised his hand to the group, and bid farewell. The signal was thus given that he had heard enough, that he was in agreement, and that the operation was to proceed to execution as planned. Just like that, he gave the order to kill, to explode, to cripple an economy, an entire society, a sacred way of life to two hundred forty million people. And like the despots who had preceded him around the world in acts of horrible enormity, he left the dirty work to those who followed him. He departed without further thought of it, having never been concerned about the consequences in the first place. He had needed to preoccupy the Americans with enough of their own troubles that he could proceed with more weighty matters. What he considered now was his real target: The sovereign state of Israel.

4.

The new president felt like he had just completed a thirty-kilometer forced march through knee-high mud, loaded with a full pack and rifle. And it was only Tuesday. The days were grueling, not only in length and complexity, but also with the kind of stress that only running an entire country's government can produce. Things were even harder because of the constant infusion of political intrigue, protocol and, of course, the ever important *spin.* Standing in front of the mirror in the bath off the master bedroom, Webb frightened himself, the apparition he saw was so haggard, so old looking, so slumped. He straightened the tired back, sucked in the midriff, squared the shoulders. A hint of a faded smile crossed his lips as he saw that the soldier was still there; he just really needed a bit of rest.

Days had turned into weeks since the firestorm that propelled him into the Oval Office, and he had, by all objective standards, done very well. The liberals on Capitol Hill were so afraid of the spin that might accompany any real hard opposition to this new, heroic, black president that they were at a loss when he began to close in on some of their most sacred cows. The most left-leaning adversaries seemed the most confused, unable, as the new President told Mac in the car after one meeting, to decide "whether to scratch their butts or wind their watches!" Reed was so bushwhacked by yet another Webbism that he nearly choked on a mouthful of very hot coffee, spewing it across the back seat of the limousine. The General was still, after all, the General.

Drying his weary face on one of those ridiculously lush towels that appointed the master suite, he chuckled to himself as he again viewed the irony of the feel of that opulent cushiness against the leathery toughness of his weathered and sun-worn skin. As he turned to walk into the bedroom and the still welcome and tantalizing presence of his beautiful Molly, the tail of that thick bath towel brushed across the top of the cabinet, sliding his watch and the toothpaste tube off onto the carpeting. The watch bounced against his bare foot, and he bent to pick it up.

Fatigue dulled even the most rudimentary of the old motor skills, and he kicked the watch against the baseboard beneath the cabinet. He bent down and, realizing that he could not see the watch without actually getting down on all fours, he got clear to the floor to complete the search. Feeling it before he saw it, he grasped the watch and started to his feet, his eyes inadvertently glancing into the corner of the small room. The lavatory cabinet and the sidewall of the bathroom met beneath the two-or three-inch overhang created by the bottom of the cabinet; there in the half light was a small object, white in color and shaped like a flat-topped cone.

Well, this guy was not paranoid, but he was pretty sophisticated about the finer points of sound bugs, and he froze in that half crouch, eyes riveted on the little object. He thought about calling the snoops, or at least ringing for the Secret Service guy out in the hall beyond the door to the master suite. "For crap sakes, Jackie," he said in exasperation, "pick the thing up. Hell, if it blows you up, at least you won't have to eat lunch tomorrow with Ted Kennedy!" He almost laughed out loud when the thing turned out to be the cap to a tube of toothpaste. Picking it up, he arose to replace it on the tube he had just set down beside the sink. Only that tube was already capped—he had just done it moments before.

He tossed the extra cap in the wastebasket, turned off the light, and walked out. Molly slid over to welcome his aching bones into the warmth of her bed; her slender legs found him, as she touched his face with her gentle hands, there in the darkness. Tolerating a Kennedy would be possible if it was to be preceded by all night with this wonderful woman.

About three a.m. Webb found himself awake, staring at the same ceiling that had provided the last texture before the eyes of his departed running mate a few weeks earlier. And it was that man who occupied his thoughts in the quiet darkness. Molly slept peacefully beside him, a long leg draped casually over his, as if to satisfy her unconscious self that he was still present and, looking over at her, he could see the elegant, sensual lines of her torso where her gown parted to reveal her beauty. An oft-repeated prayer of thanksgiving crossed his lips silently as he felt that same old thrill at the remarkable sight of her perfect ebony skin, the curves that time seemed unable to alter.

But soon his thoughts drifted to the nightly list of the insoluble; he thought of John Wesley Kincaid. The man had died in this room, in this very bed actually, although the mattress and springs had been replaced at once after his death. Every night, it seemed, the new man found himself thinking a little about Jack Kincaid. How could he have had such rotten luck, such lousy timing, as to have just *died* right in the middle of the biggest party, after the biggest political coup, of his life?

His mind said it again: *I just can't believe it. He was fine. He was healthy as a goddam horse. The docs say his whole body was fine. He just quit living. Lord, how'd that happen?* He mused to the Almighty, there in the silence. *And why, Lord? Why waste such a tremendous guy like that? And to think I about got myself killed just hauling him out of the jungle, only to have him die in bed on the first night of his presidency.* There had been many such queries from this soldier, as he had seen the loss of countless precious lives over his thirty *years in and around combat.*

*It has to have been more. It just can't be natural. It's like somebody poisoned him, or suffocated him, or hit him with something, but left no trace, no sign . . .*The thoughts trailed off again, because every one of those options had been ruled out by the best forensics guys in the business. Both eyes snapped open wide as his mind, for what reason he would never know, flashed back to that toothpaste cap. Half scolding, half-amused at the nonsense this tired mind could produce, he tried to argue himself back to sleep.

"Don't be an idiot, Jackie, you're acting like some neurotic 'wannabe' Quincy! " he mumbled to himself. He lay there trying to think of something else, chastising himself all the while for being so silly about that damned cap. But he could not dismiss it. Silently, he got out of bed, walked back into the bathroom, and retrieved the cap from the wastebasket. He opened the top drawer of the lavatory cabinet and carefully placed it in the back, first wrapping it in a tissue. Examining it again, he had caught his breath just a little, realizing there was a small bit of blue gel residue still inside. Jackie was a life long Crest man, and none of that wimpy gel, either—just the good old paste. One thing was sure: It wasn't his or Molly's.

With his tiny little find tucked away for delivery to Dickie Freeman in the morning, he slipped back into bed beside Molly and sought sleep. But tomorrow he would call that goofy little pathologist who had briefed him after examining all of Jack's innards and let him chase just one more blind lead. It was almost certainly nothing.

The Devil's Playground

* * * * *

From the first weekend, and even to some extent from the first day, of the Webb presidency, the rumblings from around the world had caused him to put enormous pressure on the intelligence community to keep updating and adding to the fund of information available regarding all these "coincidental" events. Of course, most of what was needed to find out new stuff was already in place, as the relevant agencies were in the business of constantly monitoring such things anyway. For example, that terrorist who had defected in London the weekend of Kincaid's death. When the word came that he was making big noises about big quantities of high explosives somewhere in New York, the boys and girls in the intelligence game immediately had some ideas about who and what, at least in general terms, might be involved.

In New York City, as in most big cities, the main responsibility for the identification and monitoring of suspected terrorists and their activities falls on the local FBI office. Each field office has a special counterintelligence or "CI" agent, reporting directly to the SAIC (Special Agent In Charge), whose sole responsibility in life is to know all that can be known about that particular town's population of crazies—amateur as well as professional. So either alone or with the help of assistants, he spends his time watching, listening, reading about, and even infiltrating, the ranks of every sect and faction from the Aryan Nation to the Black Muslims and the PLO. The job requires a fair amount of training, a lot of patience, a very analytical mind, a great memory, and an incredibly cynical attitude about Homo sapiens in general.

Henry Lassiter was the SA for counter-intelligence activities for the New York City FBI field office. They have more than one, including satellite offices in a number of the boroughs, but the main office is large and well staffed. Henry had been in the counter-intelligence business for almost thirty years, having first worked briefly in the CIA before failing eyesight and a broadening waistline cast him in disfavor with the beautiful people at CIA headquarters in Langley, VA. At fifty-six, he was the oldest agent in the place, and also the oldest CI officer in the country. Hardly the image of Efrim Zimblest, Jr., he was too fat, wore thick glasses, had flat feet that could only tolerate Hush Puppies and white socks, and he didn't even know where his service revolver was. That explained why he never got one of those fancy new 10-

millimeter automatic Glocks when the FeeBees automated their arsenal. But he was one brilliant sonofabitch when it came to snooping bad guys.

Sitting in a small office upstairs in the old high rise office building in Brooklyn that housed his unit, he looked like a Fuller Brush salesman or an aluminum siding rep, or even a retired bus driver. The place was strewn with piles of computer paper, old copies of the *New York Times,* crossword puzzles on top, various red file folders scattered on the chairs, the vinyl couch, and across the floor. Oh—the crossword puzzles were all filled in. Every word, every box, every day. And there was never a mistake.

A computer monitor flickered behind a dusty pile of reports from home office, the white dots of the screensaver pattern streaking away as if this little cesspool were the cockpit of the USS Enterprise and this was Spock's seat. The keyboard was not visible, buried somewhere in the mess; Henry didn't really like his computer, or anybody else's, for that matter. He had never gotten along very well with them, and now, with the vast majority of his information coming from them and being stored on them, the uneasy truce between him and that "green monster," as he lovingly called it, often erupted into ugly, loud, and potentially violent warfare.

For over a year, the unit had been uneasily tiptoeing around the edges of a vague rumor about a totally secret operation (called "black," in the trade) being run by some unknown militant group. They were quartered somewhere in the Bronx or possibly in the projects of Newark and led by some shadowy creep who supposedly was connected at the top of the terrorism food chain. Fragments of stories about disappearances, of exotic communications capabilities, had filtered through to Henry's people, always carrying with them a bit of the macabre, always suggesting foreign influence, and almost always with a hint of a large and exotic weapons stockpile.

Once, during the summer of 1996, Lassiter thought he had a strand of a lead, when a young black cocaine dealer mentioned such a place to a DEA agent who was interviewing him after his arrest. Seems he had been in possession of a briefcase full of Colombian cocaine, still in the kilo bricks, wrapped in the distinctive opaque plastic that was the trademark of the region. It went by the name of "the First," a well known moniker that designated one of the richest cocaine producers in all of South America.

The Devil's Playground

While discussing the likelihood that his future was likely to end that very night with his eternal incarceration in some federal institution of higher learning, he mentioned a report he had heard about a place in the south Bronx. Some wild man worked for terrorists there and routinely killed people; caused their bodies to vanish. The narc had called Henry, who then interviewed the kid. After getting him a ridiculously low bond over the crimson-faced objections of the Assistant U.S. Attorney handling the drug case, they agreed to allow him to wander into the general area, look around, listen to the street talk, and report back.

Lassiter hoped the kid would play ball and do as he promised; the drug charge was pretty ugly, and he was facing a huge sentence, notwithstanding his youth, if he was convicted. They briefed him, searched him, and sent him on his way. He never came back. The collective wisdom of the unit was that he had gone a bit further south than the Bronx—like maybe Costa Rica or Bolivia—on the wings of some box full of money he had stashed just for such an eventuality as this one. The risk had been worth it—cocaine dealers were as profuse as tenement rats and, had he come back with even a *little* information concerning this mysterious place, they could have begun the systematic, boring procedure of finding, watching, profiling, and infiltrating the enemy. But it failed, and the kid split. Or at least that was the opinion in the CI unit. Unless, of course, he had stepped into hell itself and been swallowed up, like the lore suggested.

But Henry Lassiter and his little squad of snoops kept this strange rumor on their radar, trying in vain to fit each stray puzzle piece found on the street into some form that would give shape and substance to the conjecture. And the news about the big explosives stockpile "somewhere in New York" only made them more interested in putting some meat on those ethereal bones. It was just so damned difficult to find a place to start. There were literally thousands of possible sites, hundreds of thousands of moving vehicles that could house such items, and over two *million* people—in the Bronx, Queens, Brooklyn, Brownsville, and several other garden spots, not to mention Newark, and even Wilmington and Philadelphia—that could really conceal such an operation. They just needed that one lead, that first fragment, to start things moving.

5.

"This is quite the hideout, Willie, if it weren't for that stinking half frozen sewer out front! Goddam thing smells like rotten shit! I'd a thought a smart nigger like you coulda found somthin' a bit more fitt'n for a hitter a my stature, 'stead a makin' me low crawl through a bunch a dead rats, trash, and smelly ice water. Hell, Will, I'as shore you'd a had yourself a highrise penthouse full a leggy whores long before now, what with all the cash you kep' haulin' in with them little trunk loads a white powder! 'Stead, I come back here 'spectin' ta get treated like a horny foreign sultan, blow jobs on demand, and end up wadin' knee deep in a landfill just to sit in this cold basement with nothin' ta look at but yore sorry puss!!"

A huge, smoke-filled guffaw followed Lester's loud tirade as he stood in the front basement room of the SPA, the faint smell of disinfectant mixed with the stench from outside. Salim smiled stiffly, forcing a guttural chuckle, while also fighting the urge to rip the white man's eyes out with a blunt object. But, the man was the best, he was absolutely trustworthy, and there was no margin for error or mistake in personnel selections when providing killers for Yasser Arafat. Looking quickly back toward the closed door to the grinder room, he smiled again, gently reproving his guest.

"Les, my good man, you must refrain from references to me by the old name. My faithful employees in the next room know nothing of my former life. As you well know, I gave up my life of debauchery and cocaine in favor of higher quests some years ago." Only the slightest edge of the sinister tinged the deep voice. "Aw hell, Will, I know—I mean 'Sallie'—it's just hard to reprogram this old computer! I still miss them wonderful hookers you always had around, too. And the good booze—what the—hey, just 'cause you got religion and can't taste the grain n'more don't mean I gotta sit here and suffer frozen toes, now *does it?* Jesus, Mary, and Joseph, Will—*Sallie*—shorely ya' got some hooch around here, just for medicinal purposes, don'tcha?"

In spite of himself, the evil one felt a smile twist his face slightly, watching and listening to the line of bullshit emitting from this colorful killer. He walked to the grinder room door and, opening it slightly, told the two gray men that he would require privacy. Moving back to the cabinet above that infamous table, he produced a bottle of—what else—Calverts Smooth as Silk, and two clean glasses; and sitting down in a chair he usually reserved for the administration of the unthinkable, he poured two drinks, straight up.

The whiskey tasted good, too good, as the Islamic convert momentarily *de*-converted slightly, sipping the amber heat. How long had it been since he had felt the warm stimulation of fine drink, smelled the sultry aroma of fine cigars, imbibed in the scent and feel of a woman's embrace. . . But that was long ago, and Allah had changed his life from emptiness and folly to the conquest of all the world for the glorification of what he now knew was the ultimate truth, Islam, and the eradication of infidels everywhere. And to that end, he now humored his highly skilled, but very necessary infidel, breaching the edicts of the faith to drink with the man only so much as was necessary to keep his confidence and assure his performance. If that meant despoiling his now purified body with a bit of booze, so be it.

Lester Monroe sat sipping the good stuff and blowing clouds of strong blue smoke from the Pall Malls he kept lighting. Sallie made small talk, reminisced about prior missions, and told the man lies about the current program until he could stand it no longer. He brought the conversation around to the relevant subject matter, the killing of Jackie Robinson Webb.

"This hit ought to be particularly satisfying to a bigot like you, Lester, killing that nigger president!" The glint and daring in Salim's eyes was not wasted on Lester, who was far from drunk and very capable of sensing the direction of the conversation. Lester's attitude toward blacks in general was no secret, but their money spent just fine, and the promised $1 million to be garnered from whacking Webb made the race of his present host absolutely irrelevant.

"Aw hell, Sal, you know better 'n that. All I'll see through that scope is *green,* no never mind what color the target is. I think I killed plenty a white boys for you before, now ain't I?" As usual, Lester was on the mark, and Sallie had to concede: Lester's bullets were truly color blind. Getting down to the business at hand, he produced a map of the lakefront area around McCormick Place, just south and east of the Loop in Chicago.

"The President speaks here, in McCormick Place, at 3 p.m.,Wednesday after next, March 20. After that, he is scheduled to attend a dedication ceremony and opening of a new exhibit area at the Shedd Aquarium, just up the street, right here." Pointing out both places and tracing the obvious route along Lake

Shore Drive, it was quickly clear that Monroe was familiar with the area. The motorcade would have to pass by Soldier Field and the Field Museum on the left and Meigs Field, over against the lake, on the right. The Aquarium was located right at the head of the drive that led into the yacht basin that bordered the small airport on the water.

"Of course, the final decision for a location from that to shoot rests with you, but our examination to this point suggests that a point atop the museum, firing northeasterly, gives you good field of fire. You'll also have plenty of observation time from concealment before actually acquiring the target. The range is right at one hundred meters, and the direction is only slightly downward, with your position and the steps to the Aquarium being roughly the same elevation.

"The museum is easily accessible for prior entry and preparation. There is very little security; nothing but a couple of rent-a-cops and some janitorial types most of the time. The stairwell and entry to the roof provide adequate privacy once you get away from the exhibit areas, and the roof has enough permanent fixtures to provide cover while you are up there. There is also a system of ductwork for cold air recirculation, vented to the roof, so ingress and egress as well as prior weapons concealment should be possible if you prefer not to use the stairs. The other locations presented problems with clear visibility, short time of exposure, and extreme distances."

The killer looked at length at the maps and aerial photographs in silence; he sipped the whiskey, smoked thoughtfully and considered the maps and descriptions for the better part of half an hour. When he spoke, his assent to the location was implicit, but his mind was looking as much at the likely escape routes after firing as at the efficacy of the firing site for target acquisition and neutralization.

"I like it, Sal, I like it fine. Now: I'll need a semiautomatic, .308, heavy barrel with flash suppressor and some noise reduction. M14, modified to handle a powder charge 15% higher than standard military specs. Leopold scope, 4x20 power, quick set and release mounting rings and, let's see. . . at that range, can I get by with a hollow point. . . No. Soft nose Hornady, lead and copper jacket. Fifty rounds. Any problem?"

Sallie was writing some of the finer points down, in preparation for the trip to the gunsmith as soon as this meeting ended. He knew the man well, and the weapon, its accessories and ammunition were no surprise. Lester always found a way to sight in his rifles, and he *always* practiced—hence the large number of rounds.

"Still like that military stuff, huh? Well, I expected as much. We have two of them here, mint condition, and they have already been modified to break down into three components for purposes of transportation and concealment. The additional powder charge does present a new twist, though; the gas operation will have to be changed, or that hot of a charge will at least cause a jam. Might even disable the mechanism. Still, I think we can get it done. Here. Look at this set of maps. You'll be driving to Chicago day after tomorrow. I'll get those two rifles. You can choose between them, then we can get the modifications and scope mounting done tonight."

The little terrorist left his infidel sniper alone to check out the best and most unobtrusive route from NYC to Chicago. Sherman was sent to fetch the rifles and scope, while the other charm school grad, Cedric, was dispatched to contact the gunsmith and arrange for Sallie to bring him the chosen weapon at once. This accomplished, he returned to find Lester folding the maps, obviously satisfied with the route and the general plan. Both weapons and the scope were examined in minute detail, disassembled, components tested, assembly performed repeatedly. Quickly, the choice was made, and the weapon was returned to its nondescript carrying case. Now for the tricky part.

They had to be certain where he would work from and when he would fire the shots. The only way to have him disposed of immediately after he had made his kill was to know exactly where he would be. And getting this wild man to report in, and to stick with the plan, was a real job. So he used the money.

"The initial five hundred thousand will be credited to the Mexican account only *after* I have confirmed from you the completion of all preparations and the location from that you will work, the time of the hit, and your anticipated escape routes. You know, Lester, we must not have you getting caught! We may need you again!!" He laughed just a bit too loud at his own nonsubtlety. But the killer agreed. Thinking through the whole thing, it was clear that he could always change things if he chose, blaming some exigent circumstance, or just being satisfied with the half mil he would already have by the time the shots were fired.

"Sure, Willie. No problem. Gimme the numbers to memorize, along with the codes, and I'll report in so often you'll wish to

"Sure, Willie. No problem. Gimme the numbers to memorize, along with the codes, and I'll report in so often you'll wish to sweet jesus I'd leave ya alone. I'll keep callin' in like a virgin at her first prom!!" Details were completed, an impressive list of facts, numbers, codes, and names was committed to memory, and he left. The delivery would be made to his hotel the next evening, in the trunk of the car he would be driving to Chicago. One thing about the PLO—they liked to go first class. The car would be a Mercedes-Benz 600SEL. Black, of course.

* * * * *

Dr. Richard Andrew Freeman sat in a private waiting room at the White House, feet almost touching the floor as his short legs dangled from the brocade chair as if he were a child waiting for the dentist. And his mood befit such a wait, too. His last "visit" with the new president had been less than congenial, and much more like a root canal than a medical briefing. Actually, he felt a bit like he'd been through an autopsy—*his own* autopsy, when the session was finished. And to make things worse, he had been so mad at himself, and so frustrated with his inability to find a cause of death after having done every single test, examination, and trick in the vast arsenal of his well-trained mind, that he sort of agreed with the irate president's assessment.

The whole thing had ended rather abruptly when the President had risen to his feet, straightened to his entire height of six feet three inches, and fixed a baleful gaze on Dickie and Jacob Steinberg, head of the pathology team that had performed the autopsy. Turning square into their faces, he spoke.

"Bullshit, boys. Just plain old barnyard bullshit. I thought I told them to get me the best and to get me some goddam answers. All I got was two pissant excuse makers from the single most overrated agency on earth, the CIA. You say there is no answer? Wrong. There *is* an answer, boys, you just haven't found it yet. That's right, gentlemen, I said *YET*. *Now you two wizards get your scrawny asses out of this building and be back here in seventy-two hours with some ANSWERS!* Oh—and if I hear anymore of this shit about not being able to figure out what killed a perfectly healthy president, you'll have more to worry about than a bad report. As you people can tell, I am *not* pleased with this poor excuse for a postmortem examination. Unless you can improve on this incomprehensible result, you may both wish you had died as small children!"

Webb had smiled only slightly, and then only for a second, as he observed that "deer in the headlights" look on the faces of these two incredibly gifted scientists. Turning away, he relaxed only a bit, lowered his voice to that godlike General intonation. After waiting several seconds, he spoke without ever looking at them again. "That will be all, gentlemen."

Dickie had not slept for two days after that; he went back to the lab and reexamined every test and every result, running many of them over again, and reexamining every slide, every sample. He ran mass spectrometry in search of every foreign, esoteric compound he could think of; he spent twelve hours in one day with Steinberg and the others, calling all over the place for ideas, reading every protocol they could find for this kind of pathological needle in the haystack. No luck. Now he was about to get his "scrawny ass" chewed *again* by this giant General, because he had absolutely nothing to report. He had visions of spending the rest of his life doing postmortem examinations on winos, floaters, and junkies in the Los Angeles morgue, where they routinely hired veterinarians to do the work.

Without warning, Webb burst into the room, slamming the door behind him. No ruffles and flourishes, no entourage, not even an introduction. The man was alone, and he was clearly on a mission.

Dickie tried to stand, but his legs would not respond. He tried to speak, but speech was difficult without air, and he was not breathing. The President saw him trying to talk, and raised his hand for silence. Not that the little guy had much chance of uttering a sound anyway.

"Doc, look, I know I was pretty hard on you and old Stienbrouner, or Steinwerner—berger—whatever his name was— there, and I'm sorry for that, I really am. It's just that every instinct in this tired being is *screaming* at me that something very bad and very wrong happened to Jack Kincaid. You guys are the best, and I know it. I just wanted you to tell me he had a stroke, or a heart attack, or something, so I could quit worrying about it, and get on with worrying about a few hundred of the other things I'm *supposed* to be worrying about." Freeman felt lightheaded, but he also felt air coursing through his lungs, as he finally was able to take a breath.

Book II – The Hounds of Hell

"Certainly, sir, I understand. . .I mean, we were so sorry, so amazed, so . . . well, so—" Webb cut him off.

"Never mind that now. Look at this." He pulled a little baggie out of his pants pocket, took out the tissue-wrapped white toothpaste cap, and carefully laid it in Freeman's hand. The doctor looked at it, then at the President's face, then back at the cap again. Just as he was about to try again to speak, Webb explained. The whole deal, complete with the paste of choice of both Webbs, and why *gel* just couldn't have been theirs.

"I know it's a long shot, and I am sure I'm acting like a complete nut. But goddamit, Doc, I gotta know what happened to Jack Kincaid; it's makin' me crazy, and I've got a few other things to do with my time! If this is a blind alley, I quit. Or at least I'll try to quit. So please, check it out, do all those high-tech things, analyze the living hell out of the thing. It's probably nothing, but I *can* tell you this much: It's not mine or my wife's, and the last person to brush his teeth in that bathroom before us was John Wesley Kincaid. After he did it, he went to bed. And Dr. Freeman, he laid down, and he died. Please try. Please."

Dickie rewrapped the cap and replaced it into the baggie, handling it like he had just been given the Holy Grail—or a live grenade. They shook hands, and he left. And even though the entire team had performed every conceivable type of chemical test on every piece and sample of the dead President, he found himself walking ever quicker as he returned to his waiting car.

That genius mind began to whir at high speed, cataloging all the tests and calculating how to get the most out of such a small sample. The Mozart kicked in again, the excitement of having just one more chance to overcome this most uncharacteristic defeat built, and he found himself half chuckling at the terror that tall ebony man had instilled in him. God, but he wanted to be tall. He had always wanted to be tall. But what he *really* wanted was to figure out why Jack Kincaid was dead. *That* was what he *really* wanted.

6.

For a financial system that accounts for at least sixty percent of all the consumer transactions completed every day in the U.S., the credit card world is surprisingly simple, and the actual mechanism that makes it all work is deceptively small. Every time a card is "swiped" through a machine by a merchant at a store or by a customer at a gas pump or a POS (point of sale) terminal at the grocery store, the same thing takes place. Transmitting by telephone lines, the little machine reads coded information on the back of the card—stuff encoded on the "mag strip"(the little brown or black line made of magnetically programmed material), and it sends that information, along with the amount of the transaction, to what the bankers and the computer geeks call a "switch." This is just a computer programmed to recognize certain of the characters that are transmitted, the numbers that identify the consumer and the bank that issued the card. It is the "authorization switch," and its only function is to determine whether or not that bank has an account in that person's name and whether or not the person is authorized to transact business in the requested amount, at the time.

A "negative advice file" is searched to see if the bank has blocked the account for any reason—like a lost or stolen card report, past due balance, or an over-limit condition on the balance. If nothing shows up in the negative file, that switch authorizes the transaction, and the merchant or automatic terminal accepts the card as payment.

The sale or payment is concluded, and the whole thing is then sent by telephone lines to another switch, this one called a "settlement switch." It directs the payment of the merchant's account with funds to be debited from the account of the bank that issued the card. There is enough information on the back of the card to identify both the customer, his bank, and the customer's account number at the bank. All this happens in a matter of seconds, with the posting of the credit to the merchant's account and the debit to the purchaser's account finished by the time the guy has left the parking lot of the store.

What is most surprising about all this is that there are no more than about five or six such switching mechanisms in the entire country: VISA, MasterCard, Discover, and a couple of multi-user networks that service a large number of smaller card issuers like American Express, Diners Club, and the department store and gas chain cards. And all these accounts, being constantly debited and credited by these few switches, get "settled"—paid—via a wire transfer system that is also operated by the Federal Reserve system. They call them ACHs, or Automated Clearinghouses. They are nothing more than miniature wire transfer networks that move information and money to cover the billions of dollars worth of transactions initiated by credit card every day.

Actually, the ACHs settle the accounts between the various banks that hold the accounts of the customers and merchants involved in all these little deals. They constantly transmit bits of information and authorize the transfer of funds to clear all this stuff and keep up with the world's commerce in "real time."

Not more than about three percent of all commerce in the U.S. is handled in cash. A substantial portion still relies on paper checks, but the vast majority of all consumer sales happen on plastic. Just imagine the instantaneous impact on American life if suddenly, without warning, they all stopped working. Pretty big mess, pretty quick. And creating such a mess requires nothing more than interrupting the flow of information over those telephone lines or, even easier, jamming the switches themselves, so that they quit issuing transaction authorization codes and settling payments.

The moment the authorization switch freezes up, commerce via plastic stops. Instantly, completely, *poof.* No authorizations, no sales. No gasoline, no milk, no bread, no nothing. And unless the consumers standing at the sales counters with their now worthless credit cards in their hands also have cash or a check to pay for what they want, they will simply do without. Of course, if the wire transfer system that moves money between the major banks has also been bushwhacked at the same time, it will only be a short time, maybe a few hours, until the entire mechanism that effects the movement of money will screech to a halt, and then the *checks* will no longer be acceptable. Nice little plan.

Willard Smalley sat back from the table in Sallie's charming little basement parlor, the top of it covered with a large piece of white paper. On it was a web of lines and boxes, arrows and abbreviations, all overlaying a map of the continental U.S. Sallie stood at his shoulder, transfixed by what he saw, slowly shaking his head as the diabolical simplicity of the whole thing became clear. "Muthafuck, Willard, pure magic. You mean, just by injecting your little evaporating viruses into each of those switch networks, you can freeze out every credit card in the country—all at the same time?!"

Willard permitted himself a rare smile, brief and subdued. "Yes sir, that is what I said. I have breached the security codes for each of them, a feat that was much easier than I ever thought it was going to be, and my tests, run just last night, confirm that I can enter them undetected, infuse the viruses, and exit their systems without detection. Just for fun, I set up accounts under fictitious names and Social Security numbers first. Then, with counterfeit VISA and MasterCards, I executed several transactions in the New York area.

"When I was confident they had all posted, I went back into each system and deleted them. Checking the accounts of the merchants, I found that every one had been removed from the merchant's clearing and settlement accounts, and the Fed had recredited the account of the issuing bank. In other words, I could do—"

"Just about whatever you wanted to do, right?" Sallie roared, interrupting those precise words before they could get out of Willard's mouth.

"Right. And if I can actually *create* not only transactions but even *accounts*, I can certainly introduce my self-destructing viruses to dismantle the whole switch, in each case. And that's not all. You see, Sallie (he was *much* more comfortable, now that his employer/host was finally realizing what he could do), this all fits in with the wire transfer crash we have already discussed. If the card systems go down and the wire transfer system has stopped moving the money around to cover all the transactions between the banks that actually *settle* all the payments represented by check traffic, just that fast, there *is* no money. Everybody rushes to the local bank or credit union office for some currency, and *voila!* You have a run on the banks."

"Most banks have less than one percent of their total customer deposits in cash on hand in the branches, or even in the central vaults, for that matter. So, when they run out of money, they close. Boom. No money, and therefore, no commerce. Like it?"

Sallie laughed out loud. He laughed uproariously, deeply, the floor shaking as his thundering voice tumbled forth, hoot after hoot, until he nearly collapsed in a heap in his chair. The ghouls peered fearfully through the back door, completely mystified by such sound and behavior from their evil boss.

"You rotten, depraved genius! Allah be praised, I think it can be done! I really think you can make the money supply vanish. You're a fuckin' Houdini, Willard, you truly are!" He laid his head down on the table and laughed until tears fell from his scarred cheeks, staining that nasty floor where so many had died.

They went through the scenario again, this time with Sallie trying to visualize the panic, the virtual pandemonium that would grip this nation over a matter of hours, once its citizens found themselves transformed into paupers by the hand of this one angry mercenary. Before Sallie could attempt to set up a defense against paying extra for this new twist, Smalley spoke. "And do not fret about additional compensation. I want you and your clients satisfied, your missions accomplished. I can do this without additional danger or fear of exposure. The five million already agreed upon will do nicely."

Salim eyed him momentarily, then hid a smile. "Insurance, that's what it is," he thought to himself. "He is guaranteeing that he'll get all that has been promised and guaranteeing that he will not find his way down our magic drain."

Then, a smile of some congeniality forcing its way across his visage; he spoke. "Most generous of you, my good man. I shall pass on to the Committee this offer, at once. But I can speak with confidence when I say that they will embrace this part of your plan, as intimated previously in our last meeting. They already anticipate the inclusion of the credit card system in your plans, and this will give some detail to that assumption. Now, tell me more. Is there not *more* that will flow from this "switch thing"—it would seem to me that there will be some impact on the merchants, as well."

"Most certainly; you have recognized one of the hidden impacts—like a sort of secondary explosion—that will result. Most merchants, and particularly the multi-location, or chain, merchants, count on the ACHs and the settlement switches to handle their money. You see, the highly automated entry systems they use to make each sale also provide inventory information and control, immediate sales reporting, and essential coin and currency monitoring. When they quit working, one can anticipate that the order will issue from all those home offices to suspend non-cash operations immediately. And just like that, there will be no electronic money, and therefore nothing to buy with it.

"Just imagine the reaction from affluent America. Statistically, the wealthier one is, the less food is kept in the house. The rich love to make one thing for dinner, above all else—reservations. And with no credit cards and no cash *and* with the restaurants closed, these rich assholes will taste real hunger for the first time in their entire pampered lives!"

The man's loathing for the genre of humanity who lived around him and populated the entire society was visible, palpable in his words and expression. Sallie could not know just how badly the banking world had treated this poor bastard. He could not begin to imagine how many times Smalley had been dealt career-stopping blows by those "cocksuckers in personnel," as he fondly named those who had never recognized his genius or enormous capabilities. But this was not just an angry man; he was a very private, very quiet man whose true venom was a complete unknown, to all but himself.

Both men laughed then, sharing an ironic bond of bloody hostility for mankind as they knew it. They went over a number of additional details about the timing and order of the planned mayhem, culminating with Sallie giving Smalley a pager. He would use it according to a preset series of number codes; codes that would first warn Willard that he should be ready, then order him to hit the networks. There would be no telephone calls and no further personal meetings. Only codes and action.

Book II – The Hounds of Hell

7.

"Henry! Henry, wake up, for cryin' out loud!" Herman Hanks shook the man by the shoulder, and Lassiter sat up with a spastic jerk that sent a pile of computer paper and crossword puzzles tumbling down in a swishing cascade of dust and styrofoam coffee cups, three of that had stale coffee still in them. A late night battle with TFC ("that fucking computer") had gone badly, and the old bones just had not been able to get out of the chair and down to the street at 3 a.m., when he finally got most of what he wanted from the cursed machine. His glasses were dangling loose from his ears as his head lay cradled on his arms atop the aforementioned pile, and they crashed, lenses down, onto the floor.

"*Shit! Domove! If I break those freaking glasses*— Oh, there. . now—what th'—*Herman! For* Crissakes, ya scared the crap outta me. Jesus, boy, don't you *knock* before you come bargin' into a guy's office?! Holy—"

"Cool it Henry, you comatose old fart—I been bangin' on the glass here for five minutes. Got tired a' mindin' my manners, since I'm just here ta try and help you sorry assholes out. Hell, you better straighten up and behave yourself, pal, er I might just take my little bit a new *info* and give it to the *Big* boys over at CIA!" Herman was ATF, a funny looking, scrawny little mope whose appearance seemed better suited to shooting heroin than guns. At 43 years old, he had been under cover so long he seldom knew when the "cover" ended and real life began. Six months of constant surveillance plus an undercover officer on the inside had finally landed a result that Herman thought might be of interest to Henry and Co.

That the counter-terrorist unit that Lassiter supervised was interested in some shadowy activity in the South Bronx was a fact well known to the folks at Alcohol, Tobacco, and Firearms; and with the movement of arms and munitions through the vastness of NYC being a fact of life, ATF saw plenty of shadows themselves. Hanks had been watching an ex-con by the name of Mosel Slaughter—the *Reverend* Mosel Slaughter, that is—proud proprietor of Slaughter House of Memories, a combination antique store, convenience store, and occasional small time drug house. It was the kind of eclectic place that shows up in the older neighborhoods and, in a large city, there is always a bit of mystery about what really goes on inside such a musty place.

The Devil's Playground

It was, however, the Reverend's background in weapons that interested the boys at ATF. His fifteen year prison term had been the result of a sale gone sour between Mosel and some visionary badboys intent on arming their multi-chaptered militant gang with Uzis, some stolen M14A1 fully automatic military rifles, and a 90mm recoilless rifle. Seems the boys had designs on a turf war of rather Byzantine proportions, to include the aforesaid shoulder-fired tank killer. It was intended for some hapless police car that might get in the way.

As is so often the case, somebody got stupid and said something they shouldn't have. Some uninvited guests attended the eventual meeting and transaction from ATF. Slaughter was convicted after a bitter and racially charged trial, did his time without incident, and came home at the age of 63 to live out his days in the old 'hood. And things had looked ever so quiet, too, with no evidence of people of low degree (except for the occasional junkie) and no real intelligence concerning the old gunrunning habits. However, the Rev was also a fine, even gifted, machinist and gunsmith, a trade he had learned compliments of the United States Army, some forty years earlier.

The activities that began to tweak the interest of Herman and his partners revolved around rumors that Slaughter was maintaining a substantial machine shop in the basement of his store. One piece of hearsay had it that he was tooled up and modifying a wide variety of semiautomatic rifles and pistols to fire rock 'n roll—full auto—and making a handsome profit at it. His reputation made it clear he was also very capable of fabricating specialty weapons from spare parts and even from parts he could fashion right there.

Nobody ever accused the man of being stupid. He could work on weapons at night, taking possession of them from customers who could deliver them under the cover of regular shipments of some of the bulkier articles he sold as antiques. And the smaller pieces, like Mac 10s, Uzis, and the many 9mm pistols on the market, could be carried right into the store in a man's coat pocket without detection.

What got Herman fired up was the result of the U.S. Attorney's grand jury subpoena on the bank where Slaughter held his business account. There were frequent cash deposits and just as frequent transmissions by wire transfer to an account in Mexico City.

Book II – The Hounds of Hell

The AUSA (Assistant U.S. Attorney) assigned to the investigation had secured a "mail cover" for Herman's convenience, a little device that allows a law enforcement agency to get copies of the return addresses on the outside of every envelope that goes to a certain address or P.O. box. They are very common in narcotics and gambling investigations, and the theory that allows this without a warrant is that a person has no reasonable expectation of privacy concerning what is on the *outside* of an envelope.

The guys also stole his trash every week for three months, learning a lot about his eating habits and his interest in pornographic literature, but also identifying every person or at least every location from that he had received mail. Banks, brokerage houses, foreign accounts, investments, and even some pretty bizarre pen pals were easily listed from the weekly trash run, and Mosel was no more careful about his refuse than anybody else. He was a lot more worried that the scholars who picked it up would scatter it all over the block than he was about who might find interest in the return addresses on his envelopes. The results were little short of astounding.

Step two of this dance was to get to the places where he apparently had financial connections and to learn what was there. They found the predictable concentrations of cash in the Mexican accounts, and there was even a pretty healthy portfolio at Prudential Bache in an amount consistent with a profit well above what the little operation on the main floor of the store would suggest. But there was more. With relations ever so delicate between Mexico and the U.S. and more importantly between U.S. and Mexican banks, Mexican financial institutions were prevailed upon to allow just a bit of "informal" discovery of certain information. This included cash concentrations from suspected drug cartels, U.S.-based organized crime money laundering schemes using Mexican banks, or suspected terrorist activities. Bingo.

The right Reverend Mosel Slaughter was no dummy. Some of his gain from the high-priced gunsmithing he was doing, turning pop guns into machine guns, was *re*-transferred by him out of the Mexican account to an Argentinean bank.

Argentina had been less than cooperative at first but, with a little help from his friends at the State Department, Hanks finally learned that the account into that some of Slaughter's gun money was going had, until the end of 1995, had a high balance of just under six million U.S. dollars. One million and change had gone into one helluva a building project in Rio, a modest little hacienda with a view of that Jesus statue, complete with indoor pool, sauna, four-car garage, the works. The rest was more difficult to trace, but suffice it to say that ol' Mosel, man of God that he was, had been the humble recipient of enough money to bankroll *several* revolutions.

The sources were still a little sketchy, but one thing was pretty clear. The guy was somehow managing to do an enormous business in some kind of contraband, banking huge sums of cash and constructing a wide array of little kingdoms for himself or someone else. All this without ever making a telephone call outside the U.S. or even running up a phone bill in excess of $50 a month, and without ever handling *anything* the Feds could identify as even a *little* dirty. To be sure, the ATF folks scrutinized every entry on every telephone bill the old bandit incurred for every month since his parole, more than four years ago.

So they watched him. And they watched him. And... nothing.

Herman even got an undercover guy inside, an older snoop by the name of Eddie Stump, a master of the "grumpy old man" disguise. Every two or three days for three months, Eddie went in to buy cigarettes, cat food, and a quart of 2% milk, always bitching about something, always feigning a cynical interest in some piece of junk, and *always* managing to talk to Mosel for a couple of minutes. Over time, Slaughter came to expect Stump and, although he never got anything of any real value out of the ex-con, Eddie did get a lot of detail out of the line of bullshit offered up by the Rev. Then one day, while attentively studying a junky old nightstand for that Slaughter was asking six hundred dollars, he snapped to attention at the low thunder that had just come from the mouth of a diminutive man at the register.

Although he could not make out what was said, he did turn quickly enough to see that Slaughter was engaged in an animated conversation with the little guy, and the customer had his hands resting on a slender brown box that was on the counter. The thing was too small for a gun—or at least for a *whole* gun—but it had the look of a package of some weight, securely wrapped and tied. "Fast Eddie" switched on the little recorder in his coat pocket and moved nonchalantly toward the two men. Excruciatingly careful and exacting analysis of the tape would reveal the words "soon" and either "surprising" or "suppression," along with a clearly audible goodbye that suggested a quick return by the customer.

Taxi records indicated that the little man had gone first to a department store, then to a shoe store, and finally to a doctor's office, before ordering the cabby to drive into the heart of the rotting core of the projects. When he got out of the cab, according to the chase car that had been following him in tandem with a second tactical unit assigned to "leap frog" the cab, he looked quickly around and was gone. Just like that.

Stump was unable to make a return visit that would not arouse suspicion before the rest of the weapon that Lester had chosen arrived. Trusty gray Cedric brought in the longer pieces, including the receiver group and the barrel, the next morning; to have returned so soon would have been to break with the ostensible habits the agent so carefully wove into his appearances. However, the surveillance camera in the attic of the building across the street had been awake and in operation when the less-than-subtle package arrived. Nothing spectacular really, just the appearance of a man not previously seen at the store, carrying a package just a little too long. Again, there was nothing suggestive of a weapon; but then, these guys were being paid to see every deviation from the norm as a possible piece of information. Cedric was only in the store for seventy-five seconds before he re-emerged, walking directly to the bus stop. Certainly atypical for your basic antique hunter.

Cops sometimes wait for years for such a simple little thread to follow. The man got on the bus headed back up town. The chase car followed that bus only a few blocks before Wallace got off that bus, hailed a cab, and proceeded *straight* into the South Bronx. He exited the cab in the middle of the street, in such plain view, and in a place of such complete nakedness, that there was no chance for the chase car to stop—or even to slow down and observe where he went. He *was*, however, in the very area of town where that young cocaine dealer had vanished and where the rumors suggested several other disappearances.

Efforts at a voiceprint match were fruitless, although every technician in the place had come into the FBI lab to hear that most unusual of voices. But one thing was obvious: A weapon had been delivered to Slaughter, granted, in component parts, but delivered nonetheless, and Mosel was doing something to it. Hanks was pretty sure the boys in counterintelligence would be interested in this new piece, and he went to find Lassiter before even going home after the long night in the sound lab.

Hanks sipped his institutional coffee from a nasty, multistained old mug that had come from the bottom drawer of Lassiter's desk. Henry read and re-read the reports, stopped to look at the maps of the city that covered the litter on his desk top, and asked again. "And *both* these guys—you *think*—were a part of the *same* delivery, a day apart. And *both* these guys were carrying parts of the *same weapon*, for this Moses guy—"

Herman corrected him, "Mo*sel*, Henry, for crissakes, Mo*sel!* Ya can't expect to find him or use him if ya can't even say his freakin' name right! *MOSEL!* Goddam gumshoe shitheads! And don't sound so gaddam skeptical, either! I don't see you scholars coming up with anything nearly this good. Why'd I bother ta' haul my dead ass all the way over here just to talk to a toad like you, anyway!? Holy shit, Lassiter, pay attention. How the fuck 'm I supposed ta help you amateurs if you won't even goddam *listen* when I fuckin' talk to ya'?! Now listen *up!* Don't sound so goddam cynical either, you old prick—this is pretty good stuff, if you ask me."

The older man suppressed a crooked smile at the mini-tantrum being thrown by his animated, mopey comrade. It was immediately obvious that the guy was off his feet with fatigue, and the product of an inopportune grin might be most unpleasant. Hanks took a gulp of the coffee, cringing at the grunge visible around the sides of the cup and, settling back in his chair, collected himself and continued.

" Now—I *said* the subjects both came in within the same twenty-four hour period, each carrying a package, and neither were people the stakeout guys had ever seen there before. *Ever.* And neither of them came back for the merchandise. Also *not the usual* for Mosel's clientele. We figure C.O.D. and personal delivery required, no intermediaries, no snitches, no middle men, no exceptions. At least none that we've observed. Again, not S.O.P. So I'm here to tell ya there's some shit 'n the game over in Slaughter's House a Mem'ries. You don't like my take, fine. Ignore me. Fuck ya. I told ya. So I'm a regular good Sumatran—right?"

By now Lassiter was awake, slurping his second dirty cup of the same coffee. The crossword puzzle genius stifled a smirk at the part about the "good Sumatran," then thought better of correcting his cranky colleague. He mumbled to himself, mumbled again, moved back and forth between the map and the narrative provided by Hanks, then offered a tired smile.

"You're a fucking genius, Herman. . . No, *really!* A bloody wizard! Or at least you're a lucky bastard. Anyway, thanks. Looks like fish to me, too. Smells like fish, and even tastes like it. And there's no question money in those quantities, and moving through such complicated channels, is consistent with some major action. . no doubt pretty high level, and for sure either drugs or guns."

He chuckled at himself momentarily, then looked with bloodshot eyes at his comrade. "Modifying some kind of long gun, high power, no doubt, prob'ly to whack some drug lord or gunrunner they don't like anymore. But you're right on about a connection with our South Bronx thing; every sense I own is tellin' me those assholes are up to a whole bunch a *no good,* and this deal about the gun heats things up." He paused, looking again at the paperwork and the maps; he stared a long moment into the steam from his coffee, then looked up.

"Thanks, Herman. Please let me know what else happens, and *do* give me a quick call if either one of them shows up again. Oh, and Herman—I owe ya one." They both indulged in a moment's grin, and the younger man was gone, his ungainly, loping, lopsided stride melting into the morning crowd in the hallway. Lassiter allowed himself a moment's reflection on the effort involved in what Hanks had just done; the man had been working for about fifty hours without a break. He went back to the map of the Bronx borough and began to apply thirty years of the metaphysics of hunting treacherous people to the facts at hand.

8.

In the world of explosives, things are less than precise. Even with the most exacting measurements in the proportions that compose the substances that actually explode, things never behave exactly the same way twice.

The physics of blowing things up is not so complex, really—just a huge version of what happens when you strike a match, clap your hands, or slam the car door. Air is displaced by the sudden creation of thrust or force in an outward direction, and that that is moved or displaced pushes the air or objects in its path away from the point where the thrust began. The air that is pushed across it by the closing of the door disturbs the dust on the dashboard and, if the other side window is open, the dust is pushed out through that opening. When a match is struck, energy is released as the phosphorous ignites and burns, and that energy, in the form of heat, moves away from the point of origin, dissipating in the surrounding atmosphere. Simple.

What makes an explosion instead of a dust swirl is the size of the occurrence and the speed with that the air and matter around it are forced away. For example, the dust on the dashboard moves about three feet in one second, and the thrust dissipates very quickly against the resistance of the surrounding atmosphere. The heat wave from the match moves away from the match head much more quickly—maybe ten to fifteen feet per second, also fading very rapidly. Of course, these two silly examples don't really explode in the sense that people associate with a bomb. Present day explosive materials create much more thrust—much more quickly—and can move exponentially more matter than such benign reactions as closing doors or burning matches. The leading edge of exploding modern smokeless gunpowder travels away from the point of origin at about 3,800 feet per second (fps), or about 2,600 miles per hour.

That brings us to the real thing: "plastic explosive" in its most powerful form, the compound the military calls C 4. This stuff doesn't explode, it "detonates." That's an expression reserved for substances that burn at speeds the human mind can scarcely imagine. The leading edge of the shock wave created by the detonation of C4 travels away from the point of origin at approximately 24,000 fps, equating to about 16,000 miles per hour, or what astrophysicists call "escape velocity." This is the speed required for objects travelling away from Earth to break the hold of gravity, exceed orbital speed, and plunge into space, except for atmospheric resistance. Pretty fast indeed and, when pushing a shock wave the size that C4, in even small quantities, creates, it simply flattens—even vaporizes—whatever it touches.

Among the many attributes that make plastic so popular, variety is one of the most important. Extremely potent compounds can be formed into thin sheets, an eighth to a quarter of an inch thick, and roping, that comes in 100-foot rolls. The sheets, called Flex-X can be wrapped around objects or slipped under stationary targets, then detonated in such a way as to take out just the right length of a linear bridge span or electrical conduit. Detonation Cord, or "det cord," can be strung along the outline of a doorframe, rolled up into a ball or cylinder, or strung out along a string of other explosives, placed in series. When set off, it will cause the serial detonation of the whole thing, at such high speed that the human eye or ear cannot separate one from the other.

One of the things that make C4 and the many forms of plastic explosive so popular and so useful is that it is so compact. The name "plastic" is just about impossible to trace anymore, but it probably comes mostly from the consistency and appearance of the compound in its many forms. A quantity of military-grade plastic the size of an attaché case, when placed and detonated by an expert, destroy will a car, collapse a small building, tear an airplane in half, or scatter the remains of many people across a large area. The amount of damage is, dependent of course upon placement and the composition of the thing to be blown up, but such a quantity *can* bring down a pretty big bridge if set by a good technician.

Another thing: It can be cut, thrown, burned, shot, even submerged indefinitely, without causing it to detonate or harming its potency or stability. Small wonder it is the weapon of choice of some of the most evil men on the planet.

* * * * *

The "back table" at Twin Peaks is the area around the pool table, and the unwritten but well understood rule and tradition is that the area is "men only," unless otherwise specified. Waitresses, clad only in tiny bikini outfits, tend the drink orders and occasional food requests, but they do not tarry unless invited—and that seldom happens at the back table. As J.D.

stepped through the doorway, cold drizzle dripping off his baseball cap and running down the back of his windbreaker, the scent and rush of warm air momentarily stopped him in his tracks. Booze, cigarette smoke, marijuana, and musty wetness were mixed with the smells of heavy, strong perfumes, colognes, and food. A strange mix, but welcome against the miseries of rain and cold outside.

Standing in the little alcove that shielded the main dining room from the street, he stood to the side of the glass door leading inside, his figure concealed by the door frame, his eyes adjusting to the light. Old habits die hard, especially when they contribute to one's survival, and the years of living in the shadows and depending on his skills of observation and concealment were as strong and instinctive as breathing and blinking his eyes. He took off his hat, shook off the rain, and quietly stepped inside, his gaze quickly catching the location and face of each party in the main room. Looking to the back, the others were visible, all silhouettes through the soft light and smoke, except for the one tall but misshapen form at the head of the pool table. Mitch was here.

"Ma gawd, ma gawd, Moses and Jesus hisself! Whiskey Jack, ma Luv—you git your cute little black ass ova' hea' and give us a great big hug—and a bil ol' nasty kiss!!" James Brown Sanderson, a/k/a Jackson Daniels, fought to find breath, fought even harder not to laugh out loud at the obvious fact that this enormous woman had just managed to bushwhack him right in the middle of the room. How her substantial self had missed his wily study of the room was a mystery. But even the time for evasive action was passed, as the woman was on him, and around him, before he could react. "Some guerilla!" he thought, as she buried him in her immense bosom. She always referred to herself in the plural "us"—J.D. had no doubt why, as he struggled for air. The air was truly thin, or at least hard to find at times, between the twin peaks.

"Tits, darlin', ya shouldn't a' snuck up on me like that, I might a mistook ya for the enemy and done ya some awful harm!" She roared with huge laughter, and all those in the room, unable to miss this loud exchange, caught the humor of the whole thing and joined in. She mashed his face in a sloppy smooch that left deep red lipstick from one side of his mouth to the other. Then she released him with such quickness that his body sprang off the mass of her upholstery, and he nearly fell to the floor. His

136

own coloring almost matched the lipstick smear as he struggled to keep his balance, and he could hear the voices of the others at the back table, chuckling at his plight.

The victim fought for words, some quip or comeback that might salvage his decimated pride and countenance; he looked back at his smiling, giant attacker and, at that range, his entire field of vision was obstructed by her huge attributes. For just a moment, he tried to imagine the bulwark that was responsible for holding the things up in such prominent fashion, discarded the thought and, smiling weakly, backed away.

"Thanks for the welcome, Tits, gooda see you, too. Nice ta be back. . ." Wiping lipstick on the sleeve of his jacket, he turned to walk to the area where the others waited, stumbling into an empty table that was piled high with a busser's pan full of dirty glasses.

The racket was enormous, as the contents crashed to the floor. Jack lunged clumsily to catch it, the laughter now out of control. One woman patron spoke a raucous commentary "Jesus, Enchante, you *still* knockin' the men off they feet!" More laughter. Then a man added to the now generalized hilarity, all at poor J.D.'s expense. "Man's knees buckled like a cheap card table! Whassa' matta, J.D., them jugs too much fo' ya? Ha! Been'ere an' dunnat, too, brotha'! What a way *to go!*"

Daniels grinned sheepishly as the guffaws overpowered his otherwise tough persona, and the blush deepened as a leggy waitress bent over in front of him to begin picking up the mess. Now his own grin was hard to suppress, but the embarrassment was far greater for him than the humor. Of course, the assembled mercenaries awaited, grins like grand piano keyboards, eager to add their own ribald one-liners to his plight.

There was a total of eight men in back, some sitting along the two walls that formed the corner of the restaurant, three moving silently around the pool table. And two stood, one on either side of the small area, their eyes subtly moving from door to window, table to stair, then back again. Neither of them mingled with the others, entered into the conversation, or even spoke, except to answer one of the others. These were the not-so-obvious sentries, maintaining an invisible perimeter around the group. Tyreese Broland, standing at the head of the table with cue in hand, flashed the aforesaid pearly smile, and intoned the inevitable— and predictable—welcome.

The Devil's Playground

"Nice *trip*, 'Whis', and great recovery! 'Cep we was scared there fer a minute you's gonna git all snatched up, so ta speak, 'tween all them tiddies and that skinny li'l ho. Y'er either super trained in the art a con-sin-*tra*-shun er you blind, that's fo' *god*dam sho'!" Laughter erupted among these heretofore-quiet men, knees being slapped, more piano key grins lighting up dark, chiseled faces—faces that seldom creased in such frivolity and almost never had reason for laughter. The volume was quickly checked, however, and the additive quips and one-liners, each received with more grins and hoots, were *not* audible outside the group.

Those in the main room could only cast sidelong, even furtive glances in that direction, quickly turning away; it was clear that these men were to be left alone, not molested or even engaged in conversation beyond short greetings. This was particularly true once they had formed up in the back table area. That deference ran deep in these communities, and such men were accorded great regard and were to be feared and left alone. The humor aimed at J.D. was only possible because of his still youthful appearance (although a full forty-seven years old, his slender stature and fine face belied his age) and the fact that he had not yet arrived in back when his calamity struck.

That same leggy waitress whose lithesome form had so captivated him a few moments earlier arrived with a Budweiser long neck bottle for him. Their eyes met as he took the beer, the man appearing nonchalant and seemingly ignorant of her presence except for the beer. But eyes locked momentarily, and her lips parted slightly as her chest heaved with her rapid breathing. She stood perfectly erect, slight of frame but tall, figure perfect in each particular.

"Thanks, Babe. . . thanks. . .now *beat it.*" The words lacked harshness to attend such a message and, turning with her as she slumped as if struck to the heart by his rebuff, he spoke in a low voice. "*Latresha—later*" then again as she subtly turned slightly back, her eyes stopping short of him, his voice little more than a whisper, "*later!*" She walked back toward the bar, away from these cold men. As she reached the end of the bar to fill another order, Enchante could see the slight smile lifting the high cheekbones and bending the corners of the wide mouth. When the young woman saw the proprietor's gaze, the countenance lit a bit further and, brushing past the big woman's flowing gown, she quietly spoke: "Later." A deep glutteral chuckle bubbled from deep within the magnificent woman, and, calling the girl's name, she handed her a room key and a knowing smile.

"You mind yo' bizness, Dan'ls, that shit a' make you stupit. . no man fit fa' duty wit ta Vanguard got time be chasin' pussy. . special that cheap hooka' kand no way, you hea' me, nigga'?" Daniels stood perfectly still as the conflict between decorum and revenge rose like bitter gall in his throat. Then, just as quickly, the conflict was momentarily resolved—the freak had gone too far, said too much, meddled too deep, not to suffer at least a response.

"Fuck off, Mitch, OK? Keep yo' freak ass the fuck outa' my face." His voice was far more calm than his message, but the full force of it hit the taller man hard. "I don't take no shit from no-shot up, halfass gang punk, can't even whack a honky cop 'thout gittin' his black ass shot full a holes! I come a thousand miles, from Cambodia ta Calcutta, 'thout takin' lead, an' I shot plenty a pissed-off gooks gittin' there. So I don't need no advice from no one-eyed amateur hitman! Just stay the fuck outta' my face, 'else I finish what that cop started." Mitchell shuddered as if suffering electric shock, as each epithet hit him. The pool cue in his hands rose and swung horizontally, the tall man smoothly sliding it through his hands until he held it by the slender tip end. The weighted butt arced at Daniels' temple, a blur of dark wood through the air; just as instantly it stopped, and Mitchell stared, his one eye open wide, as he realized that the shorter man stood holding the butt of the cue in his left hand.

If Mitchell's swing and Daniels' reaction had been blinding, Tyreese Broland was just as quick, as he stood between the two men, one hand on the cue and the other held up commanding attention. His voice a coarse stage whisper, he barked at them. "GENTLEMEN! Please!! Think! This cannot be. LaShawn, let go of the cue." Mitchell looked at him in disbelief, then in anger. Then in submission. He released the cue. "J.D., let go. This has gone far enough. We will shortly take assignments that will alter the course of history, and nothing can jeopardize that mission. *NOTHING.* Do you understand me, gentlemen?"

Daniels let go of the cue as well, and both men parted a step, eyes locked like two boxers during the pre-fight announcements. "As you have said, Tyreese. . . as you have said. We have done with it . . .We have done with it. I obey orders." He paused, his eyes snapping from Broland to Mitchell, then back to Broland.

"But I won't take no more ignorant bullshit from *this* asshole. It's just that simple. He fucks with me again you need a new team leader. 'Cause *this* one (his finger thrusting into Mitchell's face). . . he gon' be gone. *Promise.*"

Mitchell was brooding, steaming, even frothing. But there was that part of him still trying to comprehend the fact that his adversary had just stopped his two-handed horizontal butt stroke in midair, with *one hand*. Somehow, that made further offensive efforts temporarily unthinkable. Wise choice. He looked away, turned and, grabbing his beer from the end of the table, walked toward the restroom door in back.

* * * * *

While the business of maintaining electrical power and water to the tenement that housed the SPA was not all that difficult, only a bit cumbersome, telephone service was just too complicated and too risky. Phone lines were more obvious, and taps were a guaranteed fact of life if there were ever even the slightest notion by law enforcement that such an operation were extant in the building. Cellular communication, however, presented no such problems. It could be obtained in virtually any name one could support with modest fake identification, and the bills could go to any post-office box in the world without raising questions. And because Sallie only spoke in the most cryptic of codes when he used it, interception of conversations was of no concern. He also kept his cell phone turned off, the battery removed, so as not to provide even the most subtle hint of the existence of life within that not-so-abandoned building.

He sat on the edge of the bed, in the windowless center of his suite, in the center of the old building, his cell phone aglow in the low light of the room. His party answered, her deep sultry voice refraining from any identification of the place being called.

"Hello, darlin,' what can I *do* for you?" Tits grinned as she always did when answering the TP phone. Sallie spoke few words in returning the greeting.

"Will tonight be acceptable, my dear? I desire your accommodations, if that would be all right with you. Say, in an hour?" The voice was instantly revealing of the person talking, and Enchante spoke quickly and softly.

"Of course, darlin', of course! We'll be here, so feel free! You just come on over and feel *free!* An hour it is, and should I advise the rest?" Sallie smiled at the verification that the team leaders were indeed awaiting his arrival.

"Please. And say to them that I require an hour. That will be nice. Thank you." The line went dead and he was gone, the phone off, battery again removed.

In exactly one hour, the little killer sat down on the couch in Enchante's sitting room, having entered from the alley. He had been quickly embraced by her largeness, and he punctuated the greeting with a bundle of 10 one hundred-dollar bills' that he slipped down the vast cleavage in the front of her gown. She kissed the top of his bald head, smiled benevolently, and walked out the front door of her private quarters, ushering in the twenty men who, by 2:30, had gathered at TPs. The last of the regular patrons had left before 2:00.

Abdul Salim Alakmah stood before the twenty men, his heart pounding in his chest, his breathing controlled. What he saw as his gaze moved from face to face, man to man, was a resource in destruction as great as he could imagine had ever been assembled in so small a place. All combat veterans, every one a seasoned mercenary killer who had proven his mettle repeatedly; each one a true expert in weapons and explosives. They were the best. Several had been trained by the PLO at one of their several training locations in the Sudan, often with the assistance of Iran's finest teachers.

And he was about to deliver to them the orders that would separate them for all time from every other man who had ever acted in furtherance of a great cause. Not a man given to speeches or hyperbole, his voice seldom made a trivial sound. He addressed the men at once and came right to the point, handing two plain manila envelopes to each man. One was standard letter size; the other a five-inch by seven-inch that was sealed. The stack of smaller envelopes was retained by Tyreese.

"The time has come, gentlemen, so let us begin. I need not re-emphasize to you the absolute requirement that you maintain complete silence and secrecy from this point forward. Speak to no one of this meeting or its agenda; if captured, lie. If tortured, do not succumb; you will be expected to take your own life if capture is imminent and the opportunity is available. But, knowing what I do about each of you—and I know virtually *everything* about you—I think such dire eventualities are most

141

unlikely. To the contrary, I expect that anyone who attempts to interdict you or interfere with the execution of your mission in any way will himself discover an immediate need for suicide."

There was a soft rustle throughout the room, each man smiling slightly, some casting confident half smiles at comrades. The man's complete confidence and awesome command of the language captivated the assembly, but the idea of being so completely "known" left each man less than comfortable.

"Please examine the list of locations contained in each of your packets. Of course, the contents are coded, and the maps have been randomized, so that the "key" that Tyreese is now handing you will be necessary in order for you to locate each target. Keep the key in a separate place, preferably in the safe pouch that you will find within the upholstery beneath the back seat of the vehicle assigned to you. All you need is the location list; you already know what to do.

"Each target is a large electrical substation in a metropolitan area, and the schedule, that is page two of the main packet, will tell you when each station is to be rigged and set. But remember, all explosions are to be set for detonation at the same time on the same date, March 21, at 3:00a.m. eastern standard time. The timing and detonation devices that are provided are most reliable, and each of you is intimately familiar with their operation and capabilities. You will be expected to show the final settings to your assistant at each location, and you are not to start the devices until he has confirmed the accuracy of the settings."

The men sat in silence as they examined the lists and cryptographically scrambled maps of their targets. They occasionally spoke softly to each other as they applied the decoding keys to the maps, chuckling to one another as each manipulated the key to make sense of them. Working much like a child's kaleidoscope, but using various pieces of different maps instead of colored crystals, the keys would turn a map of nonsense into a very traditional looking road map, on that the target locations were highlighted. Routes to each place were also marked clearly on the decoded versions, so that identification and access could be accomplished in advance of entry each time. LaShawn Mitchell was the first to speak after the long silence.

"You a fuckin' artist, Sal, no shit. These things never make sense to the white boys in a hunerd years! But what s'pos ta' happ'm if a team gets made while sett'n the charges? We waste 'em, er whut?" Salim shook his head as if to catch up with the questioner, who had skipped down the page to a later point in the outline.

"I was coming to that, Mitch, but the answer is yes. Neutralize any resistance at once and without survivors. But you must dispose of any remains without trace and in such a way that even an *immediate* investigation will not be able to determine a hint of the presence of struggle or problem. Any casualties you inflict must not be found until *after* the completion of the mission by all teams and *after* actual detonation of all devices. In other words, avoid the problem, and try not to kill anyone. Any questions?"

Clyde Foster, a former Navy SEAL and a mercenary with twenty years experience, said what many were thinking. "Salim, m' man, why the addition of the 'assistants'? Every one of us has acted alone on big demolitions hits over and over. Why do we add new faces and therefore new *problems* now? After all these years as a loner, takin' in a stray just feels. . .well, it just feels all wrong." A quiet rumble of assent swept through their number as the man finished.

"I understand, Clyde, and I am confident many of you agree with Clyde's expression. The answer is clear. If anything happens to any of the team leaders—you in this room—the continuation and completion of each and every mission must not be compromised. The assistant permits that. And be assured, gentlemen, these are not "strays" you are taking in. They are well trained, very experienced, and dedicated to the completion of the mission. I have paired you up with great care and attention to personal detail. I have absolute confidence in your "seconds", if you will, and you may be as confident as I that they are completely committed to you as individuals and as leaders. Now, for a few details."

Sallie took them through the various idiosyncrasies of a few of the sites, offered suggestions concerning the size and type charges to be used for some of the more unique stations. He gave specific instructions concerning the use of flammables in certain locations where fire was desired in addition to explosion and destruction of the hardware. "A few of the older places, and a few of the newer ones that have been placed in close proximity to other targets of convenience, will require a gasoline additive to the mix. I know we have not tried to prescribe the placement or exact size of the charges to be used, trusting instead in your own expertise to set and activate the appropriate charge. However, where gasoline has been prescribed, the instructions are specific and must be carefully followed.

"Use gas-soaked steel wool, taped to the side of the five-gallon cans of fuel, and ensure that the gasoline, although buried, will achieve sufficient altitude and atomization from the main blast. You must be certain that the gas gets sufficiently airborne to create a gaseous fireball when the steel wool ignites. This has been prescribed only for places where an important secondary target has been identified. I think there are twenty-three total out of the entire 250 blast sites, so nobody will have too many of these to rig. Obviously, the coordination of the explosion series within each site will be important where the fire is a part of the mission. If the Flex-x goes off first and the primary transformer detonations are delayed by even a few thousandths of a second, ignition of the vaporized gas may not happen at all. Or if it does, the altitude required to achieve fires in a wide enough area will not be achieved, and the plastic insulation in the older plants will not be melted."

Sallie waited a few seconds, then concluded. "Page three of the primary packet contains the location and security procedures for obtaining the vehicles. Each is already in place, fully loaded with everything we could think of to assist in the setting and detonating of these devices. Fuel tanks are full, defensive weapons have been secreted as identified on page four, and there is a supply of currency, $3,000.00 to be exact, located as set out on page four as well. You will proceed to the first location, observe it and determine that it is safe for penetration, then wait until the date specified to set the explosives.

"And remember, do *not* permit any charge, even the smaller sets of Flex or det cord, to remain visible after installation. Once all targets have been set, you will proceed as outlined on pages six and seven. After no less than twenty days, you may begin to return to this area. But remember, it is anticipated that vehicle travel will have become extremely hazardous by that time, so exercise caution when attempting to come east.

"Oh, I almost forgot." Salim's eyes turned that murky ice water green as he fixed his gaze on the misshapen face of LaShawn Mitchell. "Mitch. You are cleared to complete the planning and to execute your requested hit in Iowa. *However,* you are to take no steps nor are you to act in any way in furtherance of that mission until *after* all your charges have been set, concealed, and a suitable place of hiding for you and your assistant has been established. Then, *and only then,* will you be authorized to visit punishment for the sins of the father upon the children. Feel free to exterminate them all."

Mitchell's jaws flexed, and his countenance froze into a Halloween mask of twisted features; his heart raced with the thought of delivering personal vengeance on the family of the cop whose shotgun had twice torn through his handsome body. The first blast had ripped through his abdomen and across his hip, the second tearing off a huge chunk of his left cheek, cheekbone, left ear and, worst of all, his eye. He had spent a year in various hospitals in Canada and Europe, all at the sole expense of the Committee, after having been transported to Sallie's care in the trunk of a car. Of course, the cop died in the firefight, but not at Mitchell's hand. The shots that felled him had come from the AK47 of one of the locals, himself killed by Mick O'Neal's 12-gauge before the cop hit the ground. Now would he come screaming out of hell, and he would methodically take out every remnant of the Irish infidel's lineage with personal delight.

Salim turned, shook hands with each of the team leaders and left. Just like that, he had ordered the disassembly of the very pulse of American society. The chain reaction created by the near simultaneous destruction of two hundred fifty large electrical stations would effectively bomb the U.S. right out of the twentieth century. The network that supplied power to over 70% of the country would simply collapse under such a strain and, with current stockpiles of transformers at only a few hundred nationwide, the very act of finding replacement parts would become a multiyear project. Experience had taught repeatedly that far less significant events were capable of creating big time power losses, even *without* damage to the intricate network that supplies electricity to the whole country.

With banks closed and otherwise affluent people suddenly out of money and without food or heat, Washington could be counted on to start bringing troops home to fight the civil havoc that would follow. That would open the door to the long-awaited invasion and annihilation of the hated Jewish State and, at the same time, the most financially wealthy nation on earth would collapse into anarchy.

The men stood talking for only a few moments before Broland began ushering them out a few at a time, some by the alley, some by the front door. He would take the rest of the darkness hours to disperse the men completely, as he maintained great discipline to avoid any show of numbers or identities. Six of the men actually stayed until the streets again filled with people in the morning; among them was J.D., who slipped upstairs to the waiting favors of the delightful Latresha. And as experienced as these people were in the realities of warfare and killing, none of them had ever experienced such feelings as those that bombarded each of them after Sallie left.

Book II – The Hounds of Hell

9.

Chicago in March can be a very unpleasant place. Although not located in a particularly northern latitude, it sits at the southern end of Lake Michigan, where it enjoys the frequent result of what the weathermen call "lake effect". That's a euphemism for wet, cold weather that turns the beginning of spring into a screaming, raging, frozen caldron of rain, snow, ice, and wind. Waves crash against the sea walls and rock piles of the beaches along Lake Shore Drive, at times spraying icy mist all the way up onto the windows of the Drake and other hotels and apartment buildings that line the historic lakefront. To call the place disagreeable is a near cosmic understatement.

Molly Webb, chilly in only her nightgown, stared out the window of the Drake, flinching at the cracking and creaking of the old building as it groaned against the ice-filled wind. She shivered and turned away, speaking with tired a voice to the back side of her husband as he lay stretched out on the huge bed in their suite. "Jackie, I swear to sweet Mary, but I couldn't be colder if we were standing at the north pole. I haven't been warm in three months. And I thought Washington was miserable in winter. Just about the time a hint of spring appears there, we come to *Chicago,* for Pete's sake, and Presto! . . . more winter!!"

The tone in her voice was sadder than the words, with the fatigue-producing tension and maddening schedule of the past months weighing on her slender form. The bone weariness was apparent even to the casual observer. But her husband was anything but casual where Molly was concerned. He had seen it, a lot of it—that wearing down of the posture, the lines around mouth and eyes, slightly creasing the perfect smoothness of her skin, muting the fire that always lay close to the surface in her black eyes.

Turning toward her, he gazed for a long moment at her form as she stood before the window, her shoulders slightly stooped, head tilted to one side, resting against the window frame. The events of the last eight months raced past in his mind like some high speed newsreel, from the moment of the call from Jack Kincaid, through nomination and the three months of punishing campaign; then the inauguration and Kincaid's death. All that, followed by the two-plus months of blinding pace since his own ascent to the presidency, made all the prior effort seem vacation-like by comparison to the speed and pressure of this new life.

Clearly he had not calculated the cost of the presidency in terms of its toll on Molly, or even on their kids who, although all grown and living on their own, were constantly drawn into the swirl of activity and stress. These were precious folks, a wonderful woman and three of the world's great young people— more precious to him than his life—and their courage and steadfastness over his thirty years of military service had been singular in his experience.

As those images streaked through his mind's vision, he saw the hard parts: The wonderful, sad faces of his children, as they moved again and again, leaving friends and schools, streets and back yards. Always there was a little fear in their eyes as they looked up at their tall, uniformed Daddy, searching his face for assurance. How many times had he wiped a tear from the little girl's cheek as she watched a friend walk away from the car, another friend left behind?

Each time, he told her he was sorry for the loss, each time trying to ease the pain with promises of new friends to come, new places and people to experience. Gentle arms would hug his neck and child-sweet breath would whisper "I love you, Daddy"; each time, if only for a moment, he would hate himself for having chosen the military and for having chosen to live it so aggressively and with such passion. Just like being president, it had been an all-consuming endeavor, leaving little time, and little self, for other pursuits.

That child was Melinda Diane Webb. The eldest of the three Webb kids, she was now thirty years old and a practicing pediatrician in Dallas, the only one of the eight cities they had called home that ever *felt* like home to her. Married to a freelance writer, who had the patience of Job and the mental toughness of a Navy SEAL, Mark was the only man on Earth who Jackie thought could have handled life with Melinda. And handle it he did.

Their first born, a girl named Emily, had Daddy around most of the time and, although the program was a bit unorthodox in Grandpa's eyes, it was working with glorious results. His heart ached a moment, again, reckoning with the distance in time and miles between those most wonderful of people and these two exhausted parents. Weariness gave way to a keener emotion; the President swung his long legs over the edge of the bed and, standing up to stretch, he silently walked over to the window.

It was at the precise moment when he slipped his arms around her from behind that he detected the soft sound of a sniffle, felt her reach up and brush a tear from her face. If the aching in his heart had been keen in the previous moments of recollection, it became a burning dagger as Molly lay back against her husband, a subtle sob pulsing the slender frame. No words were spoken as they stood there. Jackie buried his face in her hair, then gently kissed her neck. He looked past her into the gathering darkness, black water transforming into white spray, wind twisting the tall trees along the street below the window. The President of the United States felt his knees weaken, so powerful was the combination of senses and emotions attacking him at that moment. The reverie produced by the recollection of times gone by was mixed with ever-present memories of war scenes, so permanently burned into his being. All that, overlaid with the still incomprehensible reality of the presidency, combined to hit him with as much force as any of the waves that crashed against that seawall.

Closing his eyes, Jackie Robinson Webb fought the suggestion of a tear; his arms drew together, enveloping the form of his wife. And it was then that he felt the rush of love and passion this woman had always—absolutely *always*—generated within him. His hands moved around and up her bodice, tracing and caressing the fine lines of her figure. Her scent, the feel of her hair against his cheek, that still perfect skin created a medicine so strong as to obliterate every other thought. Although tall, Molly was slight of frame; although delicate, she was of dramatic proportion. And the General was a man of imposing size.

His arms so enfolded her that his hands reached far around her torso and, as she straightened to accept his embrace, he could feel the quickening heartbeat in her breasts, held gently in those powerful, rough hands. Closing her eyes, a smile chased away the last tear, as she welcomed the thirty-five year old paradox of these rough warrior hands that could radiate such heat and tenderness.

Molly turned in her husband's arms and, as he relaxed his embrace, she ran her hands up his chest and around his neck. His scent found its mark in her, and they melded together in a long awaited, badly needed kiss. The need and hunger in her man's aggressive kiss aroused the passion and desire within her, and she reveled in the miraculously balanced equation that allowed her to experience such joy and fulfillment while simultaneously nurturing and feeding her man.

In an instant, the President felt a rush of emotional heat and gratitude—emotion in the love and desire he felt for Molly, and gratitude to the Good Lord for this rare evening alone with his wife. It had been weeks since there had been a break. Tomorrow would be full of activity and stress, with no fewer than five separate appearances, including a speech before the general session of the National Governors' Conference. But now, all that could wait.

Separating momentarily from Molly's arms, he turned out the lights and pulled back the bedspread. Reaching for the telephone, he called the faithful Brooks, still the perfect minister of privacy, and simply said "Sergeant Major, we're in to stay. *No calls.*"

As he hung up the phone, he could hear the familiar response, "Thank you, sir, I'm clear."

March 19 was finished, except for the best part. March 20 would have to wait. The President slipped out of his clothes and into the waiting arms of his wife. A whispered prayer of thanksgiving vanished into the darkness around them as the waves crashed and the wind blew. Tomorrow after all, would arrive soon enough.

* * * * *

CCDPW. The string of letters across the right front pocket of Lester Monroe's coveralls was matched on the left side by the name SKIP. A well worn electrician's tool belt hung naturally from his lean hips like a journeyman's version of a pair of six-guns, and the unlined leather gloves fit the look perfectly. He pushed a small four-wheel cart into the utility elevator, having spent the past two hours busily hustling in and out of the Museum of Natural History. He acknowledged the rent-a-cops who officiously stood guard against the hordes of kids who flowed through the front of the place in a constant torrent of chatter, color, and excitement. Identifying himself as the Public Works electrician sent to check out the "units up stairs," he flashed his Cook County identification badge and walked past the teeming throng, all to the somber and knowing nod of the room-temperature-IQ keepers of the peace.

Lester walked purposefully through the first floor and straight to the elevator, having been provided a floor plan of the place in the packet that lay under the seat of Mercedes provided him by his employer in New York. The instructions also directed him to a covered garage in the Loop, the downtown area inside the circle created by the city's elevated transit system. There he found a utility van outfitted with the logo of the City of Chicago and those same letters, CCDPW, for Cook County Department of Public Works. In the van had been the required ID, the tools, the cart, and a map of the downtown area. He transferred all his own gear to the van and drove away from the big black beauty, leaving it full of gas and loaded with several changes of clothing and a variety of aids for use in creating disguises.

With just one day to prepare for an operation that would permit only a single attempt and no alternate plan for accomplishing the hit, there was plenty to do. After visiting affably with the janitor on an elevator ride to the top floor when he had first arrived, he began the business of acting like an electrician. "Just routine, Donnie, just routine. Gotta' check the pressure on the compressors and make sure the calibration on the 'stats is OK for the ol' "Swing into Spring"—Ha! ain't that a hoot!. . .blowin' like a mad bitch, 'nuff ice on the sidewalk ta make a guy fall an' bust 'is ass jis' gittin' up the freakin' steps, and I'm s'pose ta git 'er ready for spring!"

Donnie, a dopey-looking redneck with long greasy hair down to his shoulders and none on top of his head had laughed through his nose and blown a fine mist out toward Lester, in response to this little routine. Lester stepped back as if dodging hostile fire, only to watch Donnie rake his sleeve across his messy nose without missing a beat.

"No shit, ain't it great?" Donnie responded, sniffing so hard at the mess on the end of his nose that his eyes watered. "Every year the big guys think a some other way to spend more money, right? I'm surprised you ain't a A-rab or a nigger or sumthin'! *Hell*, white man don't usually get these busy work thangs! It's 'bout always some *manor-i-tee* contractor tradin' votes fer the County's money!"

Lester laughed out loud at Donnie's comment, as well as the colorful way he expressed himself. For a moment, he forgot who he really was and why he was there, as he joked with the greasy little hillbilly janitor. When he got back on the elevator and headed back to the van for the cart that would carry his weapon

151

and equipment, he did not see that Donnie's goofy grin disappeared as the doors went shut.

The work was easy, but for the misery inflicted by Mother Nature whenever he ventured onto the roof. Removing the side panel from the large air conditioning unit that sat in the middle of the flat roof and about one third of the way toward the east end— toward the target area—Lester's eyes scanned the scene with X-ray attention to detail. Using the toolbox and cart as a rest, he subtly examined the field of fire afforded by the location. Large trees occupied the space between the museum and the north entrance to the Shedd Aquarium, making the shot much trickier. "Damn sure glad for the trusty ol' .308, b'god. Fuckin' M16 round's too hot and *way* too light to survive nickin' a branch 'r two. I can reach out an' *touch* that nigger with that big bullet though, even if I nick a branch on the way."

So went the killer's thoughts and musings as he practiced moving from the big compressor over to the location from that he had chosen to fire; he plotted with growing efficiency the precise movements that would be required to walk the thirty feet from the unit to the spot, then kneel down and take a prone firing position. The precision broke down at that point.

It was impossible to calculate just how long it would take for the presidential limousine to get from Lester's observation point on the roof, as it passed by on Lake Shore Drive, to the designated stopping place at the curb in front of the Aquarium. He would have to play that part as it developed, ensuring that nothing he did was too obvious, too quick, or too abrupt.

The plan was simple, as all such plans must be in order to succeed. He would arrive on the roof an hour before the shot was to occur. Removing the panel from the air-conditioning unit again, he would unwrap the M14 from its waterproof case, remount the scope, and load the weapon with a clip of the special hot rounds that Sallie had procured.

He had stopped once on the way to Chicago, after wandering up into the hills of Pennsylvania for half a day. Finding a particularly remote area down in the bottom of a deep canyon, he had set up a range, six targets of dark red apples set at the same distance as he would face from the top of the museum, and fired at them to sight in the weapon. One shot had missed. A section of newsprint behind the first apple bore the obvious mark of the errant bullet, high and slightly to the right. A single adjustment put things right, and the other five apples exploded in a mist of pulp and water vapor. Satisfied with the whole exercise, he had fired several more rounds for a good measure of practice, packed the rifle, and continued east.

Knowing the exact placement and setting of the scope made quick assembly easy. It was not even necessary to pick the weapon up to complete the work; it would not be exposed to the elements until he moved it to the firing site. One hour before the scheduled time of arrival, he would place the weapon back in its case, wrap it in a tarp, and quickly carry it over to its final location. There he would lay it down amid a hodgepodge of tools and carts, returning to the compressor and his "work."

After thirty minutes, he would slip back down the steps to the roof and hide himself in a small janitor's closet, frequently checking his watch in anticipation of the time when he would return to the roof and his mission. Acquiring his target, he would sight carefully, fire twice, drop the rifle in place, and move directly back to the stairs. Escape would follow one of three routes and plans, dependent upon the presence or absence of interference or discovery by any unfortunate third parties.

If he was able to get down the back steps of the museum quickly and without detection, Monroe would simply exit the building in the rear, get in the van, and move back out into traffic on Lake Shore Drive. Travelling south, he would circle around back to the Loop and the garage where the Mercedes waited. The theory, often proven accurate in practice, was that there would be enough confusion at the point where the victim was hit that no one would immediately discern the direction or location from that the shots had come.

Further, the sound suppression engineered into the big rifle, although it could not silence the report of such a heavy round, would make it less obvious, and people inside the museum would not hear it on the lower floors. The tumultuous cacophony of one thousand kids would virtually guarantee that.

If, somehow, he were interdicted before he got to the truck, he would neutralize any resistance, then quickly get to the first floor and mingle with the crowd. Dressed in his coveralls and wearing his tools, he would move out the front door and, if the way was clear, go to the truck. If for any reason the truck was compromised, he would walk south across the parking lot to the other almost identical stone building that bordered the restricted parking area, enter it, and dispose of his tools. He would hide in a large room in the basement of that building, a room where the electrical panels and environmental controls formed a perfect habitat for an electrician and an excellent hiding place for man and tools alike. Again, he would wait for a short time, then head for the Loop and the garage. He might even take a cab, but walking would not pose a difficult assignment.

If things really went to hell—a specter he doubted but always planned for—there was the unpleasant but effective escape via the cold waters of Lake Michigan. Tied to the pilings of one of the yacht piers across the street was a cache of air tank, fins, mask, and regulator, along with full head neoprene hood, gloves, and boots. This was accomplished the night before he first went inside the museum. He would be wearing a waterproof neoprene suit beneath his coveralls. If he could make the water, he could dive in, hide between the piers, and make his way to the scuba gear. There was plenty of cover between the piers, even without the many boats that occupied the slips during warm weather, and he would just wait for the hastening darkness, then swim away to the south. Dry clothes and shoes awaited, tucked into a rockpile that formed part of the seawall down from the huge McCormick Place Convention Center.

Turning these options over and over in his mind, Lester finished his onsite preparations and drove the van back onto the expressway. His accommodations were far away, back at the Radisson in Merrillville, Indiana, an hour away. One of his rules—rules that had contributed mightily to his long survival in this uniquely risky business—had always been to stay far away from the actual scene of his killing. Cops could canvas the area where the hit had occurred forever without having someone point him out or express curiosity about his presence to some over-eager gumshoe. There would be plenty of time to get to the museum the next day without having to stay too close to the target area.

After just one more walkthrough, Lester finished hiding the tools of his trade, closed up the compressor housing and, walking back to the elevator, turned and descended the three floors of steps to the loading dock at the back entrance. He fought his nerves, anxiety filling his throat with tension, his bowels growling. Tomorrow he would act again. Tomorrow he would earn a million dollars. Tomorrow he would change the course of history.

Book II – The Hounds of Hell

* * * * *

The last twenty locations where explosives would be set were reserved for March 19. These were mostly some of the more important hits, harder to rig and more difficult to work on without being seen. The logic Sallie employed in ordering the target preparations was to wait until the last night before working those more sensitive sites; if a team were compromised, discovered, or even captured, there would be less time for the local authorities to start talking to their counterparts in other cities. There was no target so important as to permit such discovery, because the idea was to interrupt power over a wide area, not just to create a problem in one particular place.

The setting of the charges at the over two hundred other sites had gone extremely well, owing to both the skill and stealth of the teams and the almost incredible absence of *any* real security measures. Even the substations that were lit made little or no effort to deter intrusion. None were actively guarded. That fact plus the ease with that electrical power could be significantly interrupted made this system an easy and very effective target for the Committee.

The delivery of electricity in the U.S. is accomplished by a deceptively fragile system. The repeated wide area blackouts and brownouts experienced throughout the last decade had made it clear to the Committee that real havoc could be created for the entire country if a substantial break could be accomplished at random high power locations. The reason was simple: The delivery of electrical power is not linear. A local hydroelectric plant does not just send power to a large substation, that supplies a series of smaller substations, then supplying individual consumers. Juice gets passed around the country by an interdependent network, or "grid," resulting in the power from one place often being transmitted over high-tension line systems to places far away from where the power is generated.

The existence, intricacy, and fragile nature of this system explain much of the cause for the wide area power outages that have resulted from a single equipment failure. If that failure happens in a place where electricity is being switched for retransmission to a remote location, the power will be interrupted not only to the immediate area but also to the place where the power was to be sent. When the power fails to get there via the prescribed route and from the prescribed place, the network tries

155

to recognize the failure and provide that power from someplace else. The strategy employed by the PLO was simply to hit enough places, cause enough damage, and kill the juice to enough areas at the same time that a sort of "meltdown" would occur.

The system would have more demands for power than it could answer and, because Salim had chosen his targets carefully, there would be no alternative routes by that to supply the electricity. For that reason alone, he had determined that multiple stations would have to be hit in each target area. Simple disruption of power was not enough to create the desired effect: To remove the U.S. from the world scene and produce the instant, huge problems necessary to cause hysteria and collapse. By destroying six stations in Cincinnati, eight in St. Louis, a like number in Denver, and so on with two hundred-fifty sites, the stress on the power network would be overwhelming. Likewise, the use of alternative routing of power from remote locations would fail, because the multiple hits would break the chain of lines sufficiently that those alternative routes would also be broken.

By March 19, two hundred sets of charges were set. The last night the teams had only two objectives each, but those were of major importance and posed significant security risks to them. J.D. and his appointed assistant, a baby-faced kid from Miami named Reggie, had become a most proficient team over the three weeks they had worked together. And despite the fatigue produced by such a long assignment and the tension associated with working in exposed and dangerous places this night, they were excited and even light hearted.

"One thing sure, J.D., bein' out a this damn death trap's gonna make me sleep a whole lot better! This van's been home for 23 days, but livin' in a mobile bomb gets old after a while, even if the money *is* good."

J.D. smiled through a tired face, the stress of constant travel and fear of detection having worn him to his last nerve. "No shit, kid—fucker's been capable a makin' a crater fifty feet deep if it went off with all the C4 we been carrying— and she's *still* pretty hot, even almost empty! But we close, Reg, real close to the end. Can't wait for some time off and a little trip back to TPs!!" The memory of the lithesome perfection of his lady-in-waiting raced through him like a blast from one of the transformers he'd been rigging for destruction. "Nice ta have some cover, too. This misty shit gonna make work a little tricky—the steel's wet and slick, but we shouldn't have ta worry 'bout gettin' caught so much here."

A dense fog covered the land around suburban south St. Louis where they were working at a large substation. The place was illuminated by a half dozen mercury vapor lights, casting their orange pall over the stark geometry of wires, steel frameworks, cylindrical transformers, and big square ground units.

The garish lights reflected and diffused through the fog for a visual effect both dramatic and mystical. More importantly, the effect was a significant reduction in visibility from outside the chain link-encased compound. No one manned the place, no one guarded it. Quietly getting out of the van for that last time, their mood was almost festive, although caution and perfection of product were still absolutes. Smirking back at the elder terrorist, Reggie tossed a tease at J.D.'s fantasies.

"Fer an oldtimer, you sho' got a hot *rod,* Jack!! That li'l ho had steam coming out your ears for two weeks—an' dam if I don't see the ol' manhood wakin' up right now!!" He laughed a silent guffaw as he ducked a lightning backhand. Jackson Daniels chuckled to himself, both at the younger man's powers of observation and at his own obsession with "that li'l ho." He also noted that the kid was quick enough to avoid his blow; few had been able to do that. Maybe he *was* slowing down, after all. The two men worked almost without a syllable passing between them, the routines and thought processes having been honed to a surgical edge by practice and exceptional skill.

Working intently at the base of one of the six-foot-tall ground transformers, Reggie first dug a hole through the pea gravel and the dirt beneath it, fashioning a pit almost two feet deep. Into that hole was inserted an attaché case containing 10 one-pound rectangular bricks of C 4, charged with a powerful detonator and wired to a digital clock. The clock was set for the next night, 3 a.m., but the connection to the clock was not yet affixed. As he finished the main charge, he looked up to see J.D. nimbly negotiating a steel beam that formed the superstructure that supported a long string of transformers and connecting lines. The place hummed with sounds whining through the wires, and the terrorist moved with deliberate speed from place to place. Kneeling on one of the beams, he removed his backpack and took out a 9-inch by 12-inch sheet of Flex-X, the flat, moldable form of plastic that he would wrap around one of the four-inch-thick conduits feeding the string of transformers above his head.

Four sheets of Flex lay end to end, wrapping the heavy silver conduit in a sheath of explosive over three feet long. Pulling a long roll of detonation cord from the pack, J.D. pressed the free end of the white roping into the seam between two slabs of the Flex. He unrolled a length of the cord, sufficient to reach the ground along the vertical support at his shoulder, cut the length, and let it hang loose. The next step was to move to another location, 100 feet farther into the rigging of the station, where the target was another string of transformers. These were fed from above by heavy insulated cable; they would also get a Flex-X wrap. Again, det cord hung to the ground from the four-sheet charge of molded plastic, and the procedure was repeated at the far end of the complex. There another string of cylinders stood gleaming with mist through the strange orange light.

Reggie moved directly to the opposite end of the ground-mounted equipment, setting another buried charge at the base of one of the tall green boxes. He ran lengths of det cord to sticks of C4 that were concealed between the boxes and covered with gravel. This job had to remain hidden for only twenty-four hours, so the work went a bit faster. Once all the aerial charges had been set and connected with the exploding cord, the whole system was then connected with the same stuff, the culmination of that was a single wrap into the still exposed case of C4 in the hole with the clock detonation device. The cord was carefully hidden along its route to the detonator, either buried or pressed into the back sides of steel rails and supports; the result was an invisible network of connected high explosive, all hooked together with cord that not only would cause the detonation of each charge but would also itself explode with great effect.

Working together, the two men then dug a final hole, next to the main charge and about a foot to the side of it. This one was deeper—deep enough to hold a five-gallon can of gasoline, into the snout of that was inserted a length of det cord. A dozen chunks of charcoal floated in the petroleum. A gas-soaked pad of steel wool was then taped to the side of the can, and the whole apparatus was buried and recovered with gravel. When the big charge went off, the gas would be vaporized instantly, gaining loft and dispersion above the site. The steel wool-gasoline combination would heat to tremendous temperature at the same time, and the burst of flame ignite the vaporized gasoline, creating a huge fireball.

Because this installation was older, it had quite a bit of plastic insulated wiring and several wooden posts within the superstructure. The result of this little cocktail would be instantaneous ignition of everything flammable within a wide area, plus the launching of countless chunks of burning shrapnel, including the charcoal already in the gas. These would travel out into the woods beside the station and probably reach the roofs of the buildings in the business complex 400 meters away. Finishing this last job, they followed procedure exactly, and Reggie checked the timer and activation sequence setup. No problem. The place would go up like it was hit by a meteor at 3 a.m., March 21.

10.

March 20 dawned gray and miserable in Bethesda, Maryland, where the first weak tendrils of light through the windows of the pathology lab found Dickie Freeman mumbling nonsense into the index of an enormous volume on the sources and effects of naturally occurring poisons. Mozart had been replaced sometime during the night with Beethoven, the *Ninth Symphony,* now erupting into the wild strains of lyric German in the choral fourth movement. Nobody could understand how the guy could have music of that complexity going on inside his head while he was at the same time accomplishing thought processes that were themselves composed of multiple layers of complicated formulae. He spoke to the empty room.

"*Shit.* . .I gotta get this right the first time. . .the sample is so small. . .there's no way I can get sufficient sample for more than two, maybe three tests, *max.* . .gotta hit this one the first time." Moving back to the lab table, he finished the last preparations for the spectrography experiment that had kept him mumbling for hours. To perform it, he would have to destroy a significant portion of the sample, actually burning it while the fancy machine gathered all kinds of data about it while it burned. "If it's any one of these agents, it'll show up and the ID will be accomplished. If it's something else, the sample's gone and I don't have shit. Or if there is nothing in there in the first place. . .man, am I tired of this thing."

He remembered the two encounters with the new president; at the first, he had left hoping to be hit by a train on the way back to the lab. At the second, still alive in his mind, there were those black eyes, imperious while at the same time so goddam earnest and entreating, almost begging for help. In all his life, Dickie could not remember such a person. He had known great men before, had worked side by side with the best minds in all science. He had studied with the greatest men and women in the business; greatness was not new to him. But this new president. . .wow.

The man was a human power source. His presence was so much bigger than the big body that he seemed to create a crowd just by walking into a room. Sharp movements, piercing gaze, clear voice and diction, quick response. Dickie laughed at the memory of that recurring urge, when the man had entered the room, to soil his pants. "Gotta get this one for the General. . don't wanna have to face him again without an answer." He fired up the machine and meticulously performed the experiment, monitoring gauges, screens, and printouts constantly as the seconds passed and the sample was consumed. Nothing.

There was no match to any of the agents profiled. "Goddammit. . .but *wait*. . .no, that's nothing. . .wonder why that one parameter shows a value but no match. Now *just a minute. . ."* Back to the huge book. *Agents in this classification, while distinct and unique, bear sufficient molecular similarities to other venoms that the possibility of false positive results from spectrography exists. Specifically, where elevated values appear, but a match with known agents does not occur, additional testing is warranted and should be performed for agents found in the following:*

    a. Common wasp,
    b.   Fire ant.

These both contain sufficient histamine roperties to create violent and almost instantaneous pulmonary reaction, typically with fatal results in subjects with a previous history of overt, violent, extreme, or even moderately excessive reaction to similar agents.

Dickie sat still. He took off his heavy glasses, rubbed the eyes that now were so apparently full of sand; massaged the back of his neck, all full of knots and spasm. Eyes closed. For a moment, he could not think, could not synthesize the information or put the results just obtained into the synthesis. Looking at the clock, he tried to remember what Webb had said about calling him. Standing down from the high lab stool, he began searching for the folder in his bag where the numerous telephone numbers given to him by the President were located. Too tired and too numb for panic, he just kept digging until the thing finally surfaced.

"3/17-21JRW gone. Call M. Reed, WH Chief of Staff #202-532-1976." Freeman remembered Mac Reed, the stocky ranch foreman-type chief who had first ushered him into the room where he met the President.

Reed had shaken his hand, grinned quickly, and said, "Good luck to both of you—the General's pretty uptight over this whole investigation. He's tough, but I doubt he'll hurt either of you. . .at least I don't *think* he will." He had smiled again and left the room, closing the door behind him. He was wrong about the "hurting" part. Dickie punched in the numbers for Reed and waited, scribbling notes on a pad, outlining what he wanted to ask.

"Dr. Reed—I mean *Mr.* Reed—this is *Dr.* Freeman, out at Bethesda Naval. . .I'm the pathologist working on the—"

"I know who you are, Doctor, what can I do for you? Good to know the team is up before breakfast." Freeman fought the urge to advise Reed in clear terms just how long he had in fact been up, but decided against it.

"Yes. . .right. Look, Mr. Reed, I need a little information. I'm really close on this thing, but there is simply not enough sample left for any more near misses. The whole thing boils down to ants—*fire* ants, actually—or maybe wasps. . .at least that's the way the spectrograph sees it. . .and me, too—I mean, well, the text is pretty clear that elevated values on the result for cobra, although not consistent with that result, can suggest other venoms, such as, well, really odd. . .but, even *bug* venom. . Anyway, what I—"

"Son, you're off your feet, sounds like your random access memory went a little too *random*. Bug venom? What the hell are you talking about?"

"Yes, well, you're right, of course, sorry for the run on, but I'm just, well, really close on this one and, well, I haven't slept for a while, so I'm a little slow, but, well, here's the point. Did President Kincaid ever have a bad reaction to a bug bite, bee sting, ant bite, or anything like that, that you know about? Get back to me if you need to check it out, my number here is. . ."

"No need, Doc. Last summer, Nashville, Tennessee. We went to a picnic openhouse where the locals were having a fund raiser for Jack's campaign. He got stung by a wasp and sat on an ant hill at the same time! Funnier 'n hell, except he got really sick! Eyes swelled up, lips got puffy, almost fainted. They gave him some Benadryl, laid him down for a while, and he got better. Surprised you guys didn't know about it, 'cause it was in all the papers, even got a bit of coverage on the networks. The pundits had a real party with all the double entendres about the candidate's butt all swollen up with ant bites. It was kinda' scary, though, there for a few minutes. Really strange, I mean—"

"Thanks, Dr. Reed. . . I mean *Mr.* Reed, I'll get back to you. ."

The phone went dead, and he was gone. Reed shook his head, hung up the phone, and walked out of his office to see if the staff had gotten into gear yet. After all, it was 7:10 a.m., and there was a country to run.

Dickie felt a rush of invigoration as he stumbled over a box of files on his way back to the huge book on the table. He quickly confirmed the testing that would be necessary to determine whether or not there was fire ant or wasp venom in the toothpaste cap sample, made sure there was enough sample left for both tests, and quickly performed the first. Bingo. The chemical analysis of the sample showed a concentrated presence of the venom of the fire ant. The sample was *very* concentrated, and it was clear that, if the subject had a sensitivity to that poison, sufficient quantity could easily have been ingested through the mucous membrane of the cheek and tongue to spark the reaction. The mad scientist sat back against the supporting backrest of the lab stool, his head spinning, sparks visible behind his eyes, a loud roar in his head. Fatigue seemed to be quickly winning the battle anyway, and the sudden realization that he had found the answer to the President's death made him light headed.

Quickly coming to his wobbly feet, Dickie called Jacob Steinberg, waking the pathologist from the only sleep he had had in three days. "Jake? Dickie. Fire ants. Plain and so goddam simple, I could just cry. Freakin' fire ants!! Would you believe it? Shit, I almost burned up the whole sample before I found it. . fucking ants. Wow. . ."

Steinberg fought for consciousness, struggled ferociously against unconsciousness. The voice was so familiar, but *ants?* What. . .He sat up in bed, his voice an inhuman sound. "*Dickie? What—DICKIE?? What—*are you mad?! Jesus, Dick, *what? I—*"

"*Jake,* it's me, Dick. . .I've found it. Poison, Jake, fire ant venom. The shit's so concentrated in the sample, I'm surprised we didn't *smell* it! But *really*—I just checked with that guy at the White House—you know—Reed, the guy who worked for Kincaid and stayed put when Webb took over. Says Kincaid got stung last summer while campaigning in Tennessee, a wasp *and fire ants at the same time!!*

Got sick, almost passed out, swelled up—the works. . .except he got better with Benadryl and some decent supportive care— they didn't even hospitalize him. But you know what that means, Jake. Mast cells, IgE antibodies, perfect setup for anaphylaxis. Goddamit, Jake, but somebody was clever. . .in the freaking *tooth*paste, of all things!"

The Devil's Playground

By now, Steinberg was sitting up on the edge of the bed, fighting a pounding head and a magnum wave of nausea. But the whole attack was banished as he suddenly became clear on what happened to Jack Kincaid. They had all read papers on the subject. "Demonstration of Antivenom Antibody in Insect Sting Deaths," and other similar writings described in detail the almost instant deaths suffered by people who experienced bad allergic reactions to bee stings, wasp stings, even ants. And the problem for the pathologist at autopsy was always the same. Unless someone had seen the event or there were enough stings to be apparent upon gross examination, there was nothing—*nothing*— that suggested what happened to the subject. Except that he had died.

The synapses began to function in the sleepy scientist's head, as he saw the problem—and the resolution. "Ok, Dick, OK. . .OK. . . . *Now* it starts to make sense. Holy. . .wow. . . brilliant. . wow—*everybody* knew he'd had that reaction last summer, so they just gave him another dose. Boom."

When stung by one of these insects, some people have an allergic reaction. It's not always very violent, but it is abnormal. Usually there is local swelling around the sting site, often there is shortness of breath, even generalized swelling in a wide area around the site. But they get better, usually in a few minutes or at worst a few hours. Only that's not all. Because of that reaction, an allergic reaction occurs in the blood of the victim. That first sting has caused a sensitization that stimulates the production of what are called "mast cells," or allergic cells, but only in a limited quantity. Those tend to reside then in the pulmonary system—the lungs—lying quietly until another exposure to the venom occurs.

Both men were thinking the same things as the silent seconds passed. They could remember the articles they had read, the studies they had seen and even participated in, all revolving around the bizarre and deadly reaction that could—and all too often *did*—kill people.

"The bad news begins with that subsequent exposure," Dickie began to recite the program. "When the body senses the presence of the venom again, the mast cells instantly begin producing the hormone, the antibody against the venom, in quantities sufficient to cause the body's muscles to constrict—"

Steinberg cut him off, picking up the theme like a tag team lecturer. " The striated muscle in the lungs responds, restricting

164

then *prohibiting* breathing, and the person dies of oxygen starvation within a couple of minutes, unless a cardiac occurrence is sparked by the whole trauma. In either case, you're dead. Just like that. And there is typically nothing that can be done to save 'em!" Immediate injections of epinephrine are sometimes helpful, but usually those are unavailable, so death ensues at once. And they both knew that Jack Kincaid had had no chance for injections of epinephrine or anything else, as he simply lay down in his bed and quietly suffocated.

The forensic problem with all this is that such a death leaves no trace. "As soon as death occurs, the pulmonary muscle relaxes, and the death has happened so fast that the new sting site hasn't even had time to swell up, leaving a clue. There *are* no clues. The person looks fine at autopsy—except for being dead, that is—and the observable phenomena inside the body, even in the lungs, are so unremarkable that the cause of death ends up being declared unknown." Steinberg was mumbling, but reciting the whole program like he was teaching a class. "It's only when the presence of the venom can be inferred by what some witness reports, or where visible evidence of sting can be seen, that an accurate diagnosis is possible, and—"

"Bag the lecture, Professor, I already had the course. And don't sound so sure of yourself—you didn't figure it out either!"

"Oh, I know, Dickie, sorry, just trying to think it through. *Shit,* that's why we saw nothing at autopsy—there was nothing to see! Only there *were* clues. . .same things we always see in simple cardiac arrest. Like passive congestion in the internal organs, froth in the larynx, and focal pulmonary edema. . .all the usual. But hell, these are also present in all kinds of natural deaths, and they can be anticipated just about anytime heart failure, drowning, stroke, or even simple cardiac arrest occurs! What a bunch a' stars we turned out to be—holy shit—fire ant venom. . . ."

Steinberg hung up the phone with a groggy "I'll be right there" and got dressed for the thirty-minute drive back to Bethesda. As he drove, both men found themselves marveling at the brilliant simplicity of the way this man had been murdered. The fact of Kincaid's run-in with the bugs last summer was widely known; anybody with a forensic pathology background and an understanding of the phenomenon of anaphylactic shock that can be caused by allergic reactions to such stings could figure out that another exposure to such a venom would almost certainly be fatal.

It was the toothpaste method that amazed both men the most. What a stroke of diabolical genius. By definition, the unmarried man would surely be alone when he brushed his teeth. By putting a small amount of concentrated poison right at the top of the tube, where the entire sample would be consumed when he put the stuff on his toothbrush, there was little chance a later analysis of the contents of the tube would yield any useful information. And the venom would certainly be absorbed through the mucosa of the cheek and tongue, causing the reaction to begin almost at once.

If Kincaid had just put the cap back on the tube, even *this* clue would have been lost. Nobody thought to save the toothpaste for examination, anyway. And the reaction would then occur at a time when he was just as certainly alone, probably in bed, and death would ensue without even a remote chance of help getting to the President.

When the two got back together, they reviewed all the details of the lab findings, actually running the last tests again on the tiny amount of tooth gel that was left. They reviewed the autopsy notes, confirming the laryngeal froth, the pulmonary edema, even a couple of references to passive congestion in some of the organs that were removed and studied later.

Steinberg remembered a classified paper on the use of cobra venom by the Soviets, back during the Cold War, and they realized just how easy the whole thing could be. "Ricin," an extract of cobra venom, was coated on sharp little darts, then shot with a blow gun into the neck, shoulder, or back of the intended victim. Same result. The dart would fall off or be removed by the assassin, and the target would die. Just like that. No trace, no evidence of foul play, just a dead guy. Freeman and Steinberg quickly reduced their report to writing and decided to hand carry it to the White House for delivery to Reed.

What they were reporting was of enormous importance, it proved conclusively that Kincaid had been assassinated. There was no doubt in their minds that what they were about to tell Mac Reed, and eventually Jackie Webb, would rock all of Washington and later the entire country. But as they walked into the White House, they could not know that, before the day was finished, their discoveries would be overshadowed by events of such magnitude that it would be weeks before the discovery was made public. The White House staff was about to suffer *another* blow, the result of that would cause panic, even terror, in the hearts of all concerned.

11.

"Slugger is in place. Repeat. Slugger is in place and secure. Copy?"

"This is Control. I'm clear, Thad, we have a visual on the speaker's rostrum. Lady One is not in sight from Control. Lady Watch, please advise."

"This is Lady Watch, affirm. She is not on the rostrum—no room. She is with Tom in front of the stage, front row, seat 6. Tom is standing up, facing the back of the hall. Control, you should be able to see him, at least—"

"Roger—we have visual on Tom and on Molly as well. OK, let's run the circuit. Transport, do you copy?—report."

"This is Transport, Control. We are in place in the underground location, with the limo. Zach is driving and Lennie has the door. Local Feebs in place have confirmed sweep of the route to the car from inside and have also cleared the ramp up to the street. We're clear."

"O.K. Control to Rooftop—Glen, do you copy? Report."

"Yeah, Control, all clear. Cover is a complete 360 of rooftop, and there are two birds up and visible from here. Oh—and thanks for asking—it's colder than a well digger's ass up here. Rooftop out." And so it went, like it always went, and like it had gone for thirty years of radio-controlled security for the president's Secret Service people. Besides the obvious observation points and crucial maneuvers required whenever the man's location changed, there were no fewer than fifty FBI and Secret Service agents spread out through the 800 attendees at this main event for the National Conference of Governors. The rest of these did not speak unless trouble surfaced. They milled around, watched exits and windows, checked restrooms and elevators.

Although there appeared to be no organization to this larger corps of agents, a careful examination of their respective locations would have shown the observer that they were well dispersed over a large area; every conceivable avenue of ingress and egress was inhabited by at least one of these folks, and each one was connected to the same radio communication frequency. Trouble of any kind could be expected to evoke an instant and decisive response, with a detailed prearranged set of plans dictating backup, support and confirmation of all reports. There was even a list of no fewer than six different escape routes for removal of the

Book II – The Hounds of Hell

President, known to these devoted spooks as "Slugger," after the obvious reference to the great Jackie Robinson in his own name. The man's well-known history, personality, and reputation only served to re-enforce such a moniker.

Introductions were completed, applause was instant and deafening, and the President flashed a smile that was at once shy and confident. His gaze was both humble and assured; his stance inviting, but still imposing in its erectness and stature. Such were the many sides and attributes of this unique man, this first black President of the United States.

There had developed, over the months since his ascension to the top spot, a sort of ironic relief among Americans all over the land. This seemed to have had its genesis in having finally elected an African American to the Presidency, without having had to actually *elect* him. He had not been *elected* president, but *vice* president, and then the immediate death of the *elected* president had necessitated a sort of *appointment* of him to the top spot. Everyone seemed glad to have him there and just as relieved that it had been accomplished without all the discomfort that would have accompanied a campaign featuring him as the candidate for the top spot.

All this silliness, about that the commentators constantly ruminated in print and on the air, was to say that the time had long since arrived when a black—the right black, installed because of qualifications and devotion, not because of color or expediency—should occupy that office. So now they had him—competent, heroic, brilliant, courageous, and handsome—and folks were not just crazy about *him,* they were also glad to have gotten to this place at all. The country had him, and he had turned out to be one helluva leader; his early skirmishes with his adversaries of a liberal bent had gone very well. It was the very "unelectedness" of his presidency that seemed to make him willing to take whatever direction he thought appropriate, without so much concern over appearances, campaign tones, and all that other baggage that always haunts chief executives.

He was the ironic darling of the conservatives, the instant, de facto champion of Black America, the arch-advocate of the military, the incontrovertible leader of the country—the consequent perfect nemesis for his spend-crazy liberal adversaries. No fan of big government, he was the product of a family that had worked hard to support his education and development; his attitudes and politics hit responsive chords everywhere. And the international community viewed him with a combination of awe, fear, and relief after the two terms worth of crooks and fools who had occupied the office before him.

Molly evoked comparisons with Jackie Kennedy, with her lanky elegance and daring, even dramatic personal style. The two of them managed, in just two short months, to awaken a kind of national pride in the body politic—a sense of dignity mixed with common sense—that had their faces on every magazine cover and their names on everyone's lips.

Sixteen minutes into his speech, Webb had just summarized his whole plan of attack on the problem of soaring illiteracy in public schools, after having first addressed his impending dismantling of the IRS; this was attendant to the implementation of a national sales tax. Although many in the room had grave misgivings over the idea of a "use tax," the idea of driving a stake through the heart of the most hated institution in the history of the Republic made argument difficult. They found themselves applauding repeatedly as he outlined his plan to disband this "single most tyrannical tool for the abridgement of American freedoms ever to darken the landscape of our democracy."

Never a fan of longwinded speeches, he wound up with a quick, incisive style that was already changing the way politicians spoke publicly all over the land.

Do not delude yourselves, my fellow executives, into believing that 'the more things change, the more they will stay the same.' Maintaining such an attitude can be expected to remove you from the very enterprise for that you have all so aggressively campaigned. I promise you that things will change. Our people have demanded it, and I have promised it to them. They have announced their mandate for integrity, accountability, and the kind of true equality that is founded upon hard work and devotion to God, country, and family. And people, do not believe for a single moment that there is still such a thing as "business as usual" in the world of American government. Those days are gone.

With your help, we will return our country to the greatness it has known, and that its citizens so richly deserve. We have declared an end to the kind of sloth, the kind of duplicity, and the kind of perverse amorality that have so blighted our government over the past eight years. It remains to us, each and every person in this room who has been chosen by his or her own neighbors in solemn election, to commit every ounce of our strength and intellect to the accomplishment of this great goal. There can be no person here who holds to any other agenda: The battle for the rebuilding of the dignity and integrity of the United States of America must not falter, cannot fail, and will end in victory for the forces of good.

Let me address this duty and privilege of leadership. Yes, I have been honored to lead brave men on the field of combat. But I have also led beautiful children at play and men and women in prayer. I can tell you this much about leadership: It does not so much flow from courage as from necessity; not so much from design as from the heart. It is far more the product of love than of valor and much more the result of God's grace than the consequence of the leader's merit.

Do not trust to feelings or to emotion. Build instead on what your intellect and your soul tell you is right. Right not in terms of the moment, for the day is tossed by every swell of fad and whimsy. But right in absolute terms—the kind of right that God has given us, and the righteousness that transcends every selfish interest and exploitative desire.

Be guided by what is right, and be influenced only by what you know to be honest and faithful. And people, if you need our help, it is there. If you find yourself in need of leadership, pray with me for God's guidance, and together we will deliver that that America demands and deserves. God bless you all, and God bless America.

The last word was followed by a long moment of odd silence, as though the audience was frozen in time and place. Then, almost as one, they rose to their feet in thundering shouts of acclamation, applause instantly drowning out every other sound. Webb stepped back, shook hands with the president of the National Conference, then walked down the steps of the stage, moving along the route prescribed by the security people. Molly met him at the base of the steps, kissed him powerfully and without apology, right there in front of the world and, taking his arm, was swept away by their Secret Service entourage.

As they stepped into the long black limousine that was idling in the basement of the huge convention center, Molly turned to her husband, her eyes a mist of tearful emotion. "Jackie, my darling, I swear to God above, but you were *wonderful!* And the *people,* Jackie, they were totally captivated!! Dearest Jesus, but it was so awesome, at times the whole thing scares me to death."

171

Webb looked deep into her moist eyes, at first a bit embarrassed at her effusiveness, but then curious over her expression of fear. "Molly—what on earth do you have to be scared of—hell, they're stuck with us now. . .got almost four years before they can run us off! Seems like you—"

"No, dummy, I'm not afraid of some kind of *political* problem, Lord knows there'll be plenty of those. I don't know. . .just seems to me you're so *big* now. . .I mean. . .so visible, so decisive, and well—oh, you know—old habits die hard and, well, Jackie dear, you *are* the first black resident. . .So many have sworn not to permit that, and some of the fringes are so violently bigoted, even now, that I—"

"Nonsense, babe, don't go borrowing trouble. We got better security than Saddam Hussein, for Pete's sake!! We're fine. Hellfire, Molly, if a hundred thousand gooks couldn't get me when I was standing right in front of them and darin' 'em to shoot back, I doubt if any brain-dead redneck's gonna get the job done now. And besides, we got things to do! God's already decided to punish me by answering my stupid prayer about bein' president in the first place. Don't think He'll let the bad guys whack me now!!"

A big laugh filled the small space where they were, as husband embraced wife. Webb often spoke in metaphors of God, and Molly was pretty sure her husband, although always lighthearted and seemingly joking about such things, did believe that the Good Lord looked out for him. And after the number of apparently impossible spots from which he had been saved over the years of combat, it was really pretty hard to argue with the proposition.

They rolled up the ramp and onto Lake Shore Drive, heading north toward the Shedd Aquarium, their mood light and the flush of the thunderous reception still ringing in their ears. Another car led the way, local marked police units out in front of both cars, and two more unmarked vehicles filled with Secret Service agents followed right behind the limo. Passing by the yacht basin and Miggs Field on the right and the Museum on the left, they pulled into the drive in front of the Aquarium, stopping just a few feet off the thoroughfare. Traffic was blocked off in the immediate area, so they could allow the motorcade to spread back into Lake Shore Drive. As the cars rolled to a stop, agents poured from the various car doors like ants, each heading in a prearranged direction, taking up positions along the walk from the limo to the entrance of the building.

Book II – The Hounds of Hell

* * * * *

"Hey, Skip—what'sup, man—gonna be colder'n hell up on that roof today!! Betcha'd ruther be sippin' sar maish frum th'bottle 'uth some li'l pootang, huh!!" Donnie laughed with his mouth open wide, his few teeth pointing in various directions as he croaked at his own humor.

"Yeah, Donnie, gonna be a might chilly up there, but I'll be done soon, an' then I just may do exactly that! Anyway, just bein' a loyal gubment servant, right?" He laughed again, louder this time than the last, and Lester walked past him to the back elevator. With only an hour until the target would be in position, he had to make ready quickly and then get out of sight. The aerial surveillance would certainly see him and pay a lot of attention to his presence, once the President was at McCormick Place. So he had to set up shop, be completely ready to move back out on the roof, then busy himself unobtrusively on the top floor of the Museum until time to act.

The rifle was hidden inside the sheet metal cover of the main compressor housing, approximately in the middle of the roof. The shooting site, over closer to the edge, was a smaller unit, and it was there that Lester set up what looked like a tarpaulin covering over some work in progress. He transported the rifle to that spot in pieces, working to assemble it with practiced hands underneath the tarp. A low rest lay at the end of the covered place, and the rifle, now loaded and equipped with the scope, was ready. He moved back inside, not to return until he saw the motorcade pass by from his vantagepoint at the stairwell window, leading to the roof access.

In order not to draw suspicion, the killer had to look busy inside on the top floor. Parts from several units similar to those on the roof were spread out on the floor inside the entry to the roof stairwell, and tools lay mixed in with the parts. As he sat acting busy with a small coil assembly that was apart in his lap, Monroe had to stifle a frightened cry as the hillbilly janitor spooked him from behind.

"Hey, Don, you checkin' up on me agin? 'Fraid I won't give the city its money's worth?" His slight smile teased the younger man.

"Naw, hell, Skip—I'as just bored 'uth all them screamin' brats downstairs, so I come up ta see what ya's doin', that's all. . ." The two visited for several minutes, and the acid in Lester's stomach began to build up as time elapsed toward the passage of the motorcade. Just when he was starting to devise a way to kill the kid and hide his body if he didn't leave, Billie got bored again and wandered off. As soon as he was out of sight, Lester sprinted to the window, only to see the first flashing lights that preceded the main event. Dashing back to the place where he had just had his tense little visit with the resident idiot, he satisfied himself that the kid was really gone and ran back up the steps to the roof.

Moving deliberately but in straight lines, Monroe first checked for the location of the two helicopters that had been in the air for the last hour. The gusty winds made precision impossible for the two pilots, so there were times when both would be out over the lake at the same time; a couple of times he had seen both aircraft north of the Aquarium and away from his location at the same moment. As fate would have it, the wind picked up to near gale force just as the main motorcade pulled up to the entrance, and the two choppers had to fight mightily to maintain control. Holding close to the target area was simply impossible.

When the second of the two aircraft disappeared behind the trees between the Museum and the Aquarium, Lester quickly walked over to the smaller compressor unit where the rifle was hidden and the rest was in place. His heart leapt as he saw two plainclothes Secret Service men reach for the passenger side rear door of the black limo, and the President and his wife stepped out. His firing point was to be on the walkway up to the entrance, after both the target and the woman walked passed the limo. Lester slipped under the tarp, pulled the rifle up under his chest to his shoulder, and assumed a prone firing position.

The scope opened onto the backs of the heads of no less than a dozen people, as the President moved within a virtual shroud of bodies. For a moment, Monroe could not make out who was who, and he thought the shot would have to be aborted.

With maximum magnification through the big telescopic sight, suddenly the chaos seemed to clear temporarily, and the unmistakable profile of Webb appeared at the crosshairs. Tall, erect, hair closely cropped in military style, he was immediately flanked by a black woman. "Target acquired, Les, lock on and fire." His mind ordered his actions and steadied his nerves. "That's him—couldn't miss that nigger head in a crowd twice that size. *Hit him!*" One breath, in and out, then a second in and held—exhale slowly— "target lock, squeeze and fire. . .hold, hold, *PUMPH!*"

The target disappeared in a mist of red and pink, visible momentarily even through the scope. The wind, blowing sharply into the shooter's face, swallowed the report of the heavy .308 round, and the shock that accompanied the impact of the bullet down range kept anyone from even thinking of looking back at him. For an instant, the fallen body was visible, and the killer's reflexes at once recognized the reacquisition of the target. *"PUMPH!"* again the weapon jolted against his shoulder, and he could see the body jump as the second round found its mark.

"Mission accomplished, Lester, now *haul ass!!!"* Rolling out from under the canvas, he slid the rifle back under the stiff fabric, moved—again very deliberately—back, first to the big air conditioning unit, where he scooped up his tool belt and fastened it on as he walked away to the doorway into the stairwell. His head pounded with the enormity of the moment as adrenaline coursed through his blood and his thoughts raced ahead to the many options for escape. At the bottom of the stairs that led to the roof, he had to go out into the hallway of the top floor, then proceed to the back stairs that serviced the rest of the building.

As his hand pushed open the door leading out into the hall, the hair stood up on the back of his neck with the realization that there was slight movement behind him. There was a small, dark alcove created by the staircase, dusty and strewn with refuse and a few discarded cleaning supplies.

In the business of tactical survival, predictability is the kiss of death, and hesitation is a guarantee for failure. Lester had no intention of dying, and failure was not in his vocabulary; without so much as a flinch in recognition of the threat, he dropped straight to the floor, rolling at the same time toward the left, where the door stood ajar approximately eighteen inches. His right shoulder brushed against it, pushing it open a little further against the tension of the automatic closer. The ten millimeter Sig Sauer automatic was out of his shoulder holster and into his hand without the apparent passage of so much as a single heartbeat, and he rolled around and up into a sitting position with the door coming closed against his left leg.

Donnie never knew a man could move so quickly, and notwithstanding his own long experience in the cruel art of killing, his quarry was quicker than he could ever have anticipated. Both men's weapons seemed to fire simultaneously,

175

the lighter report of Donnie's nine-millimeter mixed with the purposeful thud of the three rounds from Lester's ten. The nine-millimeter bullets hit Lester twice, once about even with his navel, and once slightly to the left of his sternum, four inches below the top of his shirt collar.

Lester's shots found Donnie all three times. He first took a round to the chest, dead center, followed by another just above it. Those two threw him straight back against the plaster wall, a mixture of plaster chips and blood staining the off-white surface where the hollow points smashed against the wall after exiting his back. The third, a second later, found his forehead, an inch above the bridge of his nose, and the back of his head exploded up that same wall. He slid limply down the wall and lay still.

Rolling back up on his knees, the victor rubbed his chest and belly through the deep indentations of the bullet impressions in his Kevlar vest. "Never leave home without it, Don." He quietly closed the door, after picking up the three cartridge casings that lay at his feet. He was a man who attended his details.

Walking down the hall to the back stairs, he decided not to chance using them, walked past them and descended the front way instead. There was no way of knowing who might have heard these last shots, and anyone who did would almost certainly come to investigate. Slowing to a nonchalant walk as he entered the cacophony of the main floor, all full of the chatter of kids having fun, he walked across the exhibit area in his tool belted disguise and out the back to his waiting service truck. No one inside had heard a thing, and at that moment, no one had any reason to take note of one more service man in coveralls.

Outside, faint shouts could be heard now on the wind that blew in from the lake, carrying the suggestion of hysteria from the entrance of the Aquarium. Climbing in the truck, Lester suddenly realized what had just happened. "Willie, you lowlife nigger sonofabitch—*JACK FUCKING RUBY!!!* You'll pay for this one, you miserable prick. . ." Even in the midst of escaping from the assassination of the President of the United States, he found himself overwrought at the realization that Sallie and Company had never intended for him to survive this hit.

Such "loss prevention" measures were considered beyond the pale, even in this most heinous of professions, and to have been the target of such a plot infuriated Monroe almost beyond control. He had performed flawlessly for the little bastard no less than half a dozen times, a couple of that had been much harder shots and

176

in much more dangerous settings; never had he failed, and *never* had he given the man a reason to want him neutralized. He would have to have a little visit with good ol' Willie—soon.

Then another realization hit him: There was a dead man in the alcove at the base of the stairs that led to the weapon that had killed the president. *Voila`!* It would take a good while for the double-crossing assholes to figure out that it was not *he* who had been found dead at the scene. He smiled briefly at the idea that he was a temporary dead man, able to move without his new victim even being aware of his existence, much less his new mission.

Choking down the bitter bile of his fury, he turned his attentions to operating the truck out into traffic on the other side of the Museum, opposite Lake Shore Drive. Turning onto the southbound lanes, he drove back past McCormick Place, up onto Interstate 55, and out into the heavy stream of commuter traffic. After a few blocks, he merged onto the Dan Ryan Expressway, then exited it back down onto the city streets for the trip around and back up to the Loop and his waiting escape car.

By the time Lester had meandered back into downtown, sirens were screaming all over the place and the whole area was flashing with blue, yellow, and red bubblegum lights from the tops of a hundred police and rescue vehicles. He wondered about roadblocks, searches, even random stops and interrogations. Of course, he had his identification badge and his truck full of tools and air conditioning parts, so he looked pretty normal. And with the treacherous tools of his *real* trade still lying in a sinister pile on the deserted rooftop, he had no fear about such a search, anyway. As always, the weapon used for the hit was a conglomeration of parts from several stolen guns, and his gloved hands had left no prints for the crime lab boys to discover.

The trusty ten millimeter Sig Sauer automatic that dispatched hillbilly Donnie had been dropped into a trash bin beside the back door of the Museum, and it was print free, anyway, Lester having worn those same unlined leather gloves throughout the day. The weapon was an assemblage of parts from three different stolen guns, with the upper slide assembly having come from a burglary in Des Moines, the grip and lower action from a weapon stolen in Miami, and the clip an off brand he had purchased in Houston.

No search materialized as of the moment he entered the parking garage where the Mercedes awaited his return. Parking as close to it as possible, he waited until no other people were in the area, then he quickly locked the truck and, unlocking the black car with the keyless entry button, sat down within the dark tinted interior.   The smell of the cold leather welcomed his agitated psyche as he finally dared to take a deep breath and try to collect himself. After a few moments of silence, he reached into the back seat and pulled out a long dark topcoat and a wool scarf. With the coat on and buttoned up over the scarf that covered even the collar of his workman's coveralls, he would not draw attention if questioned or even asked to stand.

The big German engine roared to life as the killer glided down to the first floor and out onto the street. The attendant who took his thirty-two dollar parking fee never betrayed the least interest in him as he drove out into the press and racket of the wet evening rush hour. Where others might find frustration in the snarled mess of heavy traffic, Lester found just the kind of anonymity he needed as he drove north out of town on I-94. Finally, an hour away from Miggs Field and the completion of his mission, he considered turning on the radio to listen to the reports of what he had done. He decided against it.

12.

Lee Jefferson Medley was the kind of kid who always landed on his feet. And usually he landed substantially in front of everyone else with whom he associated. From high school football and first team All-American status at USC through six years of outstanding service in the Army, first in the Military Police and then in military intelligence, he had always led a charmed life. Six more years in the FBI gave way to his life-long ambition, when he had finally been selected for the coveted executive protection division of the Secret Service. And at six feet two inches tall and two hundred twenty pounds, it was not a matter of luck that he landed an assignment guarding the new president and his wife. Close-cropped hair, erect posture, and square, powerful shoulders made him a perfect close-in protector for Jackie Webb; the men looked like twins from a distance.

It had always been a tactic of the Service to try to keep people around a president who bore at least a vague likeness to him; typically, at least one man who fit that general description would be detailed to dress very similarly to the president, with the obvious intention that one attempting to do him harm might mistake one for the other. So when Lee Medley walked up to the left of Molly Webb as the President stooped over to pick up a glove that had fallen out of his topcoat, he momentarily replaced him perfectly next to the First Lady as they walked toward the entrance to the Shedd Aquarium. Before Webb could scoop up the glove, stand up, and return to his wife's side, the younger man's head exploded with a hollow, sickening "thwak!," and he pitched violently over on his face. The wind and street noise completely swallowed the report of the weapon fired from atop the Museum.

It had been many years since Jackie Webb heard that sound, but it snapped open a vision of the gory death he had seen countless times during his tenure as a soldier. Molly reacted like most folks who are unaccustomed to such incomprehensible horror: She looked at the fallen, bloody man without the least comprehension of what she was seeing. Then his body jerked violently off the ground, like some unseen explosive had gone off under him, and in that moment she began to realize that he had been shot—and that he was being shot again. The next thing she remembered was the noiseless sensation of being off the ground, out of control, the cold, wet wind peppering her face.

Without actually ever making the cognitive connection, she somehow recognized that she had been scooped right off her feet by her husband, and almost before she could get her feet down again, she sprawled across the back seat of a waiting car with Jackie diving in on top of her. His hands were over her shoulders and head as he forced her down onto the floor of the car, her husband's voice thundering *"GO!!GO!!"* and she was aware that they were accelerating away from the scene. She felt the warmth of the heater blowing from under the front seat as the sensation of tremendous pain gripped her throat. It was only then, with the soothing, reassuring sound of her husband's now softened voice in her ear, that she realized that she had been screaming hysterically, and her throat was raw and on fire from the strain.

The car screeched to a stop, surrounded at once by several others, their own tires squealing as they broad slid in around them. The doors flew open and the voices of men barked orders to get out and stay down. Jackie was suddenly gone, and Molly could feel harsh hands gripping her by the back of her coat and under her arms—a very powerful man ripping her off the floor and out of the back seat. The tender flesh of her soft flank burned as the hands raked across her. As she gained her feet, she at once saw a helicopter less than thirty feet in front of them on the runway of Miggs Field, its big rotor creating a whirlwind of icy, grit-filled turbulence; her husband was moving toward her, himself surrounded by no fewer than six men.

They ran to each other, joined hands, then sprinted the thirty feet and literally dove into the waiting aircraft, the ground disappearing from beneath their feet before the door of the thing could even go closed. Then she could feel him scooping her into his arms, holding her ever so tight, his breath coming in short gasps, heart pounding against her breast. Turning into his embrace, her face was wet and, touching her fingers to her cheek, she realized that tears were streaming down, dripping off her chin. She sobbed uncontrollably. And so did he.

After a moment, Webb could stand it no longer, and he pulled himself up onto his knees in the floor of the chopper. Looking back toward the Aquarium, he could see a cluster of men bent over the form of Lee Medley, their expressions clear even at the ever-increasing distance and altitude. Others, some in plainclothes and some in various uniforms, were running back and forth, taking up defensive positions or just trying to find some place to hide. Sick with helplessness and overwhelmed with grief, frustrated and already in a fury at what had happened, the new president fought a powerful wave of nausea.

No sense of time assisted him as he tried to put it together, but in fact, between the moment the agent was hit by the second round and the time the chopper lifted off, less than sixty seconds had elapsed. These security people were *very* good at what they did, and evidence of countless rehearsals for just such an eventuality was obvious. The pilot, seeing that he was looking back in the direction of the shooting, reached around and gently touched his arm.

"You're OK, General—you're *both* OK. We're headed for O'Hare now, ETA about eight minutes to Air Force One, sir, so just sit tight. I only saw a little of the mess out front as I responded to the extraction order—that goddam wind was giving us fits, just trying to keep on top of your motorcade. Guess we shoulda' stayed closer in—I just kept having visions of driving this thing into that big plate glass window on the back side of the Aquarium. . . I—"

"Bag it, Captain, nothing you could've done. Sumbitch must've had a perfect location and one helluva weapon—no way you'd have *ever* gotten a make on him. And judging from the impact, it had to have been something big, maybe 30/06 or .308, even a .300 magnum—probably semi-auto, too. That second shot hit within no more than three seconds of the first. Holy shit. . Holy. . ."

"Just try to relax a minute, sir, we'll have you back on Air Force One in about five minutes." The Jet Ranger helicopter banked around to the north of the tall buildings that filled downtown Chicago, the John Hancock building marking the upper end of the skyline. From there, they streaked straight west to the north end of the huge complex that was O'Hare International Airport, landing within minutes, right next to the waiting 747. Almost before they had time to begin to realize what had just happened, they were off the ground again and roaring back toward Washington. They could not know what cataclysm awaited them over the next few hours.

13.

"You gonna work all night? I'm sure the big boys will appreciate your devotion, but damn, Will, you been here for almost fifteen hours!" Smalley looked up from his computer screen, concealed his irritation at the interruption, then smiled weakly at one of the few men in the whole Federal Reserve System he sort of liked.

"You're right, of course, Mo, I'll just finish this last auto rec run on the Kansas City Fed clearing account, then I'll bag it. I am pretty tired." Morris Rathman shook his head wearily, threw up a hand to signify goodbye, and closed the older man's door. Mo didn't have too much of a life, but his fat wife and a couple of cats were a thousand times more than what awaited poor Willard when he went home. The halls were dark and shadowed with eerie light from the exit signs over the stairwell doors. It all mixed in with the flicker of scores of computer screens—now deserted until morning.

In fact, this solitude was what Smalley had awaited. He quietly removed the diskette that had been occupying his A drive, replacing it with the first of four he took from the bottom drawer of his desk. Inserting it, his fingers flew across the keys as he booted up the information. "Fedwire, disk 1—domestic interrupt: A drive, folder 1, task 1: ID mirror/NY.Fed." More keystrokes, then a pause. He sat back momentarily, sighed deeply, removed the disk.

It was while he was reviewing the perfection of his own personal computer virus that he stopped short, stunned by the realization that there was a subtle vibration palpable against his hip. The blood rushed to his head, his face flushed—he stopped breathing. Looking quickly back at the door to his office, he confirmed that it was closed tight; then he stood, and reaching inside his waistband, he pulled out a small black pager, its near silent buzzing sending chills up his arm and down his spine. His breath now coming in short, choppy gasps, he lay the little object down on his desk, as it buzzed and vibrated again.

In the top drawer of his desk was a small index card, on that WAS inscribed a short, innocuous series of numbers. After the last one was the word "GO." A second series, this one ending in a string of three zeroes, was followed by the word "STOP." Laying the card down beside the pager, his hands shook almost uncontrollably as he picked up the vibrating device and depressed the message retrieval button. The display panel lit up, and a string of numbers appeared. He picked up the card, comparing the numbers on the pager display to those written on the card. A sharp pain in his chest made him wince as he inhaled a short breath. "GO."

Willard Smalley sat down at his desk and waited for the pain to subside and the shaking in his hands to stop. Removing a small bottle from his shirt pocket, he placed two tiny nitroglycerin tablets under his tongue. He could feel his pulse slow down, the feeling coming back in his left arm and hand.

It took him about ten minutes to wind his way through the cybermaze of codes and false clearances that attempted to guard the Fedwire system from unauthorized entry. Although not a protocol that some high school hacker could penetrate, it posed no problem to the very man who had designed and installed a major portion of it. It did take a couple of extra minutes for the last stage of entry to be accomplished, as the security codes had been changed just a few hours before this action commenced. No problem, though, and Smalley adroitly introduced his virus-filled diskettes into the system at exactly the right place and time. Backing out of this most secure of compartments, he blasted the programs that were designed to identify the source of any attempted entry—an extra special virus just for them.

Once out of that whole program, he walked down to the Fedwire transmission terminal room, where the New York Fed's personnel confirmed all electronic orders during normal banking hours; the monitor for the main file server was never turned off; as that computer remained on twenty-four hours a day. Willard entered the required commands for a view of existing transactions in progress and confirmed that no evidence of entry—authorized or otherwise—had been recognized. A brief smile crossed his florid face, a quick sigh emanated from his heaving chest. The insertion had been accomplished without detection. He walked out, turning out the light behind him.

Again addressing the keyboard, Smalley turned his attention to the task of gaining entry into the switch computers for the four major credit card networks. Each was a bit different, but he chuckled at the transparent, juvenile attempts at security present in them all. An hour after he started with the VISA switch, he finished with the last of the four, the proprietary network switch that drove the many smaller card operations. He sat back, his pulse again pounding in his temples. Another dose of nitro was in order.

Verification of the effect of this task was not as easy, there being no local terminal that could verify the completion of the virus insertions or the effect they were to have on the continuation of transmission of authorizations and settlement. Willard had previously decided that a stop at the gas station on the way home, plus an attempted telephone catalog order that he would initiate when he got home, would suffice. Certainly no one could associate these with him in any sinister way. Collecting up all the disks for both jobs, he first re-verified that they were all there and that the A drive on his own unit was empty; then, with the complete set in his coat pocket, he shrugged into his top coat, turned out the lights, and walked to the elevator.

As the elevator whined its solitary way to the basement and his waiting car, he determined absolutely that this would be his last departure from this awful place. All that remained for him to do tonight was to dispose of the disks, pick up his bags at home, drive to JFK, and fly direct and nonstop to Honolulu. From there, he would have a four-hour layover, after that he would fly on to his beloved Tahiti and the paradise that had eluded him for over fifty years. With five million dollars safely deposited into three accounts (he had verified all three before shutting down the system), and with all the mayhem that was about to explode, there was no reason for Willard Smalley ever to come back to this hell hole again. He declared silently that he had darkened the door of the New York Fed for the last time. He was right.

* * * * *

Killing had always had a peculiar impact on Lester Monroe. Even back when it was legal in Vietnam, the adrenaline rush and almost sexual pleasure he gained from close-in combat death was always followed by a time of uncharacteristic silence and a hunger for solitude. The usually gregarious hellraiser became quiet—not sullen or mean—but melancholy and pensive. It lasted only a few hours when he was a young soldier but later, when he began to kill for money, the trend became more pronounced. Eventually, as the profit from murder for hire became more substantial (in line with his prowess and reputation), he began to actually plan for a sort of "sabbatical" after each hit, including a place where quiet was the rule and solitude was easy to find.

184

Book II – The Hounds of Hell

Driving out of the Chicago area, the reverie hit, and the time for silence arrived.

The Lake Michigan coastline, from the end of the suburban sprawl of Chicago to the beginning of the suburban sprawl of Milwaukee, looks more like Maine than Wisconsin. Beautiful homes sit atop bluffs and cliffs where commanding views of the wonderful blue water are a guarantee of breathtaking sunrises. The area is predominantly private; there are few hotels and no big time development, although the small towns along the shore do a brisk business in charter fishing. Occasional "bed and breakfast" enterprises dot the outskirts of the towns, but of bright lights and tall buildings there are none.

The big Mercedes rolled to a stop outside a quaint old Victorian edifice, where a dignified sign identified "Sunrise Overlook, a Bed and Breakfast," and a big gray cat lay asleep squarely in the middle of the welcome mat at the front door. In the midst of the gathering darkness, both outside and within his own psyche, Lester smiled at his own schizophrenic self, 90 percent hell raisin' hillbilly and 10 percent hermit. Stepping over the cat, he opened the ornate front door; leaded and beveled panes of glass in a collage filled almost the entire area of the massive wooden frame, and the scent of old money welcomed his tired senses.

An austere matron of rotund proportion and stark countenance met him with a deep, sonorous voice. "Good *eeevaning,* sir, may I *helllpp* you?" The words were part greeting, part "what on *earth* do *you* want," in implication. Monroe was unimpressed by the posturing, round old bag, but he maintained the best decorum he could muster. "Evenin', Ma'am, like a room with a view, if you don't mind." Part of the change he underwent in this aftermath of killing included a softer demeanor and an effort not to speak in his customary raucous and obscene ways. He adopted an understated effect that gave him an "aw shucks" shy appearance and tended to discourage others from serious efforts at conversation. This also helped him in the woman department, as he always experienced a rush of testosterone when coming out of this temporary funk.

After the quiet time, and after having successfully bedded one or more unsuspecting females, he would resume being the other Lester, heading back to the world of the soldier of fortune. The stuffy matron leered at him momentarily, causing the hair to stand up on the back of his neck; she looked over his shoulder in

185

a not so subtle way and reacted with widened eyes at the sleek, expensive 600SEL in the drive.

"Oh—why. . .*yes* . . .I do suppose we have such a suite available. . .let me see. . .yes, the *Flagler* is not reserved, after all. Yes, that would give you a fine view of the lake. It certainly would." Lester suppressed a stupid grin as he watched the old broad warm up after seeing the big car.

"Great. Thanks, ma'am, 'presheate it." His eyes never left the floor.

"And for how long would you *like* the suite, Mr.—"

"It's Jackson, ma'am, Alan Jackson—you know, like the singer—" Instantly he knew the greaseball in him had slipped out, as the woman looked at him with an uncomprehending stare. "I'll be here through Saturday, I imagine. . .if that'd be OK with y'all. . ."

"We can accommodate you, Mr. Jackson, no problem. *I* am Mrs. *Wutherly. That* will be fifty-five dollars per night, and that includes continental breakfast from 7 a.m. until 9:30 daily. Tea at 4 p.m., and sweet snacks between 8:30 and 10 p.m. each evening. We prefer cash." The last word was emphasized enough to make it clear that he was to pay in advance, so he quickly produced two crisp one hundred dollar bills and a $50.

"Here, ma'am—this should cover it. If I owe any more, just say the word. That be OK 'th y'all?" The "aw shucks" mode was in full swing, and the iron woman was beginning to soften to it slightly. She smiled stiffly and removed the currency from his extended hand, bowing imperceptibly as she turned away toward the elegant antique cherry secretary, the obvious location where business was transacted. She gave him back a twenty-dollar bill.

"It is almost dark now, have you eaten?" Her heavily enhanced eyebrows arched nearly into her salt-and-pepper widow's peak. Lester's almost complete metabolic shutdown had made food a forgotten subject, and he thanked her, inquiring politely about restaurants in the area for tomorrow. He knew his appetite would return with a screaming vengeance by morning, and the idea of polite little pastries and weak coffee flavored with some sissy aromatic additives was totally repulsive. The chainsaw that would be growling within him tomorrow would need stouter fare, by far.

Mrs. Wutherly insisted on accompanying him to the suite, where she further insisted on providing a wordy tour of the room. This narrative was complete with repeated references to the many mementos lying about that bore connection to the famous Flaglers, who had at one time made a habit of staying here. All this was lost on poor Lester, who just wanted the woman to leave so he could get undressed and fall asleep. She finished with an understated flourish concerning the decorative pitcher and bowl that occupied an ancient side table under the window that overlooked the back yard and lake beyond. Re-emphasizing the decorative nature of the piece, it was clear that she wanted to ensure the Lester would not try to wash in it—or worse. He got the point.

Undressing as he watched the blackness gather and consume the huge lake, he was so overtaken by fatigue that he could feel his legs giving out as he staggered toward the big four poster bed. Lester pulled the heavy comforter and soft old sheets up to his chin. As the darkness enveloped him, flashbacks of the day, and of the two men he had killed, appeared momentarily. Closing his eyes, he told himself that the time would come for a reckoning over that business with the "Jack Ruby" thing. At least the bastards had gotten what they bargained for. That nigger president was dead. Graveyard dead.

* * * * *

Sitting at a desk on the main set of *CBS News* in New York, Dan Rather was striking and somber. His suit coat long since removed, his suspenders and coordinating tie gave him an Edward R. Murrow style that kept the eye attentive and the ear attuned. By 8:30 p.m. he had been on the air for nearly five hours, since the story of the attempt on the life of President Webb had broken. Although obviously tiring from the grind, his delivery was still crisp and imposing.

"At this hour, we have confirmed that one Secret Service agent has been killed in an attempt on the life of President Webb, and that earlier reports of injury to Mrs. Webb were incorrect. Both the President and the First Lady are back in Washington, having arrived at Andrews Air Force base at approximately 6:15 p.m., eastern standard time. The Agent in Charge for the Division of Presidential Security, Lyle Davisson, has just announced a press conference and briefing for 9 p.m. tonight. At that time we are told there will be some video footage, as well as a statement from one of the agents who actually participated in the removal of the President and Mrs. Webb from the scene. Bob Schieffer, CBS chief Washington correspondent, joins us now with more on this incredible and tragic story. . .Bob—"

"Well, Dan, it's been quite an afternoon. What appeared to be a relatively routine ceremony at the Shedd Aquarium on Lake Michigan just outside of downtown Chicago turned into a nightmare of high-powered gunfire and decisive heroism by the Secret Service *and the President himself. He* was apparently responsible for snatching his wife from the line of fire of the sniper's rifle. Quick reactions by the agents accompanying the First Family, coupled with some pretty impressive maneuvers by one of the helicopters that were hovering over the motorcade, almost certainly saved the lives of the President and Mrs. Webb.

"So far, we believe the shots came from the Museum of Natural History, about one hundred-fifty yards from the Aquarium. We have confirmed that a weapon has been recovered from the roof of the Museum and, as we reported earlier, a man has been found shot and killed at the base of the stairwell that leads to the roof. He is described only as a white male in his thirties or forties, shot two or three times. We do *not* know, however, who shot him. His identity has not been determined, as far as we know at this hour. We hope to learn much more at the press conference to occur at 9 p.m. Dan—"

Abdul Salim Alakmah sat motionless in front of the television set in his sanctuary quarters, deep within the old tenement. His pale eyes fixed a frigid stare into the screen, his breathing almost imperceptible, his pulse visible at neck and temple. Exploding without warning, he hurled the coffee table and its entire contents through the air and into the wall behind the TV. "Mutha Fucker—Mutha Fucker—Lester, you miserable piece of *SHIT!!!* Dearest Allah—what now? How could he be so goddam stupid, so *fucking* inept, so totally *out to lunch!!!* Killed the wrong nigger. Probably thought they all looked alike, so he just shot the first one that appeared in his fucking ignorant scope!! *Mutha FUCKER!!!"*

He sat back down as Schieffer began the part about the dead man at the museum; he was hopeful that it was Lester they had found. "Serves you right, you white honky *cocksucker!!!* Ol' Jack Ruby gave you the *big* surprise, after all." Sallie was weak and shaky, notwithstanding the bravado of his explosion *and* his apparent confidence that Monroe had been taken out by Hillbilly Don. In only a matter of hours—if not minutes—he would start getting communications from the Committee, probably from Arafat himself, and trying to explain how the thing could fail so miserably would be difficult at best. He froze in place as the cell phone, now turned on in anticipation of the inevitable call, squawked from the table. Time to face the music.

* * * * *

Smalley looked around the garage area before walking to his car. Confident there was no one present, he turned back into the glassed-in area where the elevators emptied out into the basement and opened a trash can that stood between the two elevator doors. Reaching under his topcoat and into the pocket of his suit, he felt the stack of diskettes, grasping them in preparation for dropping them into the half full canister. He would make sure they were covered up by other trash inside. He had carefully researched this particular trashcan, learning that it was emptied every night between 12:30 and 1 a.m.

The janitor who did it was legally blind, so much so that he could not get a drivers license and could only work here because the Americans With Disabilities Act scared the hell out of his employer and kept him from being retired or terminated. Willard wanted none of that Hollywood crap of burning or throwing the disks into some river where there would be some potential for discovery. Like everything else that ever went into that can, the disks would simply go out in the daily dumpster pickup. And once they were *in* that dumpster, with no fingerprints and no way of identifying them, they would be gone. Just like that.

Turning back toward the car but still standing beside the trash can, Willard tried to relax the tension in his chest. He reached for the nitro again, attempting to soothe himself with thoughts of the black sand beaches of Tahiti and the five million dollars he had at his command, irrespective of the mess he had just made of the electronic money system in the U.S. His money was already on deposit outside the U.S., and he could go personally to Caracas, Rio, and eventually Singapore when he wanted to resupply, if necessary.

He thought of sand and surf and lithesome dark girls. Of sweet tropical tastes and smells, native foods and unfamiliar music. Breezes and salt spray. Peace.

Collapsing onto the cold concrete, he looked up through tear-flooded eyes at the pale bluish lights of the parking garage. He felt his mouth moving as if to speak or cry for help, but there was no sound. The tears were blurring the image of the light, and the stark lines of the girders that supported the ceiling began to move.

His hands and arms tried to grasp at the crushing pain in his chest, then at the searing heat of his tongue being severed by his own clinched teeth. Choking on bile and blood, the images faded before half open eyes. And then he was dead.

14.

Rain pelted the asphalt all around the roof that covered the gas pumps, as Josh Landry shivered against the wet cold. Crazy designs appeared and vanished at once, as the sheets of icy rain blew past on a vicious wind, the orange light from under the large canopy casting eerie hues through the swirling pools. It was after midnight, he was dead- dog exhausted after finishing a brief that had taken eleven straight days to complete, and he had a miserable cold. Sneezing and swearing at the same time, he tried again to make the infernal automatic gas pump accept his credit card.

"Come on, you miserable bastard, I *know* that card works! Paid the whole thing off two weeks ago, so *Come on!*" His voice echoed under the steel roof, and he quickly looked around to see if anyone had heard his tantrum. Of course not, as no *sane* person would be out in this mess, particularly without having already secured a sufficient quantity of gasoline to get home. Poor planning again.

It seemed always to be that way when a brief was due. Worse than any jury trial and more consuming than the bar exam, an appellate brief was the most excruciatingly exacting, hypertechnical mass of rules, form, and exasperation known to any lawyer. Women lawyers compared it to childbirth, and any man who heard the comparison immediately got a new and improved respect for labor and delivery.

The card simply would not take, so he went inside to pay in advance, as the screen so indelicately bade him with its not so subtle *see manager* message scrolling across the cold face of the pump. "Hi, Tony, guess I'm a bigger deadbeat than ever. Damn thing won't take my card. Here's ten bucks for enough juice to get me home. I'll fill up tomorrow." Tony, a huge young man with thinning hair and a girth the size of a fifty-five gallon drum, smiled through cigarette stained teeth.

"Not ta worry, Mr. Landry, sumbitch must be down. Nobody's been able ta git it ta work since about midnight. An' now I cain't even git the bastard ta take my call ta reconcile ma cash ta ma sales. Shit, guess it' lak they say—Takes a cumputer ta really mess thangs up *good!!*"

Josh smiled through tired lips and sighed a bit of relief that it was not his card account that was the problem. He said goodbye to Two Ton Tony, pumped his gas, climbed back in the family van, and headed out into the freezing rain. Home, bed, and Jess were sure gonna feel good tonight. He had already declared to all concerned that he would not be in tomorrow. Turning on the radio, he hunted for an AM station to get an update on the attempt to kill the President.

Although nothing really new had been learned from the press conference held by the Secret Service guys, Landry listened with more than casual acumen on the subject of snipers and long-range killing. In Vietnam, where the standard issue weapon for all soldiers was the M16 in one of its many forms, snipers had continued to use the heavier, slower, NATO round, the 7.62mm, also known as the .308. The smaller 5.56 mm (.223 caliber) round fired by the M16 was hotter by far, developing a muzzle velocity of 3,200 feet per second. But the lighter bullet, travelling at such tremendous speed, had a tendency to deflect when coming into contact with even the slightest obstacle.

The big, heavy NATO round was slower, had a more arching trajectory than the flat, hot 5.56, but things in the way didn't seem to bother it so much. Josh found himself in quiet flashbacks, seeing "targets of opportunity," as they were called in Op orders, tumbling ass over teakettle when hit by his scope-equipped M14. Shooting people through heavy grass, tree branches, even windows or walls had been almost routine. He shook his head to clear the mist of horror that still crept into his mind's eye at such moments. "Betcher sweet ass that hitter was shootin' a big round. Said the agent came clear off the ground when he got hit by the second round. Three-0-eight, sure as hell." He lectured on to nobody in particular as the miles slipped past toward home.

After keeping himself awake for several miles with his soliloquy on the subject of killing at great distances, a chill found him, hitting him with as much force as that 7.62 NATO round had hit the Secret Service agent. A surreal, tumbling array of images spun in his head as he suddenly found some obtuse connection between the hit in Chicago and the continued fear they experienced each day over the reports about LaShawn Mitchell. FBI keeps telling me there's some connection between what Mitchell has vowed to do to us and that "thing with national implications" they keep talking about.

"S'posed to be soon, and be a part of something 'bigger'—like maybe killing a president—or even more. Holy sweet Jesus, you don't suppose. . .naw. . .there you go again, Josh, getting all

192

grandiose and weird. . .still, better watch. . . The headlights found the entrance to the gravel and weed driveway, the van groaning as it thumped over the tank trap sized potholes full of icy water. The warrior's eyes fought for focus against the blindness produced by the bright lights. Eyes strained into the black night as he shut off the headlamps and slowed.

Sharp clarity accompanied eye adjustment to the darkness. Ghosts lurked in the mist and the light refracted from the one porch light. What was there? Nothing. Why this feeling of dread and foreboding? No reason. *Get a grip, Bozo, the joint's deserted. And besides, no self-respecting sniper's gonna lie around in this crap. Nope, no fun. Relax. . .*

He thought he had relaxed. He had not. Even with sweet Jessica wrapped around him, her breathing soft and steady against his chest, sleep evaded him. But the fear did not.

Night in the country. A quiet that is full of sound, no matter the time of year or the weather, accompanies darkness that always retains enough light to see in some detail, after the eyes are adjusted. It is impossible to describe night in the country to one whose life experience is limited to cities and suburbs. They cannot fathom the concept of a time so completely associated with the absence of sound and light, being so full of both. And sleeping out there takes some adjustment for those accustomed to the presence and darkness of the city.

As he lay in this country-quiet, the ceiling fan slowly turning above his head as it moved the warm air from the fireplace, Joshua Owen Landry faced a cascade of images, argued a myriad of cases. Sleep was so elusive, he had no idea when it was that he finally nodded off. He *did,* however, know when he awoke, at 3:50 A.M. according to the old windup alarm clock ticking away on Jesse's makeup table, the sense of something amiss now out of control.

Sitting upright in bed, the fog in his head cleared almost at once, as he tried to identify the elusive "wrongness" of the moment. Once, he would have been able to spin through every category of possibility almost simultaneously; he could run the whole list of stimuli in an entire environment at the same time, sifting and sorting with all senses at once, the five acting together to produce a sixth. That was twenty-five years ago, and things change; people grow older, slower.

Josh shook himself awake and began to try to isolate what it was that had his stomach in a knot and his breathing completely stopped, his heart racing at tachycardia rate. All was quiet, except for the rain. All was dark. Quiet. Dark. Very quiet. Very dark—spinning in place toward the nightstand, he glared at the clock radio, whose red numerals blared the announcement of morning each day. Nothing. It was dark.

"What—*listen*, dammit—quiet. . .*too* quiet. . .the furnace is off. . . The power is gone." The thoughts never found the spoken word, but the mind spoke in short, terse bursts. Stepping out of bed, he walked to the window and peered out across the fields to the south, where the next neighbor was brother Carl. He had a light over the north door of the barn, and in winter, that light was visible. But not tonight.

The road was deserted, and the porch light on the front of the house across the road was out. Josh couldn't remember the last time that light had been out, the old lady who lived there was so afraid of the dark. Power failures were not uncommon in the country, but they were usually accompanied by a storm of some kind. Tonight there was only the cold rain. It all added to the sense of foreboding and fear that would not go away.

A faint sound from the distance quickly became a siren, coming in from the north, in the direction of Jericho—now two, maybe three. Grabbing a sweatshirt, Josh walked out into the front of the house where he would be able to see the emergency vehicles if they drove by at all. Then, almost by accident, he looked out over the woods that darkened the horizon across the road from Carl's house, again to the south. An orange glow emanated from behind the woods, seemingly coming from a place where there was nothing to burn—only open fields. Suddenly the orange was shot through with white, red and blue, followed a few seconds later by the report of a big explosion. The orange color intensified as it became clear that some kind of petroleum had gone up in a big way.

"Carl—Josh. What's the deal—power's out, sirens everywhere, and some kind of explosion just went off way south, almost to the edge of Richland. Your power's gone, too, isn't it?" Standing at the window in the kitchen, Josh could see both west toward the road and south toward Carl.

"Yeah, went off right at 3:30, almost on the dot. I was reading in the study, and that old clock chimed the half hour right as things went dark. Tell ya' what else. I felt one helluva shock wave just after the lights went out, too. I mean something *big,* like 'ka*Boom!!*' Didn't you feel that?"

194

"Naw, hell no, it took me over two hours to *get* to sleep, probably not long before that, I was feelin' *nothin'* by then. . . maybe one of those big fuel storage tanks—" Glass shattered all around Josh's head, pots and pans careened wildly down around him as they tumbled from their hooks on the ceiling beams. Then he was on the floor, dropping the phone, low crawling away from the exploding sound of automatic gunfire that followed the several impacts, causing all the mess. *"INCOMING—INCOMING—HOLY SHIT, EVERYBODY DOWN—DEAREST JESUS, WHERE—"*

Josh was on his feet, crouched low as he sprinted for the bedroom closet and his shotgun. His mind fought back and forth between the kids upstairs and Jess, back in their room, and he was aware that they were still taking fire from at least two sources. One was right outside the kitchen window, the other through the living room window. That one appeared from the muzzle flashes to be further away.

Carl's voice cracked as he screamed into the now discarded phone. *"Josh—Josh!! what's going—are those shots—Josh. . ."* He too dropped the phone and raced to the hall closet where his shotgun and a .45 automatic were kept. Grabbing both, the older Landry stuffed his bare feet into the first available boots by the back door, and as the door went shut, he yelled back at Gail, "Call the Sheriff—all hell's come loose at Josh's—sounds like automatic weapons—get help!!" The door slammed and he was gone, the roar of his truck's engine disappearing into the night.

It had been only a few seconds since the fusillade began, probably less than thirty seconds, and already the sound of children crying and screaming had Josh to the point of insanity. But there was no time. Racking a round of buckshot into the chamber of Mick O'Neal's riot gun, he ran back into the bedroom and directly into a screaming Jess, knocking her several feet across the room and into the wingback chair in the corner. *"Get DOWN, Jess, and don't move—the kids are better off upstairs—"* With that, he slipped out the side window and vanished into the darkness.

Knowing there was at least one shooter either on the porch or right next to it, that seemed the best place to start. Coming around from the back of the house would give him just a moment's element of surprise, unless there were more guns that he couldn't see. That would have to take care of itself—unless he silenced the one on the porch instantly, someone inside would almost certainly be hit by the merciless stream of lead being poured through the kitchen windows. Barefooted and wearing only his underwear and the sweatshirt, Josh moved with a speed and purpose he would otherwise have thought had been left in the jungles of long ago.

God watched over him—the gunman was on the porch and firing nonstop into the house with some kind of 9mm machine gun—Mac 10, Josh thought for a split second. Hurdling up the three feet from ground to porch floor, the big shotgun roared into the flank of the aggressor— *"BLAM!! klak-klunk BLAM!!"* The two rounds, fired half a second apart as Josh pumped and ripped the second, lifted the man off the ground and tossed him ten feet further up the porch. The first load hit him a quartering angle into his right shoulder and chest, lifting and spinning him around facing Josh. The second ripped open his chest and spewed bone, blood, and organs up across the man's face as he landed in a slimy heap.

"Klak-klunk", the next round snapped into the chamber as Josh peeled two more live ones out of the ammo holder mounted on the side of the stock. He shoved them into the magazine without ever looking down as he leaped down off the porch and ran back into the back yard again. Next stop, gunman number two. He slid to an abrupt stop as he realized the firing had stopped from *both* locations, so it was likely that number two was on the move and looking for counterattack. Climbing back through the window, he was greeted by his wife's muffled scream, as she beheld the apparition of her man turned killer, his face livid, gaze on fire with the hunt.

He turned from her without really seeing her, running through the house to the stairs that led to the second floor. The roof over the porch would provide perfect concealment and an excellent shot if he could get out there without being seen. Luke stared wide-eyed as his father blew through his room and soundlessly raised the window onto the porch roof. *"Stay away from the window, Son—get in with your sisters—NOW!!"* The hoarse whisper propelled the boy out into the hallway. Josh slipped out onto the shingles, every sense charged with the adrenaline that now controlled him.

The corner of the roofline gave him momentary cover as he saw a flicker of movement along a line of trees at the edge of the front yard. Target acquired— *"BLAM!!—klak-klunk—BLAM!!"* A quick pause, then *"BLAM!!"* again. Josh was sure he'd hit the second man, as well.

Silence now. . .if there were more of them, he was in real jeopardy, outside, up high, exposed and with no way back to the window except across open roof. The momentary tunnel vision widened, as the sound of tires on gravel announced Carl's truck. *"Shit, dammit, Carl—I don't see any more of them—can't chance getting him in a crossfire—is it—"* A rustling sound betrayed movement at the site where the second man had gone down. *"BLAM!!"* again he fired before realizing the sound was the man's lifeless form sliding down between the trunk of a tree and the low bushes that flanked the tree line.

Josh jammed the three remaining shells from the stock bandoleer into the magazine as he slipped back through the window and into Luke's room. As he appeared in the doorway from the boy's bedroom out into the upstairs hall, all four kids stood huddled together, their mother's arms holding them close around her. They looked at him as if he were a total stranger, as though he might shoot them next.

"Stay *put* you guys—I think I got 'em all, but I can't be sure—Carl is coming. *Just stay right here!!"* He ran down the stairs, two and three at a time, racing through the kitchen so fast he forgot there was shattered glass all over the floor. The pain in his bare feet was instant and overwhelming, as the shards sliced, punctured and broke off in him. Stifling a scream, he jumped back, running to the front door.

"Carl—stay low—one bad guy down on the porch, another against the northmost maple tree in front. I think they're done for, but can't be sure—STAY BEHIND THE TRUCK!!" Each phrase escalated in volume and intensity as the younger Landry's voice barked out orders to the elder.

Josh walked painfully across the porch front and cautiously around the corner, the blood of the first gunman warm against his cold feet. Looking down at the gaping, half-empty chest cavity of the man, his eyes wide, mouth open, face covered with a thick spray of red, Josh fought back the vomit that tore at his throat. One down. The darkness beneath the trees out front made the approach to the second man much more treacherous. *"CARL— cover me—gotta see about the other one—you see where he went down?"* The elder Landry strained his eyes in the direction of the darkness, catching a bit of a form against the far tree trunk.

The Devil's Playground

"YEAH—got 'im—go in slow and holler if he moves." Wincing with the growing fire in his feet, Josh stepped off the front of the porch and sprinted across the open expanse of the yard, stopping against the southernmost tree. Moving slowly now, no sound, low profile, he came up behind the man, finding him seated at the base of that last Maple tree. "If you can hear me, asshole, you got no chance. Move and your head is gone. Throw out any weapon, to your left, *slow.*" No response. "Don't get cute, pal, this is no shit—toss the guns—" Moving in behind the man without a sound, Josh stuck him at shoulder level with the barrel of the big shotgun. The body fell over to the left, rolling back face up. Well, not actually *face* up. No face. Not much *head,* for that matter. That last round had killed a man who had been dead since the first one hit him full in the chest and neck.

"Oh, Jesus, what have I—what *is* this—what, oh *God*—how could—" The bile rose again, only this time the tide would not be turned, and the aging warrior knelt, vomiting violently into the bloody grass. Four rounds of buckshot had made an unrecognizable mess out of the whole front of the man. One arm was shot nearly off half way between the shoulder and elbow, and the damage to the torso was devastating. Carl saw Josh's reaction and ran over to his side.

Josh—you *got* 'em both, Josh—I never even got out of the truck—Jesus, holy God, what a mess—Josh, it's OK now, I—" He looked down at the grisly visage glaring up into the night and began to retch beside his brother. Death was never pleasant, but combat death was the worst, the absoklute worst.

15.

"This is KCF76, ham radio Augusta, Georgia, runnin' on batt'ries, power's gone fer good—any you feller's on the ham freq got ya' ear's on tonat?   This is KCF76, ham radio Augusta, Georgia, in the dark, over?"   Silence greeted the repeated entreaty, but Jimmy Jo Winston didn't give up. Lighting another cigarette, he again identified himself to the darkness, waited, then did it again.   It had been two hours wet blackness still hid the world at 5:45 a.m.

"KCF76, this is W6ninerC81, Tulsa, Oklahoma, copy your call, but the signal is weak—better talk fast—my batteries won't last long. We got the darkness, too. Had a huge explosion north a' town about 3:30, an' according to my cousin who lives over on the west side, they had another there about the same time. Things've gone pure black here, an' I hear talk on the network there's trouble with backup supplies. Wonder if somebody took out a big plant? Whatcha got back east—over?"

Jimmy Jo was so excited to hear another voice after his own sense of isolation had grown almost out of control during the two hours of radio silence, he nearly jumped out of his chair as he responded.   "Gawddam, Freddie, but I's begin'n ta think we'd been *nuked* er somethin'!! Shore is good ta hear another voace. I been two ahrs tryin' ta raise one a' y'all. Yeah—dark hea', too, for shore. I ain't heard nuthin' 'bout no explosions. . .hell, it's quiet as the graveyard all over town. 'Sides, nearest power station's up ta Columbia, anyways.   Doubt I'd a heard much if they's trouble that far away. My brother-in-law works fer the power company, an' he says we git all ar power from plants in Virginia an' South Carolina, anyway. No way to know *where* your electricity's comin' from, way I understand it. I saw an article in *Popular Mech*—"

Hey, you windy hillbillies, this is Xray 25 delta 4, Minneapolis, Minnesota, and it's colder dan a welldigger's arse an' dark as pitch up here, too. . .yah. . . Somebody ban blowin' up substations like Fourth a' July, an' da word I got from local fire department guys is dat da bombs had some kind a' petroleum base—spewed fire an' shrapnel a quarter mile in every direction. Got an apartment complex and da roof of a shopping mall on fire right now.   Big trouble is, dere's no juice ta run the station houses, an' the fire departments are havin' ta work in the dark— 'cep for the lights on the trucks. Helluva a mess, boys—looks like more'n a coincidence, if ya' ask me!"

The Devil's Playground

Jimmy Jo Winston of Augusta and Freddie Slater of Tulsa both started talking at once—an impossibility in the world of radio communications—with JJ finally getting the upper hand. "Sig, you old Swede, glad yore in one piece!! Me an' Freddie, here, been tryin' ta figure out what the hell's goin' on. Guess we ain't been nuked yet. Least I *hope* not. Anybody heard from Bonnie? She's always close ta the news—got that big short-wave outfit, too, ya know. . ."

"Yaah, dis is Sig, again, an' no, I ain't heard from da old woman neither. You boys hold silence a minute while I call her ID and see if I can raise 'er. This is Xray 25 delta 4, Minneapolis, calling niner Hotel 682 Indigo. . .do you copy. . .over? . . .Niner Hotel 682 Indigo, Bakersfield, do you copy, over?

"Nobody home, Sig, but this is 26 Alpha Zero 28 Zebra, Nashville, Indiana, alive, well, dark, and cold. . .Just came on the freq five minutes ago and copied all you guys—thank the good Lord for some D batteries. Talked by cell phone to my daughter in Indy about four o'clock, and things 'er black there, too. Cell network had some short-term back up power, but it's gone now. Anyway, she's got friends that work third trick at the Kroger warehouse, called her to say they'd got sent home about four, an' the whole world was dark as paint. One of them drove past a big power substation beside the expressway, said it looked like a Lego set that got crushed by Godzilla! What was left was just a big mess a' twisted steel an' smoke comin' out of a huge crater."

"Clam up boys, ladies present—this is niner Hotel 682 Indigo, Bakersfield, sunny California—an' I'm *touched* you boys was worried 'bout ol' Bonnie—oh—and yes, it's dark here, too. Happened about 12:30 local time, that would be 3:30 for you JJ." "Dammit, Bonnie, that's right on—been dark here since then exactly. Anything on the short-wave yet? We thought maybe you'd 've heard somethin' from off shore—"

"Nothing yet. I just found my battery pack and hooked up to the HAM to try to hear what you guys knew. All I can tell you is that my neighbors and I thought the big one had hit! Shook the whole house, knocked pictures off the wall, and a big piece of steel took out the whole front window and door of the house down the street. Substation's only a block away—big sonofabitch, too, been there for years. Still on fire, all the old timbers must've got sprayed with some kind of gas, or something. What a mess.

"Listen, boys, I'll sign off an' just listen to the short-wave. If there's anything cookin', I'll get back on the air an' fill ya' in. I should have battery enough for another two hours of transmission—the short-wave receiver only takes a little juice.

"Oh, and boys, seem odd to any of you that this big blackout comes about twelve hours after somebody tried ta kill the President? 682 Indigo, OUT."

Nobody spoke for a long moment, as each of them tried to assimilate what they were learning. Independent and eccentric by nature and nightowls by definition, HAM radio people tend not to panic easily. And this little society of late-night radio freaks often talked at this crazy hour. But never had they experienced a string of transmissions like this. Finally, the old retired Army radioman from southern Indiana broke the silence.

"Sig, this is Al, I know JJ's got a generator, and Freddie's got that little solar unit he uses to heat water, what about you? You got any way ta' recharge your radio batteries?"

"Ya, I got a big generator ta run the milking machines when the power goes out, an' I can use the auxiliary outlet ta charge up. . . guess we better take care to be sure an' have juice enough ta talk each night. . .may be the only way ta know what the hell's happenin'." Freddie spoke quickly, as the old Swede ended his transmission.

"Speakin' a that, I'm gonna run out pretty quick, now, so I'll sign off. Be back on the freq at zero 7 hundred—this is W6niner Charlie 81, Tulsa, out." With only Al Franklin in Nashville and Jimmy Jo in Augusta left, they agreed to save batteries and get back on the HAM net at 7 a.m. That was about two hours away, and nobody had any thought of sleep. Nobody had any thought of *anything* but finding out what had happened to the power. And *everybody* wrestled with what Bonnie had said about the connection between the events yesterday in Chicago and the multiple electrical explosions that had darkened the entire country. Probably no connection at all. Probably.

* * * * *

For generations, the pundits have declared that what came from the White House was often a lot of heat, but seldom much light. More true than anyone will ever know, but one thing they do *not* have in the White House is *darkness.* The place has more contingency plans, backup systems, and escape routes than a prairiedog town, and more guards, sentries, and barricades than Fort Knox. So, when the power went out at 1600 Pennsylvania

Avenue, less than sixty seconds passed before a backup generator, powered by a big Cummins diesel engine, was fired up and the juice was back on again.

The terrorist genius who had masterminded the whole electrical system sabotage idea had been smart enough to understand that the specific substations that served the White House and adjacent buildings were not the typical unguarded variety. They were unique, in that they were manned full time, and there were sufficient passive impediments to entry to make them bad targets. Anyway, the destruction of other stations, further out and less well attended, had the same effect. As Sallie thought, the interdependent nature of power delivery all over the country made a kind of random domino effect occur when several delivery routes were interrupted in the same general area.

Nobody even woke the President when the power first went out, because it went back on as soon as the generator was fired up and running. However, when calls began filtering in that electrical lines had been severed in a wide area around Washington by detonation of some Richter scale-sized explosions, the night shift situation room staff quickly called Mac Reed. He just as quickly awakened the President. Storming into the main conference room on the first floor, Webb scared the crap out of the bleary-eyed night owls with his instant presence and broad daylight-caliber alertness to the whole place.

"OK, people, somebody talk to me—what's this jive about bombings of electrical stations? Mac, when you called me, you said something about the affected area being wider than just the District—*how* wide, Mac and how many stations are we talking about? Have we identified the locations that have been hit? And what about casualties—bombs that big are guaranteed to kill anybody in the area—sounds like C 4 to me, somebody said some of the big ground units were blown clear out of the installation grounds—*WELL?*"

"*Jackie*—Gen—Mr. President—"

"You're stuttering, Mac, what's the scoop??"

"Jesus, Jackie—(Mac's voice now turned to a coarse whisper, all eyes upon them in the middle of the room,) Take a breath, for crissakes!" Now in full voice, and with pointed inflection aimed directly at his boss, Reed began addressing the questions. "Yes sir, there have been at least five explosions in the Washington area, none in the District, all in Virginia and Maryland. But the effect has been devastating on the power system—seems like the whole delivery system was connected. Power's out as far away as we've been able to check so far, and that includes our most recent reports from Annapolis and another from Richmond. All black. Secure radio transmissions from as far away as Memphis and St. Louis report blackouts as well."

"What the hell does *that* mean, Mac? How many bomb sites are we talking about here?" Reed turned a quarter turn toward one of the young intelligence types seated at a computer screen against the far wall of the room, his index finger commanding an instant answer to the President's question.

"Well, sir, the numbers are unconfirmed, because the huge power failure has affected the telephone service as well. Telephone exchanges usually have their own power sources, that is why your phones typically still work and even ring when the power is off. But this series of explosions appears to have caused such pervasive power interruptions that the phone companies are black, too. They are supposed to have independent backup generators, but not all of them do. So, we're stuck with military reports and, as you know, the military installations provide all their own power, anyway. They have to physically drive out into the communities to determine the situation."

The young man's intense, direct gaze was immediately impressive to Webb, who had always been a excellent judge of quality in people. His blue eyes never left the President's face as he continued.

"We have confirmed five explosions in the outlying areas to the District, two of that appear to have included some kind of incendiary component—big fires erupted around the sites at once. All are currently still burning out of control. Only have one actual visual on a site, sir. Jill took that from an MP who had been off duty and coming back from leave to Andrews an hour after the explosion at a location about ten miles from the base. Jill—?" The lad, Scott Arenson, turned in his chair and looked at a young woman with curly red hair and freckles. Cute more than pretty, her demeanor was also all business. She was wearing a headset, that she removed as she turned to address the boss.

"Yes sir; an SFC Michael Higgins, Air Force MPs, told me he had seen the site. It was a pretty large unmanned substation, about a half-acre area inside high chainlink. Higgins said the steel—wait, I have a quote from him I wrote it down verbatim— 'Place looked like a pile of pretzels, with a huge crater the size of a small meteor impact, right in the middle. All the steel was ripped apart, eight ground mounted transformers were either blown apart, turned inside out, or actually blown clear out of the area. Helluva mess!' When I asked him for a guess as to what had done it, he told me he'd never seen anything make that big a mess except C 4."

The chill that invaded Jackie Webb's spinal column blistered through him like a jolt of the now nonexistent high voltage electricity; and this was a man whose nerves had endured an assassination attempt and the death of one of his favorite men already, within the past twelve hours. The evening had been full of briefings, meetings, and panicky phone calls with everyone from the Secretary General of the U.N. to his own dear mother, whose nerves were in worse shape than his. Twenty-five years in the military had taught him to recognize an enemy offensive when he saw one, and every fiber of his being was on fire with the realization that he—and his country—were under attack.

"Mac, these kids have a good start on this, but that's all it is—a start. Get it in gear, and fire up the emergency communications toys. I want a true picture of this mess within the hour." Looking back at Arenson, he spoke without the least apprehension that his orders would fail to produce the desired results. "Son, get back to that headset, and tell General Howard at Andrews that I want an AWACS airborne within ten minutes. Tell him to fire up the whole AWACS/NORAD satellite network *right now,* so we can have whatever there is back into our sit room in no time flat."

"Jill, the report is good—*very* good. But we gotta have some poop on these explosions ASAP. Call ATF, wake up that lazy Wayne Weber, the big boss, and tell him to get his fat ass in gear *now.* I want an explosives team scrambled within one hour, dispatched to each of the area bomb sites. They are to examine, photograph, and haul ass back to the White House. I want them here by zero nine hundred. OK?" There was a high-pitched, unison "Yessir!" from the two shining faces, and they spun in their chairs so hard that each of them had to spin *back* half a turn to get to work. A second's smirk vanished from the President's face, as the enormity of the moment buried the brief comedy of the kids' reaction to his orders.

"Mac, what the hell is this? First some professional tries to make parfait out of my head, then only twelve hours later bombs take out the power all over the place. Am I missing something, or is this the beginning of a really bad day?" Reed, still susceptible to Webbisms, suppressed his own smirk, attempting to respond to the underlying rhetorical question. Then he remembered the *other* little tidbit of info he had not yet dropped on the head man.

"Well, General, sure seems like more than a coincidence. And there is a bit more. Just a bit. Been waiting for a quiet moment for this, but—"

"You've been waiting. . .you've been. . .holy God, Mac, you mean there's something *else?*" Reed felt like a total heel, instantly regretting that he had opened this other box of bad news. Webb was a man whose face seemed to defy the usual human expressions, especially things like surprise, consternation, and especially fear. But what he saw now was a big dose of all three. Turning away for a moment, he realized there was no way he could avoid it, now that he had sparked the man's curiosity.

"Dick Freeman was here this morning, about nine o'clock. He's the forensic Path—"

"I know who the sumbitch is, goddammit! He was just here! Now what did he have to say, Mac?" Reed couldn't help it. Even after twenty years, with the man more or less, Jackie Robinson Webb could still make him piss his pants. He physically shook as the president roared his impatience, took a deep breath, and burped out the whole thing at once.

"Fire ant venom, sir, concentrated fire ant venom. On the top of the toothpaste tube, and therefore in the cap you found. Jack had had a bad reaction to some bee stings back during the campaign—picnic fundraiser down south someplace—Georgia, I think—anyway, the thing was all over the media after it happened, and the whole world instantly knew the Jack was allergic to bug stings. Apparently anyone who's had such a reaction is potentially very susceptible to a fatal reaction on future exposure. So, some brilliant terrorist assassin slipped him a lethal dose of fire ant venom in his toothpaste, and he basically got asphyxiated in his own bed."

Webb stood in the corner of the room, as his minions chattered away at their consoles, his expression blank, his jaw at first slack, then knotted. Reed filled him in on some detail about the content of the final report from the mad scientists, complete with his own early morning phone conversation with the little genius pathologist who had actually cracked the investigation. He tried to find some way to ease the impact such news would have to have on his boss, especially in view of the horrors of the past day. It was not possible.

205

"I'm sorry sir, I knew it would be a hard one for you; but I also knew you'd been suspecting such an outcome. I could tell you smelled a rat from the moment we found Kincaid. I just wish I could make some kind of sense out of all this for you—I'm so sorry, General, I really am. . ."

Webb stood looking at the floor, his whole being afraid to look up, for fear of what might appear next. Jackie Webb had made a living—and stayed alive—for over twenty-five years because of his uncanny ability to assimilate and synthesize large amounts of disjointed information in an extremely short time. He could turn the apparently dissimilar parts into a unified reality that he could then use to solve problems. Whether calculating a response to an enemy offensive or determining how to react to political pressures from five directions at once, he always seemed to be able to piece together a whole, logical picture. Now, first standing, then leaning against the wall of the situation room in the basement of the White House, he tried to do it again. He could not.

The dream of leading his country in peace instead of war, of being president, seemed gone. Instead, he felt the cold sensation, as those same senses fabricated a whole from all these parts, that he was about to preside over the first true, earnest, and apparently successful attack on the United States by a foreign power since the War of 1812. Only this time, they were already here, they had killed the elected president without detection, nearly killed his replacement, and had now sentenced the most technologically advanced culture in the history of the world to darkness. For the first time in his life, Jackie Robinson Webb was lost. Totally lost.

* * * * *

The ringing in his ears was overborne by the sound of crying in the house, as Josh Landry accepted his brother's assistance in standing up over the horrible form of his would-be killer. Pain shot up his legs from the cuts and shards of glass imbedded in his feet, and he too cried out in anguish. But just as quickly, he recognized the voices in the house as those of his children, and he called out to them.

"It's all right, guys, I'm OK—just stay inside and I'll be in with Uncle Carl in a minute. It's cold out here—stay inside. . ." His voice weakened as he finished the sentence, and he leaned heavily on Carl's arm and shoulder. Two men lay dead, one in his yard and the other on his front porch, he was in great pain from the wounds in his feet, and his wife and children were terrified inside the house. The combination was worse than any anxiety or grief he had ever felt as a soldier, both because his precious family was part of this whole event, and also because this time the killing had not taken place in some remote jungle. They were right in his front yard.

Carl, now nearly carrying his bleeding brother across the yard toward the front door, became more physician than brother as he searched all over the younger man for injuries or other signs of problems. The foot wounds were obvious, as Josh left a bloody footprint with each step. But Carl was also watching to see if the indescribable stress had had any other affect on him. His pulse was visible in his neck, his breathing was short and fast—probably over 50 respirations per minute. He was shaking violently now, wet and freezing cold from the exposure to the icy rain. They stepped slowly up onto the porch, and Jess opened the door for them.

"Dear God, Joshua, what—oh my God, you're bleed—*JAN!! KATE—get some clean towels and—holy SHIT, Carl, we don't have any light!! LUKE!! Get me some candles and that kerosene lantern—NOW!! Carl, there's some alcohol—oh, Jesus, what has—*" She fell to her knees with the sight of the blood pooling around Josh's feet. Carl could see her sinking and grabbed her before she could hit the floor.

"*Jess*—he's all right, Jess. Just got his feet cut up by the glass on the floor. Hey—don't you pass out on me, Sis, I need you *vertical,* right now!! Kate, you guys bring some clean things into the kitchen, and we'll clean up your dad quick. Luke, let's see those lanterns. And Luke, run and get me that big six cell flashlight out of Dad's tool box—hurry." Jessica Landry responded to the strong, confident tones of her brother-in-law's voice and wobbled along with them as they made their way from the front door of the house into the kitchen.

Carl was the only doctor this whole brood had ever had—he had delivered Luke when a snow storm made the trip to town impossible— so his presence quickly spread a sense of calm over this terrified household. The variety of lights, assisted by the beginning of dawn, gave the doctor adequate opportunity to examine Josh's multiple cuts and punctures. All the shards of glass except one were removed, and that one was going to require some daylight and probably a scalpel and an incision to accomplish. Stitches would also be essential when that procedure was completed, so he finished with the lesser injuries and wrapped the feet in anticipation of moving Josh to his house for further work after daybreak.

Still lying on the kitchen cabinet with his feet dangling into the sink, Josh accepted a glass of scotch from Jess, who managed a weak smile as she offered him the stout drink. "Here, I'm sure it's noon *somewhere* . . . you can break training just this once—we won't tell the coach. . ." Josh laughed out loud at his wife's uncanny knowledge of him—he'd been thinking about a touch of the grain to calm his nerves and dull the throbbing in his feet.

"Thanks, babe, it'll work as well as Valium, and it tastes a lot better." She tried to laugh, but tears poured down her cheeks as she collapsed on his chest. Her sobs were impossible to hide, and the kids reacted at once. Luke slipped in between Mom and Dad, his arms snaking around his mother's legs, while one hand reached up and touched his father's sweaty face. The girls tried to conceal tears as they each in turn found some part of Josh's body to touch. In a matter of moments, the whole crowd was weeping openly, each of the kids trying to console the other while at the same time wiping eyes and noses on pajama sleeves.

Carl stepped back quietly and walked back out onto the porch. They needed to be with their dad, and he needed to see what his warrior brother had done to his other adversary. Cautiously at first, then with more confidence, the physician's curiosity overtook the layman's fears, and he took a good look at the dead man on the porch. His chest was a real mess, as the second load of heavy buckshot had hit at a strafing angle, the man having been already falling back and away when it hit him. But the man's face had been spared, only covered with blood and other goop from the chest cavity.

What made Carl stop breathing was not the gaping gory open thorax, but the badly scarred and mutilated face. Old wounds, now long since healed, had so twisted the shape of the man's countenance that he looked almost like he was wearing some kind of Halloween mask. One eye was gone, covered by a black eye patch, and a big piece of cheek bone was missing, a great depression in the face beneath the empty eye socket in its place. It took Carl about ten seconds to realize who he was seeing.

At the precise moment when he came to the recognition that the man was black, he also knew to a certainty that the man was

LaShawn Mitchell. Boy, the cops would have a field day with this one. Another unwelcome reality—no cops. Gail certainly had called at once, but no one showed. Must've been busy somewhere else. It would be over a month before they saw *any* authorities. He stood up and walked back into the house and his bloody patient.

16.

The twentieth century American mind has trouble imagining any situation that includes the absence of convenience. Ever since the end of the Great Depression, folks have really had just about all the electricity, petroleum, groceries, shelter, and even entertainment they could possibly use. The television age, the computer age made communication and the dissemination of information so easy and so predictable, that almost nobody could complain of missing out on what was going on in the world. But, as is so often the case when things are that good, the people really did not comprehend just what it was that made things so easy—and so vulnerable.

When the lights went out, the result was more than darkness. With a pervasive interruption in the power supply, the telephone system quit. Without electricity, the gas pumps stopped pumping, the automatic doors at the grocery and Wal-Mart would not open, and the stoplights all quit. But on a more basic level, fundamental infrastructure necessities ceased instantly. With the vast majority of suburban America being served by forced main sanitary sewers, the power failure meant that the big private utilities that pumped effluent *up hill* to treatment plants stopped pumping. They typically have backup generators to provide for short interruptions in power, but they only have sufficient fuel to run for a few hours. The lift stations often sit close to or right in residential areas, and the cessation of pumping meant an almost immediate overload on the lines and consequent eruption of raw sewage into every available stream and ditch. Great fun.

The hospitals, so very dependent on a huge and steady power supply, went at once into backup delivery of electricity, mostly from on-site diesel generators. Problem with that is, with a supply of diesel fuel of about two thousand gallons, all power to the hospitals would stop within about five days. Without electricity, police and fire operations would become grossly ineffective, there being no efficient way for them to learn of problems.

The absence of telephone service, traditional and cellular, meant that the delivery of all public services essentially stopped, except for what might result from ongoing patrols. And responding to emergencies, whether medical, criminal, or even sanitary, became problematic. What would a policeman do with a

person injured in an accident, if he could not radio for an ambulance or take him to a hospital where there was power for treating his injuries? Receiving a report of a crime in progress became an impossibility, and for the officer who discovered such a situation, the absence of electrical power at his station meant that he could not radio in a call for assistance.

The first places to feel the true weight of all this were the densely populated urban areas of America's major cities. Within a few hours, hundreds of thousands of people were cold and unable to get help with basic necessities. Grocery stores didn't open, because there was no light, no power to run refrigerators and freezers, cash registers and doors; there were no phones to call in orders for re-stocking depleted shelves. Then, after about twenty-four hours, meats, dairy products and produce began to spoil. An interesting phenomenon about city folk is that they tend not to keep much food in the house at one time. Instead, they shop often, almost daily, both because they have limited space to store food and because they can always be assured of buying fresh items.

So with little food available, no heat, and wet, cold weather, it took only about twenty-four hours for panic to set in. Hysteria followed panic, and violence followed hysteria, so that by Friday night inner city areas from Newark to East L.A., from Cleveland to Atlanta and Miami were enveloped in flames and rioting. Only this time, with no communications system with that to call for help, and with panic and its progeny spreading like a grass fire in high winds, nobody showed up to stop the fighting or put out the fires. Hunger, thirst, and fear grew by the hour; things got out of hand very quickly.

17.

The President sat looking straight ahead into the face of Walter Flanigan, his Director of the famous Federal Emergency Management Administration—FEMA. The poor bastard looked like he had come directly from the fires of the south side of Chicago on foot, and his blotchy, red face was exceeded for tension only by his almost uncontrollable shakes. His first visit with the new president and his first *real* emergency were not going particularly well. Webb had been barbecuing him for approximately thirty minutes when he finally took a breath. Flanigan wiped his brow with the sleeve of his coat and tried to respond to the barrage of questions and complaints he had just endured.

"I know it seems less than complete, Mr. President, but we have been so handicapped by the loss of communications that we—"

"*Horseshit, Walter,* just what the hell were you and your scholars planning *for,* anyway? Didn't all your wizards ever think of an emergency that might include a pervasive loss of electrical power? What about all that crap we heard about your ability to field a huge team of "experts" in the event of a nuclear event or a big natural disaster? Didn't any of those scenarios include something so esoteric as a bigtime power failure? Or did I miss something—are the Russians now building warheads that destroy the country, but leave the electricity on? *Well?*"

Flanigan flinched at this, the fourth time the man had commenced his sarcastic assault. All he really wanted to do was to run screaming out of the Cabinet conference room, never to be seen or heard from again. "Yes sir, we *have* planned for power failures, *big ones,* and we have planned for rioting in multiple locations at the same time. It's just that we never planned for a national blackout and generalized violence in every major metropolitan area at the same time.

"Frankly sir, and with all due respect, there simply aren't enough personnel to go around. In Philadelphia alone, where rioting, looting, and mob violence continue completely unchecked, the number of persons engaged in this stuff exceeds all the civil and military capability available in all the northeast by about two thousand to one. With three thousand sworn police officers plus another eighteen hundred reserves, working twenty-four hours a day, there are more fires and more gunfights than they can ever hope to interdict. Worse, Philly is only one of five cities within Pennsylvania where major looting and violence continues: The same conditions exist in Pittsburgh, Scranton, Allentown, and every other population center in the northeast. We simply do not have the horsepower to respond to this big a mess.

"And, to make things worse, the National Guard troop strength in some of the most critical states has been depleted terribly by the Middle East build up. Hell—Iowa, Indiana, California, and Illinois alone have committed over fifteen thousand troops to that political nightmare, and the results have been no less than catastrophic back home."

Webb rubbed his eyes, flexing his neck and back muscles to try to combat the horrendous tension that racked his whole body. In an instant, he saw in his mind's eye, a parade of bureaucrats just like Walter Flanigan, whose asses he had chewed and whose faces he had seen over the past two days. Head people from the National Guard Bureau, the Department of Transportation, the Coast Guard, even the private Red Cross, had trouped through the White House, gotten their butts reamed. They had each in turn tried to explain to this furious leader why they had been unable to accomplish their particular part of this huge mission.

Looking at Flanigan's exhausted countenance—the man was on the verge of collapse—again the General felt that overwhelming sense of frustration at having devoured another bearer of bad tidings, while having once again learned nothing about what to do. "All right, Walter, get your ass out a' here and get some sleep. You're worthless to us dead. Be back here at zero seven—I mean, at seven a.m. tomorrow, and we'll try to put something together. I've got the rest of this huge bureaucracy coming back then, too. Maybe between us, we can get a handle on things. Now, beat it. And *go to bed.* That's an order."

Poor Walter fought back a flood of salty tears at the realization that the Commander-in-Chief had just, in his own gruff way, recognized his efforts, after taking a pretty big chunk out of his back side first. And the picture of his head hitting a pillow was positively intoxicating. "Thank you, sir. . .and, well, Mr. President. . .there's nothing...I mean, well, holy sweet Jesus, Jackie, I never in my wildest dreams—I mean. . .the number of casualties, and I can't even get the goddam locals on the telephone and then there's not even any *water* in Scranton, the

213

goddam water plant is all forced mains and the power is gone and—"

His shoulders heaved as his torso convulsed, forcing his posture over into an elderly ball. He reached convulsively for the arm of the chair from that he had just risen and, missing it, collapsed to one knee. Just like when the lead had begun to fly in Chicago, Webb forgot all about being a bigshot and, with his still stunning quickness, shot across the fifteen feet that separated the two men. He blew past at least three other shocked men, catching Walter's shuddering frame under the arms. He lifted the heavy man to his feet, gently cradling his weight and turning him ninety degrees; aiming the man's back at that same chair, he lowered him and barked an order to anybody who was close.

"Get me some water—*now*. And let's loosen his tie and shoelaces. *Mac*—get that doctor in here on the double, and I want the stewards to prepare a guest room for this man. *MOVE!!*" People scattered in all directions, reacting to the orders. Even as he was himself leaping to respond, Mac Reed marveled at the unique power and authority that exuded from the man. Like ants, they all split apart into action.

Materializing almost out of nowhere, Sgt. Major Brooks appeared, his big, rough hands moving with perfect precision to loosen Flanigan's tie, then to unlace his shoes and belt. Working like one man, he and Webb slipped the man out of the chair and onto a couch that sat under one of the tall windows of the Cabinet Room, Webb grabbing a stray suit coat to cover him with while Brooks gave him a quick once-over, pulse rate, respiration, pupil dilation.

"I think he's stable, General, just spent. Seems a little weak in the pulse department, but his color's OK. Poor bastard probably hasn't been to bed in a week. Shit—looks like war to me, sir. Like some op center during a bad offensive."

"That's because that's what it is Sergeant Major, that's just what it is. . ." Webb's voice trailed off into a momentary flashback, to the days of undeclared war when occurrences like these were all too common. Only then the participants were not men in their sixties, political appointments whose jobs included paper shuffling, pointless meetings, and bullshit cocktail parties. This man had been run over by an overdose of *real* emergency, and it was clearly too much for him. But Webb had to admire his grit. He had literally gone until he dropped, overweight bureaucrat or not. Once again, the call of real duty had found some real worth in the heart and soul of a real man.

Medics soon swooped in, quickly determining that Flanigan had merely collapsed from exhaustion. Partially awake now, sat up on the couch as they prepared to take him to the guest quarters by stretcher. "Jack—I mean Gen—Mr. President, I'm OK—just a bit worn out—this fat old ass hasn't gone this hard since Korea. I'll be—"

"Bag it Walter, no explanation *or apology* needed—you've got lots of wornout company right now. Boys, escort Mr. Flanigan to the guest quarters, and one of you accompany the doctor to his room for a quick checkup. Then I want him left alone till zero six hundred. And I think Mr. Flanigan can walk. Is that right, Walter?"

The older man smiled weakly, stood and straightened his posture, again touched by the General's brusk but insightful manner. He wanted nothing to do with being wheeled out of the Cabinet Room on a gurney. "Yessir—thank you sir—I won't be needing *that* thing. I can walk just fine—just a little tired, that's all."

Webb took his arm for a short moment, just long enough to make contact. Flanigan looked into the ebony eyes, burning but now bright with emotion, nodded his gratitude, and began to walk toward the door, a young medic at each arm.

Brooks looked back at his long time leader, companion, and sometimes-biggest pain in the ass, and a sad gaze met the President. "Gen'ral Jackie, sir, sometimes—with all due respect, sir—I think you just don't know how much of a bad ass you really are. That poor ol' man 'bout popped his ticker 'cause a' you ridin' him so, sir, and, if you don't mind my sayin' so, you beatin' the crap outta the man didn't do a bit a good. You think, Sir?" Webb stood stock still, his own eyes now locked into the penetrating eyes of his most devoted supporter. He turned aside, glancing out the window into the chill air of late March.

Brooks was a frequent presence, even in the most secret of high level meetings. He looked after the President and whoever was with him, never appearing put off by even the most "waiterly" duties. He was so much a part of all the goings on around the President that he was missed when absent. If a congressional delegation or Cabinet official, or a group from Justice was in the White House, they found themselves looking for Brooks if his presence was not obvious. "Good Day Sergeant Major. You keeping His Majesty in line?" went the banter, with Brooks always smiling and just a bit shy with some good natured retort.

"I do my best, Senator, but I fear that I am incapable of accomplishing that that the entire Marine Corps failed to do in thirty years!" Laughter always followed him, accompanied with the respect that could only flow from a record of valor and devotion like that of Jonathan Montgomery Brooks. And Webb felt every ounce of that devotion, returning it in kind in his own way. The man had been to every duty assignment since Webb had become a colonel, right through and including this craziness with the Presidency.

Ironically, Brooks had *not* been at the Shedd Aquarium; he had taken the afternoon off to visit with his only living kin—an uncle and one sister—who lived on the south side of Chicago. It took him several days to stop flogging himself over being absent at that crucial moment. Webb had issued one of his famous "orders," requiring the Sgt. Major to "forget it!! Just be glad you weren't there to get your ass shot. Bad enough we lost one man. Your luck, you'd 've taken one of those .308s too."

They stood alone in the Cabinet Room for a long moment. The General addressed his aid. "Yeah, I know, Jonathan, just thinking about that when poor ol' Walter went down. I just go nuts with this great huge monster of a government being so incapable of dealing with true crisis. I want somebody to demonstrate some real leadership, figure out some answers, and help us get started turning things around. Crissakes, Sarg, the country's in the dark, freezing to death, riots run unabated, and all we can do is have briefings at that all these goddam bureaucrats tell us why they can't fix it!"

Brooks let him rave on for a minute, then brought him back to the present. "The National Guard rep is here, as ordered, sir. S'pose you better go see what he has to say?" Webb nodded, and they walked out, down the hall and into one of the sitting rooms where the next appointment was waiting.

The guy from the National Guard Bureau just happened to be an Adjutant General from Iowa by the name of Andrew Whitaker. Even with the mess in his own state, he had been summoned to Washington for briefing; he was well known to the military establishment as a bright light, a devoted soldier, and a man with the kind of combat qualifications that made his input very valuable. He had been contacted via satellite transmission at the

216

local Army base, then flown to Andrews in the rear seat of an F-15.

He stood impatiently looking at the pictures over the fireplace, dressed in the fatigues he had been wearing when the call came in. Brooks ushered Webb into the room as Whitaker turned and strode to the center of the room, hand extended.

"Andy, by god, its about time I had a visitor who could find his butt with both hands! You're a sight for sore eyes, you old grunt!!" Whitaker smiled in spite of the darkness that surrounded them all, the ebullience of the big man's greeting nearly overwhelming the younger officer. He blushed and smiled back into Webb's countenance.

"Thank you, Mr. President, I'm honored to be here—just wish the circumstances were different. Figured you must want something pretty bad to scramble one of those supersonic taxi cabs! Quite a ride... I'm still not sure I've got my legs back under me." Webb allowed himself a moment's wry smile at the reaction. He had flown in those firebirds only twice and had been deathly sick for eight hours after each trip.

"Yeah, I been there. Best proof I ever had that I belonged on the ground. If flying one of those rocket ships had been the only way to serve in the military, I think *I'd* have gone to Canada!" They all laughed loud, Webb's irrepressible wit once again releasing the tension of even this somber time.

"I'm sure glad you came, Andy—I've had about all the bureaucratic excuse making I can deal with for one lifetime. Jesus, Mary, and Joseph but these people amaze me. For all the good they've done so far, we could have simply done without every one of their programs, saved a trillion or so, and made the whole goddam thing up as we went!! But, there I go again, bitchin' instead a' fixin'! Let's talk about this thing. Before we get into the next step, tell me what's going on in your neck of the woods."

Whitaker's gaze darkened. His jaw knit, his dark, thick eyebrows furrowing into an intense scowl. He was silent for a long moment.

"Worst nightmare any leader could ever imagine and beyond the imaginations of most folks. I've got fires burning out of control in Des Moines, Richland, Iowa City, and Dubuque. There is no water in any of the suburbs of any of those cities where forced mains deliver it, there being no power to run the pumps. The hospitals are running out of diesel fuel to operate their generators, and it takes a company sized security force, complete

217

with gunship air cover, to convoy more fuel to them. Diesel fuel inventories are not only short, but also inadequately protected. One major fuel dump in Richland went up like Armageddon when the bastards took out a power station that was only a few hundred meters away. It was a county highway garage, where the state stored twenty-five thousand gallons. One of the tanks was old and weak, and the concussion of all that high explosive must have ruptured it.

"The bomb had a petroleum component, apparently thickened gasoline—gas and soap flakes, like we used to make in 'Nam—remember, called it poor man's napalm?" Webb nodded gravely. He *did* remember. Ivory Snow mixed in five gallon cans of gasoline, plus a shovel full of charcoal, and you had an incendiary device that would, when ignited by a good jolt of C4, send flaming chunks of gas-soaked charcoal hundreds of meters in all directions.

"I got entire city communities, particularly the poor ones, with no food and no heat, except, of course, the heat of burning buildings. I swear to almighty God, but I'll never understand the logic of responding to crisis by burning down your own place. Anyway, those people have been dying like flies, the kids and the old people either caught in the crossfire between the gangs and the police and National Guard units or getting quick and deadly cases of pneumonia and other bugs from being wet and cold. Once their homes have been burned, all they can do is start migrating through the streets, looking to churches, business buildings, and police stations for cover. And most of those have been hit, too."

Webb and Brooks stood stock still, their faces frozen into the countenance of this bearer of worse tidings. "I got roving bands a' rednecks and convicts who've broken out of the prisons, harassing every attempt to deliver supplies to all these freezing people. Newest little party is those assholes cruising the suburbs, shooting up the houses, killing men, raping women, and stealing their vehicles. It's those jackoffs that got the truckers so spooked they won't leave home. Hence the need for convoy movement to haul fuel and supplies for the hospitals and such."

"At last count, we had lost three hundred twenty-six uniformed civilian police officers, seventy-eight firefighters, and one hundred eighty-seven National Guard infantry and MPs. Some have been killed trying to fight fires, sixteen civilian police've been killed in car wrecks and by falling debris when buildings have collapsed; but the most have been shot by snipers or whole squads of gang members in pitched firefights."

The President looked like he had just heard a paragraph of nonsense. Then it sank in that the man had just told him about *deaths*. Not injuries, or accidents, but *combat deaths*.

"What? Andrew, are you telling me you've got almost six hundred dead? What the hell is going on?"

"General, the place is simply up for grabs. There are no less than a dozen gangs, all equipped with small arms, constantly upgrading from what they can steal, or what they take off the police or Guardsmen they kill. Ambush was the tactic of choice at first, bushwhacking marked civilian units and stealing their sidearms and shotguns after killing the cops. Then, when the Guard started showing up, they scoped out the advance parties, hit them from two or three directions at the same time and stole their M16s, grenade launchers, even one M60 machine gun.

"I'm sorry to say that our boys weren't really ready to take fire that fast. But the absence of reliable communications, caused by the power failure, kept them from knowing what they were getting into. Plus, the units I sent in weren't infantry *or* MP—they were makeshift from what was left after the big boys took all my combat troops. It's just been really hard to get people to believe this kind of shit can happen right here at home. Oh, and about that machine gun—we got the sonofabitch back, but it was expensive. Four dead, eleven wounded. Bastards had set it up inside an old stone office building in Richland, firing with great effect on everything that passed by. Bunch a' black militants, including two that appeared to have been of foreign extraction— maybe Libyan. No ID, of course. Finally, we sent in an old Cobra gunship and stuck a rack of rockets up their nose. Took out the gun, but also took out the whole top of the building. Strange stuff, sir, firing on your own buildings in your own town."

Webb felt an odd combination of outrage and grief, anger and mourning. Then, as if the Almighty had hit him with a blinding flash of the obvious, he turned toward the fireplace wall and a somber portrait of Abraham Lincoln.

A chill raced through the President's bones, shaking him almost off his feet. Attempting to conceal the weakness that at once had overtaken him, he moved to a wingback chair, cautiously easing into its soft upholstery. The picture in his mind was so overwhelming that he found himself short of breath, cold, eyes blurry. Lincoln looked down at him, face sad, countenance so uniquely homely and handsome at the same time. He had been Webb's true hero—his *only* real hero—since early childhood. Not just the obvious stuff, either. To be sure, he had freed the slaves, paving and lighting the way for all that Webb had done. But more, there was the intellect, the wit, the singular command of the language.

Lincoln had been possessed of such an understated passion for life, liberty, and the sanctity of each person. Over the years, Webb read the entire six volume chronicle of Carl Sandburg's exhaustive work on the man—twice. Now, that intense gaze looked down on the shoulders of the first black man to occupy the very office from that he had resolved to guarantee that dream to this president's ancestors. Webb found himself so overwhelmed by the moment—so torn by the irony of his present, seemingly impossible tasks—but at the same moment, and for the first time, so close to the man who had made it all possible, speech was momentarily impossible.

"You OK, Gen'ral? Here, maybe Walter Flanigan's not the only guy been pushed pretty hard. . .sir?" Webb looked up at Brooks, who was holding a glass of water. Snapping back to alertness again, he realized that both Brooks and Whitaker were riveted on his person, fear beginning to show in their eyes.

"No—no, I'm fine. Really. Just looked up at the old man there, and it hit me for the first time, actually, the *very* first time, since we took office, just what shoes I'm standing in. Dearest Jesus, holy Christ, how will I—" Silence filled the room, as the three of them stood in the soft lamplight created by the diesel generators that hummed outside the window. For a long moment, the three looked at each other, the enormity of the whole experience suddenly crushingly real.

Whitaker spoke softly. "Mr. President, things are pretty bad, for sure, and probably getting worse. . . but, well sir, I couldn't imagine a better man to lead us through it than you. Don't doubt, sir. Just don't doubt. Keep the faith and don't doubt." Another immeasurable period of silence followed, the three veterans looking at each other, around the room, at the portrait, back at each other again. Finally, they resumed their discussions of the situation, Whitaker filling the President in on other details of the current situation.

Medical supply stockpiles, as well as delivery capability, plus the immediate problem of food and water to the hundreds of thousands of people in outlying suburbs, posed huge problems, even without the crisis of continued rioting, looting' and burning in the cities. Whitaker agreed to come back for the early briefing set for the morning to follow but insisted that he be allowed to return home immediately thereafter.

Webb escorted the tired soldier to the door, where Brooks took over, leading him to another guest room upstairs in the White House. Turning back into the now empty sitting room, the President slowly walked over to that same portrait, looking with equal parts of fear and awe into the unique face. Images mixed with prayers as the newest President looked into the eyes of the one from the 1860s. And the realization that he would climb no less steep an obstacle than what Lincoln had faced humbled him, weighed on him, engulfed him with the a sense of overwhelming doubt, fear, anxiety. Whispering another prayer for guidance and wisdom, he slowly walked out of the room, turning off the light as he closed the door.

18.

Static greeted the eager headphones, listening intently for response. Freddie Slater penetrated the night skies with his Oklahoma tones, each transmission a little more earnest, then more hopeless. The radio frequency he had chosen was as dark as the black sky, devoid of even a hint of life or light. "This'll be ma last attempt until zeeero 400, y'all, so if yore tryin' ta respond without success, we'll try agin then. This is W6niner charlie 81, Tulsa, do you copy, does *anybody* copy out there. . . over?" A long moment, then another. Slater reached for the power switch on the face of his HAM transmitter, holding it, touching it, pressing slightly on it.

"*Fr—d—shshshshshs—SQUAWshshshshshs—Xra--SQUAAAAA—Delta 4, OVER?!*" Freddie keyed the mic, his hand reflexively jerking away from the power button, as if to avoid accidentally losing this connection.

"Sig, for crissakes, *SIG!   Holy shit, Sig,* I near give ya' up! Been transmitt'n fer 'bout an hour, no sound. Thought the whole crowd 'd bought the big one. Yer breakin' up bad, Sig, you got any power boost? I can't hardly copy. . ." Another silence, followed by more broken voice transmission, then real silence. Freddie tried a couple more times, hoping the Swede had a transmission booster with enough electrical power left to increase his signal. Nothing. But all was not lost. Bonnie, from Bakersfield, broke the silence, after it was clear that Sig couldn't get the required juice.

"Freddie, this is Bonnie, I think Sig's just short on power, or maybe there's some atmospheric trouble. I haven't heard the weather in almost two weeks, so I couldn't begin to guess what's up top between here and Minneapolis, anyway. How's things, Fred? I got some more news from the short-wave."

"I'm just hangin' on, Bonnie. Bunch a' rednecks been terrorizin' the whole area, day and night. They must be rippin' off the upper crust closer in ta town, stealin' their cars, then usin' 'em ta come further out. I ain't had any trouble yet. . .hell, I'm almost an hour from the city limits. But I talked ta'n old boy down the road a piece today. Met 'im back in the woods between his place an' mine when we 'as both lookin' fer deer. Said those assholes 'd come down the next road over, holler'n and screamin', shootin' things up pretty good. Said they'd took a woman an' a girl from over by Clayton, killed the man and set the place on fire. Sweet Jesus, but I cain't believe that."

"I know, Freddie, we're way too close to L.A. to suit me. Whole town's on fire, best we can tell. The BBC broadcast says there's been a pitched battle going on in East L.A. for over a week now, blacks and Mexicans squared off with the police and National Guard, fighting almost house to house. BBC says there's over a hundred and fifty thousand folks just wandering around outside, hungry, thirsty, lost. Got no idea what's happened to the rest. Apparently, the hunger thing's getting pretty serious. I just can't imagine what those poor folks who had so little anyway are doing now. . ."

Freddie listened through the vast expanse of darkness that separated him from the formless voice of Bonnie, half a continent away. The fear and anxiety he felt tried to silence him; the desire not to lose this one invisible human contact with her compelled him to continue speaking. For Frederick James Slater, although not an educated man, nor even a particularly successful man, *was* a man of substance.

He was a man who believed in God and in His creation, believed in his fellow man's basic goodness through all the flaws. In his own quiet way, he loved Bonnie, like he loved Sig, Al, and JJ. Faceless to be sure, they were anything but formless to Freddie, and his night time society with them had long been a source of happiness and learning, even beyond the fun and recreation the whole HAM thing provided.

A widower in his late fifties, his kids were grown and gone, wife dead over ten years; the man kept to himself mostly. But his shyness did not connote coolness or an uncaring personality. His farming neighbors and his many old friends from church kept him in touch with "folks," so that he was never really isolated. And he loved people—all people, really. The whole spectre of what was going on now, with the suffering that attended the loss of power, sickened him, made him sorrow within himself.

"Bonnie, I swear. . .I just cain't understand it all. . .been sixty years since there'uz suffrin' like this. An' all this violence—holy Gawdamighty—I'm fearin' folks 'er gonna kill each other off 'fore it's all said an' done. That same ol' boy I's tellin' ya 'bout told me he'd heard talk a' this gang thing from some fellers that'd been inta Tulsa an' seen it first hand. Said it looked more like Bosnia er someplace in I-Rack, ya' know? I mean *shit*, Bon, there's folks gittin' raped and killed all over the place, ta hear them guys talk.."

"Well, Fred, I wish I had a different spin for ya'. There's a big bunch a gangs runnin' loose all over southern California, way we hear it now. Apparently, there's a *big* problem all through Orange County, between L.A. and San Diego. Drive-by shootings, a lot of looting, and even what those guys told your friend—people bein' drug out of their houses and beat up—or worse. The BBC broadcast last night—no, I think it was *two* nights ago—said there was a huge problem with what that English reporter called 'random violence' in most suburban areas. He didn't explain himself too much but did say that there had been a lot of casualties resulting from some kind of 'gang related activities.' Sounds like the same thing to me—a bunch of roughnecks using all this trouble as an excuse to run wild."

"Hey, you two wind bags, sounds like a damn funeral to me! This is 26 Alpha Zero 28 Zebra, Nashville, Indiana, can you copy?"

Both Freddie and Bonnie were so surprised to hear another voice that neither of them could immediately respond. "I say again, this is 26 Alpha Zero 28 Zebra, Nashville—guys, this is Al, do you copy?!" Still it took a second for either of them to speak, then both tried to talk at the same time. All that produced was a short line of nonsense and static, followed by more silence. Freddie realized what they had done and resolved to maintain silence until Bonnie had successfully made contact with Al.

"That's affirmative, Al, this is Bonnie—how the hell are ya'? We figured the rest a' you boys must've gone to bed early!"

"No chance, Bonnie, just having trouble getting out tonight. Whole Midwest is socked in with low ceilings, low barometer, and lots of tall cloud cover. Makes it hard to transmit. Freddie, you copy now?"

"You bet, Al, an' it shore is good ta hear from ya'! Things quiet up there?" Again there was static and a long silence, as both waited for Franklin to respond. Finally, after at least three unsuccessful attempts, he came back.

"Well, that depends who ya' ask. National Guard has been strung thin as piano wire, between Indy and Gary, what with so many of them gone back to the Middle East *and* Bosnia. So all the rest of us have for protection is local police and fire. And there's damn few a' them, when you consider how many people there are to look after. Out our way, things are pretty quiet.

"We're about thirty miles from the nearest city of any size. But I talked to a local sheriff's deputy about ten o'clock last night, and he said things were really rockin' up in Indy. No electricity, a big mess of fires throughout the projects on the east and near north sides a' town, and apparently a pretty big band a' rednecks roaming the suburbs shooting things up.

"Deputy told me he had helped give first aid to a young officer from the next county north—Morgan County, that borders Indy— an' he'd been shot twice by a gang of white trash he ran into. They'd been driving through some exclusive bedroom community south of Indianapolis, draggin' people out a' their homes, beating the hell out of the men and, according to what this injured deputy said, even killing people. My deputy said the kid lost consciousness while they were working on him. He'd lost a lot of blood. Don't know if he made it or not. Things're pretty ugly, that's for sure."

They talked on into the first gray hints of dawn in the midwest, promising each other to return to the airwaves the next night, conditions permitting. What they didn't say, but what was on all their minds, was concern for the others—Jimmy Jo in Augusta, Sigurd in Minneapolis, and a half dozen other HAM operators who had not been heard from even once since the whole thing had started. No one could really come to terms with the reality that life had been so fundamentally altered, so quickly. And what they couldn't know was that it would take such a long time to ever repair the damage.

19.

Throughout the last half of the twentieth century, money has become more and more an illusory commodity. With the end of the precious metal standard that at one time had backed all currency, the ability to actually control an inventory of money pretty much vanished. Over the past twenty-five years, the entire idea of there being real green money in a vault someplace that actually represented the balance in anyone's account had disappeared. With the advent of what the bankers like to call "electronic money," all connection between any currency—or any balance in any account—and real value had been replaced with a kind of "convention" or shared fiction that whatever the marketplace decreed as valuable was, in fact, just that.

That's all fine, so long as the confidence level of all the principal players in the money business remains sufficient to permit business to run as usual. And, in much the same way that the electrical power in Maine could be affected by a series of interruptions in the power to Idaho, a loss of access to funds in the United States can create bigtime ripples clear around the world.

Even without the sabotage of the wire transfer system, both at home and on an international level, just the collapse of the credit card networks had spun the world's money centers into a huge tizzy. The same switches, accessed by satellite transmission, authorized and settled transactions all over the world for MasterCard, VISA, American Express, Discover, and others. When they suddenly quit working, a very large piece of international commerce stopped at the same moment.

It was, however, the crash of the Fedwire system, courtesy of the diabolical skills of the now departed Willard Smalley, that spun the international marketplace into havoc. Deposits held in U.S. banks with balances well into the trillions of dollars suddenly became impossible to retrieve, to settle against, or even to identify, as the whole architecture of the American-based wire transfer system disintegrated. And even without the cataclysmic loss of something as fundamental as electricity, the shock waves that crashed against the economies of virtually every foreign country doing business or maintaining large accounts in the U.S. had enormous and immediate impact.

Money simply stopped moving, in some cases in such huge quantities that entire portions of foreign economies ceased to exist

226

at all. Numerous western European and Asian banks failed within a few days, and American banks quickly saw their foreign holdings snatched up by the governments of the institutions and countries that had been hit with those losses. Of course, no one was really secure in this business, anyway, so the entire international banking world shivered against losses for that there was no possible recovery, and from that there was absolutely no escape.

* * * * *

The chill of the gathering darkness found its way through every last layer of Josh Landry's clothing, producing a shiver he had been committed to vanquishing after the last all-nighter he pulled lying in the woods. He was hidden at the edge of the clearing that defined the only vantagepoint within half a mile where a man could effectively observe Jericho Road and both the Landry driveway entrances. He sat against the base of a big maple tree, the weedy fence-row his only camouflage. The bright moonlight that would soon wash the countryside in its eerie white light would make the space beneath the tree a black hole where he could sit without fear of detection.

A low rumbling—feeling more than sound—interrupted his reverie. From the north there was the hint of presence that told his heightened senses a car was approaching from the direction of Richland. Lifting the little FM band radio transmitter to his face, he keyed the mic and alerted Carl and the others. "Company from the north, boys, sounds like a couple cars, at least. Heads up. Carl, you copy?"

The doctor's tension-ridden voice responded. "OK Josh, stay low and don't come in behind 'em until you're sure there are no more coming. We sure don't want another late surprise visitor like last night."

"All right, big brother, I'll be good. But don't expect me to wait more than half a minute if these assholes turn in for another little party. Remember, I'm on horseback out here, and it'll take me at least three minutes to get to either place. You got everybody in the basement?"

"Yep. Jess has twenty-six kids and all the moms down there. Two men beside the garage, one under the front porch, and Larry on the roof behind the chimney. He's got the Winchester and a .45 Colt. There's only two men at my place, both with 15s, but they'll never be able to hold off two carloads of bad guys. We'll drive straight through the woods and enter from the back if you report they're headed there." Sweat moistened Josh's hands, then chilled them, as he gripped the A.R. 15, neurotically rechecking to see that the magazine was seated properly, safety off.

He whispered a quick prayer for them all, adding a postscript of thanksgiving for the fortress mentality of his brother. It had been his idea to purchase a few big guns against just such an eventuality. Suffering great ridicule and unmerciful teasing, the elder Landry had bought three semiautomatics, several ammunition clips, and the tools necessary to maintain them. In the past fifteen days, those weapons had roared into the faces of some of the nastiest people in America, killing twenty-three—mostly at night. Although there was plenty of trouble during the daytime that first week or so, the frequency of the raids had slackened in the past few days. Now it seemed they only showed up at night, usually at least two carloads, driving fancy cars and trucks they had stolen from defenseless people in town—raining down terror on any household they happened to find.

The folks along Jericho Road could not know that the evil they were enduring was also haunting the days and nights of people all over the country. Vicious and intense urban rioting, looting, and gang terror continued to consume the entire population of civilian law enforcement, as well as what was left of the various National Guard components that had not been sent to the Middle East or on some other stupid adventure by Jackie Webb's genius predecessor. Now, with every available policeman, fireman, and guardsman neck deep in urban anarchy, the suburbs and rural areas were essentially without protection, except for what the people could produce for themselves.

Such was the case in the area around Jericho, where folks had banded together, pooling food, water, and weapons, and setting up fortified positions in that to protect their children, old people, and those who had been injured by these emissaries of the devil himself. The women often found themselves handling whatever weapons were available, right beside the men, as there were often too few men to go around. And in each suburban community, the men were the first targets of the black militants, the neonazis, and the just plain bad people who found this playground to be the fulfillment of a lifetime of pent up anger and really ugly rage.

Book II – The Hounds of Hell

Josh felt his stomach knot into that old but all too familiar searing, burning pain as the first set of headlights appeared over a rise about a mile away. "Carl, I got two—no three—yeah, *three* vehicles southbound, approaching your drive at about fifty. These guys are really moving out. Looks like they'll blow right on—*wait—hold it—oh shit! They're turning in at your place. Goddamit, they all three turned in at your place. Sonofabitch—just two men there!! Carl, do you copy, they're heading up your driveway very fast—*"

Josh had been constantly amazed at the coolness with that his older brother handled their many combat-like situations over the past weeks. Even though he had never even been in the military, never seen anything remotely like this, the doctor was steady, observant, calculating, and at times very quick to kill. He responded to Josh. "I copy, and we're moving out. I'll leave Larry on the roof and one AR here to cover. Jess and the girls in the basement have Mick's shotgun and two handguns. Wait until you're sure that's all of them, then come in behind. We'll take the four-wheelers and approach from the woods and fields. *Emmitt—this is Carl—do you copy that? You've got company—three loads of badboys, so stay low and hold on. We're coming!*"

A pause of no more than three seconds ended with the excited voice of Emmitt Thompson, their neighbor and longtime friend, who was with the other group of kids and adults, about thirty in all. They were inside Carl's relatively bulletproof fieldstone house. "*Yeah—COPY!! We're in position, but there's only me and Lyle, so hurry up!*"

Carl stuffed the little radio in his hip pocket, grabbed his own shotgun, and opened the door to the basement. "*Jess—come here!! We got company at my place, so you're it. You've got an automatic rifle outside and a sniper on the roof.* That should take care of things 'til we can clean up the riffraff at home. And, Jess—better come up here and bring that big shotgun. Somebody needs to keep a lookout from inside, too."

Jessica Marie Landry swept up her father's 12 gauge, spun back around and barked at the kids and other women in the basement. "You guys keep it absolutely still and listen for trouble. Bonnie—come with me. Jan, you're in charge down here. And *please, QUIET!*"

She bounded up the steps, grabbing her brother-in-law's hand as he turned toward the kitchen door. "*YOU be careful, Carl*

Landry—and bring my damn husband back with you!!" He looked for an instant into her face, eyes on fire with passion and a mixture of excitement and fear. He turned back to the door and was gone. A moment later, she heard the quiet rumble of the motors of the fourwheelers as the men raced off through the woods, behind the house. Two men were visible on each machine, rifles slung over shoulders, heads protruding forward as their eyes searched for the tractor trail that led first into the woods, then across the end of the wide bean field that separated the two houses.

For only a moment she could remember the fit she had thrown when Josh brought one of those damned machines home for Luke. "A damn death trap, that's all!! If that boy gets paralyzed, or worse, it'll be *you* I'll be killin', Josh Landry!" Carl had also bought one, and the three of them then proceeded to turn the entire farm into an obstacle course where they could race, climb, and otherwise scar the ancient fields. The only good thing about them had been that their continued operation produced a number of new trails that were just as good for horses as for machines. Jess often treated herself to a gallop through those back trails, smiling a grudging smile at the machines that had made it possible.

The men disappeared just as the dull thump of gunfire became audible, coming from the direction of Carl's place. Jess quit breathing for a moment, then whispered a fear-laden prayer for all. Bitter burning gripped her throat, as she once again tried to make herself admit the horror of what was really happening to them and to their country. At the same time, Carl and the three men who accompanied him flew through the woods and approached the open field; they felt and heard those same reports. Tightening their grip on the handlebars of the funny little machines, they hunched low, straining to see the trail through the darkness. Likewise, Josh knelt low under the big tree; like a runner in the blocks, he waited to be sure no more cars approached.

* * * * *

Emmitt Thompson slammed the door to the basement of Carl Landry's house, crouching low as he moved to the window behind the kitchen table. He reached the window just as the second vehicle, an older model pickup truck, became visible and turned off its headlights.

The third vehicle made the last turn and came into view then, a huge white Mercedes-Benz with all its windows down and men hanging out of every opening. The front car slid to a stop at the head of the circle; it was a midsize Dodge van, one like all the moms drove for car pool.

The sliding door flew open, and four men jumped out, whooping and screaming obscenities as they opened fire on the front of the house with a variety of shotguns and pistols.

Because of the stone facade, there was protection for Emmitt and Earl Stone, the other armed protector of all those in the basement. The glass in the front windows vanished in a shower of dust and shards. Stone came around into the kitchen from the end of the living room, where he had been watching for an attempted entry from the back. The intense firing in front told him there was no time to wait for such an attempt. Diving onto the floor, the aging veteran of Korea low-crawled to the other windows that faced the front of the house from the kitchen and, seeing Emmitt in position beside him, shouted, "NOW!"

Both men rolled up onto one knee and opened fire, Emmitt with the third of the three ARs and Earl with a twelve-gauge pump gun he'd used for thirty years to kill geese. The enemy in this case turned out to be a bunch of drunks, an unusual combination of blacks and whites, who had been on a wild reign of terror that commenced over three hours earlier in one of the upscale suburbs west of Richland. Several hours of killing and torturing unarmed folk plus the consumption of large quantities of stolen liquor had made them complacent, and the first four met a quick and messy death as the old men cut into their ranks with a close-in and withering counterattack.

A breath of ear-ringing silence followed, punctuated by the final groans and gasps of the four who lay dying outside the windows. As if instantly sobered up by the sight of their bloodthirsty pals lying in front of them, the rest spun into a quick retreat that took them back behind their vehicles. Two of the men in the last car were not yet in the assault, and they opened fire from about fifty feet away into the kitchen windows. A cry of agony jolted Emmitt out of his tunnel vision view of the frontal field of fire as he turned to see Earl Stone roll back and away across the floor. A thick trail of blood marked the floor as he came to rest at the base of the cabinets, the cry of pain now replaced with a low groan.

"*Earl!! You hit, Earl?? Goddammit—Carl, this is Emmitt—Earl's hit—where the hell are you guys?!*" The response was not a radio transmission but the sound of heavy gunfire from the woods at the edge of the front yard. Coming in from the deep cover that surrounded the big house, Carl and the others managed to get within less than fifty yards of the attackers before having to fire. And the roar of the previous firing had further aided their quick advance. Taking up supported positions, some leaning against trees, others lying prone in the deep grass, they opened fire with excellent effect.

Another moment of silence. Visible in the half-light created by the beginnings of moonlight, the defenders could see at least four more men down on the ground around the stolen cars and trucks. No one moved on either side, as Carl's men waited for the appearance of another target, and the wounded lay still, either already dead or too hurt and too scared to move.

Without warning, the headlights came on in the Mercedes, the engine roared, and the big car blew gravel and mud forward, peppering the wounded men who lay around it. Screeching backward and swinging wildly around to head back out the drive, the white machine sped away in still another hail of rocks and dirt. Because he was armed with the automatic, it was Carl who opened fire on the retreating vehicle, blowing out the back and right side windows.

"*Shit!—Too high!! Josh, if you can copy, badboy coming out in a white Benz—I think I missed him.* Finish it."

Josh did copy, as he hunkered low in the saddle on his favorite gelding, back in the weeds along the fencerow. He was coming in fast behind the sound of the gunfire, his horse as jittery as a hooker at a Methodist baptism, running along in the dark. Without responding to the radio, Josh drew back on the reins, sliding out of the saddle as if to bulldog an errant steer. He rolled away from the horse, which stopped instantly, standing wide eyed, nostrils spewing steam into the darkness. He ignored the throbbing pain in his still-sore feet as he moved for the cover of the fencerow.

The lights of the Mercedes were now visible, and Josh rolled up on one knee against a fence post. He breathed slowly, purposefully, quieting his pounding heart. He uttered a prayer for forgiveness. He waited as the car sped toward him.

Book II – The Hounds of Hell

Now. Deliberate, accurate, no waste. The 5.56mm rounds thundered into the speeding car, blowing out the windshield at the same time they took off the top of the driver's head. The car slowed, rolled off the drive, and meandered into the fence. It was finished—again.

20.

The aftermath of violence is really an altered state. Physiologically, the adrenaline—epinephrine, actually—that has been pumped into the bloodstream by the body's reaction to powerful stimulation leaves one shaky, clammy, chilled, nauseated, and weak. The beginnings of recognition within each person's mind of what has just happened, coupled with the relief that accompanies knowing that he is still alive and unhurt, creates a hushed environment, ears ringing, senses overloaded. The smells and sights of what is left to prove the fighting happened seem momentarily distant, foggy, as if through a fine curtain.

For the combatants, there is the rush of exhilaration that follows violent victory; often in war, it is the time when counterattack is the most effective, as the victors become inattentive to their defense, consumed with their own accomplishment. They are likely, before the quietness sets in, to laugh, boast, and talk loudly about the battle. In fact, they are reassuring themselves and each other that they are still OK and that the bloody results constitute the right. Then they begin to observe the carnage their weapons and their actions have created. Then things get quiet.

Standing up in the brightening moonlight after several minutes of waiting in the shadows, Carl Landry moved in a shallow circle around the dark vehicles that sat idling in his driveway. The others moved in the same circles, but in the opposite direction, approaching the cars and trucks and the bodies that lay beside them.

Everyone jumped almost out of his shoes as the voice of Emmitt Thompson broke the silence. His tone was shakey as he moved toward them on wobbly legs. "Doc, is that you? Oh, Jesus, Doc, I thought you'd never get here. Holy mother of Mary, what a mess. . .looks like war—I can't believe we could be—" He mumbled absently, obviously in shock after the horrors of the past minutes. Looking down at the dead men littering the ground, he turned again toward Carl and spoke with vacant, hollow voice. "Earl's dead, Carl. Shot twice. Dearest Jesus, Carl, what a mess—Earl's dead. . . Bastards back by the cars musta got 'im—we killed the ones up close. Shoulda' seen those pricks' faces when we opened up on 'em from point blank. . .Earl's dead, Carl. . .yep, Earl. . ."

The voice faded as the man's shoulders began to heave with the first onslaught of intense grief. The air hung cold, damp, quiet, the smell of gunpowder mixed with the scent of blood and death. As if moving in deep water, the others, at first snapping around at the mumbled announcement about Earl, looked with hollow expression at each other, at Emmitt, and then back to the dead around them. Carl took a deep breath, then awoke to the sound of Josh's horse approaching on the gravel drive.

"You boys know the drill; clean up this mess. Weapons first, then confirm the kills. Search 'em for money, ammo, whatever. Then gather the dead over there at the edge of the woods. I'll go see to Earl. Josh, I heard you shooting—you get that last one?"

Josh slowly dismounted, wincing as his tender feet touched the ground. "Fish in a goddam barrel, Carl. Caught him at the last bend in the driveway, down by the road. Hated tearing up that nice car. Wonder who they tortured to get it. . ." Moving slowly through this post-battle haze, he followed Carl to the house. As they walked, he keyed the mic on his radio, telling Jess they had survived another raid. "Honey, it's me. . .we're OK here. . .looks like the freakin' Mekong Delta after Tet, but we're OK. You guys copy?"

The radio squawked almost immediately, Jess responding with a relief that was palpable, even over the little radio. "Yeah, Josh, we're fine—just a bit shaky and anxious for you to come home. Hurry back." The husband swallowed a convulsion of bile and tears, the paradox of his wife's sweet voice against the sight of all these bloody corpses almost more than his exhausted psyche could handle.

"Ok, stand by. Back in a bit. And Jess—I—" His throat closed against his efforts to speak, his mind filled with a mixture of the moment and the horror of long ago. Only then it was someone else's land ravaged by violence, soaked in the blood of its people. He swallowed hard, the words needing vent. "I—Jess, this so—I can't believe it all—I love you. . ." The transmission stopped, choked off by grief that overpowered expression.

Limping inside through the massive oaken front door, Josh looked to his right, seeing Carl kneeling over a motionless form that was face down on the kitchen floor. Holding a flashlight in one hand, the physician felt for signs of life with the other. The sound of Josh's shuffling gait on the hardwood drew his attention only long enough to bark an order. "Here—*hold this*—I can't do shit with just one hand! I'm afraid it's too late, anyway, but let's try—"

"Got it—who—holy Jesus, that's Earl!—How bad—here, can we turn him over—can't see—"

"Yeah, there's another flashlight in the top drawer by the sink. Get it, and let's see—I don't feel a pulse—he's bleeding like a stuck pig—here—holy *shit,* Josh, look—neck wound! Hand me that towel!"

As Josh snapped on the second light, holding it under his arm and aiming it at the motionless man's neck and head, Carl did the same with the first light, and they rolled him over on his back. The glistening, slick appearance of his shirt told the story of a deep, deadly wound, and the smell of blood was overpowering.

"Been shot twice, at least. Looks like he must've been hunched over, probably trying to duck down away from incoming fire. One chest wound—oh, *shit*—exit in the lower back—goddammit! No way to know how much damage on that one. Entrance high on the shoulder. Track coulda gotten a lung or a big artery—can't tell—exit is low enough and off to the right—might've missed the abdomen—I wish I'd treated more gunshot wounds! I need some instruments to do this. Josh, get my bag outta the pickup in the garage!"

Josh jumped to his feet, gasping at the painful reminder of his own still-fresh injuries. He limped to the back door and disappeared into the garage. "Goddammit, Earl, the Chinese wasted a half million rounds tryin' to get your fat ass, and they couldn't get the job done. Don't go dying on me now! *Hurry up, Josh! I—*"

"At ease, Doc, here it is. Gimme that light and you do your thing." Carl ripped open the top of the old leather bag, jerking out his stethoscope and a small pen light. Jamming the former into his ears, he pressed the business end of the device to Earl's chest. Silence. Only the sound of the two men breathing. Josh watched his brother's face for a sign. Carl let go of the end of the stethoscope, flipped on the little flashlight, and pulled back one of the patient's eyelids. Josh could see that the pupils were *not* dilated, and that they reacted to the light being shone into them. Now neither man breathed at all, as the doctor went back to the chest, listening intently for signs of life in the man's chest. His eyes stared intently into the quiet face, eyes fixed on the moribund countenance. Then a little quick movement as Carl snapped his gaze to the chest.

"There—THERE!! Wait—wait. . .no. . .YES!! I got a heartbeat! Direct pressure now, Josh—let's put pressure on all three wound sites. We gotta stop what bleeding we can—he'll probably die anyway, but maybe—wish we had some blood to give him, and an operating room. . ."

Working at Carl's direction, both men affixed pressure bandages to the wounds, Carl constantly listening to the faint sounds in the wounded man's chest. After several minutes, they raised up, the intense pain in backs and shoulders making them lightheaded. "He's hurt so bad, Josh, I just don't know. If that through and through wound didn't hit anything major, didn't knick a lung or tear up an organ, maybe, just maybe. . .But we gotta get him off this floor, into a bed, and keep him warm. Hole's not very big—what'd they hit him with, can you tell?"

Josh trained the flashlight on the entrance wound in the top of the shoulder, then looked at the exit in the low back. "Too big a hole for 5.56mm, and the exit is pretty clean—no big mess there—probably nine millimeter. An AK or AR15 woulda torn his back to shreds on the way out. Maybe even full metal jacket, too—not jagged enough for a hollow point. Coulda been worse. That one asshole right outside the window—the one with no head—he had an AR. That would've torn him apart. I noticed that both the stiffs back by the van had some kind of machine gun pistols. One was an MP5, and I know that's nine millimeter."

They stood looking at the motionless form on the floor, straining in the darkness to see the slight raising of his chest as he took those shallow, labored breaths. Walking back toward the front door, they were met by Gail, Carl's wife, who walked into her husband's arms, then collapsed. "Go get some of the boys to move Earl to my bed, cover him up and get one of the kerosene lanterns to light and leave burning beside the bed. I gotta tend to this." Josh nodded and left through the front door.

Carl held tight to the form of his wife, momentarily bemused by the passion and intensity of her behavior toward him since all this had started, some three weeks earlier. Even in the midst of the horror of the moment, he felt his pulse quicken as he buried his face in the softness of the long hair at the base of her neck. Her breathing was quick and short, as she clung tight to his shoulders, her chest heaving against him. He picked her up, one arm scooping her off the floor from behind her knees, then walked to the sofa beside the back windows.

Gently lowering her to the soft fabric, he knelt, holding her close for a long moment. "I got wounded to tend to, darlin', you just rest a minute. The folks in the basement are OK for now. Betsy can take care of things. Quiet now." Pulling a knit shawl from the back of the sofa, he covered her up and kissed her.

The woman took a sharp breath, opening her eyes through tears that now began to run in great streams back into her hair. "Oh Carl, what—I can't believe all this—we can't keep this up much longer—

"One day at a time, Gail, just one at a time. So far, so good. If you can call killing thirty men 'good.' The weather'll turn soon, we can feed quite a few people with what we have here, plus what we can produce. . .just give it a chance. Good Lord hasn't let us down yet, now has He? Nope, not that I can see. You just rest a minute. Be light soon, and we got a *bunch* a' folks to feed." He pulled away and disappeared back into the kitchen, where Josh was overseeing the business of slipping a piece of plywood under the motionless form of Earl Stone. Emmitt Thompson was bent over his friend of thirty years, quiet sobs emanating from his chest, tears flowing down his ruddy cheeks.

"You just hold on now, Earl, ol' buddy, you jus' hol'—jus' hol' on, ol' pal. . .that's all, jus' keep real still an' we'll get you the bes' we can get for care. . .that's right—*see—here's Doc L. right now— gon'be fine, right Doc?—Right?!. . .*" Carl looked professionally at the dark forms of the four men who were gently moving Earl onto the board. He looked through the half light of the kitchen into the tear-stained face of Emmitt with a different countenance—this one softer, eyes bright with feeling. That trademark caring gaze was so unique to moments like these, as the man was otherwise stoic to the point of looking wooden to outsiders most of the time.

"Can't tell too much yet, Em, but we can sure hope. Awful good sign that his breathing is as strong as it is. He's lost a lot of blood from that neck wound, and I can't tell much about the other one yet. We'll just take good care of him, keep him warm and dry, and watch him. If I can raise anybody on the radio later, we might try Richland Community, but I doubt they can do anything now anyway. Just you keep prayin', Em, just keep it up. Good Lord spared us all so far—that's more'n these thugs we been shootin' at can say. Let's just hope He keeps it up." His big arm wrapped around the older man's shoulders as they watched the others pick Earl up and carry him back into Carl and Gail's room.

By about 6 a.m. the first hints of spring dawn were faintly visible through the mists that covered the empty fields. Josh rode back home after the cleanup was completed at Carl's, and although chilled to the bone and exhausted, he found sleep to be as elusive as the mists themselves. Now, standing on the back porch with a cup of coffee, he was shaken from his thoughts by the sound of his brother's four-wheeler rumbling out of the woods toward the back of the house. The elder's shoulders slumped in obvious fatigue, and Josh could tell the man was on his last calorie.

"You lost? Or just lookin' for some more rednecks to shoot?" Carl looked past him at the dim kerosene light shining from the kitchen, then on down the drive toward the dark forms of the horses grazing behind the barn.

"Helluva state, huh? Can't believe it, Josh. Must be an inexhaustible supply of bloodthirsty jugheads in this country. Do you know what it means that they keep coming and coming and coming, each time in stolen cars? Damn right you do. It means they've probably beat the shit out of the owners, maybe killed 'em or worse, and that means folks back in town are still sufferin' awful while we sit out here in pitched battles. Helluva state, that's all. . .."

Josh could hear the hint of the same specter that had been gnawing at him for several days: What was going on back in town, and especially out in the nicer suburbs. Everybody agreed that the cops and the Guard were probably working on the city itself, that, if the glowing of fires they saw each night were any indication, was a horrible inferno raging out of control.

At least three times in the last week, standing around awaiting the next night's festivities, the men had talked about the plight of all those people who had no weapons, no protection, and no fuel. Implicit in all those conversations was the notion that something should be done. It was just that nobody knew what that something might be. They were all consumed with the business of feeding and protecting the nearly one hundred people who were presently packed into five houses along Jericho Road, and the weapons, food, and fuel required to do that were not inexhaustible.

Still, all those people. What was happening to them? How were they surviving—*were* they surviving? And what were these

239

horrible maniacs doing to them before they stole their cars and food? How could all this be happening? Nobody would have ever believed the quantum of animus, greed, violence, and rage, black and white alike, that could spew forth when the opportunity arose. It was as true as it was unbelievable, as devastating as it was true. And there was simply no way to predict it and absolutely no way to stop it.

21.

The Big Apple. Gotham. Broadway—Times Square—the Empire State Building—bright lights and high times. . .the City that Never Sleeps. Right.

They weren't sleeping much, that was for sure. They also weren't eating, either. Not drinking much clean water and not living inside. And for about two hundred fifty thousand, they weren't living anymore.

Reports of widespread gang violence and near continuous firefights between authorities and large roving contingents of armed militants continue to reach the BBC. As recently as last evening, one source close to the military headquarters that is attempting to restore order was quoted as saying that the death toll would be impossible to determine for many w—SQUAWWWEEEEE—!!!—

Sallie looked with exasperation at the short-wave radio on the table in the inner sanctum of the building that also housed the little shop of horrors. The clipped English diction of the reporter had been unceremoniously interrupted by some kind of atmospheric burp that produced an earsplitting racket.

"Come on, goddammit—you miserable piece of dogshit—don't—" His tirade was cut short in midsentence by the resumption of the reporter's monologue.

. . . of the eastern seaboard, principally New York, Newark, Philadelphia, Wilmington, Boston, and Baltimore, seem to have had the most intense problems with continued violence. One observer reported that the sight of tanks and armored personnel carriers rumbling through the streets, accompanied by company-size units of military, was commonplace.

Further, gunfire continues in most places unabated throughout the day and night. Fires burn out of control throughout much of the older sections of New York, Newark, and Philadelphia, where the aging housing structures and otherwise dilapidated buildings were quickly consumed. The same fate has been met by many of the older business structures on the island of Manhattan, where structural deteriorating conditions were pervasive even before the onset of fighting.

But perhaps the most difficult and insoluble problem, even more so than the ongoing violence, is the lack of food and clean water. After approximately four weeks without the delivery of foodstuffs to the inner-city areas, the threat of starvation on a large scale has become very real. And because sewage treatment facilities have been without electrical power and personnel to operate them for that same time period, raw sewage has begun to flow into water sources as well. Suburban areas are affected by a similar plight, as most newer housing areas, even the most expensive, have been served by forced main water and sewage utilities. These use large pumping stations powered by electricity. The results have included substantial outbreaks of cholera and dysentery, both with deadly effect.

Although information concerning other parts of the United States is less complete, it is believed that similar problems exist in most major metropolitan areas. Chicago, Miami, and Los Angeles appear to be hardest hit, where large inner city and minority populations are likewise trapped in conditions of armed violence, unchecked widespread fires burning out of control, and shortages of food and clean water. This is Neville Anderson, reporting for the BBC.

Abdul Salim Alakmah's cold light green eyes stared hard into the face of the big radio console. Seated in a chair at the table where the radio was set up, he reached methodically for the power switch and turned the device off. The chill in the room irritated him deeper into his heavy sweater; he sat motionless for several minutes, lost in deep consideration of what was now happening at his direction. Faint traces of humanity were quickly snuffed out in his mind, replaced long ago, except for such momentary flickers, with the cold vicious terrorism his fearless leader had so effectively advocated. He looked at the portrait of Yasser Arafat, hanging prominently on the wall of this windowless sanctuary in the middle of the old building.

He spoke to the emptiness. "Things are just as I had anticipated. The international monetary collapse has been more pervasive than any of us could have imagined, so I am confident the whole of Europe will soon follow the imperialists in the U.S. into anarchy. Mr. Smalley was indeed worth his compensation. I only wish the Committee would favor me with more information concerning the return of troops to this country from the Middle East. I have heard nothing now for at least a week."

Standing, he moved deliberately through the dimly lit room toward the door that led to the elevators. The strong smell of diesel fumes permeated the whole place, a side effect of generated power that had never occurred to the little terrorist before he began to use it.

The power for operating lights and radios, even for hot water and the furnace fan, came from a large set of solar panels that sat on the roof. Although easily visible from above, either from aircraft or from other, taller buildings, they were relatively unobtrusive, particularly in view of the somewhat more pressing details extant on every street in New York. And the large stockpile of food and clean water seemed to be very adequate for even a long, protracted confinement. Actually, although the hours sometimes passed slowly—boredom being his biggest problem—Sallie was pleased with the whole program. The reports he received from the Committee via the exotic radio system confirmed the success of the operation, and Arafat was pleased; he had taken advantage of the distraction to mount a big offensive against Jewish settlements in Gaza and the West Bank.

Even the security of the old building had been pretty good. Early in the fireworks, a large band of blacks and Hispanics came screaming down the deserted streets of this largely vacant area, torches and Molotov cocktails lighting their way. A contingent of about twenty-five had stumbled onto the alley that concealed the entrance to the place, necessitating countermeasures. The two gray men, led by Sallie himself, took up fortified positions above and to either side of the trash-choked deadend, first opening fire with a blinding fusillade of automatic weapons fire, followed by detonation of thirteen pre-set antipersonnel explosives on either side of the mob.

The devastation was overwhelming. Every person who had entered the alley died there. Many were badly wounded by the shrapnel produced by the grenade-size mines, while others died at once from the gunfire. Sallie left them there to die at their own leisure, their cries and groans inaudible inside the fortress. Now, some three weeks after that quick firefight, their bodies lay naked and ravaged. Others had ventured into the valley of death far enough to loot and strip their bodies, while the canine population quickly found their remains. The present condition in that awful place so discouraged others from entering, there had been no additional visitors since then. Except the dogs, of course.

Alakmah filed daily reports via his radio, after first spending several hours on the roof with his binoculars and telescope. From positions behind the low wall that formed the facade of the top of the building, he could see for many blocks in all directions. Using the street maps obtained for that purpose, he continually plotted the progress of the fires and gunfights his actions and planning helped to orchestrate. He could not know just how impressed the members of the Committee were with his acumen in the area of predicting human behavior. No one had ever expected such a complete urban collapse, and there was no way they had *ever* thought the Americans would turn so violent with each other.

Sallie met Sherman at the entrance to the elevator. "Ah, Sherman, I was just coming for you. I think I'll go see how the inferno is doing. Please begin dinner preparations, and ask your compatriot to set up the satellite dish for transmission. I'll send my report after dinner."

The ghoul nodded and moved silently back to the basement room as the little man disappeared into the elevator. Each was momentarily amused at the perfect insulation they enjoyed from the difficulties outside their ghetto concealment.

* * * * *

Fury had been replaced with quiet commitment; rage with a cold devotion to a singular goal. Focus followed frenzy. Lester Monroe would find, torture, and ultimately kill Willie Calvert. Sitting on the dock of a small bay on the Wisconsin shore of Lake Michigan, he watched the fishing boats make their way in through the fading light, a cold mist evaporating from the exhaust of each vessel. Soft glowing lanterns began to appear in the windows of houses along the waterfront, as if to show beacon to the returning fishermen. Otherwise, the picturesque little town was darkening quickly in the absence of electricity to power the street lights and porch lanterns.

The bed and breakfast at that Lester stayed immediately after his failed attempt to kill Jackie Webb was only too happy to continue accommodating him after the electricity failed and the world suddenly become inhospitable to travel. The town's water supply came from a huge elevated tank that continued to provide adequate water volume and pressure, although the town fathers wondered with increasing concern how they would refill the big tank once it ran dry. A local contractor volunteered his big generator to operate the pump and, unless the hospital and the county home used up all the diesel fuel before they got to the tank, it would be filled in that manner.

The gravity-fed sewer system relied largely on sedimentation beds and gravel filtration for its operation, and the limited need for electrical power was likewise being provided by generators. Everyone feared the exhaustion of the existing supplies of fuel.

Lester had left town in a blind rage after he put together the obvious identity and mission of the man he had killed in the stairwell of the museum; connecting both with his old buddy/client, Sallie, had been pretty easy. And the fact that he had "shot the wrong nigger" did little to calm his rankled attitude, as he sped toward NYC and a date with Sallie. Heading back down I-94 two days after the failed assassination attempt and only a few hours after the end of electricity, he had but one objective: He would get back to NYC, find that scrawny little nigger, and carve him up into small pieces.

Then he got back to Chicago. Panic gripped the city by the time he approached downtown, the electricity having vanished in a cluster of explosive sparks and shockwaves all over the area a few hours before he arrived.

It took only about twelve hours for the riffraff to recognize an advantage of singular proportion, and every gang of punks, every thug, and every pyromaniac nutcase in the whole damn town had gone to work at the same time. The roadway looked like those news photos of the highway outside of Kuwait City right after the American warships finished cooking all those Iraqi soldiers who were running away in stolen civilian cars and trucks. Looking ahead around a wide turn in the expressway just north of downtown, Lester was greeted by the horrific sight of scores of cars turned and twisted in all kinds of directions; people ran wildly in every direction. It was not a sign suggestive of easy passage.

Locking up the fancy braking system on the big exotic machine, he spun the Mercedes around 180 degrees, drove back northbound in the southbound lanes until he came to the first merge lane. He roared up the on ramp, slid around the corner at the top, across the overpass and back down the merge lane that dumped on to the northbound lanes of the Dan Ryan, with truly professional skill. This was not a man who panicked under pressure. And he was not a man to become the slave of his emotions, no matter how righteous and overpowering they might be. He drove straight back to the quiet sanctuary from that he had just come.

The Devil's Playground

Now, some three weeks later, he grew restless, anxiety making every moment of each day an exercise in stomach acid production.

As he watched the people gathering along the street in front of the docks, sharing the day's events and proceeds, he knew that soon he had to leave. Soon. Very, very soon.

* * * * *

The men who had performed so flawlessly in the business of setting and arming the two hundred bombs that turned out the nation's lights were far apart and further yet from NYC when things went dark. Some, mostly the younger and more philosophically militant, found cells of the Black Panthers or other equally vicious gangs with that to associate after the bombs had done their job. They had no trouble finding fun and frolic amidst entire urban populations that were at once cold, hungry, and terrified; they quickly adapted to the run and shoot offense that pitted them against every conceivable description of law enforcement known to mankind. Killing was, after all, still killing. Jackson Daniels was one of those, although not so young as many, and he truly threw himself into the business of terrorizing defenseless people. Then one rainy afternoon, as he accompanied a small group of Black Panthers on a raid into the old neighborhood of Clayton, Missouri, he suddenly got his fill. Clayton was a small, clean suburb of St. Louis, and the population included a large assortment of students, young marrieds with small kids, and a lot of old people.

Roving through the side streets, the two carloads of armed terrorists zeroed in on a three-story brick apartment building, one of four in a row along a tree-lined boulevard. They sprang from their stolen cars, screaming like crazed banshee warriors as they blew through the doorway that revealed stairs up to the apartment entrances.

Following a couple of particularly vicious young punks who appeared to have regard for nothing and no one, he watched them drag an elderly couple out of their apartment and down to the lawn below. Stripping the old woman naked, they kicked her between the legs, then in the ribs, the blows resounding with the snapping of frail old bones.

The man fared no better, except that he made the horrible mistake of standing, lunging at one of the two punks, in an obvious but futile gesture of protection for his wife. His face and chest exploded in a mist of gore as one of the two emptied half a magazine of nine-millimeter bullets into him at point blank range. J.D. was no stranger to abuse, and the sight of violent death had become routine to him over the past years.

Even watching the commission of atrocities like this was not so unusual. But the old woman somehow conjured up an image of his dear little Aunt Hattie, who had been the only living person ever to give him love and attention as a child. She had, as he later realized, really cared for him in an unselfish and devoted way, otherwise totally unknown in his life. The old lady, her pale flesh pinking from the chill air, the vicious blows immediately swelling with discolored bruising, set off a reaction inside this man that could never have been predicted.

Without speaking, he walked up behind the kid as he stood over the dying man and, pulling his combat knife from its sheath, stuck the thing right through the younger man's back, the tip popping out the front of his jacket. The other young thug, intent until that moment on pummeling the woman, turned in slackjawed disbelief at the sight of his comrade in mayhem collapsing to the ground on top of the old man. He looked at the two bodies, then at J.D., standing there with blood dripping off the tip of the big knife; he shuddered slightly as if to turn away, and Daniels shot him.

The kid spun almost all the way around before hitting the sidewalk, then tried to start crawling away. The big .45 automatic roared four more times, the slender young body convulsing as if hit by high voltage each time the heavy slugs slammed into him, then he lay still. With all the noisy carnage surrounding them, the shots and killings scarcely drew attention, even from the remaining six hoods who were raising the devil's own hell inside the apartment building. Jackson Daniels stood for a moment, quiet, his Sig Sauer smoking in his hand, the bloody knife still dripping on his shoes. Then, moving without hesitation or pretense, he walked over to the shivering woman and covered her naked form with the tatters of her dress.

She tried to pull away, but the pain in her chest would not permit it. Then, as if realizing this was not another aggressor, she surrendered, all tension and motion ceasing. He rearranged the torn dress to cover her bare shoulders, wiped off a long stream of blood that was running from her hairline all the way to her chin. He wiggled out of his heavy coat, a well worn olive drab military field jacket, and covered her with it.

J.D. began to move her around, working to get his left arm under her legs, his right behind her shoulders, preparing to pick her up. She lay quiet in his arms as he started to his feet. Then her head tipped heavily over and away from his chest, and he knew she was dead.

There were no emotions left for this man, no tears, no real compassion. But this old woman, a *white* woman at that, had touched him, seen him, convicted him. "Hattie, dear Auntie, I am so sorry.. . ." And in that moment, he finished with the blood lust. He laid her down next to her husband and walked away, leaving her dead body covered with his coat. He didn't quit walking until he was back in New York.

22.

Standing to ease the spasm in his lower back, Eddie Griswald looked to his left just in time to see Josh Landry doing the same thing. Their eyes met as they exchanged wornout expressions. At least there was somebody else whose body was beginning to complain loudly about the demands being made for physical labor. The two had just finished offloading the last of the newest occupants of the wooded glade just back of Carl's house, a place referred to only as "the morgue."

One of the many problems that truly haunt places that endure large-scale death and dying in a short time is what to do with the bodies. In a button-down culture like twentieth century America, it's all very medicinal, with hospitals and funeral homes handling all the grizzly details well away from the public eye. Even when things have gotten ugly in far away places like Ethiopia, Rwanda, India, Pakistan, or Bosnia, the occasional nasty photo of a rotting corpse is the exception, not the rule. Death and decomposition are so very indelicate.

The folks along the Jericho Road, and in thousands of places like it all over the country, quickly found themselves required to deal on a very intimate basis with a critical question: When you kill a bunch of people, what do you do with their bodies? When people die of starvation, exposure, gunshot, or even just old age, how do you dispose of a burgeoning quantity of objects that quickly decompose, attract all manner of critters and bugs, and begin to stink almost at once? The polite world of ordinary people had no idea, any more than the folks in other places did, what to do with such a problem. But the fact became quickly irrefutable that dead human bodies had to be handled properly, just like every other disposable feature of human existence.

The only factor that bought a little time where this issue was concerned was the season and the weather. The bodies started stacking up during late March and early April, more in the cities than in the outlying areas. Throughout the Midwest, the eastern seaboard and even the Mid-Atlantic States, spring came late, so temperatures remained around freezing or just above until late April. The Landrys did what people were doing all over the country—they picked a place where the sun could be avoided and warm air was less likely to touch them, and they stacked up the dead like cordwood. Guards kept the dogs and other varmints away, while everyone hoped some kind of help would soon arrive.

The Devil's Playground

For people like those who had been fighting pitched battles with heavily armed gangs over a period of several weeks, the problem was acute. Folks who have died of gunshot wounds do not leave behind a nice, neat corpse, suitable for dressing and burial in a fancy coffin. Multiple holes leak quantities of blood and other fluids, so that even cold temperatures do not answer all the questions. And every time any of the men and women who were fighting to protect the lives and property of their neighbors were forced to enter this shady little morgue, a new reminder of just how horrible things really were was driven home.

"Goddam, Josh, we don't stop killin' these pricks pretty soon, we're gonna run outta woods to keep 'em in. . .have ta' start feedin' the stiffs ta the varmints. Ya' think?" Josh looked for a long moment at the two rows of the dead, lined up in straight order.

"We stop killing these pricks, they'll start stackin' us up out here just like this. No way of knowin' just how long this unending parade of demons can keep coming. I just keep thinking they'll run out a' cars to commandeer, or gas to siphon, or food to steal, and start starvin' like the rest of the world is doing. Can't keep up too much longer. And the raids *have* really slacked off now, don't you think?"

After thinking about all this, Eddie agreed. "Yeah, they've slacked off, all right. But I swear to almighty gawd they're gettin' better armed every time they show up! This last crowd had two MP5s, three Mac10s, and an AK47, plus the usual collection of shotguns and hunting rifles. Pretty soon somebody'll show up with a grenade launcher or one a' those big-ass flame throwers, and we'll all be toast—*REALLY!!*"

Josh swallowed a quick smile, immediately sobered by expression of a fear he'd been harboring for weeks. It was clear that some of the weapons that were showing up in these raids had been taken from military personnel. Twice they had recovered military issue M16s from men they killed in these engagements, and only three nights ago, they had found a single LAW—light anti-tank weapon—in the trunk of one of the cars used in an assault on a neighbor's place.

The guy with the M16 didn't figure out that it could be operated in a fully automatic mode before one of the roof top snipers took him out. The LAW was a real mystery. Nobody could figure how they could have gotten one of those, as it was widely believed that National Guard infantry and Military Police units did not carry them. That meant someone had gotten into an armory somewhere, which was an idea that *really* struck terror in the hearts of all. A few of these goons in an armory was like turning them loose in the terrorists' toy store, and it was impossible to imagine just what surprises they might find there.

Among the many ironies of this netherworld time, every community and neighborhood found themselves grateful for the presence of people with combat experience. Folks like Josh, Emmitt Thompson, and thousands like them, veterans of any of the last three wars, provided the only organization and logic to their efforts at self defense. Things like perimeter defense, listening posts and concealed observation points, as well as proper deployment of existing weapons and marksmen, could only come from men—and women—experienced in the real thing. And that's what everybody was immediately doing. The real thing.

The little radio in his pocket squawked, and Josh quickly responded. "Josh, this is Emmitt, can you copy?"

"I copy, Em, but talk fast—these batteries are weak, and I haven't had time to get back to the charger for new ones."

"Carl wants you to take a couple of the boys and get down to Schmidt's place—says there's a plume a' smoke comin' from behind their barn, and he can't leave Earl just now. OK?"

"OK, Em, I got Eddie with me and we got the pick up and a couple rifles—we'll check it out." Looking back at the younger man, Josh nodded toward the truck and started toward the driver's door. Eddie swung in on the passenger side, pulling an old Winchester model 94 onto his lap from the floor behind the seat. As the truck rolled away from the dark shade of the morgue, he levered a long brass cartridge into the chamber, then checked the magazine in the .45 pistol in his belt.

"Gimme that 12-gauge, Ed, and check in the glove box for some buckshot. Fill 'er up." They rolled off down the long driveway, turning north toward Schmidt's place. The smoke *was* obvious, but its origin was odd, coming from some distance behind the barn at the back of their property. Then, as they got close enough to begin seeing detail, a lone figure appeared, running away from the fire. Straining for detail, both men exclaimed at the same time.

"Holy shit, that's Becky Schmidt! HO—goddam—Josh, she's down— *LISTEN—shots!!*" Indeed, they could hear shots an instant after seeing the form of the woman hit the ground. "We gotta flank 'em Josh, can we get straight through this field?"

Landry quickly scanned the landscape, weighing options and balancing the risks. He ripped the radio out of his hip pocket. "Carl, this is Josh—badboys at Schmidt's—you copy?—Becky's down and there's a fire—number of badboys unknown—*you copy?!*" The little device went silent, the red light on its face suddenly dark. "Sumbitch, Ed, it's outta juice. Guess we're it. OK, I'm going right up the gut—no time for anything else—*look! somebody's running toward Becky—dammit, HOLD ON!!*"

Josh floored the accelerator, the truck engine roaring as the machine bounced over the shallow ditch at the edge of the road. Dirt and mud flew in all directions as the tires dug for traction. There was about three hundred yards of open bean field and one fence between them and the place where Becky Schmidt had fallen, and the big truck handled both in a matter of seconds. The man was still bending over the motionless form of the woman when the exploding sound of the truck flattening the wire fence jerked his head in their direction.

The man was armed with a revolver, and he fired it at the truck at the same time he turned to run back toward the source of the smoke. A single older model Chevy van was visible as the two men closed on Becky's body. "Swing the door open right now and jump out with Becky—take the rifle. I'll get the sprinter— GO!"

The kid flung the door open, stepping from the moving truck as ordered. Josh swerved to avoid running over the woman, then floored the truck again. At the same moment the man realized the truck was about to run him down, Josh realized the guy was turning to fire into the windshield. The distance was about thirty feet. He hurled himself down onto the seat while keeping the accelerator on the floor. The windshield popped with the sound of three slugs poking holes in it. But the safety glass did not shatter, instead just caving in slowly, hanging in place.

Josh waited to hear and feel the truck running over the aggressor. Nothing. He grabbed the wheel, at the same time letting off the gas, and pulled himself upright. Turning as he sat up, he could see the man aiming the big handgun at him through the back window, and he instantly dropped back down onto the seat. Two more shots rang out as the back window *did* shatter, followed by a third impact that came through the back wall of the truck, penetrating the seat and bouncing off the dash. Landry was paralyzed by the reality that he was now down, hiding behind a wall that would not stop a bullet, and his adversary was coming toward him without fear of return fire. In that moment, Joshua Landry knew he was going to die.

For what seemed like forever, there was no sound at all, except for the idling of the truck engine. Josh lay frozen on the seat of the truck, totally still. As if his psyche had told him to accept this end, he just lay there, oblivious to the sharp pain in his right arm as the raised rib on top the barrel of his shotgun dug into his flesh. The gun's presence sparked him as a strange voice shattered the deadly silence. "He's down—take 'im!! Go on, Jimmy, take the sumbitch out!! Jus' shoot the bastard, Jim!! He's down on the seat a' the truck, so jus' go on and finish 'im!!"

A stimulus that could only be described as volcanic shook Josh from his catatonic state. His mind assimilated the assorted information at once: The engine, the shotgun, the second person whose voice came from in front of the truck. Still lying on the seat, he floored the truck again, this time without first sitting up, and the roar was followed almost instantly by screaming and the hollow sound of something hitting the front of the truck. Holding the gas all the way down, Josh felt the truck rock up and over the body of the man he'd just hit, and without waiting even another heartbeat he jerked on the door handle while turning the wheel sharply to the left.

The centrifugal force of the sharp left turn whipped open the right door, and Josh slid out, grasping the fore end of the shotgun as he rolled onto the ground. The good Lord must have guided that big gun into his grasp, as he rolled over and up onto his knees, now facing the man with the revolver. *BLAM!! KLAK— KLUNK—BLAM!!*

The revolver tumbled skyward as the man flew off the ground from the force of the two quick blasts. The truck kept rolling, revealing the groaning form of number two, complete with a perfect tire track in gray mud right up his chest and across the side of his twisted face.

The man moved slightly as he continued to groan, and Josh shot him, too. No more groaning. He stood for a moment, the pounding in his head so loud that he thought someone was banging a bass drum behind him. Then he realized Eddie was yelling at him frantically.

Turning in slow motion, his eyes focused on his comrade just in time to see him pointing the Winchester right at him. No time to reason why—Josh dropped straight to the ground. The .30/30 roared, then again. Lying on the wet ground in complete confusion, Josh could not see the two other men who were raising shotguns to fire at him. One spun around and dropped, his gun cartwheeling off through the air, while the other dropped to one knee and took obvious aim.

In that one heartbeat, Josh knew what Ed had been shooting at, and he responded by rolling, crawling, then running, for the cover of the truck. The report of the shotgun shook him at the same time the sensation of being stung by fifty bees took his complete attention. He was hit, but the pain was confined to his right side and shoulder. The Winchester boomed again, then again, followed by four shots from Ed's .45. "Stay put, Josh, they're both down, but I don't know if there's more or not. Get under the truck!!" With no obvious targets to shoot at, and with the fire in his shoulder growing by the second, he did what he was told.

Ed's footsteps as he ran past the truck were all Josh heard before more shots rang out, followed by screams of pain from two more voices. Josh rolled out from under the truck, up on one knee, and trained the big 12-gauge in the direction of the last shots. Nobody was there. At least no one was standing. Josh winced as he stood, the flexion required to stand telling him he had also taken some shot to his butt. Peering over the hood of the truck, his heart sank, his knees buckled, and he nearly fell to his knees again. Tears filled his eyes and a shriek of anguish rushed from his throat. Eddie Griswald lay still, face up, about twenty feet from the lifeless forms of two more strangers.

Catching himself, he steadied his stance with a hand on the hood of the truck, then raised the shotgun and walked toward the pile of motionless bodies. The walk became a stumbling run almost at once as he fully realized that Eddie was down. Kneeling beside the blonde-headed kid, he felt for a pulse, looked for wounds. The young man's chest and abdomen were blood soaked, and his breathing was shallow and slow. Josh tried to stand, only to fall like a sack of mud, his own blood running out from under his pant leg and across the top of his boot. He stood back up, but pitched forward directly into the arms of Emmitt Thompson.

"Carl, this is Emmitt—get over here quick—been an awful fight here, Carl—we got three of our own down—looks real bad. You copy?"

As if he had to force himself to key the mic to respond, several seconds elapsed before Carl spoke. "You say *three of ours?*
We only sent two!! Is Josh all right?!"
"He's hit, but he standing up. Eddie's dead, and Becky Schmidt is unconscious. Just get over here OK?" The older man's voice cracked, imparting a sense of urgent begging to his last transmission, and Carl responded by grabbing his medical bag and a grocery sack that contained bandages and other first aid supplies. He yelled over his shoulder to the young woman who had taken over his practice two years before. "Faith—we got trouble—grab your stuff and c'mon—*NOW!!"* She appeared from the door of the master bedroom, where she had been changing the bandages on Earl Stone. No words were exchanged as she ran out behind him, an additional sack of medical supplies under her arm.

* * * * *

Faith Jackson, M.D., was not a beautiful woman, kind of plain, less than shapely, and at about forty, almost dowdy. But her mind was quick and orderly, her smile immediate and infectious, and her grasp of the science—and the art—of medicine, was a marvel to behold. Devoid of bullshit and possessed of a quiet courage in the worst of times, she was the kind of physician who fit perfectly into this unpretentious midwestern community. Of course, nothing in her past life or even her medical training could have prepared her for the practice of medicine in a war zone. Without hospital support, without sterile conditions, and without even a fraction of the drugs needed to treat the kinds of problems she was now seeing, it was a real picnic.
They rumbled up the gravel and raced past the Schmidt house, sliding to a stop behind the barn, where Josh and Emmitt were kneeling over the form of Becky Schmidt. "Been shot in the back, Carl, goddammit, the sumbitches shot the poor thing in the back—she ain't dead, though—look—"
Emmitt was babbling again, the carnage so overwhelming that he just couldn't help himself. Josh stood stiff legged beside the woman's body, his face vacant, ashen. Carl and Faith quickly checked the injured woman, determining that she had only been hit once, but that the wound had either hit or narrowly missed her spine, passing through her abdomen and out the front.

255

"Dearest Jesus, this is bad, Faith. You got any i.v. with you?"

Nodding while she rummaged through the bag of stuff, she quickly produced a bag of saline and an I.V. needle and tube.

"This is all I have. It won't clot, but at least it will provide some volume until we can get a better look at her. If there's any major damage in the gut, she'll bleed out and die before we can get her any help anyway. Here—help me anchor this needle, then we can take her back. *Josh—you're bleeding, for cryin'—*"

"I'm OK, Faith, just took some bird shot in the ass, that's all. Don't worry 'bout me. You guys just save this girl. It's too late for Eddie. . ." His voice trailed off as his gaze turned back in the direction where a couple of the men were loading Eddie Griswald's body into the bed of the truck.

They looked back at the barnlot-turned-battlefield, shaking their heads as they gestured at first one body then another. The fire was burning down now, still a mystery to all. The only way they'd ever know why it had been started in the first place and what part it had played in the whole mess would be for Becky Schmidt to tell them. And right now, that seemed pretty unlikely.

Becky was twenty-six years old, the only daughter of a couple who had had her late in their lives. Her dad was fifty years old when she was born, her mother forty-six, and he had died before she finished high school. The mother, a wonderful German woman with a big laugh and the best pie-making skills in all of Iowa, had been sick most of the last two years, and everyone knew she must be in the house now, bedridden and unable to get outside. Carl dispatched Emmit to the house to check on her and see about bringing her with them.

The truck rolled slowly over to where the young woman lay, and Carl, Faith, and Josh lifted her gently into the bed of the truck. Faith climbed in with her, resting the patient's head in her lap, taking her coat off to cover the wounded woman's torso and arms. Josh choked back tears of pain, grief, and rage as he slowly got into the truck. Carl drove them back, leaving the others to clean up yet another pile of dead bodies.

The scene was so filled with pathos and pain that no one could speak. The truck carried the body of one brave young man who had given his life for his friends, the gravely wounded body of another youthful victim whose only sin had been being alone in the country, and Joshua Landry, now mired in *another* undeclared war. It was truly a truckload of sorrow.

Book II – The Hounds of Hell

23.

The National Guard Armory in Des Moines, Iowa, was outside of town about five miles, an impressive layout of equipment, vehicles, and rotary wing aircraft behind a ten foot chainlink fence. The long, low main building sprouted a grand collection of antennae and communications dishes, and a one hundred foot tower at the edge of the big compound stabbed another complement of the same stuff into the night sky. Andrew Whitaker stood at the window of his office, facing into the gravel lot that was the motor pool, a half-burned Lucky Strike hanging from his lips.

A dozen uniformed personnel moved in and out of the open office, out into a large room filled with gray desks and dark green filing cabinets; the floor was a mass of twisted and intertwined wires, running to a wide variety of radios, screens and telephone-like devices, all scattered about on desks and on the floor. The place was lit with that garish pale blue cast given off by fluorescent tube fixtures, while the rumble of a big generator was audible from the direction of the back of the building. "*Sir—* Captain Wheeler is calling on the radio, sir—*urgent.*"

Turning from the window, Whitaker looked across the room at a disheveled SP4 named Brandt, who stood anxiously in the doorway, awaiting a reply. "OK, Will, I'm coming. More good news from downtown, no doubt. Lead on. . ." The chubby, unshaven specialist turned quickly, glancing repeatedly back over his shoulder to assure himself the boss was really following. Arriving at a high table that was strewn with all kinds of radios, Brandt handed a large table top microphone to the general.

"Wheeler, this is Whitaker. What's cookin', Frosty? Over." The speaker squawked loudly, the sharp pop of the relay transmitter followed, and then Wheeler spoke.

"Yessir, copy—this is Wheeler. Sir, I gotta have some help down here, before the whole freekin' place falls down. We been here three weeks, killed about two hundred crazies, and there are still places where the guys take fire if they drive through in marked units. We're out of medical supplies—*completely* out of bandage and disinfectant, and rations are about gone. I caught a bunch of the guys giving their MREs to some kids in the street earlier today; can't blame 'em though—the hunger here is worse than anything else. Anyway, that's not the reason, or at least not the *main* reason, for this call."

Wheeler's transmission stopped. Waiting for the man to continue, Whitaker wrestled with the vision of his men giving their rations to the starving population of the projects in Des Moines. MREs are "meals ready to eat," in military jargon, decent food by comparison to what soldiers faced before they came along. Finally, the general keyed the mic. "Fine, so what *is* the purpose of this transmission, Captain?"

"*Yessir,* General, what I really need—well, sir,I—one of my patrols just found a group of thirty-eight women holed up in the basement of one of the tenements that didn't get torched; cold, wet, very hungry, living in pretty horrendous conditions. Boys had to dig 'em out, because one end of the building had collapsed around them, and, well, sir, every last one a' those gals has a new baby. . .and I mean *new,* sir. They been hustling bits a' food and water, tying old rags together to make diapers, and worst of all, deliverin' each other's babies!! No shit, sir, these squirts are all brand new, all born just since the power went off and this whole mess started!!

"I said they all had babies—that's wrong—six of them haven't had theirs yet and, of those, two appear to be in labor right now. I mean, it's really amazing, the way they been carin' for each other an' all, can't believe they delivered all those rascals without help! Babies really don't look too bad, considerin' what they been through and where they are, but the moms are sinkin' fast."

Images of pain and suffering so intense he could not bear them flashed before this leader's eyes, listening to the voice of his young captain. For just an instant, searing photos of Biafra, India, Rwanda screamed at the man, his eyes tearing against the vacant faces of starving children. He shook his head, realizing Wheeler had started talking again.

"General, sir, I gotta have some choppers and get these kids vac'd outta here *right now,* or those little ones are gonna die sure. Too cold, no real food, and these moms, most of 'em little more'n kids themselves, are wastin' away quick. They're all nursin' these babies, so the little ones are just using up their mommas, draining all their strength out through the milk. It's really pitiful, sir, and we just gotta have some help.

"I could vac 'em myself, but I'm afraid to expose 'em to all that sniper fire, collapsed buildings, and crazy mobs. Hell, we don't have a big enough armored vehicle to get 'em out, anyway. Please, sir—*please. . .*"

Book II – The Hounds of Hell

Whitaker looked at the floor, wiping his face with the palm of his hand, his eyes burning from the cigarette smoke, the fatigue, and now this fresh, intense rush of emotion. He looked across the big room, only to realize the place was absolutely quiet, every one of the twenty people in the place standing stock still, hanging on every word the captain had said over the big speaker. They were now all watching their general, holding their breath, unable to imagine what he would say or how he would respond.

The problems were much more complex than just ordering a few helicopters to fly into town and evacuate some pregnant women and some small babies. Most of their choppers had been sent to Kuwait by that genius commander-in-chief, Flint, along with most of the rest of the state's real military hardware and capability. Hell, this Wheeler kid was a quartermaster jock, and he was running a battalion-size mechanized infantry force that was outfitted with a bunch of make-do hardware and manned by a collection of auto mechanics and accountants.

The same bad news had been endured by military leadership in every militia and National Guard unit in the country, with enormous demands being placed on what was left of their forces. Those forces had been strengthened over a long period of time and were for the most part, a pretty capable force. But with the "peace dividend" defense spending cuts and standing force build-down, the military establishment found itself ever more dependent on these units for off shore duty. And then along came Flint, who succeeded in emasculating what was left of the standing army, while at the same time spreading it razor thin in a half dozen politically correct missions all over the globe.

All over the place, brave men and women who were only secondarily trained for combat duty were pressed into full-time direct hostile fire roles. Usually undermanned, often less than adequately trained for such duty, and typically poorly equipped with leftover weapons and vehicles, they did the best they could. They fought and repelled armed gangs, took out snipers, fought fires. They also suffered casualties and severe losses, bleeding and dying in their own home towns, while their better trained and outfitted comrades patrolled the streets of some Bosnian town or sat in the sands of Saudi Arabia, waiting for "So Damn Insane" to show his cards—again.

Whitaker looked around the room for the face of Denny Adams, his motor pool and aircraft maintenance supervisor.

"Denny—there's six choppers out there—how many of them will fly?" Staff Sergeant Adams snapped an immediate answer.

"*All of 'em, sir!!*" An audible sigh echoed around the room, every eye still on the general. "But I only got three pilots. And only one of them is here. The other two are stuck about fifty miles from here. Their aircraft both quit and had to be force-landed *on* a highway while they were trying to support a convoy of fuel and supplies back here." Another sigh, this one filled with dejection.

"All right, go shake out that one last pilot. Fuel him, send him *right now* to get those other two off the road—transport them back here at once. Jack up the boys in flight prep, and tell them I need two other birds ready for takeoff in sixty minutes. Tell that pilot to haul ass—OK?" Adams nearly jumped out of his seat, barking "YES SIR!!" to the big man's orders, and the rest of them began to breathe again.

"Captain Wheeler, this is General Whitaker, do you copy?"

"Yessir, I do, sir, go ahead."

"Secure those women at once. Move them only as far as you have to in order to ensure their temporary safety and protection from the weather. You are to select an appropriate site for the landing, loading and takeoff of three choppers simultaneously, if possible, and you are to insure that there will be no hostile fire during this operation. Are you clear, Captain?" The Captain likewise responded instantly.

"Oh, yessir, General, I copy! We got it, sir, I know just the place, sir; there's a little municipal park about six blocks from where these kids are hiding—we'll sweep it now for any rifraff—plenty a' room to land several birds at once. I'll contact air control with the whole thing. Thank you, sir, thank you!! I can't tell you what this will mean to these men. We been watching people starve and die for weeks and, well, if we'd a had to let these babies die, I think it mighta killed us, too. Wheeler, out."

Whitaker looked around the room again, this time seeing the wet, smiling faces of a bunch of folks who had had nothing to smile about for a really long time. A young woman, dressed in her fatigues and wearing the rank of Specialist 4th Class, turned to him from six feet away, tears glistening from her cheeks. "Golly, General, you're about to be a father—I mean a *grand*father—I mean—well, anyway, things are sure gonna start hopping around here!"

Laughter erupted all over the room as people started chattering about where they would put the babies, how they would get some of the rations converted into baby food, what they would use for diapers. With all the area hospitals long since out of fuel for their generators, their patients moved and consolidated as they tried to treat the people in the most acute need, there was simply no place to take a bunch of malnourished, cold mommies with a bunch of newborns. Andrew Whitaker realized he had just increased the population of this building by seventy people.

Regulations strictly prohibited entry into the armory by civilians, and even more strictly addressed the subject of quartering them at that location. It was not to be done. But then, they weren't supposed to be without hospitals, without doctors and nurses, without food and electricity. Tough Shit. They were off every chart that attempted to address the prescribed procedures in the event of severe domestic need. Screw the regulations.

"OK, people, company coming. Somebody wake up the cook—tell him to have a full hot meal for forty people ready in ninety minutes. Medics—you call the menu. Those girls are weak and clearly malnourished, so we gotta feed 'em right. And figure out how to get some kind of formula or something mixed up. It may be that those babies are none too strong, either. Better find somebody who has some expertise with neonatal problems, too, I gotta believe some a' those squirts are gonna be in trouble.

"Brandt, you and Specialist Stickles here get moving. We got forty women in need of showers, clothing, and a bed." The young woman who had just addressed him grinned again and, wiping her eyes on her shirt sleeve, grabbed Brandt by the shirt as she drug him off in the direction of the supply room. Whitaker lifted his chin slightly, turning to speak to the small group.

"Captain was right. 'Bout time we had something to celebrate. Can't think of anything better than new life. The Good Lord's obviously been looking after these girls until now—guess He's called our number to help out. He fed five thousand with a couple loaves a' bread, and we're way ahead a' that, so I figure we'll find a way. *Let's move!*"

The Devil's Playground

* * * * *

"This is Niner Hotel 682 Indigo, Bakersfield, anybody home out there—over?" Bonnie waited a full minute, then repeated the call. Earlier in the evening, just after midnight, they had all been together for a long gabfest, Al in Nashville, JJ in Augusta, Freddie in Tulsa, and the Swede in Minneapolis, but now things were quiet, and Bonnie had news. *"I say again—this is niner Hotel 682 Indigo, Bakersfield, wake up you lazy bums—I got news—!"*

A few seconds later, Sigurd responded in a sleepy, Scandanavian drawl. "Ya, ya, I got da copy, Bonnie. . .Dis is Xray 26 delta4, Minneapolis—so wats da big news—I jus' got up to go an' milk da couws—so go ahead—I'm all ears!"

"Listen, Sig, I just spent the last two hours glued to the VOA, and we were *right!* The trouble we been telling each other about *is* everywhere—apparently, the President has ordered all our troops out a' the Middle east and says he's gonna restore order here, 'on the double!!'—and that's a quote!! Big time trouble still burning in Miami, New York, Philly, L.A., and Chicago. There's so much violence, and so many bad guys, they been runnin' over the police and Guard people, stealing their weapons, terrorizing everybody, burning everything in sight—gotta do something about it."

"'Bout time, dat's wat *I* say, Bonnie. . .'bout time. Da white trash and da black 'militaries'—er wut eber dey call dem—dey ban havin' dey own way too much now—gotta blast dos assholes outta sight—ya, dat's wat *I* say. . ."

"Well, there's a lot more bad guys than anybody'd ever thought, of all colors, and gettin' them under control without big time force has proven to be impossible—anyway, this Voice of America story says President Webb will make a speech on the radio in a couple days—gonna talk about getting out of this mess we're in. That'll be interesting, for sure—bet he's got no clue what to do next!"

"Nah, nah, Bonnie, nah, nah. . .he ban not so bad, already, I tink—man's got balls, ya know? NO buuulsheet in dat man, nosir—no buulsheet. I tink he says he gonna *do* sumtin, dat *sumtin* gonna get *done! You don' see him* standin' 'roun an' pick his nose while dat asshole try shoot his head to puddin'—nah, nah—look wat he dun, Bonnie—look wat he dun. *He MOVE AND MOVE QUICK!!* Dat da soldier in 'im, dat's right. . .don' care he black man—'bout time, anaway, don't you tink, Bonnie? Yah, you

262

tink. . .dis man got no truck wit da lazy man or da coward. . .he gon' *do* sumtin, yah, dat's right—and do it *right now!*"

Bonnie smiled at the old Swede's elongated stress on all those important words. She knew him well, as one knows another when all they have to learn from is one sense. Listening to Sigurd's voice so many nights over the last year since she became involved in HAM radio, she had formed a picture of him that was very intricate. When he began to lean hard on the vowel sounds, and when the emphasis made her visualize his eyes bugging out, she knew he was beyond chatter or hyperbole. He meant what he said. And this was one of those times.

Through the darkness and the silence of the late night, a belief in what Sig was saying began to erode her cynicism, capture her imagination. Maybe this big, handsome, ex-Marine *was* the man to lead them through this horrible nightmare. Just maybe he could find the key, the combination, which would save their precious way of life.

"I don't know, Sig, I just don't know. He sure is different, that's for sure. . .but this place is in such a mess!! What on earth could anybody do now? I just don't know—"

"*Dat's da point, Bonnie, see,* he is simply da best. . .no buulsheet, no excuses, just *action*— dat's right. You wait an' see wat he says, wat he says he wants and wat *he's* gon' do—you wait an' see. . .I jus' know *I* feel it. . .ban pray ev'ry night for all dees monts, 'oh God, see us tru' dis awful darkness, don' let da wundarfuul America die of da darkness—send us leaders, men of courage—not afraid to say and do hard tings—jus' keep us togeder', yah? *Yah?—*"

"I sure hope you're right, Sig, sure do. I pray so hard, too. Been a steady stream of hungry people wandering through here the past two weeks; sometimes lost, hurt, even some wounded in the fighting back in L.A. All so lost and helpless. Swear, I'm about out of things to give them. Had thirteen people on my back porch last night. Got really chilly—maybe fifty or less—so we just kept dragging sheets, blankets, old coats, even table cloths, out to the porch. Soon they were all asleep, kids, moms, old people. Really sad, and so many more still out there. . .don't know what to do next. This morning, my neighbor built a big fire in his fancy brick barbecue pit—started about seven a.m. Just started cooking whatever anybody brought him. I couldn't believe there was still that much food left in the whole area.

"I still don't know where it all came from, 'cause I know this community is really low on food. I'm down to the leftovers from the canning I did year before last, and if it weren't for my big bag of bread flour, we'd have run out a long time ago. Anyway, the folks stood around for a while after they all ate, talking, running the rumors, reporting what they'd seen, the things they'd suffered or watched others suffer. Then they all sort of moved on—some report about a big church up in the valley where there was food and shelter in the big buildings. Now I got a whole new batch in the same place as those guys were in last night. . .guess we'll just do what we can. . ."

They talked on for several minutes, exchanging stories they had heard, talking of what they tried to do for those in the most acute need. Living in the country outside Minneapolis, Sigurd had seen far less of the real violence, except for a couple of roving bands of thugs that cruised out that far a week before. They were rumored to have killed entire families in a small subdivision between there and the Twin Cities, but they had not molested his farm or any around them. His neighbor found an abandoned van and two late model cars, out of gas and full of scraps of food, articles of clothing, and empty cartridge casings and shotgun shells.

Each day Sig was driving an old cargo wagon, pulled by his aging draft horses, into the nearby town, hauling raw milk, eggs, and canned vegetables to the Catholic Church. Gasoline was almost nonexistent, so they turned to the old and less extravagant methods that had served them well before. Hunger was everywhere, but he was not the only one making such contributions. At least twenty farmers had made their way into the town over the past eleven days carrying such gifts. Sig said there were no fewer than three hundred people staying at the church and in the rectory, kept warm by wood bonfires in the rectory yard and fireplace heat inside, sheltered under the tall gothic roof of the old stone building. "We jus' keep on dooin' wat we can, ya know? Jus' give wat we have, an' hope da Good Lorrdd will make up da diff'rence. . ." So far, so good. . .so far. . .

24.

The first real evidence of spring came late everywhere. The tenacity with that Old Man Winter held on had produced a quantum of human suffering that was like unto life in a frozen hell. While fires, riots, and armed conflict continued to ravage major cities all over the country throughout April, cold temperatures, icy rains mixed with snow, and razor-edged winds battered the hundreds of thousands of persons made homeless by the violence. Even in areas that were spared the armed conflict, the absence of electricity quickly turned the world into a damp, cold, drafty warehouse.

Ironically, except for the most intense pain caused by urban violence, it was the more elite and economically well-healed communities that were the hardest hit. The more affluent people were, the less likely they were to have any substantial stores of food or alternative fuel in their homes. And often, the more elegant and dramatic styles of architecture associated with wealthy people's homes also created spaces that were difficult to heat and impossible to defend from hostile acts. Oblique angles, expanses of glass, and open designs were beautiful to look at and most able to impress one's fellows, but they were also drafty, inefficient, and far from bulletproof.

Of course, the loss of power had immediately shut down commerce, even before the devil's merchants began plying his stores of terror; even the few places that were able to obtain the juice to operate for the first few days could do business only in cash. The credit card networks were totally destroyed, and with the damage done to the banking system by the wire transfer sabotage, no one would even consider taking a check. So, for the elite who made his or her favorite thing for dinner each night— reservations—hunger became their immediate and constant companion.

To make things even worse, the fashionable disdain for all manner of firearms, that had been turned into a pure fanaticism by people like Jeffrey Flint and a whole host of liberal zealots, rendered most of the population virtually defenseless. Calling 911 immediately turned into a sad joke, within hours of the end of electricity, both because most telephone service was gone and because of the enormous demands placed on law enforcement by the onset of violence in the cities.

265

Those who still maintained possession of even the most modest of guns quickly found themselves attempting to defend their entire neighborhoods from the marauding bands of crazies that trolled the streets of those splendid neighborhoods. Sometimes the militia style armed gangs quickly overpowered the out-gunned, under-trained, soft suburbanite defenders, their weapons then turned on them by the bad guys. However, the man who was smart enough—or at least lucky enough—to have held on to his twelve-gauge duck gun made the immediate discovery that a whole carload of screaming thugs instantly lost interest in their vicious pursuits when the first one out of the truck lost his head to a load of buckshot.

As has always been the case with men of such low degree, courage was not in large supply among them; they relied for their backbone on the strength of their numbers and the elements of surprise and cruelty. So, when any band of these wild men suddenly beheld their comrade's brains strung across the hood of the truck, a quick re-evaluation occurred.

All over the country, where people could band together and arm themselves in a semi-organized fashion, they were able to ward off the latter-day Mongol hordes from ravaging their communities. Toughness and steel resolve quickly replaced the softness, as these folk began to fight back in defense of their homes and families. Amazing what a little reality can do to replace fantasy and voluntary stupidity with common sense and logic.

The elitist arguments about how law-abiding citizens would just suffer harm by their own weapons when the bad guys disarmed them seemed suddenly hollow when folks saw the reality that there was nobody who would race to save them. Then the idea of self-protection became instantly attractive. As so many said in unison all over the country, "at least if I'm armed, I have a chance."

Except for the areas like those that were treated to the generosity of Sigurd Johansen and others like him, supplies were slim or non-existent. People quickly began to migrate toward every rumor of food and shelter, often exposing themselves to the evil hordes in the process and facing the caprice of March and early April weather as well. Although many found ways to stay warm and marginally fed, far more ran face to face into a phenomenon unknown to white, affluent America for over sixty years: Hunger.

266

Book II – The Hounds of Hell

* * * * *

Molly Webb's wonderful face was tight and drawn, lines appearing around her mouth, her black eyes heavy with sadness and frustration. Sitting beside the fireplace in one of the elegant parlors off the Oval Office, still in her raincoat, she was dressed in jeans and a big, bulky sweater, rubber boots and gloves. Droplets of melted snow and flecks of rain glistened in her hair; streaks in her makeup betrayed the tracks of tears, still moist on her cheeks. She was awakened from the momentary quiet and comfort provided by the fire when her husband entered the room.

The President was alone, dressed in jeans and a sweatshirt that bore the simple inscription U.S.M.C. She stood and turned to him, trying to maintain composure and at least some tired form of dignity, but when she heard his deep voice as he spoke her name, she ran into his arms and sobbed hard. Aware that she had just returned from a most unpleasant field trip into the projects of urban Washington, he had little doubt about the stimulus behind the tears. Her slender body shook with grief, her tears quickly soaking the front of his shirt. He could feel her heart pounding against him. "Pretty rough, huh?"

"Oh, Jackie, it was like a trip into Biafra or Pakistan. . .so many children exposed and hungry—I wanted to scoop up the whole big crowd and haul them here for a hot meal. It seems so unfair that we should be warm and well fed while they suffer so. . And the conditions, dearest Jesus, the *conditions*. . .If I saw one, I saw one hundred people who were not only hungry and cold, but *hurt*—some of them burned, others beaten. And Jackie, there were even a few who had been shot, sitting or lying around in the gym at this high school, weak, pale, their wounds wrapped in soiled bandages. I've just never seen anything like this. Too horrible for words. . ."

Webb held his wife close, his own imagination spinning memories of the horrors of war and deprivation as he had seen it in so many places around the world. Sunken cheeks, hollow expressions, swollen joints and bellies, festering wounds, all turned into the collage of his mind; but never here, never in his own land of the free and home of the brave. He gently separated their bodies from the grip of the sorrow-laden embrace, his eyes finding her face, gazing into the passionate sadness in her eyes.

"Not a new phenomenon, if you've ever spent time away from the good ol' U.S. of A. But the idea of real hunger right here in

267

Washington, I'll admit, is pretty hard to comprehend. Wish I had some slick liberal spending program to spin at them—promise them we'd handle it and make sure their suffering ended without delay. Unfortunately, it'd be a big-ass hellacious lie, like it's been every other time somebody like me has said it.

"Fact is, things are likely to get a bunch worse before they ever start to get any better. We don't even have the personnel to protect them from the bastards that have done all this—or from each other. Like fighting a war without infantry."

"Can't we do *something* ? For the love of God, Jackie, you can't just let them freeze and starve, can you? I mean, you're the *president,* for crying out loud. Issue some kind of an order—tell the Army to take them some food, or set up some tents. . ." Molly stiffened, pulling herself from his grasp, her eyes turning from sadness to anger in an instant. The images of what she had just seen filled her mind.

"I can*not* believe you can be the goddam *President* and you can't even get some simple medical care and food to your own people!" The roaring flood of emotion would not be contained as her voice boomed and her arms sliced the air. Webb knew where this torrent came from, but the words hit like iron fists to his heart. She was not finished.

"We didn't sacrifice all these years, almost get our heads blown off, go through all this *shit,* just to stand by and let a whole city—our whole *country*—just starve to *death!!* For Cris—"

"*ENOUGH, Molly—that is enough!!* What do you think I've been doing here for forty to fifty hours at a time for the last two months, staring at the broads and enjoying the bloody *view??* There are no less than fifty *million people* just like the ones you saw today, all over the continent, in the same exact shape, and I haven't done anything for them *either!!* And they're the lucky ones. The numbers are off the chart when you start counting the dead."

He took a breath, exhaling slowly, as he tried to get his heart rate and his emotions under control. In two long strides he closed the short distance she had achieved between them when the hysteria erupted. The quickness put her in his grasp before she ever saw the first hint of movement, and he held her at arm's length, his grip firm on her upper arms, eyes piercing through her, two black lasers.

"I have prayed, thought, yelled, screamed, and prayed some more, and do you know what I have? *Do you? Well?*" His grip tightened on her arms, his features rigid, his face a mask of near insane passion. His eyes burned black and hot, angry and sorrow-laden. She looked back at him without expression, so spent was she and then so overwhelmed by the intensity of his being, alone with her in this room.

Then the President himself succumbed to the obvious fact of defeat, realized how tightly he gripped his beloved Molly, and let go. Turning away, he took a couple of unsteady steps toward the middle of the room, then, arms upraised, as if imploring the Almighty Himself, the answer to his own question thundered, cried, from his chest.

"NOTHING, Molly, that's right, not a goddam thing—nothing! They just keep on suffering and dying, and I, Jackie Robinson Webb, the great ebony hope, can do *nothing!* How you like that one, woman, *huh? Think I'm back here enjoying the goddam cherry blossoms, is that what you think?* Dearest Great God in Heaven, but I have done what I *can*—people starve, people freeze, people *die*—at each others' *hands,* no less, and I can do absolutely nothing—do you understand me, woman? I am powerless, weak, *WORTHLESS!*

"I did just fine until I got to the big dance, and then I fell flat on my face in front of the biggest challenge of my life and the most difficult moment of the century for our country. . ." Eyes suddenly deeper set with fatigue, face longer with hopelessness, the wonderful deep voice cracked as tears glistened at the corners of his eyes.

Webb turned back to face his wife after having covered most of the middle of the room in that frantic moment of defeat, arms waving, hands gesticulating in support of each epithet. Following a moment of near terror, produced by this man who she had suddenly *not* known, her eyes again saw her husband, compassion and abiding love vanquishing any remnant of fear. The sight of his tears and the comprehension that her grand warrior, lover, hero, father of her children and *only* love was himself engulfed in frustration and sorrow, filled her with a rending, torturing empathy.

Her breath came in short, painful gasps, the lights seemed to dim and brighten without cause, her chest heaved in response to the irregular, almost spastic pattern of her respiration; her heart pounded in her chest and neck. For a long moment, they stood apart, eyes locked, each searching the other for some respite from the perfect, exquisite agony that filled the room and crushed every sense. Sounds from the room or beyond were drowned completely by the pounding, roaring rush within their heads, each weak and tenuous from the outpouring of painful emotion, both near collapse from the strain. Time seemed to dilate, then momentarily to stop, as they stood apart, motionless, chests heaving, heads throbbing.

There was no apprehension of the act of coming together and no recollection of the moment of their embrace; they simply realized that they had mutually closed the distance between them in exact unison, their bodies—and hearts—melding in a powerful union.

Her arms had encircled his neck, her face buried in his chest, every inch and contour of her long body pressed into him, while he enfolded her torso, her form so tight against him that the pounding in her chest beat heavily against his own heart. Her tears soaked the front of his worn sweatshirt while, with face buried in the soft nape of her neck, his tears made shiny tracks as they ran across her smooth dark skin.

No words were spoken as their hot agony-laden sobs filled the quiet place. They mourned the way they had done after every other hard thing for thirty-five years—together, bonded, as one. The sorrow of sixty-eight miserable days of apparent anarchy after sixty more of near insane pace and workloads seemed to have crushed them both. And having just experienced a brief but terrifying moment of separation at the hand of all this, they clung to each other as they always had, each drinking in the other's grief, carrying the other's awful pain. Jonathan Brooks quietly turned the brass door handle, slowly opening the heavy wooden door without intrusion.

Ever present wherever Webb was, the Sergeant Major had responded to Webb's loud and obviously agitated voice, as it echoed around the area of the Oval Office. He averted his eyes at once when he saw the President and his wife embraced, weeping without restraint. Pain struck to his own heart at the sight, and he quickly began to back out of the room and close the big door. But Webb lifted his head from Molly as he detected the slight movement. "It's OK, Brooks—just a little venting for both of us. Molly just returned from a short trip into hell. Thanks."

270

Book II – The Hounds of Hell

"Certainly, sir, can I get you anything—or for you, ma'am? I could get some coffee, or a bite to eat?" Their eyes met, and Webb's mind whirled and spun in the realization that this body he held so tightly in his arms was significantly smaller, lighter, almost frail by comparison to what he knew of her. Another rush of pain and anger hit him as he fought the reality that Molly had quit eating, the long tendency to lose weight having begun in earnest.

"Perhaps just a bit. . .something for Molly would be fine. . you know what works—and I think a little training break might be in order for the old man here, too. Just a short scotch and some ice. Thank you, Brooks—"

Molly lifted her face from her husband's embrace, her head shaking slowly from side to side. "No, *please,* nothing for me—I'm fine, *really,* I'm fine. . .just a little tired, that's all. . .just a little—" The rough finger gently touched her lips, stopping her mid-sentence. "*Shhhh—stop.* Carry on, Brooks, I'll handle this argumentative woman. Oh—and see if you can find just a taste of chocolate. I want to see if Mrs. Webb's sweet tooth is still asleep." Brooks smiled slightly as he nodded and closed the door. As he walked out into the larger area in front of the office, he instructed the woman seated at the large central desk.

"The President is not to be disturbed, Jeannine please see that no one enters the sitting room." He turned and moved silently away. Her reaction was instant and unquestioning. This man was, in his own understated way, as dominant a persona as the man he served with such complete devotion.

* * * * *

Brooks had little family, with only a sister and one elderly uncle, still living in Chicago. Born in the deep southern precincts of Mississippi, his only avenue out of the abject poverty and historical racism of the South had been athletics. And while the hometown folk chafed mightily when he spurned the advances of the football coaches at Ol' Miss, they quickly forgave all when Bear Bryant saw fit to start the eighteen-year-old freshman at running back in his third game.

Graceful and elusive, high stepping and far quicker than his smooth stride would suggest, the kid took the entire conference—and the NCAA—by storm. By his junior year, talk of the Heisman Trophy filled the little town, as well as the campus of the

271

University of Alabama. Then, one day during the early spring of 1968, while cooling off after an off-season session in the weight room, a teammate entered the locker room, his face so tight and wooden that Brooks immediately thought the guy was about to barf. He was right.

"Jon—man I been lookin' everywhere for ya', man. . .I, well, this Sergeant and some kind a chaplain guy came to the room—said they hadd'a see Jon Brooks right a way. . . I tol' em—"

"*Jimmy—what'chhu sayin'—who's this lookin'—Oh man, oh Dear God, oh no—Where, Jim—Where??*" The visit every member of every family in the United States who had family stuck in Vietnam dreaded hit Brooks with all the fury of the entire defensive line of the Crimson Tide, as he stood, grabbing, shaking his buddy for information.   His eye caught movement at the doorway to the room, he spun to see two tall soldiers in full dress uniform, their eyes dark with sadness.

Thomas Jefferson Brooks was four years older than his famous brother, a helicopter gunship pilot for the 101st Airborne Division, United States Army. His courage and daring had filled the papers of the South with a score of stories during his two tours of duty in the Far East.   The man was the perfect combination of intellect, reflexes, intuition, and courage as he aimed his Cobra into the faces of the VC all over South Vietnam, Thailand, and Cambodia. The most amazing single fact in all the lore surrounding him was that he had never been shot down, never been hit by enemy fire in over three hundred close-in fire missions supporting the infantry in the deep canopy of steaming jungle.

But these handsome faces bore a different reality. One of them was a black major with the cross insignia of the chaplaincy on his shoulders, the other a white master sergeant whose uniform sparkled with infantry identifiers—crossed rifles, combat infantryman badge, the silver parachute of the airborne. Their demeanor was solemn and dignified, their unity obvious, their task wrought with sorrow.

Brooks sat down hard on the wooden bench, his body still shiny-wet from the shower, a towel around his waist. For a long moment, no one spoke. Then the chaplain, easily recognizing the famous youth and seeing the comprehension in his eyes, quickly and quietly delivered the message of death.

"I am sorry, son, so powerfully sorry. He was fine and brave, a man of great valor and devotion. He died with guns blazing, refusing to abort his mission, even after they ordered him away; there were still brave men on the ground who had no hope of escape unless he could get effective fire into the enemy.

"One of the men he saved told me Jeff got so close to the ground on his last pass, they could see his face through the window of the chopper. He looked at them and smiled just for a moment as he roared past their position, then poured everything he had into a fortified machine gun and mortar emplacement that was cutting the boys to ribbons. The bunker exploded just as he flew over it. That's what he did, Jon—he gave everything he had. Everything."

They sat together for several minutes, said a prayer together, then the uniforms left, the young star quietly sobbing beside his teammate on the hard bench. He cried and cried. His tears dripped off his nose and chin, ran down the rippling muscle of his chest and torso, soaked into the towel around his waist. He cried for one hour without stopping. Then he stood up, stepped back into the shower, and still weeping, stood under the soothing spray for another hour.

He dressed, packed the locker's contents in his gym bag, and walked back to the dorm, where he packed his belongings and called a cab for a ride to the bus station.

Six hours later, he was standing in the humble living room of his mother's house, her frail body held tight against him as they grieved together. They buried Thomas Jefferson Brooks on a blustery Saturday, late in March 1968; Lance Corporal Jonathan Montgomery Brooks stepped off the plane in Da Nang, Republic of South Vietnam, October 3.

He was like his brother, quick, savvy, cool, deadly. But his was not the sky to choose for his battlefield, but the ground. The young man born to the crushing heat of the Mississippi back country found quick identity in the steaming jungles, marshy fields, and narrow trails. And while he had no gunship from that to wreak vengeance upon the enemy, he had his warrior skills; the devastation he accomplished upon them was no less impressive than that that Jeff had delivered from the air.

Like Jeff, he seemed charmed, his elusive style beneath the hot jungle canopy making him almost ghost-like, at times a mere shadow bearing death to the VC. Unlike Jeff, he came home after his second tour, alive but changed, healthy yet forever scarred. By the end of the war, Jon Brooks had attained the rank of staff sergeant, he had earned his own footlocker full of medals and commendations, and he had garnered quite a reputation among the Marines as a consummate artist of infiltration and concealment.

They sent him to Quantico, Virginia, where he discovered yet another innate ability: He was a superb, natural born teacher. Most of the next ten years was then spent training the best to be better, coaching the elite and designing the curricula that produced some of the finest warriors on earth. While there, he took a class of field grade officers through an advanced course in small unit insurgency training, meeting and teaching fourteen majors, light and full colonels under extreme conditions. Among them was the most famous black soldier in the world at that time, a ramrod straight, fire-breathing leatherneck colonel by the name of Jackie Robinson Webb.

They bonded almost at once, Brooks at once star-struck by Webb's presence and simultaneously overwhelmed by the man's youthful eagerness. He possessed a passion to learn and his personal, almost shy humility when the talk turned to his heroic accomplishments belied the lore that surrounded him. When the course ended, Webb wasted no time in recruiting Brooks, by then one of the highest ranking non-commissioned officers in the whole Corps, to be his personal attache and assistant.

Webb had learned, just before entering Brooks' course that he had been assigned to a top-level position with an elite battalion-strength unit. Its mission was to include preemptive ground force strike capability as well as quick response, hostage extraction, and insurgency functions.

It was to be his command, and after about the first two hours with Sergeant Major Brooks, he knew he would not rest until he had successfully recruited him as his non-commissioned right hand. Brooks thought about the invitation for a while— approximately eight seconds—and accepted before the famous man had the chance to change his mind. That was 1981; they had been together ever since.

* * * * *

The three of them sat quietly beside the crackling fire, sharing food and that touch of scotch the President requested. These three had experienced, encountered, endured every conceivable combination of emotion and event over the years they had been together. Brooks so quickly become a part of them, that

274

every time the two Marines were called away to some assignment where the family could not go, Molly was doubly saddened by the farewell. Watching Jonathan Brooks climb the stairs into a troop transport hurt almost as much as seeing her beloved husband lead the way.

They talked more to comfort each other than to exchange information; they traded a bit of White House gossip; they spoke with the knowledge that each took strength and encouragement from the other's voice and presence. They ministered to one another for those few quiet minutes in the midst of the greatest crisis to hit America in the twentieth century, and soon their conversation turned back to the tasks—and the tragedies—at hand. Molly was still emotional about the sights and horrors of the day, both men intimately familiar with the experiences she recounted. But that was not enough.

She looked earnestly into both their faces, reiterating her passionate belief that the people needed to see, or at least to *hear,* from their president, a feat that to that point had not been possible.

Although the best technicians in the business continued to work around the clock in an effort to cobble together some kind of workable radio network, the lack of power in so many places made it impossible to that point.

She turned her gaze upon them, leaned forward in her chair, and said, in a voice that would not be denied, "So try *again,* Jackie, try again. Your people need you, darling, and if they can't see you, they at least deserve to hear your voice. So try again. And again, and again. *Please."*

After several attempts to explain the technical difficulties, both men gave up, assuring her they would press for a quick solution to the radio silence that continued to grip the nation. And the new President needed little encouragement on the subject of reaching out to his people in this crisis. Among the scores of frustrations and roadblocks he had encountered, being unable to encourage them, report to them, instruct them, and find a way for them to hear his voice was one of the worst.

Brooks looked at his watch, realizing it was time for them to attend a Cabinet meeting the President had called for 4 p.m. They rose to leave, Molly opting to stay in the warm confines of the small parlor for a bit longer. But as they started for the door, she stood, stopping them momentarily with a word.

"I know this is a horrible time for our country, and especially for both of you, but I also know we are in good hands—yours, dearest Jackie—and also yours, Jon. I thank the Lord for both of you constantly, and I pray for you in this awful time. He will not fail you—or us—we must not forget that."

Standing between them, she slipped a slender hand behind each of their necks and, closing her eyes, kissed each of them in turn; her husband first, her lips gently touching his, then Brooks, the softness of her cheek brushing against his face. "I love you both."

Brooks flushed and searched the carpet, his eyes averted from her face, while the husband took that moment to remind himself of her beauty once again.

His arm encircled her waist and, pulling her to him, he spoke in a hushed tone while his other hand found his comrade's shoulder.

"Amen, Molly. Amen." They separated without further sound, and the two men disappeared through the heavy door. The First Lady stood for several seconds in that warm silence, her mind and heart filled with the enormity of the moment, but also flooded with the overpowering reality of where she was and why she was there. Looking from portrait to portrait, from the likeness of one president to another on the walls of that place, she was, for that short time, caught up in the truth of American Greatness and the unique dream that was now in such jeopardy.

An old Bible lay on a side table, a fixture in that room for an unknown time. She sat beside it, laid it open on her lap, and read from the page that first appeared before her tired eyes. Molly Webb smiled, then blinked back tears, as the familiar, mighty words of the prophet Isaiah rang in her head.

> *But they that wait upon the Lord shall*
> *renew their strength; they shall mount*
> *up with wings like eagles; they shall run,*
> *and not be weary; and they shall walk,*
> *and not faint. Is. 40: 31.*

No stranger to the Word throughout her life, these words of comfort and guarantee washed over her like a new baptism, her mind at once recalling the moment when she stood in the warm waters of the creek behind their small church, so long ago. The little community was some fifteen miles outside Atlanta, its humility a fitting accompaniment to the integrity of its hardworking population. A huge black preacher, his hands so strong around her young shoulders, his eyes looking into the purple sky, his voice deep, had entoned the words:

"Molly Anne Jacobs, Ah nabtaze you in'a name a th' Fatha, and a' th' Son, an' a Holy Ghos. . .AMAN AN AMAN. . .Gawd Bless this purfec' chal' of the sunshine." She self-consciously gasped for air as the big man's handkerchief-covered palm came away from her small face, the tepid waters of the stream running off her head and shoulders.

How many times she had recalled that moment, one that in time became, in retrospect, a defining moment in her life and in the direction she would take her future. And although there were many other moments of greatness and tremendous joy—her wedding, the birth of her children, the inauguration of her husband as President of the United States—standing there knee deep in the waters of that stream remained at the top of the list.

The entirety of all that now rushed over her, on top of the pain and pathos of the day just past, combined to put the First Lady in a near trance-like state, except that she was still acutely aware of who and where she was. No "voices," only the memory of all she had heard. No "visions," just the images of mingled joy and sorrow filled her being as she sat there among the likenesses of these great men. Then, looking back down to that same passage, she closed her eyes and asked God to include all of them in that wonderful promise.

It was in that moment that Molly Webb first apprehended the truth of where she really was—and what she really was to do and be. And in that same moment she pledged herself to the task of leading, feeding, encouraging, and representing the whole multitude of the nation's people who stood cold and hungry, in such desperate need of help—and hope.

She could see in stark relief that this was a singular opportunity to transcend race, class, position, prejudice, in the purest pursuit of a common good. Standing, she reverently placed the old Bible back in its place and walked out of the room.

25.

"Good afternoon, ladies and gentlemen. I trust we all have news to share and some ideas to implement. The First Lady has just returned from a visit with some of our citizens here in the District, and I need not tell you, the report was far from pleasant. Chaplain, please begin."

H. Terrance Albrecht, Captain, U. S. Army, motioned for all to stand, then led them in the customary prayer of invocation. While never saying so, the chaplain found quiet humor in the intensity that accompanied prayer these days. "Necessity doth make believers of us all," he often whispered to himself.

The President motioned all to their seats around the huge table, beginning a meeting of the Cabinet that, like so many already held, had every possiblity of turning into an inquisition at any moment. "Larry, my wife has just chewed my ass again about not having found a way to address our people. What can your great minds at the FCC report? I know you have been working with the existing networks, but have you had any luck getting us onto one of those short-wave bands?"

Lawrence T. Shenihan affirmed his good news with such speed and obvious relief that the others had to stifle smirks and giggles at his ebullience. Poor Larry had been the most recent victim of the Webb cross-examination experience, having been guilty of delivering no solution to the communications problem after three separate presidential requests. The only non-humorous feature to all this was that everyone knew exactly what it was like to incur the wrath of the Boss. No fun. More than one Cabinet member had barely managed to maintain composure—or consciousness—when delivering bad news, not to mention the poor bastards like Walter Flanigan who simply collapsed on the spot.

"Yessir. We have been able to coordinate what's left of the CBS radio net with the guys at Army Signal Corps at Ft. Bragg; they've rigged up a combination short-wave frequency and standard fm and am band transmission capability and, using HAM radio operators from all over the place to test it, have confirmed they can do it. They worked out some kind of combo between the existing networks, the Comsat satellite system, and the short-wave bands, and they say we can transmit with the expectation of good reception in most locations.

"Of course, all that is dependent on the people having access to battery-powered radio reception. Almost nobody has electricity at this point. The mountains are a problem, but that's not new. And if we re-broadcast several times over a two or three day period, mostly at night, the HAM operators are telling us the word will get around and a lot of folks will hear you. We just need a good, clear master tape to work from, one that can be duped repeatedly for delivery to other locations around the country. That's so we can get the best penetration for the places where radio is always a problem anyway.

OK, General?"

Shenihan's eyes bulged almost to the lenses of his thick glasses as he leaned hard on the "General" part, imparting a sort of "there—now get off my tired ass!" message, accompanied by a crooked, slightly proud smile. The room erupted in laughter and applause, a combination of jubilation at the result and relief that poor Larry had missed his third consecutive barbecue.

Good news was a rare commodity, as well, contributing even more to the celebration of even this breakthrough. Webb found himself smiling at the obvious reference to his prior conduct toward the man, and soon they were all hooting and roaring with relief and good humor at the "complexities" of working for a man so powerful—and so powerfully driven in the cause of helping his countrymen.

The remainder of the meeting went pretty well, with reports of the first successful movement of food, shelter material, and quantities of diesel fuel buoying them all further. Apparently, the rioting and widespread violence that had continued for so many weeks all over the place were subsiding, the depletion of the fuels required to continue the horrors being the principal cause. Far from being under control, the violence was at least slowing down, making the business of transportation of relief supplies and repair to the electrical system less dangerous and problematic.

The biggest single problem impeding a fix for the electrical woes was the lack of repair parts. Those big transformers that stand like huge robots in substations, long ceramic insulators sticking out of their tops like antennae on an Orsons Welles spaceman, are expensive and relatively complex. Worse, the stockpile of new ones at any one time is surprisingly low. Well over a thousand of them were destroyed by Sallie's boys, and there was nowhere near that many available in anybody's inventory for replacement. And of course, manufacture of parts and fabrication of transformers required electricity. No one could ever have imagined the tumbling, rippling, earthquake of chain reaction results caused by this simple sabotage.

There was also the awful issue of all those troops who were sweating their asses off half way around the world in the Saudi desert and the ones playing chicken with the crazies in Bosnia. Nobel Peace Prize-winning Arafat, Daffie Khadafi, So Damn Insane, and Rafsanjhanhi, among other architects of impending Jewish extinction, awaited the American decision to bag the international scene in favor of problems at home, having gotten the maximum effect out of their terrorism in the U.S. This was in part thanks to depletion of home Guard and militia strength.

Now they waited for our troops to race back home to work on internal problems of obvious catastrophic proportions, whereupon they would swoop down on Israel with every weapon known to mankind; the result would be annihilation—finally—of the hated Jews.

With all the consternation over conditions at home, the administration found it difficult to give the kind of attention to this problem that would otherwise have been expended on a potentially global situation. Troop movements and stockpiling of material by this coalition of killers were accompanied by a constant stream of terrorist attacks, bombings, murders, and propaganda.

The caldron was as hot as it could get without exploding into full scale war, and the presence of American troops seemed to be the only factor holding back the forces of conquest from streaming across the Golan and right into Jerusalem.

Never had an American president been confronted with such an obvious threat of aggression at a time when there was such fierce competition for the use of the country's resources at home. The need for Guardsmen to be at home, running to ground the evil forces that continued to burn America's cities and beleaguer the heartland, was overwhelming; they needed to be restoring order, putting out fires, saving American lives. They were half a world away, once again nose to nose with a huge population of fanatics who wanted nothing more in all the world than to die for their holy cause. And Nobel Peace Laureates like Bloody Arafat had a great plan to permit them to do just that. Not an easy problem.

The entire military establishment was designed to handle a maximum of two MRCs—major regional conflicts—

simultaneously. Bosnia and Iraq were big drains on existing force strength all by themselves, both because of the size of each operation and because of the time during that both had continued to fester and boil. When all hell broke loose at home, a problem far bigger than *any* major regional conflict appeared, and there was simply not enough strength left to handle it.

As the Cabinet adjourned, in a moment it became clear that the biggest assignment now belonged to the President. Nobody said anything, but everybody knew that it was up to him, the untested and little known new man, to compose this first address to a nation—and to a world—in great travail. He had to build it in such a way as to successfully stem the tide of panic and suffering away from two hundred million people. He had to craft it so that he avoided the appearance of abandoning Israel. But he had to bring his troops home to help save America. He walked out of the Cabinet Room and back into the Oval Office alone, his mind already spinning toward that incredibly important message. He walked straight to the desk, sat down, and picked up a pen. He would not rise from that seat until it was done.

* * * * *

"This is 26 Alpha Zero 28 Zebra, Nashville, Indiana, transmitting, do you copy?" I say again, this is 2 6 Alpha Zer— *squaaaaawwweeeeee. . ."* Al waited a few seconds, his anticipation at the presence of someone on the HAM frequency with him mixed with frustration that they were "stepping on" his transmission— talking at the same time he was—then he keyed his mic and did it again. This time the required call sign was completed, and after the obligatory pause, Bonnie answered.

"Sorry 'bout stepping on you, Al, but I guess the signal must be a bit flukey tonight. I wasn't copying your call letters at first. What's up?"

"Hey, Bonnie—no problem. Just glad to hear a friendly voice. Seems like every time I sit down at this thing, it's like a little miracle to be able to hear from any of you at all. I just keep waiting for my battery pack to give out, or something major to go wrong with my transmitter. Hell, I've recharged these batteries about fifty times in the last two months from the gas generator we've been using to operate the electric pressure pump on the well. What's up in sunny Bakersfield?"

More squawking and static was followed by a good, clear voice from Bonnie. "Hangin' in, Al. Same problem with the battery packs, though. Got a solar panel on the roof that's been there for at least ten years. . .needs repair, but it still works well enough to heat water and operate a couple low amp circuits for the kitchen—at least when the sun's shining. Everything quit completely during the rains last week. *Oh! I almost forgot.* You hear about the President's speech?"

"You bet! I even got to help the big boys test the short wave band reception yesterday. Freddie hit me about 3 a.m. yesterday morning to say he'd copied a transmission from Ft. Bragg; they were working to get enough bands wired together to get a message from the General to the whole country. My test worked pretty well, although I was having some battery problems that affected my short-wave reception. Been broadcasting a canned message they gave me at Bragg all day. So far, I've gotten confirmation from eleven operators since I started transmitting about 6 am this morning. Whadda *you* hear?"

"Same. Good ol' Sig was on the freq this morning by 7, transmitting that same message, and I caught him when he was done, before he signed off. Guess things are pretty bad up north, too. Weather's been horrible for almost two weeks, temps below freezing every night and three snowstorms in ten days. Sig says his barn is full of freezing people. Says they started migrating out into the country about three weeks ago, headed for the farms and the little farming towns that were rumored to have food and some power.

"Sig really got kind of emotional—said the gravel road in front of his house looked like a picture of Rwanda out of *Life* magazine, all full of people wrapped in blankets, some hurt or sick, most carrying little kids. Says every farm in the area's got upwards of forty—fifty folks, sleeping in their barns and out buildings, waiting for some kind of food; Sig said some of 'em have the sick ones in their houses—"

"Noow Bonnie, der you go, stealin' my tuundar again!! I ban try get in—get a woord in edgewise for tirty minutes nooowww, an' *yew guys,* just yak yak yak. . ."

"Hey, Sig—you're back! Thought you'd lost your power, or somethin'. Where ya' been? Hell, old man winter left Nashville two weeks ago—guess he stopped by your place on his way north!"

"Ya, no *Shit,* Al. Ban freeze our Scandinavian ass off, seems like a *year* since warm wedder!! Boy, whaadaa *mess!* Bonnie was right, we got refugee like you got ants. . .Boy, whaadaa *mess.* . .so many young, an' sick. . .Doc Holmgren been come to ev'ry house in Homer Needham's horse wagon ev'ry day since all deez arrive. Can't do too much, tho', no medicine left, no hospital. People die.

"*Shit, Al,* I'm feedin' em raw meelk, *right from da cow!!* Dey look funny face when dey taste it first time, but, by Gawd it's food. We got fires goin' in da barnlot like crazy—pasteurize da meelk an' feed da' kids...whaadaa mess. . ."

Even at distances of thousands of miles, in the dead of the night, the pathos and emotion conveyed by the old Swede's singsong delivery painted pictures that made throats knot, eyes sting. But he wasn't finished. "Some dos assholes—*militia*—just redneck *criminals,* I say—harrass the shit out'a folks on the road. Jesus, dey got little bunch a freezing folks and *killed* 'em—tortured like *Bosnia.* Jesus, sounds like goddam *Bosnia.* Helmer Gaille an' some da' boys from over ta' Solvang got da bastards, doe. . .set up surprise party for dos assholes down along da creek, where woods come right to da edge of da road.

"Blew dos assholes to *ribbons,* I guess—big, nasty surprise, yah? You *bet.* . .'bout time, too. No prisoners, just a bunch a' dead assholes. . .yah—'bout time, dat's what *I* say. . ." A unison round of smirks, invisible but still present over the dark miles, preceded a moment's laughter at the colorful Swede's description of the fate of "dos assholes," then the conversation turned back to the news about the President's speech.

"Nobody thought those guys would ever even get elected, not to mention ending up with a black president. But he's one helluva a man, I'll tell you that much! Seems every group that wanders by here on their way out of L.A. now is talking about the guy. And so far, he hasn't done squat—but I guess that's sort of understandable; I mean, Washington lost their electricity like the rest of us did."

Al felt a twinge of military loyalty being challenged. "Yeah—go slow there, Bonnie, it ain' like the guy can pass a bill or make a speech and turn the lights back on. Hell, if that'd worked, Jeffrey Flint would'a been the greatest president of all time! He promised more bullshit and tried to spend more of our money than anybody since Napoleon—still got run outt'a town on a rail.

Couldn't a happened to a nicer guy. . .Give that old leatherneck a chance. Tell ya' one thing—what*ever* he says to us, it'll be the truth. No varnish, no dance. Just the plain ol' American truth. Count on it."

They talked on for a few more minutes, traded technical talk and conjecture about how the network would work when the President addressed the people. Both Al and Bonnie bragged on Sigurd for his feeding of so many folks, to which he responded with a huge run-on about not being special, and not being different than anybody else and only doing what he could and just doing the same thing the rest of them were doing and just hoping he could help a few more each day and "yus' wanna keep the fires buurrrnning an' the gooode meelk acomin' till things warm up an' the assholes run out'a gas and ammo." And two people who had never seen the guy were sure they loved him absolutely.

But Sigurd Johansen could not hide from his beneficence or his courage—or his love for whomever walked up the long lane to his plain, clean farm house. And people say there's no God.

26.

For as long as there have been people who waited out the last ferocious roaring of winter, there have been those perfect moments of peace and exhilaration when the first true breath of spring is suddenly, subtly, undeniably present. Luke Landry was awash in such a moment, the dampness of the moss cold against his bottom at the same instant that the sun kissed his freckled cheek and a balmy breeze brushed his golden hair.

The creek behind Uncle Carl's barn gurgled merrily, though its contents were scarcely fifty degrees beneath this first embrace of sunshine; the boy hung over the bank, peering intently into the clear waters at tiny fish that darted and spun through the eddies and swirls beneath the trunk of a sycamore growing out of the bank. Rolling over, his face an inch from the chilly water, he stared hard past the bubbles and into the blackness that boiled in front of him; he searched out each little artifact of winter, each particle of interest, each flash of life's first movement, free of winter's grip.

Luke Landry could not hear the sound of his father's horseback voice, calling his name with ever-increasing urgency. Uncle Carl's deep baritone thundered down the creek bottom, echoing through the trees and off the sandstone walls above the bend in the little stream. But the full-throated laughter of the riffles in the creek drowned out every outside sound. The men's voices were accompanied by half a dozen others on foot, combing the fence rows and muddy fields, walking the tractor trails and drainage ditches in search of the youngest Landry.

He had been missing for four hours, at a time when no one dared venture far from the relative safety of home; the children were not permitted out of *sight* of their parents. But it was spring, and it was warm, and for every spring since he was old enough to walk without help, this country child had wandered the fields and fences, the back lots and the stream beds of Jericho Township for entire days at a time when the first breath of warm breeze found him. Every year he wandered, climbed, dug, and explored. Every year he walked and sang, pondered and talked to himself. Every year he did it alone.

So, when the icy fingers of winter's last presence evaporated into those first hints of new life, Luke did what he had always done. And the horrors that had recently turned his young life into a sentence of confinement within the basement of his own home only served to further guarantee that those first lyrics would call him back to the fields and wood lots that he loved and that had been his habitat of choice always.

"Luke—*LUKE!!* You ok, son? *LUKE!*" Emmett Thompson stood over the engrossed boy, a gentle mix of humor and exasperation on his face, his 12-gauge shotgun now cradled in the crook of his arm. Luke jumped as if hit by lightning at the jolting sound of the old man's voice, his face a blank mask of surprise and noncomprehension. Recognizing his visitor, he rolled over and up onto his knees, the empty face now replaced with a smile of welcome and warmth.

"Em, hey, whassup? Been watchin' the minnows an' the tadpoles—there's gobs a' neat stuff in the creek already, Em— Jees, I think it's really gonna be spring now, *right?*" The excitement in his gray-green eyes so disarmed Thompson that he instantly lost all heart to scold the kid for his AWOL status. Instead, he knelt beside the wiry rascal, caught up just for a moment in the same innocence that filled Luke's joyful welcome. They looked together back into the cold water, Luke chattering mightily as he pointed out each new thing, each additional proof of the passage of winter.

After a minute, Emmett realized with a chuckle that the kid had completely taken him over, so exuberant was his enchantment with these chilly signs of new life. In a short breath of reflection, the aging latter day soldier felt a rush of emotion, the mixed images of death and suffering now overlaid with the momentary peace and welcome of this irrepressible excitement at the first warmth of spring. Pulling back from the water's edge, he took the boy's hand as they both stood.

"You're in some deep trouble, young man. . .your Daddy's been combing the backwoods for you for almost two hours now. Got the whole crowd in an uproar over your unannounced little hike. Look—here comes Uncle Carl right now—hope you don't get your bottom paddled for this one!" Carl Landry's intense gaze found Luke from the edge of the field, as he spotted the two forms standing beside the creek. Unlike Emmett Thompson, there was no hint of mirth in his expression as he stopped, recognized the kid was OK, and spun his horse back into the field to summon Josh.

"Josh, it's Carl—All clear—I say again, *ALL CLEAR.* Dan'l Boone is alive and well down by the creek below the south field. Do you copy?" After a moment, the father's voice crackled back in response, the relief and emotion clear, even through the metallic tone of the two way radio speaker.

"I'm clear, Carl. Just came out of the woods 'bout half a mile east of you, so stay put—and tell that scamp not to move! Homestead, this is Josh—Jessica, do you copy?"

An instant, quivery feminine voice responded. "Yes, thank God, I do, Josh—just get that squirt home so I can beat his skinny bottom, OK?" The relief in her voice was even more apparent than the anger and frustration that had preceded it. He swallowed a smirk, instantly thankful his son was well, but almost *more* grateful that it was to be Luke, not he, who would soon incur the Queen's wrath.

Reining around, he spurred his gelding into a canter and very quickly felt the tension within him fading as the sweet breeze swept his face.

"Son, you're butt is in real jeopardy right now—where the hell have you been? You *know* the rules, for crying out loud—how could you just ignore all we've been through, and all the precautions we've taken, and just *take off?* You dope, you're gonna be lucky to avoid permanent scarring when your mother gets her hands on you!" This entire speech was delivered with the boy completely enfolded in his father's strong embrace. As angry and scared as he was, Josh was so relieved to have found the kid in one healthy piece, and at the same time so acutely aware of what had taken the child over, there was little venom in the lecture.

Tough to punish a kid for being like his father. Tougher yet to punish him for the nature passion that every male Landry and most of the females had shared for generations. For a moment, Josh looked past Thompson, past the horse standing hipshot in the sun at the edge of the woods, and into the sunny springs of long ago. Then he had occupied this exact spot with the now long departed brother, a near perfect likeness of this child. They grew up on this land, free spirits in union with its every feature and nuance, three boys in harmony with this place.

The irony of this moment, with Josh, Carl, and Luke at the creek's edge, hit the two brothers at the same time. They looked at the strawberry blonde head of the child in Josh's arms and saw his namesake, clear as if back from the grave.

Eyes met and quickly averted, as both men simultaneously felt the overwhelming power of the moment: The sorrow of the lost brother, the lost peace, the lost innocence. Carl turned toward the field, his voice husky and soft, his reticence and stoicism threatened by his own powerful reminiscences. After a sighing breath, he spoke as he headed for the field.

"C'mon boys, we better haul ass before Jessica Marie comes after all of us." He tried to be stern toward the boy. "Luke, if you. . .I mean, son, you better. . .I mean, you gotta. . .I mean, the next time I... ah, hell, let's get on back, fellers, ok?" Releasing his enfolding of Luke, Josh stood and took the boy's hand, walking back to the horses the way these two always walked, hand in hand.

They climbed into the saddle and rode double back to their house, Luke quickly shifting into motor mouth chatter as he described in ever more excited detail all the treasures he had seen on his unauthorized walkabout. That night, after the predictable Irish tornado had passed and Mom was finished with her tirade, they sat on the porch swing, parents and kids, aunts and uncles, plus a complement of neighbors and others who had found refuge on the Jericho Road.

Deep red mixed with pink, blue, black, and purple as the sun set. Joy at the warm air was mixed with a sense of awe at the incredible beauty of the evening; but all was tinged with an undercurrent of anxiety as they constantly cast cautious and fearful glances up and down the road out in front of the house. Quiet chatter, punctuated by an occasional door slamming or the voices of the kids as they basked in this rare playtime outside in the warm air, filled the canopy of the porch. It spilled out across the yard and into the pasture where the horses prospected for the sweet, first shoots of new grass.

No lights twinkled from the windows of surrounding houses, no cars passed up and down the road; no phones rang and no televisions flickered inside. As if suspended in time, the whole environment was devoid of the familiar sounds of high tech living. And with the recent absence of evil men in search of evil pastime, the one remnant of electric technology, the two-way radio, was even quiet. Batteries recharged from electric generators had kept these places in contact with each other through the worst of times, but now everyone felt a profound relief at the absence of the squawking panic that emanated from the small radios.

There was, however, an undercurrent of apprehension, mixed with curiosity and hope, as they all sat there in the gathering darkness. Life was going to be different for a long time to come, and the glitzy materialism of the last quarter century was, in an instant, a faded memory. No jets streaked the skies with their vapor trails; no sirens screeched with the passage of emergency vehicles or police cars. The heavy drone of construction machinery was gone. Everyone wondered what would be next, how they would live. But more, they wondered if the old ways, all full of convenience and things, temptations and fast pace, would ever return. Only the Good Lord could tell. And He wasn't talking.

27.

In almost thirty years of military service, Jackie Webb had known almost every conceivable variety of fear and anxiety. The anticipation of impending combat, close in, fierce, vicious, deadly; the terror of lying wounded and sick in skimpy cover, while the enemy searched tirelessly to find him; the heart-pounding, gasping horror of running headlong from fire and capture, the sounds of the pursuers growing louder and coming ever closer; the burning, retching, rending grief that violent death produces. The incalculable weight and anxiety of watching troops he commanded move off into the lair of the enemy—moving with courage and determination at his command, only to die horrible deaths in the act of obeying his orders.

But this was different. Although always glib and comfortable speaking before the largest of audiences, the minutes before this first radio address turned this giant among men into a neurotic, pacing, fretful mess. The President had insisted that this and all future radio addresses must come from the Oval Office, notwithstanding the obvious truism that location was totally irrelevant to a radio audience. Molly sat with him, her serious countenance intense but confident, severe, yet almost serene.

The chairman of the FCC, Lawrence Shenihan, there to assure himself that the damnable makeshift "network" would finally function, moved furtively back and forth between the Oval Office and the small control booth set up at the desk of the President's secretary. Mac Reed and Jonathan Brooks were the only other persons allowed inside the big round room, both of whom stood or sat at attention, awaiting any order or request from the man. Finally, Shenihan stuck his head around the doorway between the desk and the Oval Office and spoke. "OK, General, let's do it—I'll give you the lead, you wait five seconds, then begin. Oh—and Jackie, Godspeed."

Webb stood stock still for a beat, then his countenance changed subtly, his shoulders squared a bit, and he walked a straight, direct path to the huge desk, where his manuscript and microphone waited. He sat down, closed his eyes, and prayed silently to Almighty God for guidance. "I am once again inadequate to a task, Father, and without you I shall fail. Take over here, like you always have, and just use me as Your conduit. I can do all things through You. Amen."

"Ladies and Gentlemen, the President of the United States."

My fellow Americans, greetings from your White House. I cannot know how many of you can hear my voice this evening, but I can tell you that we have made arrangements to retransmit this message every six hours over the next three days; we also will distribute three hundred taped copies throughout the country, at military bases and other government installations that are open. Federal Communications Commission Director Lawrence Shenihan has worked tirelessly for nearly two months to get this radio network put together, and we are in his debt. Although we have broadcast previously, our success has been limited, as the required pieces of this electronic puzzle have been absent.

I come before you this evening with many objectives, both informational and strategic, but my most urgent desire is simply to tell you that the United States of America is not dead, only injured by the treachery of terrorism. I will continue to speak to you via this network about twice per week, updating you directly on our reconstruction efforts and other important matters. The era of secrecy and dishonesty, at least in the executive branch of your government, is dead.

March 19, 1996, marked the beginning of a coordinated attack on this country by agents of the Palestinian Liberation Organization, with the technical and tactical support of the Libyans and the Iraqis. As you know, my predecessor in this office, President Flint, had committed approximately fifty thousand American troops to the protection of the sovereignty of Kuwait, Saudi Arabia, and Israel during the final months of his administration.

We now believe the actions of the aggressors in the Middle East were calculated to accomplish that result, so that they might then execute their plan for attack on our homeland at a time when our capability for maintaining order was weakened by the absence of our many fine National Guard and state militia units. It is my intention to bring a large portion of those soldiers home as quickly as possible, and I will address that subject later in this broadcast.

The offensive against us began, not with the attempt to assassinate me in Chicago in the afternoon of March 19, but with the successful assassination of President Kincaid on the evening of his inauguration. After some six weeks of investigation and forensic examination of the evidence, pathologists working at my direction discovered that the President was poisoned with a biological agent that was virtually undetectable after his death. We have not determined who did it, but our investigation of the events that followed clearly points to those forces previously named.

The attempt on my life cost the life of a fine young Secret Service agent, Lee Jefferson Medley, who was killed by the two sniper bullets intended for me. His devotion and courage were singular, his sacrifice supreme. To his family and friends, I can only say that you must temper your grief with pride, and know that Lee died doing what he loved to do. And know also that I miss him deeply.

Webb halted for a beat, suddenly aware that tears had filled his eyes, his throat tight, chest heaving. At this point, he had been sure there was no emotion left—he was wrong. A deep breath, then another, and he continued, voice noticeably altered.

Overnight on March 19, explosions at approximately 200 electrical installations destroyed the power distribution network, resulting in loss of electricity to all areas of the country. Our intelligence units tell us that several teams of terrorists trained in the use of high explosives set these bombs over about a ten day period prior to 19 March.

At the same time, a terrorist traitor inside the Federal Reserve Bank of New York used his position and knowledge of the system to infect the wholesale wire transfer system with a virus that destroyed both domestic and international electronic funds transfer capabilities. The reason we are sure of his identity is that he was found dead in the parking garage of that bank, the victim of an apparent heart attack. On his person, FBI agents found the diskettes containing the virus programs. We now believe it was this same traitor who also infected the four major credit card systems with a similar virus, completely disabling all four.

The impact of all that has been profound all over the world. The wholesale wire transfer system that the New York Fed operated was responsible for a major portion of the international funds movement conducted every day. Well over half of all the electronic funds transfers conducted in the international marketplace were handled by that institution. The result has been devastating to the economies of all the countries of Europe and of Japan, who were the major players in that arena. We have many other more pressing domestic matters to cover tonight, but you should know that great economic and social strife has struck those countries since March 19, producing many of the same conditions we all now face.

Of course, our own problems have been nearly all-consuming. I have mobilized all available remaining state Guard units and supported them with all the troops and equipment I could find, in our continuing efforts to restore order to major metropolitan areas. Unfortunately, because of the great depletion of our state units by the prior administration, much of the personnel and gear needed for just this kind of mission was gone when we needed them. And although I am acutely aware of the suffering and even the violence that has descended upon outlying areas and suburbs, the rioting and armed conflicts in our major cities has essentially consumed all available resources to this point.

Aside from working around the clock to restore order, we have been beset with seemingly insurmountable tasks of delivering food, shelter, and medical supplies to needy citizens everywhere, as well as the overriding requirement that we repair the electrical system as quickly as possible. That has proven to be more difficult than anyone could have imagined. Our enemies knew their business well, for the business of repairing the many devastated substations is made much more difficult by the shortage of large transformers and associated equipment needed to put them back together. In most instances, the skill of the terrorists in the application of their explosives appears to have so completely destroyed the existing structures that most have to be rebuilt from the ground up.

Our utility companies and the Army Corps of Engineers have worked constantly to accomplish as much rebuilding as possible in the shortest time; fabrication of new equipment has begun in earnest, but even that could not commence until we had found ways to provide electrical power to the factories that manufacture the required parts.

As of this date, working without stopping for approximately one month, and usually under heavy armed protection, teams of experts have successfully reconstructed sixteen of the biggest installations that were destroyed. Of course, the entire network of power distribution was damaged beyond just the physical devastation of the plants themselves, but much of that has also been remedied.

The Devil's Playground

However, the realities are grim, my fellow Americans, and it is my intention to make you aware of the true conditions at all times. Only in that way can I expect you to react appropriately, and with the kind of courage and unselfishness so many of you have demonstrated already. Know this: It will be months, maybe even a year, before we will have electrical power restored to even the most crucial areas. Hospitals, food processing facilities of all types, and trucking operations for the delivery of relief supplies are our top priority. But the destruction accomplished by our enemies has been so complete, and the consequences so complex, that we anticipate the restoration of residential power will take no less than a year, and maybe much longer.

One of the things the terrorists counted on was the onset of civil strife, once panic had set in. I am sad to report that they were most accurate in their calculations. Rioting spread throughout every major city in the country and quickly overwhelmed all civilian and remaining military capability. Our own people have essentially destroyed vast portions of these wonderful cities, and only now are we beginning to regain control, largely because of the shortage of fuel and ammunition needed for the continuation of hostilities. Thousands have been killed in the fighting or in the fires and collapsed buildings that have resulted. Hundreds of thousands have been left homeless, exposed to the dangers of the end of winter.

However, amid all this indescribable suffering, countless thousands of Americans have sacrificed self and property to care for others. In the absence of order, you have banded together to protect each other, often arming yourselves and defending each other against lawless factions that preyed upon their otherwise defenseless neighbors. Every hour brings new and more astounding reports to the White House—reports of heroism, sacrifice, and courage in the face of great danger. It is to those, and to the folks whom they have helped, that I now speak.

You have demonstrated the spirit of liberty and the love of Almighty God in ways far more powerful than I can describe. You have reached out in spite of terrible risk, often sacrificing even your own lives in your quest to save others. Do not give up. Redouble your efforts, and invest your neighbors and those you help with your own zeal and devotion. It will be many months before we can hope to deliver any kind of meaningful assistance to most areas, and until we can get this great country back on its feet, only you can keep it alive.

And to those who have exploited this horrible time through violence and a lust for destruction, I promise you, none will be spared. Those who would abuse, torture, kill, simply to satisfy the evil within them, can expect no quarter. Every person, whether law enforcement, military, or private citizen, whom you attack will pursue you relentlessly. We will not become the slaves of violence, ceding our freedom to bands of would-be warlords and gangs.

My fellow Americans, you have fought bravely; you must continue to do so. What has become clear over the past months is that, given the dimensions of these events, your governments, local, state and federal, simply could not have protected you. It has been your own courage and grit, your own resources—arms, supplies, fuel—that has permitted you to survive to this point.

I have ordered approximately sixty-five percent of our troops home from the Middle East, with the majority of those forces being state Guard and Militia units. They will be returned to their own states, where they will reinforce the brave men and women who have performed so tirelessly to this point without them. However, let me be clear to the terrorist aggressors who also continue to threaten Israel: They are not abandoned. Strategic weapons, air, sea and supporting forces remain on alert, buttressed by our most sophisticated intelligence and communications sytems. We have more than sufficient capability to defend that small country. Your attacks on our country only serve to ensure that we will be forced to use those weapons instead of ground units, if you are stupid enough to pursue your obvious goals.

And to my own countrymen, know that we are committed to you and to the reconstruction of our homeland. Your own courage and commitment to each other and to your country is a tremendous model to people everywhere. I will keep you informed, speaking to you regularly by radio myself. Continue to care for each other, to feed and shelter those in need, and to defend those who face the cruelty we all work to destroy.

This is President Webb, speaking to you from the Oval Office in the White House, God bless you all and God bless the United States of America.

The little red light went out on the control box beside the microphone, and Webb slumped back into the leather chair. His eyes closed in prayer and fatigue, as he realized he, too, was now exhausted to the point of collapse. A moment's mirth crossed his mind's eye, as he thought of poor Walter Flanigan— "see, Walter, my legs are rubber, too—we're not so different, after all. . ."

Overwhelmed by the magnitude of the task and the enormity of the position he how held, he looked up at the two photographs he had set on the desk in frames, one on either side of the microphone. One was Franklin Roosevelt, smiling through clenched teeth before the mic at one of his fireside chats, and the other of Winston Churchill, cigar jutting from resolute jaw. Both men had used the radio to reach their beleaguered people, in war and afterward; both men had refused to sugarcoat or hide the truth. Once again he felt the crushing presence of the great men in whose steps he now walked.

Turning in his chair, he looked out across the darkness where once lights had shone, seemingly in perpetuity. Musing as his pulse rate slowed and the soft touch of his wife's hands found his face, this one man, a hero, a soldier, a son of African-American beginnings and limitless potential, grieved this dark night. He felt the fire of righteous fury alive in his belly, the passionate love for his country pounding in his chest, the driving energy to overcome all obstacles in pursuit of the good of his people, pulsing in his head. Another prayer, this time with eyes open, sadly drinking in the dark seat of liberty, he breathed the words so that only Molly, her face so close to his, could hear.

"Oh God, my God, do not forsake me now. Guide me and direct me—and all who follow me —for Thy sake. Lord, the suffering so burdens me that I fear I will collapse beneath the weight. Save us...make me the instrument of good, and have mercy on these wonderful people. Amen."

BOOK III

STARTING OVER, FIGHTING BACK

1.

The dead lay strewn like bloody dolls across broken tables and against walls; dazed victims sat or wandered around on the sidewalk and in the street outside the cafe, their faces ashen except for the lacerations that bled down onto their chests and shoulders. A pair of Afghan hounds lay dead at the edge of the street, their owner a dismembered heap of flesh fifty feet away on the opposite sidewalk. For a few moments following the blast, the only sounds were the soft moanings of the wounded mixed with the crackling of small fires now burning with increasing vigor in the back of the little restaurant. Then the first sirens began their two-toned cry from several blocks away, accompanied by urgent voices, now freed from their brief muteness.

Tevi's Cafe, the sixth blast site in eleven days, accounted for only six dead and twenty wounded, although the wounds of those who survived were deep and permanent. All of Tel Aviv, along with all of Israel, shook and wept over the events. Anger and frustration were mixed with grief and cries for revenge against the terrorists who seemed ever more able to strike without warning, without detection, and without fear of capture. The government continued to retaliate, like a big, lethargic draft horse, swatting at flies already gone from the place where they had bitten him; they deported suspected sympathizers, arrested suspected conspirators, even set up a vast array of road blocks and search points. All that did was aggravate the Jews who spent hours in the long lines created by this pointless effort.

Israeli soldiers stalked the byways and alleys, the parking lots and warehouses of every city, their full battle regalia and weaponry almost humorous against the ghostly efficiency of their invisible enemies. So intense was the suffering and so consuming the fear of what would next occur that the troop movements in the deserts to the north and east of this one tiny Jewish State seemed almost unimportant.

Benjii Arakhan drove nonchalantly away from Tevi's smoking ruins, his heart still pounding, his mood light, satisfied. Another lightning strike by the wizards of the PLO completed successfully without incident.

* * * * *

"Excuse me, sir, but we have a Priority Alpha call on the secure line, sir, it's President Netanyahu—says it's *most* urgent." Webb looked up from the maps and reports spread across the Cabinet Room conference table, his eyes straining to focus on the young face that addressed him from the doorway. The kid was a fuzzy apparition through the half glasses the President used to see the fine detail of the maps, and he snatched them irritably from his face to see who it was. Pitching them across the table and into the pile of paper, the big man covered the space between himself and the soldier in three strides, the messenger turning at once to lead the way.

"We had some trouble with the encryption coding on the initial transmission—something to do with the scrambler sequence. At first, we thought maybe the net had been compromised, but the snoops say it's still secure. Here—here you go, sir, I've routed the call to your office. Can I get you anything?"

"No. Nothing now, thanks. Can I pick up here?"

"Yessir. The call is holding on secure line one."

Webb snatched up the receiver from the long table behind his huge desk, his eyes scanning the scene outside the Oval Office; heat waves rippled up from the pavement and the brown, dead grass. A second's sadness at the weed infestation and abandoned look of the gardens outside the White House—then focus on the call.

"Benjamin—what a pleasant surprise! How *are* you?" A pause while the whole thing was scrambled, transmitted, unscrambled, and received. All in a second.

"Not good, Jackie, not good at all. I am sure you are aware of the escalation of terrorist attacks, both in Tel Aviv and in Jerusalem; but did you know what was going on in the desert?"

"Well, my briefing this morning included more satellite reports of troop movements north and east of you, but it seemed to be the same things we had already observed—no new strength or approach toward Israel. What's up?" Webb

298

searched the desk top for the report, grabbing it and opening the file just as the Israeli spoke in response.

"Mossad says all that movement is just that. *Movement.* The real action is back in Iraq, just fifty miles south of Baghdad. Babylon, Jackie. *Babylon.* We had a defector slip out of there yesterday, and he supplied the missing pieces of a pretty ugly puzzle we had been working on for a month. That bastard Saddam has been smuggling missile parts into the historic restoration area where they are rebuilding the ancient city. Like using a school or a Red Cross installation to conceal munitions, only worse—and much, much more effective."

Webb sat erect at the edge of his chair, his eyes boring into the desk top as he assimilated what he was hearing. "Can't be, Benjamin, the parts are too big, and the support platform is a dead giveaway for the bird's camera. If he moved in a weapons platform that size, we'd have seen it."

"That's what we thought, too, but it appears we were very wrong. He may have moved the steel and the launch platform in a piece at a time over a two year period, not even assembling it until after they had completed a building around it. It's got a removable roof, Jackie, and they can open it, set the coordinates, and launch the thing in less than fifteen minutes!" The tension in the man's voice was obvious, even over all the miles, and through all the security measures, scramblers, codes, and protocols. Webb knew him well, having followed his career for many years. Always a student of warfare and a devoted fan of Israeli history, the American President knew well that this Jewish politician was a true patriot and a man committed to the defense of his tiny country. So hearing the concern, even the fear, in his voice, he paid close attention.

"But Benjamin, Babylon is too far away from any important Israeli targets to be a plausible launch site for SCUDS or any of the other missile systems the Iraqis have. And didn't my heroic predecessor assure you that they had no strategic warheads?"

"Just my point, Jackie. You know as well as I do that Flint could have cared less about all that. He paid little attention to the actual content of the U.N. report. Have you read that thing?"

Webb flushed, his eyes blinking as he faced again the impossibility of his job. The report of the United Nations

Commission on Nuclear, Biological and Chemical Weapons, prepared after they had completed their "examination" of Iraqi installations, had been lying on the desk in the Oval Office since before he took office. He had not yet reviewed it. Little interruptions, like the destruction of the power system in his own country, widespread anarchy, not to mention his own attempted assassination, had kept him from doing all the reading he should have done. "I have only scanned it, Benjamin, and my staff has told me it was pretty sketchy, but I must confess that I have not read its contents carefully." The president flinched at his own deception, only hoping his counterpart also faced similar impossibilities of his own.

"Well, it's shoddy, incomplete, and at times obviously incorrect, that has led us to the conclusion that the entire inspection project was compromised. Our source is telling us that this missile site is *not* a SCUD platform at all, but is a larger unit, capable of launching a fifteen hundred mile range device, with ICBM-quality accuracy. They're not that big, of course, but the technology and hardware are the same, only with a smaller, single stage rocket. And they have both chemical and nuclear warheads for it. Frankly, Jackie, I believe that part even more than the stuff about the range of the missile."

"Ever since the Russians got caught selling that big nuclear cannon to the Iranians, back in '89, we've been watching them. Hell, they *told* us they could account for only about half their nukes, after the breakup of the USSR, and that was probably a big, convenient exaggeration. I don't think they have any idea how many they have or how many they've sold. Probably lost more to the black market than anywhere else.

"The North Koreans, the Chinese, and the Iraqis all had a big interest in buying the things, and we know they tried repeatedly, because we intercepted several communications between them dealing with precisely that subject. Jackie, we need your help, and we need it right now."

Webb sat back into the leather of his high-backed chair, resting his tense neck and shoulders, eyes closed. For several seconds, he was silent, his mind struggling mightily to make sense of what he had heard, to separate this problem from the myriad others that filled his every waking moment—and all his dreams. Just as the Israeli was about to ask if he was still there, he spoke.

"Benjamin, you know we will do whatever we can; I left a big contingent of fighters and intelligence forces in Saudi, and there's a pretty visible division-size mech infantry unit making dust close by. Short of invading Babylon and blowing the thing up ourselves, I don't know what else we can do." Netanyahu leapt on the opening like a poised cobra.

"That's my point, Jackie! While we are so deeply appreciative of these efforts, they do nothing to address this horrible weapon!!" He took a breath, let the sentence sink in, the continued. "For all we know, they may have multiple tubes set up, from that they can launch a big nuke against us, then reload and blast your entire force into hyperspace— *just like that!* Don't you see? The presence of a fixed emplacement missile site with that kind of accuracy, power, and range changes the whole cosmic game, Jackie. It negates our air superiority, shrinks the distance between opposing sides, and obviates the whole necessity for ground forces.

"Dammit, Jackie, this is exactly what we talked about when I was there in February; only then we thought we were making up Draconian hypotheses, not wrestling with immediate realities." The dirty joke the politicians played on the world after the fall of the Berlin Wall had never been wasted on Jackie Webb. Even before he became chairman of the Joint Chiefs, he knew what was going on in Europe and Asia with regard to the integrity of the Soviet missile arsenal. The inventory was scattered over millions of square miles of wilderness, in no fewer than six provinces that, after the breakup, felt an instant sense of independence—and *no* sense of loyalty or responsibility regarding the nuclear weapons suddenly under their control.

With all this intelligence already well known to him, all the American president could do in response to the entreaties of his colleague in Israel was to promise a return call within the next day, after meeting with his strategy gurus. He did his best to sound hopeful, but the whole thing left him feeling weak, hopeless. He hung up, turning in his chair to once again look at the forlorn decay outside his window.

301

The Devil's Playground

*   *   *   *   *

Almost overnight, the U.S. went from having one nuclear adversary to having at least eight; from one well-known, predictable opponent to a whole array of complete wild cards, religious and political zealots more interested in power and vengeance than anything resembling "détente." At least three of the former Soviet states with nukes were Muslim, radically opposed to the West anyway, and impoverished beyond the imagination of most Americans. Selling such weapons to Islamic governments for millions and millions of dollars in hard currency was simply no problem for them.

While American presidents and world leaders drank deeply from the cup of nonsense they proclaimed as the end of the cold war, a brisk trade in nuclear warheads and attendant delivery technology was widely believed to have moved a score of the big bombs into the hands of such crazy bastards as Rafsanjannii of Iran, Saddam Hussein of Iraq, and that gaggle of wild men who ran things in North Korea. Entire cadres of highly skilled weapons designers and technicians, previously well paid and cared for by the USSR, were instantly out of work, out of money, and very short on options to care for their families.

They made easy targets for the oil rich, ruthless principals in the Middle East, where many were quickly scooped up and relocated—with large deposits of hard currency to their credit—to the warmer and more commodious surroundings of the Mediterranean.

2.

Heat is not an option in much of the Middle East. It is a reality. It is not a matter of concern. It is a constant. One is not concerned with *how* hot it is; it is simply *hot*. Of course, there is a wet and disagreeable season, briefly wrought with mud and chill, blanketed in leaden skies and low clouds. But except for that one wet season—one that does not favor much of the arid expanse of desert and wilderness that comprises most of Saudi Arabia, Iraq, Iran, Jordan, and the northern portion of Israel—the entire region is as hot as any of Dante's awful fantasies of Hell itself.

Adolpho Weidenolf knew the heat well, after twenty-five years in and around the historic "fertile crescent" where the liquid staff of life flows lazily along the course of the Tigress and Euphrates Rivers. He was an archaeologist, a geologist, a geographer. He was also a nuclear physicist with long experience in missile guidance systems as well as the many interesting uses for fusionable material. He was a reconstituted war criminal, living the life of one reborn to a completely new identity after the end of World War II.

Late in the war, he had been ordered into battle from his otherwise cushy assignment at Buchenwald—killing Jews for fun and profit—to a less enjoyable venue. He found himself with his back to Germany and his face buried in the frozen mud of the Russian frontier. From a battlefield where he lay bloody and nearly dead from exposure, he had crawled away and toward the south, feeding from the rations of the dead, stripping what clothing he could scavenge from their frozen bodies, and chancing fires only at night and in the deepest of forests. He killed civilians for their unmarked garments and scraps of food, treated his painful wounds with stolen medical supplies he took from those same peasants.

Eventually, he made it through the Baltics and into Turkey, where complicity and intentional ignorance of everyone's origin and true name was the rule. Like some outlaw hideout in the old American West, Istanbul was an easy place for the acquisition of new identities. Adolpho Weidenolf was the former Karl Isaac Wampler, mixed son of a German Catholic and his Jewish wife—a political zealot who burned with hatred for all that was Jewish, including his own Polish lineage. His appearance was that of the blue-eyed

Aryan, but for a faint trace of his Semitic ancestry, that was easily concealed amid his fanatic persona and accentuated Germanic traits. But still the nose, the shape of his high forehead, the hair texture—present—but easily missed.

Weidenolf, a/k/a Wampler, only twenty years old in 1945, quickly found work, and just as quickly found his intellect, there in the streets of Istanbul. He was quite clearly a genius. Learning Turkish and modern Greek almost simultaneously, he discovered his gift for language. By 1950, with a degree in Archaeology and another in Semitic languages, he was proficient in several of the languages of the Arab world. Migrating back to Germany by way of Italy and Portugal, France, and then Austria, the young scholar discovered another passion, physics.

Always a natural in mathematics and chemistry, his hunger for information and learning pushed him into a quest of the principles of astrophysics, quantum mechanics, and finally, nuclear studies. All over Europe, in Paris, in Stuttgart, and finally in Russia, he studied. It was there that he acquired communism, his next addiction. Adolpho Weidenolf hungered for Marx, drank in Lenin, and found himself consumed with the overwhelming iron-fisted power of Stalin. After all, concentration camps and mass exterminations were nothing new or problematic to him.

Intellectual and academic prowess, coupled with his fanatic commitment to Soviet politics and political philosophy, made this brilliant radical genius quickly visible to his hosts. An illustrious career in the ICBM business for the Soviet Union kept him busy throughout the Cold War, the great champions of the proletariat lining his pockets and pampering his every perceived need—and want. By 1970 Weidenolf was one of the leading invisible architects of the arms race, his brilliant facility for all things nuclear nicely complemented by an understanding of and genius for the implementation of sophisticated missile guidance systems.

Traveling around the great USSR, moving like some regal envoy to the ruling class of the Communist state, he spent the ensuing fifteen years designing, modifying, testing, and then re-designing the most sophisticated weapons of mass destruction on earth. But this cosmic duty still could not completely occupy the genius mind. Archeology, geology, and the old passion for ancient Babylon still called Adolpho again and again.

Every holiday, every vacation, even the weekends, were spent either in the libraries of Europe or actually on the parched ground of the "Ur of the Chaldees"—the Fertile Crescent—feeding his lifelong appetite for the antiquitous, the arcane, the mystical. And it was there, in the arid expanse of Iraq, south of Baghdad, that he formed and cemented some really interesting and important relationships with the Muslim world. The more "moderate" Sunni branch of Islam left him bored, less than interested. But the wild, death-obsessed Shiites fit his taste for the radical, the revolutionary, much better.

Over the decade of the seventies and the early eighties, Weidenolf acquired a quiet but great reputation among those who studied antiquities, his scholarship and instinct enhanced by his fluent command of the many languages and dialects of the Arab world. The tenured position at the University in Moscow, where he lectured on archaeology and ancient history, provided him with the credentials and the cover he needed to be able to move in and out of these circles without suspicion. This produced a result well-intended by his Soviet bosses, who used his connections with the Iraqis, Iranians, and Syrians to great Cold War advantage.

His trips to the Middle East were often punctuated with clandestine visits to the heads of state of those radical countries, where he helped to cultivate his country's growing economic, military and strategic connections with these lucrative markets for weapons, technology, and intelligence. And of course everyone who participated in this growing alliance, the PLO, the Hezbollah, and the Hamas, all shared at least one common goal: The extermination of every Jew on earth and the irradication of the loathsome State of Israel.

So it was a natural and quick transition from Moscow to Baghdad for Adolpho, when the Berlin Wall came crashing down and the Politboro collapsed in a mess of intrigue and anarchy. Imagine the delight that lit the countenance of Saddam Hussein when he learned that his long time Soviet envoy, archaeologist extraordinaire and top secret messenger was also a world class nuclear weapons expert; and he was attended by a whole cadre of technicians and scientists looking for lucrative work in a warm climate.

3.

"LUKE!! *LUKE, you get over here right now!!*" Jesse Landry straightened her aching back, wincing at the variety of snap, crackle and pop sounds produced by her tired spine, as she squinted against the sun. The June sky was all brass and cotton, heat waves warping the distant tree line, while the sounds of crickets, grasshoppers, and birds mixed with the voices of half a dozen women who also toiled amid the long rows of beans and sweet corn. But what Luke's mom wanted was for her dawdling son to bring her the bushel basket she had asked for some ten minutes earlier; they had produced a mighty pile of weeds and rocks for deposit at the edge of the woods.

The cornflower blue eyes looked with feigned innocence at the redheaded Irish woman whose temper he was sorely testing; there had been a necessary digression between loads of weeds. A black snake hid in the weeds along the woods, a large rat protruding from its mouth, feet still wiggling. Investigation of such a discovery could not be delayed.

"Sure, Mom, no problem—you shoulda' seen that big ol' snake, Mom, had that rat by the head and wouldn't let go fer love ner money!! Awesome, Mom, really—come see! Sucker's squirtin' blood all around his mouth! *Look!—*"

"Enough—*Luke Joseph Landry, you get your skinny little butt over here with that basket right now, or it'll be* **you** *I feed to the snakes!! Now* **move!**"

The boy's shoulders slumped in dejection, but he began to walk toward the garden again, his gaze back in the direction of the rat carnage. The smirks and giggles of the others, watching all this from the rows of beans, were punctuated by the cat calls and tauntings of his older sister, Jan.

"You *better* get over there, Luke, 'fore Mom jerks your jeans down and paddles your *beehind!*" The snake was suddenly forgotten, the boy's countenance darkening in an instant, as he took verbal aim at his mouthy sibling.

"*Shut-up, Whiner, er I'll tell* **Tommy** *'bout Sean Kingman—* fix your wagon fer sure, *Jan!* Maybe Tommy boy'd like ta know he's got competition in the spit swappin' department!! How 'bout *that*, Whiner? Huh?!" The teenager's face flushed, then blanched, a combined look of shock, anger, and terror at once flashing across her freckled mug. How could this scamp have known about Sean—about her new experiments into the world of first kisses—and how could he be so crass, so cruel, so very, horribly *Boy* about the whole thing?

Homicide seemed like an excellent idea. Then she realized that every woman in the area had heard her impudent little brother's retort, including her mother, who stood in slack-jawed amazement at the entire venomous exchange.

"**Luke**—the basket, please. Jan, best keep your smart mouth shut, unless there are no other revelations possible by your observant brother! We'll discuss this later." Her face strained mightily to maintain a severe gaze, the corners of her mouth quivered with the effort to conceal the smirk that tried to break free. Luke delivered the basket, scooping up little armloads of weeds and rocks; Jan searched the dirt between the bean rows, her face crimson, eyes wet with rage and embarrassment. Ah, the joys of family life.

Violence had given way to disappointed vigilance over the past six weeks, with fewer and fewer unwanted visitors venturing onto the Jericho Road. The havoc in the suburbs had provided most of the transportation and all the petroleum for the various thugs and soldiers of the unthinkable, but that seemed to be waning as well in recent weeks. The continued violence and visits from marauding gangs had succeeded in delaying food production and the first efforts to really begin life without electricity—or commerce.

The devastation to the electrical system throughout Iowa was beyond description. At least three major power substations had been destroyed in Richland alone, plus four in Des Moines and a similar number in Dubuque, Iowa City, and neighboring Omaha. Of course, the overall effect of this destruction was the collapse of the whole electrical power delivery network, nationwide—sort of like pulling out just the right wooden blocks in a child's castle, resulting in the fall of the whole thing.

Now it was time to face life on different terms, where lights were no longer the product of convenient plastic switches, where water ceased to magically appear at taps on the end of pressure tanks filled by electrical power, and where communications, entertainment, and even sewage treatment could no longer be expected.

A dozen homes, most of that were inhabited by families with at least part time farming operations dotted Jericho Road. A few, like the two Landry homes, housed professionals who worked in Richland, driving back to the country each evening. But they were not unaffected by their neighbors' lifestyles and self-sufficiency. Big gardens were the rule, and most had animals, too. Sam Childress, the stock broker, spent the days playing roulette on the big board and the evenings and weekends working with a small hog operation, some chickens, and eight beef cows. His kids showed the hogs in 4-H each year, and the eggs and fryers were a little micro-business for his wife, who essentially paid for most of their groceries with the proceeds from her sales of eggs and chickens to her neighbors.

All this had been a nice balance for these folks, money and prestige from profession and contentment from life in the country; they could afford a pretty affluent lifestyle because of their work in town, then avoid going nuts from the insane pace by coming home to their own farms. All this created a sort of de facto infrastructure that served to permit life to continue after the apocalypse that left the country in powerless darkness.

The biggest problem with turning all these little mini-farms into real food producers was the timing. It was March when the lights went out, and nobody could even *begin* to prepare for food production before the middle of April—for crops that would not produce food for several months after that. Then there was the violence to be dealt with.

The rioting, looting, and intensely violent rhetoric surrounding the aftermath of the Rodney King verdict, including the Reginald Denny beating and the burning of major portions of East L.A., made it pretty clear that the American version of Homo sapiens was as dangerous and volatile as any other copy, anywhere else on earth. So when everyone, regardless of economic condition or geographic location, fell victim to the same catastrophic loss at the same time, the Devil's own agents wasted no time in capitalizing on the situation.

For the rest of March, all of April, and the first week of May the only way to survive for the folks on Jericho Road was to band together, provide common, defensible positions for the protection of their families, and wait for the wide variety of maniacs to run out of gas and ammunition.

Now, with the early June sun constantly announcing that summer was in fact here again, the families ventured out of their fortified positions and into the fields and gardens. They worked with a zeal born of necessity, a purpose to overcome these challenges, and a unity that only suffering and fighting together can produce. And they worked under the watchful, concealed protection of armed sentries. Even though the daily firefights had given way first to more sporadic engagements, then finally to an uneasy quiet that saw only occasional strange vehicles on the dusty road, they took no chances.

Marshalling men, weapons, and ammunition, the guys readily accepted the directives that Josh Landry issued regarding some of the finer military points of perimeter defense and covert surveillance. The toll on all resources had been dramatic, even though "crazy Doc L." had amassed over a thousand rounds of 5.56mm ammunition, two cases of 12-gauge buckshot, and fifteen hundred rounds of .45 caliber pistol ammunition. Of course, being country people anyway, everybody had weapons of some kind. Hunting pieces, double-barreled shotguns, and .22 caliber rifles, mostly; several also possessed more high powered stuff, like .30/.30 Winchesters, bolt action .30/06s, and Ruger "ranch rifles," also chambered to shoot the 5.56.

These were sufficient to repel the many raids that so terrorized wide areas of the country over the months since the blackout commenced, but injuries were common, and a total of five defenders and seven non-combatants had died. The small band of neighbors fought a total of thirteen engagements with well-armed and vicious gangs of thugs; none of the attackers was permitted to survive.

"Boys, what we have to do is kill these people. We cannot provide the wounded with medical attention, as our supplies and personnel are insufficient even for our own. Shoot to kill," Josh had admonished his assembled ragtag defense force after the first such battle.

"Anybody you shoot, you finish. You may be confident that anyone who comes up this road or into one of our driveways, armed and shooting at us, is not here on a peace mission. We are all the law there is, and when we're gone, they'll overrun the place; I need not tell you what that would mean for our wives and children. One thing we cannot permit to happen is a big mess of bleeding bad guys sucking up our few medical resources. If they show up, they die."

And so it was. Indeed, no one who ventured into the area and engaged these people survived the experience. Thirty-eight bodies occupied the shady outdoor morgue, in the woods south of Carl's house, until a long-overdue National Guard patrol finally passed through the second week of May. An ashen faced Captain—a finance officer pressed into a combat assignment because of the absence of most of the personnel who were trained for such duty—stood with mouth agape, staring at the incomprehensible sight of all the dead bodies laid out in that shady cemetery. "Dearest Jesus, Dr. Landry, you kill all these people yourself? M'god, man, there's gotta be twenty—maybe thirty—"

"There are thirty-eight we've killed, and twelve more of our own who we've already buried. As you can see, waiting for you boys to show up was not an option." Carl's point was not lost on these men, although the astounded soldier made no response to the elder Landry's bluntness. The captain recounted similar discoveries by other such patrols, and rumor had it that such experiences were common. The next day a big olive-drab truck with a canvas-covered bed appeared back at Carl's, and a squad of Guardsmen proceeded to load the ripening bodies. What the Landrys could not know, but what the soldiers were quickly learning, was that the ultimate disposal of human remains was becoming one of the biggest jobs—and *the* biggest public health concern—of all. Carl and Josh were glad enough just to see the big deuce-and-a-half rumble off down the dusty lane and out of sight, its grisly cargo a horrific, tragic load of macabre memories that would remain with them for the rest of their lives.

Jess and the small group of girls and women working in the Landry's big garden talked and laughed, gossiped and sang, the joy of being out of those dark basements and into the sunshine over-shadowing the more stark and sad realities they faced. Two young men sat hidden in the trees, one to either side of the woods-edge garden plot, their eyes searching the roads, tractor trails, and footpaths in every direction. Twice there had been incursions by small remnants of the gangs, and twice the results were the same. Reacting to the signals they heard from the invisible guards, the women quickly gathered together, moved off into the edge of the woods, lay flat on the ground.

The sentries waited until the thugs were too close to miss, then opened fire, continuing until every one of the enemies was down. It had been three weeks since the last unknown vehicle was spotted, and five weeks since the last shootout, but the vigilance continued. Now, in the warmth of summer, working with people of common mind and shared goals, the young marksmen provided a much appreciated measure of security and sense of safety—a welcome change from the days and nights of terror, gunfire, and blood so recently endured.

They finished a final hour of weeding, watered the crops of vegetables and tomatoes with many hand-drawn buckets of water, and gathered up to go home. Tomorrow they would meet at another location, performing the same work there.

The Landry contingent served up cool drinks from the deep well that had served the place for three generations—a hand pump stood in rusty but serviceable condition, centered on a silver-gray wooden platform of boards that had to be at least seventy-five years old. A big diesel generator purchased by Josh at the bankruptcy sale of the assets of a big highway construction company some years before, provided replacement electricity for house water, also running the furnace, appliances, and lights. Of course, the supply of diesel fuel was far from inexhaustible; the big generator was used sparingly to provide necessities—heat in the coldest of times, water for drinking and sanitation, and lights when needed to work at night.

When Carl and his associate were tending to the sick and wounded at night, the generator was moved to his house to perform the same functions. Smaller gasoline generators provided power for tools, sump pumps, and lights for barns and stables. Far less than convenient, these wonders of modern science made it possible for the whole clan to continue to care for themselves and others. But just how much caring would be required, and for how long, was a dark unknown to the folk of Jericho Road.

311

4.

"You assholes gon' be toast, just like those pricks up the street, you keep trackin' this way! You hear that? We got all the guns and ammo we could steal, and now we got all those dead pricks had too, so, y'all c'mon up this street—we feed you ta the dogs jus' like we did them pricks!!" The hollow, metallic echo of the megaphone-amplified angry voice bounced off the walls of the high tenements, the origin made difficult to identify by the reverberations and the crying and screams of unseen children.

Lt. Ryan Hathaway, platoon leader of the 1st Platoon, A Co., 4th Battalion, (what was left of) 2d Division, Iowa National Guard, spun around into the grimy faces of two of his squad leaders, who were huddled with their men behind a burned out bus. The thing lay on its side diagonally across the middle of an intersection.

"Wha—where the hell did they—oh. . .bet that's *our* bullhorn they're using. . .I remember that Schockley had one in his Hummer. Used it last week to talk some refugees out of that woods in the park. Holy—they really *did* clean 'em out. ." Moments ago, they had come upon the corpses of five Guardsmen in a burned out HumVee personnel vehicle, the machine having obviously been destroyed by some kind of high explosive charge, apparently fired at them from some distance. Lt. Gene Schockley, Platoon leader of 2d platoon and close friend to Hathaway, was burned almost beyond recognition in the front seat of the truck.

Even in the midst of the intensity of the moment, the small bunch of soldiers now looked blankly, empty eyes searching each other's faces for some sense or meaning to what had happened and what was going on before them. Then the insulting slap of the bullhorn shattered the moment of lostness again.

"Hey, you honky pigs, slide on 'roun' that corner an' let us make cinders out'chore white ass, too—got some more home-made hell for all comers, boys, plus two LAWS an' a grenade launcher! SEE?—" A short pause of ear-ringing silence was punctuated by two quick reports, *"Thunk!—Thunk!"* Another moment of emptiness, then two wicked explosions within three feet of each other, landing side by side in front of the

bumper of the bus. *WHUM—WHUMPPP!!* The massive frame of the big passenger vehicle grunted, lifted clear of the ground in the front end a foot or more, shuddered a foot back into the men hiding behind it, and crashed heavily back to the pavement.

The street shook from all these impacts, the two explosions and the huge crash of the bus, and the deafening roar of all three so disoriented the soldiers that nobody initially apprehended the fact that the bus had fallen directly on the backs and heads of two men. Hathaway stared momentarily in uncomprehending shock at the violently shaking legs of both men; they first kicked, flailed wildly, as if to crawl out of the grip of the huge object, then twitched briefly into deadly stillness. The whole remaining contingent of the platoon seemed simultaneously to see the pool of blood oozing from under the bus—at the same time reacting to the realization that they were *completely* exposed, the big bus having been only a false breastwork of defense.

"Get back*!!—movemovemove—get back—scatter left and right—, now gogogo—stay low and move out—haulass-go-go-go—now-now-now GO!!!*" The men erupted in an instant ant-like scattering pattern, left, right, and straight back. One medic lunged for the two dead, reaching their exposed legs just as the Lieutenant snatched a huge handful of the back of his BDU shirt and jerked him to the ground.

"*Disregard, Doc, DISREGARD! They're gone—can't do shit for 'em now and I can't be losin' you for two dead men—now GO!!!GO GO GO!!—*"

The pandemonium went delirious as the medic scooted on his butt back away from the corpses, at first crabbing backwards on heels and hands cartoon-like, then spinning over to a hands-and-feet-running movement in a wide arc toward the empty hole that once had been the front window of a drugstore. A fusillade of automatic weapons fire strafed the belly of the overturned bus, a shower of sparks, asphalt, rocks, and miscellaneous shards of glass and bus parts tumbling wildly in a wide radius around the center of the intersection.

Hathaway flattened himself on the pavement, at first pressing his entire form against the tall expanse of the roof of the bus, then lurching away from it as his mind played the

3-D mental photo of the two crushed soldiers beside him. Jumping away, high velocity bullets whistled past his ears, a powerful *snap!* instantaneously slapping him with the reality that one of the projectiles had just ripped through his backpack. Flat again on the hot pavement for a moment, then a cry of prayer and epithet mixed as he hurled himself for the opposite sidewalk, where an angling alley cut between the buildings just shy of the corner.

Dearest Jesus, here I come—forgive me, Lord—I just can't lay here and get poked full a' holes like this—Lord—save this worthless —! He ran crouched over, long strides eating up the distance.

Fifty feet became twenty, then ten feet, as the sound of the bullets smashing into the bus frame and the street became more distant to his ears. Then, just five feet short of the cover of the corner of that one building wall forming the end of the alley, a quick breath of silence was followed instantly by a hail of bullets, brick fragments and glass over his head. Diving into the shadow of the wall, the lieutenant instinctively covered his helmeted head and exposed neck with both hands and forearms, the rain of hot shrapnel singing all around him.

Another quick pause, then a renewed roar from the automatic weapon. *Can't even see where the bastards are hiding!! How am I supposed to shoot back if I ca*—Bullets whined and whistled like metallic hornets all around the walls above his head, while the lone soldier tried to squeeze his body through the space formed by the union of the wall with the street. Then a combination of primal rage, exasperation, and frustration hit him like one of those big bullets.

"ENOUGH, you assholes, that is E-NOUGH!!!" Ryan Hathaway completely forgot himself, his human body's frailty, and any fragment of concern for his life, so passionate became his fury, as he rolled up on one knee while pulling his M16 to his shoulder. He leaned against the corner of the wall, preparing to shoot left-handed, as his now acute vision searched for the origin of fire. Even the primal warrior keeps his instinctive skills of war, and he knew without saying or even thinking it that they had to be visible in order for them to be firing at his position. Can't be any other way.

Book III – Starting Over, Fighting Back

There—he's got Schockley's machinegun! He raised the rifle to his shoulder and commenced firing at the same time, the comparatively short distance of about seventy-five yards to a glassless window of the first tenement building in that block making the shot easy. A large black man stood bare-chested in the window, a bandolier of machinegun ammunition draped over his shoulder and down into the big gun. He held it to his chest, the stock under his arm, firing steadily and with obviously practiced skill. But he was not, at the moment, shooting into the alley. Ryan Hathaway acquired him in his sights. The hail of fire from the window was at that precise second directed at the men cowering in the pharmacy on the other side of the street.

The lieutenant's rifle fired semi-auto, each shot quickly aimed before being fired, yet with the rounds sizzling downrange no more than a second apart. A subtle flash of sparks signaled that a bullet had hit the machinegun on top of the receiver assembly, the projectile, ricocheting straight up. The big black gunner's head split in half vertically as the bullet struck the exact middle of his chin. Two more bullets blew through his throat and upper chest before his already dead body could fall out of sight and back into the room. More silence now, real silence. Nobody could hear anything, all ears temporarily deafened by the thundering roar of the firefight.

As it turned out, the only origin of fire was that stolen M60, taken from the back of the bombed out Hummer. Of course, everybody knew there were more rifles trained on the street further down, and *many* more of the mixture of thugs, militants, terrorists, and crazies who had made the pacification of this town impossible for three months. Even though the Guard was armed with military weapons and support, these evil bastards appeared to have a great arsenal of surprises that kept the Guardsmen and local law enforcement from being able to root them out.

Such people had been able long ago to gain access, on the Internet and other places as well, to the formulae for a wide variety of high explosives and contraband weapons. Worse yet, the same media fomented an array of violent, even inhuman practices aimed at children and women. Over and over during the past months, Hathaway and his men had discovered the bodies of raped, mutilated and murdered small

315

children and women of all ages, unfortunate enough to have fallen into their hands.

Wading through the aftermath of what these men left as they continued to evade capture, no one could doubt that they remained purposeful in their depravities, taking obvious sadistic pleasure in these horrible pastimes.

"Red Platoon, Red 1, the machinegun is out—repeat, I have taken out the big gun. Report your status by squad." In turn, each of the four squads that formed the platoon was heard to report in, voices shaky, positions most tenuous. The only casualties in this brief engagement were the two guys crushed by the bus. Now it was time to get some help and flush out the rest of the vermin. The haunting wail of children crying, punctuated occasionally by a blood curdling scream that obviously came from a woman, added even more urgency to the moment.

"Alpha Black, 6, this is Alpha Red 1, do you read me?" A quick response at least let Hathaway start breathing again. He reported the recent results, adding the part about the screaming and crying. They promised immediate reinforcements, as everybody had been looking for these people for weeks, only finding them, as these soldiers just had, at times when they possessed insufficient information and troop strength to respond effectively. However, the Guardsmen now at work in Richland were becoming very good at what they did. Urban guerrilla warfare had not been much in the future plans of most of them, but they figured it out quickly once the fighting started.

Heat and increased mobility by the enemy replaced the frozen standoffs of the first few weeks so that now, without the need to avoid the elements, the bad guys were really getting into gear. The group now being pursued by A Company was a strange mixture of Black Panthers and local street gang members, including one band of Mexicans and a clutch of white boys who just seemed to have a taste for combat. And torture. Most of their targets were women and smaller children, making the passion to eradicate them all the more intense. Soldiers constantly marveled at the knack these awful people had for finding and controlling what few supplies of food remained in town. And of course, might made for control, and they were the only people in town who were armed, so there was little real competition for that small supply.

The lieutenant looked behind him, up the street, and smiled a mean smile as he saw two APCs, in front of about twenty foot soldiers jogging along with weapons held at port arms. Time to kick some terrorist ass and settle a particularly personal score.

5.

It was early in the night for the radio chatter to begin but, with the advent of warmer weather and the reduction in more risky endeavors for the country folk, the HAM comrades were heating up the airwaves by 10 p.m. And although the violence had tapered off for some, the net was all ears for word from Bakersfield concerning the state of near civil war that continued to burn in L.A. Bonnie reported with a voice heavily laced with excitement—even agitation—and profound sadness, as the lifelong resident of Southern California described recent developments.

"See, boys, the problem is not just that we have rioting and looting—that's bad enough. But what we're learning is that the long history of gang presence and the horrible relationships between the folks in the rough parts of the city athe nd police had already made L.A. a near perfect environment for anarchy. Even New York had a hard time matching La La Land for complete chaos!"

She went on holding forth, a firsthand observer, on the nasty sociology of life in those crime-infested ghettos. Years of gangland warfare by large groups of young men, long in the business of amassing weapons, learning to build explosives, and practicing the skills of killing, produced a very advanced form of urban guerilla. Where a town like Chicago or St. Louis might have a few hundred really militant, hardcore criminal gang members with the stomach for long-term mayhem, L.A. had thousands. Most of them had lived the life of drive-by shootings, turf wars, and police assassinations on a daily basis for many years. Therefore their evil infrastructure, leadership, and even knowledge of how to kill without fear of capture made them a pack of mad dogs the likes of that the country had not seen since the days of Cantrell's Raiders during and after the Civil War.

"Looks like what's left of the National Guard is really in over its head. Rumor has it that the President is sending a big contingent of the forces coming home from Saudi directly to Southern California; guess we're gonna get upwards of five, maybe ten thousand combat troops, including armor and some air support! Jesus, guys, but that breaks my heart. I mean, we really need the help, and if they don't hurry up, the place'll look more like Somalia—warlords and all—than anything remotely resembling my old home town. But still, the idea of tanks rolling through the streets, and all the innocents who will suffer."

Her voice trailed off, thick with sadness and emotion. A long moment passed across the dark miles, then Sig broke the silence. "Yah, yah, Bonnie, I oonnerstaand all dis. . .some a' my people moved away and lived in Budapest back in da' fifties—broke der hearts, all dat killin' an' tanks an' machinegun fire. . . dey excape—got home wit der skins, prais Got, dat's wut *I* say—prais Got, dey got out wit der skins. . ." He, too, went momentarily quiet. Then he picked up again.

"But hey Bon, don't you tink dos assholes will give up and run like dogs when the Army comes? Eh? Dat's wut happen't when dos assholes come out from Minneapolis—ya!. . .Ol' Helmer Gaille an' da boys, dey make da nice surprise for dos assholes—ran away like chickenshit, dat's wut. . .dat's right— a taste a da real ting from some bad ass G.I.s—dat's wut gon fix all *dat* shit—yah. . ."

Bonnie felt the gentle cadence of the Scandinavian's efforts to draw them closer; certainly, the experiences of his family in Europe during the '50s was more than a little relevant to what she felt now. And then there had been virtually no hope of an end or a return to peace. The communists had taken everything, including thousands of people's lives. She could only hope that the conflagration about to erupt in L.A. would end in a different result. Al, from Nashville, interrupted her musings.

"Listen, you guys, don't count us out just yet. Those last two radio broadcasts by the President have been pretty hot stuff, ya' know? Sounds like a '90s Churchill to me. No jive, and no "big brother." He just keeps telling us we gotta pull together, restore order, and take care of each other for now. It may be hot now, but winter is coming, and we may still have no electricity by then.

"He's right, for sure. So far, we've been able to keep the home fires burning around here, but there's so much to do! Only folks who're gonna survive are those who find a way to work together. Can't wait on the government to come through with supplies—hell, can't really even count on them to stop the crazies from tryin' ta burn things down!

"Biggest problem I see is what's gonna happen to all those folks who live in the cities. Dearest Jesus, but I hope they

319

can find some peace, *and some food*—soon. I hear there's folks dying of starvation all over the place; I was listening in late the other night when two guys were talking on the net. One was from White Plains, New York, the other a guy from Montreal—spoke pretty good English, but with a heavy accent.

"Get ready for this one, guys: The death toll in NYC proper, just from exposure and malnutrition, has reached at least one hundred thousand!! That's not including the deaths from all the rioting and the natural causes list. Boys and girls, things ain't pretty, and the dance has just begun. I gotta run, people. Batteries gettin' low, and I gotta roll out early to go work a big garden plot the folks in town have going. Hang in there, everbody, this is Nashville—*out.*"

The conversation faded quickly after that last mind-bending statistic, and everybody decided to save their batteries, too. But nobody who had been on the net that night could avoid the vision of death that Al described. Suddenly, all the cynical talk about meltdown, all the crass "tough shitsky" banter of prior times concerning the plight of the cities, left a really bad taste. Trying to sleep, each of them tried—and tried *not to*—imagine such an unthinkable result in the Big Apple, in Philly, Dallas, and yes, even in La La Land. Prayers into the darkness; pleas to Almighty God for mercy. Divine mercy. Lots of it.

6.

The midday buzz in the White House was at its usual level, the phones ringing, papers shuffling, the smell of a catered luncheon for Congressional leaders and the Cabinet filling the whole place with hunger pangs. Even in the midst of crisis, supplies for these events always seemed to become available, it being the President's lifelong belief that hard work was best done by well-fed troops, although the fare was much more basic, and far less chic, than was typical of fatter times. "Troops" were what the boys and girls from Capitol Hill felt like by the time they finished every encounter with General Jackie. No matter the subject, no matter the time or nature of the event, his energy, charisma, at times his overpowering intimidation, and even his unremitting line of hyperbole, was always in evidence.

There was a growing lore surrounding the man, much of that was well grounded in the truth, but some of that seemed to be growing out of a kind of powerful admiration for the man in all his incarnations—albeit begrudgingly at times. When it was his loyal opposition from the liberal side of the aisle that found itself so incapable of avoiding capture by this dynamo of charisma and savoir faire, they tried valiantly to avoid defeat, but typically to no avail.

He was Ronald Reagan without the sense of royalty, all full of self-deprecating humor and gentle banter; Jimmy Carter but with grit and a roaring energy so thinly hidden behind the gentle approach. He was Jack Kennedy with roots, devoid of "slick," witty without being arcane or condescending. More Harry Truman than anything else, his terse, linear style of analysis and problem solving took no joy in the wanderings and whinings of liberals who tried—without success—to inject those ridiculous little sociological guilt trips into every effort at progress. And clearly, he was not about to embrace *any* course that would dress the country in the hair shirt of blaming, or any solution that would create more and more immoral dependency on the government by the American people.

This president believed that the one positive result he could accomplish through all the pain and tragedy of this time was that these people were going to be contributors in their own recovery. They were going to help each other, and they were going to forge a new ethic about who they were and whose responsibility it was going to be for the architecture of the nature and content of their collective futures. So every speech, every radio message, every quotation, was laced with that singular message: Self-reliance, cooperation, care and concern for each other, and a relentless toughness toward the forces of evil that so ravaged the country. And it was working.

Every meeting was replete with reports about the neighbor-hoods, the communities, the entire cities, that had organized themselves, pooled resources, weapons, medical supplies, food, shelter, and survived the end of winter and even the ravages of rioting and terrorism. He promised—and *delivered*—food and medicine, the resources needed to rebuild. He did not foster or permit "programs" that would create additional dependencies in people already in such a mess for the precise reason that they were too dependent.

So with every meeting there was that undertone of self-reliance, that intolerance for whining, that insistence on the reward for courage, compassion, initiative; no different today. The Cabinet was joined by the joint leadership of both houses of Congress, plus Mack Reed and, of course, Jonathan Montgomery Brooks.

The subject was the use and deployment of the troops returning from Saudi Arabia, and the discussion centered on the number and types of forces to be used in the two most difficult places, New York and Los Angeles. "People, things are so badly out of hand in these two cities that I firmly believe we may lose them both, and much of their populations, unless drastic—and *dramatic*—actions are taken at once. Certainly we stand to lose the entirety of the inestimable architecture, priceless art, and scholarship this country holds dear unless we can take NYC back from the bastards that are tearing it up as we speak. Nothing less than a systematic occupation, block by block if necessary, will do.

"And with regard to L.A., it may already be too late for such measures there. I was briefed late last night by the Adjutant General of the California National Guard, who had Governor Simonson with him; they made it clear that conventional law enforcement, even with the military assistance of the Guard, has been essentially neutralized. The place is no longer up for grabs—it is firmly in the hands of the warlords whose gangs were so well entrenched even before the blackout began. Sadly, the people of California had lost control well before all this. The best advice I have received suggests that an effort to completely evacuate the population of East L.A., Watts, and much of the outlying areas, under such heavy guard and air cover as is required, must be accomplished *before* we can address what to do with the huge army of gangland thugs that now control the place. As brutal as it sounds, we may have to mount a full scale invasion of the place and take it apart, one brick at a time, if necessary."

The room was silent as a mausoleum. Eyes searched empty plates, napkins scuffed across pained faces and knit brows, a fork or two softly clanked to a salad plate. The chairman of the House Ways and Means Committee, an old conservative Republican named Emmanuel Sofsky, took a long, deep breath, the telegraphed pre-cursor to his every statement, and raised his shaggy, white-maned head in the direction of the president.

"Mr. President, I was born in the Bronx, sixty-three years ago next week; as you know, I was educated there, left on the boat for the sunny shores of Normandy right out through the East River, and raised seven children within six-tenths of a mile from the place where I was born. I am sure you also know that, although I have been proud to support you on so many matters over these past months, I am no fan of your military bravado—or your predisposition toward the use of force.

"All too often, Mr. President, *with all due respect, sir,* you seem ever too willing to turn the wrath of automatic weapons loose on our problems. And on our adversaries. I am sure there are those in this room who are confident *they* have endured that precise firepower emanating from yourself. . ." A soft rustle of smiles, smirks, and a chuckle or two moved the close air of the dining room, as yet another one of those lore-inducing references to the indominatability of this president hit home. Webb flushed for a moment, but did not speak.

The Chairman was a man to be heard completely before responding.

"Now, having said all that, I must add that there *are times* when the swift, powerful, violent decisiveness of such action is the only hope for success. And, *again, with all due respect, sir,* tell us what you propose, and let's rid ourselves of these animals before they succeed in torturing the entire population of my beloved New York City into extinction, and all her priceless treasures with them!"

A moment's stark stillness was followed by commencement of one of those low murmurings, like what they do in the British House of Commons in accord with the thoughts expressed by one of the MPs. This murmuring quickly gathered air and depth, several of the number addressing each other approvingly while still watching the Chairman and the President intently.

"Well bygod, Manny you old goat, now *that's* no *shit!* You're finally makin' some sense—'course, it's about time, too, 'fore the riffraff levels the place!" An ancient politician at the end of the table instantly had the attention of the assembly.

"All this goddam talk about 'alternative responses,' 'measured reactions,' and 'cautious progress' has been nothin' more 'n a huge waste a' time and energy. I been sorry as *hell* ta have sat through so many debates these last weeks about what ta do when the nastiest variety of Homo sapiens on earth is tearing apart our country—hell, we been actin' like a platoon a' hookers trapped in the convent—can't decide whether ta join the nuns or dance with the priest! Now let's get on with it! Amen, Manny, bygod, *AMEN!!*—Mr. President, what's the plan?"

Nathaniel Greenlea Johnstone, senior senator from the state of Mississippi, was one of the most colorful, excitable, irascible, and brilliant personalities in all of politics. At seventy-two years of age, he was the only person in the room senior to Chairman Sofsky, and the two had been terrorizing the halls of Congress together for most of the last quarter century. Although the laughter generated by his wild simile seemed to release a groundswell of tension previously choking the assembled company, his humor and unique qualities of description also helped the others see clearly just how fundamentally important this decision was. They also recognized, without exception, that it was the *right* decision. In six days, a total of twenty-five thousand Army and Marine troops would be back on the ground in the U.S., and Webb knew exactly what he was going to do with all of them.

Before he adjourned the meeting, he outlined the plans, set out the order of priorities and the time frames, asked for and received the approval of every person in the room. An entire population of heretofore-free persons were the hostages of depravity and horror, most inexplicably at the hands of their own countrymen. They had no hope without swift, decisive action, violent and deadly—so much so that the specter of some of them dying in the struggle made more sense than letting them continue to die en masse of starvation, beatings, torture, and disease. The United States would reclaim its cities and liberate its people from the hands of Satan himself. Soon.

7.

King Nebuchadnezzar ran a tight ship. A man of vision and high intellect, he was also a general whose leadership produced one of the world's great empires; he was a warrior of violent, even vicious resolve when faced with an adversary or recalcitrant captive. After twice sacking Jerusalem but leaving the Jews mostly in place, he grew weary of their pesky refusals to follow the dictates of his vassal leadership. The place was leveled, the last king blinded so that he would not have to "see" his countrymen forced into captivity—but only after slaying all his sons while the king watched. Not a man to be trifled with.

The great empire over that Nebuchadnezzar ruled was, of course, Babylon, the great pearl of the Fertile Crescent, the prized seat of the Cradle of Civilization, a city so beautiful and so wealthy, that every new, emerging power coveted possessing it. Cyrus the Persian, in league with the Medes, took it from Nebuchadnezzar's slothful, drunken descendant, Belshazzer, without a battle, simply by damming up the Euphrates above the city, exposing the fortifications' underbelly to surreptitious infiltration. They just walked in under the fortifications. The Persians had control of the city for several days before the young king even knew they were there.

The Medes, after ascending above the Persians, lost it to the great Alexander, and later the Romans took it, sacked it. But the city clad in gold, that gemstone of ancient times, where the Jews lived seventy years in captivity as their own Scriptures had foretold, has never really been gone from the mind of Eastern man. From the days of Nimrod and the infamous "Tower of Babel," when God scattered the world's people and confused their language into "babbling," this has been a place of intrigue, lust, and power. No surprise that the man who likens himself to, and claims blood kinship with, Nebuchadnezzar, Saddam Hussein, would seek to rebuild the ancient capitol to its previous splendor.

The historic halls, palaces, and battlements have been meticulously reconstructed, including the expenditure of millions of dollars' worth of precious metals and stones to restore that ancient opulence about that so much has been written. SoDamnInsane holds affairs of state there regularly, and work continues apace to expand the grandeur, to call back into being that one greatest of ancient cities—and all its mystical powers, excesses, and intrigues.

Adolpho Weidenolf lay supine, his back pressed down against the cool hardness of reinforced concrete, while his face cleared by an inch or two the awesome array of circuit boards, wires, and microchips that made up the infrastructure and micro-architecture of his masterpiece of telemetry and ballistics. There was such a perfect contrast between the almost chill sensation at his back and the intense heat in his face that concentration at times seemed impossible, lying there four stories below the floor of the Grand Palace in Babylon. Then, in one more of those predictable attacks of claustrophobia, he demanded immediate extraction.

"E*NOUGH!!* Extract me—*EXTRACT ME NOW!!*" Two young technicians instantly darted to opposite corners of the undercarriage where the old man lay, firmly grasping an ankle apiece. He was lying on a slick, thin sheet of plastic, specially fabricated to avoid static electricity, but slick and strong enough to permit movement. They simply pulled the aging fanatic out by his legs, quickly helping him into a sitting position while handing him a large jug of ice water.

"Goddammit, but I *hate it* in that carriage!! Unless we can find that one glitch that is derailing the secondary telemetry coordinates package for the number two launch sequence soon, I swear I'm going to blow the thing to kingdom come myself, then just use a case of dynamite to take out Tel Aviv!! *Shit,* but I'm sick of that maze of circuitry under there. You young men remind me, next time, not to design these things so that the most sensitive and temperamental components end up *on the bottom!*"

He gulped from the large jar of water, drained it and shoved it at one of the kids for a quick refill. Draining it again, he motioned to be helped up, and they began to follow him over to the ladder that ascended the four floor-deep cavern beneath the Grand Palace's botanical gardens. Simplicity and quiet demanded the absence of anything so cumbersome or obvious as an elevator apparatus, so the only way down into the bowels of the operation was via a narrow steel ladder. After climbing up three floors, or about thirty feet, they could walk over the floor of what otherwise would have been the basement to a flight of regular stairs, and enter the main part of the Palace from there.

There in the Grand Palace, the botanical garden architecture made a perfect concealment for Adolpho's fine weapon of mass destruction. It was covered on top by an ornate series of half domes, scalloped geometric shapes, and decorative roof designs, all held up by round columns that also formed part of the design and decor of the garden area. Very intricate, very tasteful, and architecturally accurate, and apparently very permanent. However, the southern third of the roof covering was set on pillars that only *looked* permanent. In fact, this portion of the supporting columns was set on massive rollers, the rollers in turn set in tracks connected to massive electric motors located and concealed beneath the floor of what appeared to be the basement. The tracks themselves lay beneath perfect inlays of marble, all of that could be removed in seconds, revealing the strong rails beneath.

When the proper sequence of commands was sent through a computer controlled console, and after the proper entry of authorization and encryption codes, these motors simply pulled the entire southern third of the roof line to the north about thirty feet, the pillars ingeniously moving precisely between the stationary columns that held up the non-moving portion of the roof. The height of the moving part of the cover was two inches greater than that of the nonmoving parts, so that as the pillars moved north, the southern third of the roof simply slipped over the rest, exposing the floor of the gardens to the sky. The floor then parted in thirds, fanning out and away to leave the basement open to a dimension of forty feet each way.

High, tempered-steel shielding then appeared vertically, as the floor of the "basement" also parted and the nosecone of the first of two stacked missiles pointed at the heavens. Pretty slick, really, and not all that complicated to build *or to conceal.* Oh, to be sure, there had been times when the construction activities were "sensitive," as when the deep excavation for the modified silo cavity was being dug to a depth of fifty feet; there was also the problem of satellite observation of such activities. So, much of it was done at night, during the rainy season, and in as confused and disjointed a manner as possible. Actually, the big hole itself had taken only eight days to dig and a week to shore up and support, before the footings and forms for the concrete ceiling—also the *floor* of the basement—could be set and poured.

After the completion of the deep excavation and its concealment, the rest was much easier; Saddam even invited the gullible folks from *National Geographic* to come observe on occasion, so they could tell all the world how he was re-manufacturing the grandeur of Mystic Babylon. Things like tracking and the gearing and mechanical operation of the moving floors and pillars were simply done before anybody got there to see what was going on. A temporary covering over the entire site was of no real significance from the air, or from the ground either, as the only way to keep the heat from becoming unbearable on the work area was to keep it covered with canvas. It took less than ninety days to complete the excavation, the mechanical installations, and make the place impervious to detection from outside.

From then on, throughout the last half of 1996, Weidenolf and his little band of geniuses busied themselves fabricating many of the more bulky parts for two missiles on location in Babylon. Most of the smaller assemblies were actually put together in the hole, tested and re-tested to the finest tolerances in a makeshift computer lab that sat in a cave-like depression in the wall of the excavation, down twenty feet. A series of pulleys, two hydraulic lifts, and a system of ladders and platforms descending beside the missile cylinders completed the amazingly simple arrangements for assembly of the big birds. They lay at a forty-five degree angle on their sides in the big hole, not vertical as was common in the bigger ICBM tubes of Cold War days.

"Now, my friends, let us first cool off, then return to the hole and the remainder of my adjustments. Then it's back to the computer lab to test everything. Our client has asked in the firmest of terms that we make an end to this as soon as possible. It is my profound sense that we must deliver the product within days, or suffer the ire of a man we all know to be capable of genocide. I have not lived this long just to die at the hand of *that* madman! The design is perfect, the target well within our capability and range, and the warheads well suited to the task of killing Jews. Come—we'll finish the testing, run the entire protocol of simulations three times just to be sure, then report the project complete."

They all felt the relief of seeing the end of the tunnel, the lifting of the weight of working under the demands of one so capricious and dangerous as Saddam. They spoke with increasing animation about the series of tests that would, they were certain, declare that their weapons were ready for launch. And just like that, one million people would die.

8.

Roxanne was a force never to be ignored. She was loud, impetuous, and at times plainly vulgar; she was barely sixteen years old. Her voice was piercing, her manner intense, her agenda constantly clear, whatever it might be. Pretty in her way, rather tall and shapely but too thin, this refugee from the urban wars of Richland made her presence known at once when the first helicopter full of women and babies touched down at the Guard Armory; wrapped in an olive drab blanket and holding an infant against her, she spotted Andrew Whitaker instantly.

"*HEY—HEY YOU THERE—YOU THE GUY THAT ORDERED US OUTTA THAT HELLHOLE??!!* Well, ARE YA'?? LOOK, GIRLS, THERE'S THE BOSS—OOPS!—SHIT, GIRLS, IF THAT AIN'T A REAL LIVE GENERAL—DEAREST LORD GOD IN HEAVEN—LOOKIE THERE!!" With that fanfare and announcement, she broke ranks with the line of youngsters following her, each also clutching a baby, and ran in a straight line toward the stunned general, who stood, mouth agape, as the assault unfolded. She looked like a cross between an escapee from an asylum and a kid who'd just gotten off the school bus—except of course, for the baby in her arms. Her blanket began to slip from her slender shoulders as she ran, her mouth open wide in a continuing string of squeals, shrieks, and unintelligible epithets as she ran toward him. As the covering fell away, Whitaker's attitude changed instantly from disbelief first to embarrassment, then painful sadness, to overwhelming compassion and shock.

She was frail, her dark skin mottled and blotchy, dried blood streaking her neck and fragile shoulders. She was naked except for the tatters of a pair of ragged jeans, so that only the tiny form or her swaddled baby covered her torso. Wounds were obvious across her shoulders, a crust of scabbing and nasty pieces of tattered bandage hung from numerous lacerations and abrasions all over her chest and abdomen; the jeans were open in front where the zipper had torn loose. Her thick hair was matted to her head and the back of her neck, a mass of knots, twists, and filthy, crusty blood. An old cut in her scalp was glaring through a part in the thick matting of hair. The man was transfixed, at once repulsed and drawn overpoweringly to the form of this child running toward him.

The arrival of the first chopper—actually two had arrived at the same time—drew a crowd consisting of every person in the place. Besides the medics and the women who had volunteered to assist with the moms and their babies, all the clerks, the motorpool guys, the cooks, even the communications crew that was *never* off duty, lined up to watch them unload. And nobody was ready for what they saw. Roxanne's ebullience was *not* the norm, as most were scared to death, and of the thirty-some women being evacuated, thirteen were non-ambulatory. Of the rest, there were eight more who could not walk without help, and every one of them was so weak and depleted that the one hundred foot walk from the touchdown point to the door of the building was all they could do.

Will Brandt, the Sp4 who did most of what the general needed done, stood outside the building beside him, along with a nurse and one of the women volunteers, as they watched the unloading begin. The penetrating noise emanating from Roxanne's throat was replaced with the deep, raspy, heaving sounds of sobbing, out of control, as her form fell against him. Her strength seemed to give out as she reached him, her delicate body convulsing on Whitaker's chest. The nurse caught the baby as the child-mom collapsed into the big man's arms, her arms clinging to his neck, her flesh pressed against the rough material of his fatigues. She stunk of filth and infection, of malnutrition and vomit, the combination welling up a wave of nausea in Whitaker's innards.

Then he realized two amazing things: First, he had taken her, this complete stranger, in his arms, holding her sobbing, convulsing form firmly, gently against him; second, all the shaking was not coming from her, as he discovered *he* was sobbing, his hot tears running off the end of his nose and chin, running down her neck, leaving tracks in the dirt and blood on her shoulders and back. It was a moment transfixed and frozen in the chill early April air; there couldn't have been more "wrong" with the whole thing.

Big, white general, right smack in the middle of a military installation, his arms, his body, his entire being, embracing a young, black woman, nude from the hips up, her lacerated, frail body exposed to the cold air around his strong arms. His face pressed against her bruised cheek, wiping her tears with his own; his big rough hands caressing the torn, battered, flesh of her flanks and back. Nobody knew how long they stood there, the sobbing intermingled with the sounds of his big voice, softly murmuring in her ear, "it's OK, darlin', you're safe, you're here, now, it's OK, we got food, an' your babe seems fine. . .it's OK, now, child. . Good Lord sent the boys ta' bring ya' home. . .it's gon' be fine now. . .it's just fine. . . ."

Finally, the infant cried weakly, and the nurse spoke. "Sir, let's get these kids inside the rest of the way—come on, still cold out here. . ." With that, Specialist Brandt picked up the blanket and drew it over the girl's bare shoulders, a convulsion of chill and pain resulting from the fabric hitting the many cuts and injuries on that small frame. Roxanne relaxed her embrace from the big man's neck and, in spite of his efforts not to, he looked down at her.

Looking down, he could see the results of her devotion to the child, her slight body wasted from nursing. His mind could see what had transpired in that cold dungeon these young women had inhabited over the past weeks, the pathos of their devotion, the sacrifice made by them without fanfare and with no real glimmer that what they were doing would succeed in saving the lives of their precious babes. They had scavenged, dug, fought, and prayed for each additional moment of life for themselves and their fragile new additions. The entire idea that ones so young—kids really—and inner city "welfare types" at that, could be capable of such altruism, such commitment, and such indescribable courage and grit, was beyond anything his jaded mind would have thought possible.

It was at that moment that he knew the true merit of the persons now filing into his armory. And it was at that precise instant that he became convinced, for the first time in his life, that there was no form of Homo sapiens unworthy of his supreme sacrifice. This was the most beautiful collection of dirty, sick, weak, and abandoned of the species he could imagine. Without warning, his head rang with the words of the Lord Himself: "For as much as ye have done it unto the least of these, my brethren, ye have done so unto me." The tears welled up anew, his intellect seeing how "least" the brethren could be.

The Devil's Playground

As if scooping up a sleeping child for the trip to bed, the General held one arm behind Roxanne's shoulders, while the other hand gently slid down over her bottom, behind her knees, where he then lifted her bare, frost-bitten feet from the pavement and carried her inside. And like some sleeping child, her skinny arms clung to his neck as they walked through the doors to the waiting medics.

General Andrew Whitaker laid little Roxanne Miller down on a makeshift gurney, took the baby from the nurse and laid it—a little boy—down in the crook of her arm and, kneeling beside them, kissed them both. No one moved, no one spoke. No one breathed. He stood, wiped the tears from his nose and face and, turning to the assembled force, looked self-consciously away. He walked back to his office with the single command, "Carry on."

That was April, and nothing that happened in the following months did anything to change the impact of Roxanne's grand entrance. A wild combination of silliness, raucous noise, and pathos, she stole the hearts of the whole place at once. And only Roxanne could have gotten by with calling Andrew Whitaker "General Grandpa."

Men and weapons rumbled through the armory as was to be expected, wounded soldiers, broken equipment, stories of warfare in the streets. Babies cried, cooed, gurgled, and slept in cradles made from desk drawers and in-baskets, empty artillery shell cases, and rifle boxes. They ate and thrived on a perpetual supply of formula mixed up from combinations of powdered milk, sugar, and soy bean flour, while their tiny bodies stayed warm beneath poncho covers, old blankets, fatigue shirts, and olive drab underwear.

Two of the women died, one of apparent malnutrition and the other from sepsis secondary to an abscessed laceration inflicted by a band of thugs who tried to cut out her navel. Only the one who died of malnutrition had a baby, the other girl being one of only four rescued who neither had a child nor was pregnant at the time of the extraction. And the orphaned child quickly found the efforts of all those other Mommies, plus the devotion of the staff that cared for them, redoubled in her favor. The girls named her Sofie, after her mother, and also because they all said she was "Sofie's choice." Her momma had chosen to feed her from her own body, even when, before they were rescued, it became obvious that her weakened body would not survive the demands of the infant's needs. Sofie the mother seemed to simply give up after she realized that there was someone to care for and feed her tiny baby. She died four days after the rescue.

* * * * *

"Street Sweeper 6, this is Hawkeye 6, do you copy? Street Sweeper 6, come in! Street Sweeper 6, this is Hawkeye 6, I say again, proceed with assault. Repeat. Proceed with assault and neutralization of all enemy resistance. Do you copy?"

"Hawkeye 6, this is Street Sweeper 6, copy your transmission. We have units in place and a static make on location of captured weapon. Request Cobra Support, sir—I say again, request Cobra backup for upper-floor resistance."

"Street Sweeper 6, this is Hawkeye 6, copy your request for air support. The 3-Air will get aviation support. One gunship, ETA four minutes. Execute the operation." The resonating tones of General Whitaker's big voice rang in his ears, as Ryan Hathaway looked back at his counterpart from B Company, reinforced with armored personnel carriers. The captain, Logan Pierce, was one of the only real combat arms guys in this fight. His unit was the only infantry outfit not called to Saudi this last time, and they had been doing double and triple duty ever since bombs signaled the end of civilization in March.

"Guess that means we go kill some thugs, right Logan?" Pierce smiled through a tired countenance at Ryan Hathaway, then nodded. The idea of finally being close to this cell of terrorist bastards, at a time when there was sufficient daylight and enough weapons to do something about it, made his otherwise miserable day into cause for celebration. He picked up his radio and talked in measured, steady tones.

"OK, boys, listen up, this is Bravo Black 6. I want the APCs moved to the corners of this intersection where the bus is burning. Stay out of the line of any fire from down the street. You already know where Lt. Hathaway hit the goon who had our M60, and we have make on additional bad boys in that block. Set up at the head of the street, but stay out of sight. Move-out will be oblique in both directions after the gunship makes suppressive runs. I repeat. We will have one

Cobra up for this operation. Our information is that we have treed the bad boys. Repeat, we confirm bad boys in the block. On my command, move out, and neutralize all resistance. Repeat, neutralize. Stand by."

Hathaway could feel the adrenaline rush again, this time with the luxury of some help on his side of the equation. "Logan, we can't let 'em flush out the other end and into the next block. That's a mess down there. Twice we've chased 'em into there—lost 'em. Too much cover and too many buildings to fall on us."

Pierce smiled malevolently back into the face of his younger compatriot. "Not to worry, Ry, not to worry. The other two APCs came in from the other end thirty minutes ago, along with the only tank in the area. Got a little surprise for these guys this time. Oh—and I almost forgot. We took a minigun off a busted Huey yesterday. Mounted it on top of that last Hummer from 3d Platoon. It's waiting down the street in the alley. Let's go."

Book III – Starting Over, Fighting Back

* * * * *

The heat of evening only served to permit the sounds of battle to rumble and roll from the innermost parts of the city all the way out into the country surrounding Richland. Although the families along Jericho Road were spending more and more time in their own respective homes each week, the evenings still found them congregating on the Landry porches, the chatter of the day's activities audible across the fields. That chatter stopped abruptly as the ominous thunder of heavy explosions, punctuated by the staccato of small arms fire, carried to their ears. Richland was six miles away to the northwest, but the prevailing evening breeze delivered a very clear image.

"Holy jeses, boys, sounds like the Army's doing a little urban renewal tonight. Bit late for all that, seems ta me. . can't recall them playin' at night since the first week—*Wow!— That was a big one!—*" Carl's observations were interrupted as a huge booming explosion seemed to shake the house. Josh Landry's face knit as he wrapped his arms tighter around the torso of the son on his lap. Distance shone in his eyes, and hardness mixed with pain, as the faint, familiar "whup whup whup" sound of the old Huey rotary wing aircraft reached their ears.

"Gunship. Wow. Dearest God, Guard's hittin' the bastards with air support, close in. Must be awful in there, people," he spoke in low tones, to the assembly—and to no one in particular. "Can't believe it. They're tearing the city apart, one brick at a time, rootin' 'em out. Holy. . ." His voice trailed off as he buried his nose in the thick blond hair covering the back of Luke's neck, all salty and smelling of little boy smells. Nobody spoke, as they all sat in silence, twenty-some folks, each with his own image of what was happening in their town and where it might be happening. Josh and Luke sat on the floor next to the old rocker occupied by Jess, and she reached over, gently running her fingers through Josh's hair, then massaging the tense muscles in his neck and shoulders.

"It's been so long now, too. Almost three months, with no power, almost no food, and certainly no resupply to the bad guys of ammunition or weapons. How on earth can they keep it up?" Jess spoke vacantly, amazed at the appetite for war's

337

rewards apparently held by Richland's riffraff. After a pause, during that another big explosion shook the place, Josh responded.

"After a while, killing and conflict become their own reward. The clock stops, the future beyond the next fight vanishes, and ideas apart from the conquest of the enemy just don't matter. Personalities sort of disappear; faces get indistinguishable, people lose identity. You get to the place where life is lived from one killing to the next, one op order to the next, even one chopper ride to the next. And all the ingenuity, planning, vision they possess is concentrated on that one goal. Killing the enemy. Great life. Simple, too."

No one spoke in response, there being no others in the assembled company who had been in war—at least before all this. Certainly, the awful conflict they had shared over the past weeks counted as war, but the presence of homes and families to be defended, the fear of losing them, and the passion to be rid of the bloodthirsty, evil men who pursued them kept them focused on the real reason for fighting back.

Finally, one of the youngest of the team that had been in most of the combat, a redhead by the name of Curtis May, spoke in response to Josh's observations. He had been eyeball deep in the first weekend of the festivities following the blackout, as his family lived apart from the others, at the end of a long lane. Seventeen years old and a lanky six footer with the sweetest jump shot in the county, Curtis had a gentle manner and slow, graceful gait that belied the ferocity with that he greeted those first visitors. "After that first weekend, there was a time when all I could think about was the next fight. Forgot, sometimes, what we were fightin' 'bout, just wanted to fight again. Boy, but that was a rush."

Carl spoke. "Son, must a' been the Good Lord firin' you up, for sure. You and that little Ruger were all that stood between your family and the unthinkable for several days, 'til the rest of us could come lend a hand." Carl's reference was to the .223 caliber ranch rifle that Curtis handled with such deadly success. Alone and too far removed from the others to be able to get help, he had shown real grit and a mad dog vengeance for protecting his family—all with remarkable and gruesome results. The elder Landry continued to follow his brother's thought.

"Guess what Josh's sayin' is that, if you're gonna win at war, can't have much else on your mind. It's just that, the longer it goes on, the greater the chance that the victory comes at the price of a guy's humanity. Shoulda' seen ol' Joshua when they sent him home from the Central Highlands. Whew! Pretty scary, for sure. Boy could pick a fight in a phone booth, clear out a whole tavern full a' otherwise quiet rednecks, then convince the cops the whole thing was their fault! All that made him a helluva soldier, but made socializin' a bit difficult! Fortunately, a certain Irish lass came along after a while and got him interested in different pursuits."

Jess blushed and smiled fiercely at her brother-in-law, then uncorked a deadly backhanded shot with Luke's baseball glove that Carl dodged as it whistled past his ear. His smile was so full of orneriness and love at the same time, they both laughed out loud. In fact, no one on planet Earth had been happier for her to come along with those delicious "different pursuits" that saved his brother's sanity and probably his life as well.

A long volley of automatic weapons fire froze the conversation at once, and every eye seemed to turn in unison to the direction of town; then, one at a time, those present began to sneak sidelong glances back at Josh. It was as if his face could tell them whether to be scared or not, and his reaction to all things violent was their early warning system.

"Well, people, best act a little like warriors tonight. Never know just what the Guard might flush out a' town. Let's set sentries along the road, two at either end, a relay post at the head of Carl's drive, and keep two squads ready, at least 'til dawn. Emmitt, take one AR15, then let's put one more at Carl's, with the other two at the sentry posts. Better bring the folks in from the houses at either end of the road, too. I don't want another one of those multiple venue surprises."

On three different occasions, gangs had attacked the homes along the Jericho Road simultaneously, once requiring response to three locations at the same time. Weapons and men were stretched beyond capability that day, and loss of innocent life was high. One whole family was wiped out by the bastards before anybody could get to them, and two defenders died when they responded to attack without sufficient numbers and firepower.

339

The Devil's Playground

"Be a good idea to reinforce the day guards for a while, too. We have three groups working fields around the May's house, as well as garden crews in five places. Let's set somebody in the trees, but it'd be a good idea to leave eyes at either end of the road, too. Better check the radio batteries and keep things charged up plenty. If we're lucky, maybe we'll have another visit from a Guard patrol. . .give us a little info on what the hell's going on in town." The men assented at once; but Josh wasn't finished.

"Things've gone pretty well so far, good idea not to let down now. I think the quiet of the past few weeks has begun to convince us that the worst is over—hope that's true. But, as we can hear, it's *not* over for others, and they're not so far away. If the Guard flushes 'em out, gets 'em on the run and they can find wheels to get loose, the trash that comes next time will not only be mean as a bunch a' rattlesnakes, they'll be worn out and probably hurt. Bad combination. Let's stay alert and maintain full readiness at all times. Boys, that means keeping vehicles—or horses—handy and fueled. Extra ammo on your person at all times and extra weapons, too. Ladies, be ready to drop whatever you're doing and head for the basements at the drop of a hat—keep weapons, ammo, and water where you can get to 'em quick.

"Things get ugly again, we may find ourselves stretched thin, with all the folks who've gone back to their own places. In a few days, we'll have a better feel for what might be coming from town." He paused a moment, allowing his words and warnings to sink in, then, standing up beside Jess, his voice lower and full of sadness and resignation, "Sorry 'bout all this, people, I really am. . .nobody wanted ta be done with the killin' more 'n me. An maybe we *are* done with it. Just can't tell from here. . .not now, anyway. Just don't forget, *any of you*—it's not us s'posed ta be doin' the dying. It's *them*. Same as before—shoot to kill. Pray God keeps lookin' after us like He has been."

Josh picked up his hat, an old straw Stetson with a lot of miles on it, sighed quietly, and stepped off the porch in the direction of the stable. They all sat in a long, heavy silence as he walked away, the sounds of the evening's crickets, birds, and breezes punctuated by erratic bursts of small arms fire coming from the heartland.

9.

Of all the rotten inconveniences the past months had created, nothing seemed to bother Lassiter as much as the smoke. Ever since the city caught fire, within a few hours of the blackout, the acrid, trash fire-like stink of black smoke had hung in the air twenty-four hours a day, seven days a week. Now, three months into life in an urban hell, he was used to so many of the deprivations, he seemed to those whom he led to be a man without senses—or nerve endings. Except for the smoke. It produced a nasty taste in his mouth, watery eyes, and a nagging cough that seemed to increase in intensity with each passing day.

Among the many law enforcement types in New York City, the FBI had quickly responded when rioting and looting became generalized; the miserable weather of late March had impeded the crazies a bit, but when the weather turned to warmer hints of spring, things got interesting very quickly. All kinds of federal people worked and fought side by side with local police, National Guard units, and such citizens as could be found in possession of weapons to assist in the fight. They put out fires, rescued entire colonies of stranded people from high rise buildings, delivered a few babies, and fought countless firefights and pitched battles with bad people of every description.

And while all those "other duties as assigned" were monopolizing entire weeks without a break, Washington was ordering the search for the operatives who were thought to have been at the root of the electrical problems to be intensified. Right before the lights went out, Lassiter and his snoops had gotten pretty close to the information needed to start tracking the elusive character called "Sallie," thought to be concealed in the Bronx somewhere. When the shots were fired in Chicago, killing one Secret Service man and scaring the hell out of the new president and his wife, the FBI team that had come so close to intercepting the weapon was hit by a tidal wave of anguish at the thought that they had been within a few feet of foiling that whole operation. That was as close as they got, although they worked day and night with ATF's people over the following weeks between the time Lester Monroe left NYC for his date with the President and the beginning of the blackout.

Now things were such a mess in the Big Apple, that it was nearly impossible to gather intelligence or follow up on leads that might filter in from the street; the place was a caldron of fires, snipers, rioting, rotting bodies, and great throngs of refugees wandering around in search of food and shelter. But these men were working, nonetheless. The entire team supervised by Lassiter simply moved into the FBI offices, some without even having had the chance to go home and get personal items first.

The old building where they maintained their offices had been spared most of the violence, although on several occasions there was significant fighting right in front of the aging structure. Both the Guard and the Feds were using it as headquarters, so supreme efforts were undertaken to protect it. And amid demands for help with all those other problems, they kept looking for Sallie. They shared the old building with a variety of local, military, and other federal agency personnel, including a makeshift command post for the National Guard, two other FBI offices from around town, and the ATF. A big mobile diesel generator provided power—and diesel fumes to add to Henry's cough—but with frequent interruptions due to fuel shortages.

Department of Justice communications, received by secure radio transmissions, kept them all informed about the relative conditions in and around New York, and orders regarding the continuation of the search for Sallie were constantly coming in. Although not a single mercenary had been captured or killed, the rumors concerning them were legion, and one of the many jobs handed to the New York FBI office was the tracking down of as much information about this ethereal little killer as possible. Lassiter was just standing up in front of the landfill that occupied his desk when a familiar voice spun him around 180 degrees.

"Hey, Henry, you old fat ass, how'd you keep from gettin' your bald head blown off by the bad guys, huh? You been hidin' in this sewer for three months?" The insults had no steam, as the target turned to see the mopey, bedraggled countenance of Herman Hanks occupying a small portion of the doorway to his office.

"*Shit—HERMAN! HERMAN!!! I was sure you were DEAD!! Holy—this is—holy SHIT, this is great!! Hey, guys, look, it's—*"

"For crissakes, Hank, calm down, I just been out in the provinces doing the same thing you assholes been doin'— killin' people and movin' great masses a' starvin' natives from one place to another. . .great work, huh?" The skinny agent found himself in the grip of a bear hug, the two of them laughing and trading insults and interagency barbs for several minutes before settling down to a more serious discussion. Lassiter quickly noted that the younger man had been injured, a stifled cry of pain having been produced by that bear hug.

Henry knew, all too well, of a particularly ugly pitched battle that had been fought over in Brownsville between a small mixed force of federal agents, local cops, and a squad of National Guardsmen and a much larger contingent of bad guys. Herman was among that group. They sat drinking bad coffee for an hour while the unlikely looking agent told a growing crowd of folks the awful details of that terrible afternoon, only a few weeks before. And a knot of anguish began to grow in the old agent's gut as he listened.

A pretty elaborate ambush set with the obvious intention of killing everybody and seizing as many weapons as possible had been laid by a well-armed cell of the Nation of Islam. It consisted of nearly fifty men wielding a variety of high-powered rifles, including several military pieces. The worst part, however, was the box full of hand grenades they had. Details were in short supply, but Lassiter knew the loss of life by the troops was significant and devastating, with twenty or more killed plus a dozen badly injured. As he now learned, Herman was among the luckier of those on the injured list. Lassiter knew too well how bad it had been.

The blacks, well armed and led by men with extensive combat experience, set up on both sides of the street in a densely populated area, having first completely subjugated the starving population. Snipers with commandeered M16s occupied concealed and fortified positions atop buildings, while four others, armed with M79 grenade launchers and boxes of hand grenades, waited at the windows of upper story apartments. The bait to draw the police into the trap was a fire in a small apartment building at the end of the block, where twenty-five women and small children were first tied up, then left visible in the windows of the burning structure.

The Devil's Playground

A child was sent to hail the police to assist, his own mother among those inside; the response was then predictable.

The caution that should have permeated their every move was tossed aside with the first panic-stricken shrieks from the burning building. Radio calls for help were quickly answered by all units, of whatever description in the area, and a hasty (and therefore deadly) order issued to race to their aid. Fire-fighting capability was pretty much non-existent, due to the demands placed on them during the first weeks of the fighting, the number of fire-fighters already killed by snipers while working in that flaming environment, and the lack of sufficient water to do the job. So with the screams of moms and kids ringing in their ears, this contingent of cops and soldiers raced to the rescue.

Before they could get half way up the block, the devil's mercenaries opened up from both sides of the street, an acid rain of bullets, exploding grenades, and Molotov cocktails scattering them for the cover of the downstairs building entries. Of course, those doorways were either booby-trapped or occupied by concealed, armed adversaries, so the first order of business was surviving the entry into the building. This small responding contingent left thirteen dead in the street, while eight more died in the doorways of the apartment buildings. Owing primarily to what the survivors insisted was a pure act of God, the remaining sixteen were spared, their own reflexes and uncharacteristically poor aim by the Islamic fanatics having saved them from that secondary ambush.

Their attentions quickly returned to the screams emanating from the burning building a few yards away, and just when they were about to get stupid again and try to get to those trapped inside, a huge explosion erupted in the middle of the burning structure, blowing out the whole central architecture. The inferno then immediately collapsed on itself, mercifully killing—and burying—all inside. But the explosion and collapse of the building put out the fire.

"When it was finally over, we figured they had booby trapped the entrance where the hostages were tied, thinking they could finish off anybody who got through the surprise party out in the street. They hadn't counted on an ancient gas line that ran up through the mechanical chase beside the elevator shaft; damn thing musta' ruptured—maybe even was leaking already, because the whole front of the building went.

Knocked out all the windows on the other side of the street with flying bricks. . .took out the doors, even busted the gas lines inside, too. It went up like Fourth a' July, just like the first one—only there was no fire and no hostages inside. We found a few dead, mostly old people, in the rubble, but nothing like the one with the hostages."

"We heard the Guard had'da use bayonets and stick the suckers like frogs to get 'em out'a there, Herman, that true?" The scrawny agent looked around to discover a crowd of a dozen folks, standing in the doorway and out in the hall, quiet as a bunch of teenagers in a bordello, eyes wide, mouths agape. News of Herman's presence spread like VD through the FBI offices, and they quickly let the Guard know there was a real live survivor of the infamous "Battle of Brownsville" in the house. The lore and fiction, as well as the facts, of that event had already become the single most reported—and lied about—firefight of them all, and nobody had any idea that Herman Hanks was in the middle of it. However, anybody who knew the guy would not have been surprised; his frumpy, heroin addict demeanor had long been known to be the disguise of a tough agent when things got ugly.

He flushed at the realization that he had gathered such an audience, his face red, his gaze averted. "Holy—damn, boys, what's the deal—we havin' a party?" The laughter he generated with his humble countenance was anything but derisive, and Lassiter quickly assured him they all wanted to hear the rest. "Relax, Dopey, we've just heard more bullshit and rumor about that day than you can imagine! Oh, we've all had our fun with the natives over the past few months, it's just that the "Battle of Brownsville" was—well, . . ." The older man's face reddened, the place grew instantly silent again. Henry Lassiter was more shocked than embarrassed to realize that his throat had seized up, his eyes fighting a miniature flood, his voice absent.

Taking a long moment to collect himself, every eye now suddenly on him as he sat in the rickety old wooden desk chair beside Herman, Lassiter tried to speak again. "It's just that it seems we all lost somebody in that mess, Herman. Guys downstairs in the Guard command post lost one whole squad a' riflemen and machine gunners, weapons and all and, as I'm sure you know, the body count included six NYPD uniforms, and. . ." His face reddened again. Another deep breath. "And we had seven FeeBees we never saw again."

Wiping his face and running nose on his sleeve, he paused another beat, breathed again, then continued. "Three of the guys we lost were from this office, including a new recruit named. . ." A pregnant, agonizing pall descended on the room, all eyes on the floor, all breathing stopped. The senior man's shoulders shook, his rough, meaty hands muffling the sobs that racked his heavy frame.

"Kid's name was Jake—Jacob Henry Lassiter." A brawny, obviously Irish roughneck by the name of Seamus O'Dorgan, an FBI agent who ran the HRT operation (Hostage Rescue Team) spoke. His voice husky with an anguish-beneath-toughness sort of tone, his ruddy, massive face beet red, he raised his chin slightly to fill in the blank left by Lassiter's silence.

Herman looked around the room full of grieving faces and felt the freight train of sorrow and recollection hit him anew. Ever since that day, his life had been different, twisted. Now, surrounded by a wake of sadness and the otherwise unthinkable sight of Henry Lassiter crying, he was himself nearly overcome by it once again.

"I'm—oh sweet Jesus, Henry—I'm so sorry. . .I mean, if I'd known. . .I mean I didn't mean ta. . .it's just that you *asked* me where I got hurt and I just, well, I mean, I didn't think. . .I never meant ta'—"

The big Irishman spoke again. "Not to worry, Herman, he needs ta' know—we *all* need ta' know what happened that day. Seems there's not a man in the place didn't lose someone in that hell hole, and we know so little about what really happened. Everybody who fought in that thing either got killed or came from some other place or agency, so facts've been in short supply. Ol' Henry here, all he knew was that Jake was there, and he never came back. Guard reported him killed, but we couldn't ever find out what they did with him—I mean, what they did with his body." Lassiter straightened in his chair, wiped his face with his sleeve again, and spoke quietly.

"Herman, it's OK, pal, there's no way you could've known. Kid had only been here three months when the lights went out, and the Bureau was gonna move him to Buffalo in April. Anyway, that's why I asked ya' to tell me what happened. I

346

just don't know shit about what really happened, and like Shamus says we all want—no, we all *need* to know. Please, go on, how'd you get out'a there, and how'd you guys ever flush those assholes? We heard you got 'em all, that right?"

The younger man looked around, then at Henry's swollen face, then back at O'Dorghan. It was obvious that he was now in a command performance, so like it or not, he had to re-live it—again. And besides, Henry Lassiter was probably his favorite FeeBee in the world, and he just couldn't deny such a request. He turned slightly in his chair and began again.

10.

The grandeur of the world's most famous address was certainly diminished from what it had been when they took office, but Molly Webb decided to dress things up a bit for the evening's event anyway, even if she had to produce the effect all by herself. Women were in short supply among Washington's official families, at least outside their own well guarded homes. The now almost ancient traditions surrounding formal events in the Capitol town, fancy dinners where all the bigwigs brought their spouses, were instantly suspended when the demons turned out the lights.

For several days after the initial events, the government basically shut down, except for the White House, the Pentagon, and the CIA, manned because a full staff worked in each place twenty-four hours a day. And they were also well guarded, rigged with backup power sources, and set up for emergency operation. Not so for the legislative branch, where the huge capitol building stood empty except for a battalion-size armed force, including several tanks, that stood watch over it at Webb's command until the occupants of its many high offices could return under heavy security. When they got back, at first only a few at a time, spouses stayed behind in safer environs, provided by the executive branch and delivered by the military again.

Meetings had no visitor's gallery, luncheons and evening meetings never saw spouses, male or female, in attendance. All in all, pretty dull. It's ever so hard to add sparkle to an event that is hosted by armored vehicles, observed close-up by uniformed, armed guards and, more importantly, missing even a single beautiful gown, feminine face, or hint of perfume. Except, of course, for the meeting attendees who were female, and they tended to dress down, as was the norm for those days. All this convinced the First Lady that this predominantly male gaggle of should be accompanied by at least *one* gussied-up woman this evening, since her husband had vetoed inclusion of spouses for security reasons, again. Webb had chosen this night to detail the deployment of the returning forces, back from the desert and headed for urban combat in their own country.

An audible gasp sucked all the air from the main dining room as she entered, every head spinning instantly in her direction, all conversation suspended mid-word like an E.F. Hutton commercial; one deep southern voice could be heard to utter ". . .and people say there's no God. . ." A flutter of laughter at Senator Johnstone's remark—or prayer—and a slow swell of applause began to build around the big room. Molly's face flushed, her black eyes flashing then averting toward the floor, that wide, explosive smile igniting the room.

The president appeared at her side and, taking her hand, spoke through his most devilish grin. "People, the First Lady thought the place could use a touch of elegance tonight, even if my continued stuffiness concerning the security precautions for your families prohibited their attendance."

Nathaniel Johnstone spoke again, his deep voice more forceful now. "Mr. President, I do believe Mrs. Webb has produced a house full of elegance all by herself. . .and I bet I speak for the assembled company—so seldom can I say that (more giggles)—that we are in her debt." Applause broke out again, and an impromptu receiving line formed as each person in the room sought a closer look at the First Lady and the chance to speak to her personally.

Dressed in a long, form fitting, sequined gown, jet black in color and set off by sequined high heels that put her right at under six feet tall, her hair was back and up, exposing those famous cheekbones and the exquisite detail of her eyes and high forehead. A neckline modest but slightly provocative, backless design except for crisscross satin straps, it was again slightly revealing as it exposed the long, smooth sidelines of her figure. Diamond pendant earrings sparkled against the deep hue of her face, and a row of diamond bracelets decorated slender wrists and forearms wrapped in black gloves that reached above the elbow.

Besides the instant primal instinct awakened in every man in the room, including most specifically the squad of young Marines standing sentry at each door and window, there was an immediate realization that she had accomplished her mission. She had returned, if only for the evening, the now absent glamour and grandeur of State events to this wonderful old house.

Molly quickly overcame the moment's shyness and the flush of embarrassment created by all the attention and the realization that her beautiful body had the eye of every man in the room. Just to prove she was far more than a pretty face,

349

she held up a gloved hand for quiet. "Ladies and gentlemen, thank you for your greeting—I think."

A big laugh from the assembled group momentarily interrupted her. "I do so miss the company of your spouses, men and women alike, whom I had already come to know well in the few weeks before all this occurred. Please convey my greetings to them all, and tell them I continue to lobby the President for their quick return. Until then, I guess *I'll* just have to dress things up around here!" Burst of laughter and applause; line for greeting—and staring—continued at once.

She commanded the place the entire evening, even after the dinner dishes had been cleared and the business commenced. Her imposing husband continually saw the distraction she created, as men all over the room stole glances at her while he was detailing the coming campaign. But just when he was about to get irritated by the diversion, the thought hit him in a blinding flash of the obvious: This woman is one helluva secret weapon. I could probably sell these people Manhattan Island *again* with her in the room. Filing the thought for future use, he continued, no longer bothered by the constant barrage of furtive glances his wife was collecting. He completed the details of the briefing, including much they had not heard before concerning troop strengths and deployment schemes, weapons and re-supply, and even the details of the plans for care of the huge number of refugees to be expected.

"So, as you can see, folks, we'll give the troops about seven days to rest, reload, and move out to these locations. I have, as I said, reserved the vast majority of the mechanized units, armor included, for New York and Los Angeles, as it is our firm belief those cities will, in large measure, require what amounts to a full scale invasion. Of course, the story in New York is different than the one in L.A., as the situation is not as generalized throughout the urban area there; Los Angeles is basically overrun at this point. As I told you last week, we will move first to evacuate the largest number of non-combatants possible from all areas, it being our goal to remove no less than 75% of the remaining population before commencement of military operations."

"Mr. *President!* Do you mean by this that you plan to invade the city of Los Angeles with armored vehicles and ground troops at a time when upwards of three hundred thousand people may still be helplessly confined there?" June Mendez Garza, a young Representative from southern California, was incredulous and, it was obvious from her tone, on the verge of hysteria at the idea.

"No, ma'am, please—that is not what I have said. You forget, over a million people have already left the city limits as of now, seeking safety and provisions both north and south of town. Our most recent reports indicate that churches, schools, and even municipal buildings in the smaller communities have accumulated huge masses of people, plus all those taken in by each family with a spare bed or chair. Supplies of food and medicine have begun to move with a bit more effect each week, as the hostilities in these other places have declined in frequency and intensity. We project that we can evacuate the city to the point where there are no more than thirty to forty thousand noncombatants left. And most of them are either being held prisoner by the bad guys or have otherwise aligned themselves with them."

"But *still,* how can you countenance an armed invasion of the city with even that many innocent persons to be exposed to firefights, cannon fire, and—for *God's Sake, Sir—almost certain death!! I thought that was what you were trying to stop—what are you thinking?!!"*

Webb swallowed the rise of his temper and the urge to throttle her, then realized what was happening. Another member of the remaining government had just come face to face with the truth about what had happened, and the truth about war, wherever it is waged. Before he could speak, Nathaniel Johnstone took the floor, slowly rising from his seat directly across the table from Garza. "Congresswoman Garza-June—you are right. . .absolutely right in your assessment. Thousands of noncombatants, elderly and very young, mostly, are going to die in this fight, fought in your own beloved city. It is wrong and, worse, it is reprehensible. And each person in this room has wrestled with the horror of it, coming to the exact conclusion you have just so passionately expressed.

"When I realized what the President was proposing, I determined at that moment that what he wanted to do was unthinkable, and that he was nothing more than a warmongering mercenary, and—with all due respect, sir—a mean sonofabitch." Heads nodded almost imperceptibly around the room, each face stony and intent, eyes dark and burning. "At one point, the idea of attempting to remove him from this place even occurred to me. Thankfully, I was sleeping when that occurred, and I shook the nightmare at once when I awoke. You see, June, as unthinkable as it is to imagine the sacrifice of innocent persons *at all,* that decision, the President finally made me see, had already been made by the enemies of peace when they occupied the city and subjugated its people.

"As he has so painfully explained tonight, although you have chosen until this moment not to hear him, all these people will die anyway, every last one of them, either from torture, execution, starvation, or disease, if we do not take back this place from the evil men who now control it. And, if God wills, and the President's plans can be well executed by the armed forces, many, if not most, of those persons will be rescued. Simply put, Ms. Garza, this unthinkable choice is no choice at all. It is the last imperative."

Silence filled the room for an eternity as the old man eased slowly back into his chair, reaching as he did so for his water glass. Eyes moved from his weary visage to the flushed, tear-stained face of June Garza, to Webb, and back to her again. It was clear beyond all doubt that it was incumbent upon her to speak, to either accept or reject what she had heard.

Slowly her face hardened and, regaining her composure and the dignity that always seemed to accompany this young woman, she stood. "Senator Johnstone has spoken eloquently, as usual, and clearly I am far from his equal in that department." She looked down momentarily, summoning strength from within, hands on the table.

"What the President proposes is, as the Senator has said, unthinkable. The specter of tanks rumbling through the streets of my hometown, of fires and explosions, ladies and gentlemen, I must say in all humility, breaks my heart." She paused again, commanding the tears to retreat from the wells of her eyes.

"I guess I just never thought being a member of the Congress of the United States would include within its responsibilities voting to sack American cities. That one has taken a little getting used to." A rustle of acknowledgement moved quietly around the table. "But these times must try the soul of man—and woman—every bit as much as the agony we all know has been shared by others before us since the very foundation of the republic. It can be no coincidence that this wonderful portrait of Lincoln looks on us at this moment." She then stood straight, her youth more apparent now and the sadness and pain in her eyes all the more obvious; she turned toward Webb.

"I have sold you short, Mr. President. Forgive me. The Senator is right, of course. We have not chosen this course, it has been dictated to us. I only ask that, as you enter upon this terrible mission, you—" the voice quit. She stood with head up, the battle with her tears now lost, her chest heaving against her will not to quit. The time of silence seemed eternal, as each man and woman in the room felt the edge of that sword at their hearts.

"Act swiftly, sir, and with great care. . .and show all the mercy you possibly can to my beloved people." She sat down quickly then, brushing tears from her cheeks.

Webb fought the same pain, the same tears, and felt the same eyes of Lincoln upon him. He stood, his long frame seeming to continue up and up, posture at once tired and erect.

"Ladies and gentlemen, please do not think for an instant that I desire this course, or that the vision of combat on American soil pleases me. Whatever success I have had on the field of battle has not been born of pleasure or an enjoyment of mayhem. Each death walks with me every step I take, and every lost life has left the sad mark of its irreplaceability on my soul. I have thought and prayed about this mission for many weeks now, and many times I have determined not to proceed. But each time, the answer becomes clear again.

"Our own troops will be attacking their own soil; we can be assured they will show mercy to their own. And Congresswoman Garza, I thank you. Not only for your assent, but for your objections, voiced so passionately on behalf of your constituency. Clearly, those feelings, thoughts, and observations must not be silenced as we move into this dark, dark time in our history. Pray with me, all of you, and pray without ceasing. I know in the depths of my soul that only with God's divine guidance can we have any hope of saving this republic. Chaplain, we are adjourned. Would you pray for us, please."

Everyone stood in unison as the uniformed Reverend bowed his head. Another long moment of profound quiet preceded his voice, as if the man of God knew how badly this assembly needed it. Then he spoke.

Kind and Gracious Heavenly Father, we come before You with heavy but grateful hearts at this moment, trusting in Thee not only for guidance but more, for mercy, as we attempt to retrieve our country from the grip of anarchy. We ask Thy Blessing upon every soldier who acts in furtherance of this cause. Guide and protect them, Lord, each and every one; make them swift and sure, strong and decisive, but equally balanced with discernment and mercy, Father, as they work and risk—and lose—their lives; as they fight the forces of evil that appear now to be so strong, inevitably sacrificing beyond the call of duty. God save the United States of America. Amen.

11.

The idea that the planned destruction of his homeland, the God-endowed Promised Land, was in large measure the product of a Jewish mind made Benjamin Netanyahu crazy. And while he maintained a very staid and even boring composure for the world most of the time, in the privacy of his home, where he now listened to an incredible briefing from the top dogs at Israeli Intelligence, he was near apoplectic.

"You are certain, William, *certain,* that this man is a Jew—at least *half* Jewish? How can you be sure? I mean the trails are old and *very* cold that lead back to the forties now, and many times we either have been misled or have fallen victim to just plain bad information already."

"I understand, Benjamin, but here—look at this. Tell me this is not a Jew." A 5x7 photograph was removed from an envelope in the snoop's briefcase; the Prime Minister's face stiffened, his eyes looked like dark heat seekers on the color print.

"Dearest God in heaven. He has done what he could to conceal, even to destroy, but the features are there." Shaking his head slowly from side to side, he studied in silence. "The shape of that head and face cannot be destroyed—and the eyes, dearest God, it cannot be." His mind raced, confusion and fury mixed, as he tried to reconcile this revelation in his mind. Rusty on the details of his Hebrew School education, he still could remember well the apocalyptic prophecies of Isaiah and Ezekiel, the intimations of more and more attempts to destroy the Chosen People of God. His mind went spinning out of intellectual and spiritual control at the thought that such attempted holocaust could come at a Jewish hand.

". . .and this man was a war criminal as well? How do you know this, William, how can you *know* this?!" Even people who have lived around the intelligence community their entire lives find it difficult to believe anybody can get what those guys get. And their bosses and the politicians and generals who put their information to work typically want nothing to do with knowledge of how they got it. The snoops know it, too. They provide little in the way of detail about the methods employed, preferring instead to deliver their sometimes devastating morsels without attribution or explanation, simply expecting the stuff to be accepted. Of course, they get some of it wrong; not a particularly precise business, after all. The senior man spoke deliberately, his desire to provide confirmation moving him to fill in a few of those blanks.

"We've known about Adolpho for many years, as he has had quite the career in the service of evil. We followed his rise to fame in the nuclear warhead business, even watched him snuggle up to the scholars in Iraq and Libya when things fell apart with the USSR. His publications on the archaeology of Babylon and the Fertile Crescent in general only served to confirm our belief that he was not only very smart, but also extremely valuable to all sides. What we never had any way to discover until recently was that he had a Jewish mother. And the reason for that was that we never knew he had another name, one with Jewish roots. We also never saw him. Seems he has always been very camera shy and somehow managed to stay out of pictures of any kind. Smart guy."

William Samuelson was as good as they come, and his clipped English accent only lent credence and a 007 sort of intrigue and believability to whatever he said. And he seldom said anything wrong. Born in Canada in 1942, the child of refugees from Hungary, he was educated in England. He was Jewish by birth—and by devotion—and he had moved to Israel as soon after his eighteenth birthday as he could get there. The zeal that burned within him for his homeland was seldom proclaimed and almost never obvious, but the man was an Israeli patriot of the first magnitude. The fierceness of his gaze as he continued concerning this anathema would-be exterminator of the Jews was not lost on Netanyahu.

"He was born Karl Isaac Wampler; that middle name would have given us a hint, don't you think? Anyway, the same operative who discovered the old name also identified his mother, a Polish Jew who married a German in 1921. The way we learned all this is so bizarre, I can't help but think it's good stuff. A Jewish Pole, doing research for the Holocaust Museum, was digging through old birth records in Berlin. Most of them had been destroyed during the air war in Germany, but some of the older records of the private hospitals in the area were kept off-site in warehouse facilities away from the primary bombing targets, and those were discovered only recently. Not really a 'Dead Sea Scrolls' sort of discovery, the records were just stacked in boxes on the upper floor of a small warehouse, but pretty interesting to the many families and genealogists who could use them to fill in blanks in their various searches."

He paused to take a long drag on one of those Turkish cigarettes—the ones that smell like burning horse hair and have enough nicotine in them to blow the top of a guy's head off if he inhales too deeply. Samuelson inhaled *very* deeply. The boss spoke before he could resume the story.

"William, I know this sounds ridiculous, but I remember that find. Happened in the early seventies, and I read about it. Wasn't that the one that contained some information about some of Hitler's family?"

"That's the one, Benjamin, but few people ever read the rest of those reports. There were birth and death records on about twenty-five thousand residents of the Berlin area, dating from about 1912 to 1928. Anyway, this Museum fellow found several entries for people named Wampler. Apparently a pretty common name in that area during those years. One more background detail: Before about 1924, no effort was made to conceal intermarriage between Germans and Jews. Hitler's influence really didn't gain momentum until later and, as you know, the strong push to ostracize the Jews came later as well. So some of these people have learned that old German birth records contain such interesting information as maiden names—even homes of origin.

"This young chap is looking through the birth records and comes on an entry for 'Wampler,' only the mother's maiden name is *very Jewish.* 'Ruth Weidenstein.' Even says where she is from, naming the town of Wolszlyn, a few miles outside of Zielona Gora—roughly a hundred miles from Berlin. There was apparently a lot of intermarriage across the border between Poles and Germans for several years before all that crap with Hitler started. So, the student goes to Wolszlyn, looks up Weidenstein, a name with substantial German connotation as well, and bingo! Ruth. Well, not *Ruth,* actually, but her birth records, and some of her family. Boy, what a mess. Seems the family still sees red when the name comes up, thanks to the ugliness our boy Karl performed while just a boy—a boy in the Brown Shirts!

"This was a pretty difficult boy, from all accounts. By the time he was 12, he had been repeatedly incarcerated for a variety of petty offenses, and anything his parents said or

357

believed he rejected. Then the Brown Shirts came to town, and he heard all the right stuff to convince him that everything about his family, and particularly about his mother, was bad—most specifically his mother's lineage and his father's treason for having married a Jew. He apparently assumed quite a passion against them both and made it his business to learn to hate everything Jewish. The Nazis let him continue because his features were not overtly 'incorrect.' And his family had never practiced the mother's faith since her arrival in the Berlin area after her marriage to Wampler. Anyway, he turned out to be such a fanatical Jew hater, nobody ever questioned him. Just like that, a perfect little Nazi—at the ripe old age of thirteen."

The Prime Minister stared at the picture, then let his gaze wander to the window, then back to his lap and to the floor. Prayers mixed with epithets as thoughts found confusion, so difficult—even incomprehensible—was this person about whom he now heard. Hatred for one's mother; could she have been that abusive as to drive him to embrace the ideology that would pitch the world into the most horrible events in history? Could he then hate his Jewish heritage so much that he could eventually not only permit but participate in, the execution of so many innocents? What could be the truth of such a man, or *was* there truth regarding him?

One thing was certain: He was real, he was a genius, and his talents were presently trained on the singular goal of the destruction of Israel. And Jew or not, he had to be handled— *now.* They already knew of the Iraqis' abilities when it came to protecting important people. Half the snoops and most of the assassins in the Western world spent most of the 1980s trying to find and kill Saddam, and nobody ever got a shot. Surely, this wild man with the priceless skills and attitudes was being accorded the same level of security. No sense wasting precious lives on the fool's errand of trying to take him out. Netanyahu's mind, even his soul, spun in a caldron of confusion, ideas, conflicts, and fury, as he struggled with this deadly conundrum.

"All right, William, this will take some thinking. We probably cannot hope to kill this mad half-Jew; we probably couldn't even get close enough to him to try, although you *did* get that picture—"

"More luck than skill, Benjamin, we had a look at the *National Geographic* proofs from the piece they're doing on the restoration of Babylon, and somehow, no doubt quite innocently, somebody got this one clear shot of him. And because no other photos of him were around for comparison, we weren't really sure it was him until we confirmed it with an operative who had studied with him at one of the digs up on the Tigres, several years ago."

"Well, however you got it, it was well done. But still, there has to be a way—some chink in that ice cube he calls a heart—some way to at least twist him a bit. . .maybe a way to communicate, play a mind game or two—yes. William, here is your immediate assignment. No hit men, no night surveillance. Just find me a way to get a message to him, preferably a written message, but word of mouth will do if that's all we can get. Even if we cannot actually get close to him, let's find a way to get inside his sphere, even his head. . maybe there's just a little. . .probably silly, but at least we can distract the bastard from his genocidal duties a bit. Yes, that's it. You are to create a way for written messages to get to him, and to get there on relatively short notice. If we can actually get into his residence *just once,* leave him enough unexplainable notice of our presence to make him uncomfortable, that will be a start, anyway. Thank you, William."

12.

"After the explosion, things got instantly quiet. You could tell in a flash that the huge blast had come from that little apartment building, 'cause the screaming and crying quit. Quiet like a graveyard, all at once. Not a peep from all those kids and their mommas, and no sound from across the street where the other building had gone 'boom!' right after it. Those of us who survived the reception committees in each of the doorways were separated from each other, and no more than half of us had radios that still worked. I could hear transmissions coming from out in the street, but that turned out to be from one of the dead Guardsmen's radios—kinda' spooky, squattin' in that doorway, listening to the sound of radio voices coming from a dead soldier. . ." Herman Hanks looked at the floor for a moment, his eyes distant and almost vacant. Then he focused again and continued.

"Finally—we all heard it at the same time—somebody yelled out into the street from inside one of the doorways, *'Everybody clear your own building—MOVE OUT!!!'* It was amazing, for real. Some a' the guys said they recognized the voice as the platoon leader from the Guard unit, and it may have been him, but we found him dead later, so I can't say for sure. Weird, man, no shit, so freekin' weird. . .it was like we all got the picture at the same moment. Just like that, ya' know, like we all figured, *shit, prob'ly gonna die in this sewer anyway, might as well clean out the goons on the way out!*

"So, away we went. I was with a Harbor Patrol guy who had a twelve-gauge riot gun and a pocket full a double zero buckshot and a great big revolver a' some kind. I had one a' those H&K Mp5s we got last year, with three mags of thirty rounds each. Had my 10 millimeter, too."

In the time it took to set up the story, Herman Hanks lost himself in it again. His singsong, dopey delivery reminded them of listening to Kato testify in the Simpson trial—or interrogating some junkie in a holding cell at the Tombs. But the intensity of his gaze and the quickness with that he began to spit out the sequence of events, captivated his small but growing audience. And to his own surprise, he felt a need to finally get this story told all the way through. Tossing his stringy hair back out of his face again, he launched full bore into it.

Book III – Starting Over, Fighting Back

"This Harbor Patrol guy, Tony Castilano, he looks at me with this rattlesnake grin and he says, 'this way, greaser, let's hit 'em.' And I just checked the magazine in that little machinegun and did what he said. Guy was short, stocky, swarthy some way or another—prob'ly Italian, I guess, but lemme tell you boys, he was one bad sonofabitch, ol' Tony.

"He took off like somethin' was after 'im, pounding up flight after flight of steps. Well, my lungs are poppin', I need a cigarette, and I'm dyin' on those steps. Finally, he takes a right, stops at the door to the sixth floor hallway. I'm half a floor behind, so I come wheezin' up to the doorway, just wantin' the asshole ta slow down, right? But before I can find wind to bitch about the steps, he holds up his hand like he's some Indian chief or somethin—I freeze like he says.

"He turns to me and says, 'this is six—saw two snipers and the guy with the M79 on six. You take the left side, me the right—we're at the end, so it'll be a left turn to get in the hall. And be still—stop breathin' like a beached whale, for crissakes!! Stay low. No shit, they're in rooms on the left side, 'bout half way down.' I look at him like he's lost his simple mind. The idea of going down that hall sounds like assisted suicide to me. But hell, no time and he's gone, so I go, too. Quiet like a morgue in the hallway, no talk to give 'em away, and all the doors are shut. But this Tony, he thinks he knows right where they are, so I just stay on the left and follow him.

"Sure as hell, we go down about half way, and one a' those assholes opens up with some kinda' big automatic, turns out it was an old M14A1, full auto, baby, rock'n roll!! I'm thinkin' like I been taught, ya' know? Move and listen, stop and assess, plan an entry, check for backup—you guys know the drill. Fact is, I'm scared shitless, but oh no, not Tony the bandit!! Boom! He kicks the door so hard he splits out the frame on the doorknob side *and* fractures the frame around the hinges on the other side at the same time! Swear ta' my sweet mother's gravestone, it looked like a string a' det cord had gone off! Well, Tony waits for no man, and before I could even get it through my head that he'd blown the door to pieces, he was through it and the twelve-gauge was roarin' like a hand-held howitzer.

"I jumped clear off the floor with the first blast, then went in behind him—not sure what I thought I was gonna do, but it

was over before I could even shoot. Two dead, shot all to hell
and gone, brains, blood, and big black holes all over the walls
beside the window, and that big M14 layin' beside one a' the
dead guys. The grenade launcher was still in the other guy's
hands, but most a' his head was missin', so I figured he
wouldn't mind me takin' it from him. "We found a whole crate
a' ammo for that M79—enough grenades to blow up every car
in the area, plus two cans a'308 for the rifle. Judging from
the empty cartridges all over the floor, these two were
responsible for a lot of the welcome we got when we rounded
the corner onto that block. Anyway, I'm standing there
thinking what ta do next, when Tony jerks the grenade
launcher outa my hands and stuffs the case a' shells for it in
my arms.

"'*Here,*' he says, 'you carry these, and keep up,
goddammit. There's another nest upstairs and a guy with a
big gun on the roof. Let's go.'" Herman laughed out loud
describing the wild man he was following, then raced back
into the play by play.

"We charged off in the direction of the stairway again, and
my lungs started on fire just *thinkin'* a running up more
flights. Tony took off up again, stopped on the ninth floor,
just like before. I caught up again, and in we went. Same
shit. Boom! Door comes apart and Tony wastes two more bad
boys. Just like that. No shit, I'm about ready to put my little
MP5 up for sale, 'cause I don't need a gun with Tony along!
Then he looks at me, his eyes bug out and he points that
cannon right at my head! All I can do is drop straight to the
floor and think about what to do with this maniac and *BLAM!*
He shoots a guy standing in the doorway. Sucker's 'bout ten
feet away and man what a mess. Everything from the tip of
his nose up is gone—actually I saw it against the wall when
we left the room—boy was dead before he hit the ground."

Everyone in the room, and all the rest standing silently in
the hallway, were all too familiar with gunfights and the sight
and smell of violent death, so there were many slow nods as
he described it all. The only difference was, this was about
the Battle of Brownsville. Herman tossed his stringy mane
and set the trap for another punch line.

"And guess what? Same shit *again!* Away we go, headin'
for the freakin' roof and those pricks with the big gun. So far
the score is pretty good: five a' them and none of us—me an'

Tony, that is—plus we got that grenade launcher and a bunch of ammo for it. Now we gotta get up that last stairway and onto the roof without being seen, 'cause we got no chance—I mean like *zero* chance—to survive if they see us. Tony's runnin' up to the door that leads out onto the roof and all at once, he stops and steps aside real quick. I'm draggin' my lungs behind me by this point, but I get up behind him and kneel down. He motions me to be quiet, then signals that the machine gun is set up right in front of the doorway, maybe twenty feet away.

He points at the M79 and motions for me to give him two shells for it. They're weird looking, like miniature Howitzer rounds, or oversized rifle shells. . .he takes one, waits for them to start firing again to cover the sound, then breaks open the little gun and shoves one a' those big shells in, then closes it before they stop firing. He whispers 'that's all, folks'—no shit—just like Bugs Bunny—rolls up on one knee and '*Pumph! BOOM!!*' Then nothing. He motions me over and we slip out onto the roof. Gone, baby, I mean there is simply nothin' left. There's a hole about a foot wide in the low plaster wall that sits on the edge of the roofline—ya' know, a decorative thing like they got on lots a' the old buildings—and there's a big metal box full of bandolier ammo for a machinegun, but that's it. He yells again, says 'Let's go! Gotta get down there before one a' those pricks gets that gun.'

"I'm thinkin' 'right. . .thing's prob'ly in fifteen pieces after falling 11 stories onto the pavement. . .but I was wrong. We flew down those steps and there they were. Two guys blown all to bits, and that goddam gun—no shit, now—that M60 lit right on top a' one a' them, and it's fine! I look up and realize Tony's smiling, and he's got that box of bandolier ammo under his arm. I felt like laughing out loud, but then somebody opened up on us from the other side of the street, so we scooped up the gun and ran back inside."

Herman went silent, that vacant look back in his eyes, his gaze fixed on the floor. So far, the story was very similar to a hundred others that most of the men in the room could have told, but everyone knew there was more.

Henry Lassiter had been listening intently, his own face twisting and changing with every detail, like a reflecting pool into the anguish in his soul. He tried to speak several times, wanting a detail here or there, but nothing would come out when he opened his mouth. Now he tried again, this time successfully. "We heard they set the whole place on fire, Herman, and that's what cost you so many lives. That right? Your people really die in fires?" The thinly concealed horror in his eyes was betrayed by the tone of his voice, nearly failing him as he finished the question. Hanks saw it and jumped on it.

"Naw, that's bullshit. Yeah, they torched about half the buildings in that block, but none of our guys got caught in the fires. Only ones we lost to the fires were two cops who got flushed out a' their hiding places by the smoke, then got cut down on the sidewalk when they came out. And most a' the fires went out anyway, 'cause the buildings were mostly empty, so there wasn't much tinder to start and feed 'em 'til they could get into the walls. Assholes weren't smart enough to start 'em in the stairwells. . .Sweet Mary, but *that* works. Like lighting a fire in a chimney—*WHOOSH!!*"

He could see the older man angling for information, or even conjecture, about the fate of his son, but Herman wanted nothing to do with that one, so off he went again, back into the story.

"Anyway, I'm still not sure how we got back inside the doorway without gettin' poked full a' holes. Seemed like the whole roofline of that block was shootin' at us as we ran for cover. Sort a' like John Wayne, ya' know, all that shootin', and bullets ricochetin' off the pavement and walls, but ol' Rambo—and *me*, of course—don't get hit. Well, the bad boys up top had to have seen Tony with that '60, 'cause we really drew a crowd. Almost before our butts hit the floor in the entryway of the tenement, we both heard somebody yell out— from a window on the other side of the street, I think, 'They got it! Hit 'em quick—*GET THAT GUN BACK!!*' and they opened up again.

"Now, we're pretty sure they're gone from this building, but we obviously didn't clear every floor, just went after the guns Tony had seen. So, we're figuring there's a pretty good chance somebody's gonna hunt us up from back inside. Tony's eyes bore a hole in the floor, like he's figurin' what to do, then he looks at me and spits orders. 'Get into the hallway, inside the doorway of one a' those apartments—make sure it's empty (like I'd forget!)—and cover my back. Maybe I can sweep that freakin' roofline and clean off some a' the reception committee.' I did what he said, of course, and set up shop across the hall and down a little from the entry. I could hear him snappin' parts a' the big gun into place, cussin' up a storm, then he cut loose. Wow."

"That machinegun was the loudest damn thing I ever heard—my head still hurts when I think about it. Sittin' in that doorway, not twenty feet away from Tony, I swear it shook the fillings right out a' my back teeth! Anyway, he really hurt 'em with it, fired almost without stopping for two, three minutes. Every so often he'd go *gotcha* or something like that, but that was all I could get out a all those rounds sweepin' the buildings on the other side of the street. Then I had this really sickening thought.

"When the bastards first opened fire on us, out in the street, there were at least five different origins of fire. And at least three different places shootin' those grenades, too. We had one of the grenade launchers with us now, but that left two unaccounted for, and *that* made Tony an obvious target for one of them from over where his bullets were hittin'. All at once I got this picture of one of those things goin' off in his face, and I panicked. I started screamin' and hollerin'—like he could hear me with that thing bangin' away—jumped up out a that doorway and ran over there like I was gonna stop him, then *BOOM!* That was all she wrote." His face went white, sweat appeared on his lip, the muscles in his jaws twitched. No one spoke, moved, or breathed.

13.

Ryan Hathaway stood in the middle of the street, the gathering darkness mixed with the sweat running into his eyes, making visibility worse by the minute. Heart pounding, chest heaving great gasping gulps of hot, humid air, his legs shook with fatigue and frustration. The dust cloud blown up by the big rotor of the old Cobra gunship only made things worse, and the lieutenant strained against all these impediments to see where his elusive quarry had gone. Most of the vermin lay dead in the street, or hanging out of upper story windows, or on the floors of the rooms where they'd been chased. But a small contingent, including one of the captured machine-guns, ran right out the far end of the block, just like Hathaway had feared.

Looking back in the direction of the sound of a Hummer, he saw Logan Pierce leap from the big vehicle as it slid to a stop. Hathaway spat an epithet-filled report at his superior. "Sonsabitches ran out the end, just like before, Captain—goddammit, but I knew they'd do that!! Where the hell's that chopper going, for crissakes!?. Get him on the radio and tell him to get his ass back in here and chase 'em down!! *Logan—PLEASE—they're gettin' away again, jeses, Logan, what th'—*" The older officer spoke quietly, firm. Neither of them could understand how anybody could have gotten past the ambush waiting at the end of the block.

"Too dark, Ryan, he'll crash that thing sure if he tries to get down between these buildings anymore. And besides, the dust cloud he stirred up plus all the smoke from those two buildings he blasted have made it impossible. I just got off the radio with him directly—got it from the horse's mouth. Sorry. Relax, we got most of 'em this time, and at least one a' those creeps is hit pretty good—one a' my squad leaders found a nasty blood trail coming down the back stairs of that building there—right where they came out. How many got away, any idea?"

The junior officer shook his head, his left sleeve blotting the sweat and grime away from his bloodshot eyes. He spat dryly, his shoulders slumping further yet as he answered. "Naw, can't be sure at all. Maybe six, eight. I'm just sure they had a vehicle down here somewhere, though, 'cause every time we've gotten this far, they've just vanished. And this time I thought I heard the sound of an engine starting down the street, but the chopper was so loud I couldn't really tell. If they got to a car or a truck, they're really gone. Hey—maybe the chopper could climb up and look for them from high enough not to be so risky—whatcha think, Cap?"

Pierce already had the mic keyed, his voice barking out call signs. "Cobra One, this is Bravo Black 6, can you sweep southwest from last objective? Possible vehicle escaping—over?"

"Bravo Black 6, this is Cobra One we're up, and—stand by, I'm only about twenty seconds away. . .OK, boys, got the location—negative sir, I repeat negative for personnel or vehicles. You copy, Bravo Black 6?"

"Cobra One, this is Bravo Black 6. Leader, I copy—negative for escaping vehicles. Out."

Hathaway leaned his tired bottom against the side of the idling Hummer, took off his helmet, and wiped his face with his sleeve again. Then, to his astonishment, he found himself swallowing bitter bile, his eyes welling up with tears of anger, frustration, fury. "God*dam*mit, Logan, but I cannot *believe it!!* Those skunks got away again. . .holy *shit,* but I'm sick of all this. . .we been chasing those murderous assholes for six weeks, never even gettin' close enough to return fire most of the time, and finally—*finally*—we get there and they get away."

Pierce stood silently beside him, the crackle of the fires behind him punctuated by the gathering rumble of a cave-in where the Cobra had blown the backbone out of one of the old buildings with two racks of rockets. Turning back to Hathaway, he looked for a long minute at the youthful face of this brave man. A CPA in days now gone, the kid had been jammed not only into leadership, but into combat, with only the most basic of training beforehand. Now his face had that gray, aging pall that only a steady diet of death and destruction can deliver, and ached inside at what he saw.

"Not to worry, Ry. This time we wasted 'em pretty good. Got back Shockley's guns—and his bullhorn—killed thirteen of the worst dicks in town, and saved twenty-eight hostages." Hathaway's face snapped up to meet Pierce's gaze. "What—no shit!!?! WOW!! You mean those kids screaming up the street?"

"Yep, you whackin' that machine-gunner musta spooked the ones who had the kids—that's the building they were in—'cause they hauled ass without takin' the gun *or hurtin' the kids.* Although they'd done plenty already. We're vacin' 'em right now. Got two gunships en route. And by the way, pretty nice shootin' for an accountant. C'mon, let's clean up this mess and get back to the command post. I'm thirsty, and I think the Sergeant still has a few Budweisers left in his stash." Hathaway smiled weakly, pulled forward onto his aching feet again, then followed the captain back up the street.

Neither of them heard the sound of the old Ford van as it pulled around the corner, out from the concealment of an overhead door access way into the loading dock behind a gutted department store. It rumbled down the street and into the darkness, five men huddled inside. Headed south, out of town.

14.

"Benjii—*Benjii!!* C'mon—if we don't leave right now, the streets will be so full we'll have no chance of getting to the terminal in time—now h*urry!*" Arakhan motioned distractedly to his eager comrade, still digging through a pile of weaponry and lethal accouterments. Spying the timer he'd misplaced at the last minute, he snatched it up and ran toward the little Hyundai sedan. It zipped away from the back of the garage and was gone.

Negotiating the ever-building mass of rush hour cars and trucks on the streets of Jerusalem was a matter that took extreme skill and no small amount of luck. They darted along, narrowly escaping semi-trailer tailgates and streetlight poles, stoplights, and panic-stricken pedestrians, as the young terrorist displayed proof that he had plenty of both luck and skill. The kid was staying within the Arab areas of town, speeding past residential neighborhoods enroute to the target, a commercial development that could be counted on to be teeming with people at this time of day. The streets were lined with shops, restaurants, and delicatessens, sure to be well populated with all manner of Arabs at 9 a.m. on a weekday. Young Baheer's mission was to get to the area by 8:30, drop off Benjii, then proceed to the alley behind a row of businesses and wait. Done.

"No more racing, Baheer, is that clear? From this moment on, you are invisible. Do *nothing* that would draw attention to you, right?" The kid nodded in that "I *know*, Dad" way that only a person 21 years old can do and drove away—slowly. Benjii noted that he did, in fact, become invisible.

Dressed in the ubiquitous garb of secular Jerusalem, Arakhan blended into the masses packing the streets. The small back pack slung carelessly over one shoulder was indistinguishable from a thousand others visible at the same moment, and his expression, gait, and attire were a sloppy but perfect match for the rest of humanity crowding the streets and sidewalks. After working up a sweat during the four-block walk to the drugstore, he walked in at precisely 8:55.

The proprietor spoke to him, his words more aimed at work than greeting. "Quickly now, we need stock up front in books—and there's a spill over behind the cosmetics. looks like some kind of syrup. Very messy." Benjii nodded, moving

369

behind the cash register and down the long counter that bordered one entire wall of the old store. In front of the glass case that displayed an array of watches and costume jewelry, he nonchalantly dropped his backpack and turned into the doorway that led to the back of the store. There was no hint visible in his demeanor to suggest the speed at that his heart was racing.

During the first minutes of the ride from the garage to the drop-off point, Arakhan had quickly finished assembly of the bomb in his bag. A pound of C4 lay wrapped in plain brown paper, a small detonator stuck into it at one end. A pencil was sufficient to make a perfect resting place for the small object, roughly the diameter of a .22 caliber cartridge and about two inches long. A wire fuse six inches long ran to the digital timer, that had been the last item found before leaving, and setting it to send a battery-powered electrical impulse at 9:30 took only seconds to accomplish.

The shock wave created by detonation of the block of explosive would make its own shrapnel, the pure force of the blast killing all within twenty-five meters. The glass case full of small items, including pocket knives and a variety of small metal toys and the like, would make a huge grenade out of the whole back of the store. Add to that the fact that the wall where the pack now rested was a bearing wall, holding up the center of the old four-story building, and the results are obvious.

The terrorist did as he was told by the boss, cleaning up some cough medicine, stocking some shelves with paperback books, and then checking out several customers. Until 9:20. A casual glance at his watch, carefully synchronized with the electronic timer in his backpack on the way to town, told him it was time for a small diversion. His departure would occur within three minutes. At exactly 9:24, an elderly man slipped and fell in the front doorway, crashing into first one side of the aisle then the other, merchandise scattering everywhere.

The proprietor raced to his aid, as the old man made lots of noise, cursed loudly in an Arabic dialect, threatened to report all manner of violations to all manner of agencies and public authorities. Finally he jerked his arm away from the now furious owner as he stomped loudly out of the store. The old man walked the half block to the corner and turned ninety degrees onto the intersecting street, then stepped into the waiting Hyundai, still driven by Baheer, but now with Benjii in the back seat. They drove away quickly.

They could hear and feel the huge concussion created by the exploding bomb two minutes later. The building collapsed, killing eighteen people, plus eleven more who were blown to plasma in the street. No one would doubt that the bomb was Jewish retribution against the violence recently attributed to the PLO, and the resulting addition to the polarization between the two was predictable and necessary to keep the fires of hostility properly fanned. Killing his own people for the sake of a bigger objective had never been a problem for Yasser Arafat.

15.

The President of the United States lay in an expended, quivering heap, his heart still racing, his skin moist with perspiration, his breathing quick and shallow. Mind momentarily empty, he felt faint and weak, limp.

"Old man, you still know how to please a woman, and that's a fact. Been with you at least one hundred years now, and well. . you're still the best! Unless of course, *you're* dead, too. Jackie, bless your heart, you're panting like an old hound! Goodness, man, this ol' broad too much for you?" Molly rocked up on one elbow, her slender hand gently grabbing her husband's heaving ribs in a sharp tickle.

He moved only slightly, the fatigue more intense than the tickle reflex. He turned back toward his smiling wife, the sight of her beauty again shortening his gasping breath.

"I swear, but you're a mouthy broad, Mrs. Webb. . .first you attempt assassination by suffocation, then laugh at the victim! You're a hard woman, Mrs. Webb. . .a hard woman." Without warning, the President's long body moved up and around her, his powerful arms enveloping her, rolling her back and pinning her to the pillow. A groan was muffled as it emanated from her throat and got lost in his embrace, while she once again marveled at the blinding quickness of this big man.

"Enough of your disrespect, young lady, hush and let me rest. Tomorrow starts at 0 dark thirty—OK?" Before she could answer, his face disappeared from view, as he planted a number of kisses from her chin down to her navel, and all places in between. Again the giggle, but now more like a squawk, her own tickle reflex producing a gyrating attempt to escape. As he pulled away from her, Jackie Webb stopped, instantly motionless. He pulled himself back up to the pillow and stopped, his gaze locked on the face of his wife. The grin faded to an intense visage; breathing slowed. Molly lay motionless, her eyes locked to his, their faces inches apart.

"Woman, you are my ideal, my gift from God. I love you like I did then—only more. I love you." A tender kiss punctuated the statement before he lay his head next to hers. They were asleep in seconds.

Book III – Starting Over, Fighting Back

* * * * *

"Reveille, sir, it's zero five hundred. Chopper lift off scheduled for thirty minutes from now. You clear, sir?" Brooks knew just how much voice it took to awaken the General, and what response to expect.

"Yes, Jonathan, I'm clear. Thank you." The sergeant major quietly closed the door just as Webb turned on the small lamp beside the bed.

They were on the big jet Ranger three minutes early, the dampness of morning over Washington creating a veil over the city as they streaked toward Ft. Bragg. Webb sipped strong coffee from a big mug as they flew, his notes for the upcoming address now in a neat stack on the floor beside his seat. How many times he had ridden in these craft, the sound of the rotors drowning out the churning in his stomach as he anticipated the approaching mission. Only this time, the end of the ride would not be met with hostile fire or a drop into remote wilderness. This time he would be met with honor guard, "Ruffles and Flourishes," "Hail to the Chief." Then he would speak to several thousand men who were about to attack America's two biggest cities.

Hot sunshine produced beads of sweat on the faces of soldiers standing row on row, formations perfectly set on the parade ground. Every one of the thousands of men who stood this event held his position of attention, their discipline apparent, unified. And every one hoped to catch a glimpse of "General Jackie," first foot soldier to sit in the White House since Ike. He was the man who had broken the race barrier to the highest office in the world; the man who had kicked butt and taken names in Vietnam, won the Medal of Honor and lived to tell about it. He was the commander-in-chief who brought them home from the God-forsaken deserts of Saudi Arabia—brought them back to their own ravaged country, where they could fight to recover the land for its people. This was a man they loved and revered.

Stepping down from his supported position in the back of the reviewing vehicle, a Hummer with no top, Jackie Robinson Webb strode deliberately across the parade ground and up the ten steps to the platform. Like some picture out of the past, the rostrum was draped with red, white, and blue bunting, Old Glory and the flag of the president stood flanking the lectern, a light breeze ruffling the fabric. The p.a. announcer's big voice boomed, "Ladies and gentlemen, the President of the United States."

His heart pounded heavily, slowly, as he ascended the steps, the outline for his address still back in the chopper. This would be a speech from the heart, not from the desktop. Then, without flourish, he spoke into the microphones. "Would you stand with me, please."

The huge throng that occupied the bleachers on either side of the expanse of soldiers at attention rose in unison, as Webb stepped back from the lectern; he subtly ushered a colonel in the United States Army Chaplain Corps to the front. "Let us pray together," the silver-haired officer said in a quiet, deep voice.

Heavenly Father, we come before You with heavy hearts, our beloved country ravaged by damage inflicted at the hands of evil men. Our homes and families suffer, Lord, they are hungry, exposed, injured, sick. The devastation to our cities has cost us priceless treasures of learning and art, our society torn and burned. But these men and women stand before You this day, asking Your blessing upon them and their mission of recapture, of restoration.

Guide us as we vanquish the cruelty that has killed our children and raped our women, direct our actions against the awful forces that have torn our republic apart. Make us the instruments of Thy will, and lead us safely, effectively, swiftly against the enemy, that we might liberate our suffering people and return our country to order and freedom. We ask these things in Thy name, oh Lord Amen.

A rustle spread across the parade ground as the people in the bleachers sat down; a stout Army Brigadier General spoke sharply to the Commander of troops before him: "Colonel, bring your troops to parade rest."

The colonel saluted, turned an about face on his heels and barked "Bring your troops to parade rest." Echoing across the open expanse, the unit commanders in sequence barked out their preparatory order, each addressing the unit before him, "Brigade—" *Battalion—"* or *"Company"— followed by the command of execution," Pa-Raade REST!"*

A huge rumbling swept across the hot field, and that quickly, twenty-five thousand men and women stood with their eyes forward, hands behind their backs, feet apart. The president stepped back to the podium.

The sight of all these soldiers—row on row, stretching across the open area, flags fluttering in the hot breeze—sent chills up and down the big man's back. Again he fought tears, welling up but quickly blinked away; he feared his voice would fail him. A whispered prayer and a deep breath.

"Fellow Americans, we are here today about matters most gravely important, at a time when our Country faces great danger. I have come to send you forward on missions of maximum importance to the future of the United States. But first,—" and here a smile, broad and warm, touched with emotion, broke across the dark face of the President— "*Welcome home!*"

Applause broke out spontaneously all over the field, and a huge cheer exploded from the massed formation. A band director who had been clued in earlier by a whispered order from the big man himself sliced the air with a downbeat to "The Stars and Stripes Forever," and everybody stood again. Smiles gave way to tears and back slapping hugs from one end of the giant assembly to the other, as thirty thousand people celebrated the safe return of all these brave troops from the folly that had lured them to the remote deserts. The emphatic crack of percussion that ended the "Stars and Stripes" bounced and tumbled into the distance, and suddenly the big field was quiet again.

"There is no greater joy in the life of the military commander than the moment when he sees his troops safely home again. God bless you."

I stand before you today bereft of the kind of zeal for combat that I have enjoyed these past twenty-five years as a soldier, my heart instead fearful and my mind often confused. This time I have no faraway enemy to vanquish, no foreign land in that to perform acts of military skill. Instead, it is my job to send you brave soldiers against our own land, our own beloved cities. For that reason alone, this is the most difficult mission of all.

I have ordered you to battle, my compatriots, not against some far distant enemy, not to secure some remote and distant objective, but to re-take from the forces of evil the very heart of our own land.

The Devil's Playground

When I ordered you home from the deserts of Saudi Arabia, I did so with eager desire to remove you from what now appears to have been largely a grand hoax, a huge diversionary charade, intended to deprive the United States of the very power and authority it would need to stave off the forces of evil that then attacked us in your absence. The fact that our leaders were so easily duped is the source of immense national humiliation to us all. And while you were gone, our enemies struck at the heart of our country, plunging us into darkness and goading us into the most indescribable violence against each other.

Now, with you back home where you belong, I must ask you to shoulder another responsibility, this time in the immediate defense of your own hometowns. You must recapture our great American cities and return them to the honest and law abiding-persons to whom they truly belong. Unfortunately, many of these very citizens remain trapped in the clutches of anarchy, their freedoms, their very lives now in the hands of men who would squander them as mere objects of their wanton pleasures. These are forces that must be stopped; they must be removed.

So I send you to battle in your own cities, with orders to destroy the evil that holds them, but at the same time to save the innocent persons now imprisoned by their violence and base appetites; act swiftly, decisively, but with caution and compassion for all the precious lives now in the balance. With God's help, we will drive the forces of dread and destruction out, while saving and protecting the lives of all those who await our arrival with waning hope. You must not fail them. God bless all of you, and God bless the United States of America."

As so often had happened already, the end of the President's speech was followed by complete silence. He captured, *captivated* his audiences with a forthright, almost blunt delivery, but one punctuated by grand and timeless rhetoric that rang true and hit home. But this time, no applause followed the silence. Instead, the man turned, returned the salute of the general in command of the assembly, took the hand of his wife, and quietly walked off the platform. At the command, the entire mass of uniforms

376

snapped back to attention, and the president came to attention in return.

The congregation of humanity was so enormous that the traditional "pass in review" parade was essentially impossible to accomplish, so the president was instead escorted by color guard across the massive formation and then out of the parade ground. The mood left behind was somber, even reverent, colored by the overwhelming dread of what lay ahead. But to a man, they all knew *what* to do, and they had complete confidence in the man now leading them. What remained was the accomplishment of the mission.

16.

Chaos makes things impossible for the stable, law-abiding citizen, with no way to maintain access to the essentials of life. Conventional patterns of behavior, set in the cement of lifelong habits and traditions that have worked for generations, suddenly fail; what follows is hunger, sickness, and panic born of isolation and violence. But things are different for those who live their lives on the other side; criminals, drifters, con men, mercenaries can more easily move and scavenge than their more sedentary, honest counterparts, and at times, the very existence of such conditions can make things easier for them, especially things like travel and the acquisition of weapons and information.

When Lester Monroe finally drove away from the peace and boredom of Lake Michigan for the last time, he knew he would not be able to travel by highway in his big Mercedes for very long. However, he got farther than he thought he would, driving all the way into central Pennsylvania before things got nasty enough to require him to leave the car. Gas had been tough, but he successfully siphoned enough from a variety of abandoned cars to keep going that far. Outside Pittsburgh, on I-79, he encountered a messy mixture of military units and assorted roving gangs of hoodlums that required him to get off the big roads. With his objective now only a few hundred miles away, he decided to follow other, less direct avenues the rest of the way.

The Steel City was no less racked with chaos than the other cities he'd traveled through—or around—but with his well-honed instincts for survival, Lester found his way. Using his twenty-plus years of military life as a calling card, he approached Guard units and managed to talk and con his way into long conversations with various troops hungry for information from other places. Of course, the fact that he wore his own BDUs, complete with master sergeant stripes, combat infantryman badge and Airborne wings, helped even more. The story was pretty good, too. Home on leave when the lights went out, stuck in Chicago for eight weeks, just trying to get back to NYC in hopes of finding Mom.

Wherever he went, the good ol' boy persona seemed able to glean information and even an occasional bit of food from the younger men in uniform. The upshot of all this was a decision to move directly into the NYC area as quickly as possible, and to do so without much preparation. Weapons for Sallie's demise would be no problem once into the big city, and carrying any kind of firearm between Pittsburgh and the Eastern Seaboard would be an open invitation to unwanted attention.

After walking nearly fifty miles over a two-day period in early June, Monroe hailed down a convoy of Guardsmen en route from Pittsburgh to Altoona, regaling them with a sad tale of woe concerning his poor sick momma back in Jersey. Could he bum a ride to town? Sure, no problem. Strict military regulations concerning such things were much ignored, what with the constant stream of lost and homeless persons littering every route. From Altoona to Harrisburg, from there to Allentown, then to Elizabeth by the Fourth of July, the good ol' boy drill worked like a charm. With the Bronx only a few short miles away, the time for real preparation and finding a way into the city had arrived. Weapons, transportation, some food, then go kill Sallie.

* * * * *

Things were getting less appealing with each passing day in the Spa. Rations of all but the most basic stuff were getting thin, and the air conditioning that had always kept the ancient tenement reasonably comfortable quit, although use of the generator that powered it had become too risky anyway. Now the rickety old structure was as hot and musty as any other building in the South Bronx, making the fact that they were forbidden to open windows below the fifth floor all the more painful. The two dutiful creeps that tended to his every need and whim did all they could do to keep the diminutive terrorist mollified, but the long siege was beginning to wear on him. And of course, given the bloodthirsty personality of the guy, neither of the two ghouls could be sure what might happen next. Cedric stood, shoulders stooped in that timeless posture of obeisance, awaiting the master's order.

"All right then, Cedric, fetch Sherman at once and prepare the microwave dish for assembly at dusk. That gives you an hour—plenty of time. I have to believe we'll hear from the Committee tonight. Hell, it's been almost three weeks,

379

and things are so hot in the Middle East now, they *have* to be planning something for us. *GO!*"

Cedric strove to deny his mind the unspoken objections he had to setting up the damnable space-age transmitter on such short notice. Regulations required that, once the offensive began, no portion of it was to be left visible after use. That included a platform and dish that weighed two hundred fifty pounds, a complete computer that handled the encryption and decoding required to make sense of the transmissions, and one hundred feet of heavy cord for power and data, incoming and outgoing. The stuff was also required to be stored in secure fashion, so unpacking it was also a big deal. All in all not a fun project, and certainly not one to be easily accomplished in one hour, in an environment where the temperatures exceeded one hundred degrees and the air was thick with dust and mold.

Nonetheless, the job was accomplished as ordered, and right after sunset, July 6, Sallie sat in the black shadows of the entrance to the roof, headphones in place, computer booted up and awaiting signals. Exactly at 8 o'clock, the introductory bits lit up the screen, the first sounds of audio transmission began, and the little killer sat up straight in expectant posture. "Good evening, Salim, this is Anwar. Present with me are the members of the Committee, except for the Chairman. I trust all is well with you and your team." The fact that he was actually listening to the big boys again, for the first time since the Offensive began, left him stunned, so much so that he was several seconds responding to the inquiry.

"Yes—YES, Anwar, thank you, we are well, only a bit warm and somewhat bored on occasion. And you?—"

"Thank you, Salim, we are well, if only, like you, weary of the waiting and eager for the consummation of the plan. And that is why we call this evening, my friend, to issue orders, now that the next phase is about to unfold. With the invasion of New York by American troops imminent, it is time to arm the faithful with the weapons and explosives you have stockpiled. Tomorrow, at zero two hundred, Eastern Time, a large contingent of the Vanguard will appear at your installation; their leader will only be identified to you by the code name "Striker," and all we can tell you about him is that he is tall, thinly built, Arab in appearance, and has a long, oblique scar that runs from in front of his left ear down to the corner of his mouth. Is that clear, Salim?"

Sallie blinked hard to take in this flood of information, having stopped breathing when the announcement about the "next phase" was made. This was what he had been waiting for, planning for, *living for* for almost five years. Now he would truly fight in the cause of Allah, striking deep at the heart of the infidel and, more personally, sating himself in the blood of thousands. Again, after too long a pause, he responded. "Yes, Anwar, all clear. We eagerly await the visitors. But what are we to do, here at the SPA, after arming these men? Can we not accompany them into the offensive?"

"Not at once, Salim. Be patient. Your function is to remain in contact with the Committee and provide resupply, particularly of the explosives and ammunition. We do not want too much of those precious commodities leaving the safety of your care at once. But I assure you, Salim, that you and your team will shortly wade deep into the enemy. Only be patient a little longer."

Sallie stifled a scream, swallowed an enormous, profane objection, closed his eyes tightly in an effort to control his rage. "As you have said, Anwar, as you have said. We are obedient to the will of the leadership without question."

The transmission ended without further conversation, and the NYC contingent immediately began disassembly and concealment of the equipment. Sallie moved quickly to the storage area, once more to satisfy himself of the location and readiness of the instruments of death and destruction he had warehoused in the middle floors of the old building. In six hours, he would begin to provide the soldiers of Islam with the tools of the holy Jihad, the war to capture all the world for Allah. His frustration at being temporarily left behind was overshadowed at once by his excitement at the momentous events shortly to occur.

* * * * *

J.D. stood in the rubble of what he was certain was the very store where he had wasted the old Jew, some twenty-five years earlier, the sound of military vehicles rumbling by on the elevated highway that had so perfectly drowned out the sound of his murder weapon, long ago. After ten days in

Philadelphia, he had still found no trace of his aunt, who was, at least as recently as a year ago, still living in the same place she was when he left so precipitously after killing the liquor store manager. Of course, he had not communicated with her for twenty years, since his "remains" were transported back to Newark for military burial. He had no doubt that Hattie had been there, tears streaming down her plump cheeks, flag clutched close to her bosom.

Ever since that old white lady died in his arms back in St. Louis, some four months ago, Jackson Daniels had had but one consuming goal—well *two*, actually. One was to kill that little bastard who had convinced all his brethren to bomb their own country right out of the twentieth century, and the other was to find his dear Aunt Hattie, confess the whole thing to her, and live out his life caring for her. She was, after all, the only human on the planet ever to show him any real affection, and the only person ever to make even the slightest attempt to provide for him. It had been the feel of the arms of that dying woman, clutching his neck before she slipped away, that shocked him into a passion for his only real family. A strange paradox for one who had chosen killing for money as a way of life.

The search had gone poorly, with many parts of Philadelphia still on fire and rife with violence of all kinds. Starvation and disease ran unchecked, with the dead rotting in the streets in ever-increasing numbers. Efforts by law enforcement and military alike to collect up the corpses were foiled again and again by gangs of every description who set up ambushes, using the bodies as bait. Twice J.D. found himself stuck in the middle of a firefight, being forced to take up weapons from the dead around him just to get out alive. He killed more thugs than cops in those two engagements, but each time narrowly escaped with his hide intact. And there was still no sign of Hattie.

Landing in the rubble of the old liquor store was quite accidental, but fortuitous, because it sent him back in time through the old routes he had known as a boy and teenager. He resolved to find Hattie, dead or alive, then to arm himself and pay a visit to Sallie.

17.

"'Scuse me, Henry, but I got a call for you on the secure line—big boys wantcha on the double—better come on." The assembled crowd that was listening to Herman Hanks' report on the Brownsville fight spun on this interrupter, bearer of bad news, like he'd just burped into the microphone on the eighteenth green at Augusta National. Lassiter had trouble even realizing that the guy was talking to him, so intent was he on the account being rendered by his friend, all the more so as his mind strained to hear some fragment he could attribute to his missing son.

"That's really about it anyway, Henry. When I woke up, they had me on a stretcher, my head and face all wrapped in bandage. They'd plugged a gash in my chest with a big wad a' gauze, and before I could speak, I was loaded into the back of an Army ambulance. Turned out my wounds were pretty superficial, so here I am. Found out later that the body bag lying on the sidewalk beside the ambulance was Tony. Guard brought in two gunships to clean off the rooftops and an Abrams to blow out the reinforced position the assholes had at the end of the street. That's pretty much all I know. Cost us thirty-two dead and twelve wounded, plus four Hummers destroyed by some armor-piercing ammo they had for one of their stolen machineguns. Go take your call—maybe it'll be something fun like a day off—something like that."

Henry smiled weakly at the ludicrous suggestion and grunted out of the old wooden chair. Walking down the hall, he barked back over his shoulder, "Stay put, pencilneck, I'll be right back." The room with the secure line in it was inconspicuous in every way, just what one wants when hiding such things. He sat down at the desk and waited for the signal from the communications guy that the line was hot.

"Yeah—Lassiter here, who've I got?" His face went blank, then dark, his brow knitting, his eyes boring into the top of the desk. The voice identified was one he had never heard before, but the authority was obvious. He began writing down instructions as fast as he could.

"Mr. Lassiter, my name is William LaShier, and we've not met, but I am calling on orders from the Director. I am head of counter-intelligence for the Bureau, and my assignment since the blackout began has been to coordinate domestic efforts to find the source of the power station bombings; that has also included collection and analysis of all intercepted communications coming into the U.S. from the Middle East. We have just learned that the operative your office was looking for back in January is still in business, and we believe he has access to secure communications from the PLO. He is also believed to have access to a substantial arms cache." The voice paused momentarily, the rattle of papers audible in the silence.

"As you know, Army troops are preparing to begin clearing the outskirts of the city, in preparation for an effort to neutralize the armed resistance that continues the rioting and armed conflict in the more populous areas. The information we have is incomplete and somewhat in conflict, but we believe there is a large, although probably presently dispersed, paramilitary force in the area of the Bronx, with elements also hiding in Brooklyn. They may be preparing to mount an all-out counterattack against our forces when they arrive. Unless your people can find this "Sallie" person and take him out, we can expect heavy resistance to our military operations and much higher casualties as a result."

Lassiter's head pounded and his stomach turned over and over. He knew what was coming next, and the past six months had already proven that finding this guy was impossible.

"You'll not be surprised to learn that you must find him without delay. What little information we can get suggests that he will be gone within a few days, and that his weapons stash will be delivered sooner than that. You are to suspend all administrative functions, use every available man for this assignment, and link up with the National Guard units headquartered in your building; however, be careful not to spook your target before you find the weapons. There are others who can find those things if you don't, and they will almost certainly get them into the hands of these Muslim forces without delay. That is what we must avoid. Thank you."

Just like that, the guy hung up. Oh well, no need to visit about the thing, really. What was Henry going to say? "No, thanks"? He hung up the phone and headed for the HQ offices for the Guard, downstairs, all the while running over the obvious fact that the guy had to have been legitimate, or he'd never have had access to the secure line. . .and the order to find Sallie was no news flash—hell, he'd been top of the list for almost a year already. But that business about the weapons and the secure location. . .and the intelligence concerning Muslim forces. Wow, what a wild. . .but then, those snoops, they had always amazed the rest of the FBI anyway. No choice but to move on it.

He knocked on the door to the Guard HQ and, when the door opened, saw a Colonel in the Army Guard, a real estate broker by the name of Boyd Jeffers, whose face bore an expression as confused as his own. He stood at a desk with a telephone in his hand; he hung it up as Henry walked in and said, "They just told me to expect you. Sit down, Henry."

* * * * *

The south side of Richland's urban center melded quickly into some heavy industrial development that included lots of long, low buildings and tall smoke stacks, gray warehouses and a variety of assembly line buildings, all surrounded by eight-foot chain link fencing. Keeping to the side streets and alleys downtown, the old Ford van rumbled softly along toward the outskirts of town. Light drizzle began to fall through a foggy veil that descended across the low skyline of working-class Richland. The van stopped at the edge of a parking lot surrounding a vacant gas station, rolling up beside a water faucet that stuck out of the side of the building.

A lone figure warily exited the van and stooped to try the faucet. Water gushed out of it, and the man quickly filled several milk jugs and two empty beer bottles and climbed back into the van through the side door, quietly sliding it shut behind him. As the vehicle pulled away, soft voices from inside were punctuated by a muffled scream, then another, followed by a string of epithets, then silence again. The old Ford slowly rolled through the center of this now dark and deserted industrial area. It traveled a route that had previously handled a seemingly endless stream of truck-borne commerce on this road that led, in an oblique direction, out to the Interstate highway bypass. The big highway was also black dark, and the van moved on under it and followed the smaller road out into the country.

"Snoop—hey, Snoop—*goddammit, listen to me—Tub's dead, I'm sure of it. HEY—you hear me, nigger, I said Tub's dead! What we do now, Snoop, huh—got a dead man with us and two more gon' die soon—what 'chu gon' do now?!?"*

The driver looked back through the rearview mirror, then turned in his seat to try to see into the darkness behind him; all that was visible was the sweating face of the man whose eyes were now bulging out at him like some contorted mask from a bad horror flick. Pud Millan was so hysterical the driver thought his face might explode. looking around at the empty roadway, he took the van out of gear and let it coast to a stop without ever touching the brakes—or therefore causing the brake lights to beam their red signal into the night.

"OK, Pud, chill out; let's have a look. Didn't think he was hit that bad, but maybe. . .G. boy, step out and listen good—don't want no company. . .jus' don't get silly wi' that shooter, OK?" The huge white face in the right front seat grunted as he stepped from the van, his full height of six feet eight inches projecting above the roofline. The driver put the truck in park, then stooped over and walked back between the seats, trying to avoid the three bodies that lay prone, side by side. A fourth man was stretched out diagonally behind them, his feet up by the back of the sliding door and his head against the back door. Pulling a long six-cell flashlight from behind the spare tire, he shined the light directly into the ashen face and glazed eyes of a very dead man.

"Dead sure. Well—Hey, G. boy, things quiet out there?—We got some cargo to unload—quick." The huge form of Gordon Fletcher appeared at the back door, his thick, coarse features peering through the glass. He opened the right door and spoke with soft but incredibly deep tones.

"Yeah. Nothin' but crickets and frogs. Thick as soup out here with this fog. Can't see shit." Sidney Davis, Jr., aka "Snoopy" after his chosen profession of residence burglary, was the boss, the leader of what had been a small army of very bad people. Armed and trained by the Nation of Islam and populated with a charming assortment of alumni from several penitentiaries around the country, they found cover and diversion in the growing ghetto of that midwestern city. Snoopy had the respect—and fear—of every one of them, and he had led them on a wild and bloody killing spree that began when the lights went out. This was what was left. Another dead brother in need of summary disposition.

Snoopy climbed over the body and stood down on the gravel road beside his giant sentry. Listening intently, he turned in the direction of the racket coming from the thicket to their left rear. "Frogs. There. Maybe a swamp or at least a ditch. Dump him in there. Go." Fletcher turned without waiting an instant, handing his shotgun to his leader. He reached into the back of the van and scooped up the limp, bloody corpse and hefted it over his shoulder. Four steps put him out of sight, the only sound being the swish of the weeds parting as he walked into them. He walked a dozen steps, stopped, waited. Splash. He re-appeared, his feet squishing noisily, his boots obviously full of muddy water. They got back into the van and drove off.

"That's great, Snoop, just *great! pretty soon the whole goddam squad be floatin' in that fuckin' swamp. I 'spose you-"*

Shut the fuck up, Pud, 'less you pushin' ta be next!! Nothin' to be done for him 'cept get rid of his ass 'fore he start stinkin' things up. What you want—I should dig a hole, sing some songs, say a prayer—fuck you, Pud!! We headed out'ta town, find someplace to hole up and heal up, too. See if we can't fix up these other boys 'foe they die, too. Might get lucky and find some food and a good hidin' place out here. Just chill, OK?" Silence remained perfect then, as the old Ford rolled off into the foggy night, south into the country.

* * * * *

KCF76, Augusta, this is Niner Hotel 682 Indigo, Bakersfield, I copy—how's things, Jimmy?"

"Hey, Bonnie, not bad, if you call 97 degrees and one hundred percent humidity a good time!! What's up out in La La Land? Al told me a little while ago you'd seen some big action out your way? His batt'ries run low, so he signed off 'bout two a.m."

"Yeah, things're hoppin', I just can't tell exactly that way. We got all kinds of military installations around us, and it seems there's military air traffic in all directions. Edwards Air Force Base is only 'bout twenty-five miles south of my house, there's the Naval Weapons Center just north and west of us about seventy-five miles, and Ft. Irwin is due east about a hundred miles. I got everything that'll fly zipping back and forth, from C130 transports to old Hueys and A10 Warthogs, you name it, we got it. And the cargo planes are coming and going twenty-four hours a day.

"Gotta be troop transport, we figure, with that many flights. Everybody says they're preparing to invade L.A. Today, we heard a cop who'd been down to Burbank with a supply convoy the Guard was running, said they were evacuating everybody they could find from the suburbs, setting up checkpoints and reinforced positions after emptying every neighborhood. Guess they're moving the folks up into the country in the San Fernando Valley area, where they've set up big tent complexes, with military medical facilities and food re-supply. He said they even had electricity back for the big camp; that's the first I'd heard that kind of good news."

"What the hell they doin", Bon, emptyin' the whole town?"

"Can't say for sure, Jimmy, but it's something big. If the same kind of buildup is going on down at Camp Pendleton and at San Diego, the bad boys are in for a helluva party when they all head for town!" Bonnie's weariness was only thinly veiled beneath her exuberance; the months of living in a small community that was starving and trying at the same time to care for the hundreds, even thousands of homeless people who were constantly migrating out of the city, had worn her down. Her tone changed, after the short pause between transmissions to her radio partner in faraway Augusta.

"I don't know, Jimmy, I just don't know. . .I mean, I want them to come and take the city back from the gangs and the crazies, and I want help for all these starving people—it just hurts me so bad to think of 'em fighting a full scale war right in Los Angeles, destroying the whole town. . .there'll be nothin' left of the place. . .We've fed people everything we could imagine that'd pass for food in the last two months and, even with my big garden and a huge supply of canned foods some of my neighbors had, it's all about gone."

"Gonna be ugly, for sure, Bonnie, but don't seem like there's any other way out—you keep sayin' the whole area's in the control a' all those warlords an' their gangs—how else we gonna git rid of 'em. Think the president's right. Can't be no peace, no chance fer startin' over, long's the militants an' the white trash 'er holdin' control a' the whole country. Gotta take it back. . ." His voice trailed off on the end, his own thoughts turning to the carnage with that he was all too familiar, in Atlanta, Macon, and even in Augusta, where the rednecks had run wild for months. In fact, everyone had their own stories to tell, their own tragedies to haunt their dreams forever.

Soon the radio friends signed off for the night, and Bonnie turned off her transmitter as the drone of heavy aircraft vibrated through the house, on and on.

18.

Weidenolf was resting for the first time in days, his aging frame weary beyond description from the tremendous demands the last week had placed on it. Lying back on the pillow, sleep approached at once. But before he could nod off, he thought one last time about the accomplishment now complete. He had built the best, most accurate, and well concealed nuclear bomb in existence in the world. And it would kill every Jew in Tel Aviv. Of course, it would kill every non-Jew as well but, being the good Nazi that he was, he knew such was simply a reality of war.

Then slumber came more slowly, the aging mind strangely without defense against visions of days gone by; the air conditioner hummed quietly, the soft tick of his old alarm clock marched on, and the dim half light from the bathroom all acted together to produce his favorite, most restful sleeping environment. But he did not sleep.

The Russian Front appeared, a scene pockmarked with a thousand shell craters and strewn with the frozen bodies of ten thousand German soldiers. A 1939 Nazi rally in Munich, complete with the Fuhrer's staccato speech and the strident military march music, drifted across the screen of his tired mind; then Buchenwald, its high fences and piles of dead Jews, him standing amidst young naked women, their skin sunburned, their eyes wide with terror, as he chose the ones who would work and the ones who would die.

He saw the face of his Jewish mother, that doe-eyed, dopey visage with that mess of curly hair constantly struggling free of the pins that held it back from her small, homely face. Bile rose in his throat as he watched that scene, now some sixty years gone, where he stood in the yard of their small house outside of Munich, announcing his hatred for all that was his family. Cursing his ferret-faced mother for all her Jewish inferiority, he could hear his youthful voice lashing out at his father for having begotten him from the loins of one so lowly and worthless. He saw her eyes, their tears soaking her small face and wetting the front of the plain white blouse. Chest heaving, he could clearly make out the words choking from her lips against his cursing. "Why, Karlie, *why would you do this, become this!?* I am your mother, I *bore* you, you are *mine,* my *baby,* Karlie, how could you—" In his mind he pulled the Luger from his belt and shot her, the first bullet crashing into bone exactly between the small breasts. Then another to the forehead, and another, and another. . .

Eyes wide, pulse fast, Adolpho blinked to clear his head. Straightening his back and pushing the back of his head into the pillow, he stopped breathing for an instant, in shock at the realization that he was aroused, his loins quivering, erect. Realizing next that, first of all, he had not shot his mother, but had killed countless young Jewish women in her stead while at Buchenwald, he remembered anew the thrill, the sexual rush it had always given him to take the lives of those simpering females. Some he had even used first, often repeatedly, for his more traditional sexual pleasures, so that there were even a few who began to delude themselves into the belief that their favors were protecting them from the evil within him. Wrong.

Each died at his hand in the end, each death signifying completion, perfecting the symmetry of having first used them, subjugated them in every sense possible. Then he took their lives face on, so that he could see that same loathsome anguish in their eyes as his mother had exhibited the last time he saw her.

After half an hour of this involuntary newsreel of his ancient past, he arose and moved unsteadily from the small bedroom, into the sitting room, where a wall cabinet held a bottle of Russian vodka. Surely a jolt of the grain would ease the tension he now felt, and sleep would follow. A second jigger, straight down, to quell a small tremor now subtlety in evidence in the hand that held the small, heavy glass. A deep breath, then two. There. Back to bed. Standing there in the darkness, the pale light of a full moon casting its cold color across the carpet, the old man revisited the visions that had so far deprived him of sleep in spite of the intense fatigue that now ravaged his frame.

The Russian Front passed in review again, a chill enveloping him at the remembrance of that frozen hell. He tried to replace that macabre tableau of dead Germans with the motion picture of his own viciousness in combat. He recalled his glee as the machinegun at his shoulder tore through the little clutch of Russians he had surprised in their bunker; their screams, the terror in their eyes, the sound and sight of their bodies lurching and twisting as the big bullets splattered their blood and brains up the walls of their hiding place. Then, against all his defenses, she appeared again.

That apparition of his mother. Even wide awake, and even after fortification from the bottle, she was there in his mind again. Now he could hear her cries, those insipid whinings against his fanatic passion for the Third Reich and the Aryan supremacy. His revulsion clutched him, so despicable was she—and the lineage she had passed to him. For a moment he could not banish that one cry, that one plaintiff response that she kept repeating as he reviled her. "But you *are* a Jew, Karlie, you cannot *help* it or deny it. You are of my lineage; you are a Jew by birth!" He shook his head savagely to banish that sound, that thought.

He had not had this dream for some time, maybe even for years, but its recollection was no less damning for its long absence. He had often laughed a sinister laugh at the idea that this God she called upon was probably responsible for his mother's ghostly appearance in his dreams. An absurd concept, for sure, there being no such deity, as his life had clearly proven many times. And besides, what kind of God would permit his "chosen people" to suffer near extermination at the hand of the Fuhrer? Nonsense. Pure nonsense. The double jolt of booze hit him with unusual authority, accompanied by an uncharacteristic dizziness now.

Turning to return the bottle to its place, his foot struck the edge of a leg of the table beside the cabinet. His unsteadiness, increased almost at once by the rush of alcohol into his blood, made his first step an uncoordinated movement, the skin split and the toes broke with a nasty, bloody crack. Stifling a cry of pain, then growling a string of Russian/German epithets, he grabbed the wounded toes, at the same time dropping the half-liter of booze so that it landed exactly on the corner of the cabinet top.

Shards of glass and a spray of vodka went in all directions, as Adolpho first hopped, then tumbled down onto the sofa beside the table, blood oozing between his clenched fingers as it ran from the laceration between his broken toes. The sensation of the warm liquid in his hand produced a moment's panic, and he sat up quickly, at the same time turning back toward the table and a lamp. The other leg and foot led the way, only to be recoiled by a new and even more painful jolt, as a big, jagged piece of the vodka bottle sliced into his heel and the sole of his foot.

Breathing at once became shallow and quick, the whole of his torso leaped back onto the comparative safety of the sofa cushions, and the old man suddenly realized that he was not wearing his glasses. The bottom of his foot was a blurry, gooey mess, as was the hand holding the other foot.

Sitting half on the sofa, but with one cheek of his bottom hanging off and slipping slowly toward the carpet, he struggled for a clear thought, a moment's recon. Then, at once he began to laugh, just a quiet chuckle at first, followed by laughter and then roaring guffaws. "You clumsy old drunk! What a clown you are, after all—" The laughter shook him, making speech impossible for a moment. "If you don't stop all this and sit still, you'll kill yourself right in your own apartment—what an idiot—" More uproarious hoots, then more, now really out of control.

The great scientist stood, his frame reeling and weaving to and fro as his now hysterical mind struggled for control, not able to identify the reality of his narcotic induced condition. One step onto the fractured toes was followed, after a cry of agony, by a step onto the lacerated heel; the reflex against the pain caused the involuntary attempt to lift that foot from the floor, at that point the top of the foot caught the underside of the low table, and the man pitched violently forward and to his right, his temple splitting open from front to back as the corner of the cabinet top punctured it just above his ear. The sickening sound of his skull fracturing was the last thing he heard. His body quivered for several minutes, blood and brains seeping from the split in his skull, then lay quiet.

A small light swept slowly across the motionless form, a reflection in the fixed, open eyes flashing back in the direction from that the light came. The light returned for an instant to the eyes, then moved on to the big bloody gash and puncture in the temple. A pool of blood, now growing beneath Weidenolf's head, also reflected the small light, as it continued on down to the chest. The light widened its focus to encompass the torso area, remaining fixed on that point for almost three minutes. The chest never moved. The light swept on down the body to the hands, where they could be seen folded over, the whole weight of the body resting on one hyper-extended wrist. The small light went out, accompanied by soft footsteps across the sitting room. A stout form stopped at the only window in that small area, his hands ensuring that both the curtains and the blinds behind them were closed tightly.

Walking back to the body, he turned on the lamp. He reached down to the neck, feeling for the carotid pulse. Finding none, the small flashlight then tested the pupils. "You rotten little creep, you've deprived me of killing you," were the words whispered by the intruder. "Oh well, most accidents happen in the home. . ." the man stifled his own laughter, now a rising current of convulsions in his chest. The original plan had been a complete failure, as Weidenolf had inexplicably failed to have his habitual nightcap of vodka before retiring. Entering the apartment to find the man fitfully asleep in his bed was most unexpected.

"Careful—you'll end up like old Karl, here—finish and leave," he warned himself in a whisper. The man searched about the floor for the neck of the vodka bottle, wiping out the inside of it carefully. Likewise the glass, that was not broken. Then he moved silently into the bathroom, where he poured the remaining contents of a small plastic vial into the toilet. A pair of sharp scissors from his breast pocket quickly chopped the little bottle into a dozen small pieces, that were then dropped into the water as he flushed the john. Rubber gloves, torn to small bits as the water swirled, disappeared behind the remains of the vial, and he walked out of the bath.

The post mortem examination, performed by some Iraqi pathologist of limited skill, would seize upon the huge skull fracture, resultant blood loss and damage to the brain, quickly declaring that the old man had drunk too much and fallen. The rare and undetectable chemical that reacted so perfectly with the alcohol to disable the victim, discoverable only by the most sophisticated of means, would never be suspected. And the fortuity of his accidental death, occurring before it could be accomplished by more purposeful means, would be forever hidden.

From the moment when Netanyahu determined to begin a secret propaganda war against Weidenolf until the present moment, things changed almost constantly. More and more fear of the completion of a nuclear device drove Israeli Intelligence to act more precipitously. Then they got lucky enough to discover where their target lived, and killing him immediately became the surest way to derail the project. The poison, containing an agent also useful as an interrogation tool when administered in small doses, was never intended to kill him, but only to disable him sufficiently to permit meaningful conversation before he was killed by the agent. But fate can be such an interesting ingredient in the affairs of men. The Mossad officer returned to the sitting room, took a quick look around, and exited the apartment without a sound.

* * * * *

"Mr. President, sir, I have General Keithley on the phone, sir." Jackie Webb spun around in his big desk chair, his back now to the window in the Oval Office. He nodded quickly.

"Fire away—what line?" The young Sp4 told him, and he punched the button. "What's the word, Clyde, you guys ready?" The big man leaned into the desk top, then he arose, towering over the mass of papers in front of him.

"Yessir, Mr. President, ready to go. As I told all of you last night, we have isolated several pockets of armed resistance; however, since then, we have learned that ones have any hostage capability, and I would like your agreement that we take out the ones who have no captives without further delay. We also have a pretty good make on the location of hostages in the other places, and we think we can get to them pretty quickly."

"Go. Rock and fire, Clyde, no time to think anymore. Hit them as you see the opportunities arise, and keep me posted. Godspeed."

"Thank you, sir, we're enroute." The line went dead, and the big hand quietly set the receiver back in place.

"Guide them, Lord, please. . .and protect all those poor innocents. . ." Sitting again, he turned back to the window and the view out into the weed-infested gardens.

At the other end of that line, the Chairman of the Joint Chiefs of Staff, General Clyde Anthony Keithley, turned to the assembled staff, his face rigid, gaze fixed. "All right, gentlemen, hit it. The operation is now with us, subject only to periodic reports to the president. General Conlan, deploy your troops and commence operations."

A tall, silver-haired Texan, the Two Star stood, his fatigues starched and his demeanor as hard as Gary Cooper in *High Noon.* "Yes, sir. I'll be right back." He rose from his chair in one of the large conference rooms at the Pentagon, walking to the door. He turned into the hallway and entered the next room. Picking up the phone, he spat a series of orders and a string of codes and encryption sequences, followed by a terse statement.

"Yes—this is General Conlan, give me General Hambley." After a moment, he spoke again. "Dick, it's Phil. Proceed. At once. Begin with the positions on the alpha list, and neutralize them without delay. Then hit the locations on the bravo list. Dick—the man says to make every effort to spare the civilians, are you clear on that?"

"Yeah, Phil—we're clear. Just don't know. It'll depend on where they are relative to the main emplacements. We'll do our best; it's just that we can't let these people get away. They've got enough explosive material to level several blocks of Manhattan, so we can't let them loose."

"I understand. Go to it. Oh, and Dick we need to be quick about this." The man responding to the General's order was Richard T. Hambley, a Major General who was in charge of the NYC offensive. Not a man given to eloquent or lengthy speech, his response was predictably terse.

"Roger that, General, I'm clear." Hanging up the telephone, Conlan walked back into the conference room, where the Chairman awaited. He sat down, looking directly into the face of the man he'd known since their first day at West Point, nodded his head to his chief and said, "Operation commenced." Keithley nodded back, looked intently into his old friend's face, then closed his eyes.

* * * * *

Carl Landry sat on the step in front of his house, visiting quietly in the darkness with Faith Jackson, the two physicians reviewing the now dwindling number of patients being treated in his basement. The wide variety of wounds, infections, and other trauma-induced problems were mixed with some pneumonias, three heart attacks, and the births of five babies. Earl, shot so many times Carl had thought him dead on first examination, was sitting up, eating, and now quickly becoming a substantial pain in the neck, with his incessant demands for a return to his prior active life. They

396

were both amazed he had even survived, and the energy he now displayed was a true wonder.

The radio in his pocket crackled, and Carl quickly responded.

"Carl, this is Curtis, out on the hill across the road from you. It's kinda' windy up here, so I couldn't be sure, but I think I heard small arms fire from over on Countyline Road—up towards the Allen place. Should I move over that way? I'm on foot, so it'll take me fifteen minutes to get close enough for a look." Carl thought for a moment, his mind resisting the whole idea that they might again face more fighting.

"Stay put, Curtis, and I'll try to raise the Allens on the radio. OK?"

"I'm clear, just let me know quick. If they're shootin' over there, the whole thing'll be over before I can help." Carl turned the little knob on the top of his radio to channel 26, the frequency used for communications between the various compounds throughout the area. Before he could key the microphone to call them, the radio screeched in his hands, the voice emanating from it so loud and obviously panic stricken that he nearly dropped the thing.

"*Carl it's Jake—we got a mess here—van full a' bad guys-!! Do you copy, Carl?!?*" The physician stared at the radio for an instant, then responded.

"I copy, Jake, we're on our way—how many of them?" The voice answering was still excited to the point of hysteria.

"*Looks like at least five men—wait!! Holy sh—!! They're leaving!! Brad, open up on 'em—Carl, do you copy, they have broken off with us and are heading west on Borgers Lane—I don't think we hit any of 'em—you copy?!*" The man's voice began to calm slightly, as Carl assured him he had heard and understood the transmission.

"I'm clear, Jake, check to be sure you have no one injured; I'm changing frequencies to get our people in the game. I'll be back to you, and Jake—thanks for the warning." Changing the radio back, he advised Curtis to maintain his position and listen for the approaching van. Then he called over to Josh's. The two brothers quickly agreed on a response.

"Let's stay put, but add men and weapons to both the Jericho Road sentry positions. Wake up the houses right now and double the guard at each place. Oh—and Carl, send somebody from your place up to relieve Curtis May. He's been out there since dusk. Let's get some fresh eyes and ears up on that hill." Josh put down the radio without any further discussion, and both men moved to prepare for whatever might be next.

The rest of the night was laced with enough tension to restart the lights in Richland, but the old van never showed up. In fact, by morning, there was no sign of it anywhere, and no evidence of any fresh tracks on any of the gravel roads that connected Countyline with Jericho Road. And the idea that they could not verify either its presence or learn with certainty that it was gone only made for a most uncomfortable atmosphere the next day. Josh led a thorough search of every wood lot, lane, and culvert, as four different squads of his ragtag little force scoured the landscape for evidence of the old heap. No luck.

"This is ridiculous. How the hell can a full-sized van just evaporate, right in the middle of country we know intimately, and at a time when we have every avenue of escape covered? There's gotta be an explanation for it, and we're just too dumb to figure it out." Josh spat the last sentence like bitter pills, most of the venom aimed at himself, then took a long drink from the glass of water Jess had brought him. Carl sighed deeply, then spoke without looking up from his intent study of the grass in front of the porch.

"Lighten up, they might've just turned around in the dark right out of Allen's lane, headed back toward town. No way we'd be able to tell if they did, and that would explain the lack of any trail or evidence. And if they did, we'll see no more of them. That welcome committee at Jake's probably provided a clear perspective to 'em about life in the country. We'll just keep our guard up, maintain additional night security for a few days, and not worry about them." Josh chewed on that one for several minutes, while all three watched the sun sink from sight, the small radios announcing the arrival in place of each sentry position.

"OK, old man, you're probably right. . .but tomorrow, I'm going back over on Countyline once more. If they *did* turn around, there should be some evidence of it in the gravel on the side of the road, or maybe even in the grass at the edge of the fields. Just gives me the creeps, the idea that more a' those bloody assholes could still be lurkin' around here after all this time." He looked around the porch, his eye stopping involuntarily at the stain in the wooden floor where LaShawn Williams had died just four short months ago. His feet hurt through the now-healed glass cuts his brother had so expertly treated, and the vision of the man's shattered corpse lying dead at that every spot made him weak. The older Landry saw the reaction, spoke to the moment.

"Seems like a hundred years ago, huh? So much killing since then—thought we might be done with it." Waiting a moment, then seeing Josh's gaze still fixed on the spot, he stood and walked to him. A big, rough hand rested on his brother's shoulder, as he spoke again. "Turn from it, Josh. Best thing you can do with that death or any of the others. I know what you're feeling. My mind fixates on that kid up at my place, and I can't shake it sometimes. He was so young, and we just simply tore him apart—"

"*Had* to, Carl, and you know it. Little bastard would a killed the lot of us—"

"*My point, baby brother,* precisely my point. 'Had to' is a pretty apt explanation for what you're seein' right now, too. Jess, take this boy inside a while. He's gotta cover the hilltop after midnight. See ya'." He kissed Jessica Marie gently, that one hand still on Josh's shoulder, then stepped off the porch and walked to the four wheeler. It sputtered to life, and he rumbled off toward his place through the woods behind the old farmhouse.

BOOK IV

THE GREAT OFFENSIVES

I...am a jealous God, visiting the iniquity of
the fathers upon the children...of them who hate me.
Exodus

The fathers have eaten a sour grape, and
the children's teeth are set on edge.
Jeremiah

Our fathers have sinned, and are not;
and we have borne their iniquities.
Lamentations

1.

Let's go, people, RIGHT NOW!!! You're OK, but you've gotta get out'a this building at once—LET'S GO!! YOU—forget the bag, just pick up the child and follow the others. WE—" A fusillade of machinegun fire, punctuated by two thundering explosions just a few hundred feet up the street, shook the gaggle of terrified women, children, and a few old folks almost off their feet. They staggered and continued to scurry down the back steps amid the crying of children and the cacophonous racket of one hundred people yelling and screaming at the same time. The small arms fire stopped, replaced at once with the sounds of men's voices barking out orders down in the street in front of the building.

They poured out the back door—there was no door, only a jagged hole where an explosive charge had blown away the entire frame—and broke into a shuffling, ragged line. The leaders followed a squad of soldiers who were in turn led by a large black sergeant. He was armed with an M16, held at port arms as he jogged through the alley that led away from the building, then turned right and opened onto the playground of a burned-out Brooklyn grade school. Four olive drab buses stood idling in its parking lot, themselves surrounded by soldiers in full battle dress, their positions bristling with weapons and an occasional radio antenna.

When the sentries in front of the parking lot saw the line of refugees turn the corner and head toward them, they

400

instantly fanned out into an armed human funnel; their eyes alternately scanned the tops of the buildings all around the school, the streets in all directions, and then stolen looks at the heartrending apparition that approached under heavy guard. The buses were situated at the end of these human funnels, and there were no impediments to immediate entry into them, once the people got to their doors. Inside, every third seat was occupied by some kind of nurse, medic, doctor, or medical assistant. Each was supplied with clean water, juice, and some bland food stuffs, in addition to a box full of medical supplies, bandages, and even morphine. But there was no way for these brave men and women to have been prepared for what they saw, as these terrified folk clamored up the steps and stumbled down the aisles.

A capacity of fifty refugees per bus had been established in advance, and the soldier at the door of the first bus barked out the word "FIFTY!" as a young woman carrying a toddler stepped inside. Another soldier spoke to the next person in line, ushering an elderly man to begin a new line that led to the next bus. It filled in two minutes, and the drill was repeated until the entire population of that tenement had been loaded into the string of green transports.

Chattering, barked orders, an occasional cry of pain, and a steady string of cries from small children filled the air around the parking lot, as the low rumble of a heavy fifty-caliber machinegun rolled over the area. Mounted on a light tank, it was quickly shattering the front of the upper stories of an old department store from that had poured a powerful stream of small arms fire and grenades. Unlike the smaller M60 machineguns with their 7.62 mm rounds, the big gun fired a huge, half-inch bullet that was nearly three inches long. Fired into the open windows and strafed across the face of the old building, the entire brick facade seemed to shatter and crumble to the pavement below. There was simply no place to hide from its murderous barrage.

But the people in the buses hardly noticed, as the frenzy of the medics and the hunger, panic, and pain in the faces of these American refugees whipped the atmosphere to fever pitch. The back of each bus had the seats removed and a number of stretchers set up across the width of the aisle. There the worst of the injured and sick were immediately taken, triaged, and appropriate treatment commenced at once.

I.V.s were anchored, irrigation and disinfecting of putrid wounds begun, vital signs assessed. One elderly man tried to resist the orders for his assignment to one of the stretchers, protesting that he just needed something to eat.

"Don't listen to him, Ma'am, he's hurt plenty bad—those bastards beat him awful when he tried to keep 'em away from us. *Melvin, you old goat, do what they tell you!!* Take him, ma'am, an' look at his belly—they stabbed him, too. They run off when they heard you all comin'." A stout Latin woman, her voice and face a powerful force as she spoke, pointed to the old guy as she insisted on attention for him. He looked back at her and then at the nurse, at first flushing with anger, then looking bashfully at the floor.

The nurse smiled at him. "Right this way, sir, let's have a look at that knife wound—" Melvin turned half way around and collapsed into her arms, knocking her back into the next medic. They struggled to balance themselves while at the same time maneuvering their patient onto one of the gurneys. The trauma team swarmed around him and went to work on, what turned out to be a deep abdominal wound that was causing internal bleeding. The man died on the way out of town.

* * * * *

Twin Peaks had seen better days. The front window was covered over with a piece of plywood, the door hanging forlornly from one hinge. And the once provocative sign over the corner was so full of bullet holes that the only remaining identifying marks were one of the "Peaks," a small patch of green where the trees had been, and enough of the lettering to spell "T-N P-A-S" during the daylight hours only. There was no more flashing neon burning within the sign itself.

The proprietor, without her flowing white gowns and bereft of the various accouterments of cosmetic beauty, still maintained her air of jocularity, if a bit more subdued, as she continued to roll with the endless combination of punches that this new and horrible life threw at her. When life as she knew it went dark, she opened her doors to the instantly cold and hungry folk of the neighborhood, feeding them until the food was gone, sheltering them from the wet miseries of spring in New York. At times she even summarily shot a few would-be punk warlords who were improvident enough to step within range of her shotgun.

The place was far from an oasis—there simply weren't any—but she did what she could for the unfortunates who came to her. And for some reason, Twin Peaks seemed to avoid the fiery destruction that befell so much of the rest of the Bronx, Brooklyn, Brownsville, and the whole NYC area. Enchante kept her big smile, continued to get dressed every day, and always seemed able to find a way to get her big hands on enough contraband foodstuffs to feed those who turned to her.

The "girls" who had worked for her and their various broods of children made up a substantial portion of her flock, but much to the surprise of the surrounding community, many of them also gave tirelessly, tending the sick and injured and manning T.P.s little impromptu soup kitchen.

J.D. stood in the shadows of the superheated evening, across the street from the corner location of his old hangout, watching in disbelief as Ms. Weaver stepped out into the street. White, flowing garments, now tattered and soiled but still a trademark, covered the long frame, the unmistakable voice and laugh audible at once. But the bulk was gone, the face no longer full and round. Actually, when he realized it was her, the thought crossed his mind that she looked like the old Tits from her long gone heyday as the premier black madam in the Bronx.

Looking up and down the street without seeing any immediate threat, he stepped from the shadows and began slowly walking up and across the empty space toward her. Still fifty feet away, she turned to see him approaching, and that huge, thundering, laughing voice gave him his first smile in many months.

"Holy *sweet* Jesus, but if it ain't—!! It *is* you, Whisky Jack, come home to mama!! M'god, girls, but he look good, now don't 'e? Dear *Sweet* Jesus, but he look good—!" Running to him out in the street, her soiled gown trailing along behind, she met and mugged him, still able to take his smaller frame right off its feet. Only when he got close could he see the wrinkles in her soft face, the bags under the now sunken eyes. Her long torso against him, while still upholstered with those huge trademarks, amazed him with its missing girth. The old thickness through the middle, the

403

weight she had carried on that big frame, was gone. The combination of the more shapely figure, still voluptuous and stunning, with the aging in the face, left the younger man speechless, so incongruous was the effect.

"M'gawd, son, but' cher voice is gone! Girls, look who's come home t' see ol' Tits—lookin' cute as ever, he is!" The man's eyes searched the pavement, as Enchante's line of bullshit still caused him to flush. "Git yore skinny li'l black ass in here an' let's have a look at chu'. You'll be wantin' ta see—oops. . ." Her face went slack, eyes misting over, as the reality of these past months hit home again. About to mention his favorite treat, Latresha, Enchante swallowed the words and attempted to banish the thought. She lay upstairs in bed, her lithe frame wasted by malnutrition and sepsis, the result of a gunshot wound to the abdomen. J.D. could see the reaction in the big woman's face, and instantly he knew.

"Where is she, Enchante, I want to see her. I walked a thousand miles to get back here, only three things on my mind. One was my auntie, who I can't find, another was killin' that little bastard who set up this whole mess, and the third was to come get Latresha and get her out a' this place." Tits couldn't really keep up with the entire list, with her grief and anxiety over Latresha consuming the moment, and the oblique reference to Sallie was a complete foul ball.

"Whis', I. . .who you mean, you gonna kill. . .I mean, *what* mess—I. . ." J.D. cut her off gently, thinking better of his uncustomary loss of control.

"Never mind that now, Darlin', I want to see Latresha. Now."

"Oh, but J.D., she ain't so good, no sir, no good at all. Real sick, J.D., and shot, too. She'd *kill* me fer lettin' you see her like she is now, I *couldn't*—"

"If she's here, I gotta see her. Now come on, I seen sick and shot people before—let's go." He took her arm, her eyes full of sadness and anxiety again, as they walked into the restaurant. The mercenary looked around at the hungry faces that filled the room, the place thick with the smell of disease, filth and sweat. Looking for a familiar face, he spotted his girl's best friend, a formerly plump little hooker named Jolene, still recognizable for the small scar that ran from the corner of her mouth down her chin; a drunken john had broken her jaw when she was fifteen. Enchante heard about her and carried her home from the local clinic, her mouth wired shut, sixteen stitches in her chin. The kid never left her.

"Jo—hey, wha'sup, kid—where's 'Tresh? The little scar reddened as it always did when Jolene started to cry, and she looked almost involuntarily at the stairs.

"C'mon, Tits, let's go see her." His authority was beyond question now, so the big woman led him up the steps, all the while trying to explain, to prepare him.

"Now J.D., she been through a lot, see. . .been shot, sick, and unable to eat. So, she don't look like you remember—I mean, she pretty skinny now, and pale, you know? I tried so hard to keep her strength up, but with all that infection in her belly, well, I—" They stepped quietly into one of the small rooms, the heat suffocating, even with the window open wide. Again, the smell of disease and filth. He looked fearfully toward the bed, at first unable to detect even a form under the badly stained sheet. Movement under the cover told him she was there, and she rolled over to see him. The man fought an overwhelming wave of nausea mixed with sorrow.

" 'Chante, is that—oh god, J.D.—oh god—you can't—oh. ." The thin voice trailed off in a soft sob, tears flowing from the sunken eyes, as she turned away toward the wall. Without knowing he had moved at all, J.D. was beside her, kneeling against the putrid bed. The sheet slipped away, revealing the devastation wrought by the wound, infection, and attending malnutrition. A small-framed woman anyway, she had been so beautiful because of that delicate form. Now, the elegant shape was gone, the breasts shrunken, hips like those from a picture of the dead in a concentration camp. He felt that searing pain again, the one that stabbed him as he held the old lady, dying in his arms in St. Louis.

He gently slipped his arms under her and held her to him, so like the old lady. Only she was not dead. At least not yet. Kissing the matted, dirty hair, he could feel his own tears running off his cheeks and mingling with hers. The soldier of fortune was shot through with the realization that he had played a huge role in producing this hell on earth; his grief at the appalling pathos in this tiny room was redoubled by the inescapable truth that it all started in this place, and he had helped cause it all. Never one to willingly accept much responsibility for the harm he caused, this was more than even his jaded psyche could avoid. He held his love, sobbing into her embrace. Grief so overcame him that he could not think beyond the moment. The madam quietly stepped back and out of the room, as the shadows lengthened with the close approach of evening.

* * * * *

"Ok, boys, listen up—got some news from the big guys. That was home office. We got orders. Herman, you little weasel, stay put, 'cause I want you with us on this one. When I get done, go find Gallagher, or whoever you're reporting to at DEA now; tell him I kidnapped your skinny ass." Turning to the assembled company, Lassiter began his briefing, like so many others he had already conducted but, somehow, the men and women in the room could feel a difference in his tone, his demeanor. The veins in the man's neck stood out, beads of perspiration glistened from his bald head, the dark eyes bored into each face as he barked orders.

"Balloon's goin' up, *now*. Army'll be *in the Bronx* by morning, a full mechanized brigade sweeping in along the expressway and down into the projects. That little asshole we been lookin' for with such miserable results all these months is reported to have a huge arms stash for the locals to use. We gotta find him and do it quick. He may have already passed out his party treats by now, but we can't know that from here."

Hanks blinked in his usual dopey manner, the wheels turning nonstop in his head. Tossing his greasy locks back from his balding forehead, he turned to speak. "Henry, we turned this whole borough upside down in the last year, lookin' for that guy—what's so different now? Shit, all we know about him now is rumor; no real hard evidence, except for a "maybe" ID from an old—*really* old—mug shot from the inmate records at the Tombs. Hell, may not even be him, Henry. . .nobody's ever shown me any hard intelligence that says this "Sallie" is really the same guy as Willie Calvert. And besides, it's been six weeks since there was even a stray gunshot from the area we thought he might be hiding in." Lassiter shook his head and fired back at the agent.

"I *know* all that, Herman, but this is different. With things quiet in that area, any movement ought to be easily visible. And the size of force it will take to carry out a big arms cache won't be able to just "slip by" us if we're watching. Here's the deal: We know—or at least we *think* we know—that his hideout has to be in this six block area, *here."* He smacked the end of a broken yardstick against a big street map that was pinned and taped to the wall above his desk. The area was outlined in red marker, with penciled Xs over the buildings around the perimeter that had already been evacuated, cleared by search, or had burned down in the big fire storm that attended the beginning of the festivities, back in March and April.

"Denny, you and six men you choose prepare to move back into the area, *here,* after dark tonight. Set up with scopes and radios so that you can get and keep a visual make on every route in or out. Don't go up too high in the buildings; I don't want to waste any time diggin' your sorry asses out a' the rubble of any collapsed buildings, OK? Any movement, you radio in and stand by. Arm yourselves with the whole program—flak jackets, automatic weapons, grenades. If you see 'em coming, you'll stand in place and advance from there on my order. I'm takin' orders from the Guard, 'cause they'll be handling the interdiction itself. We'll go in with them.

"Roger, you go in here with four more men. Same deal. Set up for surveillance at the best places in this area, here, and radio any activity instantly. Jeff, take the rest of the troops—and you, too, Herman—get outfitted for a fight. I'll go in with you, when they finally show up, and we'll do what the Army says. Now—" The aging snoop took a breath, blinked at the sweat running into his eyes as he was talking, paused a moment.

"Bottom line. If we intercept these guys *before* they get armed, we can just take 'em out on the spot, as long as the ambush can net the whole lot. Don't open up on 'em unless you've got 'em confined, 'cause if some of 'em get away, we've gained nothing. Oh—and no prisoners. If you see someone you think you recognize who might be an interesting interrogation, you can capture him if you like. But mostly, we just gotta keep 'em from getting away.

"If, *however,* they've already been supplied with these weapons, the game changes. They'll probably be better armed than we are at that point, so that means armor. Drop back if you're outgunned; try to keep 'em in sight, but drop back.

Radio any contact, and be goddam sure to let us know your location and the route you're taking to get away.

Hanks smiled malevolently.

"Sounds like we're bait, boys."

"That's the good news, wise ass. The Colonel has a dozen armored personnel carriers rigged with 901 TOWs, plus the Army just sent him six Abrams. We make like chickens, running from the bad guys, they follow and the Army plays taps for 'em. Just like that."

The close, stale air betrayed no sound of breathing; no one moved for a long moment. The three men assigned as group leaders moved to stand almost simultaneously, their faces frozen in identical masks of grit mixed with fear and anxiety. Lassiter raised his eyes from the floor.

"Oh—and, boys—*have a nice day.*" The paradox was overwhelming, as one of the men smiled in spite of himself. A chuckle slipped from the chest of a man in the back of the room, followed by another standing in the hallway. Herman tossed his head at Henry.

"Old man got a way with words—don't 'e, boys?" Without warning, the room erupted in laughter, uproarious, hooting, guffawing, eye-watering laughter. Like a gaggle of lunatics on furlough from the asylum, they cackled, poking each other, slapping knees and pounding backs. Then, just as suddenly, the laughter ended, and they all left, talking softly to each other as they walked down the hallway, off to prepare for war. Again.

2.

A little aerial surveillance would have been nice, or even some high altitude photography from a satellite, but no such luck. Joshua Landry sat on the back step of his old farmhouse, the sounds of the chatter of several kids mixed with the drone of a baler in the field beside the house. Again he smiled to himself at his brother's fortress mentality—that screwball mind that had insisted on a supply of diesel fuel and gasoline sufficient to operate their small farm for at least one season without resupply. Two of the younger men stood on an old hay wagon, stacking hay bales as they crawled out the back of the even older New Holland baler. Carl sat in the seat of a bright green tractor, pulling the entire operation around the field as they turned dusty, green forage into bricks of food for cows and horses.

A gaggle of laughing teenagers could be heard at the barn, passing the time between hay wagon deliveries, with their endless line of teasing ridicule of each other. The undeniably unique sound of his wife's big laugh was suddenly audible within the mix, arousing Josh from his funk. As always, Jess hung out with the kids at the barn, ramrodding the operation and providing a steady stream of banter between loads. In that moment, Josh realized that he was amid some of his favorite sounds and smells in all the world, as he sat in the middle of the twice a year ritual they all called "haybalin'."

Josh spoke to the empty back yard, his frustrated thoughts venting to a missing audience. "Bastards *must* still be around. Unless they headed back into town—a *very* unlikely possibility—they've managed to conceal that van and take care of themselves for a day and a half now. They must be hungry, almost certainly without much water. . .when they surface again we won't be as lucky as they were at Jake's. Time to dust off the ol' scoutin' skills, Josh. . .find these skunks before they find us. . ." He stood up, stretched his tired back and, casting a longing look toward the haying operation that hummed along out in the field, he walked back into the house.

Five minutes later he reappeared dressed all in olive drab and armed with a variety of weapons. He walked down the steps and out to the barn, where the whoops and screams told him the kids were dumping buckets of cold well water over each other's heads to cool off between loads. As Josh walked around the corner and into the midst of the festivities, everyone went silent at the same time, Jessica's huge smile evaporating at the sight of her husband. "Josh—what are you—"

"Gotta find our guests, Jess—they gotta be here someplace. And I just can't stand the thought of waiting for them to come calling. Not to worry, this is no seek and destroy mission. Purely recon, I promise. Here—take this and keep it on at full volume. If I find anything, I'll call at once. Tell Carl I headed back to the woods north of Jake's place, that area with the hilly pasture land behind it."

Taking the radio from her husband, her protest was immediate.

"But Josh, you've been all over the roads coming and going from that place already, and you said there was no sign of tracks *or people!!* Why go back there again, and why go *alone!?* Wait for Carl, or take one of the other men with you."

"Easy, boss, it's no big deal. Hell, I'm just lookin' for an excuse to skip *this* dusty mess—and you're doing so well, too! I'll just saddle up and take a little ride, miss all this work, and be back for dinner. Now just relax, OK?" He kissed her quickly, then walked into the barn and down toward the stalls where the riding stock was. For months they had made a practice of keeping a couple of horses up in the barn at all times, in case they determined a need for silent transportation on short notice. Saddling a buckskin gelding, he rode out the back of the barn lot without passing through the baling crew again. Riding back past the house and into the field where Carl and the two boys were working, he decided to ride up to the tractor to tell his brother what he was up to.

Although Carl had a marked tendency toward "better ideas"—after all he was older, and he *was* a doctor—he seldom questioned Josh on such matters. He nodded, expressed his predictable admonition about being careful, and let out the clutch on the John Deere. Josh could feel his brother's eyes on him as he disappeared into the trees behind the hay field.

The plan was simple: If that van was still around, the men in it had to be in pretty dire straits. Food and water were scarce at best, and certainly, unless they had been shot up too badly in the run-in with Jake's welcoming committee, they would hit again very soon. The road that ran in front of

Jake's place was paved in places, gravel in others, the product of benign neglect by the county highway department. And there were a number of fire breaks, tractor trails, and even a couple of old roadbeds that were accessible from the main road—a road that led back into town.

Josh was certain they *had not* gone back to town, as the reports concerning Richland made life out in the country, even with its occasional gunfights, a paradise by comparison. It seemed to Josh that they might have headed that way, then turned off within a few minutes, somehow managing to cover their tire tracks well enough at the point where they left the road to have avoided detection to this point. Two possibilities seemed particularly interesting, both of that were close together, offering pretty good cover. Both were gravel for a short distance after leaving the road; a little careful work with a tree branch and a foot could very easily obliterate tracks made by turning off the road. Further thoughts of a trick he had learned the hard way from the VC some eighteen years before kept his pulse elevated as he rode.

Small bands of guerrillas, operating out of South Vietnamese villages and travelling in stolen vehicles, would find a good ambush site along a well-traveled road. But instead of pulling off and concealing themselves when they came to the place, they'd drive on past it for a few hundred yards, their tire tracks making it evident they'd kept moving. Then the driver would stop and cautiously, painstakingly back up, taking extreme care not to deviate from the track already made in the dusty road surface. When they got to the ambush place—in reverse—he'd back into concealment, and then, like some wily Kiowa warrior, he'd wipe out the tracks made at the turning point. Special care was taken to repair all damage done to the tracks out in the road, so that, unless the intended victims were especially observant, there would be no way to detect the departure of the ambush vehicle from the road.

Riding along in the shade and protection of a line of trees that bordered the miles of farm fields along the way, Josh remembered just such trickery and the awful results he had seen and endured. A small squad of VC, less than ten in number and armed with a few grenades and AK47s, could decimate a much larger American unit. His mind struggled with the still vivid images of the twenty-two men he'd found

411

massacred on a dirt road that ran through the central highlands of Vietnam while on patrol with a squad of rangers in 1969. Stripped naked and rotting in the searing sun, they had been shot so many times that many of them seemed to have come apart. Their weapons were all gone, the three trucks and one jeep were burned, charred remains of the drivers, grotesque proof of the ruthless vengeance possessed by the enemy.

But young Josh had seen the roadway and its absence of tracks leading to the ambush site. Examining the tracks with an old NCO, already in the country for three tours, the man showed him how it had been done. Now, nearly thirty years later, the memory was clear, and the possibility that these men knew and used a similar method was in his mind as he rode.

The two likely exits for the van were not only close together, but they also came out in the same place, in a ravine formed by some low hills about half a mile off the road at the back of the woods. Josh's plan was to ride to within a few hundred yards of that location, then slip around into the trees and approach through the dense undergrowth that permeated that part of the woods. If he found anything, he'd pull back and radio the information to Jess and Carl. That was the plan anyway.

* * * * *

"Sherman, now listen carefully, and prepare to accommodate several men in the next few hours. They will enter by the secure doorway in back, so be certain you have released all the coded locking mechanisms in advance. There will be no time for messing with all that when there are men outside who must be admitted before they can be seen. Also— be absolutely sure the area around the disposal room is first of all completely clean, and securely locked, as well. Do you understand, Sherman?" The vacant eyes stared toward Sallie as the round face nodded in the affirmative. Speaking in his customary measured monotone, he responded.

"Yes, Salim, I will make the necessary arrangements now. The locks are set in secure mode, without any time constraints programmed in, so it will be no problem to prepare them for opening. As for the basement rooms, they are

412

secure. We have had no occasion to use them for many months now, so they are clean and locked up." His words took on a melancholy tone as he addressed his leader on the subject of the now quiet torture chambers, as if he were remembering tender bygone glory days of long ago. Sallie turned his attention to the other ghoul.

"Cedric, prepare the three storage areas. Remove the flooring, gather the weapons and array them in the hallways outside each room. There is no time for us to bring three hundred rifles to the basement. I would much prefer not to permit these strangers that much access to our facility, but it really is unimportant now. Soon we will all be leaving it anyway." The diminutive terrorist looked away, as if distracted by a distant sound or mental vision. The idea of holy combat and the spilling of unfaithful blood left him momentarily weak, his pale green eyes opaque, cloudy. Returning to the work at hand, he continued his orders to Cedric.

"Munitions are a different story. Being scattered all over the building, as well as in the sub-basement, we will have to assemble them here. Sherman, as soon as you have prepared the entry-way, assist Cedric. Begin bringing the ammunition, the grenades, and the pistols, all to this room. I believe they will fit nicely down here—stack them in front of the disposal room door. Be certain to arrange them here by type, AK separate from 9 mm, separate from 5.56 mm, et cetera. The boxes of grenades must be opened and easily accessible as the men load up to leave. It will be important to keep them moving, but quietly so. I want to get them ushered inside as quickly as possible, so as to minimize the danger of observation. I know there has been no evidence of intrusion for many weeks now, but this would be the worst time of all for discovery of our position."

The orders from the Committee had estimated the size of the force that would arrive to be armed at approximately three hundred. The very idea that so many men could approach, gather, collect up weapons and ammunition, then exit without detection in this otherwise empty area seemed ludicrous. But that was precisely what was planned. And the men who were about to execute that plan were very capable of accomplishing it in silence.

The personnel of the Vanguard who had not taken part in the initial phases of the operations were also most expert in their areas. While the explosives people were off destroying the power system nationwide, the infantry types busily prepared to first set a huge trap for returning American forces, then spring that trap with the goal of annihilating them once caught in the city, with no way to escape. And in keeping with the modern day theory of "need to know" briefing, the soldiers were not told just *how* they would destroy a huge army, just that it would happen with Allah's direction and assistance.

As Sallie directed the preparation for their arrival, his bloody mind raced with the realization that soon he would be the one to destroy the infidels himself, once the trap had been set.

The master logic of the plan was brilliant in its simplicity. Sallie smiled to himself as he worked to prepare for the arriving forces, chuckling over and over as he recalled clearly the whole plan. Unlike the ridiculous tele-dramas and UFO-filled folly of modern literature, these genius planners of the Committee knew how to plan a series of seemingly unrelated events that, while aimed as disparate targets, would act together to cause collapse. It was much like the detonation of many small explosions around the base of an old building—none capable of accomplishing the mission alone, but acting together they quickly collapsed the structure. Destruction of the electrical network had been the idea of men who spent their lives in the field of power supply, and they knew well that such an interdependent system would collapse quickly if enough of the right links were destroyed. It had worked perfectly.

In his mind, Sallie gave credit where credit was due; these men had been brilliant in the planning of such a cataclysmic event. Of course, the botching of the effort on Webb was a bit of a smudge on the whole thing, but the death of President Kincaid had been his baby. Placing the little maid within the White House staff a full year before she was called to assist him, she quietly performed her domestic functions for the replacement president, Allen Dickens. The liberal mentality of his and Flint's administrations found all that nonsense about security checks and careful background investigations all so tedious and unwarranted. Being Latin in name and

414

appearance, she was an immediate favorite of the replacement First Lady. Granted, when she was placed in the White House, he had no specific plan for her, but the very nature of her location and work duties suggested that eventually she would fill a useful role.

Of course the new administration would probably replace her when they got in gear, but Sallie counted on the inherent disorganization that attended administration changes to leave her in position long enough to do his evil bidding. Jack Kincaid really posed no threat from the detection standpoint, his own schedule that fateful day being so busy as to provide him zero time in his new quarters early in the morning hours of the next day. The simple, undetectable—and deadly— business of switching toothpaste tubes in the Presidential bathroom on the first day he was there was not difficult. He died as planned, and the little Mexican girl simply never went back to work. Her disappearance was unremarkable and, upon her return to New York, Sherman and Cedric made it complete—and irreversible.

He quieted his mind, insisting that he concentrate his every muscle and nerve on the smooth delivery of the weapons now in his possession. Soon enough he would take the rest of the necessary measures. Soon enough.

* * * * *

For men whose declared purpose in life was the killing of as many people as possible, the two young technicians standing in the sitting room of Weidenolf's apartment appeared anything but tough. The elder, an Iraqi by the name of Jaci (short for a name so long and complex even his family seldom used it) wiped his face and mouth with a wet cloth, brought to him by the investigator after he spontaneously vomited all over himself when he saw the old master. The other, a short, muscular lad in his early twenties, stood stoically, his eyes unavoidably riveted to the gruesome sight behind the coffee table. Franz Schuelman was decidedly *not* Iraqi, or any other kind of Mideasterner; he was pure German, with a hatred of Judaism that made him a perfect fit with the now dead scientist—and all Iraq as well.

Jaci tried to speak, but the bile rising in his tense throat stopped him again. Then finally, "Franz—what do we. . .I mean, we must . . .what about Saddam—"

"I *know,* Jaci, *I Know!* I mean I *don't* know, I mean—shit, we've got to finish without the old man. That's all there is to it. If we stop now, that butcher will hunt us down and feed us to his wolfhounds a piece at a time. Now stop whining—*and stop vomiting,* for godsakes, we have work to do. Unless we can assess the remaining preparations and convince him that we can complete the mission, we are dead men. Let's go." Taking his queasy comrade by the arm, he turned and made his way past the crowd of doctors, police, and onlookers in the room and out in the hallway. Jaci continued to wipe his face with the damp cloth and, as they stepped out into the hall, he turned involuntarily into the living room, where his eyes met the vacant, blood-spattered, dead gaze of his mentor and constant companion over the past year. He retched again.

They walked with quickening steps back to their little VW, sat down in the sweltering heat inside, and Franz cranked open the sun roof as he drove off toward the project site. No one spoke during the ride, as each tried to wrestle the image of Karl's split head and all that blood; each also began to attempt cogent thought concerning the remainder of the project. Just a few blocks short of the palace, Jaci broke the silence.

"The only part of the whole last phase that has me really worried is the actual pre-launch initiation sequence and the encryption entries for the target coordinates. Karl told us repeatedly about what was left to be done in the construction finish, and—oh *wow, but this is weird*—remember, just last week he kept us late on Thursday just to outline the procedures he planned to use when it was time to activate the pre-launch programs!"

"I know. I was just thinking about that little conversation when you spoke. It was almost like he knew he might not finish the project. Luckily, I wrote down most of what he said when I got home that night, and I have it in that notebook there on the back seat. Kind of stupid, I guess, to leave it lying around like that, but it's really just a bunch of chicken tracks to everyone but me. My biggest worry is that last initiation sequence—and those damnable encryption codes. How the old man did love all that mysterious shit.

"No—wrong. My *biggest* worry is old Saddam. If he decides we're too young or too inexperienced to complete the mission, we're replaced, just like that, and—"

"And dead the next day. Don't bother reminding me. C'mon, let's get busy. I don't want to waste one single—" He froze in mid-thought, his mouth open but now silent, as they both saw the same thing at the same moment. Six huge, uniformed security policemen, in two of those big, terrible, black Mercedes limos stood in the street, blocking their entrance into the private parking area behind the palace. Jaci grasped his washcloth again, trying to quell the new wave of nausea rising in his throat. Franz held his breath until he nearly passed out, then cautiously rolled up to the first uniform, a man with hand up in the unmistakable gesture STOP.

"You are Franz Schuelman—please park your car *there* and get in the limo. *YOU—follow him.*" The VW stopped in the assigned location, a public parking place just down from the formal entrance to the museum facility, on the opposite end of the complex from the palace and the project. Neither spoke as they rolled away in the big black car; it became immediately obvious that they were headed for the Presidential residence and a meeting with Saddam Hussein himself. Thought was nearly impossible as they approached the government buildings, but they knew he was there, even though his real offices and usual residence were both in Baghdad. They could not know what awaited their arrival.

3.

"This is the part I hate," the exhausted president whispered, a dry smile creasing his face at the sad humor of it all. "Waiting will kill me before any other force in the world can get to me!" Feet up on the huge Oval Office desk, he looked around the room at the small assembled group of similarly situated folks who waited for news on the progress of the offensives. Jonathon Brooks, ever present and as erect and military as ever, stood close to the door that provided access from the secretarial area off the big office. General Clyde Keithley, JCS chair, sat looking out the window, his recent arrival from the Pentagon having been the only break in the tension for several hours. Mac Reed drew deeply on another cigarette, a cloud of blue smoke following him as he paced slowly around the room, until Molly Webb stopped him with a soft but purposeful voice.

"Mac—*Mac*—you're gonna walk a rut in the floor. Or succeed in killing yourself with nicotine in short order. You must've had a huge stash of those things hidden away or, the way you smoke them, they'd all have been gone months ago. Please, sit down, rest. This promises to be a long wait. You—

"Molly, dear, you forget. . .if Mac stops moving, he falls asleep, probably without sitting down first!" Everyone laughed together as the President made reference to Reed's uncanny ability to sleep anywhere, any time. "He's just walking to stay awake. Jon, maybe you could shake 'em up in the galley, see if we can get some fresh coffee and a bit of breakfast. Then I think maybe we probably better figure a way to start getting some info from the folks in the field."

Brooks moved without response, disappearing into the hall. He was just out the door when the phone rang in the secretary's office; the Sergeant answered and immediately could be heard to respond, "Yessir, he's right here—please hold." Footsteps around the desk, then the sound of the door opening, after a firm knock.

"Sir, General Murah is on the secure line—has a report on the L.A. operation. I'll patch it to line two, if that's OK." Webb jerked his feet off the desktop, spinning at the same time to the phone.

"Mark—glad you called—talk to me." Webb's countenance knit into a deep frown, eyes closed tightly. He

418

listened for nearly two minutes before the Two Star in charge of the Los Angeles invasion took a breath. Sighing deeply, the president rubbed his eyes with his free hand, then, sitting up straight in the big chair, spoke to the general.

"All right. Sounds like things are proceeding as expected to this point. In fact, the evacuation seems a bit better than I had feared, in terms of confusion and injury. It's just one helluva lot worse than I had expected in the casualty department. General Keithley is here with me—let me put you on the speaker so we can make this next move together." Keithley, who had been standing motionless, his gaze fixed on the boss, moved quickly forward to the edge of the desk. The speakerphone clicked quietly, and the Chairman spoke to his friend of thirty years.

"Mark—Clyde here, are you well?" A short beat passed as the weight of the moment found expression in the deep sigh that emanated from Murah's chest, three thousand miles away.

"Yeah, thanks Clyde, I'm fine—just struggling like you are with this whole program of leading combat in Southern California." Then immediately, after another quick breath, he began to repeat the high points of the report he had just given the President. "Here's the deal. We had no trouble gaining access to and control of the main freeway arteries that would provide our avenues of evacuation. In fact, the plan for removal worked out particularly well—I-10, I-605/15 for the east suburbs, as well as that portion of Los Angeles proper, west of Pomoma and Fullerton. Most of that area was essentially either abandoned or free of violence, so we're using it for movement out to the staging areas at San Bernadino. That was a snap. In fact, planes are already moving the first thousand or so refugees out to the bigger sites right now.

"As you know, we've also got some pretty big camps set up in and around San Bernadino, too, and those are filling up fast. And out to the north, things were pretty easy, at least to this point. I-5 was blocked pretty badly down in town—some a' the gangs had pushed some burned out buses and semi-trailers across the whole road. We hit 'em with tanks supported by choppers, killed about thirty bad guys, then cleared the road."

Keithley leaned into the speaker, interrupting the report. "Mark, what about the Bakersfield facility and that big camp we ordered for out at the Naval Weapons Center? Are they ready for the crowd?"

"Yeah—no problem, I spoke with Division yesterday evening just before midnight. Confirmed ready and able to accept at least five thousand with shelter and a very substantial medical field facility. Anyway, things got ugly on the south side. Starting up in the area where I-10 and I-5 intersect—in the area where 610 forms the east side of that big freeway triangle that includes East L.A.—and moving south, the place is a real mess. The gang presence in the area was pretty substantial before all this started, anyway, and all that's happened in the last few months has done nothing to help things.

"Right now, I got one mech infantry battalion and two armored battalions moving in there from the south, using that part of I-5 we already talked about as a main route. However, as soon as they got close, we lost two tanks and about a dozen Hummers to some kind of anti-armor weapons. We're not sure what they all were, but at least a third of the damage was done with some old LAWs that had been stolen from a National Guard Armory about six months before the lights went out. Ground troops started calling for some helicopter support as soon as they started into the neighborhoods just north of I-105. Reports were of heavy small-arms fire, lots of grenade type explosives, and some kind of fire bomb devices coming at 'em when they approached Watts. I've sent in all the air support we have and more armor, but details are sketchy right now.

"Suffice it to say, things are not pretty in there. I— *what?? Wait a second—*Clyde, I gotta run. . .some problem with an evacuation route all blocked up with burning vehicles. I'll report back by 2200 hours." Keithley looked a hole through the speakerphone, blinked twice, then sat back in the big leather chair he occupied beside the president's desk. Webb breathed deeply, shook his head slowly, then spoke without turning.

"Busy day at the office for Mark and the boys, Clyde. Just have to sit and wait. That's all."

Book IV – The Great Offensives

* * * * *

Nothing disturbed the dank, intense presence of the darkening street, three stories below Roger Cline's vantage point, just a few windows south of a deserted, steaming intersection in the Bronx. His ear piece itched and threatened to slide out of his ear. The small headset and microphone fastened to his hat connected him to the command post and the other units now staking out all the logical routes into and out of this Dresden-like, bombed-out apparition.

The dead left from months of fighting, atrocities, starvation, and disease were still in evidence, even though armed patrols had occasionally made efforts to clean the streets. The absence of sound inside a place usually teeming with the racket of thousands of people all living on top of each other produced discomfort bordering on panic for those who sat in concealment; bellies growled, mouths went dry, pulses pounded temples furiously. Cline responded to Lassiter's request for status report.

"Yankee Clipper 6, this is Cline group. Quiet isn't the word, Henry. Like sitting in a crypt. Any activity from the others?" His coarse whisper vanished into the broken plaster walls, his eyes moving cautiously to the other side of the window where Special Agent Seamus O'Dorgan's ruddy face peered cautiously over the sill and out into the street.

"Negative, Roger, nothing. Still early, though. If the intelligence is even close to being accurate, they'll have to start appearing soon. That many men can't just materialize outta—" The transmission stopped mid-word, a single crackling sound in Cline's ear piece the only punctuation. The Irishman snapped back as if hit, his eyes locking with Cline's face, as both men reacted to the interruption. Instinct demanded more information and bade them to attempt to re-establish contact. Training told them to pay attention around them. Each of them turned silently toward his assigned direction of surveillance, hearts racing at the realization that Henry Lassiter's voice had stopped without explanation.

O'Dorgan quietly snapped his fingers, his hand below the window sill; he gestured to Cline in the direction of the mouth of an alley just thirty feet to the right of their vantage point. Cline resisted—again instinct overborne by training—the impulse to instantly turn in the direction of Seamus' gesture.

Moving deliberately, he raised up on one knee, turning just his head to look down into the darkening street. Mouth dry, eyes wide, the two watched as a silent line of shadow figures moved out of that black opening and, staying to the darkness against the buildings, filed on down the sidewalk.

These new arrivals made no sound, not so much as the scuff of a boot on pavement, their numbers increasing at a rate that, for a moment, transfixed the two observers to such an extent that no one thought to report what they saw. "Yankee Clipper 6, *this is Cline group—do you copy? I say again, this is Cline group, I have contact. Henry, are you clear—I have contact!*" The whisper seemed for a long moment to have gone nowhere beyond the hot little room, as the two men stared at each other, then back to the ever growing line of figures now pouring out of the alley. Then Lassiter responded in their ears.

"Yeah—Cline group, this is Yankee Clipper 6, I gotcha—and you're not alone. Denny's got a stream a' bad boys pourin' outta the storm sewer that runs under the projects an' dumps into the river. They're headed sort of in your direction—more toward I-95, but still. . . S*tandby—!*" The two looked at each other, then stole quick glances down into the street, now almost totally dark. The forms continued to appear at the head of the alley, then followed in succession away to the left. Lassiter came back on the radio again.

"OK, everybody listen up. This is Yankee Clipper 6. We have three lines of infiltration, all headed loosely toward the same area. Stay in place. I repeat. Stay in place until further order. Attempt to observe and advise as to the numbers you are seeing, but do not move. *Roger—*can you detect weapons? The others say they can't see weapons."

"Negative, Henry, no weapons visible. But we've seen at least fifty men file out of this alley in the past three minutes, and the stream continues. Shit, Henry, where'd they—*hold on*—Yankee Clipper 6, this is Cline. Second column has appeared right beneath us, in from the north. Same deal. No weapons visible, all dressed in dark colors. Look like a bunch a' gooks slippin' outta the jungle, swear-ta-god! Standing by."

Lassiter looked grimly at Boyd Jeffers, the Guard colonel's eyes squinting back the realization that they were being invaded; the old FBI agent tried to speak, but nothing came out of his mouth. Then, as if still not comprehending it all, he shook his head. "Goddam, Boyd, here we go. If those assholes get to the ammo dump before we figure 'em out, it'll take all the muscle we can find just to slow 'em down!"

Jeffers permitted himself a moment of wishing he was still selling real estate in Albany, then turned his energies to the moment. "Henry, time to play with the big boys. NY command told us they'd respond when they had a fix on enemy strength and location. Let's let the brass know what we've got, then they can call it. We just gotta make sure this crowd doesn't get loose with that stash of weapons."

"That's all fine, but we both got people in there, and getting them out in one piece could be pretty tough if these thugs get themselves armed before the Army shows up. Get the signal callers on the line, and let's go with part two of this program." Henry shot a glance at Herman Hanks, sitting motionless on the floor next to the radio console that carried the conversations just completed. Hanks tried to imagine what it was the guys were seeing, then moved over to the map spread out on the floor at his feet, his long fingers tracing the routes just described.

Jeffers punched in the numbers on the secure line, and the three waited while Operations Command reacted to this new information. They sat motionless while several hundred Islamic zealots headed for enough arms and munitions to create a true Bronx Zoo.

* * * * *

"So Mr. Schuelman, tell me. Just how close to completion *was* the project when last you and Dr. Weidenolf spoke? I mean, surely you and he discussed the final steps in some detail, *right?*" The moniker of "SoDamInsane" crept into Franz' imagination, despite his overwhelming fear of the man and his clear apprehension that his life, and that of his quaking friend, were in immediate danger. He swallowed an overwhelming urge to laugh like a mad scientist. The urge passed as he realized the man had an automatic pistol in his waistband. Clearly, the rumors about Saddam doing his own dirty work when the mood struck him were accurate.

"*Sir*—I mean, *yessir*—*er,* well, yes. . .of course we spoke—I mean, well we *more than spoke,* that is, well. . .we were like, well, we were *there, all the time, every day, every minute*—he kept us beside him at all times, showed us everything, every diagram, calculation, component, every—"

"*Enough*, you simpering fool—*of course* you were there, everyone knows that. But what do you *know*, fool, what do you *know*? *Can you finish what has been started or not?!*" Saddam's fingers seemed to unconsciously brush the black plastic grips of the pistol at his waist, although never really grasping it or even acknowledging its presence. But every eye was intent on *not* looking at it, either. Jaci, so terrified as to have been struck dumb to this point, found voice.

"Oh yes sir, we are familiar, intimately familiar, with the remainder of the work, and we are prepared to finish without delay—as soon as the weekend, if that would suit you. There are some calculations relative to the final launch sequences yet to be completed, but Dr. Weidenolf explained them to me and demonstrated them to both of us in detail just yesterday. Odd, don't you think? I mean, those last items, so close, and then with him dying so unexpectedly, the very night after—"

"*All right*—spare me the philosophy, boy. As much as I would prefer to, shall we say. . . *replace* you, I have no choice. If you have misspoken, or misrepresented yourselves to me, I will have you burned alive. Do we understand each other?" Without waiting long enough even for a head nod of acknowledgement, he finished.

"I need that device ready for launch within five days. No later. Can you do it? Of course you can. *Guard.* Escort these boy—I mean these young men, back to the palace and ensure that they have everything they need to complete the work. If they attempt to leave the palace without my authorization, kill them. Slowly."

The two rode back to the Volkswagen in silence, Jaci continuing to swallow the retching that attacked his insides. Franz Schuelman stared, catatonic, out the window of the big Mercedes, his mind frozen, unable to recall even the most rudimentary pieces of the remaining puzzle. Once in their little car again, Schuelman silenced Jaci's frantic rantings, and they parked in the secure area adjacent to the palace entrance. Walking into the formal gardens, they slipped through the access door to the stairwell and descended the three stories underground to the control room where the remaining work would be accomplished.

Neither spoke as they entered the room; each commenced with the last known step completed the day before, working without stopping the rest of that day and through the night. The work remaining was tedious almost beyond description, the last steps consisting of a myriad of tests, re-tests, simulations, and computer protocols that examined every facet of the complex instrument they and the old man had created.

The missile would be ready, the warhead armed, ready to go when ordered, *if* Jaci's notes of the last conversation with the old man were accurate. If.

* * * * *

At least a minute before the realization that he smelled smoke, Josh Landry's scalp began to itch, his pulse quickening imperceptibly, the horse's attitude only slightly altered. Uphill and upwind of the area that had interested him as he rode cross country, he approached the piece of gravel road that he had previously examined, determining that it bore the tracks of the fleeing vehicle. But this time he would look harder and more carefully. Josh stood in the tall grass where an old tractor trail intersected the gravel, winding away and downhill from the road. The combination of the tire tracks concealed beneath carefully arranged leaves and the faint smell of smoke stood the hair on the back of his neck straight up.

The gelding snorted softly, his head up as he searched out the cues even Landry could not acquire. They rode away at a right angle to the direction of the grass trail, keeping to the deep woods and moving through the soft, quiet forest floor for about a quarter of a mile. Dismounting, Josh tied the horse amid a clump of large oaks, the animal's form completely concealed in shadow. Enough sweet grass grew beneath the big trees to occupy the animal until he could complete his reconnaissance on foot.

It took only a few minutes to move around, upwind still, to within 100 hundred yards of the origin of the now obvious smoking fire. Low crawling to within 150 feet, he lay in tall weeds, his pulse now slow and pounding in his temples and neck. He counted three men in and around an old van, their voices quiet, their movements restrained, even slow.

Words spoken in low tones were audible, an occasional raised pitch indicative of animated, even hostile conversation. Two of the men were black, neither very big, but both quick, even sharp in motion. The lone white man was huge. Close to seven feet tall, judging from his shoulders towering above the top of the van, Josh shuddered at the thought of close-in combat with such an adversary. A moment's flashback to a desperate struggle with an enormous Chinese Army officer in the jungles of Thailand chilled him from head to foot, as he remembered the excruciating pain the powerful man inflicted as he twisted and ripped at Josh's smaller frame.

Only the blind luck of a lucky thrust with the broken blade of his bayonet saved him from being torn in half by the giant soldier. Josh fought the vision of lying in the tall weeds, the dead man's weight crushing him as he lay on him, the big man's blood flowing from the gaping neck wound that had killed him. The smell of it rose in Josh's imagination, his stomach turning.

The huge white man moved directly toward his hiding place, and present reality instantly returned. The man walked to within no more than thirty feet, then abruptly turned left, took a few steps down the slight hillside, and squatted to relieve himself. Twice more one of the others moved toward Landry's position, but never that close.

There was a short, terse conversation that produced audible fragments:—*get some food. . .water..., meds for bert. . die without it, and fucking bugs—!* After that they picked up what few items lay around the van, including several weapons. They packed them and, to Josh's great surprise, picked up a fourth man who had been lying on the ground behind the vehicle. The giant handled the obviously wounded man, cries and epithets plainly audible as he was lifted into the back of the old truck.

Suddenly it was obvious that, within a few seconds, they would be gone, off to plunder the neighborhood in search of supplies and help for the injured man. All memory of the promises made to Carl and Jessica vanished about being careful, as the predator awoke with the realization that they would be out of his reach in a few more seconds.

The sound of the old engine sputtering to life, accompanied by a cloud of gray and black smoke from its exhaust, fired the starter's gun in Josh's subconscious, and he sprang from his hiding place. Running crouched over but at top speed, the straight line course covered the 150 feet in but a few seconds. He straightened from the crouching run at about the twenty-foot mark, raising the rifle to his shoulder at the same moment he opened fire on the left side of the driver's head and exposed shoulder. The head vanished in an instant, his body lurching forward and over to the right, exposing the giant in the right seat. His enormous torso twisted away and out the passenger door, his flank and back exploding as half a dozen of the sizzling rounds ripped him apart.

Josh knew no intelligent thought, would never know the sequence or even the impact of the fire; changing magazines when the fire ceased, he sprayed the back seat and floor through openings now devoid of window glass. The screams of the dying men were inaudible over the thundering fire, as Josh changed magazines again, without counting the now forty rounds fired in and through the old machine. His last reality was the smell of gasoline that, again without conscious thought, caused him to turn and begin sprinting away from the gruesome site.

The explosion created by sparks igniting the fumes in the half full gas tank hurled Josh into the air, carried him on a fiery shock wave that slammed him into an area filled with big rocks, some forty feet away and uphill from the van. The old vehicle burned to a melted, charred black heap, the men in and around it incinerated. Only their deformed weapons and some charred bone and flesh remained to tell the story of their violent passing. Joshua Landry lay still, motionless, silent amid the rocks, his body a misshapen human doll, tossed askew in the smoke. Death was once again everywhere.

4.

Dennis Rasmussen shook his head, his vision apparently playing fatigue tricks on him, as he watched the silent line of dark figures slip past on the street in front of his position. Lying prone to the side of a two-foot hole in the face of a bombed-out, burned-out convenience store, he was tormented also by the faint remaining smell of rotten foodstuffs. The groceries had long ago been ravaged by starving looters, but what had not been stolen rotted in place. Months had passed, but in the nearly airless heat of this place, the suggestion of stinking meats and dairy products threatened his constitution at every moment. But the eye games were, at the moment, of greater concern.

The string of forms moving along beneath the overhanging canopies of store fronts snaked into and out of sight back a distance of two full blocks. They first appeared from a doorway up the street, then disappeared into another building half a block closer, then reappeared out of an alley at the head of the block where Rasmussen and his team lay in wait. Obviously these men were very familiar with a preconceived route designed to minimize their exposure to detection. And but for the coordination and placement of the surveillance units in place to detect them, it would have worked perfectly.

Then the head of the line simply vanished. One by one, eight to ten seconds apart, the front person would disappear, right in mid-stride, at a place where no visible escape existed. "*Whu—holy shit—Yankee Clipper 6, this is Rasmussen group, you copy?—Listen, Henry, Jesus, Henry—they're gone—I mean like 'poof,' they're gone!! They're walking along the sidewalk and then—like I said, 'poof'!!*"

"Rasmussen, this is Yankee Clipper 6, I'm unclear; do you maintain visual on subjects or not?"

The reporter rasped back onto the tiny microphone at his lips, trying to be clear and silent at the same time. "NO—I mean, *yes*—I mean, they're disappearing right into the street, not 30 yards from us."

A moment's pause was followed by a different whispered voice.

"Yankee Clipper 6 and Denny, this is Cooper group, a block south of Rasmussen location. I confirm disappearance, but I think they're dropping into a manhole or a stairwell of some kind. Hard to make out, it's so goddam dark down there. But Denny's right, Henry, they're disappearing right into the street!" No one spoke for several seconds, until Lassiter keyed his transmitter to the entire operation, including the military components.

"All units, this is Yankee Clipper 6. Contact lost with the long line that was proceeding south from the Interstate. Repeat. Contact lost with subjects, strength estimated at approximately 150 men. Remain in place, all ground units. Those in upper floor positions, you may move if you can do so without making noise doing it—try to detect route. This is Yankee Clipper 6." Lassiter looked across the desk at the face of Boyd Jeffers, who then immediately returned to the street and sewer maps; elbowing his way into position to look past Hanks, he intently searched for an explanation for what the men had just reported.

"Shit, Henry, makes no sense. Sewer crosses *here,* two blocks away, and there's not a manhole in that whole block. Wonder about one of those ground level stair—"

"Yankee Clipper 6, this is Cline group—O'Dorgan; I lived in the next block a few years back, Henry, did an undercover that lasted six months or more. Narcotics. I can't be specific, but I know that many of those old buildings with the below ground entrances had back exits just like the front—you know, steps up to the street. They're probably changing direction and using the alley to get to the new route."

Jeffers nodded, then shook his head in disgust. "Right there it is, Henry. Seamus is dead on. This alley parallels the street, but also intersects another at right angles, not 100 feet on down the block. We can't follow in there without exposing the men to detection. Gotta do something to keep up with this contingent or we'll never be able to triangulate the location of all those guns. *Seamus*—can you get a team in behind that line without being seen? If we lose them, too, we have no chance of identifying the stash site."

"No chance, Colonel—this whisper ain't for effect. They're processing right outside this building, like they have been for over ten minutes now. Must've been 200 or more come past already. If we so much as sneeze, we're toast." Almost without a beat, Cline echoed the response.

"No chance, guys, at least not now. Maybe when we're sure they've all passed by, we could try following them from the roofs, but that's really iffy at night, and the chances of being detected are very great. Reach in the trick bag, Henry, 'cause we're stuck right where we are, unless you want us engaging them before they get where they're going." The line went quiet, as all parties sat stuck with the same set of realities. The men in command counted themselves extremely lucky to have happened across the two still-divergent lines of infiltrating terrorists; the idea of permitting them to disappear by the same magic with that they had first shown up seemed the worst of luck and a complete failure.

Still, with the first line now nearly gone from sight of Cline's position and the second already vanished, failure seemed imminent. Detection by the terrorists was unthinkable, so following was out of the question. Losing them meant the arming of a very large enemy force with weapons of unknown quantity and description, at the precise moment when military forces were moving into the area. Lassiter reflexively reached into his drawer for the Maalox. Of course the bottle had been empty since April.

* * * * *

Being Mexican by birth had always been a mixed blessing for Miguel Sanchez. Living in Los Angeles for all but the first three of his 19 years had produced in him a strange set of values and conflicting attitudes. These were due in large part to the necessary tension between his father whom he loved, a police officer with L.A.P.D., and an older brother whom he idolized, the leader of the Diablos. Miguel, Sr., had died in a pitched gun battle with a faction of that same gang, minus his older son, brought about by the father's unfortunate presence in the middle of some warfare between two of those cells.

The younger namesake hated his father for having left him—loved and admired his courage and straight-laced mentality about law and order and peace in the streets. He also loved the hero rebel older brother, nicknamed "Pancho" by his disciples, but hated him for his association with the very gang that so violently and callously took their father's life when he happened across their bloody convocation.

430

So it was no surprise that he now slipped through the predawn quiet from the hiding place of those gang lords who held a huge chunk of East L.A. He planned to meet with his third cousin, Raul, who happened to be employed by the United States Marine Corps.

Getting loose was easy for Miguel, as his assignment these past few months had been messenger and scout for his brother's gang. His intimate knowledge of the streets and hills of most of southeastern L.A., including having worked at most of the several golf courses that lay scattered about within the maze of expressways, gave him the ability to move almost anywhere without fear of detection. He had provided intelligence to the Diablos concerning the activities of rival gangs, the movements of refugees fleeing the fires and killing in town, and the feeble efforts of civilian police and National Guard units to respond to the impossible needs of the people.

Weakened badly by the assignment of a large contingent of their troop strength to the farce in the Persian Gulf, the California Guard was largely ineffective at controlling the rampant aggression that exploded almost at once when the lights went out. Civilian police were so overwhelmed, both by the numbers of the enemy and the vast area in that the violence spread, that they mostly either gave up or got killed before they could get away. So Miguel watched and reported, moved freely and without notice between gangs and firefights, the eyes and ears of his bloody brother.

Then things began to change. Watching Pancho and eight of his thugs rape and kill several Chinese women they caught trying to escape up onto the expressway one day, Miguel was so sickened by what he saw that it became immediately obvious to him that he had to do something different. Love for his brother turned to loathing as the images of Pancho's cruelty kept him awake night after night.

As he ranged far from the Watts area about the end of June, his movements had little to do with the assignments meted out by his brother. He wandered, despair his constant companion. One afternoon, a pair of military helicopters appeared at low altitude. Instead of darting into the shadows along one of the golf courses, he simply walked out into the fairway and began waving his arms at the craft. Running up to the left side door, he shouted into the ear of the pilot, "If I can talk to my cousin, I will help you get the Diablos. His name is Raul Sanchez, and he is in intelligence with the Marines. Will you take me to him?"

The pilot nodded his head and motioned the young man into one of the web seats; first frisking him for weapons, he fastened him in, and within seconds lifted off in the direction of the Command center for eastern operations, Combined Los Angeles Occupation Force. Once inside with the men in charge of figuring out how to retake the sprawling city without killing the entire remaining population, Miguel quickly convinced them of his desire to help. He horrified them with stories of the kind of atrocities usually reserved for Bosnia, Nazi Germany, or a Stephen King movie, and the intelligence officers could not help but believe him. But he required that Raul be included for any real cooperation to occur.

Raul Sanchez was a young man who possessed so many of the characteristics of Miguel's father that Miguel had always admired him in spite of Pancho's ranting and raving about Raul's "chickenshit copout," joining the Marines and leaving the gangs. Further, street wisdom convinced Miguel that he would need an advocate. Someone would have to convince the brass that he could be trusted, or he would never be able to get them to listen to his rather fantastic information concerning weapons, munitions, explosives, and the huge number of hostages Pancho and the other warlords still held. Raul was located, an MP with the headquarters battalion, guarding the nerve center of all military operations.

The fit between the two cousins was more than just familial; they both came from the same area, knew the same geography intimately. And while the vast area engulfed in anarchy reached far beyond what they could know, the combination of Miguel's access and freedom of movement and Raul's connections to military intelligence and headquarters for the whole offensive made their work together crucially important.

Miguel spied the subtle little flag tied to a shrub at the edge of the wood lot. It bordered the rough behind a sand trap along the 12th green on Los Amigos Golf Course, a point accessible without fear of detection, from several directions.

"Buenos dias, Raul, you are early. . .you get tired of drinking the general's whiskey?" A tired smile cracked the Marine's face, as he turned to see his cousin crouching in the shadows of first light.

"You are an insolent hombre, Miguel, I should kick your
skinny butt for dragging me out here, interrupting my beauty
sleep so early. The message said to hurry—that my contact
had an urgent message. Now you only blow me shit for
enjoying the small pleasures of access to the officers' supply
stores. I think I *will* kick your—" He lunged like a cat, across
the short distance between them, snatching the younger and
smaller cousin and wrapping him instantly into an iron grip.
The kid gasped and giggled at the same time, again amazed at
Raul's quickness and strength. The hold was released,
followed a beat later by Miguel's own vengeance, a hard shot
to the solar plexus with his one free elbow.

"*There,* Mr. Bad Ass Marine. . .you see, I have learned well
from my older cousin. Gasp for air while I tell you why I
bothered you so early. You must tell the big boys to get it in
gear at once, before the entire area around Watts and into
East L.A. becomes impossible to take without tremendous loss
of life—very ugly."

The Marine stared intently at his cousin, the sharp pain
in his gut now subsiding as his breath returned. The kid
always managed to get in at least one good shot. "Miguel,
things could not get much worse—what are you saying?" The
whole place had been a fiery bloodbath, more reminiscent of
Somalia than California. The idea of something more horrible
than what already existed seemed impossible. The younger
man turned quiet, faced the elder, shook his head.

"They have agreed to join forces against the military,
Raul. Pancho's Diablos have agreed with two other cells;
between them they already control all of the Watts area and
most of Southgate. What is worse, they have reached what
Pancho calls "an accommodation" with the Bloods and, believe
it or not, that huge band of rednecks up in Englewood, the
Sons of Silence! I couldn't believe it."

Raul sat stunned for a moment, then said the whole thing
back, as if repeating it would make sense of it. "Miggie, you're
full of shit! No way the Sons would agree to a coalition with a
band of greasers like Pancho's gang. They're all white, all
completely committed to killing all of us. For as long as I can
remember, they've been raping and killing us, and we have
done the same to them— *I don't believe you!!*"

"Believe it, big boy, I was there when they met. That mob
of filthy bikers came right into Watts, rumbled up to the

433

baseball diamond outside the junior high, and sat down opposite Pancho on the bleachers. Didn't think there was that much chrome—or that much gasoline—left in all California. Raul, no shit, this changes things much for the worse. Those bums have anti-tank weapons, a ton of machineguns and, unless they're shitting Pancho, over a thousand grenades.

"Oh—and I almost forgot. One of the Diablos has finished repairing an old fifty caliber machinegun they stole from some Guard or Reserve armory back east last fall, and the Sons have five thousand rounds of ammunition for it. It's mounted on the back of a one ton pick up, welded it right to the frame. Imagine what that thing will do to your helicopters!

"Raul, unless your forces can strike quickly, this whore marriage will make retaking East L.A. more expensive than you can imagine. They have the weapons and the ammunition—and the manpower—to kill many or, as they hope, to make it so expensive that the military will seek to negotiate with them for some kind of truce. What they all want is to keep their turf, trade the hostages for supplies, and get the Army to agree they can keep control. Dumb, I know, but nobody ever said they were very smart. Just mean. And unless your people act now, many more will die. Not just soldiers, either. . .they plan to use hundreds and hundreds of hostages as shields, right out in the open, to protect their armed positions.

"The only way into them, they figure, will be *through* those starving people." The two sat in silence, while the Marine tried to make himself believe what he had just heard.

"Miggie, I need details concerning the locations of their weapons and ammunition. Also, where their personnel are hiding. Unless you can tell me that, there will be precious little to keep them from success." The Marine stood, hugged his cousin, and slipped into the woods, promising to return the next morning before dawn.

* * * * *

Molly Webb lay still on the bed, her chest heaving slowly, her heart pounding in her neck and temples. Perspiration glistened from her high forehead; brushing back the horror of the dream, she rolled up on one elbow to look out onto the darkening street. She gripped reality and convinced herself that the dream had passed and that her precious children were, no doubt, still just fine. Walking downstairs and into the area of the Oval Office, she found Jonathan Brooks.

"Any word?" His face showed the absence of new information, as he slowly shook his head. Brooks could feel the tenseness in the First Lady's countenance, and he knew the only remedy for that look was contact with her husband. He looked at her, then spoke.

"I'll find the General for you. He just finished a conference with the Pentagon on the NYC situation. I'm sure he'll be right down."

She nodded, and the man stepped into the communications room. Molly turned to see the tired smile of her husband in the doorway. The feel of his arms around her was instant medicine.

"Moms have to worry, right, *Mom?*" The President tickled her gently as he teased, then felt her grab his flank in retaliation.

"Dammit, Jackie, *not funny!!* I just had another of the *worst* dreams, and every time it's the same thing. Some mob breaks through the installation defenses, takes over the whole place, sets everything on fire, and the kids—"

"Enough, Molly. . .you'll make us both nuts, talking like that. Kid, we're a ways from getting them back here, so ya gotta beat this thing. . ." Molly had recurring nightmares about their grown children—and grandchildren, scattered from Texas to Seattle, all currently living in secure military installations where they were protected from harm. Frequent telephone contact helped, but the mother still worried constantly.

Webb was talking with his distraught wife when he caught the intent gaze of a Sergeant from communications. The kid looked like he'd just seen two ghosts, so he turned and followed the kid into the hallway. "Sorry, sir, but we got a kind of a mess here. General Keithley is talking to Command in New York, and I've got Mr. Netanyahu holding on the secure line. Says it's urgent. Better come on, sir, the Prime Minister was very insistent." Covering the space in long strides, the President was quickly seated at the desk; Keithley was seated beside the desk, on the phone and staring intently at the floor.

"Clyde—what's the word?" Webb whispered to the Four Star who was listening to the report from NYC. Keithley shook his head but didn't speak. Then he covered the receiver with his hand.

"Better go ahead and take the call from Tel Aviv, Mr. President, this will take some time. We got problems in the Bronx." Webb turned to see the Sergeant holding the receiver to the secure international line, instantly agreed with the assessment, and turned to pick up that line. Again trying to sound upbeat, he greeted the Prime Minister.

"Benjamin, good to hear from you again—I was just thinking about our last conversation. What is the progress in your investigation?" Netanyahu shot back without a second passing.

"It is difficult to put a pleasant face on this one, Jackie, so I'll be brief. One of our operatives, a most seasoned undercover surveillance specialist, found and entered the residence of this Adolpho Weidenolf—you remember, the mad scientist/ex-Nazi, ex-archaeologist/nuclear genius employed by Saddam? Well, he was attempting to incapacitate the man with some quick-acting drug so he could perform a thorough search of the apartment, but things went badly. Very badly. The drug, mixed with a considerable quantity of vodka, rendered the subject unstable on his feet, and he fell. Split his head from ear to ear. All very bloody, and most deadly.

"Now we have no idea about the condition and potential readiness of his project, and the two young men who were assisting him have been taken into custody by Saddam. Probably either dead by now or hidden someplace trying to finish the work without the master's hand. The real problem is that we had finally gotten close to this crazy man and were just beginning to follow his movements. Now we're back to square one, and we still don't know *where* he was building the goddam thing. However, all we can learn from any source worth trusting is that the project was being carried out somewhere inside the restoration area. We just don't know where, or even *if* they really built it at all. The fear is that it was fabricated inside some kind of cover, in the Old City."

"Holy—you mean you now believe they have fabricated a nuclear device *in Babylon*?? Benjamin, that seems nearly impossible. I know you said they had probably smuggled the components into the Old City over a long period of time, but a

436

rocket that big is not easily concealed, once assembled. I share your fear, but I'm not sure what we can do from this end." That was the opening the Jewish leader was waiting for.

"Jackie, we must have your immediate and full time assistance with aerial surveillance, both satellite and high altitude airplane fly overs. I know the latter is risky, but we are facing another Holocaust unless we can stop this missile before it gets airborne. Here is what my people have told me.

"They have identified some unusual topographical locations in the deserts north and east of Babylon. At first they just looked like sand, nothing big and certainly nothing resembling excavation. But they took the chance and went out there on foot, at night, and found a sufficient quantity of dirt, spread carefully over a half-mile area, to have come from a substantial excavation. Moreover, the composition of some of the dirt indicates that it came from very deep in the ground, maybe as deep as sixty to eighty feet down. What that tells us is—"

"The sumbitch has dug a silo someplace. Holy. . .hell, Benjamin, all the satellites in the cosmos won't see a silo with a lid on it. Don't see how the SR71s can help, either. They'll—"

"Hear me out, Jackie. If they have one or more missiles in some kind of silo-type arrangement, it wouldn't have to be a vertical set up. Set at an angle, equipped to raise forty to fifty degrees above horizontal, there could be more than one such weapon hidden right under existing buildings, so long as those buildings, or what *looked like buildings*, could be moved. Don't you see, they have to be hiding these damn nukes in holes in the ground, Jackie, and we've got to find them!!"

"That's fine, and I understand the urgency, but I still can't see how we can detect these holes—or silos—until they're open. And that will almost certainly be too late." Pausing only a beat, the Israeli went on.

"OK, we've been thinking about that, too. First of all, if you can position satellite surveillance over the area full time, there's a fair chance sufficient activity around the important sites will be noticeable. Second, they've got to be testing their protocols and launch sequences sufficiently to be sure they'll work. Anything goes wrong, and Babylon becomes a sand hill. . .again. All we need is one lead as to the location, and we'll blow the thing to pieces before they can get it off the ground. Now please, *please,* Jackie, order the birds up and move the satellites into the right position. The results of permitting this to continue are too awful to imagine, including almost certain nuclear war spreading far beyond Tel Aviv."

"All right, Mr. Prime Minister, I'll get on it. Be back to you within a few hours. But this is a mighty small needle in a very big sand pile."

"Thanks, Mr. President. Thank you from all of us."

Webb hung up, only to look into the hard, furrowed face of the Chairman of the Joint Chiefs of Staff, suddenly aware that, for all the horrors he had just encountered, he was about to hear some more. "So, can you top an impending nuclear strike on Israel? Go ahead, Clyde, beat that one, I dare ya!" Keithley didn't smile.

5.

The banter that goes on between old soldiers has a certain flavor, even a kind of cadence to it that only develops over years and years. Sitting in upper Brooklyn, on the tailgate of a deuce and a half (a two and one-half ton troop transport truck), its canvas top rolled forward to let in the summer sun, Lester Monroe was "smokin' and jokin'" with a few of the senior NCOs and a couple of the younger members of a group of Army National Guardsmen. They were led by a huge, jet black staff sergeant named Ullysses Washington Carver, a man possessed of the kind of bearing and authority that only those who have faced combat as a chosen career can accomplish. Carver's laugh was quick and big, his voice deep within his barrel chest. The jokes and bullshit were flowing fast and furious from Lester, as he passed around a fifth of Jack Daniels to the small assembly.

"Now this is no shit, Sarge, I been through three tours in Nam, went in early in Granada, and lived on Parris Island for six years, and I ain't never seen so much destruction as we got here! I come from over in Pennsylvania, where I was visitin' relation when the lights went out, an' we fought more firefights, killed more bad boys a' every description, and lived on less food than I ever did on hostile fire pay!" The sergeant, now warmed by the firewater so liberally bestowed by the old soldier comrade, began to respond with more and more details of the fighting in New York. Every man has his weakness, and Lester had struck pay dirt in the information department with the bottle of Jack. The small gaggle of soldiers began to swap stories and embellishments about their many shootouts with the thugs of NYC, and Lester quickly began learning the areas of densest fighting.

"Know whatcha mean, Sarge, me and the boys here been hip deep in empty cartridge casings twenty times chasin' those assholes around Brooklyn, Brownsville, up into Newark, even the Bronx! Smitty, you 'member that band a' black bastards we chased under the Interstate and into the Bronx day before yesterday? Disappeared like so much smoke when they hit the streets below the highway! No shit, *just like that!*" Lester betrayed no recognition, demonstrated no special interest, instead smiling a knowing smile, while the group continued to describe their frustrations and the carnage they had witnessed, inflicted, and endured over the past months.

After a week of similar visits, over several square miles of the perimeter of Manhattan, bumming cigarettes, sleeping under military vehicles, telling and retelling the nonsense about the search for his mother in Brooklyn, he had learned very little about the current state of things in the city. He knew even less about the conditions in and around the area where he knew Sallie had lived before giving Monroe his intended terminal assignment, and virtually nothing about impending military actions to retake the place. But now, a glimmer. A contingent of blacks, identified unintentionally by this group of soldiers, as militants who could obviously avoid contact almost at will, woke up the assassin's curiosity just when it was about to flicker and go out.

They talked until the bottle was empty, Lester having deviously succeeded in consuming but a small portion of the Kentucky truth serum, and he left them only after a back-slapping, hand-pumping farewell complete with the promise of an early return. His BDUs, complete with a variety of badges and insignia bespeaking his many combat accomplishments, had once again opened the door to places and information not available to others. And the idea that he was "in the middle of the out processing mode," retiring but not retired, as he said, gave him an elevated, senior statesman status with military personnel everywhere.

Now he knew there was substantial activity in and around the Bronx, and that activity included at least one force of urban terrorists who were accomplished enough at their trade to be able to slip into the old streets and vanish when it suited their purposes. Such men were precisely the type of well-trained professionals, mercenaries who were also zealots for Allah, that Willie Calvert would enlist and find a way to control. And if they were associated with him, they would have access to him and to the substantial weapons cache he was holding. Now to find a way into the Bronx, find that old tenement, and tear the little bastard apart, a piece at a time.

Lester suddenly realized a huge problem. He needed weapons—a handgun, a good combat knife, even a grenade or two if possible. Then he could visit his treacherous old pal one last time.

* * * * *

"Miggie, you little ghost, where the hell have you been? Shit, boy, I thought the Sons had taken you for carp bait!" Pancho Sanchez laughed loud, mouth open wide in a derisive, sneering way, his eyes cold and wet with the sting of cocaine. "I should cut you up and feed you to the fish myself, weasel, for sneaking away so early—whatchu do, baby brother, *huh??* You prowling the early morning for some pussy?? *Huh, little one—Ha!!*" That is *it!!!* You desert your beleaguered brother and leader in search of a rut with some dirty little senorita, is *that it,* well *ees it??* The elder raised his arm as if to backhand Miguel, but the younger, long the brunt of such harassment, moved instantly to the side and away.

"No, Pancho, no, no. You know better than such. I have no woman now, sad to report. I have done what I do for you every morning before dawn. I have walked the perimeter of your domain, watching for signs of movement, or evidence of attempts to invade the area of the Diablos. Nothing more, and you know it well."

The elder's anger flashed, aided in its combustion by the rush of white powder snorted only moments before the boy returned. But just as quickly, it passed. Lowering his hand, he bellowed another huge laugh, instead grabbing Miguel in a bear hug that lifted him off the ground. "Of course, bambino, of course. It is as always, amigo. You are about your brother's work. Of course." Without so much as a twitch, Pancho released him, hitting him stiff-armed in the chest with his left hand, while the right crashed into his temple and exploded his cheek in a spurt of bright blood. The boy flew across the confined space of the alley, crashed into and through a pile of trashcans, then lay motionless in the debris.

"*Dannie—watch him.* I no longer trust my little one, he has been gone too many times. If he is chasing some little bitch, it will make him stupid, and his mouth will run at the wrong time. If not, then there is no explanation for his repeated disappearances. If he tries to leave, confine him. If he runs, kill him."

A hatchet face, pock-marked and scarred by years of gang warfare, nodded, and the burly Mexican sat down on an empty crate to watch his prisoner. A huge revolver protruded from his belt, a long butcher knife carved and whittled scraps of wood and plastic from the floor of the alley.

Barely awake, his head roaring with the concussion of the deadly blow to his temple, Miguel lay still. He hoped that he could maintain this state of apparent unconsciousness long enough to learn some new information, then discover a way out to meet Raul as he had promised. But at the moment, all he could think about was the pain in his head—and the blood running out of the cut at the corner of his eye and back into his ear.

* * * * *

The several small units of federal officers mixed with Guard personnel sat still, frustration and confusion overtaking each group in turn, as the lines of shadowy figures passing in front of them either wound around and out of sight or just seemed to disappear into the pavement. They had known going in that their surveillance plan was flawed by the necessity of being stationary. Had they made any effort to follow the lines of men, being detected would have created still more problems. In addition to having a huge fight on their hands, against a force several times their own strength, all hope of finding out where the arms stash was located would disappear as well.

Back in the musty old command post, Henry Lassiter and Boyd Jeffers searched through street and sewer maps frantically, trying to accomplish some semblance of a triangulation that would show an eventual convergence of routes at the right place. With the area narrowed down to four square blocks, they contemplated moving the teams closer to that apparent destination. They hesitated to do so but at the same time knew that once these invaders got to their intended meeting with Sallie, they would turn into an even more deadly force. They decided to begin moving the teams, one at a time, a block at a time.

"Henry, that's one helluva risk for those guys. If the bad boys see 'em, the whole program's in the shitter—they scatter, get in a nasty firefight with us, we get men killed, and the arms location remains a mystery." Lassiter scratched the scrubby growth at his chin, ruminating over Herman Hanks' typically accurate assessment of the situation. Jeffers nodded and continued to study the sewer maps, hoping to recognize some hint of where the ghosts were disappearing, but more, where they were going.

About the same time, and six blocks from the place where the first line disappeared, Sallie and his pals were making final preparations for the arrival of their many guests. Weapons and ammunition were arrayed in well-organized stacks, all to permit the men to enter, be identified and armed with the type of arms appropriate to each, then returned to the street in a very short time. A small red light began to blink over the secure door in the basement room.

"Salim, *Salim*—the sensors have begun to transmit. They are close. This light is attached to the first sensor, down at the end of the block." Sallie shot a look at the blinking light, looked back at the array of rifles, grenade launchers, anti-tank weapons, and cases of ammunition, then turned away from Sherman without acknowledging the comment at all.

"Await their arrival, both of you. I'll be back momentarily. If they get here before I return, begin the delivery process at once. Each knows what he is to take, so there should be no difficulty. Be sure to get an exact count of all who enter and leave. I must attend the secure storage." Sherman and Cedric, slavish ghouls that they were, could not help but pass a look at each other as the little fiend left so abruptly. The idea of him leaving just at the moment when the culmination of all he had worked for was about to begin was in-conceivable to them. But then, Sallie had always been a study in the unknowable to both these limited minds.

He walked until he was out of sight of the men and the area around the basement storage rooms. Then he quickly shot up the stairs, four floors, and into what had once been a small janitor's closet. The door was open, and only a few remnants of supplies and a number of dead rats remained. Ignoring the smell, he stepped into the closet, reached behind a hole in the plaster and retrieved a six cell flashlight. Training its bright beam at the ceiling toward the back of the tiny room, the small man moved quickly up the wall, climbing a series of steps punched into the plaster surface.

Reaching the ceiling, he pushed aside a section of ceiling tile; a rope fell through the hole and, after first jamming the flashlight into his hip pocket, Sallie pulled himself into the dark space between the floors. He grabbed the light and aimed it across the small span of the hole, where it reflected brilliantly off the shiny surface of twelve stainless steel cylinders, bundled together in groups of four within wooden frames. The man stopped breathing. No matter how often he saw these things, and regardless of how often he replayed the plan in his head, the moment when he saw these twelve tubes of instant death always left him weak. He shook all over momentarily, then began to slide the four-cylinder crates, one at a time, to the edge of the hole.

Approximately two feet in length and four inches in diameter each, the tanks, even full of the lethal Sarin nerve agent, only weighed about ten pounds apiece. The man's wiry strength was ample to wrestle the forty-pound crates into position at the edge of the hole in the ceiling, where he tied the loose end of the rope to them, one crate at a time, and lowered them quickly to the floor. With the last one down, he slipped down the rope behind them and began breaking down the crates, standing the cylinders upright in the hallway. One at a time, he then carried them into the apartments facing the streets, all up and down the hall.

The old tenement was very big, at least by the standards of the days when it was built, stretching halfway down the block. Being situated on a corner, it had about two hundred feet of frontage on the adjoining street as well so that, properly spaced, the dozen containers could disperse a deadly mist over a total of more than six hundred feet of narrow street.

Within five minutes total elapsed time Salim had the tanks dispersed; he started back to the first room into that he had delivered one and, after first opening a window, carefully stood one of the cylinders up next to the opening. Each was fitted with a timer that operated a small detonator affixed to the end of the tank. He set the timer, then laid the container on its side in the window box that hung on the side of the building, in front of a total of eight windows on the long side of the fourth floor. The other four were likewise set in place, equally spaced apart around the corner and up the intersecting street.

Moving swiftly and with no wasted motion, the process was completed within ten minutes. With the last in place, he made sure all the windows were closed, then reached into the same hole in the wall of the closet where the flashlight had been hidden, retrieving a large, clean towel. Having planned well and for many months, he left no detail to chance; he carefully wiped all the perspiration and grit from his face, arms, and hands, then returned to the basement to find the process of weapons delivery well underway. Just before he went to greet his guests, Sallie slipped a small, rectangular transmitter into the waistband of his jeans, an object roughly the size of a pocket computer, but with a radio type antenna clipped to the side. A smile quickly disappeared from his evil countenance as he stepped into the light of the basement.

* * * * *

Richland looked almost peaceful. Well, at least compared to the raging inferno that had lit up the night skies for months, off and on throughout the summer, things looked peaceful. The departure of that unseen van full of bad guys, though still a mystery to the Guardsmen who had chased them without success, was a sort of last gasp for the agents of evil who had so terrorized the midwestern city for six months.

And part of the reason they left was that, over those months, the hometown soldiers, one building at a time, had slowly retaken the place from the clutches of terror and torture. With the neutralization of each pocket of fighting, the assets of the National Guard and local police would in turn be reallocated to the remaining problem areas, producing an ever more powerful force, constantly being concentrated into an ever smaller area. The results were slow but steady, and the good guys still had one substantial advantage—resupply. From the armory outside of town, General Whitaker's trucks and Hueys were able to provide replacement weapons, a good flow of ammunition and, of course, air support in the form of four old Cobra gun ships.

Similar success, painful, expensive, and slow, occurred around the country, in the small and medium size cities. Even places like St. Louis, Chicago, and Denver seemed to follow that scenario, as disease and starvation finally weakened even the bad guys beyond their endurance. Still, the cost was astronomical, the effort huge, and reclamation almost incomprehensible.

The units of artillery and infantry that went on President Flint's treasure hunt to the Middle East had taken the entire

445

complement of advanced technology of the Iowa National Guard with them. This included four Apache attack helicopters, the new armored personnel carriers, all the advanced tech communications equipment, and four M1A1 tanks, newly attached to the infantry just the summer before. But the old stuff was still in the arsenal at home, due in large measure to the truculent, at times defiant, then even devious devices of the commanding general.

Whitaker threw such fits about turning in the old stuff and raised so much hell about the cuts in his armaments budget that the National Guard Bureau never did succeed in getting back the "oversupply" of small arms, the old M60 tanks he still had, the inventory of spare parts for the older model trucks and weapons, and the large stash of ammunition for it all. The result was that as the months of urban warfare burned on the citizen soldiers who thought their duties would be limited to flood relief and tornado response were at least well supplied and quickly provided with needed weapons and munitions.

Logan Pierce, by this time the only remaining captain with any prior combat experience, sat at a desk under the shade of a big tent. The secure area where they now worked was an athletic field that was surrounded by high chain link fence, on the perimeter of the tenement section of Richland. The sun beat down with August persistence, but a slight afternoon breeze brushed against the flaps of the tent. The sides were rolled up to let in all the air possible.

"Captain, General's on the line. Says it's urgent." The communications specialist held the receiver of a field phone, his gazed fixed on Pierce with that "you better hurry up" look on his face. The very idea of a general talking directly with a captain never failed to unnerve him, and even though he could quickly explain to himself how it all happened—all the field grade officers were gone to play in the sand—it still had the same effect. Only when the big man had personally directed combat operations when the fighting was actually happening had Pierce been able to forget just how weird it was.

He took the phone, shaking off the nerves again. "Sir, Pierce here, how are you, General?"

"Fine, Captain, just fine. Matter of fact, *very* fine, today. Got some good news—finally. Just got off the line with the boys at the nuclear plant out on the river. They've managed to cobble together a miniature network for return of electricity to part of the city and some of the suburbs. Don't ask me how, but they tell me they were able to well, they say they *unhooked us* from the larger network that included a wide, multi-state area, repaired three substations that were blown up in March, and they think they can give us juice."

Pierce had trouble even conceiving of electricity again. And the idea of power running through the bombed-out sections of the city where buildings lay in ruins, bare, torn wires protruding everywhere, immediately raised visions of fire and electrocution in his mind.

"Wow—I mean *wow*, sir, that's great—I mean, yeah, really. But sir, what about all the places where the power lines are down, and all that bare wire is just sticking out of the rubble—I mean, are we going to have problems with fire, and —"

"I know, Logan, same thing I asked. They tell me that, as soon as you guys had the violence under control, they sent teams in to basically disconnect all areas where damage had been done to the power lines and the underground power supply. What's happening even includes some new wire running to the refugee centers, a supply directly to the University, where we have about fifteen thousand folks being cared for, and some kind of linkup to the hospitals—all five of them."

Pierce was nearly overwhelmed by the concept that the hospitals might begin to function again. They had been useless within about four days of the beginning of all this mess, as soon as the diesel fuel supplies that ran the auxiliary generators were exhausted. His mind raced through the long list of soldiers and civilians who died in the streets, in tents, some in his arms, without medical care or even modest protection from the elements.

Ending the conversation with the acceptance of some orders for conduct of inspections and patrols when the juice came back on, Pierce hung up and stepped to the edge of the tent. Looking out on the devastation of his hometown, the idea of repair somehow brought the pervasive ruin of the whole thing back to the front of his consciousness.

Trying to imagine the amount of effort, pain, and resources necessary to reclaim this mess proved to be more than his mind could accomplish; standing there in the late afternoon sun, the tent sighing as the breeze passed through it, he tried to remember how it was before. But each image of old Richland was in turn pushed aside by a score of horror scenes, fires, gun battles, and the dead. Dearest Jesus, the dead. Children, old people, soldiers, firemen, his own father, killed by small arms fire as he huddled in the recreation room of the retirement village just three miles from where the son now stood. And all his mind could say, over and over, silently until it finally slipped from his lips as low whispers, ". . .but it'll never be the same again. Never. *Never. . .*"

* * * * *

"Mr. President, you have no idea how glad I am to be able to bring some *good* news, at long last. After so many trips up here with nothing to report, I began to fear that this old ticker couldn't stand very many more meetings that failed to meet with presidential approval!" The cabinet room echoed with the unusual sound of laughter, as the gruff old bureaucrat teased the chief executive. Everyone in the place remembered Webb's barbecue of Walter Flanigan back in the first days after the nationwide loss of electricity plunged the whole country into cold darkness. The head of the Federal Emergency Management Administration, FEMA, collapsed under the General's withering excoriation for the Administration's failure to plan for big power losses.

Now the tone was different, although less than truly optimistic. Offensives were underway on both coasts to retake the largest cities from the grip of urban terrorism and anarchy that had reigned for months, and there was plenty of military power to accomplish the missions. The smaller cities and most of the outlying areas in middle America had already settled down a bit, with the major problems now more centered on starvation and disease than violence. The end of petroleum supplies had quickly spelled the end of mobile terrorism. Flanigan reported on the subject of electricity again.

"As you all know, the then-existing system for delivery of electrical power counted on a network of interrelated and interdependent sources, all connected at least indirectly to each other. When the goons blew up so many of the bigger substations that acted as the routing switches for the ultimate delivery to consumers, the result was basically a complete collapse. Moreover, the destruction of so many of the big transformers needed to store, switch, and route power all over the place produced an insurmountable problem for repair. That is, the electrical utilities nationwide had very small inventories of those transformers with that to replace those that were destroyed." Flanigan stood and moved to a chart, shaped as a map of the U.S., and began to demonstrate the locations where bombings had taken out the supply.

"As you can see, the red stars mark the locations where stations were taken out. The blue lines connecting them, show the immediate source from that power typically came for distribution from each location. Remember that the actual source of power may have been, and often was, several states away from the point of actual consumer use. The numbers in black identify how many of the large transformers were lost at each place. Here, down in the corner, is the tally. Pretty grim, I think you'll all agree. Over two thousand destroyed. Here in green, next to the number of lost transformers at each place, is the number of transformers in inventory in the general area. This tally here, next to the loss numbers, shows you that we are some one thousand transformers short of enough to do the repairs.

"Of course, the demolition of existing wreckage, running of new wire, and firing up the power plants all takes time, manpower, coordination and, most of all, petroleum to run the equipment. Probably the first real breakthrough came with the allocation by the Department of the Army of a large supply of diesel fuel to this effort."

The president studied the map for a moment, then asked the question that was on everybody's mind. "What can we do about this transformer shortage problem, Walter—looks like we're screwed, petroleum or not, if we can't replace the bombed-out equipment." There was a low mumble of assent around the room, and Flanigan lit up with true excitement at the opportunity.

"Good question, sir, and the one that stumped us the worst. Then the engineers got together by phone for a series of conferences—no small feat in a country without power and pretty much without telephone communications. Again, the military helped us. The engineers from all over were transported to secure facilities or had communications equipment flown to them, and the Army Signal Corps set up a series of conference calls, a week apart. That enabled the smart people to talk to each other over and over, compare damage and inventories, and discuss the worst of the problems. The result was *this*."

He set up a second map, looking very much like the first, but with new numbers and some heavy lines running from various of the damaged locations to power sources.

"We started with the power supply locations that were still operational, then tracked the delivery lines that were not damaged or were most easily repaired. The engineers created twelve separate WAD, or Wide Area Delivery systems, independent of each other and responsible only for power within that area. All were in agreement that one of the biggest reasons for the complete collapse was the interdependency of the whole delivery system. With this idea, loss in one area cannot by itself cause loss somewhere else. And although the result owed as much to the extremely sophisticated understanding of the network by the terrorists as it did to interdependency, the engineers felt this would make a rerun of this last mess less likely.

"Now, to answer the President's question. We allocated the existing usable replacement equipment to accomplish complete restoration of the most pivotal stations, again with the military's assistance. The Air Force has agreed to transport the big stuff from place to place for us, so we can get the identified stations up as quickly as possible. In fact, in six areas around the country, where power plants are able to do it, we are starting to re-establish juice to select neighborhoods, hospitals, and major refugee centers right now. Seattle, Richland, Iowa, Louisville, three suburbs of Dallas, Orlando, and Charleston, West Virginia will go up this week. They are more the result of local repair and redesign than from this bigger plan; local initiative has proven to be the most efficient to this point.

"So, with a skeleton framework of delivery networks in place, some of the most important locations should have power before it starts to get cold. I wish I could report that we will have power to residential areas in great numbers, but I cannot. Looks like a pretty cold winter for much of the Midwest, the Northeast, and the mountain states." That

450

sobering statement deflated the optimism in the room a bit, but they talked on with real enthusiasm, temporarily permitting themselves to forget about the warfare that still raged in America's most beloved cities.

As they broke up after the Cabinet meeting, the President sat with Mac Reed and Jonathan Brooks, who had managed to rustle up a bottle of Scotch whiskey to share. Reed had a small stack of reports concerning the ongoing status of offensives, plus an update on the CIA's efforts to get satellite surveillance turned to the trouble in Babylon. Reed blew a cloud of smoke, then moaned softly at the heat and flavor of the amber liquid. "Holy sweet— Sure tastes good. Just wish there were more to celebrate. Here, Jackie, this is the report from the L.A. Command, this is the one from NYC, and this is the—wha—Sir. . .where'd he—"

Brooks nodded in the direction of the window in the far corner of the room, where Webb stood staring into the gathering darkness. The August evening light was sufficient to show the sad dilapidation of the area around the White House, and this old soldier, this warrior leader, once again found himself nearly overcome with the unthinkable reality of what had happened to his beloved country, all while he was its president. "Boys, there are times when I fear my heart will simply break within me over all this. I must confess that I never in all my life permitted myself to even imagine being president. Never. The Joint Chiefs' assignment was beyond my wildest dreams, and I still always thought my chairmanship there had as much to do with the politics of race as with my qualifications."

He stood, glass in hand, talking quietly, almost a rasp in his deep voice. A wave of emotion came and went, his throat tightening, breathing for a moment shallow and short. The sight of a soldier out in front of the big mansion, climbing up onto the top of a tank, then settling down behind its machinegun, stabbed deep with the images of violence, war.

"We must remember that we are not saving much here, boys. We are more just trying to start over. That which was before March is mostly gone. Like it was gone in 1865, and like it was gone after the Depression. But more gone still. This time, we, at least as a people, had decided we were perpetual, permanently immune from the forces of evil. We were so very wrong. And this old man cannot begin to imagine what may arise out of these ashes. Hell, the fires are still burning, and we preside over a shambles. A republic no more. And the idea that we were so arrogant as to think ourselves bulletproof threatens to crush me utterly."

The smoke from Reed's cigarette floated lazily through the soft light of evening, and the only sound was the unison sighing of the three men. No one spoke to interrupt the president's musings; all shared his sorrow and his deep anxiety for the future of the ruins of the United States of America.

6.

He stepped reflexively on the clutch and the brake at the same time, the baler groaning to a jerky stop. The youngster on the hay wagon lurched and fell into the stack of hay bales behind him, then spun to see what had happened to the rig. Carl sat stock still, not breathing, his eyes and ears searching the close summer air for clues, information to support the urgent alarm just then going off in his head. He reached down and turned off the big diesel engine on the tractor, so that the only sound emitting from the apparatus was the slowing of rotation of the power takeoff shaft from the tractor to the baler. As the sound subsided, the boy stood still, immediately aware that Doc was intent on something.

Fully two minutes passed the chirping of birds, crickets, and the sounds of a light breeze across the newly mown hay seemed to be all there was to hear. Finally the boy could contain himself no more.

"Whassup, Dr. Landry? I don't hear a thing 'cept the frogs in the woodlot." Carl shook his head only slightly.

"Don' know, son, just heard. . .well, more sort of *felt* something—like a kind of thump, or a tremor. . .out that way—south and east, toward town a bit. Suppose the army's chasing the riffraff again. Still, didn't seem. . so far as that. ."

Looking in that general direction, Carl thought for only a moment that he saw some smudge on the horizon, close to the ridgeline that separated them from the creek bottom closer to Jake Ratliff's place. Then there was nothing.

The light breeze was blowing from behind where they sat, in the direction of town. Josh had been gone just three hours, not all that long, really, for a man moving cautiously on horseback.

Josh would have kept to cover, avoided roads completely. And they both knew the geography well enough to travel without roads. He had promised not to engage in anything stupid, and Carl believed him—well, he pretty much believed him. The man did have that unique and maddening personality quirk that could turn a walk to the trashcan into an adventure, on occasion. Probably nothing. Probably.

"Thought I might've heard a rumble or an explosion, but I guess not. Just a bit edgy, I guess." The boy smiled and nodded his dusty head, pulled on his gloves, and grabbed the hay bale that had spun out of his hands when Carl hit the brakes. Every boy in the place watched the craggy-faced physician as if he beheld Doc Holliday, and being the one chosen to work the baler with him was a big deal. Cody Jansen reminded himself that these Landry men had been successful as the shepherds of the flock for a reason; it had to have something to do with some kind of heightened senses, some kind of perception the rest of them lacked. At least that was the talk among the young men who followed their every directive, the young men whom they had led to protect a hundred people over the past six indescribable months.

Carl put the tractor in gear, started back into motion again. But he made a promise to get over there, in the direction of Jake's, if Josh wasn't back by the time he finished with this field. No matter how old they got, he was still the older brother.

* * * * *

"Gentlemen, welcome to our humble annex to Allah's glory—please find the weapons and ammunition of your choice and assignment, then make your way out through this little hallway, *here*. Cedric, have you shown the men the proper direction to take for exiting the building?"

His face uncustomarily alight with evil excitement, Cedric replied immediately that he had done so, leading the front of the now quickly moving line out of the entry area. They had been shown into the hallways where the weapons stood ready, then on into the now ancient coal bins and storage rooms that formed a catacomb, extending out under the street on the other side of the building.

Sallie smiled and shook an occasional hand as he recognized many of the men now passing through his private domain. None had ever been there, and very few had any idea the place really existed at all; now there was, even amid the grim business of arming for the holy jihad to exterminate the infidels of America, a sense of curiosity and even awe, as these Islamic terrorists first saw the extent of what Salim Abdul Alakmah had accomplished for the PLO. Some actually smiled. So impressed were they with the realization that all this had been done right in the heart of America's greatest city, right in the middle of the most populous place in the land, and immediately under the noses of the entire local, state, and international law enforcement establishment.

"Sherman—*Sherman*—come, please. Would you assist me for a moment?" The man, like his nasty cohort, was emersed in the occasion, and his attention was less than acute toward the boss's command. Turning, he walked back into the hallway, the other direction from where the men were picking out their weapons. Sallie spoke through a plastic grin, his voice deep and soft, as he did his best to maintain the host's countenance. He directed his words only to the curious assistant at his side.

"I trust you obtained an exact count of the number of men entering the facility, Sherman, as we discussed? We must know exactly how many enter *and leave* the SPA. You do remember my directives, do you not?" The ghoul could not conceal the blankness of his expression and the instant, desperate fear at having failed in a task apparently ordered by the master. In truth, he had no recollection of the order, and could only hope it had actually been delivered to Cedric.

"Salim, apologies, Salim, but I—maybe it was Cedric whom you ordered—"

"*Shut up, idiot—you were both present, I distinctly remember. If he has failed, you shall both die for this!*" The stage whisper, spat through clinched teeth and behind that now brittle smile, struck the gray man like an ax. He prayed to Allah that Cedric had heard the order and accomplished it. "Wait here, fool, and be alert. No person must wander anywhere off the precise route we have prescribed."

Sallie stroked and joked his way back to the entry room, where Cedric was purposefully directing the men into the appropriate area. "So, Cedric, how many of our guests have arrived, to this point?" The man never missed a beat, turning from the terrorist just past him, answering without a breath.

"One hundred fourteen, as of this moment, Salim. I have not yet asked Sherman to open the back exit, preferring to wait for your command. I will ask that he count the men as they leave, to confirm your requirement." The answer was forthright, confident, and matter-of-fact, so much so that the venom rising in Sallie's ugly self immediately ebbed.

"Oh—well then. . .good, well done, Cedric. I should see that no one is misinformed about the directions out of here. Thank you." Speaking those words, he touched the man's arm, requiring him to turn away momentarily from the line of mercenaries filing through the secure doorway. "Advise me of the final count at once. Is that clear?"

Cedric turned as indicated, looked for a brief moment into the cold green murk of Sallie's eyes, and responded with the usual and obligatory "As you wish, Salim." As if such pedantic ordering was necessary. Cedric swallowed his irritation with the order and turned to resume the count.

And in that brief moment two men entered simultaneously, both black men, each removing his stocking mask. The first looked toward Sallie and his assistant, a note of recognition and jovial greeting emanating from his throat. The other, passing into the room at the same time thanks to the nearly four foot wide doorway, took a soft, quick step past them and, moving with practiced skill, turned into the hallway full of men. He blended quietly and without fanfare into the small crowd. J.D. could never have dreamed of better luck.

* * * * *

Raul Sanchez stood amid company and field grade officers, a score or more in number, his face red with frustration and heat, drawn and worn with fatigue. The meeting had taken on more the tone of an inquisition than that of a briefing, ever since he told the assembly of Miguel's inexplicable failure to make their follow-up meeting regarding the impending alliance of the rival gangs. Now, with a large operation nearly underway, based mostly on the intelligence gained from the Marine's cousin, the problems created by his disappearance were obvious.

"I understand, sir, I was the one who first brought the information—*and the informant*—to you. I can only say that I was where I was supposed to be, the very location we have met now a dozen times, and Miguel never came. It is my belief that—"

"*Sergeant,* it is more than a little problem for us that he would disappear just after apprising you of what we all thought to be a pretty fantastic circumstance at best. What if this is all a ruse, an effort—successful to this point—to misdirect us away from other more realistic objectives. *Have you considered that?*" The speaker, an Air Force major in charge of the coordination of intelligence gathering efforts all over Central Los Angeles, hit the wrong nerve with his subordinate.

"With all due respect, Major Armbruster, that's ridiculous. No, it's worse than that. It's bullshit, and you know it! If you are suggesting that my—"

"That will do, Sergeant—enough. I realize this is your cousin, and a young man for whom you have great affection, but I will not tolerate such outbursts toward your superiors." Lt. Colonel Brice Wilkins spoke with less than great conviction, although he was intent on stopping the firefight before it went further. His irritation with the fly boy major less than subtle, he addressed them again.

"Major, please. I think Sergeant Sanchez has well documented for us the credentials and the background of the informant. A more plausible explanation may exist for his absence than you have insinuated. Now, Sergeant. If Miguel has been detained or somehow slowed in his return to the meeting site, what would you expect to be his next move, assuming he is free to move at all?"

Sanchez tore his gaze away from the Air Force uniform, the Latin temper pounding in his temples and neck. Turning his attention to the colonel's question, he thought for a moment. No clear answer presented itself, but the now-established practice of recurring meetings made the most sense.

"Well sir, we've met every other day, at about dawn, for over two weeks now, and I would expect Miguel to return to that habit if he's able. I think I should return to that procedure as well. Until I can find him again, I certainly think Command should continue to assume the accuracy of his reports. If those gangs have already achieved an alliance, all they have to do is move into the proper positions, fortify themselves with the weapons we know they have, move the hostages into shielding locations, and the task of removing them will become very expensive."

Colonel Wilkins rose from his seat at once, eager to speak before any further sparks could fly. What Armbruster lacked in acumen and skill he made up for in confidence, and his abrasive personality had been a problem for almost two weeks. *"Good—I like that.* Let's continue to plan for a quick strike, including gunship support and an armored entry into East L.A. and Watts, once we can get a fix on the location of these noncombatants. The informant, I remind you gentlemen, has told us the gangs intend to use them as shields to avoid just that strategy. If they get a gaggle of women and kids out in front of them, the helicopters are useless at once. Too risky. And gentlemen, let's be clear on this: *I have no desire to negotiate with a bunch a 'redneck bikers over the safety of those kids or possession of this city. Carry on.*"

* * * * *

"Jaci—*Jaci, I need you right now!! Where the hell are—*"

"Right here, Franz, only wait one second. My hands are full of very expensive components. *There.* Now. What has you bleating like some lost goat?" Schuelman crawled from beneath a small, cramped space that held a complement of wires and sequencing programs, his face red with frustration as well as heat. The temperature within the silo rose to over 100 degrees Fahrenheit, while the outside hit 120. The last bits of software installation had been more than impossible, due in large measure to the number of details that only the now departed genius had held in his head. Every time they thought they had the answers to the few remaining problems, they were beset with still more aggravations.

"I have removed the entire component, tested the programs, run a complete set of protocols, and *still* the system will not accept the commands necessary to permit firing of the main fuel cell. And without that sequence being accepted, the goddam thing will take off, climb about twenty-five hundred feet, then come crashing straight back down on top of us. Think Saddam will find *that* amusing, Jaci?"

The younger and far less stalwart member of the team, found it not at all amusing, with his own set of problems concerning the finer points of detonating a nuclear warhead ruining his afternoon.

"We've got to come to some quick solutions or this whole thing will be unworkable, whether or not Saddam kills us. Maybe his marksmen will be good at their tasks, and we'll both die quickly. Unless I can figure out the glitch in the detonation setup, all we will do is launch a great big dud that will succeed in making a small hole in the roof of some building in central Tel Aviv. I could do as much damage with a hammer."

Schuelman stood, arched his back in an effort to ease the kinks caused by so long a time in the confined space he had just occupied, then approached the table where Jaci had the notes laid out on top of a schematic of the warhead information scheme. They pored over the scribbled equations, repeatedly stopping for the younger man to decipher his own handwriting, then made their way through the remainder of the materials without ever figuring out what they were missing.

"Are you sure you have all he said? I mean, he always talked so fast, once he got on a roll about these damned programs. Or could you have misplaced any of the pages? You've got at least twenty pieces of paper just lying here. How do you know you have all you wrote? The stuff was scattered all over the backseat and the floor of the VW." Jaci shook his head.

"No, I went through the whole car when I brought them in here. Shit, Franz, if we can't crack this thing, the missile is worthless, or worse, even dangerous to the palace and the city. I remind you that there is a sufficient quantity of enriched plutonium in that lead container to vaporize the whole region, if properly detonated. If we can't make the bomb work, someone a lot smarter about weapons grade nuclear materials than me will have to disarm the thing, because I am totally clueless on that subject."

"No problem for us, my friend. If it won't work, we'll be dead long before disarming it becomes a major concern." They stood over the table full of papers, sketches, and calculations, the fatigue and anxiety turning the images into pure nonsense before them. Finally, they agreed to quit, some twenty-six hours after the commencement of their efforts to finish what Adolpho had begun. Walking out of the secure area and into the gardens, their way was blocked by a huge Red Guardsman, his rifle at port arms.

"Easy, friend. Even geniuses have to rest." He smiled weakly into the stony face of the sentry.

"Are you finished? My orders are to confine you until you have finished. Are you finished?" The two swallowed smirks at the simpleton who was empowered to kill them, if they misbehaved in any way.

"No, we're not finished, officer, only spent. Would you have us work on this project at a time when a mistake could vaporize this entire city? Does that make sense to you? Please, let us go for a few hours of rest. We'll be back before the sun, we promise."

"You will wait here. I will check. If you move, I am to shoot both of you." The giant walked to the telephone console, mounted inside an inconspicuous guard desk to the side of the main entrance. He stood for several minutes, never making a sound. Then he spoke a few words into the receiver and hung up. Walking back purposefully, he addressed both young men.

"You have four hours. I am to follow you. Unless you go only to your home, I am to shoot you. If you fail to return within four hours, I am to shoot you. Unless you finish, so that you can report to Saddam by tomorrow at 6 o'clock, I am to shoot you." Motioning toward the hallway that led to the secure parking area, he followed as they walked out.

Had it not been for the clear truth that shooting was exactly what the goon had in mind, he'd have been a perfect *Hogan's Heroes* character. Sergeant Schultz reincarnated. But the large pistol on his belt, accompanied by the automatic weapon in his hands, deprived him of his true comic identity. He spoke one last time as they sat down in the VW. "Have a nice rest."

7.

"Almost dark in New York, late afternoon in L.A., war raging on both coasts, and I'm sitting here on my butt with precious little information about any of it. You'd think I was just along for the ride. Corporal, let's try to reach General Murah again. By now they must have completed their evacuation of the coastline suburbs, unless they ran into unexpected resistance. And that whole warlord thing has had my stomach in a knot for two days. Mark may be irritated with me, but he'll get over it." Clyde Anthony Keithley accepted the nod of his communications specialist, then turned back to the desk where the commander in chief was studying an array of satellite images of central Iraq.

"Clyde, if the gangs don't kill Mark Murah, your calls will send him AWOL for sure. It's only been two hours since your last call, and I'd think he'd 've called back if he had anything to tell us. Now come look at this mess and tell me what your fine mind makes of all these sand piles. I can sure use your powers of ob—"

"Sir, I mean General Keithley, General Murah just called in. He's asking for you and the President. I'll put it through on the speaker." The two looked at each other, then at the photos on the desk, then at the phone, as it produced the voice of the Chief of Occupation Forces, West.

"Clyde, this is Mark, can you hear me all right? I need to speak with the President as well. Clyde?"

"Yes, Mark, we're clear, and the President is here with me, along with Mac. Fire away."

"Nothing is predictable except unpredictability out here, guys. Reminds me of summer camp at Parris Island, after our junior year. One bullshit dirty trick after another. The only thing that hasn't happened yet is an earthquake, and I'm almost afraid to say that. Here's the deal. We told you earlier about the G-2 we had concerning some kind of alliance between the Mexicans and the rednecks. Thought it looked pretty good, made some sense, and fit what we already knew about the weaponry and hostage situation with these people who call themselves the "Sons of Silence." Since we last talked, we have lost the informant.

"This kid was not just a shot in the dark, either. His cousin is a Marine, an MP doing security and intelligence work for Headquarters West. He met personally with the informant on several occasions, and we felt what he said was good. Then he disappeared. Failed to show up for the last meet with his cousin. I know it sounds silly, having an offensive the size of this one stalled because of one missing snitch, but we know these people have a large number of refugees essentially held hostage within the area of East L.A. Once these gangs join forces and pool weapons and ammunition, they can use these people as bargaining chips to get what they want.

"Of course, we're not about to give them some kind of possessory right to a big chunk of the city, but this thing with the hostages is a real problem. If we move in without a clear picture of where those people are and what kind of exposure they have to our fire, we'll end up killing more of them than we do bad guys. So you can see that we're pretty much stuck." There was silence in the Oval Office, each of the four men in the room staring at the floor, trying to absorb the problem.

"Mark, Jackie here. Can you get people into the area to do some covert surveillance without creating an instant firefight? If you could get some indication about the whereabouts of these noncombatants and how many there are, maybe you could make a stab at liberating them first— before the thugs can get them into position."

"I agree, Mark. This is Clyde. What about fly overs? Surely they've gotten used to the sound of aircraft all over the place by now. Can you learn anything by looking from up top?"

"Been there. There's a squad of SEALS sneaking in after dark tonight, hoping to learn something about the noncombatants. We also tried the air route, but the gangs have evidently stashed their hostages inside. I have a dozen two-man teams attempting to observe every large structure in a six-mile square, where they might be keeping a large number of people. They have to be starving by now. But we know they have water. That area is supplied by a gravity line from a couple of huge water towers that have never been damaged in all the fighting. That's all we know now."

"All right. Mark, this is Jackie again. I know it sounds ugly, but you must be ready to go in there soon. Killing a huge number of hostages is an awful prospect, but to be

462

honest about it, they're all dying anyway. No food, disease probably rampant by now, and a couple hundred Diablos using them for entertainment constantly. If you can't learn where they are within a day, better get ready to go in anyway. God only knows what the gangs are doing to them already."

"I'm clear, Mr. President. We should have recon information in about six hours, so we'll report back by approximately 0800 your time." There was a click, and he was gone. After communicating with each other from all over the world for the better part of thirty years, formalities were few and far between. In fact these old classmates were constantly having to remind themselves that one of their own was now actually their commander in chief.

"This is the same shit we faced in Somalia, Jackie. Even reminds me some of all those villages in the Central Highlands a little, back in the late sixties. Except this time they're American citizens, in Los Angeles, for crissakes. Jesus what a mess. Mark's right, though. Can't just take off and go in blazing without knowing where these people are being held. . . What a mess. . ." Keithley shook his head and walked out of the room, heading for the back steps and some fresh air.

The President looked into his empty glass, turned off the lamp on the desk, and walked out toward the private quarters. Mac Reed and Jonathan Brooks would stand "charge of quarters" until news arrived from any front or until dawn, whichever came first.

* * * * *

The low murmur of men's voices reflected the continued extreme level of discipline within the ranks of Allah's warriors, but the numbers were quickly overpowering the small basement area allotted to them in the SPA. Moving through the contingent, now fully armed and ready to move on, Sallie motioned to Sherman.

"My friend, please proceed to the back of the coal bins and show our guests to the exit. *Gentlemen—may I have your attention for a moment.* Thank you. As you pass through the back of this area, you will find yourselves at a secret opening into the storm sewer. I checked it this afternoon, and there is almost no water in it at this time. I am sure you were briefed with regard to your direction of travel when you get into it, so we will bid you farewell now. *May Allah be praised and his sword wet with the blood of many!!"*

The men responded with quiet assent, then began to move in the direction already indicated by the ever-growing line. Sherman passed to the front of that line, then disappeared into the coal bin doorway and was gone. Within sixty seconds, the line began to move into that dark hole in the back wall of the basement, each man stepping into total darkness as he left the hallway. In less than five minutes, the crowd of men dissipated, so that the remaining long line that had been crowding into the entryway, and even remaining in the alley that led to the secure entrance, was finally all inside the basement rooms.

The weapons disappeared quickly, as each man selected from the choices—most taking automatic rifles or submachineguns like Israeli Uzis, stolen U.S. M-16s, Mac 10s, H&K MP5s, and the ever popular Chinese AK47s. Every last terrorist was issued an automatic pistol, a most impressive supply of brand new Glock 10mms, complete with two twelve-round clips already fully loaded with the vicious Black Talon hollow point ammunition. A series of thefts from, of all places, the FBI training academy at Quantico, Virginia, had accounted for most of these, augmented by approximately twenty-five smaller burglaries from various FBI and ATF field offices around the country. Several burglaries of gun stores added twenty weapons, but the small supplies of such weapons in retail stores made them less attractive targets.

About ten percent of the men took only handguns, it being their assignment to take explosives, small antitank weapons, Claymore mine components, det cord and wire for rigging more exotic surprises. There were 90mm recoilless rifles, complete with twenty rounds of ammunition each—perfect for armor destruction and accurate neutralization of fortified positions. Twelve men, in teams of three, carried out the small 81 millimeter mortars and 50 rounds of ammunition for each. Once in place, these would lob high explosive charges right into the middle of enemy troop formations, scattering deadly shrapnel in a large meter circle. Ammunition resupply was not the assignment of this place, there being large caches already in place all over the city.

Sallie watched casually, his green eyes missing nothing, as the men filed through in near silence. He spoke to the many who were his own enlistees, occasionally exchanging a few familiar words with the older men he knew from his many years as a criminal on New York's huge dark side. The quiet discipline of the men was impressive, as was their direct and confident acquisition of the weapons assigned to each. His main concern, however, remained, the confinement of all these people to the narrow area where they selected their weapons and then moved on out, under the street. He could not permit any person to gain access to the rest of the building, and he constantly remained covertly vigilant to prohibit anyone from wandering off down the other hallways that led to stairs and the upper floors.

Within just over an hour, the place was nearly empty, and the last of the dark figures had processed through the basement. A strange, damp chill settled within the dirty old walls, as the late night air found its way through the open doorway and out into the big sewer. A draft, drawing the air through and mixing at times with the dank back flow of the smelly sewer, left the whole basement area most unpleasant. Both the gray men were anxious to leave it and return to the upper levels as quickly as possible, hurrying to store the empty boxes and remains of the supply process just completed. Sensing their desires, Sallie quickly disabused them of an early end to the work.

"Men, we are far from finished with Allah's work. These many crates must be stored, but first they must be disassembled, with all markings and identifying wording obliterated. Take the wooden crates apart and stack all panels from them that contain printing together inside the coal bins. I will dispose of them myself. The rest, take back to the upper story storage rooms and put them away neatly. We may have need of them at a later date." This made little sense to either of the two men, as they had always understood that their work in that nasty hole would be complete once the weapons had been delivered and the offensive begun. In fact, they both thought they were to become soldiers beside their leader at that point.

"Have you two compared numbers, so that I may assure the Committee that only authorized personnel were permitted in here?" Neither man looked at the other, a quick plan for avoiding further problems with their boss having been completed. Cedric spoke.

"Yes, Salim. Our counts agreed exactly. Two hundred eighty-two men entered at my location, and exactly as many left via the coal bin, where Sherman tallied their number upon exit." Of course, given the unavoidable confusion of having so many in such a small place made such a claim ridiculous, but it seemed to satisfy Sallie. Neither man betrayed the slightest hint that their report was a total fabrication, their attempted count having produced numbers that were apart by at least fifteen men. The two were confident that only proper persons had entered, and everyone got the weapons they came for. What possible difference could the count make?

Much depended upon the coordination of all weapons deliveries and the commencement of a well-armed counteroffensive against the U.S. forces now poised to retake the city. And while Arafat and company well knew they could not expect to prohibit the eventual occupation of Manhattan by such a large army, it was their intention to use every weapon and device they could muster to decimate those forces in the process. The fact that most or all their own would die in the fight meant nothing to them; moreover, the zealots making up the vast majority of these terrorists were perfectly happy to die anyway.

The lessons of over thirty years of true guerilla warfare, first in the Far East then in a variety of other places around the world, had made it clear that relatively small, well-armed militants, familiar with their surroundings and using civilians as pawns where indicated, could stave off and even defeat much larger, more cumbersome forces. With thousands of starving people to use as bait, shields, and bargaining chips, and with the kind of weapons that make close-in combat very expensive for offensive operations, a few hundred skilled militant terrorists were certain to make the occupation of New York City a true nightmare.

Sallie was itching to receive his orders to enter the fight personally, but he had a number of loose ends to deal with first. He stepped into the hallway where Cedric and Sherman were bent to the task of disassembling over 150 crates and, drawing a silencer-equipped .357 magnum revolver from under his shirt, shot both men. Each went down with a round to the back, between the shoulder blades, followed immediately with a second to the side of the head. The sickening sweet smell of blood immediately began to fill the basement, the doors now being closed and locked again.

"Sort of like losing a good pet, only bigger, really. I guess I should have required you to walk to the grinder room first, but the thought that you might sense my purpose militated against it. Oh well, I'll just have to drag your white asses in there. No big deal." The additional scent of released bowels, mixed with the ever mounting smell of blood, made him light headed, as he once again revelled in the macabre eroticism of violent death.

"I haven't killed in so long. You cannot imagine, dear Sherman, how many times I nearly succumbed to slitting your fat throat, just to have the scent of blood in my nostrils again. But I forbore this pleasure, knowing Allah had need of your services until now. Oh, I will have to set up the communications equipment, but you should have known that was why I instructed you to leave it in the stairwell to the roof last time. Farewell."

He dragged first Sherman, then Cedric, to that awful room full of unspeakable memories and tortures, muttering to himself about the glories to come, both in this little place and in the great jihad that would soon follow.

8.

On television and often in books, people are depicted being tied up and confined for long periods. They are shown stumbling out of darkened spaces or untying their bonds then rubbing their wrists and ankles to restore circulation. They may squint at the bright lights, shield their eyes and walk erratically. All very theatrical, very tidy, and very wrong. Twenty-four hours confined without movement, even without being tied up, leaves the victim barely able to walk at all, particularly if movement has been restricted so that circulation can be encouraged and nerve pressure can be minimized. Persons who are tied, handcuffed, or packed into the trunk of a car find themselves unable even to feel their hands and feet. Walking or dialing a phone is simply impossible.

Often, where ligatures have been tied too tightly, the victims suffers tissue destruction on a scale sufficient to require amputation of hands and feet. Not a good result for the hero in the feature length film. But another feature of this unpleasant experience is the ongoing workings of the body's biological processes. After a few hours, particularly when a significant dose of fear is part of the equation, people urinate all over themselves. Defecation, vomiting and, of course, heavy perspiration all contribute to the situation so that, in addition to being horribly dehydrated and in great pain, folks stink. So it was when Miguel Sanchez awoke, late in the afternoon, his head pounding from the fractured facial bones he sustained at his brother's hand.

Lying in the dark, a faint ray of light visible from a crack in the paint covering a window above and behind him, Miguel looked through one eye, at first unable to turn his head. He could tell that he was inside, that his hands and feet were tied, then connected by a rope behind his back, and that he was alone in the room. Abruptly, the door to the small place slammed open, and the huge and immediately recognizable form of his ugly sentry appeared. Closing that one eye, the young man prepared to be hit again.

"*Hey—muchacho—are you awake?* I might hit you again if you are. . ." The man laughed deeply, but too loud, then kicked his captive with the flat of his boot, more to move him and see if he was conscious than to inflict another wound.

Miguel winced inside, the big foot sending a shot of electric pain up both legs and into his back and neck. He was able to deny his vocal cords the pain they wanted to declare, lying still. "Sheeiit, Miggie, are you dead? Come here, little dick, it cannot be that you are still out from one stroke of Pancho's hand. Come to me."

Dannie—Danilo Fernando Rodriguez—dragged Miguel by one foot, out into the middle of the floor, away from the pile of paper, plastic, and rotten food where his body had landed when he was thrown in the room that morning. He refrained from resisting altogether, ignoring the intense pain created in his legs and back after so many hours motionless on the hard floor. The guard grabbed him by the front of his shirt one-handed and stood him up, slamming him back against the wall from that he had just come.

"*There*, that looks better, now, aren't we fine?? My god but you stink, Miguel, what—you've pissed all over yourself. Ha! Wait 'til Pancho finds out that his leetle brother has pissed on himself—he'll get a laugh from *that* one!" The boy's head bounced against the wall, causing a storm of flashing lights to go off behind his eyes, plus a renewal of the awful pain in his face. "*AAHHH! Fuck you,* you little weasel. Pancho says you must be sneaking away to screw some senorita—or snitching on him—so we will just keep you here pissing on yourself a while longer. Sleep tight."

With that, he dropped him in a heap, back into the trash from that he had just been dragged, then walked out and slammed the door. Lying still for several minutes, the prisoner listened beyond the pain that roared in his ears, hoping now to figure out enough information regarding where he was and how long he had been there to calculate whether or not he had missed his appointment with Raul. Then he looked back toward that faint stream of light coming through the painted window and realized it was becoming ever more faint. The day was ending and he had missed that meeting.

Flexing his hands, tied tightly behind his back, proved to be most painful, but he continued to exercise them until he could make a fist, open his hands wide, then ball up his fingers tightly again. The throbbing in his hands and arms brought tears to his eyes as the manipulations continued, but Miguel could sense that the bonds holding him were not so strong. The material was stretching a bit as he continued to increase movement, until finally he realized what they had used. Duct tape. It's great stuff if enough is used, but in smaller quantities it stretches over time and eventually it can even be torn, if it has not been tightly wrapped in multiple layers.

Lying there, his body stinking, wet, in pain from several sources at once, the younger Sanchez had nothing better to do than to continue to stress and worry the bonds that held him, hand and foot. The ankles were also wrapped in tape, but more heavily, and there was a length of nylon rope connecting ankles to wrists behind his back, causing his knees to be bent continually. Spasms in the back of his thighs, the muscles along his shins, and a constant aching in the knee joints added a touch of exquisite misery to the sense of overwhelming hopelessness that threatened to consume him. Efforts to continue stretching the tape around his wrists were interrupted by attacks of acute pain from the muscles in his legs, aggravated by each movement of the arms.

The rope would tighten each time he twisted his wrists, pulling his feet closer to his buttocks, encouraging deepening of the spasms in the hamstrings. Relaxing his arms and the consequent lowering of his feet shut off circulation to his hands again, sending fiery flashes of pain up his arms. Then, while this excruciating ballet was going on in the darkness, voices suddenly became audible outside.

At first the only one identifiable was Pancho, his brash bravado clear even through the wall. The faint smell of tortilla flour baking close by, coupled with his recollection of where they had been when Pancho hit him, finally told him he was at the Mexican restaurant where the Diablos had holed up and made their base of operations all summer. Of course, all the food was gone, and there was no electricity to cook with, but they had stolen everything they could find. They made do with simple traditional Mexican fare, baking and cooking on fires kindled and fed with trash and wood torn from the walls of every building in the area.

Pancho was also streetwise enough to have maintained two other locations, both surprisingly secure and difficult to find, including one in the basement of a burned-out church that no one but he and one of his women, Tricia, knew anything about. She was every bit as mean and ruthless as

470

Pancho, and her deadly appetites made her a perfect match for the young gang lord.

"So, my redneck friends, have we an agreement? I would like to fortify our positions and move the hostages into the area as quickly as possible, if we are in agreement concerning the turf to be taken by each of us when our plan comes to its goal." Interesting to Miguel that the same question he had heard Pancho ask almost two days ago was still on the table. Frustrating for him, but at the same time a relief. There would be no movement or preparation against the military until these arrangements could be finalized. Pancho intended to extract more than promises from the grimy bikers, too.

By convincing them that his stash of hostages and anti-tank weapons—items missing from the arsenal of the Sons of Silence—it was his intention to make them cede command of the operation to him. That would also include delivery by the rival gang of their 50-caliber machinegun to the location he prescribed. The Diablos had no intention of entering into a long term marriage with their hated rivals, but only forming an arrangement that would permit them to gain possession of that particular weapon and the large stash of ammunition for it and several other weapons the Sons had.

The Sons were also fierce fighters, as the Diablos well knew from years of urban combat against them. The bikers tended to be older than their rivals, and many were military combat veterans, experienced with explosives, booby traps, and anti-tank tactics. As full of himself as Pancho was, he was also smart enough to know that if they were ever to be successful in getting the attention of the Army he would have to be capable of staving off their air strike capabilities. And he would need to keep the armored personnel carriers, tanks, and truck-mounted automatic weapons at bay.

The idea of setting the big machinegun in a protected place, but one where it could fire on hovering helicopters with great effect, seemed the perfect solution to the air problem. Moreover, with the gun surrounded by a large mob of visible hostages, women and children mostly, return fire would be unlikely. It could be moved easily at night, always remaining shielded by over a hundred bodies, like having several weapons instead of just one. When supported by the variety of small anti-tank pieces they already had, Pancho Sanchez saw himself able not only to hold off a big military force but to

471

inflict enough damage from behind his shield of hostages to drive the big boys to the bargaining table. Foolish, perhaps, but plausible, and very deadly.

Miguel lay silent, listening intently for more conversation from outside his dark room. Once he heard a voice he was sure was that of the Sons of Silence leader, a nasty ex-Marine they called Fatmouth, for his enormous facial features, but the words were not clear. What was clear was that an accord was reached, given his brother's raucous laughter and the sound of clinking glasses when the tequila was passed around. As the voices faded, he went back to work on the tape at his wrists, felt it start to give and stretch, then stopped abruptly when both legs and the small of his back were stabbed with overwhelming muscle spasms. Lying in that stinking trash, pain blocking out everything else, Miguel Sanchez knew that he had to get loose, and do it without further delay.

He also knew that, once he was untied, jumping up and running out would be impossible, at least for a while. The place was still crawling with Diablos, including Pancho, and the boy's legs simply would not support him until they had first been rested from the torture most recently inflicted upon them.

* * * * *

"Carl Landry, where are you going? Stop right there, Carl. *Carl—do you hear me? Don't act like you can't hear me, Carl.* If you're going to look for Josh, I'm going, too. And don't try to hand me that crap about being needed here, either. Carl, are you listening to me?" Jessie Landry spat words like hot lead, her red curls bouncing furiously as she stomped down the driveway in pursuit of her retreating brother-in-law. After six hours of dealing with her husband's absence, alone and in pursuit of some very bad people, her nerves were spent, and she had succumbed to an attack of fearing the very worst. Carl stopped in the drive, his effort to get to the barn and saddle a horse undetected now a clear failure.

"Oh now, Jess, I was just thinking of exercising the old gelding a bit, and maybe riding over toward Jake's while I was out. No big deal, really. Just thought I—"

"Wrong, Dr. Landry. If you're riding, you've got company. Haven't been for a ride in months, myself, so I'll just tag along. Just you go ahead and saddle up, but put my saddle on Maggie while you're at it." The elder Landry stood helpless in the evening sun, the shade of his wide hat unable to conceal the expression of paralysis he now experienced. Ever since they were kids, this smart-mouthed lass had always been able to freeze all the boys in their tracks with that insistent tone and the X-ray heat of those green eyes. Her nostrils flared and her chest heaved from anxiety as well as the quick march down the drive, she was as formidable as ever.

"Now Jess, goddammit, I'll just ride over there a bit and see what baby brother has found, be back in a little—" They were both distracted at the same moment by the scuffing sound of running feet on the gravel behind them. Luke was speeding toward them with one of the communication radios held out in front of him, and he called out just as they turned toward them.

"Uncle Carl—hey, Uncle Carl—Jake's trying to raise you on the radio—he's yellin' again, *HERE*—! The boy skidded to a stop, thrusting the black box into his uncle's hand, a strident voice clearly audible emitting from it. Carl keyed the mic button.

"Jake, this is Carl, what's up? Jake?" A long pause indicated they'd both been attempting to transmit at the same time, so Landry repeated the call. "Jake, this is Carl Landry, do you copy?" This time the response shot back out of the radio at once.

"Better come quick, Carl. Looks like Josh found that van. It's bad Carl, you better hurry up." Jessica Marie Landry felt her knees begin to shake, palms sweat, breath coming in short gasps. She grabbed her brother-in-law's arm before she could fall. He spat back into the radio again.

"*Wha—say again, Jake, have you found Josh—is he OK?!*"

"Can't tell, really, Carl. Found Josh's horse tied up in the hills behind where the van was. Van's blown to hell and burned to the ground. No survivors. They're burned so bad, I can't tell who's who. But nobody's left alive. Better come in the truck. And hurry. We're at the head of the tractor trail off County 400 north—just half-mile south a' my place. We'll

473

wait out on the road for you. You should be able to get here in ten minutes in the truck. Just hurry, Carl. Please."

Jess fought to remain conscious, then her knees buckled. Carl caught her, held her to him for a moment.

"Hang on, sis, I gotta go. Luke, run and get Curtis and another of the boys—tell them to grab one of the automatic rifles, if there's one there, get to the barn in two minutes." He switched frequencies on the small radio, then spoke into it sharply. "Faith—Carl—come in. Faith, this is Carl, pick up, please." After another repetition of the call, the woman doctor's voice responded.

"Faith, grab a bag of first aid supplies—include the burn kit—get a pistol and two mags of ammo, come to Josh's in the pickup. Do it now. Be here in three minutes." She responded without inflection with a terse "OK" before doing as instructed. Four minutes later, she slid to a stop behind the wheel of a dusty Chevy pickup, and scooted to the middle of the seat, and Carl jumped in behind the wheel. Curtis May and Cody Jansen vaulted into the bed, Curtis holding an AR15 and Cody a Winchester 30/30. The right door slammed shut as Jessie Landry jumped in, the truck already rolling away from the barn. Her face was ashen, her lips rimmed with a thin line of white. Faith looked at her and instantly understood the mission.

9.

They worked for six hours with only three water breaks of two minutes each. Fighting the ever-increasing potential for error associated with overwork, they spent the few moments they were together going over the old man's notes and the long list of procedural steps he had dictated for completion of the project. Vaporizing cities had turned out to be a real job. Now, exhausted by the tension as well as the heat, Franz Schuelman and Jaci drew breath and began to recount the completed steps, leaving the list with only the last operations yet to be accomplished.

"If my interface of the telemetry program with the arming chip in the warhead is finished, all I see left to do is to set the launch sequence and coordinate it with the mechanics upstairs for opening the hatch. We have the solid fuel in place, the electronics for actually firing the missile, and I just tested the launch ramp hydraulics again to be sure they would respond to the main computer's commands for angle-of-launch and stand down after the thing actually fires."

Franz nodded, looking at the same time at his copy of the list.

"We keep acting like this were a Saturn rocket blastoff, leaving a huge crater behind it, but we must remember, the hardened silo, plus the water deluge coming in behind the liftoff will be plenty adequate to permit closing the hatch within ten minutes. Hell, Jaci, it takes little more than the propulsion equivalent of a Scud to do the job—just has to be a bit more accurate and less primitive because of the sensitive nature of the warhead. I've just retested the computer simulation for the nuclear device, and it looks absolutely perfect from every direction."

Jaci picked up the theme. "And all I have to do is retrieve the plutonium from the lead vault, set it in the explosive cell at the bottom of the warhead assembly, then button it up. Oh—and I tested the mainframe too, with the same result. The commands and sequencing with reference to the rocket detonation are perfect. Should blow at three hundred feet above the ground. Backup detonation device is tested and in place—that altimeter-operated pressure switch we hooked up to the initiation charge. Not nearly as precise as the computer-driven version that is running off the telemetry data

475

on board the missile, but certainly sufficient to make it blow if something goes wrong with the program.

"That's my big problem with these complex, elegant devices, Franz. Too damn delicate. If the onboard box dies or gets confused, we succeed only in putting a radioactive hole in the street. Kill a Jew or two if we're lucky and make a few more sick with radiation poisoning. And we're both dead within hours, courtesy of that old man. I don't see why we can't rig a radio signal-controlled backup detonator for the warhead, so we can blow the thing ourselves if something goes wrong." The German shook his head.

"No chance, Jaci, too risky. Stray radio signals, microwave, radar, or even FM band might hit the missile at the wrong time, and the thing goes off too soon, or maybe not at all. The old man was always preaching the need to stick with programming and hands off operation. Let's not get creative now." The elder shook his head in grudging assent at the logic of what his comrade had to say.

They stood, compared lists again, then agreed it was time to do everything but arm the warhead before calling Saddam to report completion of preparations. Franz finished preparing the warhead and testing the missile and warhead firing and detonation sequence; Jaci confirmed completion of the missile trajectory programming. In one hour they were climbing the concrete steps to the palace. They walked to the guard's desk and asked that their message be conveyed to the top. All that remained was the insertion of the plutonium into the warhead and initiation of the launch and arming sequences, an errand that would take less than thirty minutes to accomplish. The big guard turned to the telephone console and placed the call he had been instructed to make at this point.

* * * * *

Henry Lassiter was frantic, and Boyd Jeffers looked like he might explode, his face beet red, hands shaking as he held the radio to his face. They had just ordered two of the recon units to begin following the line of men who had just disappeared into the streets a few minutes before. They were to attempt to re-establish visual contact with the enemy, but they were not to engage them. Jeffers hoped that, by running away if detected, they might convince the intruders that they

476

were no threat or, in the alternative, get them to give chase. At least that would have the effect of taking them out when they ran into the Army's reception committee, now in place some eight blocks back uptown.

The men moved quickly but as quietly as possible. They followed the route taken by the disappearing guerillas, and both squads soon found the places where the long lines has disappeared. One went into the building Shamus O'Dorghan had mentioned, apparently emerging in the alley, just as the Irishman had predicted. From there, the line could have gone any of six directions, due in large part to the split in the alley when it intersected the next main street. At the point of a diagonal crossing point where streets came in from three directions to a central intersection, the surveillance team was left with absolutely no clues as to the direction of travel.

The other, upon discovering a large manhole with the cover off of it offering ready access to a storm sewer, was ordered to break off pursuit. Jeffers and Lassiter agreed that to enter that route would almost certainly result in the loss of the whole team. Now it was evident that the terrorists were on their way to the weapons stash, that they had not yet revealed enough about their direction of travel to give away their destination, and all contact had been lost with them.

"So much for covert surveillance, Boyd. Guess we shoulda just blown up the whole lot as soon as they were visible. No weapons catch that way, but then again, all those alleged guns don't hurt anybody if there's nobody to shoot them. Shit, what a mess. Better tell the big boys."

Jeffers shook his head, wiped the sweat from his red face, and picked up the receiver to the secure line. After establishing contact, he told his sad tale to headquarters, surprised to end up talking to the general in charge of the whole NYC operation.

"Colonel Jeffers, this is General Richard Hambley; I am the commander of the New York operation. I have been apprised of your predicament, and need your input. We have been ordered by General Conlan to move into the area without a pause, subject only to such information or cautions as you might provide us. Tell me again, Colonel, how big is this force your men have been watching?" Jeffers took a deep breath, now too tired and too worried about his own men to be terribly overwhelmed by talking to the top brass.

Had he thought about it, the whole idea of a National Guard unit commander talking directly to a task force commander would have told him just how thin they were spread. And having a guy with the reputation and rank of Richard Hambley on the line meant they were placing huge significance on the outcome of the present operation.

"General Hambley, yes, this is Colonel Jeffers. Sir we appreciate the inquiry. Our best estimate, based on visual observations of three different lines of infiltration, is something around two hundred to two hundred fifty men. Could not tell whether or not they were armed—at least none of them had weapons visible while in our sight. However, the way they progressed through the area tells us they are very familiar with it, and we are convinced that we lost them within a few blocks of their destination. Although they were still four blocks apart, the lines were headed generally toward each other. We're trying to make some calculations concerning where that might be right now."

Hambley responded immediately. "I understand, but what does all that mean to a large invading force, if we come in with fifteen hundred men, supported by armor and air cover? Can't we expect to overpower them quickly?"

"Only if you can find them, sir, and then only if they have not armed themselves with weapons that could take out both APCs and helicopters. Rumor has it this little weasel had a bunch of anti-tank pieces, including missles and recoilless rifles. And we have confirmed that an armory in upstate New York lost a case of the old LAWs last winter. If these guys are as good at getting out as they were at getting in, they could be waiting for you when you get here.

"And General, we all know that a pretty small force can make a pretty big problem for a lot of soldiers, if they are well armed, knowledgeable in the finer points of guerilla warfare, and intimately familiar with the area. These guys are all of the above. How long will it be before you can get here?"

There was a short pause, and Jeffers looked up to see Henry Lassiter's intent gaze. Nodding, the soldier confirmed what was going on. "Yep, I said G*eneral*, as in General Richard Hambley, commander of the whole New York operation. Guess we're kind of in the middle, don'tcha think, Henry?" Lassiter smiled a tired smile, shook his head, then listened as Hambley's conversation resumed. Herman Hanks

478

shook his greasy head and went back to the maps, the whole thing coming apart in his head as he sat there.

"Colonel, good point. It will take us about thirty minutes to have troops on the street in the Bronx. The contingent already waiting as your ambush component is too small to occupy that much turf. When we get there with the rest of what we need, we will have enough men and armored vehicles to fill up the streets pretty well, but we accomplish nothing if we can't find the enemy. Worse, if they have the capability of hitting us with those weapons you have described, we may lose the upper hand quickly. My biggest fear is getting into firefights with them in such tight places that we are unable to bring fire superiority to bear on the problem. Those streets are narrow, the buildings tall, and we are concerned about the whereabouts and numbers of civilians in the area."

Jeffers was amazed, shocked, and *very* happy to hear such intelligent thought coming from the big brass. Such had not been his prior experience when, on many occasions, he was told to do some really stupid things by men of high rank. But not this time. The Guardsman jumped on the opportunity to respond to smart questions.

"Yes sir, exactly. In a moment, I'll give you the locations where we have large numbers of noncombatants housed. There are at least six such places around the area of the South Bronx. Probably still about ten thousand—been feeding them with supplies from Bragg this entire last month, when we could get anything. I do know that none of the evacuation efforts have reached this far into the city yet, so there are still many people left here. They are widely scattered throughout the city, sick, starving, and terrified of the gangs and assorted armed militants that have been harassing us all summer. Our count on them is very general, but there are probably at least two to three thousand spread around in the Bronx area, still."

"All right, Colonel, here's what I am ordering. There will be one thousand troops *in the Bronx* by 2300 hours tonight. They will take up positions on the city streets south of Interstate 95. The ground units will use Interstate 87 to enter the area and will fan out from 161st Street and also from 3rd Avenue, 149th Street, and Westchester. Advise your reconnaissance units of our arrival, and have them establish contact with our people when they see them. We will use this line to confirm that contact in advance, so as to avoid the possibility of misidentification. Don't need any friendly fire problems. Air cover will be up and pretty useful with their night vision capabilities.

"We take your advice about those heavier weapons very seriously, Colonel; one recoilless rifle in the hands of a competent terrorist could make a mess of things very quickly. Once in position, we will probably wait for morning to begin a systematic sweep of every building in that end of town. Big job, I understand, but it sounds like the only way to get rid of the problem. This is a major target of our campaign, Colonel, so I cannot overemphasize the importance of interdicting this contingent and capturing or destroying their weapons capabilities. Please advise your units of all this at once. Your troops already in position close to the target area should remain at maximum ready. We'll be back to you." There was a click, and he was gone.

Jeffers recounted the instructions to Lassiter and Hanks, as the older man's countenance first blanched, then steadily darkened while he listened. They debated briefly about what to do with the men now in the middle of what would a battlefield in a few hours, then decided to put them back in the concealed positions they had occupied before the ghosts arrived. No contact had occurred, so they were presumably still unknown to the aggressors. Putting them back into hidden but strategic positions would provide continued eyes and ears, and they could then connect with the Army when it arrived.

Everybody knew, however, as they waited for the rumble of heavy mechanized infantry to commence, that they had failed in their one mission of interdiction. They had neither followed the enemy to their supply point nor had they been able to act as bait to draw them into the trap already set. Those who were to have struck the aggressors when they went for that human bait would now be reassigned functions in coordination with the incoming forces, and the opportunity for the FBI guys to finally get their hands on the elusive "Sallie" was gone. Bitterness mixed with Lassiter's anticipation, sitting there in the darkness of the August night.

* * * * *

Atmospheric conditions had been good the past few nights, so the ham aficionados burned up the late night airwaves sharing events that, in more and more places, showed signs of change and even hope. But the violence that attended every effort to retake a city and the deepening famine and disease that decimated populations everywhere tempered their optimism.

So divergent were the experiences of these late night friends that each transmission painted a collage of images bearing wide differences, but binding together in a common baseline theme. Things were bad everywhere, complete with evidence even in rural areas of the worst and lowest of that mankind was capable. Murder, torture, captivity, rape, although less frequent out in the country, still occurred enough to keep everyone armed and nervous. The cities still groaned under the oppressive weight of killing and hostage taking, but that was slowly giving way in most places to the quieter but equally deadly grip of starvation and disease. Cholera had spread through large population centers, fueled by loss of sanitation and redoubled by the quick buildup of dead bodies.

After midnight, the air across the continent clear and warm, the radios fired up again. "This is KCF76, Augusta, on the air. . .anybody turned on tonight? W6ninerC81, or Xray 25 delta 4—Freddie or Sig, this is KCF76, Augusta, Jimmy Jo calling, do you copy?" He paused, keyed his microphone again, and repeated the transmission, this time adding the call letters for Bonnie in Bakersfield. She lit up first.

"Jimmy Jo, KCF76 Augusta, this is Bonnie, niner Hotel 682 Indigo, Bakersfield, I am receiving you clear, do you copy, Jimmy?"

"Gotcha, Bon, how's tricks? Been a week since we heard from ya, kid, thought maybe the war scooped ya' up and carried ya'off!" The woman smiled and responded with reassurance, although the part about the war wasn't far off.

"Things'er hoppin' for sure, Jimmy, and from the sounds we hear day and night, L.A. is a ways from settling down. Must be a huge refugee facility north and east of here—been a steady stream of military transport vehicles running 24 hours a day past town on State Road 178, out toward China Lake

Weapons Depot. Not much of a garden spot, but safe and away from all the fighting. Also nothing but hot, this time of year. My neighbor talked to an MP who was directing a convoy out that way yesterday, and he said they got tent cities set up all over the place up there, and down at Fort Irwin, too. Interesting, 'cause all that area has been off limits to public travel for years. Guess that made it easy to set up. What's up with you? Last time we talked, you guys were hoping to get some electricity from the Savanna River plant. Any progress?"

"Naw, just the same ol' stuff. The rednecks burned up so much a' town, chasin' down and killin' all the blacks they could lay hands on, then blowin' up whole shoppin' centers, if they was to turn on the power, prob'ly just set the whole area afire. Anyway, the plant took a lot a' damage from the bombs that blew up our substations. Somethin' about a reaction to the big break in current that did bad things to the nuclear generators at the plant. They thought they had 'r handled, but the tests were all bad, so it's gonna be a while.

"Ft. Gordon has power but they have their own generating station, and there was no damage to them. Guess the terrorists were smart enough not to try planting those explosives on the reservation. Bigger problem here now is the water supply. It all comes from deep wells, pumped by electricity into the tower, feedin' the town with gravity pressure. The boys been usin' a big diesel generator from the fort to power the pump, but they had some kinda' voltage drop problem and burnt up the whole thing. Army's been tryin' ta find replacement parts for three weeks, now, and the water supply is nearly gone in the big tank."

"This is 26 Alpha Zero 28 Zebra, Nashville, Indiana—you guys ever gonna take a breath?!"

"Al!! Good ta' hear yore voice again—been weeks!!"

"Greetings, all, been busy here in the heartland. We got some help from the Army, but not much. I been out in the country every day for two weeks, putting up hay for the dairy and beef farmers in the area. Gotta take care a' those boys— they're feeding the whole town right now. Had a guy from the National Guard through here last week, told us they had precious little help for us in the way of food for the coming winter, so we just decided we'd have to make do on our own.

"Getting crowded, too. Seems word's gotten around we got a line on produce and dairy products, so folks with kids and no food just keep showing up. Mostly on foot now. Can't tell you guys what it's like to see these little ones so much of a mess. Hungry, and sick—man, I do mean sick. Cholera kills 'em so fast, funeral director's got a full time job just plantin' 'em. Crematory is runnin' day an' night. At least until the natural gas runs out. So far, we still have gas. Comes from wells right here, so maybe we'll keep it for a while.

"We got a lot of germ problems with stream water around here, mostly due to farm animals, but also because of the deer population. People with electric well supplies couldn't get water at all, so they turned to the streams. Made 'em sick right off. Apparently there've been many who died from it, what with being so weak from hunger, too. But we're better off than many, I bet. We keep a full time crew busy hauling and boiling water in big quantities, and folks come in from all over the area to haul it home. One of the bigger dairy farmers has set up a distribution site at his place, and the others are bringing meat and garden stock there everyday. He also keeps fires going and food ready to feed whoever shows up. I have no idea how many people he has fed since he got underway in June. Just came too late for some." His voice betrayed the sadness that words could not convey.

A short breath held silence before Jimmy responded to Al's report. Everyone knew what he was experiencing, and no one could ignore the tragedy that now held the land. "Guess this is one time ta be glad for livin' in a warm place. We got enough wood to keep from freezin' here in Augusta, unless winter is a lot worse than usual. I worry more about the folks livin' out in the sticks, now. Food's about gone, people been killin' off the deer population like mad already, and there's not much left. A lot of them are heading toward the ocean, down toward Charleston and Savanna. I heard the Navy is providing fuel for the commercial fishing fleet, so they can feed as many as possible from the sea. Been a good year for fishin', far as I can tell. Kind of a 'loaves and fishes thing, ya' know?"

"Boys, this is Bonnie again. Gotta go, my batteries are low. I think my little solar charger is on the blink. I charge these things for 12 hours, then end up out'a juice in less than thirty minutes. Keep up the prayers, guys, we need 'em. Army says they've moved over three hundred thousand people in the last two weeks, but the death toll is too high to estimate already. I'm signin' off."

"Night, Bon, keep yore head down!" Jimmy and Al talked on, joined briefly by Sigurd, transmitting from outside Minneapolis. His report was similar to Al's regarding the use of farm produce to feed many, but his news was better concerning power. "Yah, boys, weird ta see it, but yah, ders lights from the city in a few places. Dey got a power plant goin' an' juice ta da horspital at da med center, also got lights nort a' town in some a' da suburbs. Dos folks taken in people like crazy—da ones wit da juice, I mean. Be colder dan da well diggers ass here soon, an' people gon' freeze quick if dey can't find heat and cover. Yep—freeze *quick,* dat's wut *I say.* ."

Sig also reported continued fighting in a few places in the twin cities, where the bad guys had made great use of noncombatants for shields and bargaining chips. Not particularly creative, but effective.

The tone of these chats, after months of desperation, did possess a slight hope, but no one was deluded into thinking the fix was imminent. These people were by now face to face with a reality that they could not avoid. The death, destruction, continuing famine, and disease were far from over, and it would be years before recovery would really occur.

Book IV – The Great Offensives

10.

"Stop. Take me back two frames. *There.* What's that— that cluster in the middle?" Webb was using one of those laser pointers, the bright red dot circling a compound of buildings that bordered the Euphrates River. With the lights dimmed to enhance the images from the satellite photographs, everyone in the briefing room at the Pentagon studied intently as the sequence of pictures moved past to the narration of the CIA deputy director. The picture queried by the president was zoomed into sharper focus, then enlarged, a series of smaller and smaller squares indicating computer enhancement of the objects indicated by the red dot.

"Sir, that is Nebuchadnezzar's Palace. Saddam has been spending money like water on the place for over ten years now. Says he's related to the Babylonian king and wants to rebuild the palace to its ancient splendor, or something like that. Our people were through the area with a *National Geographic* team three years ago—pretty impressive—well, maybe opulent is a better word. Thing is huge. Gardens, gold gilt decor, jewels in the handrails, the whole program. This area here, with the dome-shaped top, is the area of the gardens themselves, and next to it, this high arched thing, is the grand hall."

Webb looked at it, his memory running momentarily back to trips to Iran for the Defense Department, when the Shah was still in power. The dramatic differences between the poverty of the people and the opulence of the ruling class had always amazed him, assaulted his sensibilities. Something about all that gold surrounded by all that hunger left him nauseated, confused. He remembered Atlanta, the city of his birth, and the struggles for basic human necessities he had known as a small boy. Snapping back to the moment, he asked about the complex of ornate buildings.

"Could that area house military stuff? Looks like at least four city blocks of buildings. What about—"

"Don't think so, sir, at least we have no reason to suspect it." The deputy director, Middle East Operations, was a young man of tremendous intellect, possessed of a quickness of wit that often compelled him to finish people's sentences for them, and often to answer their questions before they were fully asked. A mistake this time.

"*Mr. Countryman—may I finish?!* I appreciate your capabilities and command of the subject, but please. Humor me. I am no doubt old and slow by comparison to you, and no doubt you have already reached every important conclusion all by yourself. But unfortunately it is I who must understand it and then decide on a course. *OK?*" A silence filled the large room, quiet uninterrupted by the sound of anyone breathing. Everyone waited for the next blast from the Webb temper, a phenomenon well known to the assembled company and an experience not to be relished as its target. The younger man flushed, then looked back at the picture.

"Sorry sir, bad habit of mine. Please continue. My apologies." Another eternity passed without anyone breathing, then Webb spoke again.

"*Thank you, Mr. Countryman.* . .now, as I was saying, what about those big lids on these buildings here being concealment for military hardware, communications, or even a command center. You said these were gardens. Suggests open air design and, as I see here, a big open space without roofing at all. Have we any information about them?" The question was different enough from what Countryman anticipated that he had to gather himself for a moment, during that he also felt a profound sense of relief that the presidential explosion had been avoided.

"Well. . .I mean, we have watched them build the whole thing, and they have worked on it very slowly and methodically over a long period of time. I guess there could be. . ." Clyde Keithley came to his assistance.

"Mr. President, that thing has been under such close public observation, we have really never given it much consideration. It houses something like fifty million dollars worth of artifacts, jewels, and precious metals, along with a massive museum of ancient history concerning the entire Fertile Crescent. To answer your question, yes, it is big enough to house some pretty hefty equipment, but those who have examined it find no evidence that it is set up for military use.

I know what you think of Saddam—what we *all* think of him, and you're right. He's certainly not above using some big, expensive trinket like this to hide important military capabilities, but we just don't think so in this case."

"OK, Clyde. Proceed, Mr. Countryman, but let's take a good look at this area anyway. Get out the pix the bird took during construction, and have somebody examine what they were doing throughout the whole build-out. Looks like the buildings are done now, even if not finished inside. Let us know by 2400 hours what the other pictures tell us. Go back through that time period for me, would you—reviewing every picture you have of the project, from the first shovel of dirt?" The courtesy in the request failed to conceal the absolute authority in the order, and three different CIA people responded in the affirmative in unison. Webb suppressed a smile, then looked back with interest as he motioned Countryman to continue his presentation.

"This is the area outside of Babylon mentioned by the Prime Minister in his conversation with you last weekend, Mr. President. Certainly there is an area of disturbed surface soil, appearing from high altitude as a discoloration in the sand." The President sat forward in his chair, then stood, his eyes straining at the myriad of striations, shadings, and shadows that filled the wide area photograph.

"OK, help me here. If this is the city, that direction am I looking to get to this discolored area?" The red dot pointer moved back and forth between the two areas, as the narrator quickly responded.

"Sorry sir, good point. This is roughly north. The river runs pretty much north and south through the city—*here*—and we are then moving west about eighty statute miles, into the area of Karbala province. This is one of the darker spots we mentioned before and to that Mr. Netanyahu referred. Out in here, between these wadis, or wet areas, and further west toward the Saudi border, is a wide plain that is mostly sand—desert-like, although crossed in numerous places by these marshes. *Here,* out about one hundred sixty statute miles, is where the largest discolored area is located.

"You can see on this larger shot, here, that a road runs from the city of Karbala, the provincial capitol, west and south to al-Habbariya, south to Nuhaib, then on into Saudi Arabia. The two areas of discoloration are both pretty close, or at least accessible from that same road. The first, here outside of al-Habbariya, is north and west of the city, up this road and then west out into the desert, away from all this lake and swamp area they call Wadi t-Tubal. It is the smaller of the two places, the larger being here." The screen switched to a new and smaller area picture. "This is more arid yet, further from any settlement, and the area of darkened or disturbed earth is roughly four times the size of the first.

"This road that runs south and east from Nuhaib to al-Makmin is bordered on both sides by very large expanses of completely uninhabited—and mostly *uninhabitable*—wilderness. The big place is here, some thirty miles back east of that road, north and east of al-Makmin." Webb sat back for a second, his eyes blurry from all the detail he was trying to understand. The areas were in southwestern Iraq, distant from every form of habitation but, in fact, not so far from Baghdad and Babylon, making it plausible that the dirt could have come from either place.

"Fine. What is it? Benjamin told me it was there, suggested it was dirt moved from Babylon. True or false? Have we seen it up close?"

The Chairman of the JCS spoke at once. "We sent one reconnaissance plane in there from a carrier in the Gulf, low and kind of slow; don't think he was seen by any of the air defense installations in Iraq. Here are the pix of what he got. Barely made it back to Kuwait City on the fuel he had on board—long ways from the gulf to that little spot and back." More photos, but this time on paper.

The eight-by-ten glossies, thirty in all, were taken from an altitude of five hundred feet, with the last twelve from just fifty feet off the ground, although there were none from the northern location. What was plain from these additional pictures was that, over an area the size of six to eight football fields, a large quantity of dirt had been spread thinly over the sandy surface of the desert. A crisscross pattern of heavy tire prints was visible, clear testament to the dumping and spreading of the earth; some sort of rough drag had been pulled over the whole thing in an effort to mix the new soil with the sand floor or the expanse. No one could doubt that a large quantity of dirt had been spread there, and the relatively close proximity of the road that eventually led back to the provincial capitol—and to Babylon—suggested the direction from that it had come.

"Hell, boys, how much dirt is that, anyway? Anybody done any rough calculations? And what about the content of it? Seems that if we knew what kind of soil it was, or how deep in the ground it came from, we might get a feel for what and where the hole was dug."

"Already moving on that one, Mr. President. Problem is, getting in there on the ground is no small chore. That little dirt pile is approximately 400 miles west of Kuwait City, in an area that gets lots of aerial surveillance from a variety of interested parties. We've been on the line with Israeli Intelligence, and they say they think they can get somebody in there in the next day or so, but Mossad is telling them that may be too late.

"Remember that old Nazi they found dead the other day? Well, the same operative that was in his place says the two kids the old man had working for him have disappeared. Mossad also says there is such a tight lid on the whole rumor mill, they hear virtually nothing on the streets, in Baghdad, over in Jordan or Syria, or even from the snitches in Lebanon. And there's *always* a rumor in Beirut, even if its totally wrong."

An even younger intelligence officer, this one from the National Security Agency and the speaker of those lines drew a laugh from the group with his accurate observation concerning the Lebanese and their penchant for intrigue. The problem of time was now, however, on everyone's mind as the prime concern. The resident addressed the issue of the two missing assistants.

"What's the significance of those two guys? Have we reason to believe they've left? If so, seems like that slows things down a bit, unless the work was done and the missile was already operational."

"No sir, don't think they're gone. The Mossad guy who was present when the Nazi bought it says he stayed in the area, watching from close by, until after the authorities had found Weidenolf. Two young men, neither of whom was known to the Israeli snoop, did come to the apartment, then left very quickly. He lost them in traffic, but about four hours later he saw an old VW bug like the one they were driving parked in the employee lot down the street from the garden entrance to the palace project. He couldn't confirm the identity of the men or get any kind of registration on the car. Things are a lot less organized on those kinds of things in the Middle East. The VW didn't even have a plate on it."

"So, we've got a probable nuclear device hidden somewhere in the area of Babylon, just a few miles from Baghdad; the guy who's been assembling it and mounting it on some kind of delivery platform is dead, but his sidekicks are still around—we think. There are two big dirt piles out in the desert, hundreds of miles from nowhere and, although they can be said to be close to a road that leads to Babylon, we have no real connection between them and the Israelis' fears of an imminent attack. I have a head of state who is certain of that attack and the location from which it is to come. However, I have no proof the thing even exists, and only the *surmise* that it may have something to do with the historic area around the Euphrates inside the Old City. But nobody knows what.

"It is six hundred statute miles from Babylon to Tel Aviv, a distance too great for any missile known to the Iraqi arsenal at the present time, right?" Heads nodded, then Keithley spoke.

"Correct, sir, but that six hundred miles is less than challenging for any number of missile systems they *don't* have, including several known to have been in the stockpiles of the old USSR. And that's where this Weidenolf comes from. Remember, his cover was archaeology, and he hailed from the University of Moscow, although we have known for several years that his real claim to fame was missile guidance. It's been almost two years since anyone has seen him—that is, until he broke his head last week—and we have to believe his budget, if he was working for Iraq, was without limit. Six hundred miles with a very powerful nuke was just no problem for the Soviet missile arsenal. We must believe that it would pose no problem for one of their best people, either."

An eternity passed before anybody spoke again. Then Webb stood up. "All right, gentlemen. Assume the threat is not only real, but immediate. Use every kind of surveillance we can get, turn up the intelligence network heat all the way, and prepare every defensive system we can use to try to stop this thing if it gets airborne. We must assume a nuke, not just chemicals or bugs; gotta take it out high enough and far away enough from population centers to avoid most of the fallout problems, if possible. Of course, if there is some way to neutralize it before it is fired, that answer is best. I hold very little hope for that one.

490

"Picking it off with a Patriot on the outskirts of Tel Aviv won't help. If we can intercept it close to lift-off, the only people to get burned will be the Iraqis, but we can expect that they'll just claim we nuked 'em and then God knows what happens next. People, unless we can keep the thing from going off at all, every answer I can think of is a bad one. Oh— and one more thing. We know that almost every nuclear warhead ever made was set to explode well above target. And in recent history, they have been programmed only to become fully armed right before detonating. If we can get it before the arming sequence is completed, all we get is some radioactivity, and no boom. See what you can do."

He started to walk out, then turned around. "And we still have to try to retake our own cities from the devil's agents, so we are otherwise fully employed. Mr. Countryman, keep us informed." The President shook the young man's hand, then walked out into the hallway and disappeared, Mac Reed, Jonathan Brooks, and General Keithley following closely. Everybody in the place knew that, if the Iraqis succeeded in bombing Israel with a nuclear warhead, the problems of New York City, L.A., and the ever-approaching winter would pale by comparison.

11.

The sounds of wild celebration, mixed with the screams of someone who was being tortured, continued to batter Miguel's senses throughout the long evening. Long after the scant light afforded by the cracks in the painted windows had vanished, the raucous laughter of his brother and several of his lieutenants in the Diablos continued to fill the small building that was currently used as their headquarters. The pitiful moans of those being abused stopped abruptly, as did the ridiculous hoots of the men of the gang. The almost instantaneous silence so shocked and scared Miguel he quit working the tape at his wrists and feet for several minutes.

"Panchoooo. . .I think you have keeled him—ahh. . .he has no pulse now—maybe he had a heart attack or some—"

"Shutup, idiot—just another nigger, anyway—take him away. And where is the woman—that nigger woman who was with him? Bring her back to me. I need some relief from the boredom of these weak ass nigger men who die too easy. . *HURRY!!*" There was a momentary pause, then the scuffling of feet and that of something—or someone—being dragged away could be heard.

Doors slammed, after that he heard his brother vomiting out the back window. Miguel knew he was retching at having killed the man; in fact, Pancho reacted that way often when he killed. But the deep burning hatred that for unknown reasons raged within him, kept him always vicious, taunting and, too often, killing anyone who crossed him, or whom he perceived to be different or a threat. And even at the moment when his body retched at what he had done, Pancho was no less likely to continue his merciless torture on the woman now being led to him.

It was while he was listening to all this surrealistic horror that he suddenly realized that the tape around his wrists had come loose. Pancho was, to a certainty, now too drunk to consider, or even remember, his brother's presence in the makeshift cell. His passions lay in wait for yet another captive. Miguel began to slowly, quietly massage his wrists, forearms, and biceps, the pain in the middle of his back almost too great to bear as he pulled his hands around in front of him. Soon he was able to coax his throbbing muscles to let him reach down to his ankles, where aching fingers began to pick at the duct tape that bound them together.

Within minutes he had his feet loose, being slowed only by the fear that the sound of the tape being pulled off might get into the outer room. Then he heard the door from the street bang open, accompanied by the cry of a woman as she was obviously thrown to the floor. *"Shut up, bitch—!* The nauseating sound of a boot connecting with a human body shook the whole place, and Miguel could tell the woman was gasping, choking.

"She still has on her miserable clothes, Dannie—strip her so we can see her tits—goddam skinny—!!" The next moment, clearly as if he were in the room with them, Miguel could hear the remnants of her garments being ripped from her body; she cried out so sharply when it happened that he knew at once the sound had nothing to do with being stripped. She was no doubt hurt very badly.

His hands and feet now free, the feeling coming back into his spine and upper body, it was time for Miguel to find a way out of the place. The window was the most obvious answer, but it appeared to be painted shut, had no visible latching mechanism. And he already knew, it led only out into an alley where any number of drunken Diablos might be hanging out, no matter what time it was.

The best direction for departure was right out the front door. At the moment that was not an option but, given the amount of fire water apparently already consumed by Pancho and his friends, even the presence of another female prisoner might not keep them awake much longer. Without a watch, and having been unconscious so long, he could only guess at the time, but his sense was that it was sometime after midnight. Raul, if he had not already given up on his younger cousin by now, would be at the golf course again at six a.m. The rendezvous was only about a thirty-minute walk away, assuming he could walk at all.

The woman began to cry, then screamed like she'd been stabbed. Whimpering followed the scream, then she went silent. "Shit, Dannie, these niggers got no grit—another one dead, and I didn't do nothin' but burn 'er legs a bit with the cigarette!"

"Maybe she ain't dead, Pancho, just weak. She pretty skinny, this one, you know? Or maybe she fakin', think you

493

go 'way if she play possum a while. . ." The heavy thump of Pancho's boot against bare flesh sent a wave of sickness through Miguel, his passion to break through the door tempered by the greater need to survive and get to his meeting. She made no sound when kicked. The idea of another dead black girl made him sicker still; his brother had a taste for them, but he always managed to kill them eventually.

Although keeping track was impossible, he could remember at least eight or nine such young black women who had been Pancho's captives already, and all were dead. Two even apparently rose to a sort of temporary preferred status, being for a time squired around with him as he flaunted his prowess among the throngs of people imprisoned in the Watts area by his goons and the famine and disease that made travel or escape impossible. In the end both died, one of some kind of illness, but only after a particularly severe drunken rage of Pancho's left her beaten unconscious. The other he became displeased with while completely sober, shooting her down in the middle of the street, after first stripping her naked and forcing her to perform for him in front of his "men." Big brother had turned out to be a real son of a bitch.

Pancho's only long-time woman was a Latino madam whose only known name was Tricia, short for some mixture of Spanish and Irish, from that interesting mixture in her lineage. She ran a whorehouse in the midst of Diabloland, and the only relational connection visible between Pancho and her was his occasional trip to her establishment, where he saw only her, and his cardinal standing order that nothing— *absolutely nothing*—was ever to happen to her or her girls. Like some mysterious vixen, she appeared only rarely in his company, and then for the briefest of periods, had nothing to do with his business or his other associates, and treated him with cool restraint at best.

Lore had it that he so hungered for her he would permit her the haughtiest of misconduct toward him without reaction; that she could and had beaten him, slapped him, even run his men out of her place at the point of a long dagger she kept strapped to a shapely thigh. Possessed of long curly dark tresses that were uniquely touched with shades of red, she was short and marvelously constructed, in the purest of Latin traditions. But she accepted trouble from no man and wielded her dagger—and the shotgun beside her bed—with total, fatalistic abandon.

The conversation grew quieter between Pancho and his faithful Dannie, the talking lapsed, then the door closed. Voices barely audible outside the window in the alley faded, and within a few minutes, the place was totally silent. There was no sound from the front room, so Miguel could only assume the girl had been taken with them or that she was dead—the more likely possibility. He rolled up onto his knees, testing his back and stretching his shoulders and arms. Bracing against the wall while trying not to rustle the trash he was lying in, first one foot then the other came under him as he painfully stood up. Not too bad. Lightheaded and weak from 24 hours without food and smelling like an open sewer, shaky and filled with dread at the prospect of what must be in the front room, he stood for long moments in the darkness, fearful that his trembling legs might immediately give out under his weight.

He took small steps, cautious and quiet as possible, leading to the doorway, the knob, and the terrifying act of opening the door. It was locked. He sank back, catching himself by holding onto the doorknob, then went to his knees as the pain in his back returned. The door opened out, away from Miguel, so there was at least the potential of throwing his body against it. It was old and loose, like the rest of the rickety building, and he had no doubt that under ordinary circumstances he could knock it right off its hinges if he tried. But these were in no way ordinary circumstances, given his condition and, more, he feared the noise he would make, whether or not successful.

Moving painfully, slowly, he worked his way through the darkness, back to the window, where he stood for long moments, listening for sounds in the alley. He heard none, so he headed back to the door. A whispered prayer was all the help Miguel could muster, his fear of detection now overpowered by the immediate need to get away. His legs quivered from the combination of anxiety and spasm as he slammed his shoulder against the door, tumbling head over heels out into the darkened main room. His mind could hardly comprehend the soft landing, as he crashed to the floor on top of the motionless form of the naked woman left for dead by Pancho. Lying still for a few moments to determine whether or not the noise had been heard by anyone outside, Miguel quickly realized that the woman was not moving, had not reacted to his body falling on her. But although she smelled awful, her body was not stiff, and her flesh was warm to the touch.

"Holy sweet Mary, but I think she's alive. . .can't tell how bad she's—" His whispers, spoken only to himself, were cut short by a low moan coming from the woman's throat. He moved up to her face, gently placing a hand over her mouth. "*Shh—you must make no sound—please, be still. Can you hear me?*" The whispers appeared to make no impression for a brief moment, then the swollen face slowly turned up and toward him. No light assisted the young man in his efforts to tell how badly she was hurt, and the addition of a few soft sounds only confirmed that she was still alive. Somehow he sensed that she opened an eye, as her lips moved against his fingers. The words were incomplete, and the frail effort to speak quickly disappeared back into her.

"Great," he thought to himself, his hands now trying to examine her in the darkness. "Can't see shit, she's not dead, but they'll kill her for sure when they come back. I gotta get out of here right now, and this chick sure can't walk. Now what?" Moving down from her face and around the back of her neck, sticky, partially dried blood greeted his searching fingers. He fought a wave of nausea, the feel of the blood mixing with the stench of infected wounds, urine, sweat. A deep gash in her scalp accounted for the bleeding and, moving down over her shoulders and torso, he felt no other open trauma. There was thick swelling in the skin below her breast, so obvious that no medical genius was needed to identify broken ribs. Quickly he weighed the possibility that he might kill her by trying to move her at all. No problem. Left there, she was as good as dead anyway.

More open wounds and blood greeted his hands as they felt along her flanks and down her legs. The gross sensation of feeling the round lesions where cigarettes had been pressed against her inner thighs sickened him again. But the legs and feet seemed sound, with no palpably broken bones or major lacerations. The decision was quickly made. "Sister, you're going for a ride. Maybe Raul can take you out of here—if he even shows up."

With that, Miguel Sanchez, racked with agonizing pain in his legs and back, moved around behind the motionless form, now lying on her side. Up on his knees, he put an arm around her waist, the other hand under the arm that was against the floor, and scooped her up.

The most powerful sensation as she came clear of the floor was how light she was. Although she was a tall girl, Miguel realized she weighed little more than a hundred pounds—a relief in view of his decision to carry her out, but sad testament to the condition she was in. For a brief moment his mind struggled with the fact that she was completely naked, and he started to reach for the tattered garments beneath and around her. The idea was instantly discarded, as she was so unconscious that dressing her in the dark would simply be impossible. He stood, his arms now around her midsection, then rolled her around and up over a shoulder.

Pausing only long enough for his eyes to adjust and focus on the vacant street in front of the building, Miguel slipped out onto the sidewalk, taking the extra moment to close the door behind him. He wanted to leave no obvious evidence of his departure, and he knew that unless alarmed by some clear sign, the men who populated this dump would not return until after the sun was well up into the morning sky. As he began to quicken his pace, the pain in his back first worsened, then began to subside slightly. The girl slung over his shoulder bounced and constantly began to slide off, requiring repeated short stops to adjust her and try to improve the balance.

Half a dozen blocks into the dark trip, they rounded a corner, out of an alley and onto the biggest thoroughfare he would have to cross before approaching the area of the golf course. Miguel froze in his tracks, then backed around into the complete blackness of the alley, the low voices coming from a gaggle of armed thugs uninterrupted by his approach. The thought of dealing with at least eight, maybe even ten of these scholars, even without a half-dead naked woman over his shoulders, was far from pleasant, but the fact that their conversation continued uninterrupted at least let him know they had not seen him.

The sound of his cargo groaning softly added extreme urgency to the task of getting away from this welcoming

committee. They backtracked the entire length of the alley
went two blocks up and then back over to the main street
again before chancing the crossing of Long Beach Boulevard,
into the central part of Southgate. The entire walk to Los
Amigos Golf Course was over five miles and included crossing
I-605. They waded the shallow, filthy backwash in a big
drainage ditch under the expressway to cross into Downey
and the edge of the links. It was at the end of that ditch, just
a few feet from the boundary of the golf course that Miguel's
shoulders seized up so badly that he had to put the girl down.
He lay her as gently as possible on a bed of weeds growing out
of the concrete, and, in the first light of predawn, realized that
she had quit breathing.

* * * * *

Smelling like a cross between a barbecue and a fire in a
junkyard, the area surrounding the burned-out van was
scorched to a brittle white crust. Smoke hung in the close,
late afternoon air, a sense of shocked confusion mixed with
overwhelming grief among the small clutch of Jericho Road
folk responding to the explosion and fire that had been
touched off by Joshua Landry's fusillade. Everyone was once
again amazed at the destruction that gasoline explosions
could produce. The only human sounds were the low tones of
hushed conversation and the sobbing of Jessie Landry.

"Sis, we haven't found a sign of him yet, now hold on—
can't just give up without doin' some lookin' first. Now think
a minute, Jess, he's—" The woman's sobs exploded into a
screamed indictment of everyone in sight.

"*Goddammit Carl, you know that's bullshit—he's not here,
but his horse is—his gun's right there, there's all these dead
bodies—enough to account for my—*" She beat on Carl's face
and chest amid sobs laced with bitter tears; more than one
blow with the small fists landed with painful effect on his
cheeks and the bridge of his nose. Screams of hysteria
tortured every ear, as the grief poured from within her. The
elder Landry tried to control her explosion, but first had to
control her hands, as the damage she was doing to his face
was instant and getting worse. Knowing what to say was
difficult, if not impossible, and the fact that he was
overwhelmed with the same feelings only complicated his

498

efforts. Carl Landry simply could not make himself countenance the idea that his brother was among the horrible apparitions encrusted in the remains of that burned-out van. The denial was, at least for the moment, more powerful than the evidence.

He also could make no sense out of the rest of the evidence or argue with Jessie's reckoning that he was dead. Curtis May appeared at his side, touched his shoulder as he held Jessica. "Doc, you better come back here a minute. I don't want to sound silly, or to give false hope, but you gotta look at these boys again." Landry turned to see complete bewilderment in the young man's face, and just when he tried to find some way to disentangle himself from Jess, she fainted. Lying her down in the tall grass beneath the trees at the edge of the clearing, he left her in the care of Faith Jackson. There was certainly nobody else there a doctor could help.

"What the hell are you—we've already done this, Curtis, they're so obviously dead, I can look at them for a week and that won't change." Saying the words produced the first wave of the reality of his brother's death, and his own knees began to give way. But before he could say another word, or collapse either, the kid broke in.

"Doc—DOC—listen to me. We've held our noses and gone all through that wreckage and all over those bodies. What's left of their clothing, particularly the shoes and belts, are all so obviously different from anything Josh woulda' been wearing, there's no way he's in that mess. And Doc, all those corpses've been shot repeatedly, a couple of 'em four or five times a piece. We counted more'n thirty empty cartridge casings—all AR15—around the driver's side of the car, too, an' none anywhere else.

"Doc, this was no firefight. This was an ambush, an' it sure looks like Josh's kind a' work. Thing is, he musta ruptured the gas tank and blowed the sonsabitches up. Judgin' from how close the casings are to the van, I'm afraid he got blowed up, too. Just that he ain't here."

Landry stood next to the smoldering wreckage, walked around the front and looked at the trail of empty cartridges, then looked again at the bodies. The boy was right; no sign of anything consistent with his brother's presence. No belt buckle, no sheath knife, no ammunition belt. All made of metal, they would certainly have remained. And the condition of the bodies made it pretty easy to conclude the Josh had done the shooting. Even though they were so badly burned that some were little more than bones, the flesh that remained and the obvious bullet damage to the bones told Carl that they bore his brother's trademark for devastation. The fact that all four men were hit repeatedly also made Carl shudder, imagining that Josh had gone on homicidal auto pilot when he commenced his ambush. Another wave of emotional conflict hit him between the eyes, his psyche having just made its first efforts to begin dealing with the fact of his brother's death. Now, although the odds were still awful, it was clear that he was not among these dead, and they now were faced with trying to find him. What they needed most was not to panic, but to conduct a search with absolute and quick effectiveness.

"Dearest Jesus, Lord God—maybe he's not. . ." Carl Landry closed his eyes tightly for a moment, the sting of the acrid smoke mixed with the storm of emotion within. That was as far as the prayer got. Forcing his eyes open, he spun away from the carnage inside the van and began barking orders.

"Curtis, Jimmy, you two start right here. Walk circles around this thing, each one three feet bigger than the one before, until you have corkscrewed yourselves clear to the top of the ridge. *Jake.* Take me to where you found that horse. But let's move back and forth across the direction of travel Josh would have taken; maybe we can cut his track and learn something from following his route. *Faith—keep her here, keep her as quiet as possible, and when she wakes up, tell her to start praying!*"

* * * * *

The two headless bodies lay side by side on the floor of the very room where they had carved up and disposed of a score of hapless victims over the past two years, the irony of their present state darkly humorous to their leader/executioner as he laid them out. There would be no time for such procedures on them, as greater and more urgent tasks awaited Sallie. Pulling the small digital apparatus from the waistband of his jeans, he began punching in a series of numerical sequences. These were required to program the time for explosion of each of the cylinders of Sarin resting in the flower boxes on the face of the building.

The chemistry of this agent, made famous by its use in the crowded subway in Tokyo, is hardly complex. It is easily made from formulae easily obtained, and its effects are as predictable and efficient as they are horrible. One of the most useful "depopulating agents" of the non-biological variety, Sarin is delivered typically in one of two ways. Densely populated areas that lack significant ventilation are best hit by a process of explosive vaporization, turning the liquid into a fine mist that is then ingested by breathing and contact with the skin or eyes. The other method sprays the agent in a maple syrup kind of consistency, producing a sticky droplet-size chemical rain that adheres to the skin of its victims.

In either case, the highly toxic nerve components of the substance travel through the blood stream, attacking and almost instantly paralyzing the nervous system. Victims are immediately incapacitated, quickly collapsing, then dying within ten to fifteen minutes. The cause of death is most typically asphyxiation, although the impact of the drug on the autonomic nervous system also creates conditions that behave much like cardiac arrest in some people—the lucky ones. Death is slow, the pain excruciating, the results horrible to observe and impossible to reverse, absent high doses of atropine; that is often unsuccessful and, for those who then survive, nerve damage may leave them helpless anyway.

Sallie had chosen to use the maple syrup concoction, and the elevation from that the cylinders would be exploded would permit coverage of the street and sidewalk surfaces, doors and stairways, lamp posts and window glass with a lethal glaze that would remain effective for several days. One such cylinder of Sarin could, in the proper environment, easily kill over nine hundred people, and the effects of covering the streets with the gooey poison were numerous.

First of all, driving a vehicle over a surface covered with the poisonous droplets would cause the tires or tracks to throw the stuff up into the air around it. The mist of poison created by the spinning tires would fall on the exposed skin of the occupants of that or following vehicles, and everyone hit by it would be dead within a few minutes. This would include anyone in the immediate vicinity who was not in some way protected from contact. The almost incomprehensible killing

501

power of the stuff is due in large measure to the high degree of concentration achieved in its manufacture. Exploding one of those cylinders produces millions of deadly droplets of poison, and contact with just one of those will almost certainly be fatal.

In addition to the awful problems created by covering the street surfaces, any person brushing up against a door, wall, window, or step is likely to contact the sticky substance. When any amount of it comes in contact with exposed skin, the poison penetrates and does its job—immediately. So, even if there are no enemy troops present when the cylinders blow up, the combination of airborne mist and sticky syrup will make the entire area uninhabitable—*and deadly*—for about a week. Decontamination is tricky, slow, and expensive, and it cannot be accomplished effectively under conditions of hostile fire or unpredictable winds.

Sallie's detonation sequence provided for the best—or worst—of all circumstances, it being his belief that within a short time government forces would indeed be rumbling through his quiet little neighborhood and, with a little luck, they would experience his surprise of acid rain first hand. For those who came along after the fact, the wide variety of problems created by having covered the whole street with poison syrup would keep those forces distracted for quite a while. The detonation sequence was set to explode the cylinders two at a time every two hours for ten hours, beginning sixty minutes from the moment when he completed the programming. That meant he had no time to indulge his autopsy skills. Aside from running the two severed heads through the big grinder, he would leave the bodies.

Placing the little programming device down the same hole into that he had just put poor Sherman's head, he ground it to silicon pulp. As he stood up, his mind turned to the business of quickly arming himself and proceeding to the roof and his last report to the Committee. Within the hour, he would join the force that had just left the SPA, and they would commence festivities with the approaching military. So preoccupied with the remaining activities now to be accomplished, Sallie nearly failed to recognize the form that blocked his way out of the grinder room.

"Hello, Willie, my old pal. Greetings from Jack Ruby."

12.

"Do you have the young men there at this moment?"

"That is affirmative, sir, both are standing here with me."

"Put Mr. Schuelman on, please. Now." The big guard handed the receiver to Franz, his face betraying no emotion, and not much intellect either.

"He wants to speak to you." The young man fought the wave of anxiety that tried to overtake him, took the phone, and spoke as calmly as possible. It didn't work. His greeting to the President consisted of a voice that refused to produce sound. He swallowed, inhaled, tried again. Still nothing. In a panic, the younger man grabbed the receiver away and spoke at once, although his voice cracked so badly that he sounded like he'd just inhaled a gulp of helium.

"Sir—Mr. President—this is Jaci. Karl's voice is gone. . just the fatigue, I think. We are finished with preparations, sir, and reporting as you ordered."

Saddam, humorless as always, ignored the terror in the voice speaking to him, responded at once. "I want you to set the liftoff for midnight tonight. That gives you just over eleven hours to finish, test, recheck everything, then report to the guards again. When you have confirmed to me that these measures have all been accomplished, the guards will escort you back here to wait. We will prepare to celebrate your success, *yes?*" The kid tried to swallow, then tried again. He tried to speak, tried that again as well. Another deep breath.

"As you wish, Mr. President. We will complete the remaining work within two hours. We will call again when we have finished."

"Thank you, Jaci, and give my regards to your voiceless friend. Oh, and Jaci—do not fail in this mission. Is that clear to you?" The kid's voice cracked again, but at least it worked.

"Yes sir, we'll call as soon—" The line went dead with a soft click. Jaci handed the phone to the guard, then walked back toward the door to the basement, Schuelman following at a slow pace.

"Man's probably gonna kill us, whether this thing works or not, Franz. Never saw colder eyes in my life. Carrying a goddam gun, even. You'd think a president would at least have somebody else to do his killing."

"I don't know about that, but he'll kill us for sure if it *doesn't* work. Sorry about the thing with my voice. The guy just turns me inside out, and I could *not* utter a sound. I'm OK. Let's get this over with and hope Allah is good. I know it's the supreme honor to die in his service, but I much prefer the idea of serving and living on as well." Both managed half a smile at the thought of their own remaining desire for survival. They descended into the deeper recesses of the silo, where they suited up to handle the richly radioactive centerpiece of their Islamic surprise.

These last steps were supremely difficult, not so much because of their complexity, or even because of the physical skills required to do them. It was because of the enormity associated with them and the fact that the enriched plutonium they were to carry and install was so very dangerous if mishandled. After months of steady and intimate work with the various systems and more, after having been taught by one so much the master of every facet of the project, there was nothing about what remained that called for great skill. Moreover, the whole thing had been tested over and over, computer models run one hundred times, and there was simply nothing left to chance or luck. Except for electricity.

Anyone who has ever worked around computers, and especially those who are familiar with highly volatile substances, such as fuels and explosives, knows the dangers associated with sparks, no matter the source. And most of the likely sources for sparks can be avoided very easily. Not so static electricity. Elegant and complicated subsystems are built into the components of all fabrications that include such things as solid or gaseous fuels, explosives, even grain bins, where the microscopic, thick dust can blow up like the Fourth of July. A stray spark from the ignition of an engine or even the tiny ones that snap against one's legs when a garment accumulates "static cling" can turn such places into instant infernos. Great argument for fabric softeners.

Every precaution available was built into the hidden missile installation beneath the Babylonian Palatial Gardens, to include a network of what were really just high tech lightning rods, intended to gather and diffuse every conceivable millivolt of static that could get into the intricate equipment. Of course, the thing runs on electricity, so the risks cannot be excluded and, with temperatures often well above 100 degrees Fahrenheit within the maze of wires and circuits, the dry air made conditions nearly perfect for an occasional such spark. Not every occurrence is destructive, but the problem is always significant.

The standard electricity that lit the rest of the palace provided the power to the rocket assembly itself. But once the launch sequence began, it went on internal power supplied by a series of very strong batteries. They were not intended to last long periods, but only to run the sophisticated guidance and arming systems once the launch had been accomplished. The last act to be done before the initial firing began was to switch the missile to internal electrical power, a step that had to happen without electrical overload, back feed, *or sparks.* The two men moved the small cylinder of plutonium out of its lead vault, carrying it still encased in a lead container that weighed enough to make them strain mightily getting it to the warhead assembly.

The clock seemed to race away from them as the last preparations were completed, and they knew well that the old man would have been able to finish much more efficiently, more quickly, and with more certainty of the result. Truth was, for all their intellect, training, and even with all the notes left to them, these were mere boys doing a man's work. Such a missile, of that there had been thousands in the once great Soviet arsenal, was not hard to design or build, if the parts and technical support were available. What had made such a big job out of this one was the location and the requirement that all its assembly and most of its parts had to be fashioned on site.

They finished, made their call, and waited to be taken away as ordered. The missile was operating on internal power, the final commands entered, the warhead completed and ready. Five minutes before launch, the mechanical and hydraulic components on top of the rocket would automatically begin to move, rotating the canopy back and sliding the sections of the floor to the side of the cavity beneath. Then the missile tip would be elevated into precise firing position and, at exactly midnight in Babylon, it would fire, rise from the silo, and streak off to the south and west on a trip that would take just under eighteen minutes. Maximum altitude of just five thousand feet would be achieved in twelve, then the rocket would tip over and acquire its target, plunging down at speeds increasing to well over mach

3, until it reached an altitude of three hundred feet above the target.

A relatively short-range piece, the rocket assembly was more notable for its accuracy than for the distance it could travel. The warhead, in fact weighing less than two hundred pounds and easily fitting inside the space available for it in a device so compact, was nonetheless powerful. If properly detonated from an altitude of five hundred feet, most of the target city of Tel Aviv would be reduced to ashes, if not vaporized. The crater expected to remain after the blast would equal the size of the island of Manhattan, and no life would survive within those confines. Destruction worse than that experienced by Hiroshima and Nagasaki would stretch miles beyond the crater, and the capacity of the nation of Israel to govern itself would be severely compromised.

While the two understudies finished their work, Saddam reflected on the events yet to come. He had only a few more nuclear warheads, small tactical pieces, but his ability to strike with thousands of tons of chemical and biological agents was great, as was well known to the fundamentalist regimes throughout the region. All the talk of a peace process was just that—talk. The remaining Muslim allies would respond in kind, and the final annihilation of the hated Jews would become reality. The existing arsenal of Scuds and the fighter aircraft he already possessed were sufficient to deliver the rest.

He stood and walked to the intercom on his desk. "Contact the Committee. I wish to speak to the Chairman at once." A response indicating compliance followed, and he sat down at the desk to wait. Speaking softly and to the empty room, he thought aloud. *Yasser, my friend, the time has come. Your offensive has the Americans completely out of the game, so we can now strike the ultimate blow. I must confess, old man, the plan has been brilliant, surpassed only in its execution. Soon the blood of the Jews will paint the sand, and Jerusalem will belong to Islam for all time.*

At six o'clock p.m., a knock at the door preceded the message that his call had been completed, and he turned in his chair to take it. "Hello? Ah, my friend, good to hear your voice. Your efforts have borne much fruit; I have asked for this call to confirm that this night we shall make the contribution reserved for us."

* * * * *

Clyde Keithley was as close to overload as a general can get. The agents of anarchy on both coasts had not only discovered the viability of using noncombatants as shields, pawns, diversions, and bargaining chips, they had apparently mastered that art first effectively demonstrated by the Vietcong some thirty years ago. Briefing this frustrated president, also a close friend of thirty years, was far from pleasant, and the small group in attendance saw clearly just how awful the results were likely to be.

"OK, Clyde, we all know just how powerfully the presence of a large number of hostages can alter the game in any urban area. And there is no doubt that, particularly in Los Angeles, these gangs have done one helluva job of stacking that deck. What happened to the rest of the effort? Have we this same mess all over the city?"

Keithley shook his head and stepped to the big map of L.A. being displayed on the wall of the Cabinet room. "No, Jackie, not everywhere, but the fact is, there are more places than just East L.A. and Watts where this problem is present. We have already had to stop advancing *here*, *here,* and over *here* in these areas because of armed resistance that we could easily have overwhelmed, except for the presence of noncombatants. Problem we have in these places is one of imminent starvation for the hostages, more than their use as shields.

"These bums over here are holed up in the middle of a densely populated area where the residents seem to have lasted longer than in other places, probably due mostly to the fact that *this*—" He poked the pointer into a spot indicating a water tower.— "kept several thousand people in clean water clear into June. Intelligence says over 20,000 folks from all over the place migrated in there, just for the water, even though there was almost nothing to eat. The result was a really big captive audience for the gangs."

"Now *wait* a minute, Clyde, you can't tell me that 20,000 people can be held hostage by even a really big gang—no way. All they have to do is start moving and the gangs get overwhelmed." Keithley shook his head that same way again, anticipating the argument.

"I understand, Jackie, but see, these bums were smart. They had a guy who knew how to operate—and therefore to *shut down*—the water facility. Once they had control of it, no one wanted to argue anymore. And control was no problem, because the only armed force in the whole place was them. Plenty of automatic weapons, military and civilian, and no citizens with the capability of fighting back, especially after they killed off just about all the police and most of the small number of National Guard left at home. Can't give you any better explanation than that, but it's not a unique story, by any means."

Webb nodded, his face a mask of pain and anger mixed. All over the country, those who were ruthless enough to try it and well enough armed to accomplish it had done the same thing. Food, supplies, water, shelter, even in a few instances pharmacy supplies formed the stuff of power in the hands of a few. In Chicago, it was water and a big supply of grain stores, seized in place by the thugs in the gangs, then guarded by well-armed men who had the capability of destroying the whole thing if the people failed to comply with their demands. Not exactly the higher and better parts of humanity at work.

"The long term results were different, depending on how well armed the bad guys were and how big the population was. In many places, whatever was being used as the bait eventually ran out for everybody, as was the case in New Orleans, where water had to be treated by desalinization before being drunk, and St. Louis, where a large grain storage facility exploded and burned when hit by lightning. Once the medium of blackmail was gone, the game quickly changed, and the people, good and bad alike, quickly succumbed to starvation. And wherever the supply of clean water dissipated, disease and death in great quantity soon followed."

Walking over to stare out the tall window at the end of the room, Jackie Webb's mind was flooded with the memories of horrors long ago; of children bearing hand grenades, of old men wired up with enough explosives draped around their frail bodies to vaporize themselves and a whole platoon of Marines; of babies left in the road as bait for the innate softness of western man toward ones so small. Of course, their bodies were booby trapped with high explosives, so the babies were already sentenced to die anyway. As soon as a GI touched the infant, both were blown to bloody bits.

"I remember that line of school children outside of Da Nang, all walking toward our formation with their hands in the air." The Sergeant Major's head set back, like some invisible punch had caught him by surprise. His eyes blinked, misted, flashed, darkened. Then he closed them momentarily before responding.

"I remember the story, sir, and had one of my own."

Webb continued. "I'd been in country just eleven days, had seen not that first speck a' combat. Changed my life for all times, General—what happened there. I swear. . ." Webb turned around, his gaze now intent, fear, anxiety, and still burning anger boiling in the black eyes. Keithley knew the story, had seen similar events in Vietnam as well; but the others, including many who had never been in the military service at all, could only wait, clueless, for the punch line.

"I had just arrived a few minutes earlier, there to observe a staging area then in use for combat missions into the mountainous areas to the west, before assuming command of a company of Marines. We were all rookies then. Locals were everywhere in the city itself, but their access to the military installation was supposed to be limited. Well these kids, all looking to be grade school age, came marching up the road, getting to within fifty yards of a platoon-size formation that was preparing to move to airlift into the field. The kids were carrying a couple of packages in their arms, and they just kept walking and waving as they approached. We were standing some 150 yards away, when several of the men in that platoon started yelling, screaming, waving their arms in the air. We could only make out a little of it, but they were clearly trying to keep the children from getting any closer." Webb stopped. A deep breath, then two. Still he could not continue. Finally, he spoke again.

"A lieutenant seemed to appear out of nowhere, probably from within the ranks of the men standing in the formation. He barked a couple of orders that we couldn't hear, and two riflemen stepped out and stood beside him. Just then, the kids started running toward that bunch a Marines, standing there against a fence, and the two riflemen knelt down on one knee, taking aim with 16s. The Lieutenant screamed at the kids once more, then we heard his voice crack as he ordered

509

the two to open fire. Goddammedest thing I had ever seen in my life, those kids tumbling back, flipping over, then rolling on the ground as those slugs tore through them."

"The Marines started running away, toward *us,* and not in the direction of the dead kids. Then, in the blinking of an eye, the whole place went white. A huge explosion knocked everybody within a hundred yards off his feet, and the air was filled with dust and smoke so thick that the entire area around the children's bodies disappeared. I remember trying to stand up, falling, then finally getting to my feet and seeing the others in my group doing the same drunken routine. Sirens were everywhere, and five or six ambulances roared up into the mess of men. There were several Marines down, some moving a little, some still. The ones who had not been hurt were trying to help, scrambling for bandages and yelling for corpsmen to assist.

"I looked back at the others—none of us really knew what we'd just seen. We ran down to where those Marines were hit, started to do what we could. Nobody killed, although the guys closest to the explosion were hit pretty bad. Back where the kids had gone down, there was nothing but a big crater, black smoke, and almost no sign of any of those little ones. When the dust finally cleared and we had a chance to ask a few questions, it was pretty obvious." Webb sat back down at the table, rubbed his face with his hands.

"That lieutenant told us the VC made a habit of sending little kids into camp, all wired up to grenades or even high explosive charges, with orders to find the GIs and give them those packages. The kids were good as dead, anyway, so shooting them really was just an attempt to keep them from taking a bunch of us with them. I never could verify it, but Division reportedly had no less than 150 confirmed events just like that, at a cost of more than three hundred dead GIs. An enemy who is willing to use women and children as deadly pawns can really make things difficult. So, gentlemen, believe me, a pretty small gang of well-armed men can make one helluva mess if they have control of a big crowd of hostages. American soldiers are ill-equipped to kill kids—especially Americans—or to engage an enemy who is hiding behind them."

There was a long silence in the room, as each person sought to imagine in his own mind what he had just heard—

then to apply it to the present realities. Finally, Clyde Keithley resumed the briefing.

"As the President has just so graphically demonstrated, these are very difficult situations." He took a breath, looked back at the map of Los Angeles and pointed to the area of East L.A. again. "This area in here is really the one that has the most attention right now. Many of the others are bad, but this one is the worst. Two gangs have joined forces, apparently in an effort to use hostages and firepower to convince us that they should get some kind of special treatment, including the grant of continued occupation of this area.

"Intelligence efforts were never very successful, as our presence in the area has been so brief, and prior civilian and military forces were pretty much overwhelmed by the gangs months before we could get there. We now find ourselves in the difficult situation of having to rely on very few inside sources, without any real track record on the trustworthiness of the few informants we now can use. Up here, in the Long Beach and even Santa Monica areas, things were not too difficult, as the gangs tended not to range that far out of the central city. In fact, Santa Monica was pretty quiet, although there were very few people left there, mostly due to lack of water and food. We are using existing facilities, including a water treatment plant that we restored to working order and two large high school gymnasiums, to start housing refugees and treating the sick. We just today learned that a big delivery of diesel fuel has been made to the hospital there, and it should be operational within about a week."

"What happened to the efforts to interdict this gang alliance you told us about on Friday, Clyde? Can we keep them from consolidating forces? I know enough about East L.A. and Watts to fear a very long, difficult, and no doubt deadly problem if they can accomplish that, especially in view of this whole noncombatant thing." Mac Reed was no stranger to combat or to urban strife, having first seen both in Siagon, 1968. Keithley nodded, lifting a blowup of that area's map to the easel.

"Right, Mac, things have gotten pretty sticky there. You will remember that we had an informant, a Mexican kid whose cousin was a Marine MP attached to HQ for the Los Angeles operation. We talked to him—or at least the cousin did—every

511

day for over a week, learning from him about this intended Diablos/Sons of Silence alliance. Last we heard from him, the actual pooling of weapons and hostages was imminent, and the big card the white trash was bringing to the equation was at least one refurbished 50-caliber machinegun, mounted on some kind of truck or jeep. Obviously such a weapon, if protected by a large number of hostages and highly mobile—especially at night—would create a helluva problem for our choppers."

"No picnic for mechanized ground troop efforts, either, Clyde. That thing, if it's got AP ammo loaded in it, could kill any number of armored vehicles attempting to advance into the area. Jesus, boys, if they could place it right, cover it with women and children, and provide it with good ammunition, it could keep air cover *and* ground troops at bay from quite a distance. *Shit, what a mess. . .*" The president sank back in his chair and looked away from the map.

"We're trying to re-establish contact with the informant in the morning, going back to a meeting point in a golf course outside of the area, *here,* at Los Amigos. The kid failed to appear for the last meeting, and we even took the chance of several low-altitude fly overs with the contact person on board, trying to find him. If we can't learn the extent of their hostage count and where the Sons are coming from, we will take extreme risks of harming those people they are holding—if we try to go in with an invasion-size force. Mark wants to send in a Delta Force unit tonight, try to snoop without detection, and maybe set up stationary surveillance sites, at least one in Watts, and one over here, next to I-605 somewhere. They think they can use the listening devices—that thing they call 'big ears'—and spotting scopes to get a feel for the population. The debate there is not just for the safety of the unit, but what will happen to the whole situation if they get discovered."

The men spent little time discussing the whole idea before deciding the Delta Force infiltration was the right thing to do. They also ordered a unit of Navy SEALs and a Special Forces team to do the same thing, all entering from different directions with the most sophisticated communications and covert surveillance equipment they could carry. At least there would be a chance of intelligent direction of the invasion with some eyes and ears on the inside. That is, so long as they didn't get caught. The stories of mass killings and torture were so numerous, complete with eyewitness accounts and many bodies seen by aerial reconnaissance already, that everyone knew there would be a horrible price paid for getting caught.

* * * * *

"All units, this is Yankee Clipper 6—Col. Jeffers—*all units, listen up.* Remain in concealed positions. Repeat. Remain in concealment until further order. The aggressors have apparently escaped via unknown routes, probably using sewers and some of the old tunnels that connected buildings in the area. We're told there were some that are not mapped, as they were closed off and condemned back in the fifties. We expect military to arrive within 60 minutes, mech units with armor and covered by air support. You are to contact us immediately when you make visual contact with them. Then, on my order, you will join up with them and follow their directives. All units respond."

One by one, in the order preset before they started the operation, the combined FBI/National Guard surveillance units reported their understanding, each in turn identifying its location to the guard commander. They were spread over an area of about ten city blocks, with two of the two-man FBI teams hiding within a block of the SPA itself. No one had a clue how close they were, but the fourth floor flower boxes on that building were actually visible to Roger Kline and Seamus O'Dorgan as they lay behind glassless windows on the second floor of an old department store a block away.

No more than a mile away, over two hundred mercenaries, now well armed and temporarily out of harm's way, began to congregate in the darkness under the maze of expressway interchanges, city streets, and burned-out buildings. Each man moved to a prearranged site to become part of a unit for that he and his weapons were designated. Lifelong Palestinian terrorists, trained over long periods of time at installations in the deserts of the Sudan and experienced through hundreds of bombings, guerilla infiltrations, and outright firefights with Israeli police and soldiers, waited at each site to take command of their specialized units.

Working in small groups of no more than ten men, they would move to pre-identified locations all over Manhattan, setting up in concealment until the appropriate time for their various missions to commence. Like any well-conceived, well-trained guerilla operation, patience was paramount, second only to ruthless disdain for life, and they would wait, each of these little groups, until just the right moment to strike.

Six of these squads were armed with recoilless type weapons that were capable of taking out helicopters, armored personnel carriers, and even tanks. They carried less ammunition, and their weapons were more cumbersome to move, so their missions would be surgical in nature and executed in such a way as to permit them to evacuate their locations at once after striking. When they ran out of ammunition for these pieces, they would return to one of the underground locations with the weapons and receive new assignments, assuming there was no resupply available for them. All were highly skilled guerilla fighters, capable of immediately changing roles and assuming new assignments.

Ironically, the nasty little surprise set up by Sallie for the invading forces was one of his own making. The PLO had no use for such agents as Sarin, because of its lingering effects and the likelihood that its presence might cut off lines of escape for the highly mobile units employed in such operations. While the whole idea of dying for Allah in the great jihad sounded good, the pragmatism of men like Arafat and the rest of the Committee suggested that winning a guerilla war was much easier with live troops. Needless loss of troop strength was to be avoided where possible. Moreover, the whole idea behind the operations in America was to so preoccupy U.S. military resources with problems at home that there would be nothing left with that to assist the Israelis when their travail began. Clearly, the downsized armies of the United States, even with the assistance of their now all-important state militias, were stretched far too thin to provide adequate personnel to the problems now facing them at home.

It was Sallie's passion for killing that drove him to obtain the poison and set it in place, not any order from his command. He was so driven by the evil that possessed him that concern for loss of life among his own forces never entered his mind. After all, killing his own had proven to be nothing more than a momentary enjoyable diversion anyway.

Implementation of the dispersion plan was not difficult, given the careful planning and skill level of those responsible for administering it. The PLO had smuggled fifty command-level terrorists into the United States over the twelve months prior to the commencement of operations, with the destruction of the nation's electrical system. Each was carefully placed, well hidden, and completely briefed periodically as to the progress of preparations. Every one of these leaders had the luxury of anonymously moving without impediment through New York City, studying the layout of the streets, walking through the buildings to be used, even climbing the staircases, examining the elevator shafts, memorizing fields of fire and avenues of escape.

By the time they went into hiding in early March, every one of these men was an expert on the city of New York, having spent several months stashing weapons, ammunition re-supplies, even medicines and fresh water in scores of locations, each memorized and often checked to assure its continued secrecy and integrity. The result was just what it was supposed to be. The enemy knew the place better than the home team, and the operation combined intelligence, experience, planning, abundant resources, skill and, most of all, ruthless determination born of fanatic zeal.

As these men moved silently into positions all over Manhattan, the foggy darkness enshrouding their ghostlike progress, a hundred deadly traps were set for the invading American forces. And a thousand escape routes and points of safety and resupply awaited the agents of evil as they prepared to welcome the troops home to the Big Apple.

13.

"These are piles of dirt, William Samuelson. What am I supposed to tell the world? That we are justified in commencing a world war because my men have discovered piles of dirt one hundred miles from Baghdad? That piles of dirt mixed into the sand in the middle of the most Godforsaken place on the planet justify bombing a museum of ancient history? William. . .*William, you need a rest, my friend.* . .Wait, I'll call President Webb and tell him that we need to bomb Saddam's monument to his own ego because you have found some dirt in the desert!" The face of the Israeli prime minister was deep red, almost as red as the face of the head of Mossad, his most trusted and venerated paramilitary/intelligence establishment.

Samuelson had been the one to first report Weidenolf's presence in Iraq, and it was his men who finally discovered his precise location, ironically enough, in Babylon. They were the ones who connected him up directly to the palace/museum/archaeological project that Saddam had commissioned on the Euphrates River, and it was one of Samuelson's men who spiked the vodka in the old man's flat with such unexpectedly deadly results. These two men had known each other for thirty years or more, and being taunted by Netanyahu, even if he *was* the prime minister, was more than he could stand. He exploded from his chair in the small briefing room at the head of state's offices in Tel Aviv, his gaze so fierce as to prompt stifled gasps from the eight men in the room.

"*Do not patronize me, Benjamin—this entire investigation was your idea in the first place, and what we have found, each and every fact, has proven to be reliable!*" His tone softened only slightly as the prime minister stared back at him, his own countenance one of intense fury mixed with just the smallest dose of hidden surprise, so powerful was his friend's reaction. "We told you Weidenolf was there, and we were right. We told you he was one of the top Soviet missile guidance, ballistics men in the whole red empire, and that was right. We even told you he was working on that bullshit museum thing on the river—*in BABYLON, FOR THE LOVE OF ALMIGHTY GOD—and you mock me in this place, as though I were some snot-faced cub reporter trying to convince you that Godzilla had returned!!"*

The snoop sat back in his chair, working hard to relax the muscles in his shoulders and neck. He looked down at the tabletop, closed his eyes hard, rubbed his ruddy face with both hands, the meaty paws kneading the craggy features, as though attempting to scrub off the sweaty frustration carved into it. He drew breath, exhaled, looked back at the unmoving face of his boss. Sitting straighter in the chair, the fierce black eyes again locked on Netanyahu, the voice now quieter, but still deep with emotion.

"Benjamin, do not mock me, *please*. And do not mock the product of this work, done at such great risk and cost to all involved. Three men died in that damn desert, caught in a dust storm and lost to the heat, trying to get samples of that pile of dirt you are talking about. Four more men are still hidden out in Babylon, including the operative whose actions resulted in the death of that old half-breed bastard. They will eventually be recognized, tortured, and killed unless we act at once. But there are bigger problems. Those men accept that fate when they volunteer for such assignments. Dying for Israel is nothing new to the Mossad." Forward again in the chair, he began to address the assembly, as well as the prime minister.

"What is more important—a quantum leap more important, gentleman—is that if what we believe about this Palace thing is true, that madman is sitting on a weapon that could erase this or any other city in Israel, and he could do it at any time. And *that,* my old friend, is far more than just a "pile of dirt." The thick hands went back to the face again, then up and over the balding, massive head. Massaging the back of his neck, he looked away toward the others at the table.

"What do you suggest, William? It is clear that more surveillance or more investigation is probably out of the question, if you are right about the preparedness of this weapon. The Americans are watching the whole area with both satellite and high altitude atmospheric reconnaissance, and they have expressed their willingness to provide air support. But their problems at home are greater than at any time since the 1860s, and we cannot expect Jackie Webb to commit to much more. I have asked about Patriot

517

installations, but it appears all we will get is what is left over here from their preparations just past, and I doubt they would work effectively in this case, anyway."

Samuelson looked around the room, got up and walked to the door, asking the guard to step outside and close the room as he left. Moving back to the table, his voice strained with fatigue and frustration, his mind overloaded with the enormity of the occasion, he seemed unable to ask the next question aloud. Finally, he looked back at Netanyahu, now standing next to him at the display board where the satellite pictures were displayed.

"What about the Arrow, Benjamin?" No one moved. Most of the nine faces in the room looked blankly at the two men, except for the head of missile defense, Zachariah Weiss. An older, smallish man with Einstein hair and quick features, he spoke at once.

"NO. Too soon. No testing, beyond computer simulations and one set of demonstrations performed last spring in far less than optimum conditions in the South Atlantic. If it fails, the Arabs will know about our efforts; they will then know that Arrow exists *and does not work,* and we will be compromised far worse than we are at this moment. Absolutely not, Benjamin."

"Oh, come on Zac, that's lame," Samuelson countered without a breath. "If we *don't* use Arrow, we're one helluva a lot more compromised when Tel Aviv is in radioactive ashes and two million Jews are dead. Holy—Benjamin, that is no argument. And besides, Zac is too modest. The tests were very impressive—target acquisition on drones at mach 2 on all five tries, good telemetry and tracking on all but one, and two out of five kills. I can appreciate our colleague's passion for perfection, but my god, men, this is hardly the time for requiring it."

"William is speaking, gentlemen, for those of you who are not familiar with the project, of an antiballistic missile weapon, code named Arrow, that Zac and his people have developed to neutralize the larger, longer-range rockets such as the one we now fear in Iraq. It has been top secret for obvious reasons until now, and we are pretty confident none of our enemies knows about it. Even the Americans have not been apprised. What even I did not know until this moment is just how successful the tests were last spring." The headman cast an intent look in the direction of the Einstein look-alike, then, his voice heavy with concern and mounting upset, he spoke.

"Zachariah, my reports said nothing about kills, and the information regarding target acquisition was different than what William suggests here. If you have withheld—"

"Benjamin, I have withheld nothing, only attempted to refrain from encouraging too optimistic a reaction to such limited testing. Honestly, although the tracking was very positive, the dissimilarities from actual aggressor weapons were manifest, as we could not mimic real ICBMs or intermediate range missiles without every spy satellite in the skies locking onto them and instantly reacting. You must remember, all atmospheric testing that looks, acts, or pretends to be similar to a nuke-bearing device is instantly visible, and just as quickly draws a huge international crowd.

"I am hardly versed in international diplomacy, but even I can imagine the kind of reaction that spineless Jeffrey Flint would have expressed to the world, had the Americans discovered we were firing off a weapon of that size. So we tested on a small scale, a scale that was, I admit, exactly configured to produce a miniature of the real thing, but different, nonetheless.

"So, when William says we had positive tracking on five drones, he is right, but the drones were smaller, closer to the earth, and slower moving than the real thing. Also, because we could not permit the testing to be discovered, we had to work with much shorter distances, in addition to the lower altitudes. So, were you told only more generalized results? Of course you were. Did I deceive you? Absolutely not. I merely tried to maintain a real measure of caution when attaching significance to the results."

Samuelson shook his head back and forth quickly, his face now less intense and devoid of recrimination. It was, he could see, time for conciliation, not confrontation. To win this debate, he could not permit the discussion to become an inquisition of the scientist. "Please, gentlemen, it is not my intention to cast doubts on the efforts—and God knows, not on the integrity of my old friend here. We all know of Zac's efforts and the success he has had with the very foundation of our defenses against our enemies. After all, it was Zac who retrofitted the American F16s for our use, turning them from wonderful weapons platforms into the super fighters our men now use to maintain Jewish ownership of the skies. It is only his modesty, and even more, his passion for perfection that has been at work here."

He turned to face Weiss again. "Understand me, please. I respect your caution. There is just no time for any more of it here. That damn thing will work, and I believe you know in your heart that it will work. And we simply cannot refrain from employing it. Period." The prime minister spoke again to Weiss.

"I have been considering it for this problem in the past days, but its less-than-ready condition makes it very much a long shot. Frankly, Zac, I have to agree with Mossad on this. Arrow does work and, if you can field it in time, it should be engaged here, if possible. If we don't—"

"Benjamin, you don't understand. The weapon does work, but only in the most controlled of situations, and given more time than we have to set it up. Our target date for final assembly and full readiness has been previously set by you for the spring of 1999. We are therefore months from completion of testing; moreover, we only have one copy now fully assembled, and it is hidden in a remote location. A second is close to completion, but we lack parts for it to be finished at this time. We could not possibly expect to use it on such short notice."

A quiet voice took the room, a small visage at once in command of all eyes, although silent until now. "I am unaware of this 'Arrow' device, gentlemen, but if it has worked, now exists, and can have *any* likelihood of success against a nuclear attack, I must respectfully disagree with Mr. Weiss and concur with William. As usual, my friend is too much the perfectionist. These times demand response and action, whether or not perfect." The oldest man in the room, and one of the oldest in all Israeli government spoke with such authority that the discussion seemed to end before it got a good start.

At seventy-six years old, Andrew Irsansky was a patriot of Israel whose contributions had already spanned over sixty years. His forearm bore a Nazi concentration camp tattoo, and his entire family had died at Dachau. Netanyahu quickly acknowledged the remarks, adding his vote at once.

"Andrew is right, Zac. Gentlemen, Arrow, if it works, is the only weapon we have that might hit and destroy a guided missile; it is also the only one able to do so early in the flight of such a device as to kill it before its nuclear warhead is fully armed. Not that we care particularly, but that means, if it hits the missile early enough, little or no nuclear reaction will occur, and there will be little radioactive fallout over Iraq. At least then the madman won't be able to claim a nuclear strike had been made by Israel. If it fails—" Samuelson finished the sentence.

"If it fails, we're no worse off—a Patriot might kill it before it detonates, and, even if the warhead is armed, the explosion might not have as devastating an effect as if it went off over its target. We have no other option—*none*. Hitting the thing before it launches requires firing a huge warhead right into the Old City—and that assumes we're right on where it's located. Politically, we simply can't do that. Please, Zac, I understand the scientist in you wants a finished product, but this is no perfect situation; without Arrow, *Israel* may be finished." Silence greeted the end of that speech, not only from Weiss, but from the rest of those present. Over the past months of hand wringing and countless discarded plans, no one wanted to face the truth of what might now be about to happen. Even as they now dealt with it, they could not know the web of destruction already wrought by the Committee of the PLO, having to this point failed to see the link between Iraq, Arafat, and the bad news in America.

Samuelson seized the moment, afraid Weiss would still attempt to take control of the meeting. "Zac, I know what you are thinking and I have an answer. Of course Mossad knows where the Arrow is hidden, and we also know you have it set up to test again. It can be fired from there, and fired with great effect, if we can find a reliable source of early warning of the impending launch of the Iraqi nuke and proper telemetry information as it begins its arc toward the intended target. Benjamin, we only need the help of the Americans—and Jackie Webb can accomplish this for us with one phone call to NASA—to immediately program that bird they have sitting over Saudi to home in on Babylon, make positive contact with Arrow *on its present site,* and put in place the high-speed communications by direct transmission to talk to it when Saddam fires that missile."

All eyes were on the scientist, now studying the white knuckles of his clenched fists, resting on the tabletop. Netanyahu spoke in that quiet, deep voice reserved for only the most important moments of necessity. "What about it, Zachariah Weiss, is William right? If I can obtain the assistance of the Americans, can you do it? I understand your reservations, but you must tell us—is William correct?"

His eyes never left the backs of his hands, although one hand unclenched, the thumb moving up the wrist of the opposite hand to begin rubbing the dark blue numbers stamped into the aging flesh of his own body. For a long moment, he sat otherwise motionless. Taking breath, eyes never leaving the tattoo, soft words captured every nerve ending in the room.

"I only want what is best for Israel, Benjamin. That is all I want. The weapon has not been sufficiently tested, and I simply cannot tell you that it will work. Computer simulations and small-scale tests are nice, but they are not atmospheric reality." Exhaling slowly after a deep breath, fists knotted again; both hands relaxed, and lay flat, palms down on the table. Still no one spoke to argue or make response. The gray head shook side to side again.

"I simply cannot say. You must understand, Benjamin, that as a scientist, I simply cannot say. . .But William is correct in this much. Arrow is assembled, hidden but ready, in the hills north of Jerusalem. The installation is small, unobtrusive. If you can get the Americans to communicate directly between their satellite and Arrow, we can try to use it, if the need truly arises. It will take about two hours of testing and interface between the satellite and Arrow's computers to make ready." He sighed again, shoulders slumped in resignation to the now unavoidable realities. His every fiber had been committed to the completion of the project, this survivor of holocaust, passionate defender of the Chosen People. The thought of firing Arrow before it was ready, having it fail, thereby permitting genocide of his people, racked him with pain and frustration.

The only worse thought was that unless they tried it, such a result was certain. Netanyahu stood beside the old man's chair, waited a moment, then placed a hand on his shoulder. "Come, Zac, we'll call the American president right now. Gentlemen, please stay close by. I will report as soon as possible."

* * * * *

The smell of stale water mixed with the smoke of fires smoldering all over East L.A., efforts by those left standing to boil water or cook whatever fragments they could find of the things that now passed for food. Miguel Sanchez lay in the weeds beneath the expressway, his sides throbbing from the spasms created by his many hours tied up on the floor in his brother's makeshift cell. That pain was accompanied by invisible knives piercing the muscles of his legs and shoulders, from carrying the now motionless form lying beside him. The faint starlight, aided only slightly by a sliver of moon, cast an eerie pall across her slender torso. He strained in vain to see the chest rise in breath.

Goddammit, woman, do not do this to me—I have carried you all this way, and you cannot die on me now!! Rolling up onto his knees, the young man slid a hand behind her neck, lifting her shoulders and upper back a few inches off the ground. Wrenching pain shot through his own back as he turned and leaned down, placing his ear against her chest. No sound greeted him, no sense of any swelling of the lungs was apparent. He dropped her abruptly, whispered curses spilling from his mouth as he moved up to her motionless face. Blood, tears, vomit, dirt mixed across the small features, her mouth slack, lips now parted. Miguel was in an instant overcome with the reality that she was dead.

Death was no stranger to him by this time, the constant companion of all who had survived the past six months. But *this* death, the apparent loss of *this* life, an unknown black girl added to the list of his brother's victims, somehow hit him with high voltage. Carrying her, constantly checking on her, risking his very life to save just one person from the hell that had become life since the lights went out, somehow she was more than just another faceless loss. Tears welled up in his burning eyes, sobs racked him, as he scooped the lifeless naked form up in his arms like some injured child, this total stranger, one with whom he had absolutely nothing in common except for the horrors of this time.

In that moment, the stench of her open wounds, the filth matted in her thick hair, even the repulsive crust of blood covering her loins and breasts seemed dissolved away, as if washed by his tears. He held her tightly against him, her body absorbing the convulsions of his sobs. She lay limp in his arms, eyes closed; Miguel held his breath, attempting to quell his crying, and turned his face to hers. With energy from no known source, he prayed aloud to the God he was certain had forsaken them all, his voice weak, a choking rasp. "Oh dearest Lord God, Jesus Christ, why have you left us? Must this one die, too?" Then with a voice too loud, heedless of the danger, he began to moan and cry out.

"Oh Lord, my God, are you gone?! Can you watch and let this one die too—and at the hand of my evil brother, like all the rest—WHERE ARE YOU?!!" The voice rose up in his chest, a harsh roar against the still darkness, and he pulled her around to lie beside him, at the same time pressing his mouth against her parted lips. Drawing breath, he breathed into her body, the illusion of respiration caused by filling her lungs from his own. He pulled away, and she exhaled.

He did it again, now a bit more forcefully. Now he laid her back against the weeds, blowing into her yet again, at the same time placing the heel of his hand on her sternum. Clumsily at first, then with increasing speed and success, Miguel alternated between filling her lungs and pressing down on her chest. She took a breath.

Tears flowed off the end of his nose, running across her face and down into the grass beneath her head, his pace now frantic, spurred on by that one breath. For each one he gave her, she took one on her own, then stopped. Repeated, she took another, then stopped again. "God, she is trying!! Enter in, God, *please, do not abandon me here!!"* Then two breaths, then three. She stopped again. No response as he continued to press his mouth against hers, oblivious to any sensation of smell or taste, intent only on that breath that came back to him. More pressure on the breastbone, more repetitions, now more breaths, more and now more. He stopped momentarily, breathing so hard through his sobs that he felt he would faint.

It was at that moment, in the near blackness of the predawn, that his eye caught movement, his hand rising and falling as it lay against her chest. Turning her face back to his again, the warmth of her breath against him was confirmation that she was breathing again, on her own and without further encouragement. A whispered prayer of cautious thanksgiving, followed by another, more loudly announced in the stillness.

There was no way to know her real condition, the extent of her internal injuries, or why she had stopped breathing in the first place. Could she still be dying, even as she began to breathe more regularly? Maybe. Or the way he carried her, her head down for so long, might have cut off circulation, inhibited breathing, or encouraged fluid to fill her battered lungs. He knew nothing at that moment but that she was alive. The young Mexican man gently but firmly embraced the fragile nakedness of a nearly dead black woman, bonded to him only by the circumstance in which they lived and the bearing of wounds inflicted by the same evil man, his brother.

Long minutes passed before Miguel became aware of the first hint of light in the eastern sky and, with that discovery, the stark imperative that he move at once to attempt meeting with his cousin. The woman lay still beside him, her head resting against his chest and shoulder, her breathing now regular and apparently strong. The immediate problem was twofold: to get to the golf course and meet Raul, but at the same time to protect this precious life, so passionately rescued but still so tenuous. He could not risk trying to carry her again, especially in light of almost certain internal injury. But leaving her there, chilled, naked, badly hurt, seemed also unwise.

Looking around, decision time was immediate, so he took the best of the poor options available. He stripped off his tee shirt and jeans. Lifting her closer to a sitting position, still limp and comatose, he managed to pull the shirt over her head and to wiggle it down over her bare torso. The jeans he pulled on and up over the slender hips so that, after a couple of minutes, she had some covering to protect her from both the present chill and the intense sun that would shortly penetrate everything. Weeds that surrounded them made an acceptable camouflage for her body; they would also provide some scant shade, at least until the Southern California sun rose directly overhead. Standing over her, he uttered another prayer and, in those few syllables, sensed that they and the cries for help before were being heard.

"Raul, I have much to tell you, but you will learn nothing from me until this woman is safely lifted away from this miserable sewer. I *will* save at least one." He turned, clad only in his under shorts, and began running in the direction of the rendezvous point, each stride longer and quicker than the one before.

* * * * *

Janice Elaine Landry stood in the weeds of a fence row, the house and barn a cloudy visage distant one quarter mile at least, dust from the driveway like the contrail of some high flying jet or heavy smoke from October's leaf fires, all strewn in a line and lit with kerosene. Of course, she knew what she was seeing: The dust left behind any vehicle during the August dryness, the same her whole life. So familiar was the sight of that billowing cloud tumbling along the lane that at first her mind could make nothing extraordinary of it. But then the uneasiness set in—at the familiar more recently made rare, of the commonplace now so uncommon—and she began to move with purpose from the fence row's berry bushes directly back to the garden and house.

"Luke—come here. . .Luke—c'mon. Something. . .*Hey LUKE!* Somebody just left the driveway in a car, or a truck, moving fast. Must be some kind a' trouble, they're in a car. Luke, dammit, where—"

"What are you babblin' 'bout, Whiner? It's just Uncle Carl's truck—*oh. What's he. . .C'MON, SUMTHIN'S UP, JAN, LET'S GO!*"

Grabbing the two pails of berries, both kids found the bare dirt between the fence and the cow path full of muddy manure and rocks. Bare feet raced at once in the direction of home, as young instincts honed by harsh realities breathed purpose into every stride.

They returned to a buzz of anxious conversation, all full of half-information, fragments of things observed, liberally sprinkled with the instant product of a shortage of facts. "Carl got a call from Jake, over on the county road—found men on fire, and Josh's horse running down the lane. Said Josh was calling—"

"Did not—Josh's missing, along with his—or somebody's van—bunch a' bad guys chasin' him and Jake. . .or something." None of the facts fit together, all a mix of truth and speculation, fear and anxiety, plus a measure of pure hype.

The two found their sisters finally and got precious little comprehensible information from either, but all knew at once that something awful had happened and it involved their father, whom they had seen ride off into the woods many hours before. Consensus was impossible among them, Luke demanding to go on horseback to find them, Jan taking seniority's place to decree that, as was the fixed rule, no one was to leave the farm without permission and plenty of company. Four miles away, reality was not difficult to comprehend. It was impossible.

"Here's where he dismounted, tied the horse. From the mess a' manure and trampling, looks like the mount stood here a good while—maybe an hour or more. Ate every stitch a' vegetation, grass, weeds, tree limbs, sombitch musta' been part goat. No sign a' injury or even hard riding, though. Saddle clean and dry. Found 'im right here, just like I said, gettin' jumpy. Musta' been the smell a' smoke and that big explosion. Knot in the lead rope was hard as a rock—'bout had ta cut the thing ta get 'im loose." Jake talked spare and to the point, while Carl Landry scoured the ground with his eyes then responded.

"Josh was wearing riding boots, I remember that, spurs and all. But the tracks leading away from here are different— look. Like sneakers, and sure as hell no western toe and no spur marks dragged in the dirt. He must've changed out of those boots, left them close by—*there!*" Carl bent into a clump of weeds growing around a low rock pile, stood holding Josh's boots. The spurs jingled quietly as he held them up, a knot building in the older brother's stomach again.

"Goddam, Carl, you might's well gone with 'im, close as you are to the track and all. What you make a' all this, and where the hell *is* he, anyway?" Jake spoke quietly, his curiosity momentarily overtaking his concern. The doctor shook his head absently, distracted by competing thoughts and options. He was unaccustomed to having to *think* about what Josh would do. He just always pretty much *knew.*

"Got me stumped, Jake, sure as hell. Curtis was right, because none a' those barbecued stiffs were him. And his signature was all over that killing. Shit, but he goes nuts sometimes. Let's follow this track back again, find out where he set up and see if he moved around at all before introducing himself to his victims." They walked back slowly, finding each print made by the soft shoes, often stopping to back up when the tracks seemed to end. Finally, after several such retreats, they came to where Josh first lay down, up the hill about one hundred yards away from the van.

"He lay here a while, see—grass matted here, here, and *here*, where he moved back and forth. Look. The van is visible from both of these points, but not from this one over here. See? From that one he was looking into that clump a' trees off to the right and downhill from it. Let's go see what he might've been watching in there. Maybe if we—" The sentence was interrupted by shouts from the boys, who had started their search at the site of the fire. Curtis May's big voice called, excitement evident in each word.

"Doc. *DOC!!* Found where he's been, c'mon *Doc— hey you guys, over here! Come here, quick. . .*" Landry and his companion moved without a word, arriving to a circle of the youngsters who'd found a depression in the dirt, pock-marked with foot-long rocks, many of that were spattered with liberal amounts of blood.

"Holy *shit*, Josh, what did you do to yourself? Jesus, boys, if this is my brother's blood, he's hurt plenty. How. . . . far. . ." Carl stood and looked back in the direction of the smoldering remains of the old van, estimating the distance at nearly seventy feet. "If that explosion blasted him this far, it's hard to imagine how he could've survived it. 'Specially, if he landed in these big-ass rocks. All that blood on them, seems pretty clear that's exactly what happened."

"Gawddam, Doc, but that's a helluva ride. . .although I seen more'n one car blow like Mt. Saint Helen's, enough gas and enough vapors in the tank. If that piece a' cheese had half a tank a' gas in it, warm day with plenty a' vapors inside the tank, a direct hit from that rifle a Josh's coulda' blown 'er to hell. . . But where is he? If he flew this far, hit in these rocks, can't imagine him gettin' up and walking away. . ."

"My brother has a very hard head, Jake, *very hard indeed.*" The slightest trace of a half-smile crossed the knit face, and in that moment Carl Landry was sure his brother was still alive. "OK—*OK—EVERYBODY OVER HERE—QUICK!*"

The small band of men and boys, everyone but Faith and the still semiconscious Jessie, immediately responded. Carl began talking without ever turning back to face them, his eyes scanning every direction from where they stood.

"Listen up, boys. He's out here somewhere and, judging from the amount of blood on these rocks I doubt he's gone very far. But, knowing Josh—hell, who knows. You three move out, thirty—*no*—twenty feet apart, out *this* way, keep each other in sight, and keep your eyes down on the ground. It's really rocky through here, so tracks will be hard to find. Look for a blood trail, too. We've looked right around here already, found nothing like tracks. But, like Jake said, he's gone sure as hell, and there's been no one here to carry him off. I want four more of you to head out, up and over that ridge, and do the same thing. Keep each other in sight, pay particular attention to the gullies and washes where Josh might've fallen. That's where the white tails hide out, up there and over the top of the ridge, so there are plenty of places to fall.

"The rest of you fan out and cover from here out and back around to the road. Same deal. Heads down. Jake, you bring Josh's horse back here from the road. Think I'll just let him take me for a ride. Josh raised that nag from a foal, he's a total pain in the ass for anybody else to ride, but maybe we can get some horse sense into the game, if he'll behave himself a little. I gotta talk to my sister-in-law. OK, boys. Let's go find Josh."

14.

Tracked vehicles make a sound all their own, even the little ones. But main battle tanks, self-propelled artillery pieces, and even the smaller APCs, or armored personnel carriers, shake things up in a unique way. Long before O'Dorgan and Cline heard anything, or even realized that they were feeling anything either, skin began to tingle, stomachs tightening, palms moist. Looking out through the glassless opening in the old building, they stole looks at each other as well, each trying to allay the sense of expectation that came from a yet unknown source. Then the Irishman snapped around, a movement totally out of the discipline he always exercised.

"Roger—hear that? *There*—I *knew* I could feel something—*There again!! Tanks.* Been awhile, but that's what that is, close by. Hit for Henry, tell him the Army's here. See if they want us to make contact before they get them on the radio." Cline nodded without moving, pressed on the transmitter key in his pocket, and spoke softly into the mic that hung at the corner of his mouth.

"Yankee Clipper 6, this is Cline group—Henry, do you copy?"

"This is Yankee Clipper 6—Jeffers—Roger, go ahead."

"The Irishman says he hears—*oh shit, so do I—WOW*—yeah, we got armor close by. They're here. Advise if we should initiate contact. I don't need any more surprises. Over."

"Stand by. *Henry,* Cline group has military contact." Then the Guard colonel picked up the telephone and quickly began talking to his liaison with the invading force, down at Ft. Bragg. A short pause was followed by Jeffers scribbling down a series of numbers, including a radio frequency and giving the liaison his call signs, then signing off. Without explanation, he reached for their own radio set, turned the LED display to the frequency dictated by Ft. Bragg, keyed the mic, and made contact with a battalion commander who was riding in a tank close to the front of the force that was rumbling into the Bronx. The commander responded to Jeffers' transmission.

Yankee Clipper 6, this is Range Rover 6, U.S. Army, we read you."

"Affirmative, Range Rover 6, you're clear. I have a scout team very close to the front of your units in the Bronx, so I'd like for them to make contact at once, if that's OK. Just don't want any mistakes—everybody's no doubt a bit jumpy right now."

"Roger that. Advise their location, and I'll have my people marry up with them." Jeffers reconfirmed the address and physical description of the location where Cline group was hiding out, then repeated it back to Willis.

"OK, Yankee Clipper 6, this is Range Rover 6. Roger, good copy. Tell your men to move into the doorway of their building, then display red gel flashing light when the first vehicle is fifty yards away. Jeffers responded, then advised his team. Five minutes later, Seamus O'Dorgan and Roger Cline were kneeling atop an M1 tank that idled in the middle of a burned-out street, the Bronx, New York City, United States of America. The same drill was repeated for each of the advance teams of various federal agents and National Guardsmen, until all of Lassiter's and Jeffers' men had made contact.

Similar parties occurred all over the city during the next three hours, until the entire advance party of the occupation forces was set up in various locations, prepared to move through every borough of the entire urban giant. It was the plan essentially to occupy every block of the whole town with men and equipment, hoping within about four days to obtain control by virtue of sheer numbers and superiority of firepower.

The insurgent guerillas however had other ideas, as their welcoming committee, composed of hundreds of surprises, watched from concealment. The formations and placement of the incoming forces set up in perfect conformity with what the Committee had predicted. One of the weaknesses of a free society is the ease with that information can be obtained. Several copies of the military field manuals on urban unrest and pacification had been thoroughly examined and digested by appropriate terrorist leaders before they even got to America, in the months before the operation commenced.

Miniature fiber-optic, cameras, set in place weeks before by the enemy's advance teams, observed each formation in the initial force as the units set up to begin occupation. Small, high-tech listening devices prepared to eavesdrop on communications between units, units and their command centers, even conversations between tank commanders. Notwithstanding the imagination of Hollywood to the contrary, military units do not typically work with combat communications in an encrypted mode. In fact, it is virtually impossible to do so with a large force, in the field for any significant length of time.

The PLO had huge resources, had planned well and equipped its men with the latest technology, and was blessed to have been permitted to prepare for battle by stacking the deck on the very field where the fighting would occur. In a very real sense, New York had been redesigned and wired into one huge booby trap.

A few minutes before dawn, lead vehicles, mostly tanks and armored carriers of various descriptions, began to spread out through the streets of New York. And as they began to rumble forward, they began to explode. In no fewer than a hundred places, from Brooklyn and Queens to Yonkers, to Jersey City and over into Newark, either by means of mines set with huge explosive charges or with tank killing missles, millions of dollars worth of heavy vehicles came flying apart, their crews and passengers incinerated to the last man in every case.

Radios began to crackle with more and more reports of hostile fire, cries for medical attention, demands for air support. And when unit commanders responded to the calls, the results were even worse.

Four helicopter gun ships exploded in huge fireballs as they exposed themselves to hidden attack from the tall old buildings that surrounded the men they attempted to assist. Medical teams responding to calls for evacuation were cut down by machinegun fire and an unmerciful rain of grenade bombardment. Then, in each case, while the pandemonium ran out of control, with thousands of soldiers trying to sort out locations and sources of fire, and in the midst of hundreds of new fires and destruction, the guerillas slipped out of their positions. In addition to their powerful and deadly weaponry, they were armed with the supreme edge, surprise. Typically, they took with them the weapons used to accomplish this awful result, escaping through basement windows, into storm sewers, or, in a few cases simply disappearing into prearranged underground hiding places.

Book IV – The Great Offensives

A city as old and as frequently renovated as New York leaves behind each facelift a variety of empty spaces, walled-off rooms, discarded coal bins, even an occasional ancient water cistern. Equally old sewer mains, repaired and often rerouted, leave behind dead end spurs that are sealed off and forgotten. All these create vast resources for the hiding of men and the long-term concealment of weapons and ammunition. So while the airwaves screeched with calls for help, demands for reports, and orders for resumption of movement, the terrorist army disappeared into the vast recesses of underground New York, preparing to move on to the next location.

And all over the huge town, in advance of the first American units to move into the tangle of streets and alleys, PLO Vanguardsmen moved silently, setting high explosive charges, arming preset mines, preparing ambush locations. The first twelve hours of daylight operations proved to be the most expensive day of combat for the United States armed forces since Korea. As the day progressed, even maintaining control became difficult, so numerous and so devastating was the contact with the guerillas. The insurgent PLO terrorists mostly hit with unmanned traps, using small arms fire or manned high explosives only when necessary to neutralize targets or troop concentrations that were not exposed to mines or booby traps. And only lead or trailing components were fired upon, so that by the time the targets could react, identify origins, and seek to respond, they were gone.

It was during the first hours of the fighting that the most deadly events occurred, in the South Bronx. Flower boxes four floors off the ground greeted two hundred men with lethal surprise.

* * * * *

"Not expecting visitors? I'll bet. Quite the little operation you got here, Willie—oh—almost forgot, it's *Sallie,* right? Wouldn't want any of your disciples to know who you are, *or were,* now would we? They might lose their heads and do something. *Oops!!* Goddam, Willie, they already have!!" Lester roared and hooted a laugh that might have awakened the dead, except that it didn't, and the bizarre little tableau seemed to become more fantastic by the second, with Sallie

533

standing over his two headless cohorts. His own face was blank of comprehension for long moments, the shock in his eyes no more complete than if Cedric or Sherman had sat up and begun talking to him. He looked in utter disbelief at the face of a dead man, but a dead man who pointed a .45 automatic at his chest.

"Just had to come by and pay respects to the goons, here—had a notion they might be feelin' poorly by now. Guess I'm a bit late, huh? Oh well, never liked 'em much, anyway, ya know? Not much for conversation. Ugly fuckers, too. An' I never had much truck with men who'd take orders long term from a greasy little nigger. But, since I'm here, might as well rest a little, then maybe I'll just feed you to the ol' grinder there—how'd that be?" Huge laugh again, a real knee-slapper this time, accompanied by paroxysms of cigarette coughing; in that moment, Sallie saw his opening. Spinning just a quarter turn to his left, an incredibly quick hand produced that .357 magnum revolver, spitting fire in the blinking of an eye. The sound of multiple shots within such a confined space created deafness at once, there being no place for the roaring concussions to go except into unprotected ears.

Lying on the floor, fire screaming from his chest, sweet, metallic, sickening blood assaulting his taste buds, eyes glazed over, the dim light in the little room now moving slowly round and round. Speech was immediately impossible, both because of the quantity of blood filling his mouth and because his larynx was gone, a big slug having taken it out through the gaping hole in the back of his neck. Hatred rose up as bitter bile and mixed with the fluids spilling out the corners of his mouth, his head tipping slowly side to side as if to deny the obvious. After all this time, all this planning, all this sacrifice, the distances consumed, could it end in this moment? Thinking was so very hard, as was comprehending, in the ever dimming half-light. Gunpowder mixed with the smell of the dead and yet another loosening of bowels.

"Amazing how stupid people can be. Surprise is such a powerful ally to the aggressor. And to underestimate the skill of an adversary, is just really stupid. Pisses me off though you dyin' so fast. Had to react too quick. . . couldn't place my shots like I should have. You might've survived the gut shots, but that mess in your throat, gonna finish you quick. Maybe just a *little* torture, before you go. . ." The handgun roared, striking the dying man between the legs, then another and another, one to each kneecap. Convulsions of pain, incomprehensible, searing agony as a slow line of holes began to form behind each new round, stitching a line of bloody splotches from groin, through abdomen, left shoulder, right shoulder, then click.

"Hell, Sal, I'm out a' ammo. Oh well, I think you've got my point by now. Same mistake that hillbilly asshole you sent to punch my ticket made in Chicago. Musta' been trained by niggers. Turned around when I came down the stairwell and there he was. But just like you, he thought he could take advantage of surprise—jus' didn't count on the old man's quickness. Arrogant asshole—how you coulda thought you could beat me, with my gun in your face before you even started.

"Oh well. . .oh, and sorry about the president. Guess I killed the wrong nigger—look so much alike, and all. But boy, what a shot! Clean as a pin—like he was struck by lightning—and a second round for insurance, too. I was off and down the steps before they could even look around at me. Can't know for sure, but I bet with all that wind and people screaming and all it took "em a good ten minutes to figure out the direction of the shots. By then I'd already plugged that hillbilly, shucked my backup piece, and beat feet for the car. Oh—thanks for the Mercedes. Nice touch."

The end of the soliloquy was for no one's benefit in particular, as Sallie's open-mouthed, open-eyed stare demonstrated that his suffering, at least in this life, was finished. Lester bent over, picked up the dead man's handgun, rifled his pockets for extra ammunition, and stuck a handful of magnum rounds into his hip pocket. Ejecting the empty clip from his .45, he drove home a fresh magazine into the butt of the big pistol with the heel of his hand and turned to walk out of the foul-smelling tomb.

Stepping through the doorway into the main room, he was confused by what he saw, looking down in the direction of a sound he could not place. He was surprised to see the leather-bound handle of a Marine combat knife protruding from his chest, a dark forearm withdrawing from it at the same moment. At the same time, he felt a warm, wet trickle running down his back, from between his shoulder blades, and still unaccountably, his knees gave way. He pitched forward, hitting the floor on his left shoulder; even in the act of dying, the warrior tried to protect himself from falling on the object sticking out of him. The big automatic slid from his fingers and skidded away a foot, and he looked up into a dark, grim countenance above him.

"Bad enough you deprive me of killing that bloody bastard, Lester, now I find it was you tried to kill General Jackie. That's just too much. . .just too goddam much, Lester. And all that nigger talk in there, standing over poor ol' Sal. Don't get me wrong, Lester. I mighta let you alone if all you did was kill that little snake. . .I just couldn't forgive you tryin' to kill Jackie. Thought I was done killin'. . . maybe I still am. But you, you're just too bad, Lester. I mean, I know I'm a rotten asshole, but you—you're like Sallie there—in a class all your own. Too damn bad. See ya'." J.D. pulled the knife from the lifeless form, another open-mouthed, open-eyed face sightless in that place of death. Jamming both guns into his waistband, clips and loose rounds into pockets, he walked out the big door, wiping the big knife on his jeans. He thrust it back into the sheath on his belt.

* * * * *

Molly seemed to have appeared from nowhere, her long fingers finding the knots and pulsing spasms in the big man's neck and shoulders. When she worked her way up to his temples and the back of his head, it was as though her tenderness tipped over his last vestige of defense against utter disconsolation. The overwhelming sense of impending doom and collapse of what was effectively the entire existing world order, combined with the apparent eradication of large segments of the American population, seemed to break the man's last hint of defense. He wept. Quietly, from a place out of sight of the Oval Office, Jonathan Brooks closed the only door that had been ajar, and they were alone.

What stabbed the heart of the woman was the indescribable agony that her husband endured at that moment. An entire life spent in selfless, courageous, and even reckless defense of freedom and the dream of its perpetuation had come to this moment of defeat. And, as if the workings of some cruel and monstrous jokester, the decorated, oft wounded zealot warrior was thrust to the helm as the world's ship slipped deeper and deeper into oblivion. Head laid on arms, face into the desktop, the man wept. Sobs and heaves of grief, sorrow for millions, the massive shoulders shook. No longer could the pain be held in check.

Molly tried to lift him, her voice little more than a whisper in his ear, but the weight of the man was too great, his strength absent to lift his head to her. Tears pooled on the desktop. Molly continued to speak in his ear, to caress with a tender word, but the softness seemed only to tear away every fragment of restraint, torrents of sadness rushing from the great chest.

Minutes passed as the woman ministered to the man, first an arm around his shoulders, then hands to his neck and back, then kneeling beside him, her body and face snug against his side. Her heart beat heavy and slow against him. Still no sign of the great man's pride, his trademark battlefield-like counterattack resurgence. Then finally, a lessening, quieting, softening of the outpouring of grief. Tears now without sound. She spoke again, unaware until that moment that her own face was awash in hot, stinging salt. Her breath came at first in short gulps, but she held a course away from despair, willing her voice to speak, her chest to support her words with a steady flow of air against the impulse toward sobbing.

"My own heart is breaking, Jackie, you must know that it is, you all broken up like this. I been listening when I could, and Jonathan told me what happened today in New York, all before I came in and heard what you just said to the Israelis. Oh, Jackie, but I do feel it with you, you know I do darling, every stitch. Only I know what you can't know at this moment. . .that God will not forsake us, trusting as we do in Him. I know He will not do that, Jackie, I swear I know it down deep in my soul. His heart breaks with yours my love at what man has again done to destroy himself. But I am as sure as I can be that He will guide you, and help you to lead us through this awful valley of death; only He needs you to heed His counsel, and to stand tall as you always have.

"I have prayed this whole day, Jackie, from the first report of those awful events in New York until this very moment. I have prayed without ceasing, like Paul said to do, and I continue to do so, my darling, and I know He hears my prayer—not just for you, or for us, but for all who are in such terrible straits at this time. Please, Jackie, do not despair, please. Believe in Him, and in yourself. How many times has He snatched you harmless from the very jaws of death, my love? And for what purpose? To have you crushed beneath this present evil? I think not, my husband, *I know not.*"

The man was silent now, except for occasionally sniffing back his running nose and wiping his face on the sleeve of his shirt. Man heeded woman in those moments, mindful of the times in their lives together when, that one tone in her soft voice, she had guided him, chided him, exhorted and entreated him, each time on a course without error. A chill met his right side, aware that she had withdrawn from contact. Head lifted from forearms, he saw that she had walked over to the bookcase and was returning, the shiny black leather of an aged Bible in her hands.

"Look. I know it's typically nonsense to think you can just open this book and have your finger land on the perfect wisdom for the moment, but this is what I found this afternoon, right after I learned that Clyde had ordered the occupation forces to pull back in the city. I couldn't go and fight, and God knows I would've been in the way down here, so all I could do was worry, and pray, and worry some more. Then I picked up my own Bible, and this is what I saw—swear to God, this was the first phrase I saw when I opened it." She laid the old volume in front of her husband and, pointing to the lines with a long finger, she read from it.

"'*He who watches over Israel neither slumbers nor sleeps. . .*'

Now what did they teach us, ever since Sunday School, about the Jews and Israel, *huh?* Don't tell me you forgot—I'll call Matilda Mae Webb right now and tell her so, if you do! You know what I'm saying, Jackie, don't you? There is simply no way that the Good Lord is gonna let His Chosen People— whether they know and deserve it or not—be struck down, removed from that land, once they have gotten back there. For the enemies of the Jews to prevail would make a lie out of everything your mother taught you from this book, and you know better than that. The Jews *are* watched over by The One who never sleeps, and with help like that, they simply cannot be destroyed again. Not if the multiple prophecies in this book are true. Now you *have* to believe that, right? Of course. So all you have to do is help them, as I just heard you say you would, and leave the rest to Him. Period."

Her husband began to look at her, his face slowly turning toward her as she spoke. His face swollen, his nose still running furiously, her words bade him listen carefully.

"I know it's all so very complicated politically and every other way, but I am telling you plain and simple that if you believe in the content and architecture of this book, there is no way, devil be damned, that those people are going to succeed in destroying Israel." She stood straight, her own back knotting, shoulders burning knife-points into her neck. He looked at the passage she had pointed to, then looked up into her face again. His own countenance was swollen, wet, misshapen, unfocused. Back again to the page.

"But what of the cities here? Even if we avert—by some miracle, for sure—a nuclear exchange over there, Molly, we have lost our own cities, most particularly New York and now apparently L.A., to what must be a very well-armed and powerful force that is already in place, waiting for us with great advance information on our attempts to retake the place. . ."

She bent back into the desk again, rifling pages, stopping deep into the text this time. She spoke again, but this time more softly and with less firmness.

"Not so clear, but this is what I saw and, frankly, what I kept thinking all day. Unless we believe that that dark age is a reality, and there is no way, with all our resources, to avoid it, we simply must continue. Look— 'Come to me, all ye who labor and are heavy laden, and I will give you rest.' You were all talking about getting those starving people out of the way, but you can't see a way to spring them from the bad guys who have them confined. Maybe you should just ask them to come. Can't you broadcast to them, drop leaflets, get the word to them some way, just to get up and walk out? For crying out loud, Jackie, there can't be enough criminals—or enough bullets—in New York to shoot everybody!

"If you tell them you are waiting for them with food and clean water, medical attention and shelter from this awful heat, won't they be likely to just break ranks and move in a mass too big to stop? I mean, if I knew I was dead anyway, either from warlord's weapons or disease, why would I not?"

Webb sat up in his chair, spoke before she could go on, a big hand wiping his face.

"And if we had AWACs up, plus gun ships and Warthogs, we could hit 'em at once when they attempted to fire on those who flee—be like flushing the bastards out, turning the bait into ours, not theirs. Sounds crass, but they're all dead unless we do this, anyway. Still, there's all those surface-to-air pieces to think about, but they've gotta be pretty close-in. . . Babe, you've got my—this just might be a way—*c'mere,* Molly. . .just like always—the true brains of the operation." He stood and enveloped her slender frame in a huge hug, barking for Mac Reed over her shoulder. He kissed her over and over, his face still damp with the bath of sorrow so recently taken.

"Mac—get Clyde on the line at once. And tell him to have Dick Hambley on with us. They should have information available relative to methods of mass communications with noncombatants—everything from leaflet drops to megaphones—stuff that can fire them up and get 'm moving on short notice. Enough of this shit of feeding priceless men and expensive equipment to the booby trap brigade. HURRY UP."

* * * * *

A smog of a typically August variety lay on the hills that define Los Angeles in most directions. A light dew blanketed the unkempt grass of the golf course, mist hung in the trees and low spots, the sun just at the rim of the eastern horizon. Miguel Sanchez no longer had breath to utter prayer or epithet, so completely spent was he, body and soul. Worn sneakers strode at a slow run, mind nearly out of gear now except for the constant image of his hidden secret, the delicately clinging life, hidden under weeds at the edge of the expressway. Clad only in under shorts, he looked like some marathon runner who was lost from the true race course, long since lost in the delirium of fatigue, heedless of the pace or direction of his fellow runners.

Any remaining caution was discarded now; no effort made to keep to shadows or tree lines. Miguel ran right down the middle of the fairway, a direct line of sight between him and his meeting point with Raul stretching less than five hundred yards ahead of him. Then four hundred. Then three. He faltered, bronchial spasms piercing his lungs as if with burning spears, knees folding beneath the quivering weight of his small frame. He lay a moment, then struggled and grunted his way to his knees, a pitiful figure on all fours in the open, first light strafing his heaving flanks like cold steamy pointers for all to see. A final lunge and he was on his feet again.

The next collapse found him in the small enclosure of palm trees and low shrubs that surrounded the fourteenth tee. Rolling down and over onto his back, Miguel groaned and gasped, his mouth forming the sound of his cousin's name, but without success. Lying back, eyes into the slate sky, the first realization was that he was alone. After almost stopping altogether, his heart raced and he found the energy to sit up, even quickly. The voice found air, *"Raauull—dearest Jesus Christ in heaven, Raaauuull—oh God what have you—"* He ceased to breathe. Lungs flexed with the chest wall to no avail, as though banded about with steel, tightened to prohibit even slight inflation. The sensation of total asphyxiation, to tissues already so badly deprived of oxygen by the dampness of the morning and the extreme exertion, inflicted on a body already depleted by dehydration and hunger, led at once to black. A strong rough hand was clamped over his mouth and nose, suffocating the heaving body.

"Miguel, *Miguel—wake up, cousin—but make no sound— for the love of sweet Jesus, boy, keep still.* I am here, Miguel, wakeup. Wow, but you are spent, son. . .what. . .where the hell are your pants? Here, sit up and drink. . ."

Lifting him in the cradle of his arm, the Marine first splashed water from his canteen across the unconscious face, then poured a small amount into the slack-lipped mouth. Gurgling was followed at once by a wet cough, then retching, although the empty stomach could produce nothing but a spume of watery mist through the gush of air.

"Now be quiet, Miguel, I am here—what did you think, that I'd be standing by the blue tees, taking practice swings while you were putting out? For crissakes, boy, I was waiting where I always have, there in the bushes behind the ball washer. Now, what explains this mess you are in? You look like sweaty dogshit, boy, and you smell worse." Miguel could only manage a negative shake of the head from side to side, between long pulls on the tepid water of Raul's canteen.

Finally, the soldier took it away, gently admonishing him of the need for caution against making himself ill from too much at once.

"You must speak quickly, Miguel, I will have to leave momentarily. Tell me what's happened—and what has happened to you, Jesus, you're a wreck! When can we expect the Sons to—"

"*NO!! I tell you nothing—you get not a word from me, Raul—not a fucking word, until—.*" He coiled into a fetal posture, stabbed by cramps from the too-large quantity of water in the empty stomach. He gasped, retched, but did not vomit the liquid, his every sinew committed to keeping the precious stuff inside him. Raul looked at him as if observing a lunatic.

"What are you talking about, Miguel? What the hell do you mean, 'not a word,' anyway—you're not making any sense. What've they done to you, boy? Did they send you here—*are you being followed—?! Tell me what the fuck is going—*" Miguel shook his head again, realizing there was so much Raul did not know.

"No, I mean, no, they did not follow and do not know I am gone. OK, but you must hear me out and do as I say, or I cannot tell you what is next—*promise?*" The Marine looked without comprehension at his babbling cousin, at his watch, at the sky, and then in the direction of his evacuation route. He could, or at least his imagination thought he could, hear the faint *whup whup whup* of the chopper that was coming very soon to pluck him up.

"Ok, cousin, but hurry up. I don't relish squattin' in this free-fire zone forever, so talk fast. I'm listening." Miguel pulled up into a sitting position, his hand reflexively grasping the strong shoulder of his cousin. All the while the younger man was spinning from within, the pain in his chest and abdomen vying with the burning and throbbing in his legs and back. So recently had he been bound and gagged, so completely trussed, tortured. He took a breath and looked with every ounce of passion he could muster into the eyes of his comrade cousin, drawing a bead on the skepticism he could see in the Marine's eyes.

"I must have done a poor job of covering my trail, or maybe I just got crossways of Pancho's wacko side, who knows. . .but all at once, out of a crack in the sidewalk, he turned on me. And just like that, I'm tied up, drug off into a dark shithole of a holding cell in that cesspool they call headquarters. He had this big goon hit me in the head a few times, but used duct tape to tie me. Stupid asshole. Anyway, I'm out all day, wake up when it's getting dark. I heard what they were gonna do next, and I think I can piece it together enough for you to react in time, but you gotta help me first—that's what I meant a minute ago." The kid's eyes started to fog up, his breathing short and shallow. For a moment, they both thought he would pass out. Then the fire in his eyes grew ever more intense, and he moved closer to his cousin's face.

"I finally got the tape off sometime during the night, after listening to Pancho and some of his pals kill a man in the other room. The dead guy was apparently black—Pancho hates them so—and had a woman with him. They worked her over after the man was already dead and drug off, sounded to me like she was probably dead, too, but they left her right where she was, on the floor in the front room. When I finally got out there, she was out cold, bloody, burned with cigarettes, blood all over her face, between her legs, the whole Pancho thing, and—-I don't know why—I just couldn't leave her there. So I didn't. I picked her up and carried her out with me."

"*You what?! You mean you carried a girl over here—with you?? Jesus, Miuguel, you lost your mind? Where. . .I mean, you brought her. . .what have you—*"

"She tried to die on me over by the freeway, right after we got under it through the aqueduct. Don't know what it was, if I was carrying her too rough or if she's bleeding inside. . .don't know. But I got her breathing again, and covered up with some weeds an' the rest of my clothes. And cousin, I'm not telling you *shit* until we get her outta those weeds and outta this mess. Guess I just want *one* person saved. . .I watched so many die already—many at my brother's hand."

Raul thought for a moment. The kid had information crucial to the whole operation in East L.A., information that could make a huge difference in the loss of life, the expenditure of resources needed to pacify this vast, populous area. Without Miguel's help Raul knew they faced a protracted, deadly debate with some of the worst specimens of humanity anywhere. With his help, they might strike quickly and save many.

He thought about the girl. A nameless black girl, hurt, probably dying anyway. The idea of finding her, evacuating her, seemed cumbersome, completely outside his mission. From a military standpoint, all he could do was say no. Miguel would eventually help them anyway; he was just smitten by the idea that he could play hero for some little tramp. Then he shook his head. How far from humanity he had come. The young man before him had just performed an act of incredible heroism, had expended himself to the point of complete collapse, even death, to save a life. Surely they had time to finish the job.

"All right, Miguel. Here's the deal. I can't leave you here, anyway. No clothes, no food, no water. Gotta 'vac you outta here, so we'll just swing over where you stashed this kid, take her with us. OK?" Tears welled up in Miguel's eyes, just as another spasm hit his midsection. He rolled over on his side and vomited until all the water he'd drunk was gone, spilled out on the weedy grass of the tee surface. Raul knew in that moment the kid was finished helping as an inside informant. Without I.V. fluids he'd be dead in a few hours. The only answer was to get him—and his patient—out and into some competent medical hands. Standing up over the convulsing form, he keyed the mic on his radio and called the chopper in to pick them up. The pilot was an old friend, so prevailing on him to make a quick additional stop on the way out would be no problem. Raul said a short prayer that the second stop would not be to pick up another dead body.

15.

The time difference between Baghdad and Washington is ten hours—the wrong way. By the time the sun hits the White House, it's late afternoon in the Middle East, 4 o'clock p.m. The timer on the missile moved soundlessly toward a midnight launch, its target a mere five hundred miles away to the southwest, total time of flight less than fifteen minutes, most of that would be supersonic. The warhead would finally arm only two minutes before detonation, which would occur at an elevation of three hundred feet above ground level. The short arc of its flight path made telemetry easy to plot, made interception exponentially more difficult. The combination of low trajectory, supersonic speed, and short distance produced a physical and mechanical nightmare of huge proportions for any technology intent on stopping it before it exploded—and vaporized Tel Aviv.

At such speed, the warhead would arm only after already penetrating Israeli airspace, a factor designed in specifically by Weidenolf to prevent widespread radiation damage if anything went wrong with the operation before the missile achieved target proximity. He was extremely cautious to ensure that neither Saudi Arabia nor Jordan would suffer any radiation exposure if there was a problem of any kind. This meant getting to within one hundred miles of ground zero, at a maximum altitude of no more than twenty thousand feet, at a speed of at least mach three. At that combination of values, interception by any known weapons system was nearly impossible, even by means of a Patriot missile. While Patriot could do it if everything worked properly from its perspective, all known units were set too close to the target area to hit the incoming rocket before the warhead was armed. So at worst the nuclear reaction would just take out a huge chunk of Northern Israel *before* it hit Tel Aviv—there was plenty of power to take care of both.

At the other end, although they did have the advantage of surprise from two perspectives, the problems of hitting the guided missile at just the right time were immense. Of course, there was the leg up of having a weapons system the enemy did not know was there. Arrow was brand new—not even finished, really—and it could hit the streaking missile well before it penetrated Israeli airspace. Also, it sat in a location from that no one knew it might come, north and east of the target area enough to permit interception at a place unlikely to result in significant harm. In fact, the hit could be expected to occur over the huge unpopulated desert of northern Saudi Arabia, or maybe Jordan.

But those who worked frantically to train Arrow on its expected target knew they had to hit the warhead, not only before it was fully armed and capable of full-scale nuclear reaction, but also at an altitude sufficient to ensure that all parties would see the collision. The world had to recognize it for what it was, and not mistaking it for a nuke fired by the Israelis that simply went off too soon. The satellite technology, in addition to the capabilities of the Saudis and the Jordanians to observe with great accuracy the events that occurred in their airspace at all times, made it crucial that the impact occur in such a way that there could be no misinterpretation of what had happened.

Only by permitting the missile to gain altitude—and therefore speed—and to reach a place where the impact would be readily observable, could Arrow show the world that it had worked and that it had killed a nuclear device that came from Iraq. And all this had to happen over uninhabited space where fallout from the warhead components would have little or no impact on people below. Israel simply could not permit any of its neighbors, with whom it continued to enjoy a peace that was tenuous at best anyway, to suffer nuclear fallout as the result of this interception. And one thing was sure: Saddam would not bother to try all this without a warhead of sufficient size to secure the utmost devastation, and therefore, advantage.

The clock inside the missile moved on silently, digitally chronicling the passage of each vanishing second that remained in its short life span. Initiation sequence began at six o'clock p.m. Baghdad time, just an hour after the commencement of Day Two of the bloody efforts of American troops to retake the city of New York. With a day of horrible losses and indescribable frustration behind them, military forces cautiously probed around the edges of what they had now learned was a city turned into one huge booby trap. A more profoundly successful diversion could simply not be imagined by the forces of Islam, intent on destroying Israel without further delay or the wasting of any more empty words with the likes of the United Nations or the scholars of appeasement in the Israeli Knesset.

But Jackie Webb did exactly what Benjamin Netanyahu asked of him; he hooked him up with all the right people at NASA and CIA, working feverishly with the architects and technicians who built and operated Arrow. They fed vast amounts of information, codes, contingencies, and optional reactions to each other, as the hours silently clicked past within the missile hidden in Nebuchadnezzar's Palace in Babylon. Technical problems abounded at first, but within four hours, or by 4 a.m. New York time—four hours before the initiation sequence began in the missile—the Israelis and NASA were speaking the same language and had a lock on all the relevant potential launch sites and target locations and a solid satellite fix on Arrow.

All that remained was to see if the world's only real long-range, high-speed, high-altitude, antiballistic missile system would do what it was designed to do. They planned a number of computer simulations to be programmed and carried out over the following days, each intended to better refine the accuracy of the system when used in conjunction with satellite tracking and telemetry that was different from what the Arrow had been designed to use. None of the men and women who bent over screens and consoles producing these tests could know that before the first test could be run the real thing would rise out of a cleft in the banks of the Euphrates River. It would be aimed at Israel and intent on removing two million Jews from the face of the earth.

* * * * *

"Now listen, pal, I've about had it with your tricks. Been at this game for four hours now, and you been a pain in my ass the whole way. You're s'posed ta be using those mystical equine powers of observation the Indians talk about to find your beloved master—as if you *had* a master. Even Josh spends 'bout half his time contemplating putting you in an Alpo can. More like an arrangement with a crazy man than anything else. . .I mean *you,* not him. Well, maybe I *do* mean him—hell, description fits you both! *Now,* what are you—"

Carl sawed the reins on the old gelding, a buckskin blind in one eye and equipped with a unique disposition that was part racehorse, part cow pony, and part ornery old man. At 26 years old, he had seen better days, King George was a tiny bit sway-backed, but still athlete through and through. And although it seemed to be a love/hate kind of arrangement, Joshua Landry still preferred the old nag to any of the younger stock available to him, although he was the only one who felt that way. Carl often declared his preference for walking barefoot over hot coals to riding the cantankerous mount "any further than to the front end of a high-powered rifle."

After hours of trying every trick in the book to make friends, the elder Landry was at his wits' end; his intention had been to use the neurotic bond between the horse and his brother as a force that would turn the old buckskin into a bloodhound. No luck. When he tried to let him have his head and just wander where his nose took him, he stopped. Eventually, after minutes of maddening motionlessness, King would commence grazing fastidiously on the sweet grass shoots that peeked from the shade of trees in the rough woods. All the while, Carl's blood pressure continued to rise, anxiety over Josh's location and condition driving him to the point of near hysteria—except that Carl didn't get hysterical. It just wasn't in him.

But he did get mad. Over and over, a string of uncustomarily profane epithets spat from his dry mouth, and he'd jerk the old head away from its absentminded nibbling. Again, with the old horse apparently willing to stand in the shade the rest of the day, the ritual was repeated "You miserable old sonofabitch, I could'a covered more ground on my hands and knees, *with my eyes shut!!* Now get your head up and *help me find Josh—you piece of cheese—*" Then, mostly to himself, grumbling to no one, "Can't understand how a supposedly intelligent animal like this one can be so far out to lunch. Hell, every other time I sit down on him, he tries to kill us both. . .now, with a life—*Josh's life*—at stake, he stands like he's ready for the glue factory. You'd think he was married to this bug-infested jungle or some. . ."

He stopped without finishing the word. . Jerking his wide hat from his head, Carl quit breathing, turned slowly in the saddle, ears ringing with the presence of summer in the woods. Eyes strained into every crack and shadow. "Landry, you *idiot*—that's got to be it. The old horse is standing still in

548

here, and there has to be a reason. He's gotta be here, *close even,* and I'm not—" Looking back from where they had crested a low ridge that forked into two deepening ravines like the shafts of a huge divining rod, he tried to picture the route from the burned-out van to this point. It was a rough, sticker-filled, and overgrown mess of typical midwestern woods in late summer. Carl dismounted, pulled the radio from a saddlebag. Time for some help. Standing down beside the horse's head and neck, he dropped the reins in a ground tie position and keyed the mic.

"Jake, this is Carl—you copy—?" Immediately, as if he was holding the radio in anticipation of the call, the response came.

"Yeah, Jake here—you got anything Doc?"

"I don't—I mean I think. . .can't say. It's just that this horse has taken up residence in this thicket, and he just won't leave. Can't say it means anything, it's just that it's the only time in the twenty years I've been trying to ride the old fart that he has failed to take off like the devil with feet. Gotta mean something. I'm pretty far from you, maybe a mile or more, and that seems awful far for Josh to have traveled, hurt as bad as he must be. But still, it's so thick up over that ridge and down into this canyon fork, if he's here and if he unconscious maybe I just can't find him. And one thing is sure—if he *is* here, King can't get to him in this mess of stickers and grapevine."

"Where are you and how do we get to you quickest?"

"Go straight back and over that ridge behind where we found all the blood. When you crest the hill, bear right down and through the creek bottom—it's dry now, but overgrown to beat hell. After you cross it, bear back to your left again into an open space that's scattered with big rocks, and climb straight up 'til you hit the top. Wide open there, nothing but gravel and sandy soil. Not even many weeds. Back right again and across the head of that fork, then—"

Carl snapped around, his eyes flooded with tears, blood instantly running from both nostrils, the pain in his back intense. He was on the ground. Through the veil of blurred vision, the struggle was to make some sense of why he was on the ground and what had put him there. Coordination was suspended by a blow to the face that knocked him nearly unconscious, and the pain in his nose and backside where he hit the ground competed with every effort at logic. Above him was the fuzzy form of King George, his head pointing in the direction beyond where Carl was lying.

"Carl—*Carl*—*do you copy*—*Doc, are you still there?!*"

Landry fumbled for the radio, at the same time his vision cleared enough to see that King was glaring intently in the direction of the bottom of one fork of the big ravine behind them. Ears perked, nostrils flared, he blew hard and began to step over Carl. Nothing will clear a foggy head faster than the sight of an eleven hundred-pound horse stepping squarely into one's crotch. Carl rolled down and away from King's feet, at the same time entangling himself in the reins that dragged behind. He grabbed them and stumbled to his feet, at that moment understanding that the horse had taken him off his feet with a blow to the face when the horse's head jerked up and around in response to some stimulus coming from down in the gully.

Anticipation overtook pain as the horse began dragging Carl into the thicket. "Jake, think the old nag's onto something—get your ass up here on the double." He put the radio in his hip pocket and followed the horse, wiping the blood and tears from his face and chin as he stumbled after the ever-quickening pace. The men at the other end of the trail broke into a run as they crested the first ridge, Jessica Landry right in the middle of the pack. Faith Jackson matched them stride for stride. It was at least a mile to where Carl was located, through rough, thick woods.

Sweat-streaked faces fought cobwebs and low hanging branches, hands and arms bled from the tines of multi-flora rose, burned from the tiny penetrating spines of sting weed. The air was punctuated constantly by the curses of those who brushed against the big needle-like thorns of the hawthorn and honey locust trees; mosquitoes, wasps, spiders sought every patch of exposed skin. Likewise, Carl fought rocks, grapevine, and deadfall tree trunks encased in tall weeds and cobweb, at times looming in King's intended path like great tentacled beasts draped in veils of cotton. Carl ran directly into the wide sweaty expanse of the horse's ass when the horse stopped abruptly, his head again held up, ears forward.

"God*dammit, George*, but can't you do *anything* the easy way. You need some brake lights. A little warning would be-" Peering down into the ravine in the direction the horse was looking, Carl stopped breathing, knees weak, pulse shallow and short. *Oh dear God, my holy God, don't let this be. . .Oh my dearest. . .* "Jake, got 'im—north split of that double ravine that comes off the top of the second ridge—looks bad, Jake, Jesus lord my God it does. . ." The mic went dead, the radio back in the hip pocket. Tying the horse to a low-hanging branch by his reins, Carl made his way the last twenty yards into a cut in the rocks that was filled with the misshapen form of a blood-covered body. The one visible sneaker identified it as Josh.

Carl fought nausea for only a moment, the physician taking over almost to the exclusion of the familial reality at once. Mumbling to the obviously absent medical emergency staff, "Pulse weak, slow—b.p. must be falling. . .pupils non-reactive, but it's dark in here, still. . .must be deep in shock. Let's see. . .*oh*—open fracture, left fibula, dislocation, left ankle. Shit, ankle's been broken more times than I can count. . .abdomen soft, non-distended. . .no apparent internal bleeding there, so—*wups*—*oww!* Ugly laceration behind left ear, extending laterally back to occipital region, don't know how he kept from fracturing his skull. Sure wish we had x-ray. All this blood, where's it—*oh.*"

A huge laceration wrapped around the side of Josh's head and ended in his cheek. Carl pored over the wounds, constantly rechecking vital signs, listening to the slow, fading heartbeat, moving to begin first aid. Minutes passed as he worked carefully, intently, until the crashing sounds of five people breaking through the thicket pulled him from his trance.

"Whatcha got, Doc, good grief, he's *covered*—*where the hell did all that come from?*" Faith knelt beside him, automatically testing pulse and examining pupils for herself as she spoke. Then they turned him slightly to his right, exposing the massive laceration that ran from up in his hairline, down all the way past his cheekbone and into the soft flesh of his cheek. "There—bled like a stuck pig, that one did."

"That's not the worst of it, Faith, look here—leg's broken and compound. Can't say that is worse, the fracture, or the blood loss from that big bone sticking through the skin. Or the potential for infection, even into the bone itself. He needs fluids, he *really* needs blood. Of that we have none. Great. OK, let's get him immobilized and out of here right now." At that moment, Jess came stumbling and falling into the midst of the already-close quarters, chest heaving, eyes uncomprehending of the carnage that was her husband. She fell on him without words, wiping blood with her hands and hair, kissing his face, feeling for the sensation of breath from his nostrils. She never spoke, just looked up at Carl for the answer.

"Don't know, sis. Depends on what's wrong inside and on how much blood he's lost, not to mention the potential for head problems. Big laceration in back there, suggests pretty significant trauma. Only thing is, if he had a closed head injury, it's very unlikely he could have crawled this far. Skull fracture is immediate lights out. Let's just get him out of this mess and back to the house. *Jake*—the closest location to get to the truck is really right back there where the fire was. Cut me some poles for a travois and we'll make us a quick stretcher. Boys, get me two—make that *four* flat sticks, two feet long, very straight. And I need everybody's belt."

"Carl, give me that little bottle of alcohol in your shirt pocket. Let's at least try to kill the bugs we can on those wounds while he's too far out to care about the pain it will cause. And here—let's make a tourniquet for that leg with my belt, right now." They worked with great efficiency, given the nature of the injuries and the miserable conditions. Splints held in place with a combination of lead rope, leather reins, and men's belts were put in place after a partial reduction of the fractured leg, then they lifted him out of the ravine on a stretcher fabricated from strong hickory branches and grapevine. The men sweat great rivers, soaking into already wet clothes, the rest dripping off noses and chins, running into belt lines and down into socks and boots.

Carrying one who is so badly hurt through rough terrain is never easy, harder yet when the injuries are unknown in degree, worst of all when the load is beloved family and friend, leader and comrade. Anxiety raised the temperature to fever pitch; twice one of the men carrying the stretcher collapsed, sides heaving, vision vanishing to white. Another would step instantly to catch the corner before the motionless gray body could tip into the ground, while one of the others attended the newest casualty. It took almost an hour to get back to the carnage scene and the waiting truck.

In the bed of the old machine, Jess sat at Josh's head, while Carl and Faith hovered over him, jostling against the side walls as they checked tourniquets, adjusted bandages, communicated in intense, technical fragments about what they would do when they got him home. Of course, home would be Carl's, as that was the place where they had the most to work with, although that was little enough. No antibiotic left, very little antiseptic beyond a few small bottles of alcohol and hydrogen peroxide and, worst of all, no blood. Of course, there was no blood; there was no way to preserve it if they had it. They talked of transfusion, knowing they had two donors—Carl and Luke—who shared blood type with Josh. Collecting units for transfer was difficult if not impossible, as they had none of the really big needles and apparatus typically used for that purpose in hospitals.

Vital signs weakened as they neared the house, and the looks passing between the doctors told Jess there was only waning hope of saving him. Her eyes closed tightly in earnest, imploring prayers, already conveying entreaties for miracles. Which was what would be required if her husband was to survive.

* * * * *

When Jackson Daniels slipped out of the cesspool at the secure entrance to the SPA, his intention was to make his way back to TP's and spend the remainder of his foreseeable future tending to the flock of sick and dying that Enchante Weaver now housed. The idea, mostly fantasy, that his love might be nursed back to health over time occupied center stage, but he knew he might be called upon to use his guerilla skills to defend them, if and when violence rose up to terrorize them again. That was fine with him, although he had no desire ever again to raise a hand in anger or to spill blood.

His psyche wrestled with the indescribable scene from that he had just escaped, as he blinked back the vision of headless corpses, blood-spattered floors and ceilings from the brutal shots fired into the dying body of Willie Calvert, and the deadly surprise on the gaping, empty face of Lester Monroe. As if to signal the end of his career of killing in one moment frozen in time and mind, the stark tableau filling his mind spoke and described what words could not about thirty years of violent death. So distracted was he as he rose out of the alley and into the empty street that he did not at first comprehend the alarm his senses were sounding.

Only a few seconds before the first armored vehicle rumbled into view at the head of the block, his blood-soaked reverie was interrupted by the realization that the street was shaking beneath his feet. Daniels expelled the horrors from his mind in favor of more immediate problems, darting into the doorway of the very building that housed Sallie's shop of horrors—and his grave as well. Two APCs were followed by a tank, which was followed by a platoon-sized unit of soldiers on foot. They moved past the doorway, their movements furtive, cautious, their spacing adequate to guard against explosion that might take too many at once. The guerilla fighter summoned old skills, his body pressed against the narrow sliver of darkness in the entry to his sanctuary, while a practiced eye counted men and machines, calculating the size of the force that now occupied his avenue of escape.

He knew they had not been in the area when he arrived with the others, so his immediate deduction was that the Vanguard was safely beyond detection for now. Although retaining no affection for them and what they were about to do to the city, he also held no love for these invading forces. And it occurred to him that they could not know what was about to greet them in the streets ahead, come dawn.

J.D. was just coming to the quick judgment that he needed to slip back through the building to exit the other side when a thundering explosion rocked the old tenement around him. Men and equipment tumbled like stick figures, mostly crashing to the pavement. The lead APCs could be heard accelerating on down the street, then revving up as they turned to respond to the huge noise. Shards of brick and glass rained down on the street, although—and this thought immediately struck the terrorist as odd—no walls collapsed and no one appeared to have been injured badly by the blast. Another observation piled in on top of the last, when he determined that the explosion had been high up on the building, not down at street level as one would expect with booby traps or mines, set for antipersonnel purposes.

Book IV – The Great Offensives

Soldiers shouted and scurried to their feet, the first up at once seeking any shelter, searching the walls for enemies, for sources of the explosion, or for small arms fire to strafe them behind the first blast. Then a small clot of men, those who had been in the middle of the street when the concussion occurred, seemed to react to unseen stimuli, jerking heads and torsos first left, then right, some spinning almost out of control, marionettes on fine invisible strings. Helmets were ripped from heads, hands grasped chests and throats, knees buckled. Those who ran to their aid instantly took up the same ballet, many losing leg strength at once and tumbling into the stricken comrades, bodies bowling over convulsing bodies, all landing in heaps of retching, vomiting humanity.

"*GAS—GAS—GAS—MASK UP—MASK UP—GAS—GAS—!!!*" The traditional cry of alert that a chemical was released could be heard up and down the street, but only briefly, as the acrid smell of the small C4 charges mixed with the sweet scent and syrupy feel of the deadly nerve agent. Men breathed the vapors created by the atomization of the chemical as it was dispersed by the small but powerful explosions from the face of the building. Inhalation produced immediate results, and the entire force, consisting of one hundred ten men on that street and the intersecting route covered by the canisters placed on the adjoining side of the building, was down in a matter of seconds.

Daniels could not understand why there would be such a release of chemical, but his every instinct told him what it was—and that he had to get away. The sticky poison did not drift into the entryway, instead falling in an invisible film on every exposed surface and object in the street. But the deadly vapors, swirling around on the turbulence created by the blasts and all the reaction of people and vehicles on the ground, were more pervasive in their immediate penetration. Even as he moved to sprint down the long tenement hallway, silent dust found the sensitive membranes inside his nose and mouth, the grip of death clasping itself around his now-constricted throat and chest.

He fell to the filthy floor, fingers spastic in their quest to free his windpipe from the clutches of the lethal choking that wracked his diaphragm. The last image his eyes saw before losing consciousness was that of a dozen big rats, lying on the floor around his face, each twitching, flopping like puppets, their squeaking choked off at the same time Jackson Daniels sought to suck his last breath through clenched teeth and frozen chest wall.

The Fact Sheet on Exposure Limits for Sarin (GB), July 1997, identifying Department of The Army Field Manual #3-9 as its source, advises, in matter-of-fact style, that "Death usually results within 15 minutes after absorption of a fatal dose." The amount of Sarin present in the air and on exposed surfaces on that dark street in the South Bronx, August 26, 1997, was several thousand times that that the Army describes as a "minimum lethal dose." And not only did everyone who was present die, the first back up troops to arrive, driving their Hummers through both streets, spun additional clouds of the sticky death into the air, resulting in thirteen additional immediate casualties and the incapacitation of twenty-nine more. When reinforcements arrived in proper attire, employing appropriate precautions and moving quietly through the litter of dead men, they began a cleanup process that took three days to accomplish.

Every corpse, every vehicle, weapon, boot, helmet, radio, and every square inch of every exposed surface bore sufficient lethal residue to kill any person who permitted it to touch exposed skin. What they could not know at that moment was that the man who had orchestrated the whole huge ambush, including all the carnage they would endure as the night and morning melded together, as well as this awful chemical surprise, lay dead within a few yards of his final expression of hatred for all living things. Indeed the devil was at play, and Salim Abdul Alakmah had been his most faithful and zealous disciple.

* * * * *

"All right, people, show me again where Intelligence says the biggest concentrations of noncombatants are located, both in Jersey and over in New York. Give me numbers and what we know about each place." Clyde Keithley stood over a huge, detailed map of the area, spread on top of the conference table in their war room at the Pentagon. Troop locations and unit designations were already marked with little banners that stuck out from their positions, along with a big chart mounted on an easel at the end of the table. It was correlated with the insignia on the map, telling strengths and equipment for each place. An Army major grabbed a long pointer and began to move through the map for his commander.

"These red circles—there are twenty-nine of them—represent what we believe to be the most significant populations left in the City. They are identified by number and listed here on this legend, indicating what Intelligence has told us is their approximate population in each case. The ones also marked with a green circle are already in the process of evacuation, not believed to be presently controlled by hostile elements. There are eleven of them, out of the total of twenty-nine. Our only problem with them is their huge population numbers and the fact that they are so sick and weak as to be very difficult to move. The vast majority are only marginally ambulatory and so weak that we have not been able to get them to walk very far."

Keithley moved around the table, looked at the charts, then back to the maps again. "OK. That's got to end. Instead of moving them out to these already overpopulated centers, how about we start going the other way. If armed resistance is low in any area, we go to the people, not the other way around. I know the disease problems are awful, but the medics and our burial people will just have to move quickly to establish sites that can serve as collection points for people—both dead and alive—and the supplies they need." Colonel Seth Wallitch, a career soldier with a quick manner and the ability to assimilate things at once, responded with a nod and additional ideas.

"Right, General, and we can use these facilities here, the ones marked with black circles, as a base for each of them. They are high school gyms, football fields that we can cover with big tents, and a few are convention-type buildings, or at least convocation structures as big as the gymnasiums. With generators and fans to produce some ventilation, we can work with the people day and night, deliver some food and water to larger crowds and even some medical help at once. But you're right, sir—the bodies gotta go. Everywhere you have corpses, you got more sickness instantly."

"Exactly. So let's move on that one. Seth, I want you to stay here with me while we figure out what to do with these other places, so get somebody in gear right now, moving into those areas we think are safe—do it now." Wallitch turned to his left, looking back at Sergeant Major Emily Conover, a stout, square woman dressed in BDUs and displaying immediate command of what was required.

"Done. I'll have the orders drafted as soon as possible. Shouldn't take more than an hour to figure out the personnel end of it and make assignments by unit; the routing and outfitting will take a bit more time. But we'll have them moving on every location you've just highlighted before dark." She moved without a sound out of the room and into the hallway, the door closing behind her.

"Now for the fun part." Wallitch turned back to the big table, his gaze searching out the remaining large concentrations of civilians. He resumed without looking up, Keithley simultaneously following the pointer and glancing up at the charts. He needed to know, and to memorize at once, the situation at each of these places, a total of eighteen locations where large numbers of people were congregated and probably held hostage by one or more armed forces.

"The rest of these red circles identify areas occupied by several thousand noncombatants each, exact numbers unknown to us. These—*here, here, here,* and over *here,* in Newark, were all places where we encountered heavy armed resistance yesterday, and all of them have been identified to us as extremely dangerous locations.

"All through lower Manhattan, clear up into Yonkers and here, over into Brooklyn, the Bronx, and Queens, we caught total hell yesterday. Lost tanks, APCs, Hummers, choppers, and at least three hundred men. Like one huge trick bag, with preset bombs and mines, booby traps and some kind of obviously well-conceived plan for mobile small arms fire that just *wasted* exposed personnel in great numbers. Worst mess I've ever seen, sir, and I survived Tet, 1968." There was no bravado in his voice or his delivery. It was as though he was reading the weather report to his commanding officer. But the effect was powerful.

"So now what, Seth? Not only do they have fire superiority and an apparently unending supply of preset devices, they have all these miserable people as buffers to *any* effort by us to go at them with big stuff. This is where the President wants to try to use an information flood to mobilize them. But I'm afraid they will be too sick, weak, or scared to test the resolve of their captors, who have already demonstrated incredible appetites for killing."

"I know, General, I know. I've been thinking about that idea ever since we got your call last night. The old man has more of a solution there than you might at first see. Look, sure there are a lot of bad guys in there, and obviously they're not all just local punks with big guns. It's pretty clear we were set up to take the big hits yesterday, and reports identify the vast majority of those preset charges as having been very professionally constructed and set. More, they were very big. Some were ammonium nitrate/fuel oil type devices, but most were C4 and other high explosive stuff, small, but very powerful. Again, very professional."

Keithley grunted like he'd been hit in the groin. "Terrorists—well trained and equipped—is what you are saying, and I agree. Problem is, we don't know how many there are and how complete a job they've done littering the whole town with more deadly surprises for us. Can't just keep blowing up tanks until we use up all their tricks, now can we?"

"No sir, but what I meant to say—if we can get a majority of those noncombatants out of there, we can start bombing the place with a vengeance, and their numbers *have* to be finite. I personally think, from what I heard from the troops last night and what I saw yesterday, that the pros involved in this thing are not so many in number—they're just very good, and very well equipped. If we could orchestrate a mass exodus of civilians—get them pouring out every major artery that we can identify—there's no way the bad boys could have enough numbers to stop them. They'll try, and they may kill a bunch in the process, but like the man said last night, they'll die for sure if they stay put. The question is, how do we get to them, *quickly,* and convince them to start moving?"

Keithley shook his head. "I understand, Major, I understand. . ."

16.

Pancho Sanchez sat on the edge of an old table in the front of headquarters, a waif-like and very young black woman seated on an empty orange crate at his knee, her slender hands stroking the inside of his thigh, her eyes searching his face and body for signs of his ever-changing mood. Behind and to the side of him were a phalanx of swarthy young men, each bristling with weapons, their shoulders and arms draped with bandoleers of ammunition for the variety of guns they carried. The momentary tableau looked more like a scene from a Che Guevera movie than a summit conference with the enemy, but the assembled company was all business.

"Look, *Pancho,* we all know you got control in East L.A. and plenty of help back in Watts. No problem. But you got *shit* for dealing with heavy stuff—*comprendes amigo?*" The huge biker made no effort to conceal his contempt for his newfound ally. Fact was, even with all their fancy big weapons, they had a real shortage of manpower to carry off any attempt at control over a large tract of the city. And one thing the greasy Mexicans had was people, lots of them. Fatmouth spat his words like venom, his confidence in the armament he could deliver apparent at once. Pancho slid forward, off the edge of the table, and stood; his movement directly toward the bigger man, produced a quick tightening of the space, and each man on either side of the equation moved forward to take positions behind their respective leaders.

"I thought we were finished with the bullshit sales pitch, my friend—or did you feel the need to insult us again before offering something of more value than your usual empty talk? Do we move ahead, or do you continue to spray your ignorance until we kill you and dump your fat ass in the canal?" More rustling, a dozen young men moving closer together in the small, hot space, mumbling in two languages to each other and to the opposition. For what seemed like five minutes—it was really only a few seconds—no one spoke; eyes remained riveted, torsos tense, fingers nervously stroking weapons, safeties. The young woman looked from Pancho to his men, then into the gross features of Fatmouth, then back. Finally a swollen, crooked smile crossed the biker's face, and he spoke.

"Hey, *Pancho,* just fuckin' with ya' a little, OK? No big deal. Boys, lighten up a minute. Smoke 'em if ya' got 'em. . .sit back. . .visit with our friends a minute. My pal and I need to talk." He stepped forward a short step, then moved slowly toward the back room, where Miguel had been captive a few hours before. The smile broadened in an effort at conciliation, and he moved to invite the smaller man in.

"Step into my office, amigo. . .let's get done with this talk and get to work, whatcha say?" Bigger smile still, grand gesture to usher Sanchez into the back. Stepping in ahead of the biker, Pancho abruptly spun half way around, his hand firmly stopping the door from closing between them and the front room.

"Let's leave it open, Mouth, shall we—might get stuffy if we close it." Their eyes met again, but only for a moment, before the huge head began wagging up and down in acquiescence, the smile bigger and more ridiculous than ever. They moved to the back of the little space, both taking seats. Pancho sat on another orange crate while Fatmouth dumped the trash from an old aluminum chair that lay tipped on its side in the corner. Now opposite each other, pretenses dissolved quickly, and the talk proceeded in earnest. A huge finger began pointing out the locations on a wrinkled map where arms and ammunition were currently located, while Pancho listened and watched intently, nodding appropriately.

"We got good storage and a straight line into Bell Gardens from back up here in Huntington Park. There's twenty 4.2-inch mortars, six ninety mill recoilless rifles, and thirty a' those little disposable anti- tank things. Take out a chopper in a heartbeat if they're close. Plenty of ammo for all of 'em, and oh—almost forgot—the fifty caliber is fixed and mounted in the bed of a pickup. Got three thousand rounds for it, too." Pancho hid his excitement at having such power at his command, focusing his attention on the proper placement to achieve the best result.

The young Mexican began to identify the areas of note in his domain. "Our people have control of a large population here, in Southgate, as well as here, in Bell Gardens. They're pretty quiet now, still have water, and we stole a little food for 'em a week ago—they're so starved they don't argue with *nobody.* Once we have the weapons in place, both here and back in Watts and up in Huntington Park where you already have control, every attempt at infiltration gets a surprise welcome. We just have to keep the weapons moving and hide them inside the areas where the people stay."

Fatmouth nodded, the hostility between them temporarily lost in the excitement of the coming battle.

"Right. That's why it's so nice havin' all these old soldiers in my gang, Pancho. They learned all about guerilla tactics— *the hard way.* We move in tonight, set up where you say, get concealed and ready to go. Then we need for you to send us some men to do the same thing back in Watts and HP. We figure if they get the shit knocked out of the Army right off the bat, and if they can't hit back because of the number of people in the way, maybe we get control and they make a deal for the hostages. Gotta believe they want those people outta here bad." Pancho instantly warmed to the intended result, forcing the military to talk over that great huge human chess board.

"Trick will be, once we're in place and hitting them hard, to press the advantage and make 'em talk to us. Figure we just have to wait and play that one by ear." Soon the conversation wound down and they stood. The leader of the Sons of Silence, redneck and all, stuck his huge paw out in a unique gesture; Pancho took it, shook it quickly, then turned to leave.

"One thing, amigo—what happened to your prisoner—the one who was in here last night? Did he die, or did he escape?"

Pancho jerked slightly, as if struck from behind. A smile forced its way to his face as he spoke.

"Not a problem, Mouth, just my little brother, needed a bit of rest from his quest of young poontang. The boy has pussy in more places than you have guns! Just thought he should stay home for a while, you know?" The smile seemed less forced now, enough so that the gorilla seemed satisfied with the answer. No one needed to know of the repercussions already felt over his escape, or the efforts to retrieve him from his early morning sojourn with the injured girl.

"Let's move, Pancho. We can begin as soon as it's dark tonight, whenever your people think it's safe. The weapons should be here and ready to go before first light."

"I agree. We've had very little fly-over problem in the last few nights, but you must pick your routes well and have plenty of places to hide along the way. We've already talked that through. Start when our messenger reaches you—

562

probably after ten o'clock. As soon as the weapons get here, we'll send one hundred men back to you for placement. Agreed?" The big man smiled again, stepped into the front of the room, and motioned for his entourage to follow him out.

Their departure was followed by the rumble of a dozen motorcycles, and they were gone. Pancho always marveled at their continued stash of gasoline for those hogs they rode, but the fact that they had it at a time when he could find so little only served to convince him all the more that he needed their help. He could not know what would really happen next, but his thirst for power and turf drove him to near hyperventilation as he considered the possibilities. Tomorrow he would beat the Army. Tomorrow he would control it all.

17.

It was Thursday, August 27, 1997, ten o'clock a.m. in Washington and New York, nine in Richland, Iowa, seven a.m. in Los Angeles, and eight p.m. in Babylon. Hot in all those places, a cosmic meter of impending disaster measuring tension around the globe would have exploded trying to calculate the enormity of independent forces and conflicts at that point congealing into reality. And all, though remote to each other, were on disparate courses into cataclysm, that would alter the course of history for all time.

The combined forces of the Eastern Offensive began day two of their efforts to retake New York, trying to avoid the catastrophe of the previous day. In L.A., military intelligence pieced together data—rumors, speculation—from informants, aerial photography, and reports from Delta Force insurgents who had infiltrated the most volatile areas in the huge city. The president sat—or paced—with the Chairman of the Joint Chiefs of Staff, studying maps, listening intently to reports from the various field personnel engaged in operations on both coasts, while one ear remained attuned to the activities at NASA in Houston.

Spy satellites and high-altitude reconnaissance aircraft fed information to a special unit that was connected by secure line to a remote missile outpost in northern Israel, where an unproven device called Arrow sat poised for firing to the northeast, its mission the interception and destruction of a nuclear bomb. No one could know that the missile carrying that bomb was set to launch in exactly four hours. And the preparations for detecting and intercepting it, although completed, had not been tested, simulations had not been run, and nobody in the whole operation knew whether they could react successfully.

Jackie Webb straightened his long frame, attempting to release the tension in his back, after bending over the huge map table for nearly an hour without looking up. "OK, Clyde, let's run these things in order, beginning with New York. Gentlemen, please speak up when you think appropriate, but remember, this fancy squawk box can only accommodate two people talking at the same time. Identify yourselves when you speak. Go ahead, Clyde."

Keithley, along with Mac Reed, plus two members of the White House staff who worked in the situation room and, of course, Jonathan Brooks, occupied chairs in the White House with the president.   General Murrah in L.A. and General Hambley in New York were conferenced in by telephone, their voices emanating from a big black object that looked like a miniature UFO in the middle of the table. Keithley began.

"Dick, since you've had the most daylight so far today, let's begin with you. Have you been able to begin the process we discussed last night, regarding evacuations and information delivery to the noncombatants?"

"Yes. The directives you gave when we talked have been implemented. Luckily we had some troop concentrations, complete with large, portable medical units, pretty close to those areas we determined might benefit from on-site services, without the people being evacuated first. So far we have three of those operations underway, out of the total of eleven locations that Seth identified to me after your meeting last night. Three more will have personnel and supplies in place by dark this evening and, of the other five, two have already completed evacuation anyway.   Of course, all this is in addition to the evacuation process we began earlier. Those folks are filling up every available site we have at an incredible rate."

"Any problem with resistance from those welcoming committees?"

"Only a little. The first contingent to move into one of the areas designated for on-site assistance encountered some small arms fire, but it turned out to be a couple of freelancers—none of the hard core nasties that hit us yesterday. MPs took them out with return fire and a grenade launcher.   No sign of booby traps or bad guys in the populations we have so far, but everybody is searched and surveillance is intense."

"Well, so far, so good.   What about getting information into the areas held by the guerillas?" A rustling of papers, audible over the speaker, was followed at once by resumption of Hambley's voice.

"We whipped up a pretty big advance party overnight, gentlemen, dressed them in civilian clothing, sent them into the worst areas a few at a time, starting around 0300. Approximately three hundred volunteers, unarmed, moved into the most volatile, densely populated neighborhoods, using the best routes we could identify on such short notice. They are really naked in there without weapons, radios, or even food. We figured the only way for them to be able to infiltrate and then deliver information successfully was to make them completely impossible to identify. As I said, we took only volunteers, and the problem was choosing who to send. One hundred were chosen to go, and we had 1,100 volunteers.

"Those with knowledge of New York were our first choices, including twenty-two soldiers whose homes were actually in the areas into that they went. They were to act as quickly as possible, spreading the word without attracting attention to themselves, making sure they stressed that there was safety, food, medicine available.

"What we couldn't tell them was how quickly they had to move. We're hoping the people will be interested enough in the idea of getting out that they'll start a mass exodus that we'll be able to see coming. As you know, until they get out of there, we're really stalemated against the paramilitary force and the gangs that now control them—and therefore, the city."

"Dick, Clyde here, how do you find out whether or not your people get the word out? Seems to me that once they're in there, we have no way of knowing whether they've even been able to talk until we see if the people start leaving—or start getting shot."

"That's pretty close, Clyde. But they are under orders to get out as soon as they have determined that the rumor mill is really working. They're to come out the same way they went in, and hopefully, they'll come back with some intelligence for us. Seems like we should have had more of this already; problem was, civilian informants, the ones talking to the FBI and Guard units that have been here all along, have been susceptible to the same deadly problems the rest of the population faces. Over ninety percent of our sources have died, either from violence or disease, and sending soldiers into that cesspool was a pretty clear prescription for immediate cases of dysentery or cholera for them as well.

"We're hopeful these troops can get in, fire up the rumor mill, then get out before they start getting sick. As of now, no one is back that we know of, and we're concentrating on the areas that are less violent until we can get a handle on this civilian thing."

The President spoke, thanking Hambley, then moving to question Mark Murrah. "Mark, what's the score with East L.A.?" The west coast operations commander spoke with the sharp, clipped diction of an eastern educated man, his bearing so much a part of his persona that only those closest to him knew different. Mark Murrah had come from nothing, repeatedly nearly failing to make it out of childhood, the product of parental abuse and neglect in the worst neighborhood Cleveland had to offer. Charged with a number of violent crimes before he was twelve years old, it had been the Boys Club, Golden Gloves competition, and a Catholic priest that pulled him from the clear threat of a life of street crime. Boxing led to wrestling in school, where he was all-state and later NCAA champion at 162 pounds—at West Point.

The men listening to him now were all long time comrades, including Keithley and even the President. And each one knew the passionate other side to this man of letters, the general they often called "Montie," after his ever-so-formal, even stuffy demeanor. His military record, back as far as Vietnam, was full of stories of heroism, great courage, and a fair mix of sheer insanity in the face of long and dangerous odds. The only other living general in all the armed services to have been awarded the Medal of Honor, besides the President himself, no one doubted that Mark Murrah would have things in high gear, a plan in mind regarding the complex mess that was Los Angeles.

"Good morning, Mr. President, gentlemen. Greetings from sunny California. We find ourselves with a problem similar to that described by General Hambley, as regards the noncombatant situation. However, our version includes a much larger geographical area, although now probably less densely populated. Disease and starvation have taken a heavy toll here as well, and the problem of rotting bodies is extremely severe, due to the heat. Temperatures are at or near 100 degrees daily, and that makes for rapid decomposition. What we cannot hope to control is the effect these rotting corpses have on the remaining population.

"The business of evacuation has been pretty easy in some areas, but impossible in others. The suburbs to the north and those down in Orange County and on toward San Diego have gone well. To the south, we were able to move in with supplies and water, removing bodies and the gravely ill while caring for the remaining population with evacuation. Again, the real problem was disease. Over half the people have died. The task of disposition of the bodies is so huge it is hard to describe. I have ordered immediate cremation at a number of sites in an attempt to minimize the necessity for transportation of the disease-ridden corpses.

"We remain at stalemate in East L.A., Watts, and several of the Mexican enclaves where the population is controlled tightly by well-armed gangs. Hard to fathom the number of powerful military pieces they have and how good they are with them. We lost eight helicopters last weekend when we tried to move in force into three different locations. Much like what Dick described, the remaining noncombatant population is completely dominated by the gangs. They are weak, sick, terrified, and demoralized. And the gangs control the tiny amount of food and the only clean water supply, consisting of a few tanks that still have any supply left in them."

"Mark, this is Jackie. What about the intelligence that the gangs were forming alliances—any truth to it, and if so, how big of a problem is it?"

"Yes sir, it appears to be true. Our informant, a young Latino whose cousin is a Marine MP out here, was extracted, along with a female companion, earlier this morning, and what we can get from him indicates that the largest Mexican gang, the Diablos, has in fact formed an alliance with a motorcycle gang called the Sons of Silence—mostly white, almost all with long criminal records, and with a large number of older combat veterans in their ranks. One can never be really certain about such arrangements, as the egos and ethnic differences between such groups are tricky, but we believe they are now preparing to move together to set up some powerful military weapons and to attempt to force us to deal with them."

"Right. When hell freezes solid. Mark—Jackie again—can you interdict this merger? Seems to me if they get it accomplished before you can stop it their ability to hold us off will be pretty substantial, particularly if they hold as many civilians as you have suggested."

"I agree. Right now, we are setting up some surveillance locations from higher altitudes, hoping to watch for movement of larger groups of people or vehicle traffic, without our presence being seen. The problem with that is the smog.

Visibility, even with the more powerful cameras, is miserable most of the day. They are no longer creating carbon monoxide from auto engines, but fires continue to burn in enough places to create the same effect. Delta Force also has operatives in several of the localities where movement might be expected, and they can advise by radio. Our problem with them is supply. They are moving in pairs to avoid detection, and all the food and water they can get is what they are carrying with them. If they get sick, we lose them, too. So with the heat, we expect them to run out of water by tonight, when they will have to return to extraction points.

"Our biggest fear is that the heavy weapons will get in place. It is reported that they have at least one fifty-caliber machinegun, vehicle mounted, and several recoilless rifles, even half a dozen 81millimeter mortars. With a large number of hostages to use as shields and knowing as they do that we are aware of the locations of those hostages, they can inflict great damage on any aircraft or ground transport we attempt to deploy. And of course, our source tells us they will not hesitate to turn those guns on the noncombatants if they feel it necessary to demonstrate their resolve to us. We can only remain in position for quick reaction and immediate assault if the opportunity arises; we have gun ships at the ready, only a few minutes from the area, in the event we spot movement that looks like merger of their forces."

They discussed troop strengths, deployment based upon known hostage locations, and the ever-present problems of handling hundreds of thousands of sick and wounded people at the same time, once they had neutralized the resistance. And everyone knew just how difficult and how expensive that neutralization was likely to be. The vision of a fifty-caliber machinegun mounted on a truck and sitting in the middle of hundreds of noncombatant civilians made for almost certain nightmare results. Such a gun could take out helicopters at ranges of a thousand meters or more, especially if it could continue without fear of return fire. One of the tremendous attributes of the old fifty-caliber was that great skill has never been required to be effective with it. With a white phosphorous tracer every fifth round, all the operator has to do is follow them, guiding effective and killing fire into any target, in the air or on the ground. Further, no pilot would chance firing into a crowd of civilians, and the idea of launching rockets at such a target was unthinkable.

18.

The United States of America saw innumerable military occupations over that summer, but none as difficult, nor against as intractable a foe, as what lay in wait throughout New York City in August 1997. Chicago had been pretty awful, but the presence of fresh water right there in Lake Michigan made caring for the population easier, although it had to be purified before it could be used. The gang population was less well-organized there, and although well armed, it folded after a few days of skirmishes with the Army's bigger force. Likewise St. Louis, Atlanta, Dallas, Denver. But even though the armed conflict lasted a shorter time, thousands and thousands died violently or from the rampant disease that swept the land. A few places, like Richland, Iowa, San Antonio, and Pittsburgh, were still experiencing sporadic violence into August, but not on the scale that had plagued them in the spring and early summer.

Heavily populated areas felt instant terror, immediate deprivation, certain death for entire populations as water was exhausted or unavailable; there was simply no electricity with that to fill the municipal tanks or purify existing reservoir supplies. Suburban populations quickly used up existing food supplies and, without access to electronic funds—plastic money—they were just as quickly reduced to looting and total panic. Even worse, the huge reliance on forced main sewage removal and processing turned entire communities into instant cholera epidemics, and water supplies were quickly contaminated. Hundreds of thousands of homes were unable to use any of those utilities.

Water disappeared, heat was gone, and the first sixty days of the blackout resulted in millions of deaths due to exposure, as well as disease. So, as Jackie Webb oversaw the offensives intent on retaking two of the largest cities in the world, his administration was also at work nonstop trying to stem the tide of death and collapse that daily destroyed more and more of the civilization that had been almost three hundred years in the making. Reports stacked up on administration desks about death tolls, continued violence, intense suffering. And winter was ninety days away for those millions who lived in the North and Midwest.

The Devil's Playground

Almost certainly, the winter of 1997-98 would be a season without electricity for most Americans. That meant no heat for most. Even for those with natural gas heat, their furnaces required forced air movement—air that was moved by electric fans. What was painfully clear as Webb and his people tried to prepare for cold weather was that FEMA had been much more the political tool of those who angled for excuses to control people than a real resource to help free people survive such a cataclysm.

Entire programs of the Federal Emergency Management Administration were tied up with concepts that required people to be removed from their home areas and kept in relocation camps. A ridiculous idea, even on a smaller scale, but ludicrous beyond description when the whole population was at risk of freezing to death.

Webb ordered every available resource to be redirected into the task of providing thousands of regional and local points for the distribution of food, medicine, fuel. He rejected any proposal that required moving people far from their homes, and he ordered every member of his administration, military and civilian, to work with existing local governmental personnel in delivering assistance. He told everyone, every day, that their most powerful resource was the people, not the bureaucracy.

The problems that beset America were well known around the world, as well. For although there had been no terrorist-initiated interruption in the electricity supply in Europe, the devastation created by the sabotage of the wire transfer system created instant panic and plunged the already over-loaned and thinly capitalized banks around the Continent into insolvency. Depression, along with its attendant violence and the interruption of services, sent the major markets and population centers into an ugly reprise of the 1930s.

Webb stood at a window in the Oval Office, his mind nearly exploding with the number and weight of the many issues facing his crumbling, beloved country. It was one o'clock p.m., and soldiers were positioning themselves for a desperate battle to recover two great cities. And inside a deadly hole in the ground by the Euphrates River, half a world away, LED numbers flashed within the components of a big missile, now exactly sixty minutes from lifting itself out of Babylon and into the night sky.

19.

There were no monitors blinking, no little beeping sounds associated with carefully measured vital signs, no muffled voice paging some AWOL doctor to call the information desk. There were no white-clad nurses moving soundlessly in and out of clean rooms, their stethoscopes draped around their necks. No I.V. bottles hung from metal stands beside the patient's bed. There was only the bed in Carl Landry's master bedroom, that although clad in clean linens,
was drenched in blood.

With all the wounds cleaned off and clothing removed, the condition of the patient was only slightly less a mystery. A compound fracture of the left leg below the knee was ugly and the source of not only significant bleeding, but also a huge concern for infection. There being none of the high tech antibiotics routinely used to stop the kind of bone infection that is associated with open fractures, he could be expected to lose the leg, and maybe his life, too. Deep lacerations in his scalp and face were lesser problems, stitched up after being cleaned with the antiseptics available. But he was still out cold.

"Gotta be shock, Faith, only thing I can figure. I know he looks like he's busted his head, but there's no way he could've crawled over a mile in that rough country with a fractured skull and a closed head injury."

"Unless he developed a slow intra-cranial bleed when he toppled down into that gully, Carl. Sure looks like a closed head thing to me. His blood pressure is way low, he's breathing so shallow. Needs blood, and quickly." The woman physician felt Josh's forehead for fever, noting at once that he was heating up.

"OK. Let's get Luke in here and start collecting blood from him and me. Two units ought to help, and we can get more out of me if necessary. Jess, take a break and go out for Luke. He was waiting on the porch with the other kids when I came through a few minutes ago. And sis—let's just keep up the prayer line. At least he's stable for now. Got the leg set and closed, all the holes plugged. OK?" The heat of early afternoon held close the scent of blood and sweat in the bedroom, although windows were open wide. And whatever might have been happening elsewhere, the universe bounded by Jericho Road was consumed completely in the seemingly futile struggle of one man to wrest life from Death's reach.

Jessica Landry smiled only slightly, blinking back tears of exhaustion as well as anxiety. She nodded and walked out to get her son. In the three hours since returning with the unconscious man, both doctors and two nurses among their number had worked nonstop. The broken leg was a real job, the bone sticking through the skin, jagged and covered with dirt, as well as the ankle so obviously misshapen and fractured. The long bone set pretty easily, although the danger of infection was very high. The ankle begged for open repair, but such surgery was simply impossible. So they straightened it out into the configuration that looked best to their trained eyes, then immobilized it with sterile splints, hoping it would heal itself into the right shape.

Carl Landry had beaten himself over and over during the past months for not having made enough preparation for the delivery of medical attention under such conditions. "If I was so damn sure things were going to fall apart this way, why didn't I prepare better for the area in that I was best trained? Instead, we have no blood collection equipment, no osteomyelitis antibiotic, very little surgical equipment, and not enough painkiller. I might as well have spent the time playing golf." Such was the lament heard repeatedly. But they made do, and they figured out how to collect blood, if only too slowly to suit Carl. There being no way to type and cross-match and no way to preserve blood once drawn, all they could do was to collect from those with known types, then use it immediately.

By evening they had two units into the still-comatose Joshua Landry, and when his brother's blood pressure continued to stay dangerously low, Carl quickly decided to collect and transfuse an additional 1000cc quantity from his own body. And fever also became an issue. With the patient in shock, no I.V. antibiotics available, and a fever of over 104 degrees, the options were all bad. There was no ice for administration of an ice bath, and shock made that a bad choice anyway. All they could do was wait, watch, and pray. His breathing became shallower and slower, and both physicians started looking at each other with that "it's all over" look. Jess had seen enough death in her time to know her husband was sinking deeper and deeper into his coma, and that the infection was raging out of control in his body.

Book IV – The Great Offensives

They could not know what drama was playing out beyond the confines of Jericho Road, or that the continued existence of the world's population at large was at risk. Concerned only with the immediate problem of this man's struggle to survive, they hovered over his vital signs, waiting for the opportunity to move against the infection. "If his BP starts up with this third unit of blood, I say we dunk him in the coldest water we can find, at once. Unless we get control of that fever, he'll go into convulsions or neurological meltdown, and he's gone for sure. We dunk him now, he'll code for sure." Faith Jackson nodded her assent to Carl's proposal, then stood up to start collecting clean water in the bathtub off the bedroom. Carl checked Josh's blood pressure again, noting just the slightest elevation.

"Get moving, Faith—got a little improvement in the BP. Jess, this'll probably kill him, but he's a goner unless we try it. And if he survives the bath and the fever goes down, infection may make a comeback at any time and take him before we can even react. You understand where we are, sis?" Tactful as ever. Sitting on the edge of a straight chair beside the bed, hair matted and full of stickers and grass, eyes deep in despair, she could not remove her gaze from her husband's motionless face. Finally, she turned ever so slowly to meet Carl's eyes, nodded almost imperceptibly, then pitched over onto the floor.

* * * * *

Babs Morgan sat motionless at her terminal, she and the entire complement of technicians at the Johnson Space Center in Houston, oblivious to the heat of the day. Because of its ongoing importance to national security, all installations having to do with the operation of intelligence gathering systems, including satellite photography and interpretation, computer enhancement and data transmission, were favored with what might have seemed like lavish expenditures of precious resources.

Although Houston was just as dark and sweltering as the rest of the nation, a nuclear power plant, one not severely damaged by the destruction of power stations around it, provided a direct source of electricity to the Center. Food was in ample supply from stores maintained for just such

575

purposes, and air filtration augmented powerful air conditioning systems to provide the proper climate for maintenance of all the delicate equipment.

Her tiny, childlike voice seemed totally at odds with her round persona, crinkley red hair framing freckles scattered across a face that could only properly be described as fat. Chubby fingers poked at a keyboard, while small eyes darted across the three screens that surrounded her place in the huge control room. But her seat was in the upper deck, her location indicative of some position of ascendancy, authority. Although the visage seemed almost petulant as she moved with sharp, harsh strokes across the keys, that squeaky voice was more reminiscent of Shirley Temple than Roseann Arnold. And every word she spoke prompted immediate response from whomever she addressed at the moment.

Babs was in charge. Director of Satellite Intelligence and Analysis for a consortium of NASA, the NSA, and the CIA, she enjoyed the unqualified allegiance of all in the vast system of information gathering and dissemination. It was she who could, by depressing a single key, speak directly to a guidance and tracking officer of the Israeli Air Defense Command, himself seated in a sweltering sandy bunker in the middle of nowhere. His location was unknown to virtually everyone in the world, with the exception of his own command and Babs Morgan. She chirped into the tiny mouthpiece at the corner of her rosebud lips, a series of flashing images appearing on her screen.

"Arrow Base, this is Houston. . .Avi, do you copy?"

"Houston, this is Arrow Base, copy fine. Hotter than the bowels of hell, dear Babs, and the scenery is a perfect fit with the climate, but for the musical tones of your sweet voice. What do your cosmic eyes have to report?" A quick smile flashed across her round cheeks. She depressed the button again.

"Avi, you fill the atmosphere with sheer poetry. But alas, we have no news, as if we had any idea what we're really looking for anyway. The bird is in place over the suspected area of origin, and we have high-resolution pix of the palace location in particular. Looks a lot like an old city in the dark to me." She could hear a soft chuckle as Avi Reisman prepared to respond again.

"Ah. . .this is a *good* thing, my lovely, as what you see is just that. An old, *hot* city in the dark. Seriously, the best we can figure, there must be some kind of launch location, either a covered silo type arrangement or maybe even an above ground structure—although a missile big enough to carry a nuclear payload five hundred miles will be pretty big. Hell, the Scuds would go almost that far, but they were less accurate than throwing rocks. We just think they'd design and build something bigger and much more accurate. Too many Arabs in Israel for them to be sloppy, although Arafat has never been troubled by killing his own."

Babs looked at the digital clock display in her computer screen, then up at the wall, where all relevant time zones were visible on a series of clocks, set in consecutive fashion. It was 12:24 p.m. in Houston, 10:24 p.m. at Arrow base, and 11:24 p.m. in Babylon. A nagging uneasiness turned over in her stomach, her mind living in the darkness of the Iraqi night while her body sat in Houston's midday. Attributing the feeling to that old aversion to working nights, she shook it and keyed her microphone again. Never one to trust hunches or intuition, Barbara Marie Morgan was, notwithstanding the voice and appearance, a complete professional. Still, that feeling, that unrest so atypical of her usual aplomb, control, as if, even with her cosmic eyes open and producing newsprint clarity at hundreds of miles' distance, there was more to see, yet denied even to her seemingly inexhaustible vision and resources.

"I have new images every three minutes, Avi, and the whole area around the place seems quiet. Like I told you when we started, the place is nothing like trying to watch Baghdad or Teheran; it's really small, contained. They've rebuilt the old city wall some, and that thing really makes identification easy. Just keep seeing the same—*what's that?*—hold one, Avi, repeat, *standby.*" Reisman felt the fire of acid rise in his throat, the change in tone and demeanor of Babs' voice instant and unmistakable. The last two words, 'repeat, *Standby,*' conveyed none of the chatty chirpiness that had been her audio trademark during the previous sixteen hours they spent communicating. In a single breath, the voice went metallic, sharp.

"Jimmy—com'ere--quick. Take that console keyboard and pull me up the images from the last set of shots. Hurry up.

Zero in on this quad right here, the restoration area, and *right here—see that?* I want that rooftop, *right there—quick.*" Avi could not hear that command, or the strident tone in the voice that delivered it. But the technician assisting the Director heard it and responded instantly. Seated some fifteen feet away, he vaulted a desktop and slid into the chair next to his boss. Spinning a keyboard that sat on a movable base, he slapped a short series of keystrokes that then within about ten seconds lit up a screen adjoining the one Babs was studying.

"Here you go, boss, right here, and—*zap!*—enhanced. Whatcha got?" She reached without looking for the screen, turning it and moving it on the extension apparatus that held it suspended above the desk surfaces that comprised her position. By swinging the first screen toward the second, she immediately had them side by side, both people now studying the two images.

"See this—*here*—this is the view five minutes ago. All white across the top of that building—the palace gardens area, right?"

"Uh huh, that's what the schematic says. And I've been looking at that big lid for 12 hours now. So what's new, Babs? Looks the—*oh yeah—that shadow on the right side—oh yeah—what . . .?*"

"Arrow base, this is Houston, do you copy?"

"Houston, this is Arrow, go ahead, Babs, what's up?"

"Arrow base, we are transmitting images now, for you to compare. Circled area highlighted by enhancement will show you a shadow—a dark space, really, just appearing on the top of the palace. Can't identify it, or even say it means anything yet. Only I can tell you it has not been there until now. Next set of pictures, plus enhancement on suspected site, available in 90 seconds. Transmitting now—do you confirm receipt?" The line was silent. She shot a hot glance at Jimmy, who burned holes in the keyboard and his program screen, looking to assure himself that the data had been sent. He nodded his head in affirmation that all had been done properly, then was interrupted by the distant voice.

"Confirm, Houston. We have images on screen now. Roger the change. Clearly a new shadow on the roof of the palace. What's the next image look like?" They breathed steadily, but with great effort. The very first moment of any kind of change in the dark landscape, and it was happening in precisely the place they were to watch. The dark mounds out in the desert had been totally unremarkable, no movement of machinery or military units had occurred throughout the hours of watching the whole region by satellite. Nor had there been anything to raise questions from the fly overs done by the SR71 Blackbird. Now, at once, everyone froze on a single rooftop, no longer considering the long hours of tedium that proceeded this moment.

One of the great tests of the accuracy of intelligence has always been the absence of visible change that contradicts known information. So either there was no missile at all or it was already in place. If already set, all that could be learned consistently pointed at the same location, itself possessed of all the right indicators. And with no evidence of any kind of portable weapons platform, or even another venue where suspicious activity might suggest that type of activity, focusing on the palace not only made sense, it demanded careful execution as the priority surveillance target.

"OK, Avi, we have the new pix coming up right now. Do you agree that there is a visible change in that rooftop?"

"Absolutely. It's small, otherwise unremarkable, but the night is clear, there are no buildings above it to cast shadow, and the definition is too sharp to have been a plane or even temporary cloud cover. I can tell tha—"

"*Avi, it's bigger now. Twice the size.* Repeat. The shadow is increased in size to . . . let's see—Jimmy, hit the scaler for that spot—how big is that hole and what was it before?" A series of strokes, and some calculations appeared, completed on the small ancillary screen that sat atop the computer-enhanced photo display. The technician spun the little screen around to face Babs.

"Wow. Scale says that roof surface is sixty by one hundred forty, or just under nine thousand square feet. The shadow was sixty by twenty on the first take and is now sixty by eighty—holy shit, Avi, they're opening up the whole structure. *Jimmy, transmit this set and the calculations at once.* Avi, the next set is on its way, along with those numbers. See what you think, but from here, I call it confirmed. Repeat, Avi, we confirm opening sufficient for exposure of weapons platform. Do you copy?"

The Devil's Playground

"I have it, Houston. Here comes the new stuff. Damn. All right. I have alternative intercept telemetry for six potential targets in Israel, all punched in and available. We assume Tel Aviv, but can only wait for liftoff and trajectory to confirm. I am arming Arrow and ordering immediate prep for launch. It's in light concealment out on our range and will be ready for fire in three minutes. Please advise."

The voices continued their measured, deliberate tone and tempo, although the anxiety levels began to rise exponentially, because the idea of hitting one supersonic projectile with another, even under laboratory conditions, is complicated. Stretch the distances over hundreds or thousands of miles, add the speed of both the missile target and the intended interceptor, include a weapons system that has yet to be tested in final configuration, and the whole thing becomes a very real shot in the dark. Patriot missile installations manned by U.S. personnel were on the line in northern Israel as well, but their range was insufficient to make an intercept before an incoming nuke would be armed. The eventuality of hitting it with a Patriot was about as bad as permitting it to land untouched, as it would just detonate at a higher altitude, scattering its radiation and shock-wave even further. Not a good alternative.

Babs and Co. knew well the cost of a mistake here, but all they could really do was to pass on the best information and calculations possible from the satellite. Avi Reisman fought waves of nausea, even terror, as he knew he and his unproven weapon, alone in the vastness of the desert night, stood between his beloved Israel and certain nuclear annihilation for an incalculable number of Jews.

The clocks seemed to race at super speeds, minutes flying past as each new set of satellite images showed continued increase in the size of the hole in the top of the Palace of Nebuchadnezzar, until the thing gaped open to dimensions of sixty feet by over one hundred feet. A reflection at first, then a form appeared in the hole, rising higher in the dark spot with each additional three minute time span, the time between images transmitted by the satellite now in consonant orbit with Earth and therefore stationary over Babylon.

The sleek nose of the missile looked like a circle of white in the dark rectangular hole at first. Then, as it tipped over several degrees to adjust to an appropriate angle relative to its intended flight path, it produced what looked like an ellipse, with one end sharpened, the other disappearing into the blackness beneath the edge of the roof-line at the end of the opening.

Probably the only real advantage available to the U.S. and therefore to Israel was its monopoly on spy satellite technology. Except for what they could get from the Russians, now gripped by depression and violence themselves, Iraq and the PLO really had no such capability. However, the whole thing remained a thinly wrought theory and hunch, even with these new and unexplained phenomena in the darkness and, if evil was afoot, only the PLO could really know what was in store.

"Standby, Arrow. We have attempted to further enhance remaining pix; have lost contact with bird momentarily. Standby."

Babs Morgan spun in her chair, her bulk suddenly standing amid her many screens and display boards. "Guidance—guidance—we have a problem! No transmission from bird in response to enhancement commands—Jack. Howard—run the diagnostics now. Jimmy. Redisplay each of the last four screens on the bid board, use highlight for suspect area. Hurry up, people, the bastards are up to no good, and we just lost our eyes!!"

* * * * *

Hysteria is interesting stuff. Alone or in small groups, people seldom experience such phenomena, absent substantial provocation, combined with factors such as confinement, threat of great harm, starvation or other deprivation of basic human needs. It happens to be sure, but it is more often the product of larger numbers. There were those wild and deadly riots in South America at the soccer games, the bedlam that followed already violent demonstrations in Watts and, later, in East L.A. after the Rodney King verdict. And while owing for their initial impetus some untoward event, all really went totally nuts only with the presence of big crowds. A dangerous thing always, the idea of playing on hysteria to incite thousands of people to spontaneously explode out of squalor and captivity was very radical indeed.

The Devil's Playground

With over a hundred undercover operatives slipping through the populations of Brooklyn, the Bronx, Queens, and Newark, the predominant passion of all people to gossip got a big time workout. A few of the insurgents died quickly, having been unfortunate enough to talk to the wrong people. Eleven disappeared, never to be seen again, and twenty-eight quickly got sick and had to crawl out to extraction sites for help. Of those, cholera killed six of them, while the rest eventually recovered.

Sister Anne Marie, a Roman Catholic nun who tended a flock of captive folks in Brooklyn, was bathing a slender young woman with some of the clean water she maintained on hand at the St. Michael's Rectory. The water was boiled and then cooled by her and the other nuns who used a solar panel arrangement that had been given to the church by a utility company several years before as part of an energy experiment. The thing worked like crazy as long as the sun shined, that it did a lot in August. Gently turning the girl onto her side, she grimaced at the nasty sight of open, running sores that tortured the patient. They were the result of burns inflicted by a gang of madmen who had spent the first three months of the blackout on a rampage of rape and burning throughout the borough.

Soft moans slipped from the small woman, and the sister mumbled her prayer/epithet against the absence of antibiotic. The girl would die, as most burn victims had done all summer, only this one had taken longer, as her injuries were not quite as severe as some, and the overall condition of her health had been somewhat better than most when the devil's boys found her. A movement in the window above her head distracted her from her procedure just enough to result in spilling a large splash of the precious water across the woman's flank. Snapping her head around in an angry reaction to both the distraction and its result, she drew quick breath at seeing the face of a clean shaven, stout young black man, vaulting through the open window and down onto the floor. The distance down was over four feet, but the man landed so lightly as to make little noise.

"Sister, please do not scream or run away—I have news and need your help. I have come to try to get as many of your people out of here as I can. I—"

"Young man, first of all, my screaming days are over, long since, and secondly, I am running nowhere. This is my home. Now, you have startled me and caused me to spill precious clean water. Unless you make more sense with your next statement than you made with your last, I shall put down this pitcher and beat you with that broom handle until *you* run away. And you are certainly not local to this place—far too healthy and clean. Your disguise will get you cut in many pieces unless you do something about it. . ." She betrayed not the slightest trace of goodwill toward the soldier, neither did she move to disclose his presence or do him harm. The sum total of her reaction to him told him to speak quickly and to make things very clear.

"My name is Stanley Long, Sister, and I am an explosives specialist, fourth class, U.S. Army. I volunteered to come here to tell you and as many others as I can that there is food, shelter, medicine and military protection just up the way about three miles, waiting to feed and treat as many of you as can get up and walk out. We have tanks and armored vehicles to escort you and busses to haul you to safety, but you must move quickly, and in large numbers. We are—"

"You are crazy, Stanley Long, that's what you are. We start moving, the bastards—forgive me, Lord—start shooting or worse, lobbing cans of gasoline into our numbers. If you are the Army, why are you not driving in here and liberating us from these vermin who do *this* to innocent people." She gestured dramatically at the raw meat that was the backside of her patient.

"That's exactly why we *can't* come in. They will use you for shields, firing at will into our units as we try to advance. They showed us yesterday that they will use you, knowing that we won't shoot back if noncombatants are in the line of fire. I know it sounds pretty goofy, but we figure that if enough of you beat feet at the same time, the gangs will lose their protection and advantage. We are sure you are right about them opening fire. But we have scores of choppers standing by to take them out when they show themselves. Your people just have to get up and haul a—I mean, get out and go in numbers sufficient to make stopping you impossible.

"All I am asking you to do is to spread the word to as many as you can. Tell them to start right away, before it gets dark, and to make a mass exodus out of it. Get off the city streets and up onto the Interstates immediately, then move north and west until our units can see you and lead you to safety. I know I sound like a lunatic, but I swear I just came from back there, and it's all true. I've seen the medical setups, the tent shelters, clean water and food to care for thousands. Besides, we've already evacuated over a quarter of a million people from the city in the past week, before we launched the invasion night before last.

"Things just went to hell—sorry—when we came in with the big stuff. They were waiting for us with more deadly surprises than I can name. Booby traps, mines, mobile sniper teams, even a whole city block set up with Sarin nerve agent. Killed everybody who got close to it. Must've been trained terrorists; too good and too well executed for a bunch of gangland thugs. This is the only way we can fight back, for as many of the noncombatants as possible to be evacuated so we can turn loose the big stuff. Honest, Sister, we're waiting for you all in force, if you'll just go in big enough numbers."

The wiry old nun looked away, her frail shoulders stooped under the weight of all she lived with every moment. Too much to contemplate, this business of mass exodus. Her head still turned from her uninvited guest, she spoke with a weaker voice, betraying a resolve waning more each day in the midst of the accelerating collapse of what was left of her parish. "What you ask is madness, my son. Purely. These are men more wicked than you can possibly imagine. As God is my judge, they must come straight from hell to this place. They are indifferent to the suffering of thousands, and they use us for evil sport like we were objects, not people. They laugh and celebrate blood and death. If we even hint at such movement, they will kill us in huge numbers."

"We fear the same thing, Sister. Only it is what you have just said that convinces us this is what you should do. Unless we get you out of here, you will all die for sure. We know there will be losses if you try this, but many—probably most—will make it to safety and a chance to survive. Look, there are a hundred of us having this conversation with people all over New York right now, and every one of us talked to the general who's running the whole show, just last night. He met with the volunteers personally before we moved out, and he told us to make sure everybody we talked to knew he meant business. He's good, Sister, and he backs up his talk. We saw the preparations before we left, and I swear they're waiting to help." She looked back at the young handsome face now, her own countenance blotchy red, tears streaming down her face, chest heaving.

"You cannot know what we have endured, soldier. No one can. I have watched as thousands of my city have perished from torture, wounds, disease. We thought you would never. . oh Dearest Jesus, forgive my faithlessness, I—we all just never. . ." The soldier was across the small, hot room in a single quick move, the distance between them gone in an instant, his powerful arms enfolding the old nun as she heaved and sobbed into the fabric of his shirt.

For a long moment no one moved, and the only sounds were the muffled crying of the frail woman and the soft moaning of the unconscious burn victim on her soiled pallet. Stanley Long shook his head as he discovered tears running down his own face, his nostrils filled with the smell of infection, rotting flesh and sweat. He closed his eyes tight against the sting of tears and sorrow.

* * * * *

"Mr. President, I have General Hambley on the line, patched through with General Keithley, who's at the Pentagon. They want to report some developments ahead of the scheduled conference call that we have on for 1600 hours. They're on secure two, if you could pick up, sir?"

"Thanks, Sergeant. Gentlemen, tell me something good! You're almost three hours early for our call, so let's have it."

"Jackie, this is Dick—I'm at HQ right now, but I just came in from a fly over into Manhattan and the Brooklyn area. I called Clyde because I thought you should be brought up to speed sooner than 1600, as planned. We both agreed you'd want to know what's happening. Just before noon today we started seeing a few little bunches of civilians climbing up onto the elevated highways leading out of the central boroughs. First reports came from just north of the Bronx, but then we got one from Queens, and more important, one from Newark. People are out on the highways, moving pretty steadily, and to this point without much panic.

"Problem is, we don't have any way of knowing who's left, so we can't come in behind them with offensive capability. Air cover is providing security for several hundred five-ton trucks and large busses on their way to meet these folks and carry them out of town, but they haven't gotten in yet. Once the people get up onto the expressway surfaces, they seem to be able to move without impediment, but those we have talked to tell us there are lots of snipers and gangs with small arms who are firing on them as they try to get out."

"Dick, this is Clyde. What are the casualty numbers for those trying to escape? Can't we get choppers or ground assault teams in there to cover their exit?"

"Can't chance that yet, Clyde. I ordered two birds into one escape point in Brooklyn, and some bastard with a recoilless rifle got 'em both before they could react. And the ground fire was coming from good enough concealment that it was hard to get a fix on it for return fire. That brings my chopper losses to eighteen since yesterday morning. Pretty expensive lesson."

"All right, boys, Webb here. Let's get right down among 'em, and do it right now. We need those bullhorn loudspeaker things you told me you were rigging up the other night, Dick. Get as close to the perimeter of all hostile areas as you dare and *turn it up!* I want those highways full of people as soon as you can do it. I can't decide whether darkness will help or hinder us right now. Certainly, moving that many people without panicking the whole crowd will be hard, but the bad guys won't be able to fire as effectively either. And Clyde— can't we get a handle on those goddam recoilless pieces? Send in drones to draw fire, then hit 'em with Cobras or Apaches? Hell, one terrorist with a 90 millimeter seems to be able to ground our entire air capability!"

"Roger, Mr. President. Just called Bliss, and they're moving some cruise missile look-alikes that the air defense people use as targets. If we can get the bastards to fire on a couple of them, we'll get locations fixed and neutralize them quick. Great minds, Jackie."

"Right. OK, let's get moving. I'd like some tape of this exodus, if the fly boys can get it. Wouldn't hurt to be able to study later for origins of fire or evidence of enemy movement. Besides, we'd love to see what's happening."

"scuse me gentlemen, but I just got the signal that things are picking up out on the Bronx River Parkway. We're moving back in with air cover—call ya' back." His line clicked dead, leaving Keithley and Webb on the call. From the silence, it was obvious to both that neither was breathing. Finally, the president spoke.

"*Breathe,* Keithley, that's an order." The Chairman of the Joint Chiefs laughed at them both and at Webb's unique method of diffusing extreme tension.

"Yessir, affirmative sir. Breathing resumed. What time ya' got, Jackie? Oh—never mind. 1330. I'll be back up to the White House in about ninety minutes, unless I hear otherwise from   you."

"Done. Just call me if things pick up in New York. I got complete silence in L.A. so far, like a big calm before the even bigger storm. Stalemate right now, with the same problems, just different venue. Hurry back." The call ended, and Webb turned, standing again to look out into the grounds, when that same communications sergeant burst through the door, without the customary military decorum.

"*Sir—NASA on the secure line, sir. They said to tell you it was code red, sir. Line three.*" Webb stopped breathing again, spinning back to grab the telephone receiver almost before it could cool off from the last call. An unspoken prayer seeking divine intervention against a nuclear event was followed by commencement of the next call.

"Webb here, who've I got?"

"This is Barbara Morgan, Director of Satellite Intelligence here at NASA, sir. They told me to report to you directly about this."

"Thanks for the call, Ms. Morgan, I've heard of you in glowing terms. Tell me what's going on."

"Sir, it appears the Iraqis have opened a large aperture in the roof of the restored palace in Babylon, and I think what I'm seeing in the hole is a missile. We have advised Arrow base, and they confirm readiness in the event of launch. As you are aware, we just don't know if that interceptor system will actually work or not."

"Dearest Jesus, couldn't it be just an exercise? I mean, if they have hidden silos, they sure wouldn't test them in the day time! Maybe that's—"

"We hope so, sir, but the feeling of the personnel at Arrow base, as well as that of the Intelligence people here, is otherwise. Sir, we have made arrangements for you to have transmission of the pictures we continue to get from the bird; if you will transfer me to the proper technicians, they'll handle it. I have to get back to the screens. Sorry sir."

"Sure, get to it. *Bruster, pick up on this call and get us hooked up for video reception.*" Then he spoke to no one but God. "Oh Lord, my God, what next. If that thing gets past this single defense effort, we're looking at a multiple party nuclear exchange for sure. I cannot believe this, oh Lord. It flies in the face of all we know of your promises. It's in your Hands, Father; work your will."

Suddenly weighing hundreds of metaphysical pounds, Jackie Robinson Webb sat down hard in the chair behind his desk, too scared and too weary even to speak the 'Amen'."

20.

Richard Hambley had just been told that the first of his volunteers was returning from their gossip mission into the city. There were eight of them back, all in good health, but all shaken by the horrors they saw among the population being held at bay by the gangs and terrorists. Then it hit him.

"Corporal—get in touch with those returning soldiers and ask if they think they could get back in again, this time with radios. We need some eyes on the ground in there if we're gonna kill any of those terrorists!" A crisp yessir was followed by a flurry of calls and conversations, after that a total of thirty more volunteers, including every one of those who had come out healthy, were over the following two hours equipped with small, high-powered radios, spotting scopes, and pistols. They would then be reinserted into the most dangerous of areas, the plan being to use the new diversion of all those people who were starting to flee the boroughs to permit strategic placement of these folks as ground observers.

Even if they saw nothing until the next day, they would be able to call in exact and killing return fire on the locations where heavy weapons were being used on helicopters and armored vehicles.

Hambley sat in his mobile trailer, dozens of people buzzing around him, trucks and other war machinery rumbling in every direction. So anxious he could hardly contain the pounding in his head, the man was awash in a mixture of visions and awful fantasies. Hundreds and thousands of people evacuating, then panicking from being shot at, running over each other, pushing each other off bridges, out of windows. Or friendly fire, raining down fire and death on those who couldn't get out of the way. And the vision of more and more helicopters being incinerated in midair by the rocket fire coming from nowhere, inside those empty buildings. All in all not a pleasant afternoon for the commanding general. Then his communications sergeant appeared in the door way again.

"Sir, things are picking up. Better come down to the op center, they've got some video contact with one of the Cobras. Looks like Moses leading the flock across the Dead Sea, I swear!"

589

Hambley was on his feet, a smile quickly splashing across his face for a moment as he took the steps out of his trailer two at a time.

"It was the *Red* Sea, son, but I get the picture. Lead on." They jogged, then ran the one hundred yards to the big complex of semi-trailers and communications trucks that made up the operations center for the New York command. The doors were opened by a guard who snapped to attention and saluted as the general strode through behind his sergeant. They made their way through the maze of wires, cords, screens, tables, and chairs, suddenly aware that the room was quiet, but the area surrounding the big 60-inch video screen jammed with at least seventy-five silent faces.

"Dearest sweet baby Jesus. . .you were right Sarge, just like Moses and the flock. There must be fifty thousand people on that bridge alone, and—*holy mother of*—*look up ahead of them!! Somebody get me a secure line to the Pentagon, patched to 1600 and the President. And get busy rigging transmission of this video to Keithley and 1600 as well. Lord God in heaven, here they come. What—hey—look back there on the Manhattan side—THOSE PEOPLE ARE TAKING FIRE—HOLY—*"

The entire group stood frozen as if hit by liquid nitrogen, silence following the collective gasps that accompanied the general's epithet and the video clearly showing people scattering in every direction. Some half a mile back toward lower Manhattan from where the picture was focused on the masses on the George Washington Bridge, a scene from a bad movie was playing out to the silent horror of all who watched the screen. It was obvious that small arms fire from fully automatic weapons was strafing through a throng of at least two thousand people, as they moved west toward the big bridge and across into New Jersey. The helicopter on which was mounted the camera that transmitted the images visible on the big screen turned and headed toward the east end of the bridge, where invisible guns poured fire into the crowd from buildings along both sides of I-95 and, still further east, from the far end of the bridge over the adjoining Harlem River.

Nose-mounted video cameras served a variety of important functions, much like those used in police cars. The lens recorded and transmitted back to a control point high resolution, digitized information wherever it was aimed. The

590

camera could even be operated remotely by those who were receiving the images, so that possible targets, troop or weapons concentrations, civilian populations, even suspected escape routes being used by the terrorists could be recorded. The images were then computer enhanced, blown up to increase detail, compared with known grid maps. There was even a powerful zoom capability that could also be operated by the people watching from control positions. Presently, the camera was being operated by the pilot, who had the device following his own eyes by connection to the gunsights mounted in his helmet.

The whole scene, unobstructed from the vantage of the now attacking Apache, portrayed events too awful to imagine happening in the United States, with or without electricity and clean water. Some people broke and ran ahead, a huge stream of humanity pouring onto the big bridge, while at the back end of the line, a thousand or more scattered in every direction as the fire cut through them. People fell, hit by the powerful bullets, and others fell over them as great piles of writhing humanity appeared in the street. Then another chopper came into view in front of the first, banked around, streaking toward the source of fire.

Unable to speak, the crowd watching the screen suddenly reacted together, almost in perfect unison— *"THERE—THERE THEY ARE!!"* as sharp, white flashes of light could be seen coming from upper story windows of the buildings above the helpless refugees. The two aircraft banked hard one way, then hard back the other as they turned to acquire these targets. And at the very moment that the camera could clearly make out the origins of fire, a rack of rockets lit up the front of two of the buildings, three floors worth of brick, glass, and steel erupting up and outward. What they could not see was the effect on the back side of each building, where the entire exterior wall exploded out, hurling brick and other shrapnel through the empty windows and walls of the buildings facing them.

Cheers erupted as the emplacements disappeared in two fireballs, but the silence returned as the other helicopter, still visible in the camera on the first, disintegrated in a huge conflagration, the victim of one of those hand-held recoilless rifles. Gasps replaced cheers and, just as quickly, all who watched felt the deadly exposure being experienced by the pilot of the remaining gun ship, his eyes frantically trying to follow the smoke trail made by the projectile that had just taken out his friend's aircraft. Through the flying debris and smoke there was a trail to see, and the pilot found it.

All caution to the wind now, the pilot stuck his nose into the smoke trail, turned, and chased it right to the top of an old office building. Atop that structure was the faint remnant of a smoke cloud, created a few seconds before by the firing of the big weapon, the modern version of the old bazooka. Slight motion on the rooftop was all he needed, as he poured a long fusillade of mini-gun fire into the surface. The attack helicopter was only about one hundred feet above the top of the building, so the angle of fire was shallow, leaving a margin of safety for the riflemen on the roof behind the low wall that ringed the top of the old structure. The pilot cut loose with a string of grenades, the masonry wall vanishing to dust as a series of explosions took it apart.

Another collective shout from the observers, as three men were suddenly visible running for the access door in the roof. A second rack of rockets roared out from under the Apache, and just as quickly all three men were blown apart, burning appendages and other body parts tumbling through the air, torches of chemical fire raining down a macabre refuse on the street below. No cheers this time, as some were forced to turn away momentarily. All were glad for the hit, and unavoidably sickened by the incomprehensible carnage before them.

The chopper then swooped low, coming in behind the bedlam in the street, dropping to within a few feet of the pavement, his hands expertly manipulating the cyclic and elevator controls. He spun around 360 degrees, looking for additional hostile fire, almost challenging hidden foes to fire on him. Of course, he was also attempting to draw fire away from the people on the ground and to let them all see that he was there, shielding them with his guns, his aircraft and, indeed, with his very life. Without warning, the craft spun ninety degrees and opened fire with its mini-guns again, this time cutting down a cluster of four armed men who were attempting to sprint out of the building just blasted by the rockets, across the street and into another.

Although the pilot could not know it, they were running for a building where there was hidden access to the underground system of hideouts and escape so carefully put together during the months before the offensive began. He keyed his microphone as the men tumbled away from the murderous fire and contacted the forward command post. "New York Pitcher, this is Apache Red 2, copy coordinates and description on the building in the picture right now. Those assholes were running for it sure as hell, so there mighta been more there than just a place to hide from me." The communications officer in contact acknowledged, and the location was added to the already growing list of such places to be cleared, once ground troops could get in at all.

Pulling up a hundred feet, the Apache made another sweep of the faces of all the buildings on both sides of the street, daring more aggressors to fire on him, while at the same time showing the innocents on the ground that he was staying with them. Again the radio transmitted, this time to the aviation element. "Red Bird, this is Apache Red 2. I've got a situation to exploit. Can you send more gunships and all the medivacs you can find? I got maybe a hundred people shot down there on that street and, at least for right now, I have control. Could use some more eyes, too. Keep waiting for one of those recoilless things to light me up. Anyway, scramble some help, you copy?"

Several seconds passed. However, Richard Hambley was standing in the op center listening to the whole thing, so he barked at his own people, "Sarge, get Red Bird on the line and tell them I said 'Hell yes'! And hurry up. That pilot is right; the bastards may open up again at any time. I want that man out of there safely. *GO!*" It was 1:50 p.m. in New York and Hambley had to know if the boys in Washington had seen this spectacle, so he grabbed the secure line which already had both Keithley and Webb holding. "Whatcha think, boys, pretty fancy?"

"Dick, this is Clyde, that was some pretty special chopper driving, absolutely. And it looks like we may really be making some progress getting large numbers out of town, as Jackie— *and all of us*—had hoped. But we gotta get that mass of humanity off those bridges and into secure status or we'll have more of those ambushes for sure."

All three men were still watching the video screens, and the picture next panned back to the west and the direction of travel being followed by the huge crowd as it crossed into New Jersey. Of course, that crossing hardly constituted safe haven, as the climate there was still tense and dangerous as well. But it was a phenomenon they all hoped would shortly be repeated in several locations around the huge city, as thousands of people still remained the captives of gangs and self-styled, well-armed warlords. Those men were themselves the puppets of the mercenaries and zealots who had so perfectly orchestrated the resistance to U.S. military efforts to retake the city.

Webb spoke in response to Keithley's comment. "Couldn't agree more, guys, we just gotta dig in wherever we make a hit like the one we just saw. Clyde, can your people come in behind what was just accomplished, establish a secure area, and protect it with enough surveillance and firepower to keep it in place? I mean, you're *in* the South Bronx right now, and Harlem is less than a mile away from the south end of that perimeter as it stands. If we could—"

The President quit talking mid-sentence, the audible sound being his reaction to a message obviously conveyed to him from his end. When he returned, his voice was so tense he could hardly speak.

"Gentlemen, we're about to have a nuclear exchange in the Middle East. Carry on."

* * * * *

Shakey fingers traced a gentle description of fine lines across the motionless face, a countenance itself framed by the bright white of gauze and tape that wrapped her head. One eye was swollen badly, while the other bore no injury but shared the puffy aftermath of brutal blows. The hand cupped a smooth cheek and jaw line, then brushed the full, dark lips, now tenderly following contours over the chin, down the neck. Miguel's hand opened stiffly, his fingers still wooden from the trauma suffered by twelve hours of lost circulation and nerve impulse. Deep grooves in the wrists accompanied shallow lacerations across the back of his hand, as it came to rest flat on the chest of his recent burden. Pressing softly down on the small frame, hand against the worn fabric of a hospital gown, his eyes stung from a wave of salty tears, his mind now overwhelmed at the miraculous feel of the woman's heart beating against his hand, her chest rising and falling slowly with each breath.

"I have no idea who you are, girl, but it gives me more joy than you will ever understand to feel your heart beat. I thought you were gone for sure, there under that stinking bridge. Thank you, whoever you are, for not dying. Thank you, God, for letting me help save just this one from my brother's murderous lust." He leaned over, above the hand still resting lightly on the frail woman, and, steadying himself with his other hand on the I.V. pole beside her head, he bent over and kissed her, first on her forehead below the bandage, then on a cheek, and finally a brush against her lips.

"C'mon, cousin, before you go down again. I'll get my ass chewed if they find out I let you in here at all; you collapse with me and dump her out of that bed, I'll end up in the brig for sure. See? She's fine, Miguel. Just fine. Doc told me she was negative for internal bleeding, vital signs were strong. She's got a helluva big laceration in the back of her scalp, and another over her ear—probably some of Pancho's handiwork, and that face took three or four pretty good licks, but she's OK." Taking the younger man by the arm, Raul Sanchez helped him stand up, feeling at once the shakiness in Miguel's stance. As they turned to leave the tent that served as a recovery area for incoming trauma patients, the girl moved a little, one leg bending slightly at the knee.

A soft cry of pain froze them in place, turned them toward the movement under the sheets. Raul pulled his charge on toward the door to the tent, but he resisted, turning further back toward the bed.

"Raul, *shit, Raul,* that's blood, there on the sheet—*see*— right there beside her hip—goddammit, Raul, did they— god*dammit, GODDAMMIT*

RAUL, but she's bleeding from—!" A long breath, and Miguel grasped the side of the bed, his knees threatening to buckle. He swallowed a sob and another epithet, fought off the urge to vomit, felt his stomach turn a second time, swallowed hard.

"C'mon, Miguel, I told you, she's gonna be fine. You can't be surprised that they raped her, right? That's a given with Pancho—nobody knows that better than you. Report says she has some pretty bad vaginal tears, probably from some kind of foreign object, but she's too weak now for any effort to do a surgical repair. Hell, she's lucky to be alive. At least she's stopped hemorrhaging. Let's go. I'm supposed to be taking you to G2 for debriefing—the Intelligence boys need to pick your empty brain a while. She'll be OK, so let's go."

Miguel Sanchez moved stiffly, slowly, steps more like an elderly arthritis patient than a youngster of 19. The walk to the Intelligence unit was short, but the intense afternoon heat turned it into a demanding task. They stopped several times, and each time Miguel took small drinks of the Gatorade-like liquid the nurse had assigned him to drink in as large a quantity as he could keep down. Finally they stepped through the door of a long trailer that was bristling with antennae and communications dishes, a large, sweating soldier standing armed guard at the entrance.

Inside, they felt the rush of cool air, as the reality of air conditioning hit them hard. Nearly blacking out from the relief against the heat outside, Miguel and Raul were led into a small conference room lined with a variety of television monitors, computer consoles, and an enormous mess of wires and cables, all strewn about the floors and up the walls like a great twisting pile of dark snakes. A young sandy-haired Army captain, dressed in unpressed fatigues, his feet in dirty white sneakers, a Chicago Cubs cap backward on his head, smiled quickly at them and closed the door after they entered.

"Raul, I see you have retrieved your cousin for us— Miguel, sit down. My name is Peter DeCamp, Army Intelligence."

They shook hands briefly, as the officer already knew what painful condition his informant was in; then, with quick, direct movements, he rounded the end of the table and seated himself across from Miguel.

"Look boys, I know you been through a bunch today, and I am advised of the pleasures to that you were treated by the Diablos before you escaped. I'm sorry as hell about all that, but I gotta war to fight here, and the big boys want us to make some good intelligence chicken soup out of this chicken shit we have here, so bear with me, OK?" The question implied no opportunity for an answer, comment, assent, or objection; the man lit an unfiltered Pall Mall, blew a huge cloud of blue gray smoke while unfolding a large map on the table in front of the two younger men.

For almost an hour, DeCamp grilled Miguel about every conceivable detail of the weapons buildup that was anticipated to be commencing at any moment. He wanted to know the precise locations of all noncombatant concentrations, the likely routes to be used to move men and weapons into the East L.A. area, and also the same for Watts. They talked about the conversations overheard by Miguel while he was locked up in the headquarters of the Diablos, about the known strengths and weaknesses of Pancho's forces, and the stated capabilities of the Sons of Silence.

Of course, of prime concern were the heavier pieces that had been the subject of so much conjecture already. Miguel confirmed the conversations regarding the single fifty-caliber machinegun, and he also had a clear recollection concerning the numerous LAWs, light anti-tank weapons, held by the bikers.

"What we need most now, guys, is some hard information as to the timing and routes to be used to get the weapons in and the man-power out. We have at least twenty different sub-operations going on, so this isn't our only problem today, but this one has the big boys interested, because of the big concentration of noncombatants in the mix. They tell me the folks in New York are facing similar problems , but that thing is some different than what we have here. Miguel, I know you said they'd probably move tonight and that there'd be a motorized convoy of sorts to get the heavier weapons into East L.A. But can you help me with the routing? It's really gonna be hard to watch a thousand miles of streets, especially when chopper surveillance is out of the question, at least at lower altitudes. And can we get someone in there to observe, without getting caught?"

Miguel thought, looked at the big maps spread out on the table in front of him, thought some more. He shook his head. Then looking first at the maps again, then at Raul, he tentatively outlined at least the beginnings of a plan.

"If you could get someone *here,* in this little block of old houses that sits against this block that used to be shops, and *if* that person could stay out of sight long enough to watch and listen to Pancho's afternoon meeting with his punks, you might get enough information to figure out where the weapons were going. That would narrow down the options for how they get them there, and you only have to watch them. Problem is, who do you send?"

"Right. We got nobody who knows the area, and inserting a Delta team, even a pair of SEALs, accomplishes nothing unless they can get in without being compromised. Worse, if we do send somebody in who gets caught, they're likely to figure out why Miguel split and call off the whole deal. That doesn't hurt my feelings, except that they'll just re-do the deal and execute it a different way." He stood and moved over to another table, where a pitcher of tepid water sat sweating a puddle that spread slowly across the surface. Looking without seeing at the bank of monitors depicting various points of concern around the area, there seemed to be no clear solution.

Raul sat motionless throughout the whole exchange, eyes focused on the maps, jaw set, his breathing shallow. The aerial photos exploded in his head into all the dimensions, smells and sounds that had been home so long ago, before the Marine Corps swept him out of the ghetto and into military reality. "I'll go."

Miguel snapped his head around into his cousin's face, eyes for an instant uncomprehending, then blazing with immediate anger. He tried to speak, but words were absent, so stunned and horrified was he at the two-syllable answer. The captain grabbed for his cigarettes, moved two steps back to his seat at the table, sat down. A plume of blue smoke lifted over the table, as the snoop bore in on the motionless face of Raul Sanchez. Of course it was the answer, and of course, if anyone could slip in and listen up without getting caught, he was it. And of course, if he were discovered, death would be the least of his worries and an eventual welcome relief.

Miguel responded with more energy than anyone could have expected. "You're as crazy as you ever were, Raul, and dumber than you are crazy. *Fool*, you won't last ten minutes in the old neighborhood. Place's crawlin' with Pancho's hoods, *and they all know you on sight!* This is no gang full a' snot-faced kids, Captain, these are full grown badasses. Killers, men who've done hard time already, the kinda people that do what you saw in that girl we brought with us today. They so much as s*mell* Raul, he's toast. And before they kill him, they'll cut him up plenty, and you still have *shit* for intelligence. *No good, Raul, no goddam good. Stupid piece a' Latin grandstanding, too. Bullshit, that's what I think a' that idea.*"

The elder cousin knew the source of the outburst, so there was nothing about it that either surprised or angered him. But his solution was as perfect as it was dangerous, and Raul Sanchez had more than a few reasons for wanting to be in the middle of this operation.

"Calm down, Miguel, I'm not about to get caught or killed by Pancho and his goons. I was born on that block, lived nowhere else until the day I enlisted in the Marines. Besides, if I come in the way you came out, through the golf courses and under the freeway through that ditch, I can get most of the way in before anybody has a chance to see me. I'll wait for dark, move quickly, and carry a bird dog transmitter and radio, so they can come snatch me outta trouble before they can start carving me up. Captain, let's do it. Word is they want to move the big stuff tonight, so I should be hiding in the trees along the golf course by 1800. Take me an hour to get close enough to transmit information after I start moving, that I can't do until dark. That's about two hours later. Whaddaya say?"

Miguel started to speak again, tried to stand up for emphasis, then felt his knees give way beneath him, sending him back into his seat with a thud. Again words would not come, and he sat still, waiting for what he hoped would be a quick veto by the snoop captain. No luck.

"Nobody ever said Marines were interested in the easy way. OK, Sergeant. I'll have to clear it with your CO, cover your duty assignment while you're gone, and arrange equipment and figure out an infiltration setup. Take Miguel back to sickbay, go back to your area, and wait for my call. But plan on being back here, *with your cousin,* by about 1500." Just like that, the meeting was over, Miguel's favorite cousin was about to get himself killed, and he was supposed to rest. They walked slowly back to the big tent in the rest area where Raul had secured continuing care for him.

Sending Miguel back into East L.A. was out of the question, not only because of his weakened condition, but further because he would be killed immediately if discovered by any of the gangs present in the area. And after talking it through with Raul for a while, he had to admit that, if they were to have any real opportunity to interdict the influx of all those big guns into the home area, Raul was the one to do it.

Miguel even bought into the idea that he could accomplish the mission without getting killed in the process.

He lay back on an old National Guard canvas cot, shaded from the afternoon sun by an open air tent, while a light breeze moved through occasionally. Lying there looking up at the plain covering, his mind moved, again and again, over the soft lines of the girl's motionless face, tracing the softness he had touched with his rough hand. He fell asleep in the middle of that vision.

* * * * *

"Houston, this is Blackbird Command. Repeat, Houston, this is Blackbird Command, do you copy?" Babs Morgan's head jerked around from the computer screen she was watching, as the voice was not coming from her headset but could be heard over the speakers all over the large room. Turning instantly back in the direction of the communications desk, she shot a deadly look at the man whose console received and directed all incoming transmissions, just as he scanned the whole array of information in front of him. He was about to confess that he couldn't place the origin of the voice, when his eyes found a flashing light on the master control panel in front of him.

"Got it, Babs, patching to your console and headset—*now.*" She hit the transmit button and spoke into her mic at once.

"Say again, Blackbird Command, this is Houston. We have your transmission, but did not copy the entire message."

"Houston, roger. This is Blackbird Command, and we are advised of satellite transmission interruption. One of our planes is passing over target area now, altitude 80,000 feet. Please stand by while we patch you direct to pilot. We cannot transmit pix just yet, but pilot has camera visual on suspect area, so you can get description from him. Blackbird one, this is control, you are patched to Houston, go ahead."

Babs shook her red curls furiously at the idea that she could not resume photo observation of what was so clearly about to be the launch of some kind of a missile. *"Jimmy— why can't we get a feed from that plane via satcom transmission—for crissakes, Jim, we gotta see what's going on over there!!"*

"Houston, this is Blackbird one, do you copy?"

"Roger, Blackbird one, this is Houston, you are clear. We are attempting to establish link with satcom net to receive photo images from you, but don't have it yet. Do you have visual on the Palace location?"

"That's affirmative, Houston, through my lens I do. Control transmitted me the pix you took from the bird before losing contact with it, and I confirm that aperture in the top of the long building. I'll be having to turn and make another pass in another twenty seconds, and I'm losing my visual on the suspect area right now, but—*stand by. Repeat. Stand by one. HOUSTON THIS IS BLACKBIRD ONE, AND I HAVE INTENSE LIGHT AND SMOKE AT BASE OF THAT HOLE. REPEAT. I HAVE CLEAR LINE OF SIGHT ON IGNITION. DO YOU COPY?*"

Babs whacked the keyboard in front of her and was instantly in contact with Arrow base, while still having contact with the pilot of the SR71. *"Arrow base, this is Houston—Avi, we have ignition. Repeat. We have visual confirmation of an ignition at the suspect location, per aerial high altitude observation. Do you copy?"* A silence that seemed like hours followed Babs Morgan's call to the Israeli interceptor station, but just as she was about to retransmit, he responded, his voice strained but calm, calculating.

"Babs, this is Avi. I copy ignition from suspect location. Do I have audio communication with the pilot?"

"Affirmative, Arrow. This is Blackbird one. My visual is gone for two minutes. Repositioning via steep turn right now. Stand by. But I repeat, Arrow, the bastards have fired something out of that hole."

"Avi, this is Babs, I just got new image from the bird. Confirm ignition, and this picture clearly shows a missile lifting off out of that hole. I repeat, liftoff confirmed, as of— *shit—Jimmy—advise elapsed time since this image was taken by the bird—NOW."* Again seated at the next screen, the young technician beat the information out of the keyboard and responded immediately.

"Avi, Babs. Images depicting liftoff now forty seconds old. Do you copy? Missile airborne since liftoff now forty five seconds ago."

"Roger, Houston, the missile is still too low to show up on Arrow's tracking screen from line of sight, but the satellite is transmitting telemetry data right now—got it. Repeat. I have tracking and a lock on the missile. Pray for Israel, Houston, Arrow out."

The huge room was dead quiet, but for the soft whishing sound of the air conditioning. Like some reprise of an old Apollo mission when the lunar module lost signal before reentry, everybody stood motionless. Avi Reisman was fully occupied, and there had been no time to establish any kind of capability for monitoring activities at Arrow base. Then, without warning, the big screen in the middle of the upper wall of Houston control lit up with a sharp picture being transmitted from the Blackbird. No one moved or breathed, as a series of computer images flashed across the screen, each clearly depicting the bright point of flame that was the Iraqi nuclear missile as it rose into the cloudless night sky.

"Houston, this is Blackbird one, and I have visual on the missile right now. Repeat. I can see it climbing to, let's see—yeah, my screen tells me it's up to twenty thousand feet and leveling off. Must be heading—wow—here comes Arrow, I can see its light. . .heading for intercept—computer says twenty seconds. Goddam but that's a fast bird—can't give you any numbers, but looks good to this point—ten seconds to intercept—I have visual, now, I'm about one hundred miles—"

"*Blackbird one—break off!! If Arrow makes contact, we expect a nuclear reaction—do you copy?!*"

"Yeah, Houston, I'm back and pulling away but my camera has a lock on the missile. You forget, Houston, mach three gets me space—*quick*. Four, three two one—Dearest Jesus, Houston, they missed it. I repeat. They missed it. *Arrow base, this is Blackbird one, repeat, no contact. Arrow did not intercept target. If you can destroy your interceptor, you better do it quick, 'cause it's headed for the ground, according to my onboard computer, not far south of Baghdad. Confirm, Arrow base.*"

"Blackbird one, this is Arrow base. Affirmative. Ours will destruct in five, four, three, two, one—"

"Confirmed, Arrow. This is Blackbird one, and your bird just lit up a big piece of the sky west and just south of me;

about sixty-five thousand feet below my present altitude. Sorry, Arrow. What now?"

All breathing stopped after a unison gasp. Babs barked into her headset again. "Patriot base, this is Houston, Arrow has failed to intercept. Prepare to launch. Do you copy?"

"Roger, Houston, this is Patriot base. We have lock on the missile. It's still too far for interception by Patriot but we have trajectory fix and solution. Stand by."

21.

There were a total of ten television screens in the situation room in the White House, although only two of them were lit up as Jackie Webb sat watching with Mac Reed and Molly. He turned from the view of the George Washington Bridge, the vision burning in his mind of thousands of panic-stricken people running from the deadly strafing fire of automatic weapons being fired from the tall buildings back at the edge of the river. Flashing across the next screen, directly to the left of the first, was a series of images obviously transmitted from some kind of high altitude device, whether affixed to a satellite or an airplane unknowable at that moment.

"There it is, Jackie, right there. See? Big hole in the top of that building, just like Morgan told us a minute ago. Looks like—*hell, lost the picture—CORPORAL, GET HOUSTON ON THE LINE—WE LOST OUR VIDEO OF THEIR OPERATION.*"

"Relax, Mac, those people are busier than a bunch of one-armed paperhangers right now. Keeping us in the loop is not the most important thing, anyway. Besides, by the time I could get enough info to get in the decision making game, the whole thing'd be over. Let 'em work." Just as the President finished his thought, the screen lit up again, this time with pictures of an obviously different origin. The audio feed suddenly kicked in, and they were ringside to the drama being played out in Houston, on the desert floor in northern Israel, and some 80,000 feet up in the sky, from the nose camera of an SR71. In perfect unison with the rest of the players half way around and above the globe, they held their breath as the intercept failed to hit the big missile and, with his pulse pounding in his temples like multiple small explosions, Jackie looked at the ashen face of his wife.

"Dearest Jesus, Jackie, is that thing going to go off in Israel? Can't we get to it with something? I mean, if that missile can—"

"Don't know, Molly, at least not yet. We have a Patriot installation that will probably hit it, but God only knows what will happen when it does, especially if the nuke is armed when contact is made." Reed stole a glance back at the view from the belly of the Apache that was blasting away at some terrorists on a rooftop, then looked back at the face of incipient nuclear war. Suddenly it seemed so ridiculous to him, all that screaming, yelling, running across that huge bridge. In a matter of hours, the whole city might be a smoldering radioactive heap, if the Arab world—or the Chinese—decided to include the U.S. in the party.

It was impossible to know how these wild men would behave, unlike the predictable, calculating Soviets of Cold War days. And Jeffrey Flint had sold enough multistage missile technology and guidance system intelligence to the Red Chinese to have set them up with excellent capability for hitting most of the major cities in America.

All in a moment, he remembered the quickly stifled cries of treason when Flint overruled his own National Security Agency decision not to sell such potentially deadly information to ones so bent on world domination. Of course, the simple coincidence of the transfer of about two million dollars from the Chinese to the Democratic National Committee had played no role. None.

In an instant he was snapped out of the momentary musing, as the radio transmission from the SR71 confirmed that the Israelis had successfully destroyed their own errant interceptor. Looking again at the screen of the big bridge, he noticed that the scene had changed to another location, further east and north, where a like mass of humanity jammed Interstate 95. The area depicted the junction of 95 and 895, right in the heart of the Bronx, with Interstate 278 just visible when the helicopter with the camera turned to the southeast.

"Holy shit, Jackie, looka' *that*, would ya? Must be twenty thousand people up on those roads—and look at all those choppers. *Shit,* must be fifty of 'em swirling around—firing, too. . ." Both of the Webbs turned back to that screen, their minds attempting mightily to absorb the drama now spinning across the two displays. The President looked over to see his wife cover her face with her long, slender hands, then lay her head down on the table in front of her. At first thinking he heard her crying, he stood and started toward her, then stopped, realizing she had simply surrendered to the stress and was reciting the Lord's Prayer.

Touching the back of her neck for a brief moment, he whispered against her cheek. "Best thing to do now, Babe, keep it up. Looks like the whole thing's up to Him now, no matter where you look." The wide shoulders turned back toward the two screens, the psyche torn horribly between the passion playing out on the streets of New York and the devastation about to be rained down upon Israel. A flitting thought stopped him for a beat. Would God permit this to happen again, and on the sacred soil of the homeland of his Chosen? Then a pair of helicopters blew apart almost simultaneously, obviously hit by some kind of powerful weapon, and he again tried to focus for a moment on the awful plight of his own people. The tension was beyond calculation, the torsion between the two simultaneous horrors exquisite. Only Molly had sense enough to pray.

* * * * *

Since the advent of what the medical world calls "intensive care" or "critical care," people in the West have forgotten all they ever knew about just how hard it is to survive active infection, particularly when accompanied by substantial blood loss. Modern man gets so much good supportive care, so fast, and with such comprehensive attention to all aspects of any problem that in most trauma cases blood loss is minimized by quick response time when the injury occurs. Moreover, with such quick access to trauma centers and on-call qualified surgeons in command of large and technically proficient teams of supporting staff, sources of bleeding are just as quickly repaired. Immediate transfusion of that which has been lost helps to avoid the kind of shutdown that otherwise would occur.

Infections, even in people who are weakened by injury or disease, are attacked with immediate powerful intravenous doses of antibiotics that can eradicate even the most virulent of bugs in a matter of hours. And with great attention to sterility and ongoing efforts to keep wounds clean and the treating environment virtually germ free, this civilization has become accustomed to surviving all but the very worst of traumatic injuries. That is, if there are such facilities, and such professionals, and such supplies and tools to deliver that result.

Joshua Owen Landry was not so fortunate. And his physician was now very aware of just how far short of delivering that kind of care they really were. Over the past months, they had lost a score of other patients to infection and blood loss, several of whom were not hurt as badly as Josh. Faith Jackson sat at the foot of his bed and recited the situation, like doctors are wont to do—sometimes as a method of sifting through the various considerations in hopes of tripping over another idea, a forgotten remedy, a procedure to try when all else seemed hopeless.

"Don't think I understand how he could've lost that much blood, even with those two scalp wounds, Carl. The compound fracture was really ugly, but the hole it made was not so very big, and we saw no arterial involvement when we repaired it and set the bone. But his BP is in the pits, and his pulse is so slow and weak, maybe that owes more to the effect of infection. And if he's into rampant osteomyelitis, we have-."

"We have nothing to treat it with. I know, Faith, I know. Look, I found this one vial of injectible Ampicillin, enough for an i.v. if we can mix it with some saline. Let's blast the hell out of him with all we can give him, pour the fluids to him, and maybe we can boost that blood pressure a little. Keep attacking the fever topically with those towels the rest of the day and overnight, then try to get him awake enough to get some kind of nourishment into him by morning." She nodded, then shook her head as another huge problem occurred to her.

"We gonna fill him up 'til he pops, unless we can rig some kind of catheter to drain his bladder. You know what kind of problems that creates, and we have nothing to do that with, except some small plastic tubing." Without speaking in response, Carl Landry uncoiled his long frame from the floor and walked out into the main house. She was right, of course. Unless they could answer that problem, a whole additional set of problems, this time including the potential for kidney failure, would likely kill the patient, even if the infection and blood loss didn't.

Faith moved back to the head of the bed, where Janice Landry continued to bathe her father's face, neck, chest and abdomen with a wet towel. The bath in cool water had been a huge job, extremely dangerous and difficult to accomplish. But it had made a significant difference in his temperature, which was down to 102.8 degrees. Fearing the potential of deepening shock, he was removed from the water and returned to bed, where various adults and kids took turns constantly cooling him with the wet towels. Jan looked up into the doctor's face, fear branded deep into the girl's young eyes. "He's heating up again, Faith, I'm just sure of it. And his breathing is so slow and shallow now." The voice tried not to crack, went hoarse, then to a whisper. *"Oh Daddy, my sweet Daddy, please don't let go, Daddy. . .please. . .please. . ."*

"Carl, Jan's right, he's getting hotter again. I think he's losing ground. If we're gonna do anything, we gotta do it now." The elder Landry had reappeared, a long length of clear tubing in hand, along with a container of lubricating jelly and an empty bucket. Under one arm he held two clear plastic bags of saline solution to replace the now empty one that hung from a picture nail above the bed. Without speaking, they ushered everyone out of the room, pulled back the sheet that covered the patient, and went to work. Long odds, deadly problems, no supportive care available. And Joshua Landry's condition was headed south.

22.

Everyone already knew what it meant for a Patriot missile to intercept the incoming nuke, after a whole day of contingency planning and alternative war gaming. A hit by a Patriot missile would prohibit the nuke from making it to its destination, but almost certainly would not happen before the warhead was fully armed, as now it was only four minutes from its intended target. Men and women in the big control room in Houston stood ashen, faces slack and tear-stained already, knowing that, in the most fundamental sense, all hell was about to break loose.

Communications Director Morgan sat still in her chair, eyes trying to focus on the now blank screen, the transmissions sent by the SR71 having ceased. As she hit the keys to connect with Arrow base again, the whole room gasped in unison as the voice of Arrow base broke the silence.

"We have fired our second interceptor, Houston, and it is—"

"HOLY MOTHER OF GOD, HOUSTON, WHAT A FIREBALL!! HOUSTON, THIS IS BLACKBIRD ONE, AND ARROW HAS KILLED THE MISSILE!! REPEAT, HUGE FIREBALL, KILL CONFIRMED!!" After a moment of total silence, cheers exploded all over the room, hugs and backslapping were exchanged, while Babs hit the mic key again, her voice piercing over the din.

"Blackbird one, this is Houston—do you have a nuclear reaction? I repeat, *can you confirm nuclear explosion? Did the warhead arm, or did Arrow hit it soon enough?*" While the celebration was understand-able, the question was more than of passing importance. If a nuclear reaction was spreading over Jordon, southern Iraq, and northern Israel, the fallout would be deadly, and the reaction of all states would almost certainly end in a full scale nuclear exchange. If the warhead was not armed when hit, the wreckage would be dirty with radiation to be sure, but there would be no significant impact in the area. Just as fast as it had erupted, the jubilation stopped, and everyone again stared at the empty screen and the speakers placed around the walls.

"Houston, this is Arrow base. We confirm kill, and there was no nuclear explosion. Repeat, no nuke. I guess God just couldn't let it happen. Babs, this is Avi, do you copy?" Barely breathing now, but finally truly exhilarated, she responded at once.

"Avi, this is Babs, copy. Congratulations, Arrow, nice shot! I guess I didn't know you had a second interceptor ready to go. And I'm amazed the nuke didn't detonate. Where was it when you hit it?

We just got number two finished about an hour ago. It wasn't supposed to be ready until Monday. Don't ask me how they did it, but they did. When I hit the second launch switch, boom. Oh—the point of interception was just west of Amman. We can't believe the warhead wasn't armed. Conventional wisdom is that warheads are always armed by the time they reach maximum altitude, and this one was well beyond that. I think they must have set a low trajectory for the rocket to minimize the likelihood of early detection. The elapsed time for the entire route would have been only a few minutes. We are in your debt Houston, the people of Israel thank you. This is Arrow base, out."

"Jimmy, where's that champagne? This old broad needs a drink and a long night's rest. Go get that booze, while I call the President. He's been monitoring this whole thing, but I better make contact. Sixteen hundred, *this is Houston, do you copy?*"

"Houston, this is the President—we heard the entire exchange. Thanks, Babs, you were all great. . .wish I had something more presidential to say, but I just started breathing again about sixty seconds ago. This is 1600, out."

The deadly missile was gone, reduced to scraps of hot trash that fell to Earth outside of Amman, Jordan. But the shock waves felt around the world at the first attempt at a nuclear strike in over fifty years were, at that moment, incalculable.

* * * * *

Afternoon raced by in blinding heat, thousands of military personnel totally overwhelmed, not so much by enemy forces that struck from perfect concealment with deadly effect, but by the mass of sick, starving, even dying humanity that had responded to Molly Webb's idea for stimulus. I was beyond the wildest imaginings of all.

610

To be sure, the punk warlords and gang leaders who had so effectively held the large populations in manageable groups for the past months were appalled at the effect of even such a small impetus to escape. These people, since March, had sat in captivity, frozen by fear of the weapons and unspeakable cruelty that typified the conduct of their captors. And the terrorists who continued to execute their plans for long term urban warfare used the moment of the great escape to murder as many Americans as possible.

While the military necessarily had to expose itself to close-in hostile fire to provide cover for those who poured out of their imprisonment, the masters from the PLO made optimum use of the opportunity. Firing every weapon and projectile in their substantial arsenal, the terrorists killed tank after tank, helicopter after helicopter. American soldiers and pilots faced them down between the buildings, where innocents flooded the streets, a great human sea of sick, injured, terrified refugees. But the effort overall took a heavy toll on the guerillas, primarily because they had never expected U.S. personnel to evidence such a willingness to sacrifice themselves for the sake of those on the ground. When a helicopter was hit by recoilless rifle fire, others around him were poised to identify the source and respond at once.

The result was a great loss of enemy manpower and weapons, far larger than the PLO expected. And the ultimate source of power and the perfect shield against attack—the presence of a whole population of defenseless civilians—was quickly dissipating.

Sister Anne Marie clambered up the embankment to the massive expanse of interstate highway, two hundred refugees in front of and around her; her usually soft voice cracked and barked a barrage of epithets and sharp encouragement, as small children, old men and women, pregnant girls, sick and injured adults grunted, cried, pulled each other up the weed-infested slope.

A rainbow of ethnic mix, a slight blond girl tugged on the hand of a fallen Puerto Rican man, his arthritic, rough old hands struggling for a grip on her slender wrist. Three young black men, two of whom bore obvious and severe injuries that impeded their efforts up the hill, were making the climb, each with a small child wrapped around his shoulders and a second being held by the hand. The children were likewise a collage of white, Hispanic, and Asian. A priest and two more nuns followed, toward the back of this human surge, each carrying children, pulling, pushing, and prodding weak, sick adults.

"Stanley Long, wherever you are, you'd better be right! And Lord, my God, if he has sent us to die in this heat, burn his miserable soul in hell for eternity—*forgive my unbridled tongue, oh Father—*" Anne Marie crossed herself, releasing her grip on the hand of a black-eyed five-year-old boy whose Mexican lineage was obvious from great distance. *"Come on, Father Bill, Sisters, we must make the road surface before the Bloods find us. We can expect no cover or protection from the Army until we are up where they can see us clearly. Sister Louise, look behind you! There are the old ones from back in the warehouse—I completely forgot them!!"*

Releasing her firm grip on the little guy, then turning downhill and moving below an old Polish woman named Gertie, the nun placed her bony shoulder right up into the older one's bottom, driving her uphill like an offensive lineman attacking a blocking dummy. At the same time, she barked grunting orders to both the boy and the old woman before turning again down the hill. "Rickie, take her hand—and Gert, you gotta keep your feet under you—GO! You were fat for too long, you silly old Polack, but this tribulation has made you thin—only you still walk like a fat woman!! Now MOVE!! Rickie, you must make it to the top quickly, then follow the crowd, and do not go on without this old woman, do you understand?!"

She never looked back up the hill to see the wide-eyed, tear- streaked little face nodding furiously in the affirmative, his visage a passionate mixture of fear, anxiety, and miniature determination. She did, however, hear his little voice in the din, a string of Spanish exhortations peppering the aging lady he was now dragging up the embankment. But as that passion play continued with ever-increasing intensity, there were more and more tragic persons appearing from the old buildings, alleyways, and side streets, each making his own valiant effort to catch up to the ever-burgeoning throng that poured onto the Interstate.

Stumbling to the bottom of the slope, Anne Marie cursed the cumbersome garments that were an emblem of her occupation. She caught her balance, then, hiking the long skirts enough to lengthen her stride, she ran toward a small clot of folk who were shuffling in a loose formation toward the highway. "George—*George! OVER HERE— Come on, you guys, we have no time to waste, and there are others who can help you up to the road—now HURRY!!*"

A group of about twenty-five elderly black men and women, along with eight children, responded to her entreaties, and George, a handsome, silver-headed man who towered above his people at almost seven feet, waved a huge hand in the air, acknowledging the call. As they moved closer together and headed toward Anne Marie, she could see one of them, a stout old bricklayer named Ezekiel Rhodes, in their midst. Face set in an intense frown, steps purposeful but short and just the slightest bit erratic, he carried in his arms the form of a small woman, her arms limp, face jostling against the powerful chest. Recognizing the burden as that of Carvella Rhodes, the old man's niece, the nun felt a weight within, a sadness too bitter for reflection.

Carvella was dying, only a bit at a time, from abdominal injuries and unchecked infection suffered at the hands of gang members who held her enslaved in unspeakable confinement for almost a month before the old man figured out where she was and slipped her out of their clutches.

At twenty-two years of age, slender and beautiful, "Velvetta" was a woman over whom fights, even wars, might be fought. And the attention she had always garnered, without any apparent effort on her own part, long ago convinced her that her graces and favors, calculatingly bestowed only upon such men as could keep her "well," were in all situations sufficient to provide for her needs.

Then the devil came out to play, the conventions of even partially civilized society were discarded, and quite literally overnight she went from a pearl of great price to the prey of vicious pursuit. The fights were indeed fought over her, but not for her favors. Instead, gang members did mortal combat for her body, while she lay bound and gagged in a freezing janitor's closet for two days. When the victors, members of the local Blood franchise, finally prevailed, they found her semiconscious, her body a putrid mix of urine-stained garments, rat bites, and a convulsing, pneumonia-driven cough that sounded like the barking of a dog.

Drunk and already out of their minds in the blood lust, these fine young men ravaged her brutally for a day and a night before pitching her into a different cell in the old rooming house, where at least there was a mattress and some warmth from the sun as it shown in through the lone window. There she was defiled over and over, tortured and beaten off and on for almost two weeks. They fed her a little, brought her water occasionally, ravaged her at will.

Rumor led to rumor repeated and finally Ezekiel, Carvella's only remaining relative, took advantage of the zenith of a huge fiery riot that erupted some six blocks away and slipped into the building to carry her away. One sentry stood at the door to her room, but he was asleep, and the powerful old hands dispatched him silently with a single twist of the neck. He wept all the way back to the rectory with his burden, her face no longer recognizable, clothing all but gone, and the smell of rampant infection from the awful injuries between her legs threatening to asphyxiate him at every moment.

Somehow the small woman held on through the summer, but she took a turn toward death just before the evacuation began. Only Ezekiel cared not for death. She was his flesh, and he would carry her out.

"Zeke, come here—let me see her!" The broad shoulders turned to the voice, and he walked with short, choppy steps, meeting the nun who had nursed his niece so faithfully. A tender hand touched the face and forehead of the motionless form in the old man's arms, pulled back abruptly, pausing a second too long. The hand went back to the face, then pressed gently against the side of Carvella's neck. Head and shoulders slumped, again only slightly, and she shook her nun's headpiece from side to side. Voice now soft, hoarse, her face moved close to the sweat-drenched countenance of the brave old mason.

"Oh, Ezekiel. . .oh dearest Ezekiel. . ." She genuflected, whispered a prayer, pressed her lips with a tightly clenched fist. Again the soft voice, the cacophony of bedlam clattering around them.

"Oh my dearest Zeke, but your burden has passed. She is dead—I am so sorry, Zeke. . .her suffering is—"

Book IV – The Great Offensives

"I know that, Sister. I am old and full of hate and denial, but my senses are not gone. She died only a while ago, sometime after sunup this morning. See—she is still soft and warm. Only I could not leave her, this only piece of humanity that is left of my family, except for my own old bones. They will find her and violate her body, even in death, you know they will. We have seen them do it over and over before, Sister. You have stood in the window with me and watched them do it. I cannot permit that. I will carry her to the Army, so they can see to her proper."

With that, he walked past Sister Anne Marie, angling back into the group that moved now more quickly toward the embankment that led to the highway. The old nun swallowed a wave of convulsion, her chest in combat against the sobs, seizures of grief screaming within, demanding vent, expression. She could quell the expression, but not the tears, and the world gone mad was now gone to a blur, eyes afire with salt and sorrow. The end of the ragtag line came and went, the last of her lowly flock now between her and the route to help, but still she stood apart from them all, neither facing the way out nor taking a step to follow.

Like Lot's wife who saw too much, Sister Anne Marie stood in the middle of the street that crossed under Interstate 95, her ragged garments ruffled momentarily by the hot breeze that blew with such unpredictable and unreliable caprice. Blinded by tears, the agony of mourning so much loss, rage fought grief within her, and she stood still in the street. Seeing in her mind's eye the quantum of human suffering wrought at the hand of man over the past months; feeling the agony of unquenchable fatigue, knowing that order and peace were more than gone, indeed erased, the sobs broke the dam of her will. Alone there in the intersection, she could not hear the screaming entreaties of the priest and the other nuns, quickly joined by shouts of many, calling her to the roadway above the street.

Cries of alarm in addition to calls for her to hurry mixed into the superheated air of the Bronx, but all was drowned in the rending, overpowering grief that poured from the small woman. She could not see the phalanx of gang members approaching at a hard run, weapons held high, faces twisted in evil rage. Even the first shots fired into the crowd that made its way up the grade to the expressway were insufficient

615

to penetrate the roar within.   When she finally turned in response to perceived movement to her left a few feet, three men were on her before she could so much as turn her head.

23.

The smell of deep bleeding filled the air between the buildings. Small groans and gurgles audible only within the confines of the alley turned Raul Sanchez' head back and forth among the three bodies around him. His chest heaved, temples pounded, the detail of objects around him went white as he fought to retain consciousness. Sitting down hard on a stack of wooden pallets, he pressed the microphone key to permit transmission through the headset he wore. The confirming click in his ear told him his mic was open, and he started to call for extraction, code one. Then he released the button, breathed deeply a few times, decided to see whether or not there were additional problems to be encountered.

"Red Dog, this is Control, we show you attempting transmission. Transmission not received. I say again, transmission aborted. Please retransmit. Are you in emergency status? Over." Raul ignored the voice in his ear momentarily, as he bent over each of his assailants, checking for vital signs. The first two were clearly dead, one with two ten-millimeter slugs to the chest, fired from his silencer-equipped Glock, and the other with one to the chest and one centered in his forehead.

The third was the big surprise visitor to the event, a huge man Raul now thought he recognized, a giant who had crashed into the alley right when thug number two was hitting the ground. The Marine's pistol went spinning into a pile of trash against the far wall of the little passageway, as he went down beneath the massive weight of the man's body. A brief wrestling match followed, featuring a huge advantage to the aggressor in size and strength and an equally huge, even unfair, advantage to Sanchez in training and weapons. Raul never stopped moving, used the impact and bouncing of the big man's body as his impetus to roll them both over and into the center of the alley.

Momentarily free of the three hundred pound weight, the waning twilight could not catch the glint of the seven-inch Kabar combat knife that caught the big man under the sternum, then opened him, up and to the left toward his shoulder. To his surprise, Raul discovered it was this one who was still making noise, although his wounds would have dictated immediate incapacitation, and death within moments. Just as Raul leaned over to cut the man' throat, he breathed his last and was silent. Light-headed again, he sat back down on that same stack of pallets.

"Red Dog, this is Control, do you copy. Your transmission inaudible. Are you in emergency status? Over." Looking around him at the carnage that he had wrought in a matter of less than thirty seconds, then into the dark buildings on both sides of the alley, he knew from the quiet the danger had passed.

"Control, this is Red Dog. Negative. Repeat, negative for emergency status. Continuing operation. Tell DeCamp resistance has been encountered, but neutralized to this point. Out." When he came out of the ditch that served as an open storm sewer for the transport of flood waters under the freeway, the first half mile of somewhat exposed travel was uneventful. Then, as he entered a commercial area that he recognized as what had once been a string of shops and restaurants, a welcoming party of two appeared out of nowhere. They were armed with handguns and seemed to handle them with some ease, so he began by trying to bullshit his way out of trouble. Dressed in civilian clothing that was as putrid and filthy as they could find for him, his appearance did not produce any immediate alarm in the men.

Then one of them saw the ear piece in his right ear, and the fight was on. Raul hit them both at once as they stood close and directly in front of him. The heel of a hand to the point of each nose provided sufficient diversion to permit him to run right between them and into the alley, where they chased him to their respective deaths. Fair play not being an option, as soon as both were well within the cover of the narrow place, he spun and stopped, shooting both so quickly that the second had no time even to stop running before he was as dead as his partner. Now to dispose of this evidence well enough not to tip off his presence, and then continue his travels to the area of the Diablos' headquarters. Both were dragged into the back of what had been a small restaurant.

The contents of its large freezer had long since been looted clean, and it stood open, as if awaiting fresh produce. A moment of black humor flashed through Sanchez' head as he covered the bodies with what trash and junk he could find. Closing the door to the freezer, the thought of what awaited the first person to open the freezer, given the heat and the time likely to pass before discovery, made him immediately sick. Back in the alley again there was a bit of clean up to accomplish. A small flashlight helped him recover all four empty cartridge casings, and he scattered three of the pallets into the narrow passage to cover up the big bloodstains soaking into the dirty pavement. No time for more effective concealment.

It took almost two hours for Raul Sanchez to make it the rest of the way to the block that contained Diablos headquarters. But once there he quickly scaled the back wall of a building directly across from them, setting up on the roof in the black shadows of an air conditioning unit that stood close to the front. Whispered contact was maintained with his own commander for the mission, Peter DeCamp, who stayed on the line with him continuously. Not ten minutes after Raul attained this concealment, Pancho arrived, obviously agitated and even more obviously in a hurry. He arrived in an old Chevrolet Camaro, a sight surprising to the Marine, there being absolutely no petroleum left in the whole of Southern California. Fact was, Pancho walked mostly, but had saved the small car for use only when absolutely necessary. It still had most of a tank of gas in it from the last one he stole in the spring.

"*Where the fuck is Dannie—DANILO FERNANDO— WHERE*—I cannot wait on his fat ass. You. Marco, you will go with me tonight."

Just that fast, the huge man who now lay dead in the freezer of a restaurant some ten blocks away was replaced as *second* to Pancho, the leader of the pack. "Fatmouth will be here in ten minutes, and he will expect a show of strength consistent with the numbers we promised. And I can promise you, he will not make good on his promise to move those guns in here tonight unless we can show him our men and convince him that we have safe routes for moving the weapons into position.

"*Marco*—go inside and set up the table, lay out the map. Find one of those bitches and get us something to eat and drink. If they say they have nothing, kill them and get someone else. *Move.*"

The Devil's Playground

*　*　*　*　*

The afternoon melded into softer light, but the heat persisted, and Jericho Road had troubles enough, without knowing that nuclear warheads were being hurled through the night sky half a world away. They also knew nothing of a half million people pouring across the main arteries of the City of New York facing deadly enemy fire, themselves the objects of incredible acts of valor in their defense. Joshua Landry lay still, naked except for a sweaty sheet draped across his loins, a small plastic tube running from under the sheet to a gallon milk jug on the floor. Faith Jackson bathed his torso, neck, and face constantly with a wet towel that she constantly shook out, then laid back in place again. Carl Landry moved quietly between the pair of i.v. bags that hung from nails in the wall above the bed, then back to the catheter, each time constantly reassuring himself that all this plumbing was accomplishing its particular mission—fluids and antibiotic in, waste fluids out.

"He may be dying, but his kidneys don't know it yet. Boy's a human sanitation plant. Jesus, but he's hot, Faith. This fan seems to be blowing a blast furnace across his skin. Check BP again. I don't like this puny pulse a bit." She moved away from the bedside long enough to retrieve the blood pressure cuff, the drone of a gasoline generator, burning up precious fuel to power the small fan, audible outside through the window. Wrapping the limp arm in the well-worn cuff, she pumped pressure against it, stethoscope pressed against the crook of his elbow, then watched the calibrated dial as she released it.　The look on her face spoke the result before her dry mouth could form words.

"Eighty over fifty, Carl.　Down again.　He was one hundred over sixty-five an hour ago." The woman's shoulders slumped, curls shaking slowly from side to side as she looked at the instrument again.　Too long a physician not to know what it meant when vital signs continued to devalue in the face of treatment, they both could see Josh slipping away, the blood loss combining with powerful infection from his open fracture and multiple lacerations.

Outside the big bedroom, a watch of stoic faces filled the great room, soft voices occasionally interrupting silence. Luke nodded off to sleep, his head resting on his sister's lap, Janice

Elaine absently brushing a fly from his face; the others moved through the room, always casting quick glances toward the entryway into the master suite, then turning just as quickly away as if fearful that looking too long might produce bad news.

"Let's pray together again, kids. Hand me the Bible, too. I know it's frustrating, but it's what Uncle Carl told us to do. Here we go—*The Lord is my shepherd, I shall not want, He . . .*" Her soft voice again recited the psalm, as much for those around her as for her dying father. The evening wore on, prayers from exhausted lips the only sounds to come from Carl's place, against the background noise of that one generator, humming in the back yard. Bull bats swooped out of the sky, their clicking sonar sounds faintly audible further out toward the clean-swept hay fields, while barn swallows drew three-dimensional designs of indescribable complexity as they feasted on the endless supply of insects that filled the evening air. The first owl hoot of night overlapped the last soft song of the mourning dove that sat in a maple tree south of the barn, over against the woods that bordered the grounds. It was as close to a true time dilation as anyone could imagine, so much so that, before he fell asleep, Luke repeatedly looked over at the big grandfather clock, afraid he would see that the shiny disk at the end of its pendulum had simply stopped swinging left and right.

In the bedroom, even the doctors were deprived of any additional work, both of them commencing their own bone-weary prayers. Carl stood over the face of his only living immediate family, his best friend, his truest and best partner in all his life. Tears came and went as the physician gave way to the brother, replaced again by the physician, then pushed away by the friend. The ultimate irony for the healer, replayed throughout the life of every physician, was again before him. Capable of truly miraculous feats of healing much of the time, there was that moment when, in the face of simple, straightforward human sickness, there was absolutely nothing else to do. Life would remain, or it would depart. Just like that.

The Devil's Playground

* * * * *

From long hours of deadly quiet relieved only rarely by fragmentary reports, to the chaos that followed the moment when the Iraqi missile was destroyed in the night sky over Amman, one could not imagine a greater contrast. President Webb did not wait for the call from Netanyahu to come, instead immediately placing it himself; he wanted to be the first voice that declared the crisis past, not merely beginning. Of course, the exact opposite was obvious, as the entirety of the civilized world knew just how quickly response in kind might occur. And the Jews possessed a much bigger weapon and a far superior delivery system to anything held by the long list of their ethnic and political adversaries.

"I understand fully the passion you must feel at this moment, Bibi, terrorists continue to slaughter *my own* people while we watch helplessly from the air. Certainly, the very concept of a nuke landing on your soil is sufficient provocation for a retaliatory strike, but you must know that this is the most critical moment in time—a moment when restraint and circumspection are essential. Please, Benjamin, reconsider this order." The Oval Office was badly overpopulated, all eyes on the man behind the desk whose gaze remained riveted to the desktop as he spoke, then listened to the response. What seemed like the whole White House staff stood listening intently to the President's end of the conversation, foreign policy advisors and Secretary of State Burton seated on the edge of the big desk.

In fact, an equally large number remained in the situation room, where screens depicting evacuation efforts in half a dozen locations around the New York area continued to show masses of sick and injured people running away from the horrifying gunfire often being trained on them as they fled. Clyde Keithley stood watch over that venue, his observations often interrupted by calls from General Hambley or members of his staff. Reports came via e-mail, telephone, fax, and of course, rumor. The combined military forces of all branches of the service, plus National Guard units and hundreds of federal and state law enforcement personnel, tried to protect the refugees—and tried just as hard to figure out what to do with them once they were out of range of hostile fire.

The president clearly had his hands full, as calls began to stack up from every other chief of state in the western world; even the Chinese, Koreans, Indians, and Japanese placed calls in their efforts to determine what might happen next. Of course, none of them had gotten through to the Israelis, as Netanyahu was talking at length with Webb and, no surprise, Saddam Hussein wasn't taking calls. Probably busy executing a couple of young missile technicians and seeing to the covering of the launch site. The Palace Gardens roof quickly moved back into place after the brief cooling period was completed, so that now, in the dark of night, the place looked innocent of what had just been committed within it.

The conundrum was complex to the point of defying even a broad description. Would Israel, that possessed sufficient nuclear capability to vaporize Baghdad, respond in kind or would they choose a lesser magnitude of warhead and simply erase the restored palaces of Babylon? Might they rely instead on a swift and brutal strike from their large fleet of F15s, driving smart bombs down every smokestack, in the door of every power plant, and through the roof of every government building in selected major population centers in Iraq?

A full scale response of thermonuclear proportions would almost certainly provoke response of a like kind by Iran, although nobody was really sure they had a deliverable nuke anyway. Problematic for sure. But both they and the Jordanians had substantial chemical and biological capabilities, and Israel was reachable by both with existing unmanned delivery platforms.

A lesser nuclear response was not as likely to provoke Iran, although they seemed very ready to seize upon any excuse to initiate hostilities against Israel. Further, before the worldwide economic crash precipitated by the American power failure and the collapse of the electronic money system, nuclear tensions between the China and Pakistan against India had been mounting quickly. Some fear had been expressed by experts as long as a year before that the Chinese were bellicose enough in their antipathy toward India that any excuse would be enough for them to launch a preemptive strike. If they did so and the Indians responded, bombs would no doubt hit Islamabad in addition to Beijing.

The British and the French, both of whom had substantial nuclear capabilities and large enough interests in these areas of the world to be nervous, were the least likely to react quickly. However, no one could be sure how the Russians would behave, as their interests were ever more closely aligned with the consortium of Middle Eastern states that opposed Israel. Long the adversary of everything Jewish anyway, the fact that a now-collapsed Russian bureaucracy still possessed such a dangerous stockpile of weapons over that they had little control had stomachs in knots in London, Paris, Bonn, Rome, and the rest of western Europe.

The president and his staff spent the rest of the afternoon and into the night in Washington, telephone diplomacy maintaining a tenuous hold on a fragile status quo, peace being ever-so-delicate a balance to maintain. Then, early in the morning in the Middle East, a pair of Israeli F15s blasted an Iraqi aircraft out of the sky, and the calm was broken again. The Israelis reported the plane to be a spy craft, equipped with photo-reconnaissance equipment but also armed with rockets under each wing. The Iraqis denied even owning such a plane, screaming that the Israelis had shot down a passenger airliner, a DC10 with over two hundred persons on board.

There was no easy way to confirm any of this, as the formerly comprehensive worldwide aircraft and airline monitoring system that also was responsible for reservation information, flight times and routes, and cargo delivery data was now gone. There was simply no way to determine whether or not such a commercial flight ever existed, and Israel vehemently denied it, showing in support of their claims photographs they swore were taken by their fighters immediately before contact. Saddam fired up his crazy rhetoric at once, Saudi Arabia decried the killing of innocent persons, Iran announced expansion of its no-fly zone to include most of the Middle East in general, and a quick resumption of nuclear conflict seemed imminent. Morning in the White House came with no one even noticing.

24.

Mark Murrah had great difficulty with snoops in general, and the fact that they paid absolutely no attention to military decorum did little to improve their image in his mind. He stood looking at the unconventional attire of Peter DeCamp, the dirty sneakers adorning sockless feet, the Chicago Cubs baseball cap crowning an upper body clad in a Harley Davidson tee shirt. The shirttail slouched unevenly over the top of a pair of filthy fatigue pants, no belt of course, pockets bulging with cigarette pack and lighter, small pad of paper, a calculator, and a two way radio. He looked more like a reject or runaway from the YMCA homeless shelter than a captain in the U.S. Army. The general quelled a gag reflex, held his breath momentarily against the urge to skin the man.

"Oh—sorry 'bout the duds, Gen'ral, been up for six days now, ever since those beaner assholes decided to marry up with the biker crowd. Guess I could use a fresh suit a' clothes for a visit from the top brass—I mean, the big—aw hell, Gen'ral, I know I must look like dried shit, but if we could just get to it. . ."

"A capital suggestion, Captain, I must agree. We'll ignore the missing orthodoxy for the moment. I trust you will find time to address the problem of your uniform before our next visit. Proceed."

Amazed at the painless end to what for a moment had the potential for a real disaster, DeCamp tore into the details of the situation in East L.A. "Yessir, sir, I mean. . .yes, well here's the scoop. Our operative, Marine Sergeant Raul Sanchez, is located *here*, exactly where that red mark is. We know because he's got a bird dog—homing transmitter—on his belt, and we're locked on him. Also have radio communication with him right now. I spoke with him right before you came in.

"The bikers showed up an hour ago, right after 2100 Pacific Time, came in with a small group of six men, including the apparent leader. Sanchez couldn't hear them well, but the conversation did produce enough information that we think we have a fix on the ultimate location where the weapons will be hidden until they are deployed. Also, because of the need for concealment enroute, we think we know how they will get there. Here is the hideout, a Catholic school and church compound up in the Bell Gardens area—St. Pius X. Place is crawling with noncombatants, mostly Latinos and mostly very sick. Our informant has told us they have several hundred old people, a huge bunch of kids with a few parents in the mix, and they're all essentially hostage to the water supply. Diablos have it tied up; bring in enough to keep everyone alive, cut it off if anybody gets brave."

Murrah looked at the map for a long moment, his mind racing back over the reports he'd just heard from Dick Hambley about the fate of hostages in New York. "Can't let this happen, Captain, you understand that? They get those weapons, and *especially* that fifty-caliber machinegun, into place with all those people around it, there will simply be no way of getting rid of it, unless we just continue to let them shoot at us until they run out of ammunition for it. A very poor option, wouldn't you agree?" DeCamp never missed a beat.

"Right, sir, exactly our conclusion. That's why we have *this*. See? This is Florence Avenue—*right here*. This is I-710, and they intersect *here*. We can have Apaches about three air minutes away, stashed in these five locations, all up and down the Interstate, moving them right now, so they can land and wait. Got two Warthogs ready to go up—waiting for assignment, as well. They're up here, at Bracket Field, a small airport over next to the L.A. County Fairgrounds. Fortunately, those things don't need much runway, so they're just twenty miles away— no more than about six minutes from the target area, once they lift off.

"We have a SEAL Team right over *here,* hiding in an empty hospital building, and they report visual on this interchange between the freeway and Florence Avenue. The street goes under the Interstate there, and it makes sense that they'll use it for cover, checking their back trail before moving into position. There's also a stretch there that has a road surface under the expressway, running with it, so they can move without being seen from above. So, the SEALs confirm their presence, we call in the Apaches and the Hogs, and poof! toasted bikers and no more marriages made in hell. OK?"

Murrah stifled what wanted desperately to be a big, wide, approving smile, not only at the excellence of the plan, but at the picturesque delivery. But then, Mark Murrah didn't smile. Not at times like this. Ever.

626

"Captain, what is the noncombatant situation at this proposed ambush site? If these people have as much ordnance as your sources suggest, this engagement will light up a wide area around the interchange you have just identified. As you have been told repeatedly, we can't be killing the people we are supposed to be liberating, *OK?*" A short pause found DeCamp waiting just a moment before responding, as if not to appear smug at the general's question.

"Good point, sir, and one that gave us a lot a' heartburn until we realized that this area has no—repeat *no*—water. Water tank that supplied that particular garden spot went dry two months ago, and everybody's gone. Snitch confirmed that as well. The water ran out, then the thugs moved up north of Commerce, up here, and the people all went, or died. Whole place is a ghost town—really. So, we can blow the livin' crap outta things without hurtin' a soul except for the Sons a' Silence."

"Good. I like it. Just be sure those wild men in those aircraft don't destroy that bridge. Division Supply tells me they need 710 open at all costs. And if you blow that bridge, 710 is closed for good. Let's get that little detail covered without delay."

"But Gen'ral, what if they hide under that overpass? Choppers'll swoop down and blow 'em right outta there. But that might damage the—"

"My point, Captain, precisely my point. They are not to engage these people at any location where injury might occur to the bridges over 710. Is that clear? Now. I like the plan, so advise the players and carry on. Oh—and Captain. If you have a Marine in place at the Diablos HQ, don't you think he should neutralize it and all its occupants before we extract him?" Murrah's eyes were gray flint, his breathing shallow and slow. It was obvious he had already thought through this piece, and he was intent on taking the President at his word on the subject of dealing with gangs—and taking prisoners.

"Thought you might see things that way, sir. Sanchez has a sniper rifle in his backpack, broken down but quickly assembled. He's planning to take out everybody he can get his scope on, then run like hell for an LZ we have right up here, two blocks away. He'll leave a second bird dog on the roof of this building, across this street from Diablos Estates, and as soon as we have confirmation that he's off the building, boom. One of our Cobras, a California Guard chopper, will blow the thing to hell. OK?" Then it happened. Turning completely around to face the Sad Sack captain, the General smiled.

"OK, Captain, OK."

* * * * *

Heavy dew saturated everything in and around the woods south of the house. Not a breath of air stirred in the deep stillness of night, even the owls and other night birds were silent. A pair of does rustled through heavy underbrush some fifty yards outside the bedroom window, stirring the old black Labrador to momentary life. He woofed a couple of obligatory admonitions to the invisible intruders, then settled back down under the porch off the back of the house. Crickets and bullfrogs tuned occasionally, their percussion more a feature of the silence than a sound to break it.

Carl Landry was standing before he was awake, head swimming from the quick start and the heavy, hard sleep that had overtaken him some three hours before; the quiet approach of the deer, plus the dog's reaction, brought him to life too quickly for his mind to get good control of his body. Panic gripped his chest and throat at once as he began to comprehend the total silence in the room. His feet got tangled up in the light cover that had lain over his shoulders as he slept on the floor beside Josh's bed; he tripped and stumbled into the corner post on the bed, inflicting an instant red goose egg over one eye. But even that pain was insufficient to overpower the reality that there was no sound coming from the bed where his brother lay.

"Faith—*FAITH!! Come here—there's no sound—FAITH—*"

A match struck in the darkness behind Carl Landry, a lantern then began to increase its glow to shed some light toward the motionless form on the bed. They had left Josh to wrestle the giant alone, some five hours ago, every last trick and treatment by then exhausted, the fever still ravaging him, comatose, vital signs weak and fading slowly. Prayers had replaced practice, every last drop of available antibiotic already used, remaining supplies of I.V. fluids anchored in a last effort to provide sufficient volume and coolant against the fever. Finally, after nearly two more hours of sitting beside the bed, bathing his torso, each time lifting the wet towel then hot to the touch, the brother left his patient

Carl finally committed it to the Almighty, said one more prayer, laid down on the floor to rest a moment. Three hours later, the struggle appeared to be over. Still lightheaded and woozy from the shot to the forehead inflicted by the bedpost, he sat down heavily on the side of the bed, near the patient's feet. At once he knew he was about to vomit, lurched toward the adjoining bathroom, collapsed over the stool. The noise he made, heaving uncontrollably into the porcelain, was sufficient that he could not hear Faith calling his name, over and over, each time louder than before until finally, between heaves, he heard her screaming at him from the bed.

"Carl—*PLEASE—GET BACK IN HERE—LOOK AT THIS—!!!*"

The waves of nausea persisted but, summoning strength from an unknown source, he stood and wobbled back into the doorway, arms spreading to hold himself erect on either side. "What—Jesus, Faith—I'm sick as—"

"*CARL, HE'S NOT DEAD, HIS FEVER HAS BROKEN, AND HIS PULSE IS MUCH STRONGER. Still comatose, but I'm doing a BP right now, and—yup—100 over 65, up on both ends!! He's—*"

She was bulldozed by half a dozen bodies clamoring over and around her to get to Josh's quiet, cool body. First among them was Jessica Marie, who had his head cradled in her arms in an instant, her hands probing, feeling, sensing all over him.

"*She's right, Carl, he's not dead, and he's cooled way down—Dearest Jesus, he's broken the fever—Oh Carl—*" The woman spoke no more, not for several minutes, her sobs, at first audible, ebbing to quiet sounds that muffled into her husband's hair and skin. Tears ran down from his motionless face—her tears seeming never to end. Gently, quietly, kids began to appear, moving up and around their mother, arms and hands constantly feeling Dad's flesh, reassuring themselves over and over that he was still there, still living, no longer on fire with infection. Over and around all these arms, hands, legs, and heads the physicians did their best to determine their patient's condition.

"Weak pulse still, Carl, but lots better than when I left him three hours ago. I came in to check on him, found you asleep there and covered you up. He was still so hot, BP unchanged from the prior reading. I almost let myself think the steady pressure was some sign he was holding his own, then told myself that was stupid. Here, look at this." She held up the thermometer just removed from the corner of the patient's mouth, her face half shadow in the dimness of predawn; the lantern flickered as the fuel ran low. "One hundred point five. Down almost five degrees since we gave him the last of the saline." His BP is up, pulse weak but steady and up to forty-eight, respirations shallow but better, up to fifteen."

Carl again fought the battle between physician and brother, emotion vying with medical acumen and experience, a war between hope and cynicism born of long, painful learning. "If I didn't know better, I'd have to say he was coming out of the woods. He can still crump on us at any time, but he's coming, anyway. Sis, hey—let's not glom onto him too long. You kids kiss your father then go to bed. *And don't forget those prayers—of thanksgiving, this time!!"*

Kids began pulling away, then kissing Mom on the way out, until only the two doctors and Jess remained. She looked at Carl, her gaze fatigued beyond description, but a resolve apparent as her lips parted to speak. "My brother, you have saved my husband and your best friend, both of you have done it. If I try to thank you, I will only cry again, and I simply do not have the energy for more of that. But I must stay here—it's where he wants me, Carl, and you know that. I cannot leave. He knows I am here, and I cannot leave, do you understand that?"

"Easy, sis, you took the words right outta my mouth, right Faith? He wakes up without you here, it'll be my ass for sure. So you just snuggle up and go back to sleep. I just can't believe what I've seen this time. Never had one pull through under such circumstances—hell, never had such circumstances before. Guess Josh was just too ornery to let the bastards get 'im, after all. Lord God, but that was close. . Lord God, but it was. . .sure was. . ." Taking up one of the damp towels that had provided a cool touch for his brother over the past hours, he buried his face in it, as if to wipe away the crushing fatigue and stress. The rag was filled with sweat and spotted with blood.

Silent sobs filled the towel, broad shoulders heaving without sound; Carl Landry felt the gentle arm of his cohort around his waist, and they walked out toward the kitchen. The intense presence in that room lay still and thick, as the air out in the house so quickly drew contrast to the closeness in that sickroom. The devil had been cheated this time, at least for the moment. The family still had Joshua Owen Landry, though his weak, broken condition left him vulnerable to all manner of danger yet. No more the leader, at least for the present, others would carry that burden.

Jessica brushed aside another tear that ran from her cheek to his. She kissed the rough face again, touched his lips with her fingertips, and was asleep.

* * * * *

The Oval Office desk looked like a telephone and TV repair shop, screens, receivers, and wires strewn about the top in a tangle that defied logic. There was a monitor that kept displaying satellite pictures of the entire wide area around Babylon, up to Baghdad and then west and south out into the deserts and desolation of southern Iraq and northern Jordan. Another screen flickered with live video from numerous locations throughout Manhattan, New Jersey's sprawling urban complex, and north on the many main arteries being used to move the enormous flow of refugees out of town to shelter and safety. A third lit up early in the day with a view of the Bell Gardens area around East L.A., and there was also a monitor that provided the President with visual capabilities for meetings with the Joint Chiefs of Staff at the Pentagon.

Phone sets of various colors provided communications with the heads of state who kept a constant barrage of calls flowing into the White House. Every leader in the western world, the Orient, and the Middle East was seeking reassurance concerning the moment to moment heightening of the tensions that paralyzed a world terrified of nuclear exchange. Deepening economic depression and the privations that attend such phenomena were suddenly less important, the fear of imminent devastation taking all available energies.

But what the rest of the world had that the Americans did not was electricity. They had telephone service, heat, and in some places still, air conditioning, and they had radio and television for the delivery of information. The Internet, although still extant in some minor form, was essentially vapor in cyberspace, thanks to the end of telephone lines and satellite communication uplinks in North America. Canada and Mexico were hit with a pervasive loss of electric power as well, many areas of both countries being part of international treaties and consortiums for participation in the now defunct U.S. network grid of power delivery. That put them in the dark and also took away their communications capabilities.

Only the military was able to produce real telephone and radio communications for the most essential purposes, using AWACS aircraft, the military satellite system, and some of the more exotic space age toys they don't talk about very much. A network of sorts was cobbled together to keep the administration moving and in touch with the rest of the world. Jackie Webb spent the entire twenty-four hour period after the moment the Israelis destroyed Saddam's nuke doing an international telethon, threatening, cajoling, pleading, even occasionally bluffing one or more temperamental heads of state; the result was pretty impressive. After the Israelis splashed the one Iraqi MIG, things froze in place for several hours.

The Palestinians stopped blowing up restaurants and buses full of children, suddenly aware that their own interests were very much exposed; the Israeli Army and Air Force were on full alert, combat patrols searching for any excuse to pick a fight with their enemies. Of course most of the Arab world had absolutely no clue that Saddam would act in such a monstrous way, and most were unaware he even had a nuclear capability at all. A second period of incalculable stress commenced with the bushwhacking of a PLO contingent caught out in the open in the Golan Heights, some ten hours after the MIG incident, the Israelis voraciously decimating a force of almost a hundred armed men in a matter of minutes. That fired up Arafat's windbag momentarily, but even he found real propaganda a bit risky in view of the botched nuclear hit that he had so eagerly awaited and so aggressively encouraged.

By 2 a.m. the following morning, some twenty-six hours following Arrow's big score, things seemed to have frozen into a sort of tense standoff, with the Arabs, Egyptians, and even the PLO quietly satisfied with a fragile status quo that did not include the kind of swift reprisals, both air and ground, for which the Israelis were so famous. Truth be known, even Arafat could not deny the Islamic world's consistent failures when it came to doing real combat with the Jews. The big bomb was to have changed that balance, giving them the kind of advantage that only such devastation can accomplish. No luck. Instead, air superiority mixed with a substantial measure of righteous indignation and holy rage began to spook the less rabid members of the Arab community, and moderates like King Hussein of Jordan, the Saudis, and even the Egyptians were all too happy for things to cool off without the Israelis dishing out a few doses of their fury.

"Jackie, it's been thirty-eight hours since you slept and, frankly, dearest husband, you look like hell. Mr. Reed, would you assist me in a little temporary takeover? Jonathan, please take my husband into protective custody and deliver him to the private quarters at once."

"Now *wait* a minute—I should be hearing back from London and Paris on a conference call within the hour, and I told—"

"Bag it, General, your wife is right. With all due respect, Mr. President, the last three conversations you have had, all since midnight, have been a re-hash of the same conciliation speech you've been giving for twenty-four hours and, honestly sir, that visit you just had with King Hussein made absolutely no sense. Time for the boss to rest. You are hereby placed under spousal arrest. Take him away, Sergeant Major." Reed smiled through tired lines and two days worth of beard, nodding toward Jonathan Brooks, the tall slender form of the Marine moving to the president's chair.

Webb knew they were right, and he doubted his ability to resist their entreaties any further. After refusing to leave the helm no less than a dozen times over the past hours, it was clear they were right; in point of fact, he was unsure of his ability to lead or govern *at all,* without some rest and a good meal. He stood, dropped his glasses on the desktop, turned and followed Molly out of the Oval Office and into the hallway. Turning back into the room, he squared his aching shoulders to the maximum height he could muster, spoke directly to Mac Reed.

"Mac, if anything—and I do mean *anything*—untoward occurs, you are to summon me at once. Is that clear to you, Mac?"

"Yessir, you know it is. I have no desire to play acting president for you or anyone else, General. I'll just tap dance with the intermediaries and try to keep the temperatures steady while you rest a bit. *Promise.*" Reed smiled again, and Webb responded in kind, then turned and was gone.

The chief of staff looked at the mass of wires, screens, monitors, and telephone sets on the big desk, shook his head slowly, then sat down in a side chair and closed his eyes.

"Best medicine for the present condition just might be a small dose of benign neglect." No one was there to hear the thought expressed in low tones to an empty room, but the prescription was right on the money.

25.

"Red Dog, this is Control—DeCamp—we have activity over on the other side of I-105—SEAL unit says they hear auto engines. It's the right area for the Sons to be in, and they should be moving by now if they're going at all. My watch says it's 0300. Do you have activity at Diablos HQ?"

"Neg—oops—spoke too soon. Yeah. They've been in there all evening, in and out, mostly some of Pancho's groupies and a couple girls, but just now two big bikers have shown up. One is *really* big and nasty look—*oh—shit, that's Fatmouth. Damn.* OK, Control, got a pretty good crowd. Maybe it's time for a party. Request permission to fire on targets of opportunity."

Peter DeCamp responded at once. "Negative, Raul, stand by. Gotta wait until the weapons are all out in the open, on the street, so we can hit them before they can react to the presence of Cobras at your location. Sounds of your strike might scare 'em off."

Sanchez lay motionless against the side of the air conditioning compressor, his heart pounding slowly, little intense arguments raging in his head about where to shoot first. And there were women among the group now visible in the building and out in front, on the street.

"OK, Red Dog. The Sons are confirmed to be enroute, headed just where we thought they were going. Headed up through Southgate now, no more than three miles from the ambush site. They're too far away from you to hear your rifle."

The captain looked around the now busy room, a gaggle of intelligence and combat types, all mumbling into headsets, telephone receivers, microphones. The snoop captain raised his hand for quiet and was accorded immediate attention.

"Red Dog has both the leader from the Sons of Silence *and* Pancho Sanchez at the location right now. Unless someone has some excellent argument against it, I intend to order him to take out everything he can hit, then scram." There was a short beat of silence, then DeCamp turned back to the console.

"Red Dog, this is Control. Fire at will. Repeat. Fire on all targets of opportunity, then move to the extraction point. Stay no more than sixty seconds. I am scrambling your chopper ride right now." As he spat those last words, he turned part way around in his chair, pointing and nodding at the same time in the direction of a Sp4 who was seated at another radio console. The youngster acknowledged the signal, keyed his mic at once.

"Air Control, this is Liberator Command. Air control, do you copy?" The radio squawked in response, the kid immediately resuming his transmission. "OK, Air Control, we have confirmed extraction of Red Dog. Repeat. Extract Red Dog now. He will be at the LZ in five minutes. Do you copy?" Again the quick confirmation.

"Air Control, this is Liberator Command—again. Contact both Apaches and Warthogs at Bracket field at once. Commence operation. Also order the Cobra to proceed. The bird dog is in place, transmitting on prearranged frequency. Transmitter is sixty feet directly south of target, directly across the street. Apaches can lift off in two minutes, but the Hogs need to hit it right now. Over." DeCamp confirmed all this back to Raul Sanchez as he heard it being ordered by his staff.

"Red Dog, your chopper is in route. Be advised we have also scrambled Apaches and Warthogs for the weapons ambush and a single Cobra to light up the Diablos location, so the place will blow in six minutes. Commence firing and hurry up."

Raul Sanchez essentially ignored the last words from DeCamp, busying his hands and skills with a quick check of the compact little sniper rifle now at his shoulder. Mumbling into the stock, he reacted only within himself. *Right, Captain. Like I'd stick around for a smoke. Ready Set Go.* A confab of the big boys found itself interrupted as they stood on the dark sidewalk outside the little cafe, thirteen rounds of exploding bullets thundering through their number in nine seconds. So unexpected and devastating was the attack that all but two of the eleven persons who were standing on that sidewalk died without moving.

Bodies tumbled and fell over each other, a spatter of blood instantly glistening in the soft light coming from candles inside. Loaded with twenty rounds, Sanchez focused and shot, shifted focus, fired again, all in what seemed to be slow motion. In fact, he emptied the first clip in just over fourteen seconds, the sharp report of the 5.56mm rounds deadened by the suppressor assembly on the barrel of the short rifle and the remaining sound being swallowed up in the close confines of the narrow street. Reloading almost without pause, the second clip found the only persons to attempt escape and killed them.

A sharp click caused Raul to draw breath quickly before realizing his second ammunition magazine was now empty. That was the signal to withdraw, so he hit the quick release button on the side of the receiver of the rifle, broke it down and jammed it into his backpack; at five thousand dollars a copy, Uncle Sam took a dim view of abandoning such exotic weaponry. Standing part way, he permitted himself a moment to peer into the dimly lit pile of bodies, his eyes searching for confirmation that both Pancho and Fatmouth were down. The big white man was easily recognized, his bulk accentuated by his position, sprawling half on the sidewalk and half in the gutter at the edge of the street. Head, neck, and torso were essentially exploded, the only remnant of now-gone life being the sporadic twitching of one leg. That too ceased while Raul watched.

For a moment, panic gripped the sniper, as he was unable to find his cousin in the grisly mess. Then, as if by magic, he was there, standing amid the dead and the dying, his shirt and face one huge splash of glistening color. Without so much as a thought in advance, the boxy, efficient Glock automatic appeared in Raul's hand, at the same instant spitting three rounds down into the bloody torso of his cousin. The man was not large, and the impact of the big, fast bullets hitting the sternum jerked him off his feet and hurled him back into the dead behind him. The Marine turned, shouldered his pack, and slipped down the drainpipe and into the alley. Three minutes of steady running found him diving into the floor of a small helicopter, then lifting off in the direction of Liberator's command post. He permitted himself no reflection on what had just happened, or that it had included killing a relative he had loathed since childhood.

* * * * *

The business of coordinating forces, men and machines coming from different locations, bearing various weapons and having separate missions, is not simple. With the addition of one or more air components, things really get complex, as the speeds at that they can travel enroute to targets are so much greater than for any ground troops or vehicles. So, when Liberator Command prepared to hit the Sons of Silence as they moved weapons toward the protection of a vast human shield, it was paramount that the air strikes not occur until ground units were in position to come in behind them at once. The whole idea of such timing is to follow the shock and fire superiority that happens when gun ships strafe and blow up targets immediately with ground attack, while the enemy is either still retreating from the aerial barrage or is at least cowering within whatever cover they can find.

That being the logic, and such coordination not being within the acumen of Peter DeCamp, he eagerly stepped aside when Sanchez reported completion of his mission, and an erect, shaved-headed colonel took his place at the control console. Thomas Joseph Travis, U. S. Army Air Cavalry, stood about five feet eight inches tall and weighed all of 138 lbs. The voice was deep and confident, bearing such as to discourage any approach other than one of deference, if not supplication. Adjusting the headset against his ears, he moved the mouthpiece into place, examined the short list of frequencies in use, then began by addressing the aircraft.

"Warthogs One and Two, this is Liberator Command, please respond and confirm liftoff." The terse transmission produced immediate results, both pilots affirming their airborne status, direction of flight, speed, and time of arrival over the target area.

"Apaches, this is Control. We have confirmed airborne status of tac air. Please advise radar contact with two Warthogs and your status at this time."

"Roger, Control, this is Apache One. We have two birds up ourselves, and both Hogs on the screen, plus radio contact on this frequency." Colonel Travis had copied the initial communication between the airplanes and the helicopters, but protocol required confirmation by the aircraft as well.

"OK, aircraft, standby One. Warthogs, proceed on current course, but approach no closer then one mile. Repeat. One mile. Apaches, stay low and out of sight until further order." He clicked the little knob on the upper left of the console in front of him, the red LED numbers scrolling to the proper frequency for his next transmission.

"Ambush Leader, this is Liberator Command, do you copy? Please advise position and status."

"Control, this is Ambush Leader, and we copy all. We are in position as per your order, Colonel, three platoon-sized units on line, one a block off the line of travel, awaiting your order. We have two tanks, one in the front unit and another with the reserve. We are prepared to attack from both sides of the interstate bridge on your order. Over."

Travis paused for a breath, nodded his head, and looked up at his assistant, a tall, slender master sergeant named Longley. Flattop haircut and pockmarked face identifying him as all business, the man tipped his head imperceptibly after reviewing a map laid out on the table next to the console. "Roger, Colonel. Right on the money. Where are the targets?" The boss shook his head, hit the button to transmit again, this time changing frequency to the surveillance unit in place close to the bridge.

"SEAL Spotter, this is Control. Please change to tac frequency with the others and confirm."

Control, Seal here, changed as ordered. Sir, we have visual on the first elements. Looks like about eight or nine older model passenger cars and two vans, dark in color. Standby." Travis and Longley exchanged a quick look, then the speaker squawked again.

"Control, this is Seal Spotter, we have visual on that big gun. Repeat, what looks like a fifty-caliber machinegun is approaching, mounted in the bed of an old one-ton pickup truck. Over."

Longley lit a Camel, shook his head affirmatively, jabbed a finger into the map he was now holding up for the colonel to see.

"Bingo, sir. Here they are. They can't be more'n ninety seconds from the cover of that overhead." The diminutive officer never acknowledged what was said, only turned from the map and hit the button again.

"OK, people, this is Control. Let's dance. Apache One and Two, move into position, west and north of the target intersection, prepare to engage targets from the front as they travel northbound. Copy?" Instantly the chopper drivers responded, then orders were given the Warthogs. "SEAL Spotter, this is Control. Advise distance to overpass by lead elements."

"Roger, Control, lead elements in the area—now about a block from the bridge. Over."

"Hogs, this Control. Maneuver south and east, come in behind the column now. Maintain altitude not less than eight hundred feet and confirm radar or visual contact with the Apaches."

"Roger, Control, this is Warthog One. We have the choppers on radar, and I can see the lead bird off to my right about one mile. His tail rotor light is visible from here. Moving into position and—OK, Colonel, we're in position and have visual on the targets. They can't be more than a few hundred feet from that bridge and the road that runs under it."

"Apaches, maintain altitude of not more than five hundred feet; acquire targets and fire. Repeat, commence fire mission. Over." The helicopter pilot flying the lead aircraft quickly confirmed the order, and the two swooped down and into the windshields of the old cars, the first hint of their presence a stream of smoke, fire, and steam as rockets streaked from beneath their bellies into the cars. The second bird approached right of the first, his mini-guns and rockets lighting up five vehicles at once before both of the dark craft pulled up sharply, banking away for a second pass.

On the ground, bedlam reigned supreme, as the men in the cars and trucks not hit by the first volley turned wildly in the street, engines racing, tires screeching and smoking as they moved desperately away from the conflagration in front of them. A van and a pickup truck collided at low speed, momentarily blocking not only their own route of escape but also that of three other cars that were closer to the first impact point. Like a deadly game of bumper cars, they banged and crashed against each other, screamed oaths and epithets into the darkness, backed up, squealed tires again, roared away from the horror behind them.

Although there were many older combat veterans among the number of the Sons of Silence, none had seen anything like this since the late sixties, and many had never been chased by aircraft at all. Panic was boss as they searched the darkness for avenues of departure, some so scared that they turned on their headlights to see what lay in front of them. A sharp cackle smacked the ears of all on the assault frequency, as one of the Warthog pilots saw the lights.

"Holy shit, Control, some idiot just turned on his headlights. Goddam—there's another—permission to commence fire mission, Control." The tall master sergeant grabbed a headset, spun the dials, barked into the microphone.

"Ambush Leader, do you have any units in that block, and are they stupid enough to have their lights on?!"

"Negative, sir. Negative. Light 'em up, sir."

"Warthog One, this is Control. Commence firing." Tipping the stubby stick to the right and slightly downward, the pilot banked his slow-flying jet into position to acquire two of the vehicles, a string of red and white sparks signifying tracers and hot rounds that streaked down into the street and through the tops of the old cars. A huge explosion erupted out of the trunk of one of the two, confirming a large supply of ammunition as the cargo; the other simply flew apart as cannon fire punctured its gas tank, spattered the walls of the buildings on either side of the street with body parts, molten steel, gore, and burning fuel.

"Hogs, this is Control. Pull off and prepare to hit the convoy again, this time from behind. Apaches, move in from the northeast and strafe again. Ambush Leader, prepare to move out."

Three confirmations followed on the radio, followed in about fifteen seconds by two parallel streams of fire that sliced up and down the flanks of the now motionless vehicles. Then, without warning, white phosphorus tracers appeared, ground to air, not the other way around. "Jesus—Control, we're taking fire from that fifty—thought we got him first. He's—" The transmission ended, Apache One now pinwheeling, augering into the side of an empty apartment building along the street.

"Control, this is Apache Two, One is down!!! Repeat. One is down!! I'm up and out of the immediate line of fire, but the fifty is in place, and there are men on foot running toward it for cover. That makes the lead vehicles now empty, so they'll be easy, but that machinegun is a real problem, sir. Can the Hogs get to him?"

"Control, Warthog One. I got a glimpse of a couple of tracers, but that's all. He's down along the interstate, can't see where he's hiding unless he moves again. I'll sweep out a ways, get out of range, try to get a make on him with the infrared. Give me a minute."

"Ambush Leader, this Control. Move in from the west side of the expressway, send in units to take out that gun. Go up and over the highway, engage him from behind, and hurry—that bastard gun is a real problem for air cover. If nothing else, find him and mark him with smoke or a flare. Then the other chopper or the Hogs can hit him. Over." An excited voice responded within a few seconds, and orders moved through the units of ground troops hiding in and around buildings that bordered the elevated freeway on either side.

The shock effect of such a devastating air attack was sufficient to demoralize and totally confuse the remaining drivers and their companions from the convoy of old trucks, cars and vans, while both ends of the long string of vehicles were reduced to burning wreckage. The middle of the column, however—those travelling in close proximity to the truck bearing the fifty-caliber machinegun—followed it back into the cover of a clump of trees that grew up against the embankment that formed the foundation of the expressway. An overpass provided direct and pretty significant protection from aerial fire, and the trees concealed their positions, if only briefly. But all that could do nothing to permit the Sons of Silence to hide from the night scopes operated by a SEAL unit positioned atop an apartment building a few hundred yards to the west of their hiding place.

"Control, this is SEAL Spotter. Ambush Leader, do you copy this transmission?"

"Affirmative, Seal, this is Ambush Leader. Go ahead."

"We have an infrared visual on a little party of subjects now hiding under an overpass a block south of Florence Avenue on 710. Spotter reports six men and the big prize. We have visual on the truck with the machinegun. Can you get in behind them and engage?"

"Seals and Ambush Leader, this is Control. We have to protect the integrity of all overpasses—that highway is crucial. Do not use any explosive that might damage the bridge. Are you clear?" Both units confirmed, then the ground force leader ordered a close-in assault from the opposite side of the highway. Again, high-tech warfare permitted those in the command post to actually watch what was happening, via the cameras mounted in the nose of the Apache.

"Control, this is Apache Two, and I have infrared visual on the location described by Seal Spotter. Can you pull it up on your monitor?" The tall master sergeant was moving even before Colonel Travis could turn to look at the screen next to the radio console. Within a few seconds the strange, artificially colored background was visible on the monitor, and just as quickly, although at some distance and off to the north at a pretty severe angle, the forms of a small group of men crouching around a pickup truck were in the picture. The chopper lifted up and away, back over onto the east side of the expressway, the camera then observing a squad of dark forms approaching the overpass from the south. No one moved, scarcely breathing as the soldiers slipped closer and closer to the short tunnel under the highway.

"Ambush Leader, this is First squad, and we have the subjects. Will move in with small arms only, but request permission to use the grenade launcher on that truck."

"Negative, First Squad, this is control, do not light up that truck. No explosives under the overpass, do you copy?!"

"Control, this is Ambush Leader, sir. Colonel, the round from that M79 is too small to hurt a bridge of that size, and we need to take out that gun before our men enter the confined space under the bridge. Request permission to—" The long, lean figure of Jimmy Lee Longley appeared beside his commanding officer, and the brass spun as he felt his sergeant at his shoulder.

"Sir, that soldier's right. The explosive charge in an M79 round won't hurt that bridge, and sending a squad into the tunnel with a fifty- caliber waiting on them is crazy. I've blown plenty of vehicles in close quarters with that round, and it's safe enough, even if the fuel in the truck goes up. Please reconsider, sir. Gonna lose some troops if you don't." Travis' jaws knit, his dark eyes darting to the monitor that showed his men approaching the entrance to the short covered area where the enemy was hiding. Each passing moment increased the chances of detection, as they had to expect that very quickly the Sons would realize the need for cover at the opposite end of the tunnel that was formed by the highway overpass.

"All right Jimmy, but if that highway crumps, we're both dead meat. *Ambush leader, proceed. You may employ grenade fire to take out the gun.* "

In no more than ten seconds following the order a sharp, furtive movement could be seen through the infrared eye of the hovering Apache, a single soldier crouching at the edge of the entrance to the short tunnel. His body reacted to the concussion of his short grenade launcher bucking against his shoulder, and a second later, a flash at the other end of the bridge was followed by a huge fireball, signifying ignition of the truck's gas tank. Ten men poured into the tunnel behind the explosion, and the sounds of automatic weapons fire filled the darkness around the bridge. A squad of four more men scaled the steep embankment up onto the expressway, scurried across, opening deadly fire down onto the small clot of men now cowering among the trees at the edge of the street.

"Control, this is Ambush Leader. Unit leader reports gun seized—destroyed, actually—no survivors. Believe we have the whole crowd now. Have set up perimeter surrounding the entire length of the convoy, and we'll watch it until first light. At that point we'll move in and clean up. Suggest you move on that hostage location, sir."

Thomas Joseph Travis began breathing again, his mind stopping scarcely long enough to realize that they had just averted what would have been a truly horrible situation, had the recoilless rifles, automatic weapons, machineguns, and ammunition just destroyed gotten into position. He changed frequencies, ordered immediate move out of three lines of troops that were waiting to extract over four hundred hostages from the location identified by Miguel Sanchez the evening before.

Jimmy Lee Longley nudged his commander slightly, drew on a Pall Mall, smiled imperceptibly. Bending at the waist just a bit, he turned his head to speak quietly in Travis' ear. "Nice job, sir. Got 'em out without a hitch, except for that Apache. Oh, and sir—about that M79—told ya' so." Travis smiled back, equally imperceptibly, then turned to the console and his next objective, several hundred sick, starving Americans held captive in their own neighborhood for five months.

644

Book IV – The Great Offensives

* * * * *

"Zero nine hundred, sir, we have the conference call set up with JCS Chief and theater command. Can you come to the situation room, sir?" Jonathan Brooks waited patiently as Jackie Webb turned from his seat in the Oval Office. Smiling through tired eyes, he nodded and stood. They walked together to the big room on the lower level of the White House where Mac Reed and several of his staff were waiting.

"Good morning, people, do we have everyone?"

"Everyone but our president, and he's here now, so I guess the answer is yes." Reed grinned at his boss, the anticipation in his countenance anything but subtle.

". . .the hell you smiling about, Mac, you just swallow *another* canary? Look at him, Sarge, looks like he just left a private audience with Cindy Crawford—*hey—you haven't been gropin' the help again, have you?!*" Reed's face reddened, then the grin got broader as he prepared to respond.

"No sir, Mr. President, you must have me confused with President Flint—and besides, nobody left to grope except old Jon, there, and I'm afraid he might hurt me!" The laughter was quick and tension relieving, but was quickly followed by silence, as the president sat down in front of the conference call microphone-receiver apparatus.

"General Keithley, are you there? Let's get started."

"Yes, Mr. President, we are all here, General Hambley in New York, General Murrah in L.A., and my staff here at the Pentagon. Good morning. Sir, as I believe you are aware of the continued progress in New York, I would like for Mark to lead off, if that's OK. Mark?"

"Good morning, gentlemen, and greetings from sunny California. At last we have some real news. I can report that at about zero three hundred hours this morning, elements of air and ground forces interdicted a convoy of civilian vehicles, about fifteen in all, enroute to a suspected base location in the area of Bell Gardens, where two gangs had already moved several hundred noncombatants. These persons were to provide human shields for a cache of weapons and gang members, who would then in turn fan out into secure positions throughout the community, each place being similarly fortified with hostages."

There was a short pause, uncustomary for the clipped, often curt delivery so much the trademark of Mark Murrah. When he resumed, his voice was softer, obviously shot through with fatigue and tension, but somehow also much more transparent to the man.

"Boys, after almost a month of shadow boxing with these people—a month in that our most pervasive mission has been the effort to dispose of dead bodies—things are finally turning around. North, up around Santa Monica and further out, the engineers have cobbled together a sort of power grid, using a combination of generators and two small power plants they were able to fire up, and we have hospital facilities and even restoration of electricity to a few small communities.

"The bad guys are really losing their grip, as much from the effects of disease and starvation as from anything we have done, but I can report that our engagements with criminal elements have been picking up and yielding some serious results. But the best news is that ambush this morning. Mr. President, we have started moving what turned out to be almost two thousand noncombatants out of the Bell Gardens area, and word of them being freed has started a flood of refugees that seem at times to be coming out of every crack in the sidewalks. We are certainly a long way from anything that looks like success, but I can say that, for the first time since we arrived here, I see some hint of progress."

The reports from Hambley's venue were similar, and nobody dared declare victory, particularly in light of what would be left when the fighting finally ended. But there was that sense that maybe before the weather turned from fall to winter real attention might finally come to beginning the process of reconstituting, reconstructing, the devastated republic of the United States of America.

BOOK V

CONCLUSION

1.

It was what the military has always called a "field hospital." Long rows of low tents filled the athletic field from goalpost to goalpost, two rows that ran parallel the entire length of the field, an aisle way between the two wide enough to permit vehicle traffic. In the middle of the whole complex sat a doublewide tent with access via wide flaps on all sides, where motionless patients were constantly being wheeled in and out--surgery facilities in the midst of what other-wise could only be described as medieval circumstances.

The rest of the tents housed the sick and injured, those suffering from malnutrition and exhaustion, and an area just for the old folks whose bodies were simply worn out by the strain of the past months. Down close to the end of the line of wards, in an open air collection of the elderly and those who were stable and mending from wounds or illness, was a small gaggle of kids and young women, plus a couple of the aforesaid old guys, sitting around the bed of a frail, slight figure. She sat up in bed, bandages around her chest and shoulder, through that could be seen the obvious stump of an amputation above the elbow of her right arm. The head was decorated with three small bandages that covered laceration repairs now nearly two months old. She was pale, but her voice was strong and deep, just a hint of cigarette rasp adding texture.

"You have *another* visitor, Sister, a young soldier who says he knows you from the day of the escape. Or do you have *room* for another one?!" A large, stout Army nurse was ushering a tall, handsome black sergeant into the tent, his eyes wide with anticipation, his expression a mix of surprise, awe, and joy. Specialist Fourth Class Stanley Long, U.S. Army, blushed and smiled self-consciously, the relief on his face radiating throughout the room. "You may have to take a number, soldier; Sister Anne Marie seems to know at least fifty percent of the patients and most of the soldiers, in the entire city! Let me know when you're ready to leave; I'll need to sign you out--Sister has her own guest registry!" There was no edge to the wisecracks, and the big nurse smiled broadly as she left.

"Well, Stanley Long, it seems your advice was accurate after all. I guess we are in your debt. People, this young man is the soldier I told you about--the one who visited me the morning before we made our great exodus. I was treating Theresa. . ." The soft lines of her small face froze, clouded, then the jaw set, she blinked back a tear.

"Stanley, you may remember the girl I was treating for her burns when you so rudely interrupted us. Her name was Theresa Oldham. Father Dave carried her out himself. She died up on the express-way."

There was no way to know what to do next. Tall and bulky, the soldier towered over the smaller people, all of whom sat on or around the nun's bed. At once, he felt out of place, a rush of pathos and sorrow coursing through him. Stanley Long knew the operation he had volunteered for had been a success and that noncombatants by the thousands had responded to the message delivered by Stanley and others that running away from the gangs was the only hope. He also knew many had died. Snipers murdered hundreds, firing from concealment with horrifying effect at the throngs of refugees fleeing hopeless confinement. And many more simply could not make it. No doubt, Theresa Oldham was one of those. But that still did nothing to allay the feeling that somehow, in some way, he and the others were responsible for their deaths.

"I do remember her, Sister, and I am so very sorry. . .many died that day, and the next, too. But you are here, and the nurse tells me you were able to get almost your entire parish out in one piece. I--"

"You misunderstand, my son. I do not tell you of Theresa to lay blame, but to let you know that because of your brave message I could bring her out, not leave her to rot like the others. Come, let me look at you." Stretching her one remaining arm, palm up entreating his hand, she beckoned the tall youngster to her side. Two kids and one older woman moved quickly, making room for him on the side of the bed, and as he moved forward, his hand reflexively reached for hers. She pulled him gently toward her and, as he sat, she slipped a slender hand around his neck and held him close.

Book V - Conclusion

The soft light in the room helped conceal another tear glistening from the corner of her eye.

"Oh Stanley, I had so hoped you might know what you accomplished that day, and I have hoped and prayed against despair that you were well. Being able to see you again is a joy beyond words." The voice quieted even more, deeper and huskier now, emotion clutching her within. Speaking softly into the front of his fatigue shirt, her face resting against him, she wept heavily for a moment. "Look at me, *would you*--a soppy old woman, after all. I must control this, for the love of --it's not like we haven't already cried!! It's just that the moment of your visitation signaled the only ray of hope we had seen in six months, and I have been so afraid I would never be permitted to see you again and thank you myself. Lord knows I was less than cordial the last time you saw me!"

They both smiled, remembering the terse method the old nun had used to dispatch her messenger when he first approached her about encouraging her flock to break ranks and run for help. Stanley began at once attempting to find Sister Anne Marie, as soon as it was clear that her area was in fact evacuated. The evidence of ambush and atrocities committed both by gangs and by the well-armed terrorist force was ghastly for American troops who came in behind the exodus or swooped in to provide cover for the sea of helpless people that responded to the call to leave their captivity. As he moved through that area that included her parish, Long found piles of bodies, mutilated corpses, scores of dead who had been shot down or beaten to death, and many whose bodies had simply been too weak to respond to the demands of the trip.

"I looked everywhere for you, Sister, even went back through the church and rectory, all through the convent and the school, only to find the place empty. Can't say I was surprised--never doubted you'd find some way to move all your people. Then we came on an awful scene under the Interstate, where it looked like a thousand people had run up the embankment to get away. We removed thirty-eight dead, found almost a hundred more injured in the block around that location, and lost almost half of them before we could get them to medical help. Never found any evidence of you, but in the middle of all that mess, nobody could be sure. Just heard a rumor that sounded like it could be you last night, and here

I am." He smiled again, at the same time enveloping her fragile frame in another hug.

As he released her, the soft voice began again, her head shaking slowly from side to side, eyes tightly closed. "The last thing I remember is the sight of armed men coming at me from two sides, the sounds of people screaming and shouting behind me as they made their way up onto the highway, and a sense of being knocked off my feet. The next thing I remember is the sound of the helicopter that brought me here. I passed out again, remember nothing else until waking up in a recovery tent, just a few yards back toward the entrance of this compound. The Lord wasn't finished with me yet, I guess. But so many didn't make it, and I have heard many stories about what happened to those who did not get out. It. . ."

"Leave it behind, Sister, please. Just let it go. What we have seen in this city in the past six weeks cannot be described, and none of us will ever recover if we dwell on it. You are safe, your life was spared, and I can only say that this is one prayer of mine that has been answered." Embracing her again, he laid her gently back against the pillows, shook hands or hugged the gaggle of the devoted who surrounded her, then walked out into the October sun. Promising to return was easy; actually coming back to see a face that so powerfully reminded him of a quantum of sorrow and horror that haunted him now for months was another matter. Then suddenly the truth of where he was overtook him, and he hurried out of the compound and back into the street.

* * * * *

October stayed warm and inviting on the West Coast, although the intense heat of August was thankfully absent. Miguel Sanchez was convalescing from a bout with dysentery that had laid him waste for nearly a month. His assistance had been the decisive factor in derailing the coordinated effort by his brother's gang to entrench themselves in East L.A. permanently. Now, for the first time in months, food tasted good, and he was enjoying a singular treat. Raul had just smuggled into the tent/ward of the infirmary where he was staying a single one-quart Budweiser, cold and refreshing, and the patient was so overcome with delight he could not decide whether to laugh or cry.

But other stimuli assaulted him as well, knowing his brother was dead and in fact dead at the hand of the cousin who now visited him daily. A time of separation then a couple of long talks had cleared the air, and there was even an odd sense of completion in realizing that the family had taken care of its own business, even in the midst of all that chaos. However, none of that could compare to the real source of his broad smile as he drank from the beer bottle. Seated on a folding chair beside the bed was the elegant, though frail, person of Lucinda Parker.

Her hair was still short, and careful inspection revealed long scars in her scalp. Her dark skin still lacked the sheen of health, but a look at her chart would tell that she was in fact gaining a bit of weight. The doctors who examined her after she survived the first hours following her extraction from hell discovered that the damage done to her by the multiple rapes endured that one awful night was more superficial than at first feared. Walking was still painful, but her slow movements only seemed to accentuate her elegance in Miguel's eyes.

The affinity they shared for each other blossomed almost at once into romance, interrupted during early September by his struggle with dysentery. But she stayed close by, coming daily to see him, even if she had to sweet-talk a nurse or friendly soldier into pushing her to his bed in a wheelchair. Only in the past ten days had she begun to walk the hundred yards from her ward to his. And while his own weakness continued to define the narrow boundaries of his world, his growing passion for this one lovely face, this life the Lord had permitted him to save, urged him ever more quickly toward recovery.

"You stare at that girl any harder, you gonna burn a hole in her, Miggie. . .for crissakes, boy, you act like you'd never seen a pretty face before!!" Lucinda's black eyes averted toward the ground beneath her bare feet, a soft blush of color passing across her cheek. Miguel smiled with great abandon, so full of joy was he at the sight of this person.

"Shut up, Raul, you wiseass--every time I look at her, I see reason to rejoice in the middle of all this tragedy, and you know it. And don't act like such a tough guy--after all, who was it risked his neck to go pick her out a' that sewer, anyway, huh? You not so bad, after all--now *is* he Lucy?" Her eyes still studied the floor, a self-conscious grin impossible to conceal from either man. They watched her for a moment, then all three burst into laughter. Glasses clinked together, as the three shared the rare bootleg beer Raul had brought in an empty ammo box, and all knew they were slowly, gently knitting together that alchemy all people seek, the bond of family.

Lucinda Parker's people were all dead, the man killed by Pancho her only relative, an uncle on her father's side whom the Diablos had mistaken for her man. Twenty years old and unmarried, her large family was all gone, lost to starvation, disease, violence. And her short life had already been filled with years of harsh realities shoved in her face on the streets of East L.A. So the soft voice and tender eyes of young Miguel Sanchez felt to her like a gentle shower of God's love, the first and only tenderness ever to touch her.

As they talked and confessed all in those long hours, she learned of his criminal past, he learned she could not read. She pronounced her own and the Almighty's forgiveness of past wrong-doing, and he taught her from the tattered Bible that lay on the stand beside his cot, from old newspapers and magazines, even what was left of billboards and signs visible from the hospital grounds.

And they knew, as their relationship grew each day, that they resided in an artificial environment, where electricity and clean water were delivered by the Army, and where medical attention was immediate whenever they were threatened by illness or relapse from injury or malnutrition. The two of them were to the medical staff what they had become to each other--miracles of spirit and survival, evidence of success amid failure, of life in a valley of death.

Raul embraced his cousin after downing his beer, lifted the small face of Lucinda Parker in his hands, kissing her gently on the lips, then on both cheeks and, in a gesture now become ritual among the three of them, turned as he stepped into the doorway and said, "I love you both." Every time it happened, the same way each time, the girl was so overcome that speech was impossible for long moments. In her life, no man had ever touched her face, and no man had ever kissed her mouth except in that rude and licentious way that attends lesser appetites. The acceptance signaled by the touch and the familial but intimate kiss, when followed by an expression never before spoken to her, transported this woman to great joy.

Raul was not her man; Miguel was the passion she had always dreamed of, even if still ravaged by malnutrition and disease; but Raul was older, the head of this family they had knit with blood and suffering, risk and commitment. His strength and resolve, and that tenderness and earnest passion for connection that was so engrained in his gaze, inscribed across his countenance, gave them both hope for better days. It chased away that nagging fear that clutched the throats of all persons, that fear of being lost, torn from all they held dear, important, relevant. They would survive, thanks to Almighty God and His emissaries of mercy within the confines of the sprawling medical facility that was now home. And they would bond themselves, so different in some ways and so alike fundamentally, into the family they all so desperately wanted and needed to be.

Lucinda Parker stood slowly, deliberately, stepped across to slide onto the bed beside Miguel Sanchez. She sat looking into his shy face, his eyes glistening as he permitted himself to see her up close. "I love you, Miguel. And in all my life I never thought I would hear myself say those words." He reached up and pulled her face to his, kissed her gently, spoke so no other could hear.

"I love you, too, Lucy. Only promise me never to die."

* * * * *

One thing autumn could do that even anarchy was unable to stop was to paint the nation's capitol with nature's paint brush and brighten its disheveled countenance, at least for a few weeks. Because of the brilliant splash of color now decorating the area around the White House, the President had taken to requiring every meeting and conference to be there, and always--every time, if it wasn't raining--the curtains were flung wide and the windows open. Expressions of concern for security or secrecy were dismissed at once, often with the retort that "any sumbitch who wants to know what we're doing bad enough to get this close without getting shot is welcome to all he can hear."

The Devil's Playground

The Cabinet met twice weekly, "at zero seven hundred", their combined energies and skills taxed beyond description by the continued awful problems facing the country and the sheer number of issues to be addressed. To say that the Middle East was at peace was a laughable overstatement, although the month and a half since Saddam's botched nuclear strike had seen only relatively minor flare-ups between Arab and Jew. In fact, the brush with nuclear war had scared the hell out of all sides so badly that nobody wanted to risk an action that might suggest another such reaction. The expression around the White House was that "everybody over there is breathing again--occasionally."

". . .and again we ask Thy blessing and Thy holy presence within this room, oh Lord, as we strive mightily to save our homeland. Use us as instruments of Thy will, dear Lord, and guide our every step in furtherance of Thy kingdom. Amen."

"Thank you, Reverend, and good morning, everyone. Let's get to work. As we know, there was a great deal of activity in New York yesterday and the day before, so let's begin with General Keithley. Mr. Chairman, what's the news?"

Clyde Keithley stood and walked to the end of the long table, where an easel displayed a large posterboard map of the Manhattan area. Next to it was another, this one full of categories of weapons, personnel, and equipment, each with a string of numbers beside it.

"Thank you, Mr. President. As most of you know, after almost five weeks of hit-and-miss skirmishes with the PLO Vanguard, last week we finally found one of their major underground routes of escape, in the form of an abandoned spur of storm sewer that is marked in red *here*. Instead of filling it with troops, or even attempting to clear it at all, we set a number of fiber-optic camera lenses in various places, each wired to a transmitter that would send back video when the cameras were activated by motion sensors. You have seen some of that footage.

"Day before yesterday, we observed a particularly large troop contingent moving through one section of the old main, and they were going in a direction that we had already determined to lead to a large storage facility set in place during the year before this whole thing started. We decided to let them get to that location--one in that we also had a camera lens in place, thanks to the skills of our own snoops--then to

654

cut off their escape from every direction but one. It worked, and the result was one helluva fight, starting yesterday morning about dawn and running almost all day." He reached for a stack of additional poster board displays, these covered with large photographs of the area where the fighting occurred.

"General, why did you engage them only *after* they got to their weapons and ammunition supplies? If you had interdicted them beforehand, it seems they would have been less able to fight back." Webb already knew the answer, but it gave him some perverse sense of satisfaction to have the explanation given again. Even in the midst of military conflict, there were some on the Cabinet who fancied themselves as rear echelon commandos, well schooled in their own imaginations with the lore of street warfare.

"Yessir. We were unsure of the extent of the supplies located in that place, and we also still had no clear indication of the number of terrorists we were fighting. Their continued expert use of urban guerilla tactics had defeated all efforts to engage them in force. The numbers we saw moving through the tunnels the other day finally gave us some reckoning, and the force was larger than we had anticipated. With so many of them all in some kind of unusual, if not unique, meeting at one location, we felt it essential to let them congregate before striking.

"Here are the results." He lifted the boards full of pictures up onto the end of the table, a series of gasps and expletives circling the long surface at once. "As you can see, there are seventy-eight bodies laid out along the street here, and *this*-- this disturbance in the pavement--is where we blew up half a block of the sewer at a time when it was full of these people. Their bodies have been recovered with heavy construction equipment, after we were sure they were all dead. And *this*--" He stood a second large display on the table. "This is what's left of these buildings *here*--" Pointing back at the schematic of the streets of Manhattan-- ". . .after we cut off the escape of all these terrorists--" A third poster was set on the table, depicting another huge string of bodies. ". . .and engaged them in a firefight that lasted almost six hours yesterday afternoon. As you can see, we took no prisoners, there were no wounded to attend to. We have recovered one hundred eighty-seven dead from these buildings."

Silence reigned for nearly a minute, as people began to rise from their chairs, moving among the several display boards, easels, and schematics. The room started to fill with a soft cacophony of voices, as they talked among themselves, asked questions of Keithley, or commented to the president. "Gentlemen, let's move ahead. Please take seats so Clyde can complete his report; we have much to do today. General?"

"Right, sir. What is visible in this last set of pictures is this particular row of older commercial structures along *this* block in lower Manhattan. We first flushed the force that was in the sewer out onto the street, having left them only one avenue of escape and knowing they had to come up in this building, *here*. These three are connected by a tunnel--we think at one time two of these buildings--*these two here*--were actually only one structure, and when it was demolished and replaced by these two, the foundation was still in good enough shape that it was used for the new construction. All this was done shortly after the turn of the century, and such practices were much more common then than later on.

"Anyway, once we confirmed they were contained, we hit them with Apache cannon and machinegun fire, followed by close-in tank bombardment, until all three buildings looked like *this*. As you can see, there was little room left for concealment or protection. We think we got 'em all. I only wish I could report that we are now finished. However, it appears that the PLO ordered each of these men to continue fighting, setting ambushes and explosives, and employing snipers until all are dead. All in the service of Allah, I guess. So we continue to patrol, clearing one building at a time, engaging them with more success now that this big escape route is gone."

The rest of the day's meeting seemed anticlimactic after that beginning, but reports continued of slow, at times painful progress, oftentimes coming too late for millions of Americans. Efforts were nothing short of heroic in the area of fuel and shelter for all those about to face a winter without electricity. Water was becoming less of a problem, the Army having attacked the problem of sanitation and purification of water supplies with a vengeance. But Jackie Webb lived every waking moment--and through constant nightmares--with the spectre of great suffering for his people in the months ahead. Walking back to the Oval Office after the meeting, the awful picture of winter in the North and Midwest again consumed him.

His eye was caught by movement in the small garden outside his secretary's office, and he turned to identify who and what was there. The scene transfixed, even paralyzed the President of the United States so that he stood motionless, trying to assimilate what his eyes were seeing.

2.

"*There*. That should do it. If the current is too strong to allow the bobber to stay upright, add another sinker, and put it right there--*like that*--right next to the one we already put on. Twist the line through the bobber, *like this,* so it won't slip down too close to the bait, and don't forget to loop the worm over and over, hooking it through those light colored bands, like we did the other day. OK?"

"Ok, Dad, thanks. Jan and Kate said they'd go yesterday, but Whiner is too much of a sissie to stick the worms, and Kate says she has to help Mom with the canning. Can I go by myself, if I take a radio and promise to come back by six? *Pleeaassse, Dad?*" Joshua Landry smiled in spite of all efforts not to, leaned forward and drew his son against him, a sharp sensation firing up his leg and into the small of his back as he did so. Holding the child close for a moment, he reveled in the smells of the little boy, the sweaty skin of his neck, the scent of clean but wet hair, a hint of rich dirt. The emotion that rose up was willed aside in an instant, the hug relinquished to face the freckles and cornflower blue eyes that begged for release and freedom.

"Tell ya' what, son. It's about 3:30 now. You be back here at 5:30 *sharp,* take a radio, and promise me *ABSOLUTELY* that you will stay on this side of the creek, only north of the road, and under no circumstances leave the creekbed, and you can go now. But you gotta walk, you must radio me every thirty minutes, and you have to guarantee at least five bluegills and two bass--*deal?*" Luke's smile was exceeded only by the sincerity of his promise to accomplish all things, as he first flung himself into his father's arms, then pulled away with a flourish. Then the hook on his line snagged in the flannel of Josh's shirtfront, and the father cried out with the pain in his leg and the back of his neck, moving to avoid being stuck.

Luke froze as if dumbstruck, turned slowly, protecting against increasing the tension on the thin line. Jess appeared instantly in the doorway, the fear in her face produced by her husband's voice evaporating into a huge smile and laugh as she immediately recognized the real problem. "Stand still, son, or you'll undress your father--maybe that way I could get that nasty old shirt off him long enough to wash it! Now, back up here, slow--stand still. . .hold it--*there*. I take it he has finally beaten you down enough to permit him to go to the creek alone. Well, Luke, I guess your father has run off the last of the snakes and the farm is probably safe again, but *BE CAREFUL, YOU HEAR ME?!*" He was gone before the rest of the last admonition could escape his mother's lips.

"Old man, you look a bit the worse for wear. Boy's a handful, now isn't he? Let's have a look at that bandage. Been a day and a half since we changed it." She sat down on the porch swing, first lifting Josh's legs enough to permit her to rest them in her lap. The rich hues of changing trees, backlit by the sun's new, shallower angle, warmed the afternoon beyond the scant sixty degrees showing on the big thermometer by the back door. A pile of books and old magazines lay beneath the swing, a pitcher of apple cider sweat a pool that soaked into the wooden floor. A stray honeybee droned by, then sampled the bright display of zinnias that invited him to them, while a flight of geese cooled the air with the sound of their conversation.

She worked silently for several minutes, carefully removing tape, unwrapping the leg that continued to heal from its awful trauma. Dry and clean now, the last vestiges of infection had fled some three weeks ago, and what was left was a narrowing scar where the bones had protruded through the skin when they broke. "They're dry and clean, husband. Can I just put them back on?" He nodded, his gaze reluctantly returning to the porch from a long sweep of the horizon into that Luke had just disappeared.

"Jess, I've about had it with sitting around this damn porch. I've missed baling *again,* the gardens need to be manured and tilled under, and Carl continues to butcher the horses' feet, trying to put shoes on them. Don't ya' think it's about time I got to working just a little? I mean, at least I could--"

"You so much as step off this porch and I'll make you wish for a seat in that van you blew up, Joshua Landry." Her face was intense, reddening into a mask of unmistakable and indominatable Irish temper. Tears welled up in the green eyes, then momentarily her angered softened a bit. "I'm sorry, Josh. . .I do understand you well enough to know how hard it is for you to stay still for so long. You just have to let us--let

The Devil's Playground

me--care for you now. Carl says it'll take six months for you to be out of the infection woods, and every bit that long to get your strength back." He took her hand, reached over to brush the single tear that had slipped past her resolve and down onto her cheek.

"OK, boss, you win. And no fair crying. It's just that the pace was so furious, and the stakes so high these past months, I have a really hard time finding neutral. Maybe I just need more time with my wife, huh?" She scooted closer, lifting the tender leg out of her way, then got up and moved to sit against his torso on the swing. Kids' voices were faintly audible out in the pasture where two cows were heading toward the back of the barn, and another flight of geese added momentary chill as a breeze brushed against the side of the house and across their faces. They sat in silence for a while, sharing the sights and sounds, pensive with thoughts unspoken. Finally, after a deep breath, the wife spoke to her man with soft but earnest voice.

"I don't think I've ever really said this to you, Josh, through all these awful months, mostly because I've been so busy barking out caution and fear. I think the way I coped with the violence was to hate it, avoid it, deny it, and sometimes to blame you for it. But that was stupid, and I knew it when it was happening. What I want to say is, thank you for your bravery, my husband, for your leadership and, God help me, for whatever it is that makes you such a lunatic when you have to be. We'd all have died at the hand of those awful men without you and your leadership. I know it; Carl knows it. Everyone knows it. There have been many times since you got hurt that I have heard people doubting themselves, without you out front." He quickly deflected the power of her words and the intensity of her gaze.

"But they've been fine, Jess, just fine. Matter of fact, looks to me like we've grown a pretty good brand of troop out here, after all." His eyes averted at once then, as though distracted by some cue inaudible to his wife. Looking again toward the new coloring of the afternoon west horizon, there was a moment of time dilation, silent, rich and full. Emotion filled the air, but without expression, tear, sigh. A voice heavy and deep with subtle passion croaked from the man.

"Jessica, these months have been fired with a passion I could not check. . .at times fear of harm to you guys kept me awake for days on end, I forgot to eat, almost to breathe sometimes. And when that truck blew up, flying through the air toward those damn rocks, just for an instant I thought that if I was about to die, at least that fire in my chest would finally burn out. Well, I *didn't* die, but ever since I first realized I was back in Carl's bedroom, after the fever broke, I've been without that burning. Finally. So many times, back in the sixties, I thought I was about to die, but it didn't happen. This time I was sure. Wrong again, wife. Wrong again. And when it comes to courage and leadership, what we got from you glued this whole program together from the moment of the first shot."

Turning his face from that far place, Jessica Landry kissed her husband. Like a woman kisses a man, she kissed him. Her mind's voice expressed her constant prayer of thanksgiving that he was still there to kiss; that they were still together; that the worst was over. The breeze brushed her hair against his face again, cooler now as the sun's hue slipped behind a billow of cloud that swept across it. His arms pulled her close against his chest, the flannel shirt soft against her shoulders, even as it warmed them both.

Reverie spoke of redemption, of reclamation, essence and the return of joy and simplicity. And in that moment, Joshua Owen Landry, the lawyer, the soldier, the politician, died; the father, the husband, the farmer, the Christian were all reborn, living again and still. But living in a world as foreign to its past as it was unknown to its future, a world no longer in love with itself, its stuff, its appetites. And in that moment, man and woman both knew with one accord that they would not miss it.

3.

A song, soft and deep from within her chest, escaped only a short distance out into the garden in that she was kneeling, her hands busy in the soft dirt so filled with weeds and trash. Jeans wrapped around her slender hips and waist, a USMC tee-shirt tight across her torso, dirty sneakers on her feet. The First Lady of the United States was pulling weeds in the small garden outside the office of her husband, the President, and the melody to her favorite hymn, *In the Garden*, became audible to him as he approached without sound.

A whole row of formerly weed-infested perennials stood bright against the clean dirt around them, a pile of wilting greens drying in the morning sun at the end of the row. The incongruity of seeing his elegant wife working in the dirt was conflict and resolution at once; for although she was fine and beautiful, every place he had ever taken her to live had produced a garden of some kind. Even the balcony of the high-rise apartment they lived in for an entire summer in New York City years before had boasted flowers, green beans growing on poles, and fat tomatoes. So seeing her amid plants and dirt was not so strange, after all. And the irony of this sight, so closely behind the pictures of violence and death, destruction and war, in the Cabinet room only a few feet away, was palpable as he stood there in the garden.

Jackie Robinson Webb turned to leave his wife to her peaceful pastime, the press of a thousand matters overcoming every other impulse. She had not seen him, and her song continued into another verse as he approached the door back into the White House. Then another chorus. . . *"and He walks with me, and He talks with me, and He tells me I am His own. . And the joy we share, as we tarry there, none other. .has ever. . known."* He was beside his wife now, inches from her hip as she knelt and leaned into another row of weeds. Her song stopped, her head turning up to meet his gaze, then humming the next verse. The smile captured him at once, black eyes full of passion and sunlight, face glistening sparkles of heat, breathing quickened by the struggle against the deeply rooted weeds that tried to choke precious flowers.

In that moment he was beside his wife, knees in the dirt, powerful hands searching in the soil for the root of the weeds that marred and overtook the lively colors in the nation's homestead garden. His deep voice found the melody, while an arm pulled his wife against him and into a kneeling embrace that she responded to at once. The music stopped, throats gripped by silence born of strong emotion. They turned their faces down to look together into the soil of the garden.

The clutches of the day's cares dissolved briefly for our President, there beside his wife, and he found momentary peace, as if signifying his soul's hunger for some visible, palpable evidence of redemption for self, and for country. The song ended and was replaced by another, *This is my Father's World,* another of the old children's Sunday School pieces so deeply woven into Molly's spirit, so much a part of the fabric of the home she had made for thirty years for husband and kids. They sang with increasing zeal, fingers digging purposefully into the complex maze of weeds and roots that permeated what had once been so beautiful a place, minutes passing into an hour, shoulder to shoulder, voices raised while backs bent to the task of reclamation. And when Jackie Webb finally stood and straightened his back, brushed dirt from his knees, he took his wife in his arms again, prayed thanksgiving in her ear, and listened to his heart's reminder of the power she gave, the light and direction she embodied for him and for many.

They looked at the product, at each other for a moment. Smiles turned to grins, then to laughter, hugs and more grins. Then as if by some unspoken cue, they turned back to the garden at the same time; the President of the United States and the First Lady bent to the earth again and attacked another row of weeds in the garden of the White House. Her voice led his, back into hymns that filled the small space and echoed through open windows and down ancient hallways, past pictures of great men and women, in the house of the people, once again.